A PERFECTLY PARANORMAL EASTER

A PERFECTLY PARANORMAL ANTHOLOGY VOLUME 3

MARNIE ST CLAIR   SAMANTHA MARSHALL
HELLUCY HOWE   LEISL LEIGHTON

LOVE PNR? JOIN OUR PERFECTLY PARANORMAL PARAMOURS FACEBOOK GROUP

If you want to get to know the Perfectly Paranormal Anthology authors a bit more, get sneak peeks of what's coming up as well as giveaways, special offers and just some PNR fun, then join our Perfectly Paranormal Paramours Facebook Group.

Find us here:

https://www.facebook.com/groups/251663560162131

CONTENTS

SWEET HEREAFTER

MARNIE ST CLAIR

SWEET HEREAFTER

An Owlscroft Coven Novella
Book 3

Marnie St Clair

Sweet Hereafter

© 2022 by Marnie St Clair

Australian Copyright 2022

New Zealand Copyright 2022

Edited by Leisl Leighton Author Services

Published by Marnie St Clair. For more information, email marnie@marniestclair.com

First published 2022

❀ Created with Vellum

ABOUT SWEET HEREAFTER

To be reborn, you must first die ...

Future witch Everly Jackson knew wizard JJ was the one for her the moment she first saw him. But then she interpreted a vision of the future wrong, causing JJ to be inhabited by a demon – and ruining his life. Now, with guilt weighing heavily on her, she and JJ can barely breathe the same air without finding something to fight about.

But one night, on her way back from the future, Everly meets an alternative version of JJ in a most improbable place ... and realises she's been given a chance to fix what she's broken. First, she'll have to figure out all his secrets – and somehow keep her own – before he puts himself in mortal danger ... and she's forced to make the ultimate sacrifice.

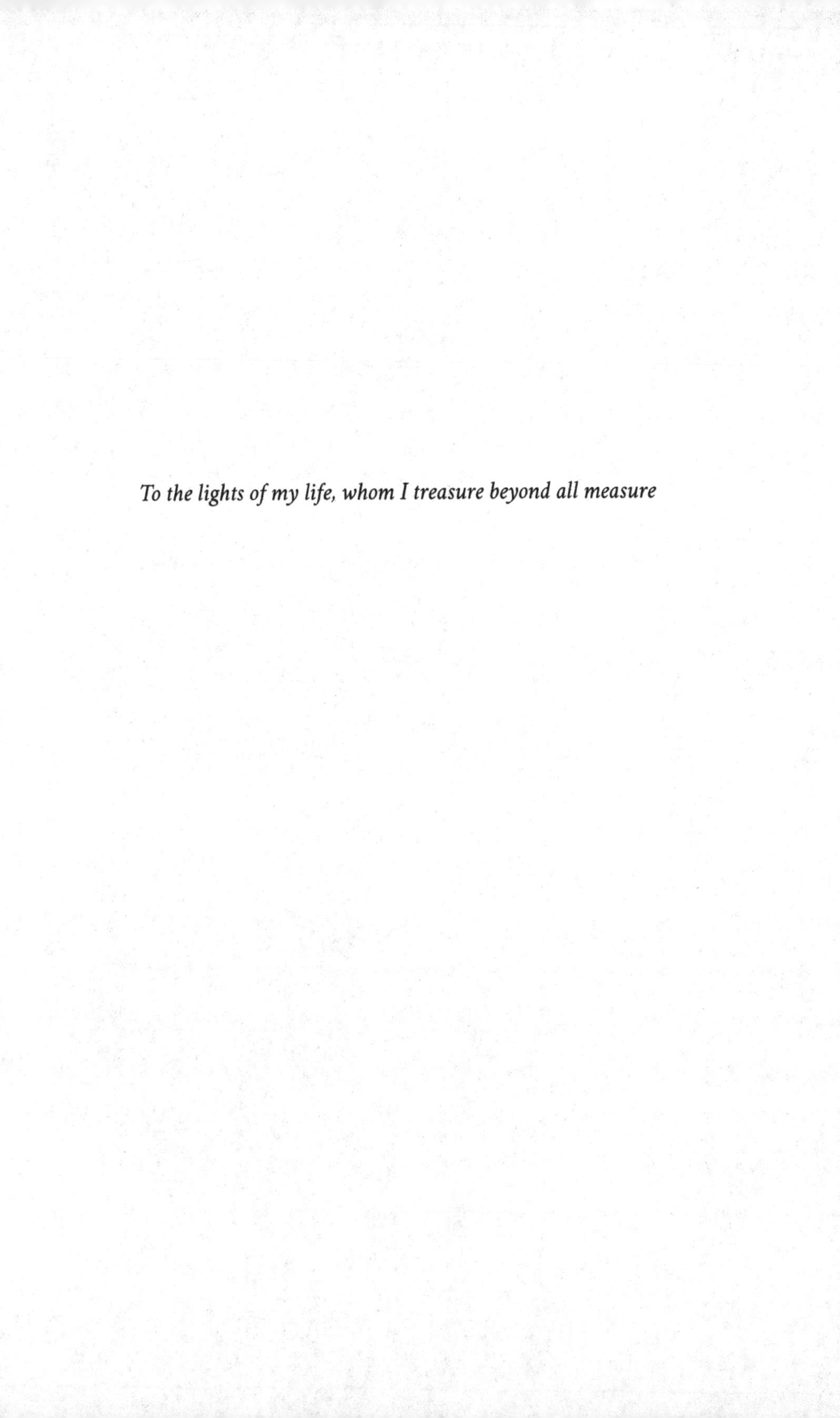

To the lights of my life, whom I treasure beyond all measure

I watch the bird swoop across the lush courtyard and land on the bronze statue of Juliet. Head cocked, he peers at me with a keen black eye. Waiting.

"Your boyfriend's back, Evie," Chloe says.

"I see him," I reply, but I'm under no illusion. That bird only loves me for my food. I'm training him. Taming him.

The five of us come here almost every day to eat lunch. It's our secret place, hidden among the throng of the busy campus; a serene sanctuary at the centre of a recital venue that only comes alive in the evening. My little avian Romeo, so named because he's always hanging around the statue of Juliet, is smart. He knows when to expect me. And he knows he gets to share.

But today, I have chips, and they're not his favourite.

Next to me, JJ is peeling the wrapper from his burger. Fluffy white bread with seeds on top. Perfect.

I tear some off.

"Hey!"

Romeo is used to our chatter but that was too abrupt. He bounces around in alarm, ready to flee.

I glare at JJ disapprovingly.

"What if I happen to be hungry?" he grumbles.

I shove my paper cup of chips into his chest. He breathes out like it's a blow, like it hurts, and his gaze shoots to mine. The edge of his stare presses against my skin, and as always, I'm arrested by his sparse classical beauty, his even features just sharp enough to create shadows. I push harder against his black t-shirt. "Yours."

His hand slowly rises to take the cup. I release it just before we touch, then turn and walk to the centre of the courtyard, extending my palm high, chunk of bread on top. I stand as still as Juliet and wait.

There's a lull in the conversation as everyone stays quiet enough for Romeo to gather confidence. There's a flutter of wings, then little scaled feet are hopping around on my hand – a sensation as unnerving as it is cute.

I swap a grin with Emma.

"Literally eating out of the palm of your hand," she mumbles around a mouthful of panini.

"When Everly Jackson casts her lovespell, no living soul can resist," Felix intones in a dramatic movie trailer voice.

It's a joke. Except for JJ, they don't know I'm a witch.

"I'd never cast a lovespell." It's true.

"In fairness, though, Evie, you don't need to," Felix replies.

The whole lovespell thing dates back to first year, when twenty-three guys asked me out on a single day. I'd just come from a strict Catholic girls' school and although that doesn't necessarily mean you're clueless, it did in my case. The joke never gets old, no matter how much I wish it would.

Besides, it's not true.

Some people have no trouble resisting me.

I don't mean to, but I turn my head and my gaze catches on JJ's.

He looks back, chewing slowly, dark eyes fathomless. Then swallows. "You're not supposed to feed birds. It ends up killing them."

The rough edge to his tone chisels through suddenly thick air, and the other three shift uncomfortably, focus their attention on their food. For six months, they've tried to ignore the tension between us.

When we're all together, that is. Individually, each of them has asked me what happened. They've probably done the same with JJ.

Of course they want to know; we were inseparable. Halloween was a hurricane that came in and flattened everything in its wake, leaving the vibrant landscape that used to be my life colourless and desolate. Now, we can barely breathe the same air. But there is nothing either of us can say to explain the wound festering between us. It would be easier if we left each other alone, but I can't bring myself to do that and apparently neither can he.

I look up. "Don't listen, Romeo. That's an old wives' tale."

JJ is intent on his burger, like he can't hear me.

"I read an article in *Nature*," I continue. "Feeding birds is just a snack to them. They don't rely on it."

"Did you have any pets in Singapore?" Chloe intervenes hurriedly, no doubt desperate to move the conversation to lighter, airier climes.

After a moment, JJ swivels to face her. "No. But I'm thinking of getting one."

Singapore is where he used to live. Before he found an ancient amulet – effectively making him a target for every murderous, power-hungry wizard in the world. Which is pretty much all of them.

Did I mention he's a wizard?

So is his uncle, Aiden, who's been responsible for JJ since his parents died, and tried to protect him from the brutal reality of wizard life. When JJ told Aiden about the amulet he'd found, Aiden made him swear not to tell anyone. JJ didn't think that included Jonathon – his other uncle. He was wrong – as soon as he saw it, Jonathon attacked him, wanting the amulet for himself.

JJ managed to escape and took the first flight out, and Aiden followed soon after.

But Melbourne is Owlscroft Coven territory, and magical visitors aren't automatically permitted to stay. In return for refuge, Aiden offered to help my sister Harlow with her demon-hunting duties, and now, they're a couple.

Which doesn't make things any easier for the two of us.

Finished, Romeo flies back to Juliet. He jumps around a bit, squawks at me. He knows there's a round two.

I head to JJ, hand out for more. He looks at it, before breaking off another chunk and dropping it into my palm. I return to position, hand in the air again.

"A dog maybe," he says, glint in his eye as he answers Chloe's question.

I flash an unimpressed glare in his direction. He's only saying it to get to me – witches and dogs do not mix – but he's gone too far. "Like Aunt Bernie would allow that. You'd have to move out."

Aunt Bernie, our Head Witch, is his current landlady. After everything that happened at Halloween, she offered him a room in our covenstead. As far as the others know, Aunt Bernie is just my eccentric aunt who lives alone in an old mansion in Hawthorn. They probably wonder why JJ is living with her, but they haven't asked.

"Speaking of … Have you heard back yet?" Chloe asks him.

What is she talking about?

My heart stutters and my throat goes tight. I look from JJ to Chloe then back, trying to limit my movements so Romeo won't freak out.

JJ's chewing; he doesn't respond immediately.

"Heard back about what?" Emma asks – and I want to kiss her.

"JJ applied for a job with McKinsey," Chloe says for him, tucking a strand of hair behind her ear.

I exhale on a squeeze of my insides.

He's applying for jobs?

He told Chloe but not me?

We had a plan for our future. It didn't involve McKinsey.

I slowly swivel a quarter-turn to stare at Juliet. In an artistic choice that is completely unfaithful to the play, the sculptor made her serene and contemplative. I try to channel some of her energy.

"The management consultancy?" Felix asks. "Aren't you studying English Lit?"

Felix's confusion is justified, though not for the reason he thinks. What does a wizard want with that kind of work?

JJ swallows and shrugs. "They take all types of graduates actually.

And they have offices all over the world." He faces Chloe. "I got an interview."

A heavy feeling sinks through my stomach.

"Yay," Chloe says.

"Yay," Emma echoes. "But I thought you wanted to stay in Melbourne. Do you have to worry about visas or something?"

He shakes his head. "I have dual citizenship." He takes another bite.

JJ has everything citizenship. Wizards don't respect national borders; they go where they want and do what they please, magicking away any obstacle in their way.

But maybe not anymore. Not for him.

He's refused to use magic since Halloween. I thought at first he was waiting to turn twenty – a wizard's coming of age – but that happened two months ago, and he still hasn't started. Does the job search mean he plans to continue like that?

There is a sudden bitterness on my tongue. I don't know anything about him or his life anymore. I swivel back.

Chloe extends her phone. "This is Maxie. He's a Scotty."

JJ gives it a quick glance. "Cute."

"You can come and meet him if you want. Maybe during the Easter break?" She's phrased the invitation casually, but I know she has more than a casual interest.

JJ doesn't. He has no idea of the effect he has on people. Even those who don't know he's a wizard – which is most everyone – are drawn to the power and subtle glamour that radiates from him; a glamour that will only increase as he grows into his heritage. He's going to field a lot of offers.

The realisation stabs at me. I remind myself that I don't own him, but it doesn't work. "You shouldn't get a dog if you're not staying."

Our gazes lock. I go taut, and that thing happens, like it always does – something inside me starts to vibrate, like I'm a tuning fork and he's my exact frequency.

It's been the same since the first time we met, just over a year ago, when all I could think was I'd found him. Or rather, he'd found me.

My equal and opposite; the half I didn't know was missing.

But if I ever did have some kind of claim to him, I don't anymore. Not after what I did.

He's broken. I broke him.

And I don't know how to fix him.

For a moment, I think I see something in his gaze – something like an invitation to go with him, to *be* with him. But then a flush spreads across his cheekbones. "You're right. I should wait."

Round two is over. Romeo flies off, this time into the branches of a small tropical-looking tree. There is no round three, but he always lingers a while, singing and making love-eyes at me.

"He's just so cute," Emma mumbles around her final mouthful, looking at Romeo.

I smile because it's expected, but inside I'm dying.

JJ and I knew exactly how we were going to spend the rest of our lives. Dreamed it up over countless feverish late-night hours, talking about how it was going to be, all we were going to achieve. Me, a rare future witch. Him, the crown prince of the wizarding world. Together – no limits.

Despite everything that happened, despite the way things are between us now, deep inside I've been assuming that somehow, those plans would come to fruition. That eventually, I would be made whole again.

For the first time, I'm forced to confront the possibility that it's not going to happen. That it's too late. That the damage I did is irrevocable, and our endless, earnest talks have come to naught.

My heart is an avalanche – breaking apart, crashing down, the last vestiges of hope disintegrating to rubble and dust.

"Argh." Emma stretches her arms above her head. "Class in five. We should motor."

Chloe jolts to her feet – she hates being late – and links her arm through Emma's. They walk out of the courtyard.

"You two should get a room already," Felix murmurs under his breath as he brushes past me to follow.

I sneak a glance at JJ, compressing his wrapper into a ball. He's not looking back. I don't know if he heard but judging by the whites of his knuckles, I'd say he did. I wait for him to say 'As if' or 'I'd rather die'. But he doesn't. And neither do I.

Maybe we should have. Before. But I thought we had forever.

He tosses the rubbish into the bin and leaves.

Then it's just me, arms wrapped around myself, like poor doomed Juliet.

The life of any witch is highly regimented, and future witches only more so. There are many restrictions on how I should use my ability. Only when under direct supervision at Owlscroft. Only to detect threats to the people of Melbourne. Only to travel a certain span ahead.

But I've never been one for rules, and I know that, even though I shouldn't, I'll be travelling far into the future tonight.

2

*E*very week, right after all-coven, I talk with Aunt Bernie. We go to her office, so it's just the two of us, uninterrupted by the many calls on her attention, and she checks, within the space of our allocated fifteen minutes, that I am still *compos mentis*.

They say future magic chooses the witch; it doesn't choose many. Future witches are rare hothouse flowers; freaks who engender as much fear as they do fascination. Technically, all witches should demonstrate some base level of skill – it's taught during the neophyte year and it's part of the exam. But few have an affinity for it – even witches get twitchy at the idea of breaking their soul into pieces – and a blind eye is turned to any deficit.

No one is at ease with a future witch. We are valued, we are respected, but we are not liked. We don't need to be. Much of the general coven work is done in small teams, but there is no way to visit the future in an ensemble. I work alone.

All the horrific possibilities that most people try *not* to dwell on, that is what I search for. I sent the weightless part of myself a few days forward in time, looking for spikes in emotions that indicate something is very wrong – terror, agony, excruciation, anguish, dread. The events that are most certain; those we have the greatest chance of preventing. Traffic collisions and gas explosions. Drownings and snakebites. Child kidnappings and twisted stalkers taking that final step. I enter that darkness, experience it fully, so I can bring back the details and Owlscroft can stop it happening.

It sounds terrible, and I suppose it is, but it's not my whole self that feels it; just that part that travels to the future. The weightless part. I don't bring the experience back to my present self – or, at least, that's the theory.

Still, burn-out rates for future witches are high.

Which is why, every week, Aunt Bernie makes me peppermint tea, sets out gourmet choc-chip cookies on floral fine bone china, and works her way through a set of questions.

Am I maintaining my schedule? Eating, sleeping? Keeping up with regular activities, engaging with my friends?

Have I partaken of any illicit substance?

Have I had thoughts of harming myself?

She doesn't ask that exactly; she puts effort into rephrasing, guising it as normal conversation. But after almost two years, it's not hard to pick the pattern.

Every week, I smile and I lie.

Oh, not about most of her questions – eating and sleeping is a little iffy at the moment, but not because of my power. I know she cares but she has no right to my deeply personal emotions. Just like she has no right to know I don't exactly stick to the rules where my power is concerned.

If she found out, she'd try to stop me – and I can't have that. Travelling to the future by myself, for myself, is the only time lately that I feel okay. Like I could be happy again.

But a lie of omission is still a lie – and I've become very good at it.

I watch as Aunt Bernie pours steaming green liquid into delicate teacups, mesmerised.

"How are you, dear heart?" she asks when she's finished.

I meet her gaze. "Good. The same. Coven. Work. Study."

"It's your last year, isn't it?"

"Yes it is, and reality's hit. We've been talking a lot about what comes next." I keep my smile bright, despite the twist and pinch those words cause. Some of us have been thinking harder than others.

She nudges my cup and saucer a little closer to me, and sits her long, lean form into a chair. "And what are you thinking?"

"Postgrad maybe? I wasn't really considering it—" I thought I'd be travelling the world, hunting for magical artefacts with JJ, but that's not on the cards anymore. "But I want to write – poetry, I think – and I could do with more guidance. I'd apply to Melbourne, of course."

The barest hint of a frown furrows her brow. "You don't have to stay here."

"I know." Witches move all the time, join other covens. But losing a future witch would be a blow to Owlscroft.

"You don't have to do anything you don't want to," she reiterates.

"I know," I repeat. "I want to stay."

She lifts her cup but her expression turns serious and she places it back in the saucer without bringing it to her mouth. "Now, you know I have to ask …"

I roll my eyes. "No drugs, Aunt Bernie. We're English nerds. We're tame. We go to a grungy pub once a week and talk Shakespeare." That's not quite true. Emma is in no way tame and Felix is not far behind, but Aunt Bernie doesn't need to know that. And I really don't touch anything beyond the occasional beverage. I can't, and I know I can't.

"So you're seeing your friends regularly?"

I nod. "We share classes and catch up outside as well."

"And Elijah?"

Aunt Bernie is the only one who calls JJ Elijah, his English name. His Chinese name is Jun Jie, but no one calls him that either. Except Aiden when he's cranky.

"Him too." I try to maintain my cheery façade, but the narrowing of her eyes lets me know she's not buying it. I let my face fall. "I mean, he's … you know what he's like now. But he still hangs with us."

Aunt Bernie tilts her head. "He's got a lot to work through. He'll get there."

I nod. *He* may; *we* may not.

She takes a sip of her tea, and so do I. Then reach for a biscuit. After a few moments watching me munch, her tension eases.

I have, apparently, passed.

"Now," she says. "Are you happy to do some work tonight?"

"Of course."

"Only if you're up to it. I realise we've been leaning on you quite heavily lately."

"It's fine," I say. "I'm fine."

How can I say no? Everything I learn helps. Sometimes it's delivered as an anonymous tip to the police. Sometimes another witch will cast some kind of spell to counter the situation. Sometimes more direct, non-magical steps are taken.

Bad things still happen. It's difficult to live with the knowledge that there's things I don't see, things we can't change. But I do my best. And I can't not do it.

~

No one knows about my nocturnal activities. Except JJ, and even he doesn't know the current extent. Every night I fly. Not through space; through time.

I'm not supposed to – future magic is considered dangerous. But it doesn't scare me, it never has. It's pure exhilaration; a freedom most will never know.

How many people – witches or otherwise – can truly say they've left themselves behind?

I taught myself when I was fourteen; four years before I joined the coven. I don't begrudge Owlscroft my service, but they don't own my ability, nor my soul.

JJ used to hassle me to stop; he hated it, called it 'numbing out'. And maybe he had a point but that doesn't make it any less necessary to my sanity. I gave it up for a while. It was easier – everything was easier – when he was in my life. If he knew what I get up to now …

Since Halloween, driven by guilt, by grief, I've been travelling more and more often; going further, lingering longer. Hours at a time, lost in a world of feelings-infused sensation, until my here-and-now self drags me back.

The future is my drug of choice; an addiction I make no attempt to fight.

I only do it at home, in the comfortable Californian bungalow I grew up in, and I wait till late at night. If disturbed, your awareness will yank you back pretty darn quick. A casual observer might assume I was dozing or daydreaming, but Mum will know immediately where I've been. I could move out – Harlow did the second she turned eighteen – but I'm still studying and only work casual hours. Besides, I get on with my parents and Camberwell is close to work, close to coven and a short train trip to campus.

Still, I'd be in a lot of trouble if anyone knew. Mum's on the Coven Council, and Aunt Bernie of course, as well as Aunt Lettie and my cousin Avery. Given how my family packs out our coven, it's amazing I get away with what I do. People see what they expect to see; what they want to see.

Tonight, I need to escape to the future more than ever.

Lying on cool sheets, I stretch out and reach for a batch of magic. It descends on me, caressing my temple, my cheek, my neck, winding and twirling around me like a ribbon. Other witches say they have trouble tethering magic, but it comes to me when I call like a lover just waiting to be beckoned.

I cant the words.

To the future
I will go
Until it's time
To come home

I feel the spell at work, fragmenting and lifting that part of me. I add my will, my intent, flinging myself high into the stream. The higher I go, the further I travel, and I want to travel far. I join the parabolic kaleidoscope – a rush of colour and feeling that's both instant and eternal – and then I'm descending at speed, on a crash course with the millions of souls of a future Melbourne.

When I do this for the coven, I search out negative emotions, but when I do it for myself, it's different feelings I chase.

I go in search of love.

When I see it flare – bright, compelling, true – I swoop like a swallow in spring.

And find myself at the Studley Park Boathouse; a warm evening, all inky lilacs and dusky rose. I see but not with my eyes. I taste but not with my mouth. Everything is filtered through the lens of feelings. There is no sharp clarity in the future – everything bleeds into a unified whole that is somehow deeper, more poignant.

The river flows – serene, happy – and geese paddle past – busy, content.

People move around her, but she doesn't notice them. She only sees *him* – her safe harbour, her fount of tender joy.

They are picnicking. Their three-month anniversary. He offers her a strawberry. It looks like a heart, smells like spring, tastes like love. She laughs at something he says and they sip champagne – lovely, bubbly, golden with delight.

Their love – giddy infatuation, devotion, wonder – surrounds me, permeates through me, until I drown in it. I linger in this dreamy future half-existence, sliding in deep, letting go, letting the multitude of sensations flow through me.

I am so profoundly immersed that the gentle pull of home at the edges of my awareness is painful. A forced wakening from the deepest slumber.

I want to stay with the running water and the paddling geese. I want to drown in sweet-tart berry sensations that are not my own. But the pull grows more insistent. Soon it will become a desperate clawing thing – dragging me back like someone drowning struggles for air.

I let go. Let my life-force tug me to the stream. Back through the blur of colour and senses.

I am almost home when something catches my attention. Off to my left, a light.

I slam on the brakes with a gut-wrenching jolt.

Tiny pinpricks explode when I realise where it's coming from. The snow globe that sits on my bedside table. Harlow brought it back for me when she went to Moscow at the end of last year.

I have never left the stream – nothing's ever distracted me like this – but I drift closer. And find myself inside, descending slowly through snow that is soft, dry and spellbindingly pretty.

I float down past trees covered in pink and white blossom, through air that carries the scent of cherry blossom, almond paste and powdered violets.

It is spring in the Moscow of my snow globe.

My feet touch down on pale pavers. In front of me is a castle, made in the same white stone. That's where the light comes from, but in some trick of physics, it bounces around the globe, lighting the whole scene.

I dust off snow as light as sugar and realise to my surprise that I am wearing clothes. Not the plaid pyjamas I am wearing in my here-and-now but a black jersey dress that hangs in my wardrobe. Unlike my travels to the future, I am corporal.

Strains of violins reach me – a dreamy waltz – and I head for the high arch of the entrance to the castle. It looked small from the outside, but inside, it's cavernous. I pass through arches from one empty room to another, following the music, collections of tall, pale candles lighting the way.

I pause outside a set of wooden doors with no handles or latches – like those of a saloon. They're ornate, with different shades of wood cut and fit together to show a huge full moon shining over a river. The music is coming from inside. I push them open with a sweep.

A man in a shirt of pure snowy white sits at a piano, back to me, playing the refrain with dramatic flourish. I draw in a sharp breath. I would know him anywhere. "JJ?"

He stills, hands high above the keys, then swivels on his seat. "You're here."

He smiles at me like he hasn't in a long time; my stupid heart softens and swells.

He stands and I walk closer, studying him; gaze devouring a face that is open and expressive, like it used to be before Halloween, when I would watch the moods shift across it like clouds across an autumn sky.

We stop when we're close. He shoves his hands in the pockets of his black pants.

"What are you doing in my snow globe?" I ask.

A hint of a smile plays at the corners of his mouth. "Waiting for you, of course."

I let out a small, shocked laugh. "In my snow globe?"

"Where else?" His gaze turns soft and serious. "It's next to you all night."

His words spark a warm glow inside but I step closer, eyes moving all over him, still hungry for the details of this other half I've so longed for. "Is it really you?"

He cocks his head. "I want to say yes but what do you think?"

The flop of his fringe, the glint in his eyes, the relaxed confidence of his stance. It's unmistakably him. I smile, then look around the room in wonder. "I don't understand. What is this place?"

He gives me a 'we've-established-that' look. "Your snow globe."

"But ... are we in the future?"

"Ah ..." He pushes a hand through his fringe, holding it back off his forehead in a movement that is so characteristically him, I have witnessed it a million times. "Not really ... It's not really any time. Or place."

He lets go; the fringe cascades back down. "Why are you here? Why am I here?"

His hands come to his hips. "You could do me a favour. I'm having a package delivered. To the apartment. Can you pick it up? Keep it safe for me?"

A frown forms between my brows. "Of course. But ..." My gaze flicks from one of his eyes to the other. "That's it?"

"Yeah. I mean ... for the moment."

He smiles; I smile back. Happiness spreads through my veins like warm honey. And then it's stupid, but all we're doing is staring, staring like we can't get enough of the sight of each other. Stars burst inside me, my grin gets wider and wider. And though we haven't moved, I feel we're somehow leaning into each other, merging into one.

He reaches; the backs of his fingers brush lightly across my cheek. "I'm so happy you're here."

I tilt my cheek into his hand, my heart growing heavy with the weight of my longing. These past months have been hard; I have needed to hear words like that for a long time.

His hand falls from my face, palm up. "Dance with me?"

The music is still playing I realise, and it's back to violins. A fresh grin breaks across my face. "Since when have you danced?"

He shrugs. "Since now. Since you're here."

I place a hand in his and the other on his shoulder, and before I know it, we are gliding across stone pavers. Sweeping around the room with unnatural speed, the light of many candles blurring behind his head. Our feet cannot possibly be on the ground. I don't understand what is happening, but I don't care. With his hand on my waist and the warmth of his body close enough to wash over my skin, I'm happier than I've ever been, swept around in a whirlwind of speed and joy. Everything feels right. Like the past six months never happened; like we are back to normal.

Better than normal. We've finally entered the silvery grove I'd always believed we'd end up in – and then, after Halloween, feared we'd never reach.

When my body – my corporal body – pulls at me in a visceral psychic tug, letting me know in no uncertain terms it's time, I fight it.

But he brings us to a gentle swirl of a halt, hands shifting to my shoulders. "You have to go."

"I don't want to. You're here."

A funny look crosses his face. He studies me for a long moment, eyes turning serious. "I'm not really. You know that."

The tide of good feelings crashes down. "What do you mean?"

A firm hold drags at me, trying to pull me back, but I dig in my metaphorical heels, stubbornly refusing to heed the call.

He takes my hands in his, runs his thumbs across my knuckles in a way that makes my pulse jump. Then he lets out a sigh. "Everly. I'm sorry."

A rash of goosebumps sweeps over me. "What for?"

I cannot last much longer. I squeeze his hands, trying to hang on, but survival instinct, raw and primal, wins as it always will, taking away all choice. "JJ!" I yell as I'm wrenched away. "What are you sorry for?"

I lurch upward in my bed, heart pounding. I drag in ragged pulls of breath around the body-jerking sobs that escape from my mouth – animal and uncontrollable. I put a hand to my cheek, feel the wetness there, then crush it against my mouth to try to contain the noise. I rock, desperate to calm myself. The last thing I need is Mum coming to check on me.

What was that?

What was that?

I twist to the side and grab my snow globe, shaking it, turning it upside down, trying to see inside. Hoping what? Hoping he falls out?

I press it to my chest and wait long moments for my breathing to calm. Then I place the snow globe back on my bedside table, and hang forward, arms around my knees, chin on top.

Bad things are coming.

3

I usually catch a tram when I'm going to coven from work – a second-hand bookshop – but tonight I walk. I need to process, and walking is how I ground myself. I can walk for hours, arms wrapped around myself, thinking – or not thinking. Just living in the rhythm of my shoes hitting the ground. Step after step after step.

I love Book Haven; the shelves and shelves of books, the smell of ink and wood, and the dust of the ages. But today, I'm distracted, unable to settle.

I still don't know what happened last night; what it was.

The whole snow globe thing was surreal. I should dismiss it, put it down to stress. I've been travelling too often. Going too far, staying too long. Most likely, the whole thing was fantasy, born of the longing of my heart.

But I can't quite believe that. It felt real. *He* felt real. I even went into the city before work, to Harlow and Aiden's, but their mailbox was empty. I told myself my disappointment was ridiculous. Did I really think there would be something waiting for me? Clearly some part of me did.

I need to see JJ. I need to find out what, if anything, he knows.

I turn off just before I reach the river, heading into the quiet street where Owlscroft is located, behind a high red-brick fence with a looming conifer hedge. Midway along is the gate – an ornate cast-iron beauty of uncertain provenance. It is old – much older than the red-brick Queen Anne mansion within – brought over from somewhere in Europe when Owlscroft was founded.

There's no way to open the gate; it either recognises you or it doesn't. It admits every member of the coven. And now JJ.

It swings open for me and I walk up through the gardens. They are lovely in every season, but the colours of the autumn stillness – the bright yellows and greens, the reds, the browns – provide a special kind of solace.

It's not all-coven tonight, so it's quiet. The huge foyer is empty. I head up the wide sweep of mahogany stairs and along the corridor to JJ's room. Aunt Bernie put him right at the end, as far from the general thrum as possible.

Before he moved in here, he lived with Aiden. He was only supposed to stay at Owlscroft a couple of days – while Aiden and Harlow were dealing with the Halloween demon drama – but he's still here. And now Harlow's moved in with Aiden.

JJ wouldn't want to third-wheel them, but they're away most of the time, travelling the world talking to other covens to learn as much as they can and help out with any demon-related problems. JJ would mostly have the apartment to himself.

I asked him just after Halloween, before things had deteriorated to their current state, why he stayed at Owlscroft. He said it was peaceful. It's a massive building – there's something like 20 bedrooms – and most of the time, it's just him and Aunt Bernie here, so I can see why he thinks so.

I rap on his door but there's no response. I try again. Nothing. I bite my lip, wondering where he is. He's almost always at Owlscroft when he's not on campus.

I hear footsteps coming up the stairs and a quiet murmuring followed by a chuckle. If I'm spotted here, I'm likely to be asked to do something. I mostly wouldn't mind but I don't want to get dragged into coven business tonight.

I open JJ's door and slip inside, closing it after me quietly. When I turn, I see his prone form on the bed, stretched like a sleeping angel.

For a moment, I am frozen. Then I move closer, allowing my gaze to rake over him like I no longer dare when he's awake. He's adopted the Melbourne uniform of black, black and more black; today, he's in black jeans and a long-sleeved black t-shirt with slashing white writing.

I draw closer, my eyes trailing over the dark sheen of his hair, the fineness of his pale skin, the elegant lines of his body.

He's so still.

Too still.

My stomach drops and I halt. Then quicken to sit at his side. The mattress dips and he tilts, but even then, he doesn't stir. Sucking in a breath, I lean over him, grip his shoulders and shake. He moves like a ragdoll under my hands, no will or force of his own.

"JJ. Wake up," I say, an undercurrent of urgency in my tone. I place a palm on his cheek and it's warm, but when I draw back to watch his chest, I can't make out a rise.

I lean down, ear to his nose, his mouth. One hand searches his neck for a pulse, the other I shove under his shirt, across his chest, to where his heart should be beating.

I cannot hear or feel anything.

I raise my head a fraction. "Wake up, wake up," I plead, hands tight claws on him. But his eyes remain closed. A hum starts to ring through my ears; a throb of pressure squeezes in a brace around my skull. Dread is taking over. I squeeze him tighter. "Wake up!"

My sharp tone cuts the air. His eyes snap open, lock on mine, so close to him, and he drags in a breath.

We rise as one, till we are both sitting upright. Close as sin, curved around each other. One of his hands is flat on the bed next to him, propping him up; the other is around my waist. My arm is still caught between us, hand splayed against his chest, moving with the frenzied in and out of his lungs.

His gaze moves between my eyes, searching for answers. A flurry of emotions passes over his face – shock, confusion, something that might be yearning.

I snatch my arm back from under his shirt. "You weren't breathing. You were so still. I thought you were—" The words come out in a shaky rush, adrenaline still coursing through me, speeding my heartbeat.

He shifts. His arm, firm around my waist, tightens. "I was asleep."

My eyes track between his. That was not sleep. Was it? "I couldn't find a pulse."

His gaze drops to my hand, the one that was under his shirt but is now on the bed near his. He looks up, dangerous glint to his dark eyes. "Want to check again?"

My breath catches in my throat. He's … inviting me to touch him?

Heat rises up my neck, warming my cheeks to a burn. I look at his mouth, so close to mine, then jerk to my feet, standing so quickly my sense of equilibrium is off and it takes a few moments to find my bearings.

He leans back against the headboard with an easy grace, one knee pulled up, arm draped over it, like he hasn't got a care in the world. "That's a no?"

Still feeling off-kilter, my hands come to my hips. It wouldn't be a no, ever, but I don't know what this – any of this – is. The casualness of his posture, the note of amusement in his tone … There is no hint of real emotions I can read; everything feels wrong.

I need to think. I turn, walk to the window, prop my hands on the sill and look out into the fading evening light. Then force my voice to match his lightness. "Ask me again some time."

He doesn't respond. I breathe out, try to relax my shoulders. The gardens are serene in the dim evening light, everything a shadow, a ghost, of its daytime self.

He's fine. He was sleeping.

I was spooked by whatever it was that happened last night and I overreacted.

"Want to tell me what you're doing in my room?"

I turn, bottom against the frame, hands still propped on the sill behind me. "I wanted to ask you something." Does he know about the snow globe? Was he there with me? "It's—" I stop, words caught in my throat. Last time I disclosed something I wasn't sure about, it ended up ruining his life. I scramble for something else to say. "The essay that's due before the Easter break ..." I start, but my gaze travels to an open jar of dried red berries on his bedside table. In all the drama, I hadn't noticed them. "What are those?"

He follows my gaze, then frowns, reaches for the jar and screws the lid on. "Hawthorn berries. An acquired taste." He leans in a fluid motion and shoves the jar in a drawer in his bedside table. "Which essay? There's a few due."

I drag my attention back to my excuse. "Keats. I thought you might need some help." JJ started English Lit halfway through the degree. He hadn't studied it before. He used to ask for my help all the time.

He shakes his head. "I'm almost done. Thanks though."

"I can read over it for you if you want."

"That's okay. Thanks though."

The words break stiff and awkward from our lips. There are many things JJ and I can be to each other, but study partners isn't one of them.

I will ask him – I have to – I just need to be subtle about it.

I drift over to his desk and pick up a book. *Gravitation: Theory and Practice*. Management. Science. So many interests I didn't know he had.

I flick through it as if I also have an interest. "I had this weird ... dream ... about you last night." It wasn't a dream, but I don't know how else to describe it. My gaze flicks to his, but all I see is mild curiosity.

"What happened?" he asks when I don't add anything further.

"We were in my snow globe." Even the memory makes me a little breathless. "The one that Harlow bought me when she and Aiden went to visit Firebird Coven. You remember it?"

"Sure."

He is waiting for me to get to the point. I am suddenly sure he doesn't know what I'm talking about. I turn, replace the book on the desk, the heaviness of his gaze prickling my skin.

I want to tell him everything. That he was there. That I don't know what it was but it wasn't a dream. That I know with dread certainty that something bad is going to happen. Something that involves him and me.

But what am I supposed to say?

You liked me like you used to. We danced and I've never been happier.

And I'm cautious now; more cautious than I was before Halloween. I'm not going to do harm by speaking too soon.

"Just one of those weird dreams that make no sense. Did Harlow end up getting something for you?"

"No." He shrugs. "There wasn't anything I wanted."

I suppress a grimace, remembering the conversation when we drove Aiden and Harlow to the airport. "A new life, wasn't it?"

He tenses, then gives me a forced half-smile. "Something like that." He stands in a liquid movement. "I better finish my essay."

He's tossing me out.

Because he can't stand my presence? Or for some other reason? I search his face, then exhale. "Let me know if you want me to read over it."

I head for the door. He stops me as I brush past with a hand on my wrist.

He studies my eyes, my face, then makes a disapproving tut. "You're doing it again."

It's not his problem anymore. *I'm* not his problem anymore.

I tug free and leave the room, closing the door behind me. Then rest against it, trying to breathe through my disappointment. That conversation, like all attempts these days, was an exercise in frustration.

I am not just frustrated. I am disappointed. Desolate.

I wanted last night to be real. I wanted here-and-now JJ to greet me like snow globe JJ did.

I wanted him to love me again.

4

ednesday night is two-for-one jugs for students. Cheap beer means the pub is filled with flannel shirts and ripped black jeans as far as the eye can see.

It's a warm evening for April and we're sitting at a table in an outside courtyard, surrounded by olive trees in wine barrels, herbs draping over the side. Emma is talking through plans for an upcoming Easter Moon electronic dance music gig she's trying to rope me into going to.

"The guy I really want to see is Easter Thursday. It may finish late – it probably will finish late – so I was thinking … I mean, I hate to invite myself—"

"Liar," Felix interjects. "You've got zero issues with inviting yourself."

"Shut up, Felix. I was thinking, if it's free, we could crash at Aiden and Harlow's."

Emma, Chloe and Felix have known Harlow for years, and they know she's now with Aiden. When JJ first turned up and I introduced him to my friends, I had to come up with some story about how we met; I couldn't say he was an on-the-run wizard my coven had taken pity on. We told them Harlow met Aiden through her work as a security guard – she's a demon hunter, so that's not too far from the truth – and they then introduced us.

"If it's free," she repeats.

I am not sure I even want to go to the gig, but I say, "Great idea."

At the same time, JJ says, "It's not."

I turn to eye him. Harlow left a key with me and Aiden left one with JJ. We both have carte blanche to use their place whenever we want while they're away, and he's never cared about anyone staying there before.

He meets my gaze and then turns to Emma. "Sorry. I've invited some friends over that night."

"Oh." I can see Emma's more-the-merrier brain working through that – she'd literally sleep twenty to a room – but she just smiles. "Of course. No problem."

"What friends?" I ask.

"You don't know them."

I think he's making it up, but I can't be sure.

"Seriously, not an issue," Emma says. "We'll just Uber home, Evie."

But I'm still watching JJ. "What friends?"

There's an uncomfortable silence.

Why am I even asking? He doesn't owe me an answer, and I'm not sure I want to hear it anyway.

His phone buzzes – timing that strikes me as convenient. He looks at the screen then excuses himself and moves to stand against the wall, not too far from our table, in the elegant slouch of a movie star.

I stare down at the table, shoulders hunched.

Felix leans close and talks low, so only I can hear. "You shouldn't push like that, Evie. He might want some privacy. It might be—"

I push my chair backwards with a screech and stand. I know what he's going to say. A date. A girlfriend even. "My round. Same again?"

Emma nods enthusiastically. I take that as an overall yes and head down the narrow side alley that leads to the bar at the front. Once there, I put in my order, pay and wait, hands fisted on the gnarled wood of the bar, trying to get a grip.

What else would I expect? It's been months since we've been in any way okay. If he's moved on, I have to accept it. Better still, get over him.

I repeat the words, but they stay just that – words without meaning or relevance; words that fail to penetrate in any way.

I suddenly long to be home and travelling fifty years in the future.

A guy rests his forearms on the bar next to me. Close. He's tilted towards me, angling for attention. I don't meet his eyes, but I can feel his gaze like a coat of grease.

"How's it going?" he says when he realises I'm not going to look.

I force out a tight half-smile without making eye contact. My order arrives and I grab the jug. I pass through the door into the alley to the courtyard. From a side door, the guy steps out in front of me. His hand goes to the jug. "I'll carry that for you."

"I've got it."

His hand remains on the jug; he's blocking my path. "I'm just trying to help."

Why are guys like this? Why don't they realise women don't like it when they don't listen? It's not gallant to provide 'assistance' that's neither needed nor desired.

"Thanks but I've got it." I inject steel into my tone.

His hand drops but he's still in my way. He smiles – he probably thinks it's charming. "What's your name? I've got to know."

I give him 'what the hell?' eyes and try to step around.

His smile fades to nothing and his hand lands on my arm. "Don't be like that."

I look pointedly at it, then back up at him.

His face, his mouth, turn mean. "You know, you're really stuck up."

Sometimes I wish I looked more like Harlow. She's tall and athletic and fierce-looking. Guys never mistakenly think she wants their attention. I look younger than I am. People take me as innocent, fragile. The blonde hair and blue eyes don't help. Sometimes I think I should change my look. Cut my hair off, dye it black. Swap to combat boots and ripped jeans. Add a few piercings for good measure.

But I am not the one who should have to change.

I am about to ask the guy to move again when his mouth opens and a strange sound escapes. A stream of pinkish-red runs down one side of his face, his neck, spreads to his chest and arms.

Shock ripples through me. For a moment, I think it's blood, and he must too because he stares down at himself in horror. But following the stream up to the balcony above, I see someone's Red Bull and vodka is more horizontal than vertical. It cascades down, landing square on the guy's head. Some bounces off, but despite our proximity, not a single drop lands on me.

Like I have some kind of shield around me.

I breathe in. The air carries the signature of magic. An energetic vibration that burns like fresh ozone – metallic, sharp, abrasive. My stomach shifts. I look past the guy, to where JJ is now in view, heading in this direction, hands in pockets, expression as calm and still as a pond on a windless day.

Something tightens in my chest, whispers through me, twists my stomach in knots.

He did that. For me. He didn't have to – he shouldn't have – but he did. It's a shot of dark gleeful joy.

The expression on the guy's face morphs from shock to anger. "Hey," he yells, looking up. The red stream comes to an end and a woman's face appears above the railing. She looks from her empty glass to the drenched man and the red puddle in confusion.

"Look what you—" He's cut off by a pair of divebombing wasps, and alternates between trying to protect himself and swatting at the attackers.

"Sorry!" the woman calls down.

Her face disappears from view; she's probably on her way down to apologise in person. I'm not sure he deserves it – especially not from her – and I don't want her facing his anger. "You should go home and wash that off," I say matter-of-factly as he continues to swear and swat.

He stares at me – face beetroot, eyes livid. I reach for some magic in case I have to add a little compulsion to get him to leave, but after a second of furious blinking and another round of batting, he shoves through the side door back inside.

JJ reaches me, expression flat, like he didn't just manufacture that whole situation.

"You didn't have to do that," I say.

He just shrugs.

I drop my gaze to his chest, looking for a tell-tale lump.

Wizards don't use spells like witches do. They store magic in their amulet, but I can't see that he's wearing his. I taught him the basics of how witches draw down and tether a batch of magic – no one told me I couldn't and Harlow was teaching Aiden. But I know witch magic – I know what it feels like – and that wasn't it.

"I thought you needed your amulet," I say as he takes the jug of beer from me.

He frowns slightly. "Not always." He turns and heads back to our table.

I catch up and walk at his side. "You never told me that."

He shrugs. "Didn't come up."

"But—"

"It's not a big deal, Everly." His tone is sharp.

We reach the table; this conversation is over for the moment. I watch as the others swap eyerolls at what they assume is another fight.

He puts the jug on the table but stands, hands on the back of his chair. "Something's come up. I have to go. Enjoy the rest of your evening."

The others send a stream of goodbyes in his direction and he walks away. I top up everyone's glasses then sit, but the mood's shifted. Everything's different when he's gone. Less, somehow.

I can tell the others are annoyed with me. They're assuming I've pestered him into leaving. But after a moment, Emma continues talking about the German DJ she wants to see the Thursday before Easter. The event runs over the whole of the Easter weekend – she wants us to decide on ticketing options. I don't – can't – take any of it in.

Yesterday, I found him without a pulse.

Now, he's using magic again. Without telling anyone. Without an amulet.

And there is still the mystery of the snow globe.

Something is going on. I try to work out what but all I have is a collection of observations that don't make sense. I can't form any coherent picture.

I pull my phone from my bag and bring up Harlow's number. They're in Thailand, where it's the middle of the afternoon. I don't want to involve them – Aiden worries about JJ as it is – but I need answers. I'll just have to tread carefully so they don't jump on the next plane home for what may be nothing.

I type a message. *Question for Aiden … Arguing with JJ and want to prove him wrong … Do wizards 100 per cent for sure need their amulets?*

I know now the answer is that they don't, but I need more information. Anything will be useful, and me arguing with JJ is not going to raise any alarm bells.

A reply comes through almost straight away. *Hi. Aiden says, and I quote, the perennial question …*

I frown. *Is that a yes or a no?*

He says lots have tried, few have succeeded.

But JJ has. *So it would be a big deal?*

Aiden says yes.

I knew it. I knew he was downplaying the whole thing.

A further message comes through. *Mongke experimented. He's one of the few who've been able to do it.*

Mongke is JJ's idol. According to him, the greatest wizard the world's ever known. And the one who owned JJ's amulet before him. So … that makes a weird kind of sense. I type back. *Thanks!*

Did you win?

Oh. The argument. *Of course.*

There's a pause this time before Harlow responds. *Go easy on him.*

I read it and frown. *Was that from Aiden?*

No.

Harlow's my sister; shouldn't she be on my side? *Sure. Thanks again.*

I pocket my phone and try to act like I'm engaged in the discussion, but really, I'm sifting through previous conversations, searching for any relevant fragment.

A memory pops and I jerk to rigid.

Mongke was the most powerful wizard of his time. Until one day, he'd had enough. He hid his amulet in a cave, where it stayed lost for a thousand years before JJ found it, and threw himself off a cliff.

5

I lie on my bed, snow globe cupped in my hands on my belly, its weight somehow comforting.

I need to get back. Here-and-now JJ might not want to talk to me – about his life, about anything – but snow globe JJ … he appeared for a reason.

The problem is, I don't know how to get back. Last time, JJ lit the castle up with candles and it was enough to attract my attention. But I've tried to repeat the process three times, travelling to the same day in the future, hoping to see a glow on the way back, but … nothing. And with nothing to stop me, I'm back in my body with no chance to leave the stream.

I lift the snow globe, shake it around. "Why won't you let me back in?"

I lower it again, watch the flakes re-settle. It's pretty, this snow globe. I asked for something nice, and Harlow came through. Real glass for the globe, real wood for the stand, fine delicate flakes. But it is nothing compared with the real thing.

The real thing.

The world that JJ created. And then I recall his words.

Not really any time or place.

How does one get to a time and place that does not exist?

I close my eyes and recall, in clear and visceral detail, everything about being there. The white gleam of the stone, the plaintive strains of violins, the smell of sweet violets in the cold air. The expression on JJ's face when he turned and saw me.

I call for a batch, almost levitating off the bed it's so potent, and going on instinct, cant a new spell:

Special place
Made for two
Blossom falls
For us too

I say it three times, absolutely and totally focused. I am so deep in my imagined snow globe sensations that when I open my eyes, it is no surprise that I am once again falling through soft blossom-snow.

I touch the ground, brush off stray flakes, and hurry into the castle.

"JJ?" My call echoes through its cavernous spaces. "Where are you?"

But there is no music to guide me this time and I run from room to room, feeling like I'm going around in circles. The thought that he might not be here hasn't occurred to me. He must be, mustn't he? He said he'd been waiting for me.

I round what feels like the hundredth door and literally bump into him, coming from the other direction.

It startles me – and him too evidently – because he steps back, dropping into a lunge and raising a sword, sideways fashion, to chest height. It's aimed at my heart.

I freeze. The only thing I can move is my eyes. When I look up, there is a red glint to his.

"JJ?" I squeeze out.

"Everly!" He stands upright, dropping the sword and planting its tip into stone pavers. A broad smile splashes across his face. "You found your way back. I knew you would."

I stare at the sword. My legs are jelly; they want to buckle.

He grimaces and steps forward, his hand landing on my upper arm. "Are you okay?"

I manage to nod.

"Sorry about that," he adds, releasing me now he knows I'm not going to topple over. "I didn't know it was you."

A frantic kind of laugh huffs out of me. "Who did you think it was?"

He shrugs, looks away.

My gaze returns to the shaft of heavy metal resting in his hand. "Is that the beheading sword?"

"Ah, yeah," he admits. He seems a little embarrassed. "I just ... like having it around."

The sword JJ stole from Owlscroft and took to confront the demon with at Halloween.

Six months after JJ fled to Melbourne, his uncle Jonathon finally tracked him down. Aiden and JJ thought he was still chasing the amulet, and that was bad enough, but then it turned out he was inhabited by a Red. The rarest and worst of the demons, who come to wreak as much violence and devastation as they can. There's only one way to kill them, and that's with the beheading sword. JJ attempted it but when he went to face Jonathon, the demon decided to jump to JJ instead. It's gone now, but he was inhabited for hours, and he's never been the same.

"Just a moment, I'll just ..." He heads for the side of the room and deposits the sword into some kind of tailor-made stand. "Better?"

"Much." I walk into the room, looking around. "What is this place?" I've never been here before but it's strangely familiar. And then I realise why. "It's Owlscroft, isn't it?"

"Yeah. A room in the cellars."

I turn, confused. "Why's it here in the castle?"

"It's up to me to decorate the place. It being my creation and all. So it's just what I'm feeling, you know?" He brings a hand to the back of his neck. "Anyways. What brings you back?"

I let out a sound. He's got to be kidding. "I need you to tell me what's going on."

"Going on?" He looks puzzled. "Like what?"

"Like …" I lift my hands in frustration. "Like you're using magic again."

"How else would I be here?"

He's right. I should have realised.

But I wasn't even talking about him, I was talking about the other JJ.

The other JJ. What does that even mean?

I cross my arms. "Who are you really?"

He frowns, head tilted. "You know who I am."

"But …" There is no doubt in my mind that this is JJ, but he's not the here-and-now version. "He doesn't know about you."

He laughs. "He knows about me. He *is* me."

I wave my hands in a wide circle. "Well, he doesn't know about this place."

The smile drops from his face. "You can't tell him."

"I haven't."

"I know. We wouldn't be here if you had. But don't."

"Why?"

He runs a hand through his hair, holds it off his forehead, then lets it go, paces a step, two. His hands land on his hip, he eyes me uncertainly. "He's trying to kill me."

My stomach drops. "But he is you."

"Yes."

A crushing weight steals my breath. "He wants to kill himself?"

"No. Of course not. But—" He breaks off, exhales heavily. "Look, promise me you won't tell him about this. If you do, he'll find a way to prevent me being here. This place won't exist. And I won't be able to help you when you need it."

There is something foreboding about his words. A chill sweeps over me; I'm cold enough to have to wrap my arms around myself. When I squeeze them close, I feel them press against my ribs. It reminds me that when we were dancing, his body was solid and warm.

What is this place even? I was so desperate to get here, to get answers, but it's hard to know what to ask. "I don't understand," I say. "I don't understand any of this."

He slides his hands into his pockets. "Don't worry, you will."

Again with the vague foreboding. I shoot him an unimpressed look. "You're just as exasperating as the real thing."

He laughs. As he looks at me, his expression softens. "I've missed you."

I've missed him too; I've been so cold in his absence, a numb empty cavity inside me that threatened to spread and swallow me whole.

But the timbre of his voice is warm and now I feel myself softening, melting like chocolate would in his palm. His eyes are the darkest brown on mine; the longer I look, the softer I get. All my feelings over the past six months rise to the fore. My grief and my loss. My regret and my guilt. My worry for him, and for myself.

I look across to the sword, securely nestled in its stand. He would never have gone to confront that Red if not for me. I told him Aiden was going to die. I thought we would go to Aiden and Harlow together, tell them to be careful, to come up with a new plan to evict the demon. I should have known JJ wouldn't go along with that, would try to stop it by himself some way. ""You must hate me for what happened. You wouldn't have been inhabited if it wasn't for me. It's my fault."

I've felt that truth constantly these long months, but I've never said it. Not to JJ, not to anyone. His face has gone blank. He probably doesn't know what to say.

"It's okay," I say. "I understand. I hate myself for it too." I'm a future witch; I'm supposed to stop bad things from happening, not make them happen.

"No, Everly. You've got it wrong." He unfreezes and steps forward, hands coming to cup my upper arms. "I could never hate you."

"I see the way you look at me."

"Do you?" he responds slowly. It is not hate I see in his eyes. He runs his hands down my arms. "What happened wasn't your fault. I asked you to look; you told me what you saw. How could I blame you for that?"

"I got it wrong." It was night; dark. Everything was distorted by the presence of the demon. It was hard to work out what was going on. All I could see was two guys face down on the ground. I thought Aiden was going to die trying to evict the demon.

He shakes his head. "It wasn't wrong. You just didn't understand what you were seeing."

His denial is a balm to my soul, but in the end, it doesn't matter. What happened, my fault or not, had a terrible effect on him. "You're still so … angry." It's not the right word – JJ's state goes well beyond anger – but it's a start.

"Not with you."

"Who then?" I look at him, unblinking, trying to work it out. "The demon," I say eventually.

He makes a funny sound and turns away, pushing a hand through his hair. "It would be easy to blame the demon for everything. But it chose me. It chose to inhabit me, and I let it. And then I couldn't get rid of it. I wasn't strong enough."

He blames himself for being inhabited? For not being able to evict it from himself? That's ridiculous. "It was a Red. No one is strong enough."

"Aiden was," he counters immediately.

"He didn't do it alone. He had Harlow. And she had your amulet."

He just shrugs, like I've missed the point.

I try to imagine having something that evil inside you; knowing that it's evil but not being able to fight it. Not even being able to choose to try to fight it. But it's no reflection on JJ, except that he's powerful enough to interest a Red in the first place.

"I wish I hadn't said anything. I wish the whole thing had never happened." My voice is small, I don't know what else to say.

His gaze darts fast and sure to mine. "You know what? I'm glad you told me what you saw. I wouldn't change what happened. The way things worked out, Aiden and Harlow evicted the demon and they're alive. Any other course of action might not have had the same result."

My eyes smart; I can't find a single word to say in response. I've never thought of it like that. Against all odds, Harlow and Aiden came out the other side, not only in one piece but stronger than ever.

For JJ though, the repercussions have not been so positive.

I feel the pull of my here-and-now self, tugging at me. It's subtle but it will grow. I don't have long. I shake my head to clear it. We've got distracted and there's so much more I need to know. "I've got to go, but I'll come back."

He shakes his head. "Don't."

My mouth opens, a huff of breath comes out.

"It takes a lot of energy to maintain this place. I don't want to run out too soon. Only come back when you need me."

Come back when I need him? I need him now.

My eyes snap open. I am back in my bed, staring at the ceiling.

Whatever I was expecting to learn tonight, it wasn't that one of the JJs is trying to kill the other. Why are there two of them? Which one am I supposed to trust?

I somehow know less than before I returned to the snow globe.

And I still don't understand what I'm supposed to do.

6

When I get to the courtyard, JJ's the only one there. He's sitting on the bench, legs crossed at the ankle in front of him, arms along the back of the seat. His eyes are closed, his head is tipped up. He looks … peaceful.

His eyes open and his face tilts towards me. I see him register that we are alone. We are never alone anymore; he avoids it. I half-expect him to launch to his feet, come out with some excuse to leave, but he doesn't.

Still, the atmosphere is instantly tense. Nothing like the ease I feel with snow globe JJ.

Who I shouldn't even be thinking about right now – this JJ can't know about him. Or he'll kill him. However that works.

Still, I'd like the option of keeping the snow globe version around. Not that either of them tells me anything useful. I'm going to do my own digging.

I deposit my bag at the other end of the bench, then walk around the courtyard, hunting for Romeo but he's nowhere in sight. I glance quickly towards the entry passage to check no one's there, then turn. "I asked Aiden about whether wizards can do magic without an amulet."

His jaw clenches, then releases. "What did he say?" He asks it casually but I pick out the sharp steel under the surface.

"That a lot of wizards would like that ability but it mostly doesn't work."

He shrugs, the movement lithe, and looks away. His face is absolutely expressionless. "Like I said."

That's not quite true. He downplayed how rare it was; how difficult to acquire. And if he's been working for it, if there's some reason he needs magic again … "I don't get why you wouldn't just use your amulet. It's yours."

When JJ found it, he was too young to learn to use it properly. He shouldn't have been able to even find it, but he's too powerful for his own good. Aiden convinced him to lock it up in a bank vault until he was ready. Which should have been when he turned twenty a couple of months ago, but he's shown no interest in retrieving it from its safe storage.

His arms come across his chest. "Have you forgotten how I lost my mother and father?"

My heart squeezes. "Of course not." His parents were murdered when he was 12. A much-feared Icelandic wizard, Torben, came for his father's amulet and ended up killing them both. JJ was at soccer practice or he might have ended up the same way. If Torben, or any other wizard, knew JJ had found Mongke's amulet, if he started using it and it came to anyone's attention, he'd be targeted. Relentlessly. "But you and Aiden were talking about how you could protect yourself."

The plan was, once JJ came of age, he'd use much of the power of the amulet as a shield to allow him to stay under the radar. If he's careful, and a little lucky, no wizard will ever know he has it.

But that was before Halloween.

"You couldn't wait to turn twenty," I say softly. "You were so keen to start."

He shrugs again. "I was a fool." The bitterness in his tone makes me jerk. He sees it, looks away. "It's not worth the risk," he adds.

"So why don't you just get another amulet? Like Aiden's." Aiden deliberately chose an average amulet; he's not interested in playing the wizard amulet death game. "Why work so hard on being able to use magic without an amulet?"

He makes a clicking sound, a humourless wry smile touching his lips. "Everly."

"I'm just trying to understand."

"There's nothing *to* understand."

I know he's lying. There's a lot more to it, but he's not going to tell me what.

At least we're talking. The sad truth is that this is the most time we've spent together and the most in-depth conversation we've had in six months.

I decide to drop it. For the moment. This fragile truce we now have between us, I don't want to ruin it.

I look around for Romeo again but he's still MIA. The busy life of a small, black bird. I don't want him to miss out. I retrieve my sandwich from my bag, break off a chunk and walk back to Juliet, leaving it on her shoulder.

I turn back to JJ. "If you—" I suck in a sharp breath at the hunger in his unwavering eyes. I cannot think. At all. He looks away and I breathe out. After a moment, when I can function, I sit at the other end of the bench. "Last night. You said you'd invited people over Easter Thursday ..." My words fail me. This is hard. "Felix pointed out that you might ..." I swivel to face him, draw my knee up in front of me, bite my lip. He's watching me closely. "If you start seeing someone, can you just tell me?"

His eyes are burning coals on mine. His mouth tightens, but he doesn't say anything.

"If that's too ... awkward, can you say something to one of the others?" They'll tell me. They might hate bringing it up, but they'll make sure I'm prepared. "I'd prefer to know."

He looks at his hands.

I drop my chin to my knee, wishing I knew what he was thinking. "I know I'm not supposed to care anymore. I'm trying."

There is a long silence, broken only by the sound of some small creature rustling in the leaves across the courtyard. He sits with absolute stillness, face like stone.

"I'm not seeing anyone." His words are quiet, unremarkable, but I almost tremble with relief. Then, with a slight curve of his lips and a quick glance in my direction, he says, "I'm trying, too."

It takes a moment for that to land, but when it does, I'm hit with a maelstrom of emotions I can't place. I stand without meaning to.

How have we ended up like this? I don't even know. It's been six months and we haven't talked properly about any of it. That's got to change. "I know it won't change anything but I want you to know I'm sorry for everything that happened."

His head jerks back. "You don't have anything to apologise for."

It's what snow globe JJ said, and while it's nice to hear and even more tempting to believe, it doesn't fix anything. "Yes, I do. Because what happened at Halloween changed you. And it changed us. You said you don't blame me—"

"I don't."

I raise my hands, palms up. "Then why are things like this? Why aren't we together?"

He has no answer for that. My frustration, my distress mount. "Why won't you tell me what's wrong? Why won't you let me help?"

His expression closes off, goes inscrutably distant. He looks away. "Because you can't help."

"Chalice, JJ!" The words rip out of me. "How do you think that makes me feel? If you don't blame me, let me apologise. For my sake, if not yours. Then say 'Everly, I forgive you.' So I don't have to feel like this."

His gaze shifts over my face, taking in the wet on my cheeks. Shock mixes with concern in his eyes. He stands but appears unsure what to say. Fists clenched, I turn and stalk across the courtyard.

I wipe roughly across my face, a sound of frustration breaking free. I will the stupid tears away, wishing again I were more like Harlow – I can't see her breaking down like this.

I hear a heavy exhale behind me, then footsteps. An arm snakes around my collar bone, holding me as his energy, his nearness, the heat of his skin, flow through me, warm and comforting as the sun.

His breath is against my ear, the back of my neck. My breath comes out in a rush and my head tilts to the side, as if to give him better access. "Everly, I forgive you." His voice is deep, low.

Just because I asked for those words doesn't mean I don't feel them in my bones. Something that's been knotted tight inside me loosens, I swell with it, and all of me feels softer, less brittle.

I turn but I don't want to leave the circle of his arms. Our fronts are not touching but they almost are, and having him close like this is heaven. I latch on to the back of his waist; I'll keep him here if I have to. He looks down, gaze raking over my face. His mouth skews, and his thumbs sweep gently under my eyes. Then his hands skim my arms, collecting mine on the way. He doesn't let them go; they hang in the space at our sides. For this one moment in time, it's all good between us.

"I should have said something sooner. I didn't know you felt like this."

We've been stuck in our own hell. Assuming the worst. Of each other. Of ourselves. I vow we will not go back to that. Whatever happens from here, we are in it together. "What you did at Halloween … It was really brave."

His eyes narrow, mouth skewing again. "It was stupid."

I squeeze his hands, shake my head. "Brave." He was willing to die to save Aiden and Harlow.

"It didn't work."

I feed his own logic back to him. "The Red was evicted; Aiden and Harlow are alive and well. Who knows how things might have played out if you hadn't done what you did?"

A strange expression crosses his face.

"You can't compare yourself to Aiden." I know he thinks Aiden is impossible to live up to, that he doesn't experience the same struggles as JJ – or just overrides them with pure strength of will. But Aiden's older – by the time Halloween arrived, he'd had time to think about what kind of wizard he wanted to be. "You hadn't even reached maturity when it happened. And he couldn't have got rid of the Red without Harlow. Or your amulet."

His eyes move between mine. I know I'm drawing on what I learned from snow globe JJ, that it's perhaps a risk to do so, but I can't leave him beating up on himself. And if he should have realised how I was feeling, the same could be said for me.

"You can't blame yourself for being inhabited. No one can stop a Red. And you're probably the only person in the whole history of the world who was possessed by a Red demon for any length of time and didn't hurt anyone."

His mouth skews again. "I wanted to."

"*The Red* wanted you to. But you didn't. And that's amazing."

He blows out a breath. "You give me too much credit."

I shake my head fiercely, look him in the eye so he knows I'm completely serious about what I just said. And he finally does what I've been waiting for, for what seems like an eternity. He steps closer and wraps me in his arms, holding me close. My arms come up around him.

We were so close in many ways before Halloween but not physically. Not that we were uncomfortable around each other, but we didn't hold each other like this. Like there wasn't a hurricane in the world strong enough to tear us apart.

I think it was me. When I met him, my feelings were so sudden and so big … Guys are always interested in me – until they get to know me, realise I'm more than blonde hair and blue eyes, and the more is kind of strange and intense. I've never been much interested in return; not like the plummet from the heavens that was my instant overwhelming feelings for JJ.

It's not that I didn't want something to happen between us – I knew it would – I just needed a little more time. I wanted a chance to enjoy it, not have the force of my desire body-slam me to the ground.

I don't need time any more. There is nothing I want more than this.

I hear violins.

It's so fitting it take me a moment to realise the sound is coming from the recital venue. A rehearsal.

And then I recognise the tune. A wave of gooseflesh sweeps over me. I draw back a little, eyes wide.

A confused smile breaks over JJ's face. "What?"

This is the waltz we danced to in the snow globe.

He has no idea. He has no idea we've already danced to this.

As the music plays, and I look up at him, a deep and overwhelming longing builds in me. I want to feel like I did then. Free, happy, in love. The words are out before I know it. "Dance with me."

He gives me a puzzled half-smile, draws back a little. "I don't dance. Two left feet."

But in his eyes, I see the same yearning I feel. I assume the position, left hand on his shoulder, right hand out, waiting for him to take it. "Please?"

He lets out a huff.

I move his hand to my waist. He squeezes, but he's standing firm, resisting my efforts to move him. "It's a no. Even for you."

"Come on," I say, taking his other hand in mine and attempting to move him. "You're a great dancer."

"Seriously, Everly. Over my dead body."

I go still; I go blank. Everything in the courtyard disappears.

My hands fall to my sides. I can do nothing but stare at him as the skin around his eyes and mouth tightens, and his expression changes from good humour to concern to something like suspicion.

A tingling sensation travels from the base of my spine to crawl over my scalp, bringing me back to life. I draw in a sharp breath. "What did you just say?" My voice is high and thready.

Emma and Chloe walk into the courtyard. They pull up when they see us – standing so close, staring so intently at each other.

Without looking at anyone, I go to the bench, collect my bag and sling it over my shoulder. "I've just remembered I've got a medieval poetry essay due tomorrow. I haven't even started."

None of them take that class; none of them can call me out on my lie.

I exit the courtyard and am halfway to Melbourne Central when I stop abruptly.

The JJ in the snow globe … He's dead.

7

I rush home, frantic.

The more I think about it, the more I know I'm right. Snow globe JJ – he's a ghost from the future. He's trapped himself in the castle, rather than … voyaging on, so I can make sure he doesn't die.

It explains everything.

He's already lived through this afternoon; he knows what just happened in the courtyard. That's why that music was playing when I first arrived in the castle, why he asked me to dance. He was sending me a message I wouldn't – couldn't – miss when it happened in the present.

Over my dead body.

It *was* over his dead body.

But he's not dead yet.

I'm going back to the snow globe. He said not to return until I needed him, but isn't that now? What could be more important than asking him when and how he dies, so I can stop it from happening?

It's still day time but there's no one at home and I'm not waiting until tonight.

I use the same technique to get back as last time. I fall through blossom-snow, touch down and run into the castle, searching from room to room. When I find him, he's lying on his bed, in a room that looks exactly like the one he has at Owlscroft.

He's dead again. Like he was that afternoon last week when I went to see if he knew anything about this place. I shake him, expecting to go through the same routine but he wakes immediately. I step back, and he rises in the bed, rubbing at his eyes.

"You're dead," I say, crossing my arms. "And no, I don't want to check again."

He yawns, back of his hand across his mouth. "Good afternoon to you too."

"Why didn't you tell me you're dead?"

He stretches, then rubs at the back of his neck. "Relax. It's only temporary."

Only temporary? I want to shake him again. I am not in the mood for this. "You need to start talking. When. Where. How. Why. Tell me everything there is to know so I can make sure it doesn't happen."

He scans my face, then taps the bed next to him. "Come. Sit down."

"I don't want to sit down. Why didn't you tell me you die?"

He shrugs. "We all die, Everly."

Understanding dawns slower than it should have. "You're not going to tell me, are you? No matter what I ask, you're not going to tell me anything useful."

"You more than anyone know how dangerous it can be to say too much about the future."

That's a stab to the chest I didn't need right now. "How can I prevent your death if I don't know anything about it?"

He looks at me as though I'm the one who doesn't get it. "That's not why I'm here."

I blink at him. "Then why did you make this place?" My frustration rises. "Why did you get me to come here? What are you trying to achieve?"

He nods, slow and serious, thinking it over. "That's actually a very good question."

My face screws up as I shout, "You don't know?"

He shrugs. "You know what time's like. Change one thing, change everything. Things get confusing."

Chalice! I don't have time for this. "You have to give me something. Even if it's just a date."

"I can't."

"Yes you can. You have to."

He shakes his head. "I can't. He'll know. About this." He tilts his chin to indicate the room.

His words are like ice against my skin. "He's not going to know."

"Everly. Of course he will."

"I won't tell him."

"He'll know," he insists.

What does that mean? It's some horrifically gory death and I'll burst into tears the second I see him? I want to throw something. "You have to talk. Seriously. I need your help, and you need mine."

He leans back against the bedhead. "You don't need me to tell you anything."

I tilt my head back and groan. That's simply not true. I have no idea what's going on. All I have is my rapidly growing and desperate sense of impending doom.

I pace the room. All he gives me are obtuse, useless fragments that don't help. Why are we in this room this time? It's his choice; he said that last time – the decor's up to him. So it's deliberate that we're in here. My first visit, we danced and then it happened in real life. This is the opposite – it's something that's already happened and is now happening in the snow globe. But why? Did I miss something first time?

I mimic my movements of last Tuesday evening. I head to the bedside table, picking up the small stack of books. The gravitation book I've seen already, and another one. Ancient, judging by the binding. I open it, handling it carefully. Inside is incredibly thin, textured paper, coloured with age and covered in elegant Chinese characters. A spike of adrenaline releases through my gut. I know what this is. What it must be. JJ's described it to me; his father brought it home after one expedition and JJ used it to find the amulet. Mongke's diary.

I hear JJ get to his feet behind me.

"What are you looking at?" He sounds protective, like he doesn't want me to look at it. Even though he put it here. I can't read it without a translate spell and I don't have time anyway. I deposit it back where I found it. Then crouch and open the small door of the bedside table. Inside is the bottle of hawthorn berries.

I draw it out and stand to face him. My hands are quick as I twist off the lid, reach in and pop one in my mouth. I haven't got long here; I need something to happen. Even if I have to make it happen.

He's frowning. Good. And he's right, it's an acquired taste. But I chew and swallow, and then pop another two into my mouth.

"Hey," he says sharply. "Cut that out."

"Why? Are they going to kill me?" I shove another one in my mouth, then another.

He moves so fast I almost choke, and I just manage to turn before he gets to the jar. I hold it out in front of me. His chest is solid against my back, arms reaching around, trying to grab it. He's going to succeed before too long. I duck under an arm but he moves with me and now we're chest to chest.

Pulse racing, breathing fast, I fling my arm out behind me … but he's got a longer reach. He moves across me and grabs the bottle, lifting it high. One arm wrapped around his waist for balance, squashed against him, I jump and try to grab it back, but he's too tall.

I give up. And wrap my arms around his neck instead.

Is this part of my plan? I have no idea.

There's a hiss of indrawn breath. He goes still as a stone. Then throws the jar across the room.

An arm winds around me, a hand comes to my jaw. I catch a glimpse of his eyes, dark and smoky with desire, then his head ducks and he kisses me.

I thread my fingers through his hair and kiss him back. Pleasure sweeps through me, making my heart race and my blood turn to hot liquid gold. The room spins. I bloom with light, this snow globe body as real as anything can be.

I feel the tug but I cling to him, still holding his head close, wanting the kiss to go on forever.

But it can't. The pull is building.

He releases me, stumbles back. His gaze is still on my mouth, his colour high, breath uneven. He lets out a groan and takes my mouth in another kiss.

Too quickly he tries to draw back again, but I don't let him. My hands grip at his arms, as if I can anchor myself here. How is it time to go again? I've learned nothing. I'm going to lose him.

"You can't die," I say. "I can't do without you."

His gaze softens. He raises a hand to my cheek. "Why do you think I'm doing all this?"

I'm wrenched away. "I'm not going to let you die," I shout.

"I know." I hear the faint reply before I'm in my bed once more.

I sit upright, fingers pressed to tingling lips.

Our first kiss, but does it even count if he isn't alive?

8

"*P*erhaps you should talk to Aunt Bernie."

This is the third day I haven't turned up to class or work or coven. I told Mum I'm buried under essays and personal issues, and I just need a break. She's been great but she's starting to worry.

The downside of living at home is that Mum is not only a member of the Coven Council but the hypervigilant type. This used to be directed at Harlow – the OG problem child. She was wild as a teenager and can still be prickly, but her heart is solid gold. She's the most steadfast and honourable person I know.

Me, on the other hand … I'm the one everyone thinks is an angel. Maybe it was having Harlow as an older sister – I felt I had to be twice as good to compensate. But that all changed at Halloween anyway. The same time Harlow got her shit together, I lost mine completely, and since then, Mum's turned her eagle eyes on me.

"I don't need to talk to her."

She hovers nervously, hands wringing. I'm curled up on the couch, waiting for her to leave for work so I can get back to what I need to do.

"But if you feel this … unwell …"

Witches don't often get sick – some weird side-effect of working with magic – but I haven't slept beyond a snatched hour here or there in three days and my exhaustion must be showing. "I'm fine, Mum. Really. I just need to rest."

To find when JJ dies I've been travelling to the future non-stop looking for the usual markers, trying to pinpoint the time, the place, the circumstances. But there's so much pain and fear out there and I don't even have a specific day to help me. I'm searching for a JJ-shaped needle in a Melbourne-sized haystack, and I can't find him.

This is what I do. I identify bad things so that they can be stopped. But now there's this one specific bad thing and I can't find it.

I would know him from a single hair on his head, so why can't I find him by the light of his soul?

All I can do is pray it's not today and keep looking.

"We need to have a serious talk with Bernadette. Reassess your load." Mum presses her lips together, fighting her urge to say more.

I probably look as hollow as I feel. I have pushed myself hard; I'm reaching my limits. My fatigue is more than physical, more than mental. My very soul is tired and aching. "I'm getting there. Once I get my work done, I'll feel better. And it's the last week of term; I can rest next week."

There's a knock at the front door. After another concerned look in my direction, she disappears to answer it. I slump down further on the couch, phone in hand, staring at Aiden's number, mulling over for the hundredth time whether to contact him.

If I tell him JJ's in danger, he'll fly back immediately. Take over.

And I don't have any details to share; I don't know how to explain what I know. If I mention snow globe JJ, he'll disappear for good. What if I still need him? He said I would.

I hear Mum laugh. Someone from the coven, finally having worked out what I do in my free time? No. If that was true, she wouldn't be laughing.

Then JJ is standing under the arch to the room, feet in socks, black backpack over a shoulder, plastic bag at his side.

My stomach drops out the bottom. We've kissed.

Or have we?

"I'll get going. I'll be home after lunch." Mum is much happier now I've got company.

JJ pulls a huge plastic cup and an oversized straw from the bag. "Delivery." It's bubble tea – brightly coloured liquid with chunks of jelly. "Peach green tea, double glass jelly, no pearls."

My favourite. I honestly didn't think anything could make me smile today. "Thank you."

He deposits the drink on the coffee table in front of me, and drops onto the other end of the couch, black backpack falling to the ground.

I lean and retrieve this treasured gift. Then sit, knees and drink against my chest, and sip. It's cold and sweet and perfect.

He swivels so one knee is cocked against the back of the couch and the other leg is out in front of him. For a long moment, we just look at each other. I see him take in my hair, cascading around my shoulders in a wild mass. I haven't brushed it since … I don't know how long … but JJ's looking at it like it's spun gold. For just a moment, I catch the naked yearning on his face.

My cheeks heat. My gaze drops to his lips.

We haven't kissed. I've kissed him, but he hasn't kissed me. I don't know how that works, but it makes for a weird dynamic.

The front door clicks closed behind Mum.

"You haven't been in class."

I shoot him a quick look then drop my head to take another sip, push the jelly in my drink around with my straw.

Am I going to tell him?

Would he want to know?

What can I say?

You're going to die soon. I don't know how, where or when.

That wouldn't be fair. "I haven't been feeling well."

His mouth skews. "What kind of not well?"

"The kind I don't want to talk about." My tone is sharp and dismissive and he flinches. I make it gentler. "I'm dealing with it." Hopefully that is true. I cannot lose him. "You came to check on me."

"Yes." He watches me sip my drink, eyes fixed on my mouth. "Are you okay?"

I don't know what to say. I nod without meeting his gaze.

"I keep thinking about the other day. In the courtyard. I shouldn't have said no. I should have just …"

He thinks that's what this is? That my feelings were hurt by his refusal to dance with me? I almost laugh. I have much bigger problems. *We* have much bigger problems. "It's not that."

I can see the question in his dark eyes.

"Not just that," I amend.

The air is ripe with tension. I know he knows there's more to it, but he doesn't press. He's got secrets of his own. I take another sip and change the subject. "Are you really applying for jobs?"

My insides tighten again at the thought of our abandoned life. We had plans. JJ's father was a treasure hunter, and he was going to take up the mantle, search the globe for magical artefacts. He'd already made a start; he found Mongke's amulet. I was going to join him, explore the world, work on my poetry.

"Yes." He says it quietly but unapologetically.

"What about …" I clench my teeth so hard, it's almost painful. What about us? "What about all those treasures waiting to be found?"

A slight frown forms between his brows. "Some things should stay buried."

"Think of all the good they could do."

"Think of all the bad they could do."

But we always knew they had that potential. We would have taken care, thought long and hard about what we did with what we found. We wouldn't have let anything fall into the wrong hands.

I stir my drink with my straw, make myself say something I know is going to hurt. "So you're leaving."

He takes a while to formulate a response, then gives a jerky nod. "I need to move on. I'm going to find a job and …" He breaks off, looks away.

"Pretend to be … normal?" The word feels strange in my mouth.

"Something like that."

"No magic? Ever?" Could he be happy without magic? What will happen to all that power when he signs up for a 9 to 5?

"That's the plan." He looks away, then back again. His dark eyes search mine. "You could do the same."

With him? Is that what he's asking? I look down at the peachy-green liquid. Try to mentally catch up with him. To where he is, having run ahead and outgrown me and our plans. "I can't leave Owlscroft."

"You were going to."

While we travelled. Not permanently. "I'm an Owlscroft Coven witch. It's who I am. I can't leave it behind."

His expression hardens. "It's not who you are. They can't ask you to stay."

"They don't. They don't have to."

"Then that's your choice. But it's not mine."

There are momentary spots of black in my vision, then everything is perfectly, blindingly clear. I jolt. My drink comes down on the table with a rough splosh. "You're breaking up with me. That's why you're here."

He lets out a long breath. "I'm not … Everly, we're not—"

"Yes we are," I say fiercely. We were – we are – together. Our bond is not always easy, but it's unbreakable. Regret rises, swift and sharp, over all the things that haven't – won't, if he gets his way – happen. If I could go back now, I would do it all with him.

"Everly—" His tone is gentle; he's trying to be kind.

Something snaps inside me. I have feelings but I don't need them handled with kid gloves. "You can break up with me but I'm not breaking up with you."

"I should have done this earlier. I didn't know you felt like this."

The words burrow into my heart; dig and claw painfully. "You feel it too," I insist. He doesn't deny it, and something in me eases. "If you want me to accept this is over, you're going to have to make me believe that you don't have feelings for me. But you can't, can you?"

His gaze traces the shape of my lips. "It doesn't matter how I feel."

"Of course it does! What else matters?"

"Who I am now." His face is marble; his tone would be dead if it were any flatter. "I'm never going to be who I was."

"I know. I don't care."

"You would. You would if you knew." He throws the words back at me. "I'm nothing you could want." The words are less than a whisper.

How can he say that? "You're everything I want."

The silence lasts for long seconds. My breath catches. I'm mesmerised; I can't look away. My gaze traces his pale skin and the dark glint of his eyes; his sharp, elegant features; his clear and pure beauty that cuts like a diamond.

"Don't freak out." Eyes locked on his, I crawl over the couch to him, lean over until I'm flush against him. My hands come to his shoulders. His are brands on my hips.

His mouth is skewed in confusion, but I don't give him time to work it out. I place my mouth on his; a gentle press that sends all the butterflies in the world on a mad flight in my belly.

I dip my head, taste the warm skin of his neck. He smells good. Fresh as rain with a bite of pepper. The feel of his fingers tightening steals my breath. When I draw back, his lips are still a little parted; there's a hint of vulnerability in his eyes. Then he curls a hand around my neck and pulls me forward. When our mouths meet again, it's nothing like the first gentle press. Pleasure flowers across every inch of my skin. I tremble with the sudden force of desire that rises and spreads through me like hot, dark honey.

Bitter-sweet and desperate. It is everything and more – everything from the past we share, everything from the future we won't have. It's every secret we've shared. Every adventure we'll never take. Every time we've found each other across a room and known we're home.

When I finally pull back, my heart is staccato, my breath uneven. "That," I say, "was our first kiss."

A few moments while he drags in oxygen, gaze locked on mine, hands still firm on my body. Then he is standing, leaving me alone sprawled on the couch, looking down at me, eyes wild, colour high. "It shouldn't have happened."

"You can't take it back."

His jaw sets. He looks furious – not with me, with himself. "I wasn't joking. What I said—" He breaks off, grabs his backpack and slings it over his shoulder. I think he's about to leave, but he crouches, and cups my jaw. "Take care of yourself." He issues it like a command, then kisses me, almost roughly, on the lips, before walking out.

He's wrong. That was always meant to happen. And now it has.

9

I need help and I know who to ask.

I see my cousin Amelia at coven, but I don't want to approach her there. I don't want to risk anyone overhearing our conversation, and I don't want her thinking about coven rules. But she's a graduate student with a thesis to work on; she probably won't be taking the Easter break like us undergrads. I text her and ask if she can meet me in the courtyard.

I turn up early, even though I know Meels will be exactly on time. Not a minute early; not a minute late. I've brought a snack for Romeo. I call for him, wondering if he'll come even though it's not my usual time and I'm not with my usual crowd.

He swoops in and my heart lifts. He settles on a branch and I approach slowly, talking sweet to him. I don't have anything for him to eat, but I stick my hand up then grin and brace when he lands and hops around.

He flies off when Amelia enters – at ten on the dot – in a long buttoned floral dress and brown lace-up boots. She has a vintage-looking brown leather doctor's bag slung over one shoulder, a couple of takeaway cups in her hands, and a smile on her face.

Amelia's the calmest person I know. Nothing phases her. Shit can be going awry all over the place, but to her, it's all good. She comes straight for me, hazel eyes sparkling, and despite the cups, manages to envelope me in a quick hug. "Vanilla pecan almond chai," she says, passing me one.

I immediately feel better – whether it's the chai, the hug or the bountiful positive vibes, I'm not sure.

"How did I not know about this place?" She sips her drink, looking around, then groans. "Thank Chalice for chai. We should do this more often."

"We should," I agree, with a twinge of guilt. I wish I'd arranged this as a random cousin catch up rather than a desperate plea for help. My mouth screws up. "Meels, I need to ask you to do something for me."

She takes in my face and her eyes fill with empathy. "What is it? Lay it on me."

"I wish I didn't have to …" I start.

She just smiles. "It's okay, Evie. I'm used to it." Chance magic is in high demand. It's just so effective. Especially when the witch in question is as talented as Amelia.

"I … I probably shouldn't even be asking. It's why I wanted to meet you here, away from coven, because …"

"It's not exactly something Aunt Bernie would approve of?" There's a wry smile on her face.

"No. But I just don't know what else to do."

She raises her brows in that encouraging manner. And I try to tell her what the problem is, but nothing comes out of my mouth. I bring the cup up instead, with fingers I now realise are shaking. I'm hoping a second shot of sweet, hot spice will offer the same sense of comfort as the first, but I overshoot and burn myself.

A sound escapes me, my hand comes to my mouth. "Ouch."

Amelia is there a second later, arm around my shoulder. "Don't worry, honey. We're going to sort this out. What's going on?"

I can't answer. I just look at her.

"Did you see something?" she prompts.

"Not exactly." How can I explain without revealing anything about the snow globe? "But kind of." I take a deep breath, hold it, then release it. It's like saying it will make it real. "It's JJ. He …" I look away. "He's going to die."

She draws in a sharp breath, cup held high and still, eyes wide. Her shock reverberates through me. It's as bad as I thought.

"Okay. Okay." She paces back and forth, attempting to calm herself. "We're not going to let that happen. Obviously. Tell me everything and we'll work out what to do."

Snow globe JJ didn't say I couldn't tell someone like Amelia, but I don't want to risk it. "I can't say much. I …" I raise my hands. "I don't know much. But I'm pretty sure it's going to happen soon." Snow globe JJ said he can't maintain that space for long, and why would he come early?

She narrows her eyes. "You want me to cast a spell that sends JJ's chance of dying down to zero? I'd need specific details to be able to do that."

"I know." I have nowhere near Amelia's skill with chance magic but I do know how it works. "That's not what I was going to ask. I need to know when and how it happens. I've been scouring the future but I can't find it. That's what I'm hoping you can help with."

Her gaze is searching. "You haven't seen it?"

I can see her other question – if I haven't seen it, how do I even know about it? I can't answer so I just shake my head. "I know it's against the rules. I don't want to make things difficult between you and Avery."

Avery is Amelia's twin. She's now part of the Coven Council, the youngest, newest member.

"Everyone breaks them a little. And believe me, Avery's no saint." Amelia blows a breath out. "Besides, she wouldn't interfere with an attempt to save JJ. None of them would." She bites her lip, tilts her head. "You don't want to tell Aunt Bernie? Get the coven on board?"

"Maybe." I'll do whatever I need to keep JJ alive, but at the moment, I wouldn't know what to say. "Once I know what's going to happen … if I can't stop it myself, I'll get help."

"Okay. Fair enough." She sips thoughtfully. "Does he know?"

"No." I turn away, hands on hips. "I need to know what I'm dealing with before I say or do anything."

"And when you do?"

I look at Juliet, shoulders slumping. "I don't know. Once I've said those words, I can't take them back. They're out there, and they change everything. What if I tell him and it makes him do the very thing that causes it? I don't want to change the future in ways I come to regret."

Her hazel eyes fill with empathy. She knows what happened at Halloween. "Yeah, I get that. Well, let's get this spell cast so you can find out what you want to know."

That's exactly what I need. "Thanks, Amelia."

She closes her eyes, concentrates on tethering some magic. Then opens them again. "Argh. Patchy batch. Horrible."

"You want magic? I'll get you some." I close my eyes, call for it, and it descends in a rush, twining around me. I push it gently in her direction.

I hear her intake of breath. "Wow. Is it always so willing for you?"

"Yes," I acknowledge.

"Lucky witch." She starts to cant.

<blockquote>
Change it up
Change the chance
Let Everly see
That which she seeks
</blockquote>

I keep sending magic to her while she repeats the spell three times for maximum effect.

When I open my eyes, she's looking at me. "Thank you," I say. "I owe you. Anything."

She tilts her head. "I might hold you to that."

I wrinkle my nose. "Except your stats assignments. You're on your own with those."

She shakes her head in mock consternation. "Everyone's always hating on stats." She's trying to appear upbeat but I can see her under-lying concern. "Keep me up to date."

I nod. "I will."

~

I DON'T WANT to watch him die, but what choice do I have?

I go straight home and close my bedroom door. I don't think about it too hard – not how far into the future to travel, not exactly where to land. I let Amelia's spell do its thing, guide me to the right time and place. When I feel a light tugging at my attention mid-descent, I know it must be him.

I swoop.

But as I enter the scene and the picture sharpens, it's not JJ that I see, but myself.

But I look … strange. I'm wearing a fake-fur coat and a face full of make-up; more eyeliner than I ever wear. My hair is teased out in a golden halo. I'm running through the dark, through scrubby bush. The path is narrow and uneven, the dust and pebbles under my feet pale in the moonlight. I am scared, terrified – the acrid taste of it burns my tongue. My heart is pounding, my breath is being drawn in and pushed out in a broken mess of a rhythm.

It's so odd, and so uncomfortable, I pull back, hover uncertainly. I've never visited myself in the future. I hadn't considered the possi-bility that I would be there when it happened.

But I must see. I sink deeper into the sensations of the night.

The scrub clears briefly. In the light of the moon, I see I am running along a cliff edge. There is water below that looks like the green-gray murky depths of the Yarra.

My heart lurches as I stumble; the adrenaline of a missed step shoots through me. I do not know how long I have been running but my legs are burning; I am fatiguing.

A bridge comes into view ahead, shining as light reflects off the water.

The world wobbles at the edges when I see JJ standing on the rail, hand on a supporting beam, looking at the water below. The night is dark but he is a bright and vital presence. I watch as he tips his head, pours something in. My tired legs put on a burst of speed, frantic to reach him.

He becomes aware of my presence, turns to face me, eyes going wide and face freezing in horror. I can't make out what he's saying but it's evident he's not expecting me and doesn't want me here. He shouts something but I ignore him. I cover the remaining distance full-pelt, shuck off my jacket, revealing a loose tank and shorts and heavy boots, and haul myself up to join him on the rail. I look at him – defiantly? – and then at the Yarra flowing below.

The two of us stand in the inky night, solemn as superheroes. The darkness shields much of his face, but his eyes gleam, the whites luminescent.

He starts talking – low, fast, intense – and I see myself reply in kind. He reaches out and touches my face, my hair. I am not great at reading lips but I make this out.

I love you.

Pain – agonising, excruciating – sears through me.

We are still in intense conversation. Then I watch in wonder as I draw his amulet from around my neck. I am wearing his amulet – why? Something fierce rises in me – then a great peace. A peace I see spreading across my face. I say something and throw the amulet high; it spins through the dark, the burnished gold gleaming in the moonlight.

Then I watch myself dive off the bridge, disappearing from view.

I see JJ's face, stunned, then the vision blacks out.

I lurch to a sitting position, heart pounding in my ear, dragging in ragged breaths around chattering teeth.

It's not what I thought.

Nothing is what I thought.

It's not JJ who dies.

It's me.

10

I stare at the stream of green liquid as Aunt Bernie pours and try to marshal calm. I have to convince her that everything is fine, and she's already predisposed to think the opposite. I made it to this week's all-coven, but I skipped last week's – a big no-no. I've had little sleep over the week; add to that the energy I've drawn on in my relentless searching of the future and I probably look like shit.

But maybe everything *is* fine? I don't know anymore.

I dropped Amelia a text to say thanks for her help, that the spell worked but it's not what I thought. I didn't specify in what way, but I heavily implied everything is okay. During all-coven this evening, I gave her a wave and a sunny smile across the ballroom. I could see her temptation to corner me and get the details, but it wasn't the right time. It's the first full moon after the equinox on Thursday night, the Paschal Full Moon – a special event with a particular energy – and Amelia was quickly drawn into all the plans. I won't be taking part – I'm not required and not really welcome, though I'm sure everyone would do their best to include me. And besides, Emma's still bugging me to go dancing with her and Felix. So I slipped away to wait for Aunt Bernie while Amelia was distracted.

She's not generally prone to overreaction; I hope my smile and wave were enough to satisfy her.

I am nowhere near being ready to talk about it. I've settled into a weird internal struggle between what I saw and my own disbelief. Why are we on that bridge? Why am I wearing his amulet? Why do I jump? I was expecting answers; all I got was more questions. None of it makes sense, and I don't have a clue what to do. But I need to work it out soon. I don't know exactly when it happens – I let Amelia's spell handle how far to take me into the future – but I've travelled enough times to be able to gauge an approximate date, and I'd say it's no further ahead than half a week.

Not tomorrow, not the next day, but shortly thereafter, I am going to plummet into the cold water of the Yarra. Am I supposed to stop it from happening or bring it into being?

I don't know, and now I have to eat choc-chip cookies and pretend I'm not losing my mind.

"You didn't make it last week. Nettie said you weren't well."

She's looking at me kindly, with such gentle understanding, that I almost fold. I ache to tell her, but if I do, the whole thing will be taken out of my hands.

And all I can think is … I choose to leap. I have no idea why. JJ and I were arguing, but there wasn't a tussle. I didn't fall by accident. I wasn't pushed or coerced. I'm not suicidal.

I have no idea why … but I choose it.

It's not like I don't know what happens. It's not like it's something I can't control.

When – if – the time comes, I can always choose not to.

If I tell anyone, they'll find some way to stop it. Which I get – I'd do the same – but I don't know if I want that to happen. For some reason, in the near future, this is what I choose. I need to make sure I still have that option. I need to trust my future self; I can't see the reasoning now, but I need to trust it will become apparent in time.

And whatever this is, it's between him and me.

Still, I just watched myself die; it's hard to pretend everything is fine. "I'm worried about JJ," I admit.

"You've been worried about Elijah for a long time."

I see the question in her eyes: what's changed? "Aren't you?"

I've never seen Aunt Bernie smile at anyone the way she does at JJ. She certainly doesn't shower us witches, even those of us who are truly her nieces, with that type of attention. She's kind and she's fair, but she's tough. Maybe she has to be.

"Less than I was," she says.

"Really?"

She inclines her head. "I sense a new strength in him. A new resolve."

I take a moment to consider that. "He's looking for jobs. With … companies. Normal companies." I manage a half-smile. "Like he's …" I break off, head shaking.

"Ordinary?"

"Exactly."

"Maybe that's what he wants to be."

A breath of air escapes my mouth. "He'll never be ordinary."

"Because he's a wizard?"

"Because he's JJ."

"Then that's what he'll learn. And you?"

My pulse jumps for reasons I don't understand. I look at her for a long moment, trying to work out her question.

She doesn't want to stress me; she graciously diverts. "He came to see me about you, you know."

No. I didn't. "When?"

"Oh, a long time ago. Not long after he arrived. He was angry. Very angry."

"Why? What did he say?"

"That he was taking you away from us."

I blink at her. "He never told me that."

"Didn't he?" she asks quietly.

"We talked about travelling. I didn't realise …" I thought it was about the artefacts.

She takes a slow sip, puts the cup back on its saucer. "I think about you often, Everly. The life of a future witch is hard indeed. It's our most valued but most … difficult of gifts. You must take a break if you need. A total break if that is what is required."

I don't meet her gaze. "The coven needs me. We need to know."

She gives a little shake of her head, as if she's irritated. "The needs of a city are not greater than those of a single witch. I have a duty to care for you as much as anyone. A greater duty. And I know all too well—" She breaks off, grips the handle of her cup fiercely. "Did you know my aunt was a future witch?"

I shake my head.

"Your mother and Lettie didn't know her. It was before their time." Aunt Bernie is at least a decade, possibly two, older than Mum and Aunt Lettie. She smiles sadly. "So I know future witches. I know they walk to the beat of their own drums. I know there is much they don't tell us."

I want to look away but I can't.

"I won't lose you like I lost her."

I want to say, "You won't," but I can't.

"Is there anything you want to tell me?"

Yes, but again, I can't. "Not yet."

She nods briskly. "If you ever need help, Everly, I am here. No strings, no questions. I'm sure it doesn't always feel this way to you, but we are at your back. Always."

JJ's LOST in his own world; it's not hard to follow without being seen.

It's Easter break so he's unlikely to be on campus, and he wasn't at Owlscroft, so I've been skulking outside Aiden and Harlow's apartment for hours, waiting until he shows so I can trail him. At this point, I don't know what else to do. I still don't know what to make of my vision of the future; snow globe JJ won't tell me anything useful; and I'm overwhelmed with everything I don't know. Only one person knows what's going on, and I'm stalking him until I find out too.

He enters Flinders Street Station – thronging as always – takes an escalator down and gets on the waiting train. The line means nothing to me but I hop into the next carriage, positioning myself close to the door so I can exit when he does.

A few stops out from the city, he disembarks. I've got my cap pulled down as far as possible but I need not bother. He doesn't even glance in my direction. It's easy for me to exit once he's past and follow him down the ramp and out of the station.

It's a windy day. Ahead of me, he has his hands in the pockets of his burgundy hoodie. He seems calm as he walks through the streets of this close-to-inner suburb.

He cuts through a park, and I realise we're heading to the river. I have a moment of panic, then remind myself it's not going to happen now – it's the middle of the day and I don't have his amulet. Still, I'm left feeling uneasy.

Around the park, it's a happy scene. Young families on the play equipment, dogs fetching balls. It's hard to reconcile with the frantic running and jagged breaths of my vision.

Past the park, we join a narrow dirt and stone track that winds through gums and scrub. I lose sight of him, but it doesn't matter. I know where he's heading. I look down, through the gums lining the bank, to the silty river below. From this height, it looks placid.

When I reach the footbridge, he's standing in the middle, forearms resting on the railing, gaze on the water below, reading … I don't know what in its murky depths.

I linger, considering whether to approach.

I was hoping to learn something by following him but he doesn't appear to be doing anything more than looking. I could wait until he's finished, follow him again, but it's time to stop our dance of avoidance. I join him, rest my arms on the rail next to his.

He flicks a quick glance at me but doesn't seem surprised by my presence. A long and weighty silence stretches, during which I contemplate the scene. The bridge is high; at least twenty metres above the river, perhaps thirty. I try to banish the memory of the event that has not yet taken place, but I feel the inevitable pull of the water below, taunting me. *One day, you will fall.*

If I do, it seems unlikely I will surface.

"I wish you'd just tell me," I say.

I can feel his eyes on me, but he doesn't insult me by asking for an explanation.

He looks back at the river, brow draws down, his eyes a storm rolling in. His body is taut with tension. "I can't."

"You can. You can tell me anything."

Again I sense he's considering it, but then he shakes his head.

It hurts; the distance imposed by the secrets he insists on keeping. "You used to trust me."

He meets my gaze. "It's not that I don't trust you."

"What then?"

He takes his time answering. "It wouldn't be fair."

I give an exasperated half-laugh. There is much I haven't told him on those same grounds, and I can see the humour of having my own logic tossed back in my face.

What if I did tell him? *It's not you who jumps, it's me.* Would he confess all then?

I lean lower on the railing, chin in my hands.

I draw in a breath when I feel a gentle tug. He's maintaining a solid couple of feet between us, but he's twining a strand of my hair around his finger. He has imposed this distance, but he doesn't like it any more than I do. That at least I'm sure of. I turn my head, then draw in another breath. He's so beautiful it hurts.

"Do you wish you were normal?" I ask.

He goes still, like my question has shocked him. Then releases my hair, hand falling to his side. There are shadows haunting his eyes. "Why do you ask?"

"You're looking for jobs. You still won't touch your amulet."

"What if I were?"

I tilt my head at him.

"Would you even look twice at me?"

I would always look twice at him. And I'm not the only one. He has no idea how he draws people. But I just chuckle. "You won't answer any of my questions, but you want me to answer yours? That's not fair either."

He smiles. "I suppose not."

"We could do a swap. Secret for a secret." I wait, tensed, to see how he takes that.

He looks back but I can't read him. "Secrets need to be kept."

"You keep mine; I keep yours. Like always." I turn to face him, elbow on the railing. "You first."

"I've asked mine."

I keep my eyes on him. "Jun Jie Lee. International student of mystery. Arrives halfway through an English Lit degree, never having studied it before. Current intentions in pursuing a degree unclear, as is his enrolment status. Problematic lack of passport, or any documentation, also evident. But one look across the lecture theatre and I'm swooning."

He gives a slight shake of his head. "Thanks, Everly. Great answer."

"You're welcome." I bump against his shoulder. "I assume you had a point?"

"Maybe all we have between us is magic."

"I'm a totally magic being and so are you." Our mutual fearlessness when it comes to magic has always been a source of joy. "If all we have in common is magic, it's still everything we are."

"What if I'd lost my magic, like Jonathon?" When his uncle recovered from being inhabited, he found he'd lost his magic altogether.

I look at the river, then back at him. "I'd still be looking." His lips tip up a fraction. It makes me glad to see. "What about me? What if I wasn't magic?"

"Is that your question?"

"No."

His mouth quirks and he shrugs.

"What if we were together no matter what?" It comes out more serious than I intended, bringing a sombre note to the conversation.

"What if we were," he responds quickly. "Ask your question."

I think what to ask. It's tempting to ask about the significance of the bridge, why I'd jump off it, but I don't want him shutting down. I think instead about how all this started. Halloween. "What was it like? Being inhabited by a Red?"

His head snaps up, a sudden tension in every line of his face and body. The look he gives me is scorching.

I've gone too far. "Stupid question," I say. "You hated it."

"Hated it?" he echoes. His expression is beyond my ability to read. "You think I *hated* it?" He looks down at the river again, hands clenched on the wooden beam of the railing. "I don't have words for how good it was."

The words, his tone, stroke like a nail across the skin of my neck. I try to swallow but emotion wraps around my throat, choking me. "I didn't know," I stammer.

"You want to know what it was like, Everly? I could have had anything in the world." His eyes have a wild tinge. "I crave it, that feeling, every minute of every day. And I know I could have it again. Any time I want. All I need to do is put on my amulet."

His words chill me from the inside out. At least now I know why he won't touch it. "Why didn't you tell someone? Why didn't you tell me?" My voice catches on the last word.

His shoulders are angled away from me. "Because there's nothing anyone can do."

I don't – can't – believe it.

My heart is heavy as I absorb the burden he's been carrying. I knew he was struggling, but to live with that … that constant temptation … I move closer, unsure of what I plan, but needing to offer him support somehow. He shifts back immediately. One hand grips the railing so his knuckles are white; the other he holds out, stopping me from coming closer. "I can't. Not now."

Stupid to take it personally, but the rejection hurts. "My mistake."

He makes a sound. "It's not you, Everly. It's …" He shoves a hand through his fringe, holding it back off his forehead. "Halloween changed me, unleashed something in me. Something I can't pack away again." His gaze rakes over my face, then travels down my body. I feel it like a physical touch. "I want things. Things I'd be willing to do anything to get."

The way he's looking at me … Maybe I should be scared, but something flares rich and deep inside. "Like what?"

"Things I can't have. Things I don't trust myself with."

That's why he's pulled back as hard as he can without actually leaving. "I trust you."

"You shouldn't. You wouldn't if you knew how I feel every day."

My mouth goes dry. "How do you feel?"

He takes so long to answer, I'm not sure he's going to. But then he speaks in a voice like gravel. "Thoughts of violence and domination beat through me like a drum. It's a voice inside that compels me to take the amulet, put it on, rule the world. Sometimes it's a whisper, a promise of everything I could do, everything I could be. Sometimes it's an overwhelming pounding desire, urging me to take my revenge."

I turn, stare at the river again. "Torben?"

The wizard who killed his parents. JJ's always wanted to avenge them; it was one of the reasons he sought out Mongke's amulet in the first place.

"Yeah, Torben. Aiden thinks I've let go of it but I'm not as pure as him. I think about my parents and I want him to die. I want to crush his heart."

My stomach turns over. Odd choice of phrase.

"I can't be like Aiden. I'm not as strong as him."

"He says you're stronger."

He grimaces. "Right. He's the one who evicted a Red." He shakes his head, mouth curving slightly. "Even now, I don't know if I'd want to; if I'd even try. Or if I'd welcome it back like a friend."

Something inside me clenches viciously. "You'd fight. That's what you're doing. Every day."

"I'm tired of fighting. And I'm not winning. Mongke had the right idea. About the amulet. About everything."

My soul goes ice-cold. Mongke. Again. "I'm going to help you, JJ. I'm going to find a way to fix this."

"You can't. This is who I am now. Until—" He breaks off. "You should stay away from me."

"Why? Do you want to crush my heart too?"

Electric energy prickles in the air between us.

"No. That's not what I'd do with you."

I stand, mouth gaping, as he walks away.

11

*M*ongke's diary is not *a* puzzle piece; it's *the* puzzle piece.

It took me too long to get to this point, but this much is now clear. If I'm to figure out what I have to do, there are things I need to know, and I will find at least some answers in the diary. I start with JJ's room at Owlscroft.

I know now why he stayed. Our covenstead is wreathed in layer upon layer of protective spells. Even we witches don't fully know its powers. Those voices, those urges … they'd be quieter here.

There's no lock on his door. I choose a time when I know he won't be there and simply enter. I don't feel great about invading his privacy, but what option do I have? I put my reluctance aside and turn the room upside down.

The diary is nowhere to be found.

Maybe he hid it at Aiden and Harlow's. That would make sense. He used to live there and still has a room. We're the only ones who have keys.

I rush to their place, hoping JJ isn't back yet. As I cross the lobby, pass the wall of mailboxes, something twigs; I draw in a sharp breath, swivel and head back. Anticipation has my hands trembling as I open their box. I tell myself it's crazy, that there's no way … But inside is a slim package addressed to Elijah Lee.

Is this what snow globe JJ asked me to pick up? Keep safe?

It's a small, white rectangle, originating from Tuscon, Arizona, from a company called Universal Elements. The potential of it whispers through me. I press, trying to identify what's inside but I can't tell through the bubble-wrap. I bite my lip, consider ripping it open, but I've already rummaged through one room and I'm about to do the same to another. In the end, I just tuck it into my handbag. I'll give it to him later.

I take the lift up, shivering in the empty corridor to Harlow and Aiden's door. The layers of protection that Aiden has put in place slide against my skin but I'm not judged a threat – I've been here many times before – and the strange probing pressure eases.

Inside, the place is empty, eerie. Wrapping my arms around me, I head to JJ's room. It's sparse now – he arrived with nothing a year ago and he's moved a good proportion of what he's collected since to Owlscroft. I don't like dredging through this room any more than the one at Owlscroft, but I don't give myself a chance to hesitate. I offer him a silent, useless apology and start.

I search with grim purpose. It's not on his bedside table; that would be way too easy. I turn to the set of shelves attached above his desk, full of class texts from last semester, then the drawer below.

Which holds two things: the business card for the café in the city where we first met and a key.

I can't believe he kept the card. I hold it in my palm, kiss it, then put it back.

The key on the other hand … Does he have a secret locker somewhere?

Of course he does. His safe-storage unit at the bank. Where his amulet is stored.

The amulet I will soon be wearing.

It's not what I came for but I add it to the collection of pilfered JJ belongings in my bag and keep looking. Through drawers of clothing and under the bed. In backpacks and in shoe boxes. Every nook and cranny.

Nothing.

I turn, hands on hips, biting my lip. It's not here. But I've got somewhere else to look now.

I hear the door to the apartment open. Chalice. JJ.

I exit his room quickly and find him at the door, toeing off his shoes.

He stops still when he sees me. "Everly." Strands of black hair fall across his forehead. My fingers curl with the desire to stroke them into place. "What are you doing here?"

I go to pull the package from my bag, but … What did snow globe JJ say exactly? "Keep it safe for me." Do I give it to here-and-now JJ or not? I allow my hand to fall to my side. "Harlow asked me to check on something for her."

"Mail?" There's expectation on his face. He's clearly anticipating it to arrive.

I shake my head, working to keep my face blank. "She was worried she'd left milk in the fridge."

It's a bad excuse. Harlow couldn't care less about sour milk. And JJ senses it.

He frowns. "I could have dealt with that. I told you I was using the place this week."

"Right. I forgot." His gaze is hard and sharp; he's assessing me, trying to judge whether I'm telling the truth. About that I am. "Don't worry. It's all yours. I'm not staying." I'm increasingly and painfully conscious of what I have in my bag. "In fact, I better get going. I've got things to do."

I walk past his dark, suspicious stare, holding my breath until I'm at the door. "See you," I call, trying for casual cheer.

I hear a grunted goodbye in return and shut the door behind me with relief.

Outside in the bright light of the sun, bag clutched to my side, I walk fast. Past a new wine bar, lush and dark, an elaborate display of expensive-looking shoes, and a bookstore I make a note to return to when I have time.

And then I'm outside the bank.

I push through the heavy doors into a huge Victorian-era room. The ceiling is double normal height – possibly triple – with elaborate plaster cornices. An eager-to-help woman at the information desk waves me towards a counter at the back when I tell her what I'm here for.

Banks are supposed to have good security but this isn't an issue for wizards or witches. I turn to face the officious-looking man behind the desk and mutter a spell under my breath as I approach.

> Believe, believe
> Believe what I say
> No need to think
> Just believe what I say

By the time I get there, he has lost some of his stiffness. I explain that I have something in a security unit. Instead of going through the normal checks, he beams at me and leads me out the back, down a set of stairs, into the dank dark chill of the vault.

It smells old down here; musty but not mouldy. At the rows of units, the attendant inserts his key and waits for me to do the same, then draws out the box and carries it to the viewing table, saying he'll return in fifteen minutes.

I wait until I hear his steps on the stairs, then open the box, lungs tight. Relief washes through me like fresh spring rain when I see a battered rust-coloured cover.

Mongke's diary. I've found it.

I draw it out carefully, revealing a little black-cloth-wrapped bundle – the amulet – and a few folded letters underneath. Ignoring those for the moment, I turn to the back cover of the diary, and flip through. Elegant Chinese characters fill page after page, stopping only a few pages from the front.

I bite my lip, considering. I had planned to read anything relevant here and return it to its safe space, but these are Mongke's words – and he's JJ's hero. Now that I'm holding it, I want to read the whole thing. Which would take much longer than my allocated fifteen minutes. Plus I may not pick up everything I need to know first time through; I may need to check details later. I nestle it into the bottom of my bag, protecting it as best I can.

I pick up the box to return to the unit, but looking into the contents, I pause.

In my vision, I have the amulet. Should I take it too?

Can I even touch it?

It's a risk. Amulets are serious business and I'm not sure what will happen if it doesn't like me. But if I have it on in my vision, I must be able to wear it.

Besides it saved my sister. Without it, Harlow would have had her heart crushed by the Red. And she said it helped evict other demons.

I draw it out, place it gently on the table and unwrap it. It's an unassuming piece to the uninitiated; small, with a gorgeous red-orange stone in its centre set in a decorative surrounding of old gold. It's impossible to put an age on, or a place of origin. But it's old. Ancient. I can feel the history of it, the number of setting suns it has witnessed.

I cover it with my hand. Heat enters through my palm and travels up my arm, rushing like satin through my veins, searching … me. I'm not sure I could stop it even if I wanted to, but I don't. I want it to see and feel everything. I need it to know how much I – we – need its help.

I let it see the first time we met. When I walked into that café and met his gaze across the room. He smiled, like he always used to – broad, open and full of life and joy – and I'd known – *known* – that I'd come home.

I let it see the first time we opened up to one another. Not long after we met, walking through city streets, as we did for hours on end. I told him about how I travel to the future – he said he wanted to come with me. Before he realised why I did it so much.

I let it see the first time we kissed – three days ago on my couch.

How my heart exploded with light and my whole body felt alive. How, for the first time, I felt like everything in my world was right.

I feel it slow, settle.

"So, you see, he needs us. Can I take you with me?"

There's a gentle buzz in my bones and I decide that will do as a yes.

I pick it up and put it around my neck. My eyes close and my head tilts to the ceiling as I absorb the shift in energies; the power that warms and invigorates like the sun, feeling somehow like JJ.

The amulet's small, flat; if I tuck it under my top, it'll be invisible from the outside. But JJ doesn't have to see it to know it's there. He'll be able to feel it. "You have to hide from him until the time's right."

There's another buzz.

If it's one thing this amulet knows how to do, it's hide. It stayed hidden for a thousand years, despite multitudes of wizards searching for it. The only reason JJ found it was because it wanted to be found by him.

That leaves the folded letters. Aiden's name is scrolled on one; mine on the other.

My heart crunches into a ball and drops to the floor. There's only one reason people leave letters like this. To express their final wishes. To finally get out everything they haven't been able to say.

To say goodbye.

I pick them up, revealing another sheet of paper below. It's a map. A set of instructions for Aiden on how to find Mongke's cave. So he can return the amulet and the diary. Where they then stay buried for eternity.

I put the letters back in the box and close it.

Anything JJ has to say to me he can say in person.

12

To be reborn, you must first die.

My heart freezes in my chest; frost crystals work their way through my veins.

It's taken me reading through the night to get this far, devouring the diary in one sitting, cross-legged on my bed. I had thought it might be dry or difficult to absorb, but it's not. It's a fascinating account of Mongke's life; full of thoughts and feelings he generously shares. He's intelligent, curious and sensitive, with a joyful vitality that reminds me of JJ. How he used to be.

But something happens. Something changes. He enters a downward spiral; tires of being a wizard. The kill or be killed ethos. The constant fight against the corrupting influence of power. He decides to live the remainder of his days differently and develops a ritual to get rid of his 'magical self'.

I read with growing horror. I don't understand all the details – the calculations, the materials – but I get the gist.

First, the magical self must be separated out; a difficult feat that is impossible to maintain for long. Then a potion is taken. There's a number of ingredients but I immediately focus on the hawthorn berries, magically manipulated to temporarily freeze the heart.

Finally, it's necessary to jump from a height into a body of water. Due to the now differing densities between the magical and non-magical selves because of the gold in the potion—

Gold. An element. Something twigs. Putting the diary aside a moment, I rummage through my bag for the package and rip it open. Platinum flakes. Same purpose?

—the magical self will not be able to follow into the water. As the wizard's heart is no longer beating, it will assume the wizard is dead (which he is at that time) and ascend.

The wizard, if he survives the impact of the jump, the poison that stops his heart, and the time spent submerged, will rise from the water reborn. Non-magical.

If he survives.

I pause, eyes squeezed shut, whole body rigid.

The parallels are clear. The berries … When I couldn't find JJ's pulse, he *was* dead. He'd manipulated the hawthorn berries so they froze his heart. The platinum flakes; the instruction to keep them safe. Even the book on gravitation – light background reading on what happens when you fall from a height. And of course, the bridge.

At least I now know why we end up there. JJ's planning on jumping off. Not to die – or, at least, not forever. But to be reborn as non-magical.

Relax. It's only temporary.

Snow globe JJ's words now make sense.

But reading on, I fear the actuality may be very different. Mongke discusses the risks; states that he believes it's likely he'll perish in the experimentation process. The greater the height, the stronger the potion, the more likely the ritual is to work. However, both these things are also more likely to result in death – of the permanent kind.

Mongke lives long enough to make several unsuccessful attempts, after which he remains magical. He continues to increase the height he jumps from, the strength of the potion.

And then the diary stops.

A heavy ball of dread gathers in my belly. I let the diary fall against my crossed legs, slumping over the top, head pressing on my forearms. Mongke did not succeed. Why does JJ believe his fate will be any different?

He doesn't. That's why he left the letters. But he's trying anyway.

His breathtaking fearlessness, which I once loved, has become the trait I hate the most.

He cannot do this. He cannot do this. As I repeat the words over and over in my head, my breath builds, coming faster and harder, and with it rises an anger that travels through me in hot licks of flame.

How could he be suffering like this and not seek help from anyone but a long-dead wizard? How could he come to this decision without even telling me? How could he risk himself in this way? Does he not know what it would do to me to lose him?

I won't let him do this.

I rise, pack the diary back into my bag, and walk out into the morning sun. Determined. At least I know now.

I enter the apartment in a fury of energy.

He is sitting cross-legged on the loungeroom floor in a meditation-type pose. Preparing, no doubt; practising separating out his magical self. His eyes flick open in response to my entry but the rest of him stays still.

I grab the diary from my bag and hold it out in front of me. "You can't be serious!"

He doesn't seem surprised that I'm here, nor that I'm holding his diary. Perhaps he knew, given the way I've been following him, hounding him, that I'd work it out. His jaw sets. He unfolds and stands. "You can't tell anyone."

It's the confirmation I was hoping not to hear. I let out a sound and throw the diary on the coffee table. "You're not going through with it."

He takes a step towards me. Stops. "You know what it's like for me now." His voice vibrates with tension.

"But this?" I point to the diary. "Mongke died!"

His jaw sets in a stubborn line. "I've been studying the ritual for months. I've made some changes. What we know now – the physics of it. The materials that are available." His hands are out, as if appealing for understanding. He lets them fall; I am not interested in the tweaks he's made. "I've got a better chance than him."

"A better chance?" I echo incredulously. "That's not good enough."

"It's going to have to be." He turns a little, arms coming across his chest. "I don't have a choice."

"No." The simple denial shoots from my mouth.

"I have no choice," he repeats, enunciating slowly. His hands come to land low on his hips. "It's getting worse. What happened at the pub last week—"

"The wasps?" There's disbelief in my tone. "You're risking your life because some creep got a drink dumped on him?"

"It's not what happened. It's what *could have* happened." He pauses a moment to let that sink in. "I didn't mean to do it. I couldn't control it."

"He was fine!"

"He got lucky. Next time … " He shakes his head. "There can't be a next time. But there will be. That's why I need to …" He starts to pace. "The cravings, the urges … they're getting worse. One day – soon – I'm not going to be strong enough. I'm going to collect my amulet and …"

I shake my head. He won't. He won't do that. "Aiden and Harlow will be back soon. They'll know what to do, they'll—"

"No." His face takes on that rigid, distant look again. "I've been thinking about it for months. This is the solution."

"This isn't a solution. It's suicide."

"I'm not planning on dying."

I can feel how wide my eyes are. "But if you take that poison … If you jump—"

I stop abruptly as realisation crashes through me. It's not going to happen like that. It's me who's going to jump. I turn before he can see my face and knows there's something big I still haven't told him.

Do I jump to stop him? I don't see how that would work, and surely that's not the best I can come up with. I'm no sacrificial lamb.

Am I?

"There must be a better way," I say finally.

"Mongke didn't find one." His voice is wooden, lifeless.

I've read the diary. I understand why Mongke felt he had to try the ritual. It took him decades to become the wise and gentle soul he was in the end. At the start, he was as violent as any wizard. He'd taken amulets by force – killed for them – and he lived with deep regret. Even after he'd changed, other wizards kept coming for him. It was kill or be killed.

And he was alone in the world; he didn't have family, he didn't have friends. He didn't have someone that would stand by his side no matter what.

JJ hasn't done the things Mongke did. He's never killed. And he wasn't planning on attracting adverse attention so he's forced to either. Before Halloween, he hadn't wanted to be non-magical. That was when things changed. "There must be a way to go back to how you were before."

His eyes are raw. "How? I can't un-feel the things I've felt. I can't box up those urges and pack them away under the bed. This is who I am now. But if I can get rid of my magic …" He pushes a hand through his fringe, holds it back, off his forehead. "Hopefully, I won't feel the same. But if I do, I'll be powerless. I won't be able to do anything about it."

I turn away again. He's so sure he is right. I need to talk him out of it, but I don't know how. "I can't let you do it."

His eyes harden to onyx. He steps towards me. "You promised you'd keep this secret."

I exhale in outrage. "I didn't promise. You didn't tell me about this. But I won't; if you agree to wait. Just till Aiden gets here."

He becomes agitated. "I can't. I don't have that luxury. I'm just waiting for—" He breaks off, turns from me.

His delivery to arrive? He can't do it without the platinum flakes. No doubt it's being tracked; he probably knows it's in the country. It won't be long until he realises I've got it. He can order more but they'll take time to arrive.

"Besides," he continues, "the timing is perfect."

I think to my first time in the castle – the moon over the river on the doors. Of course. "It's tomorrow night, isn't it?" The first full moon after the equinox has a power of its own; same for wizards as for witches.

He's hesitant to confirm details, but then he nods slowly. "Mongke suggested it. It'll help."

It may; the Easter season aids in rebirth and rejuvenation. But will it be enough? "I won't let you do it."

His eyes go full with something like pity but there's a hard core of intractable there too. "Everly … It's not your choice."

I want to throw something. "I won't let you do it."

He exhales. "I can't go on like this."

His quiet words break me, carve a hole in my soul. I stand, with my gaping wound, unable to say or do a thing. I can feel the weight he's carrying, how bone-deep tired he is. I understand the desire to be free of it all. But this is not the answer.

"I saw the letter." I'm not giving anything away; he knows I visited the bank vault.

"Did you read it?"

"No."

He nods slowly. "It's good you know."

It's good because I'm going to stop him. I almost say it out loud, but instead, my shoulders slump. I've learned a lot but not what I need to know. Not how to stop him. Not how to fix him. I am utterly and totally defeated. For just a moment, I let myself feel the full brunt of it.

I don't hear him move, but his arms come around the top of my chest, pinning me back against the warmth of his body. It's a comfort that's also an agony.

His forehead touches the crown of my head. "It's going to work. I have to believe it's going to work." His voice is harsh with withheld emotion. "I need you to believe too."

I wish I could. I turn, hands bunching at his waist, forehead on his collarbone.

"Promise me you won't stand in my way," he says against my ear.

I can't do that. "I won't tell," I say. That I can promise. More than ever, I feel that this is between him and me. There must be some reason snow globe JJ came. There must be some chance for me to change what happens. There's more I have to learn – there must be. I draw strength, and tilt back to meet his eyes. "But this isn't over."

His gaze narrows as realisation dawns. I have not – will not – accept his decision. His jaw clenches. He is starting to think, maybe, about what I know, and how. Starting to wonder, maybe, where his platinum has got to.

I step out of the circle of his arms, collect the diary in case I need it and walk out the door.

It's only once I'm out on the street that I remember what's around my neck, hidden under my layers of clothing. He didn't notice it. He probably thinks that I wouldn't dare touch it. Not many would.

"Good job," I say, pressing it against my heart.

He has no idea the lengths I'll go to for him.

13

I want to scream until my voice breaks. My throat feels scraped raw as if I have. It is Wednesday; tomorrow night is the Paschal Full Moon. I walk the paths along the Yarra – walk and walk – turn it over a million times in my mind, but I still don't know how to stop him.

Inevitably, I wind up in front of Aunt Bernie's door. I'm not thinking – I can't think – but I need my coven, my covenstead. I knock, opening it when I hear her "Come in."

Her smile falls as she sees my face. She gets to her feet and rounds her desk. Her hand is a gentle squeeze on my forearm, her gaze full of concern. "What is it? What's happened?"

When I don't answer, just look at her, arms wrapped around myself, she turns, pulling me gently towards my usual seat. "Come. Sit."

I allow her to lead me, deposit me in the chair. And wait, stiff and silent, as she takes her own. I don't know what to say; I have no idea what I'm hoping for. "I thought you might need me to do something. I know it's busy right now," I say eventually.

Aunt Bernie's gaze is intent on me, her body tilted forward, elbows on the table, hands clasped in front. "That's not why you've come."

My shoulders slump. It's not why I've come. I've promised not to tell. And if I thought it would help, I would break that promise, but it won't. "I can't say anything," I get out finally. "But it's bad. This time it's bad."

Her gaze turns sympathetic, but she doesn't say anything.

"What do I do, Aunt Bernie? I don't know what to do." My voice is getting higher, pitchy. "He's going to do something dangerous. And I've tried to talk him out of it, but he won't listen to me. I don't know how to stop him and I'm scared he's going to—" I stop. "I don't know what to do." I thought that once I'd gathered information, once I knew what he planned, that the answer would be obvious. It's not. "I know I have a role to play – I even know what it is – but I don't understand it. I don't know what to do."

"Let him go." Her voice is precise as a blade. Her brown-flecked green eyes are calm and strong on mine.

"I can't. He's making a mistake." I think of the goodbye letters, the map so Aiden can hide the amulet away from the world again. "He knows it might go wrong. I can't."

"You must. Everly, you've been a friend to him all these months – and I know that hasn't been easy. But that is all you need to do, all you need to be." She looks at me for a long time. "Sometimes, we have to let the people we love make their own choices."

I stare at her while the words sink in, while they twist in my heart. Then I let out a sob. "I can't. I can't do that." My voice gets louder, higher. She doesn't understand. She can't possibly understand. "I can't let anything happen to him. I can't—"

"Everly. Listen to me now." Her voice is sharp-edged flint; it cuts through, shocking me out of my freefall. "You are not responsible for Elijah. You are not responsible for anyone but yourself."

A raw sound escapes my mouth and I lurch forward. She might be right but it doesn't help. "I don't want anything to happen to him. I can't give up on him."

"I know that. None of us do. And I'm not suggesting you give up. But you must let go. At least a little. Take a step back. Be patient."

What she's suggesting is the opposite of my approach to date.

"You know what makes this season so special? Faith and hope. Faith in the future, hope for a new beginning. Show a little of both those things. For him, and for yourself."

Faith and hope. She is right; I have little of either. "I don't know if I can."

"Sometimes it's all we can do."

I draw in a shaky breath. The idea of trusting – not blindly, not passively – but in myself, believing that I will know what to do when the time comes, brings a sense of strength and calm.

I see my face as it appeared in my vision; the peace that came over it right before I fell.

I know, then, what I need to do. I have no fear, no doubt.

I exhale, then swipe across my cheeks. "Okay," I say.

"Good." She nods briskly. "Give yourself some space to breathe. You don't know what to do right now? I suggest you do nothing. For a little while, at least. Spend some time with your friends, think about other things. Gain some perspective. If you are right, if there's something you're meant to do, it will come to you."

This is why I came – Aunt Bernie's phlegmatism. Something I could do with cultivating.

I feel clear-headed, calm, strong. I rise to my feet, walk around the desk and lean down to hug her.

I can tell by the sound she makes that she wasn't expecting it. But I don't think she hates it. "Thanks, Aunt Bernie."

I will take her advice. And when the time comes, I will be ready.

I'D COMPLETELY FORGOTTEN about the EDM gig until I get a text from Emma saying she and Felix are running late and can we meet an hour later than planned. I'm sitting in a café with Chloe, hot chocolates in front of us, after a day perusing bookstores in the city. I'd like to say I was able to shut out all thoughts of full moons and bridges, but I switched off as much as possible, handed the problem over to my subconscious, allowing everything to dissolve and reform in endless combination.

The break has done me good. I feel rejuvenated; ready. How else would I have spent this time? There is nothing left for me to do but wait. I could have spent the time alone in my room, stressing, or travelling to the future to escape. That's what I would have done before I spoke to Aunt Bernie but where would it have got me?

And who am I to fight fate? I've seen what's to come. I might not know everything there is to know, but I keep picturing the look on my face before I fall. I am sure and I am at peace. I'm going to let fate lead me there and somehow make it work.

The thought is freeing. And a dance is exactly what I need to help me not think. I'll lose myself in the music, and when I come back, it'll be time. I'll know what to do.

I reply to Emma then turn to Chloe. "Why don't you come too?" I want them all there. For all I know, it'll be the last time I see them.

She makes a face. "A twelve-hour rave? Not really my thing."

"It's four days actually."

She makes an 'Oh God' face. "So Emma."

"So Emma," I agree. "I won't stay long. Just an hour or two." That's all I'll have before showdown. "We can get ready together. It'll be fun. Please?"

"I don't know, Evie."

It's closer to a yes than I thought I'd get. "It's the Paschal Full Moon. Time to get a little wild."

She shakes her head but she's smiling. "Is JJ coming?"

"Doubt it." He has other plans for this evening.

A funny expression passes over her face. "Oh. I just remembered what he said at the pub the other week. Sorry."

I give a little grimace. Now I know the truth, I'd prefer he did have a secret girlfriend.

"I've actually been meaning to talk to you. About him." Her cheeks are flushed; she doesn't quite meet my gaze. "I know that ... I'd never ... I mean, I do like him but ... I know you two are ... And I don't even know why ..."

I do. It's wizard glamour and it's potent. I smile. "I'll ask if he has a second cousin or something. Maybe he can transfer too."

It takes her a moment, then she laughs.

We catch the train to my place and spend an hour or two going through my wardrobe for options. In the mood to dare fate, I ask Chloe to pick my outfit.

"A little wild, did you say?" she asks with thoughtful mischievousness, and pulls out dark, patterned tights, black shorts, and a loose pink tank. Fate 1; Everly 0. But there's a certain comfort in knowing it's still on track. Who am I to fight this? I dress in Chloe's picks, keeping the amulet around my neck.

"Oh, you'll be cold on the way in," she says. "You'll need—"

I go to Mum's closet and return with the dramatic fake-fur coat.

"Yes. Perfect," she says.

I pick something equally out-of-character for her, and tease out my hair and add a tonne of eyeliner while she dresses.

We catch the train back into the city, getting out at Parliament.

I smile when I realise we're walking through the square where the demon portal is located – an innocent-looking stone fountain covered in moss that demons use to pass through from their world to ours. Aiden and Harlow used to work here every night, evicting demons from the poor passers-by they chose to inhabit. Claire and Lucinda are training for the role now; they stand fierce and ready a short distance from the fountain, monitoring for any demon presence. I give a quick wave.

"Who are they?" Chloe asks.

"Friends of Harlow's."

As we pass the fountain, curiosity flames in me; I wonder what, if anything, is staring back. The Red that inhabited JJ? I want to linger, to dare it to try it on with me.

Chloe pulls me on.

When we reach the venue, Emma and Felix are waiting outside. If I was worried that Chloe and I had overdone it ... we are tame compared with their sequins and neon and general lairiness. We swap hugs and go in, leaving our coats and bags at the counter up front. The music is already pounding.

Felix offers to buy drinks, but I don't want one. Emma grabs our hands and leads us through the crowd to the dance floor. Right to the front, near the DJ and the speakers. The music is so loud that I can't hear myself think, and I love it.

We dance and dance and dance. Emma and Felix try to teach Chloe and I how to shuffle and we do our best as they spin and float like clouds around us, almost falling over in laughter trying to imitate them.

I don't know how long we've been out here dancing. An hour? Two? I wanted to lose myself, and at the very least I've lost time.

There is a prickling over my skin. I stop dancing. Something – some sense of urgency – makes me look up. In the dark balcony, standing in solitary splendour, JJ is there, watching me. His skin is so pale it glows; his eyes are embers against snow, burning into me. Strobe lighting sweeps over him, turns him a thousand shades of red.

My breath catches in my throat. I am the only still thing on the jostle of the dancefloor.

The lighting shifts, leaves him in darkness again.

I grab Chloe's wrist, and she follows my gaze, but the next time the lighting sweeps across the balcony, it's empty.

He's gone. Or maybe I imagined him.

Chloe is looking at me for an explanation of my sudden change of mood.

I lean in close. "I'm done. Want to take off?"

She looks at Felix and Emma, still dancing.

"Stay. Have fun," I say. "I'm fine. I'll Uber home."

"Sure?"

"Absolutely." In fact, it's better. Better than better; it's right.

Something is happening. It's time.

I hug them goodbye, then make my way through the throng of heated, undulating bodies to the front of the venue. I retrieve my bag and coat and head outside into the refreshing crisp bite of the autumn night.

I take in shouted snatches of conversations and drifts of competing songs, the sweet popcorn-doughnut smell, the energy that swirls in the air. There is something I am so close to understanding.

I close my eyes.

I see him when I surprised him in the snow globe – tip of the beheading sword inches from my chest, red glint in his eye.

I see him on the bridge, saying he wants to crush Torben's heart.

I see him on that balcony, the red strobe lighting sweeping over him.

Red, red, red – it's all I can see.

I open my eyes.

There will never be anyone else for me. No one will ever see me like he does. And I will never know anyone like I know him. Inside and out.

I know him; I *know* him.

A voice in his head urging him to crush hearts?

That's not him.

And if it's not him … Is that Red still in him in some way?

I reel at the thought.

When he took the sword to confront Jonathon, the demon could have killed him instantly. Instead, it chose to jump ship and inhabit him. And it wasn't forcibly evicted, as is normally the case. Aiden invited it to inhabit him; the demon had plenty of time to leave something in JJ before it went. Like a … mini-portal. A door through which it could return. Demons always want to come back – and of course it would want to come back to JJ. Someone with the potential to fulfill its biggest plans. Every day, it's been trying to tempt him to open the door. That's what he's been living with. That's what we need to get rid of.

I don't know much about demons, but I have a sister who happens to be the world's foremost expert. I start walking, pull out my phone.

"Hey," I say when she picks up, working to keep my tone light and casual.

"Hey yourself," she replies. "Another 'debate'?"

I force out a laugh. "How'd you guess?"

"So what do you need to know this time?"

"It's about eviction."

"Demons R Us. Go right ahead."

I laugh again, a little more genuine this time. It's good to hear her voice. "What I'm wondering is, is there any grey area when it comes to demons?"

"What do you mean?"

I pick my words with care. "Can someone be inhabited and not inhabited at the same time? Like, if there's just a little bit of the demon there but it's not in control."

"That … is an excellent question." I can almost hear her pensive frown.

"Have you come across anything like that?"

"No. But that doesn't mean it isn't possible." There's a loaded pause. "I think you better tell me what's going on, Everly."

I bite my lip but there's no point not telling her. Whatever's happening, it's soon. "I think that's what's happened to JJ. I think the Red left something in him. Like a remnant of itself or some kind of door between them. Something that it can use to get back."

"Did he tell you that?"

"I don't think he knows. But we've been talking more lately and … He's really struggling with something that's urging him to … It wants him to put on his amulet."

"The amulet?"

There's a silence as she thinks about that, and I feel it vibrate against me. I hold my breath, hand pressing it to my chest, waiting.

"He should put it on."

The amulet vibrates again. I exhale in a rush. Is this the answer?

"Yeah," she says slowly, warming to her idea. "He should put it on. That amulet is a bit of a freak. Probably because of its long association with a very unusual wizard."

"Mongke."

"The one and only. Anyway, it hates all things demon. I have first-hand experience."

Harlow was wearing the amulet when the Red demon attacked

her. It protected her; it's the only reason she's still alive.

"But JJ thinks if he puts it on, he'll succumb to his ... lust for power. That he'll turn into some kind of evil magical warlord. Whether it's the Red or not."

"Aiden was always worried about that too. But I forced him to see he'd be fine. I think JJ would be too, but ... I suppose it's a risk. Wizards are ... you know. Susceptible. And JJ's inexperienced. Wait till we get back; we'll deal with it then. Maybe we can do some kind of modified evict spell? I'll look into it."

He won't wait. It's happening tonight. I don't say that. "What do you mean it's a risk?"

"The amulet belongs to him. It'll take its cues from him."

I turn that over in my mind. "So when JJ was inhabited by the Red and the amulet was protecting you, it was really JJ?"

"That's one way to look at it."

Even while inhabited by a Red demon, he was fighting against it. I wish he could see it.

"If JJ wants the ... what did you call it? Remnant? If he wants the remnant gone, the amulet will banish it for him. If he doesn't ..." She leaves it hanging.

I hear JJ's words in my head.

I don't have words for how good it was. I crave it every minute of every day.

But at the same time, he's been fighting it successfully for months. He's so sure he doesn't want it, he's pursuing a risky ritual to get rid of his magic altogether.

We won't know until he puts the amulet on.

And if we make the wrong choice ...

"Thanks, Harlow. That's been helpful."

There's a long pause. "So you'll wait till we're back."

"Of course," I lie.

"Okay. Good," she says quietly. "Everly. Take care."

"Always." Another lie.

I return the phone to my bag. And notice there's something missing. The platinum flakes.

14

I run in heavy but thankfully flat boots the short distance to Aiden and Harlow's, praying I'm not too late. He may have taken the platinum, but he still has to make the potion and he doesn't have that much of a head start.

I let myself in, expelling a huge breath when I hear movements and sense his presence. I find him in his bedroom, putting on a jacket. I wait, hand on the light switch, while his movements still and he turns, face set with determination.

"Hold still. I need to check something."

I plunge us into darkness.

Though my speciality is future magic, witches share themselves around – we all do a bit of everything. My sister's a demon hunter. I know how to cast a reveal spell.

I reach for some magic and whisper the words, fast and barely audible. I'm not sure that anything will show up given JJ's not inhabited per se, but subtle wisps of Red haze around him, flowing out like an invitation.

Violent fury rolls through me. Six months he's had that thing in him. "You've got strands of Red around you." He sucks in a breath, and I switch the light back on, revealing his shock. "You said you can feel it there, in the wings. It's still in you."

He shakes his head. "I know what being inhabited feels like. This isn't it."

"It's not a full inhabitation. But it's left something in you. A way to communicate. A way to get back. That's why you've been struggling. You've been fighting it all this time."

He crosses his arms behind his head, his gaze travels my face, then searches the corners of the room, as if he might find an answer there. I give him a moment to process but his reaction doesn't evolve into the "okay-great-what-next" I'm hoping for.

I push on. "I've been talking to Harlow—"

"You what?"

"I didn't tell her. But I needed to ask about the Red. She said something we can use. Your amulet hates demons. If you put it on—"

"I can't put it on!" The words explode from his mouth.

"If you put it on and ask it to, it'll wipe any trace of the demon from you."

"I. Can't. Put. It. On." He grinds the words out.

"She said you can. You should." At first. Before she'd had a chance to think.

"She wouldn't know." His colour is high, his tone dismissive. "She knows demons but … I don't know how to explain it to someone who isn't a wizard, but having access to that kind of power … If anything's going to push me over the edge …"

I set my jaw. "Harlow said it's guided by you."

"Yes." The look he gives me is almost pitying. "Exactly."

I want to shake him. "You'll choose to get rid of it."

He doesn't respond. But his hand goes to his backpack.

"I'll be here. I'll help you. Like Harlow helped Aiden."

His face turns to disbelief. "You think I'd put it on with you anywhere near me?"

"You'd rather risk the ritual?"

"Yes."

He'd prefer to put himself in danger than me. But he's got it wrong. I have more to fear from him going ahead with the ritual than him putting on his amulet. I consider telling him but it'll take time for him to take in and I've already thrown a lot at him. I don't want to say anything that might sway him away from trying with the amulet.

His hands are behind his head. He's been thinking things through, just as I've been doing. "You might be right about the Red," he says, in a calm, flat tone I hate. "But if I get rid of my magic, I'll lose my appeal for the demon. It doesn't make any difference to my decision."

"You don't have to do it." My tone is one of strident protest. "We'll work together. We'll find a way to get rid of it. If you still want to lose the magic, I'll help you find a safe way to do it. I won't stand in your way."

He looks like he's considering it, then shakes his head. "It'll take time I don't have. It has to be tonight."

I think of how the red lighting shifted over him in the club, the red flame in his eyes in the snow globe. Maybe he is right. Maybe he is that close. "I'll do it. Right now. I'll use your amulet to get rid of the Red."

"No. Everly—"

"I just need you to help me with what to do."

He shakes his head furiously. "It's too dangerous. It's not going to want to go. And I don't know what will happen if I'm that close to the amulet."

"You've been close to it the whole time." I pull it from under my shirt. It buzzes in joy at being revealed to him, but JJ hisses and steps back.

"You didn't even know it was there."

His eyes are fixed on it. His body has gone tense, rigid; the strain of holding back cuts lines on his face. But he holds himself back.

"How?" he bites out.

"I asked it to hide from you."

"It did what you asked?" His mouth tips up in a humourless smile. "Of course it did."

"Let me use it on you." I can finally right the mistake I made all those months ago.

"You've never worked with one before." He is looking at me, and it, with an intensity that I can feel. I can feel how hard he's working but he hasn't moved an inch. He's been fighting to maintain control for six months. He might be tired, but he's got strong. So strong. Why can't he see that?

"It knows what to do. I'll just … set it free. It'll let me, I know it will."

He doesn't look convinced.

"Please, JJ. We have to try."

He shakes his head. "I won't risk hurting you."

"You won't."

"You don't know that."

I do actually but he doesn't believe me. He doesn't believe in himself. I sigh, rub at my temples. "Can you set some kind of failsafe? Something I can use to stop you if things go bad?"

"Yes."

It's asking a lot; particularly from someone who's been inhabited. Who's been powerless in their own body. And now I'm asking him to give me that control over him. "I won't use it unless I have to."

His expression softens, just a fraction. "I trust you. It's me I don't trust."

"That's why I'll have the failsafe. Please, JJ. I need to know we tried."

He looks at me for a long time. "We try, and when it doesn't work, you let me go."

I can't make myself nod in agreement. How can I when I know where we end up?

His gaze narrows on me, but he doesn't push the issue.

I sit cross-legged on the floor, wait for him to join me. He drops in a fluid motion, sits so close our knees touch. "Set the failsafe first."

"What word do you want?"

"It's Easter. I like chocolate."

"Chocolate." The corners of his mouth grudgingly tip up. He closes his eyes briefly.

I reach for his hands. Face to face, hands intertwined, knees touching – this feels like how it should be for the two of us, always. "I like this," I say.

It makes his mouth tip up just a little more.

"So how do I start?"

"Close your eyes."

I comply.

"Can you feel it?"

"Yes." I felt it the second I unwrapped it, placed my palm on it.

"Let it come to you. Into you."

I open to it, feel it unfurl. Tendrils snake around me, through me, lighting up my veins with energy like the sun. JJ's hands tighten on mine. Maybe he can feel it too.

"You're a natural," he says.

I smile and open my eyes. He has an odd expression on his face. To say wizards are protective of their amulets is the understatement of the century. They die for them. "Do you hate seeing it on me?"

"No." I pin down his expression to something between bemusement and tenderness.

"Is this hard for you?"

"Yes."

So we should get started. "What's the first thing wizards learn to do?"

"I don't know. I just worked it out on my own."

Wizards don't have formal structures for learning like we do. They barely even have teachers. If you're lucky, you find a mentor. "Colour change it is." It's the first thing witches attempt. "What do I do?"

"You want it. And you believe you're going to get it. Don't force it. Just believe."

I close my eyes, and I picture him. The dark velvet of his eyes. Not hard to want them. I open my eyes.

The smile drops from JJ's face. "Change them back."

I bat my eyelids at him. "Not a fan?"

"You've destroyed my favourite thing in the world."

Laughing, I close my eyes and change them back. I open them again and turn serious. "I'm going to look for it. Ready?"

He nods, eyes intent on mine.

I touch lightly into his consciousness, feel his answering shudder. I go slowly, carefully, wary of triggering any sudden response. I travel through the recesses and plains of his mind. I can feel him all around me; the strangest but deepest intimacy. I brush up against something and gasp at the sensation. Pleasure floods me; like stepping into a warm bath on a cold winter's evening, satiny soft and languid. "This is …"

"Yes." He swallows thickly.

"I can't believe you want to take this away from us."

"Maybe I'll change my mind."

"We could do this every da—"

I sense the Red, a hideous, malevolent presence that roars like a scream toward me.

A memory flashes – the two of us in the courtyard, me trying to get him to dance.

Before I can control it, it forces one from me – my waltz in the snowglobe.

JJ's breath stops. I feel his sudden keen interest.

I cannot let him learn of the existence of—

I try to hide it, bury it. But he chases, sensing the presence of another man, the intensity of my feelings. I feel his all-encompassing inner drive to know who.

Chalice no. He cannot see. But the more I try *not* to think of waltzing my first time in the snow globe, the harder he tries to burst through to my conscious.

I duck; I weave. "Stop. JJ, you have to stop."

His gaze narrows to a sharp obsidian blade. "Who is he?" His voice is rough gravel.

I pull everything of myself back, retracting and retreating as fast I can go. I race away from him, trying to put some distance between us. Trying to hide in any crevasse I can find. He follows, hunting me down.

I call for the amulet. But its attention, its loyalty are divided. It will do what JJ commands, and all he can see is my supposed betrayal.

"It's not what you think." Oh, that most classic of lines. And it isn't, but I can't explain why.

I have to leave. Before he discovers the truth. But he counters my attempt to escape, holding me there like he's holding my hands. Power crackles through the air. How is he this strong? No wonder he fears himself.

My voice is husky with the effort required to push back against his will. "JJ. Stop."

He is not listening. "You love him."

I do. I do.

He feels that truth. It reverberates through him, a massive shock of hurt, coalescing into a ball of fury. The moment of weakness is exactly what the Red needs. It flares in him.

The full force of its fury, its thirst to return, to wreak havoc and devastation, to dominate everyone and everything, is overwhelming; terrible but glorious. The furious battering force of it, the relentless crushing pressure.

But it is not yet in control. JJ holds it back, prevents it taking control with a grim determination borne of months of practice.

And then, like a shift in the centre of balance, the pressure changes. To surround – cage – my heart. It does not hurt, but it's an unfathomable horror. I sob. This is what it is to be at the mercy of a Red.

But is it the Red or is it JJ? I can't tell anymore. I can't tell the difference.

I know one thing for sure. It's not that JJ cannot resist but whether he will continue to want to. Everything he has said is true.

I remember the failsafe. "Chocolate."

15

He collapses, curls into himself, breath coming heavy and uneven. I crawl close, hover over him, also breathing fast. I reach a hand to his shoulder; he turns on the contact, looks up at me. A wave of relief washes over me when I see he is lucid again, no longer in the grips of the Red.

I sink back on my knees. "Are you okay?"

"I will be." He lies back, still breathing heavily.

"Are you hurt?"

He shakes his head. "The failsafe's like an electric shock – searing enough to short-circuit my system, but the pain only lasts an instant. I just need to … get my breath back."

"We should try again," I blurt.

He huffs something that is almost a laugh, but too low, too bitter to ever be taken for amusement. "Everly, you're crazy."

"It was there. I felt it. If you hadn't seen—" I pull up sharp. He flicks an intense sideways glance at me, but after the effort I made to conceal the truth, he must know I won't – can't – tell him. "It would have worked," I say instead.

He rises in a fluid movement, one knee raised, arm draped over the top. "I almost killed you."

"No you didn't." But he could have. I feel my heart in his grip again. The squeezing pressure of it. My undeniable fear. But even then, in the grips of a Red-induced jealous rage, he hadn't hurt me. "That proves it. We try again. Now that you know …" I break off. I can't tell him what he saw. The vulnerability in his eyes almost kills me. I curl my fingers to keep from reaching for him. "You know you're the only one for me, right?"

He looks away. He knows what he felt in me – how completely my heart is given to the man I'm dancing with; how deeply in love I am. The rage may have subsided, but the hurt … the hurt is crushing. He meets my gaze again. "We had a deal. We try, then you step aside."

"I never agreed to that." And he knows it.

"Promise me you'll stay here, wait for me to return."

"I can't do that. We have to try again."

He shakes his head slowly.

I feel the moon rising; its power swelling. Soon, he will be at the bridge and I will run to him, and I still don't know how or why. We look at each other a long time. Then he stands.

This is it. He's going. His mind is set. What am I planning? To crash-tackle him to the ground to get him to stay? Unlikely to work. But there is one thing that might get through to him. I take a deep breath, look up at him. "You should know something. It's not you who jumps. It's me."

He goes statue-still; his face blanches. "What?"

"I looked for you in the future. I've seen what happens. I'm the one who jumps."

"How? How can that be?"

"I don't know." All my frustration comes out in that expression. "But I've seen it. It happens. And I don't think I've done anything to prevent it happening. Unless you just don't go." He twists, says something low and intense under his breath in Hokkien. "We have to try with the amulet again."

He shoves a hand through his hair, paces away, then back. It is not just his own life he is risking now; it's mine too. I see the moment he comes to a decision. He stands in front of me, hands low on his hips. "Okay."

Relief floods me. "Okay?"

He nods slowly. His hands come behind his head. He turns, walks to his window. "One thing I don't understand," he says into the silence. He turns to face me. "How'd you know about the platinum flakes? I've been thinking about it, and you must have got them before you'd read the diary."

The change in subject takes me by surprise. I'm still kneeling. I steeple my hands in my lap, study them, thinking very carefully about what I say. "I went to Harlow and Aiden's to look for the diary. I was walking past the mailboxes in the lobby and I decided to check if there was anything to collect. I didn't know what the package was, I just took it to give to you later."

Everything I just said is true, and I'm able to meet his gaze fully.

"But you didn't give it to me."

I shrug. "I knew you were up to something; I thought the package had to come into it somehow. But I only opened it and realised how after I read the diary."

His arms come across his chest. "And how did you know to look for the diary?"

"It was obvious. In retrospect, I'm surprised I didn't think to do it sooner. Ever since we met, you've talked about Mongke, and he kept coming up. You mentioned him when we were on the bridge. Harlow mentioned him when I asked about you doing magic without an amulet." My words flow quickly as my confidence grows. I thought it would be hard to explain without referring to snow globe JJ, but I have no reason to.

"You said you knew I was planning something, that you looked for me in the future ... I don't understand how you knew to do that."

Even now, I can avoid mentioning him. "It was when we were in the courtyard, and I asked you to dance, and you said 'over my dead body'. And I just knew. I got this ... feeling. Maybe because I'd found you lying dead in your room a few days earlier. I never believed you were sleeping; I knew that wasn't the truth. Even if I didn't know what the truth was."

This is why snow globe JJ didn't tell me anything. This is why he left his confusing array of clues that I had to follow up in the real world. Because now, in this moment, I can meet each of JJ's question with a response that has nothing to do with the snow globe.

Which means my first instinct was correct. I was right not to tell JJ about the snow globe.

Because I still need snow globe JJ.

Because this is not over.

I look at him, he looks back. His face is totally expressionless. My stomach bottoms out. Dread rises in my chest. "What have you done?" There is already a note of panic in my tone.

I try to stand but my legs won't move. My arms in front of me are trapped in a prayer-like position. I struggle but I am bound tight, wrapped in a web of invisible magical silk.

"What have you done?" I repeat in horror. There is awe in my voice, but also fear. He had no interest in my explanations. He asked all those questions to keep me talking, to keep me distracted ... then bound me so I cannot follow him.

He walks to me, crouches at my side and gently tucks a strand of hair over my ear. "I'm sorry. I had no choice. I had to keep you safe."

"Don't you dare leave me like this."

"I've instructed the amulet not to help you. I'll remove the bindings when I get back."

When he gets back ... My chest squeezes so tight I can't breathe. "Don't do this. Please don't do this."

"I love you. I'm always going to love you." His hands are on my face, my jaw. His fingers brush my lips, his touch soft on my mouth. He leans forward, presses a soft kiss to my lips. Despite everything, I tremble at it. He whispers, a flutter of breath at my temple, "See you on the other side."

He takes his backpack and leaves.

Oh Chalice no!

He thinks that by binding me like this, I can't follow. That if I can't leave this room, I can't jump. That I'll be here, still trying to free myself, when – *if* – he returns.

But he's wrong. He is magic but so am I. I'm a witch, and I can unravel this.

I call some magic down and make the bindings visible. There are red cords running all over me, looped and knotted in a beautiful and complex pattern. I use some magic to loosen one strand but it only tightens another. I try again, and the same thing happens. And then again. It's Shibari-level intricate, and every attempt to free myself only constrains me more.

This will take too long. I will be too late.

I need help.

I need help.

I close my eyes and project myself into the snow globe.

He's waiting for me outside the castle. Everything about him, and this place, is somehow faded, lacking the vitality of my earlier visits. He hasn't got long.

"The binding. How do I get out of it?"

He exhales. I have finally come at the right time. "I'd never leave you without a quick release. At your left ankle, there's an extra loop. You'll see it if you know what you're looking for. Tug on it and the whole thing will unravel."

I know I have to get back, but I'm reluctant to leave. "Is this the last time I'll see you?"

"Here? Definitely. Ever? Maybe. It depends on him. Tell him I'll do what he wants. If he calls, I'll come home. If he doesn't want me … I'm gone forever."

"You're his magical self," I say. "You're here because—"

I come to in my own consciousness before I can finish.

But I know I'm right. As part of the ritual, JJ separates out his magical self and keeps it from returning to him.

I cannot – I do not – prevent that.

I look for the loop at my ankle. I never would have noticed it, but now that he's pointed it out, it's an obvious deviation from the pattern. I use some magic to tug firmly and the whole binding loosens. I unwrap some so I can stand, then cast off the remaining vanishing strands.

I head straight for the door.

I don't think about whether I'm too late. I don't think about how to stop him. I definitely don't think about jumping off the bridge.

I tuck the amulet under my shirt and I run.

I RUN. I run. I run.

I run to the station, catch the last train out in a daze, and somehow manage to jump off at the right stop. I run through the streets, through the park. I ignore my heaving lungs and my aching muscles, and I race to the bridge.

I still have no actual plan to stop him. I will do anything. Anything to keep him from doing this.

I run. I run. I run.

Clouds in shades of grey and violet pass over the moon. Looking down, I see the river below, light playing across the crests; the heavy weight of familiarity has a rough sound escaping my mouth. The scene is identical to one I've seen before. I know how my face looks – a perfect reflection of the terror that courses through me. I know where I slip, almost fall from the path, but I don't catch myself in time to prevent doing it again. A spike of adrenaline courses through me, but I right myself and run on.

I know what's coming next. It's a horror but also a comfort. Because if nothing has changed, then despite JJ's head start, I will make it in time. All I need to do is keep running.

Under the moon, through the scrub, further and further from the lights of the city. My heart is pounding, my breath is ragged, my muscles ache, but I am almost there.

Whatever is going to happen will – must – happen.

Faith in the future; hope for a new beginning.

I run through the night. My lungs are set to bursting with the pace I set, but I don't stop. And finally the path clears. In front of me is the bridge. Standing high on the rail, like he's been waiting for eternity, is a dark, shadowy JJ. I watch his outline as he tips a bottle high, swallowing the contents.

The potion. It has started.

I make no effort to hide my presence. He turns when he hears my steps. He's beautiful as the moonlight cuts shadows into his face; blistering planes of light and smoky depths.

His eyes go wide with horror. He had thought my escape impossible; he didn't know about the snow globe. He doesn't waste time asking how I did it. "You need to leave." His voice is sharp and heavy with fear.

I can't. I won't. He had his chance to stop this.

I lose my jacket, wrench off boots. When I reach him, I grip the rail with one hand, wrapping the other around the nearest support beam, and haul myself up to join him.

We are high; so very high. My heart is in my throat, I tremble at the water rushing below, at the peaks of glinting moonlight reflecting back up.

"Everly, get down."

I don't respond. I cannot look away from the water below.

"I'll get down too," he tries frantically.

But it won't stop him; it would merely delay his plans. Tonight is optimal, moon shining high and bright above, full of the energy of the recent equinox, but it is not the only time this can happen. He will wait and he will try again.

"Please, Evie. Get down." He reaches, touches my hair, my face. "Please. I love you."

My heart fills, but I shake my head. "No. We do this tonight."

His eyes go wider at my use of 'we'. "There's no 'we' here. There's nothing you can do. You can't stop it. You can't save me. You just need to get down."

"I'm not trying to stop it anymore." It's what's supposed to happen. I draw the amulet from around my neck. "Put it on."

"You know what will happen." He sways a little, eyes bright with poison. Soon, his heart will stop beating. "I'd rather die."

He would. So convinced is he, he'd rather die than put his amulet on.

But he would never let me die. No matter what it cost him.

And I know now what I have to do.

An incredible calm comes over me. I know what my face looks like; I have seen it.

"If I can't save you, then you'll have to save me."

I throw the amulet in his direction, high in the air, and I let myself fall.

I feel total peace. Time slows, loses all meaning. I float; a snowflake drifting on the wind. The water, I know, will welcome me, arms wide open. Hold my soul in its watery bosom.

It is not until I see JJ above that I realise that this is not some near-death illusion.

I am not falling. Or at least, no faster than a feather. He has frozen me; stopped my descent.

He leaps to catch the amulet, slings it around his neck mid-air, and dives to save me.

I shouldn't be able to make it out, not with him falling at speed towards me, but somehow I see the intent, the determination in his eyes. His arms come around me, and I am released from my freeze. We tumble the final distance into the river, the water an icy rush as we slam through. He's cushioned my fall, but it's still a damaging violence. His arms go slack, I feel him sink down, away from me. The potion has taken effect. His heart has stopped. He is dead.

I grip him tight, hold him to me, and when my feet hit the bottom, I push us up with as much force as I have in my legs.

I surface, gulping in air in a shocked rush. I struggle to haul him up, get his face above water. It's hard; he's heavy, the sodden weight of our clothes acting to drag us down.

I tread water with everything in me. Glance quickly at him to see his eyes are closed, his face slack; he's a deadweight in my arms.

I need to get us to shore. I will not be able to keep his head above water for long. I hold him under his arms and start, half-swimming, half-dragging us through the water. The Yarra is narrow – thank Chalice – but it seems to take an age to get there.

It's a relief when it's shallow enough to put my feet down. I drag our drenched bodies half up on a bank and lean over him, dripping everywhere. Hands on his face, I will him to wake up and live again.

"Please. Please wake up."

His eyes snap open. A sob escapes me. I lean forward and press against his cold, wet lips.

His arms come around me, pulling me in tight against him. Joy floods through me, giving my cold, tired limbs warmth and life. I keep my mouth pressed to his, unable to get enough of the feel of it. Of his mouth on mine, of mine on his, of his arms around me, of him being here with me, alive. He kisses me until I lose myself, and I am lit from within with the brilliance of the moon.

I finally lean back, breathing hard. And listen to the sound of him doing the same. My teeth are chattering, my clothes are sodden rags, and I won't be able to move my muscles tomorrow. But I have never been more grateful. Through gum leaves, the moon sails bright overhead. He snakes an arm under my head, drawing me closer to his warmth. Then takes my hand in his, brings it to his lips, then holds it against his chest. "I made a mistake."

I draw in a breath, roll my head towards his. It's not what I was expecting to hear. "What?"

"I thought I could swap the gold for platinum, but the interaction with the berries was off. I felt it just before I hit the water." He looks down towards the river. "I would have drowned."

I look at his clean profile, lit by the moon. "So I did save you."

He raises my hand to his lips again. "You save me every day."

And he saves me. "The Red?" I make myself ask.

"Gone."

"You got the amulet to make it go."

He rolls to his side, brings his hand to my jaw. "I didn't even think about it. All I thought of was saving you."

So much heat is rising from his skin, I am no longer cold. I touch the amulet where it hangs at his collar bone. I feel something I can only describe as a ... purr. "Something else is happy to have you back."

He looks down at my hand, and a slight frown breaks across his brow. "I can't feel it anymore. I can't ..." His smile stretches to something I haven't seen in months. "It worked. I'm free."

He goes to kiss me again, but I hold him back with a hand to his chest. "Only if you want to be."

His eyes are wide.

"Your magical self ... He isn't completely gone. He's waiting to see if you want him back."

"My ... What?"

"I couldn't tell you but I've been meeting with him. That guy you saw, the one I was dancing with. It's you."

His mouth parts, but nothing comes out. His gaze scans my eyes, searching for answers.

"Do you remember me telling you I had a dream that we met in my snow globe?" He nods. "It wasn't a dream." I look at the amulet again, trying to put the pieces together myself. "I think when we hit the water and your magical self couldn't follow, instead of ascending like it was supposed to, it went into the snow globe. To help me. To help us."

He draws back a little. "That ... sounds like something I would do."

I smile, run a hand across his chest. "He's waiting for you to decide if you want to be magic or not. He can't hold on much longer."

"Would you miss him?"

"I couldn't *miss* him. He's you, and I'd still have you. Jun Jie Lee, international student of mystery."

He grins. Then turns serious. "Decision time. One I thought I'd already made."

I roll closer. "Now you can make it properly. Without a Red hounding you."

He places a hand over his amulet. "If I wasn't magic, I wouldn't have been able to stop you falling just then."

"No. But if we weren't magic, we wouldn't have been in this mess in the first place."

He looks at me, thinking through this decision that will affect the rest of our lives. "You were the one who reminded me of all the good magic can do."

"But imagine if we were normal," I say quietly. "Imagine if we were just two ordinary students. Stressing about finals, trying to find jobs, complaining about how hard it is to find an affordable rental."

He links his fingers through mine. For a moment, all we do is drink in the lively flow of the river in the background, bathe in the gentle light of the moon and the stars.

"I mean, I still own a palace in Singapore," he says. "We wouldn't have to worry about renting."

I laugh, wrestle with his hand. "Oh, the palace. I forgot about the palace."

"You want to see it?" His gaze is sly.

Something goes ping inside. "Of course. And maybe we wouldn't be searching for magical artefacts, but we could still travel the world. I could still work on my poetry."

"I could learn how to cook."

A laugh bubbles out of me.

He grins. "I'd make you a feast every night. If I knew how. I've never even boiled an egg."

"Of course not. You're the crown prince of the wizarding world. Why would you trouble yourself with such earthly concerns?"

He pulls himself up on an elbow. His gaze travels down my body. "Earthly concerns," he repeats, one finger slowly and deliberately following the trail his eyes just made.

I shiver and fist my hand in his still-wet t-shirt, tugging him down to me, but he resists.

I watch as his eyes go serious, tender. He sees me, like he always has; my light but also my dark. "What about you? Do you want to stay a witch?"

I look down at my hand, still gripping his shirt. "My coven needs me."

"I don't care what your coven needs. I'll call back my magical ability just to take yours. Tell me to and I'll do it."

I know he would. And a future expands before me just as we've been imagining. A future without the terrible things I see and feel. That scar my soul even though they shouldn't.

The burden is heavy but so is the benefit. I feel those things in some small measure so others don't have to. I shake my head. "If I have you, I can bear it. I can bear anything. I might have saved you tonight, but you saved me first. When you came into my life. I can't even think of who I was before I met you, who I'd be without you."

His eyes soften. "You will always have me. No matter what—"

"We're together," I finish.

He cups my neck. "You sure about keeping your magic?"

"Yes."

"Okay." He leans down, lands a kiss on my jaw. "But they don't get to overwork you. I *will* drag you away whenever I think you need it."

I smile. "I can live with that."

"Then so can I." His decision has been made. It's not a physical change, but there is a swooping through the air of energy. His magical self has been called back home. "I wouldn't want to live this life without you. It's you, Everly. You're my fire. My truth. My everything."

I feel it in the strength of our complicated, tough, unbreakable bond. I sneak my hands under his t-shirt at the back, relishing how he shudders at the contact. Despite the wet clothes, his skin is scorching. "Show me."

His gaze heats to velvety chocolate. "Here? Now?"

"Yes. Definitely."

And then we're in a bed. Still on the river bank, secluded under the gums. But we are on a bed. A four-poster bed with a canopy across the top, draping down the sides. "Show off," I say, delighted.

His chest is bare. I can't resist. I lean forward and press a kiss to the muscle of his chest.

Then realise I'm also no longer in clothes. I look down and laugh-shriek in outrage. All I have covering my modesty is strategically placed black lace.

I put a hand on my hip. "A skimpy negligee? Really?"

A smile breaks over his face. "Have it your way …"
The next time I look down, I'm completely nude.
I laugh again.
Oh.
This is going to be fun.

~

ENJOYED READING about the world of the Owlscroft Coven witches? Join my mailing list and receive *Bad Batch*, the first in the series, for free! Simply click here to sign up:

https://dl.bookfunnel.com/h2t9161g5d

ALSO BY MARNIE ST CLAIR

If you enjoyed this story, you may enjoy my other works:

Bad Batch

An Owlscroft Coven Novella, Book 1

(In A Perfectly Paranormal Valentine)

Good Riddance

An Owlscroft Coven Novella, Book 2

(In A Perfectly Paranormal Halloween)

Sweet Hereafter

An Owlscroft Coven Novella, Book 3

(In A Perfectly Paranormal Easter)

No Place Like You

A sweet but sizzling rural romance

Blue Steal

A witty and suspenseful romantic mystery

ABOUT MARNIE

After years of forecasting the price of tea in China, Marnie St Clair finally shut down the spreadsheets and got serious about her passion for romance, especially the kind that blends charm, humour and a dollop of magic and mystery.

A country girl at heart, Marnie now lives in Melbourne, Australia, with two surprisingly civil teens and a weatherman husband. She likes prosecco, cottage gardens, driving at night, sandalwood-scented anything and a really strong cup of coffee. Or preferably two.

You can contact Marnie through her website www.marniestclair.com, where you can also sign up to her newsletter to be the first to find out about new releases, special deals and exclusive giveaways.

And if you want to get to know the Perfectly Paranormal Anthology authors a bit more, get sneak peeks of what's coming up for the APP Anthologies, as well as giveaways, special offers and just some PNR fun, then join our Perfectly Paranormal Paramours Facebook Group.

Find us here:

https://www.facebook.com/groups/251663560162131

ACKNOWLEDGMENTS

A big heartfelt thanks to the *A Perfectly Paranormal Anthology* contributors – Hellucy Howe, Leisl Leighton and Samantha Marshall – and former contributor Georgia Tingley for inviting me to be part of the group. *A Perfectly Paranormal* has been a blast to be part of and I look forward to future instalments.

Thanks as always to lovely Mady (no sister like you) and my writing group pals Leisl and Frana for the continued support and friendship.

A million kisses to my biggest support and own personal weatherman.

FOILED

SAMANTHA MARSHALL

FOILED

A Merged Worlds
Novella

~

Samantha Marshall

❀ Created with Vellum

ABOUT FOILED

Everything has a dark side... even chocolate.

Taylin Colkannis has never questioned her place as head Sentinel of Evergreen Waters Retreat - until the night an intruder sneaks into her home and attempts to murder her mentor right under her nose. Before she has a chance to change out of her pyjamas, Taylin's kitchen is overtaken by an entire department of Easter Bunnies and a darkly handsome man claiming to be the only god capable of saving her mentor's life.

Drift was once the Primal God of the Vernal Equinox - until Ostara, Goddess of the Spring and Dawn, stole his powers, his staff, his duties as the Easter Hare and, if that wasn't enough, his dignity. Countless centuries later, a nameless thief has snatched the Staff of Easter from Ostara's domain and is using it to wreak havoc across the land of Mu. To regain his birthright, Drift must catch the thief... and nobody, least of all the enchanting Taylin Colkannis with her moon-touched magic and beguiling smile, is going to stand in his way.

Desperate to save her mentor, Taylin offers to help Drift recover his staff - putting them in direct competition with Ostara and the Easter Bunny Conglomerate, who will stop at nothing to prevent Drift's restoration. With the balance of the Merged Worlds at stake and danger around every corner, Taylin and Drift must learn to trust the primal attraction blooming between them... or tear each other apart.

For those who helped me through one of the toughest points of my author career, which just so happened to coincide with the writing of this tale. You know who you are, and I remain eternally grateful.
Thank you.

THE UNFORTUNATE FATE OF GREAT AUNT ETHEL

A crinkle in the dark.

That's all it took for Taylin's eyes to snap open; no gentle, lazy lash lifting but a brutal, immediate awareness that had all the fine hairs on her body standing on end.

With careful deliberation, she forced her fingers to curl around the top of the bedsheet. One. Just a dream. Two. Dreams fade. Three. She was safe. Four … a wild, riotous flash of fury slammed into her brain, forcing her teeth together and bowing her spine before it cut off with the finality of a slamming door.

Taylin's heart rabbited in her chest as the very *real* slamming of a door echoed from downstairs.

Someone was in the house.

Get up. Get up. Get up.

But she was made of stone, her bones a weight too great to lift, her lungs inadequate tools with which to provide oxygen to her body.

No.

She was not helpless. She was Taylin Colkannis, triple-banded mage, Sentinel of Evergreen Waters Retreat, and she would never be helpless again.

Throwing the covers back, Taylin rolled out of bed and crept to the door. She hesitated with one hand on the knob, her senses ranging the house for signs of the intruder.

Nothing – except for an odd patch of static downstairs and to the right, in the kitchen. The strange cloud didn't give off any emotion, no hint of life … and yet there was *something*, some kind of lingering residue that made Taylin want to scream and scream and scream and scream.

"Not helpless," she whispered, pulling open the door. "Not. Helpless."

Her steps were slow and deliberate down the landing, the rasp of her breathing the only sound in the choking silence. Shadows prowled beyond the faint luminosity of her skin, snickering as they awaited an opportunity to pounce. She took the stairs one at a time, one eye on her route and the other examining the magic woven into the very bones of the estate. Both Taylin and Great Aunt Ethel worked to recharge those wards every day, pouring love and strength into them until there was very little that could endanger Evergreen's residents – and no way the residents could endanger anyone else.

Taylin paused at the foot of the stairs. The back door stood to her left, limned by moonlight … and ajar, as though slammed with such force it bounced off the frame before the lock had time to engage. She cracked it enough to peer into the night, the moonlight painting a blessing across her glowing skin.

A faint breeze whispered across the manicured lawns, causing the ever-blooming flowers in the garden to bob their heads hello, hello, hello. Beneath the outward appearance of peace crept a lingering echo of thwarted rage and driving purpose, a memory that faded more with every passing moment. Whoever had come was now gone.

She scanned the rest of the estate. Evergreen Waters Retreat had several buildings, of which the two-story home she shared with Great Aunt Ethel was the crown jewel. Since none of the wards were disturbed over the rest of the property, whoever had entered the house had known exactly what they wanted and where to find it.

Though … Great Aunt Ethel hadn't raised the alarm, and the wards, whilst reflecting the intruder's passage, remained intact.

Perhaps this was no more than a late-night visit by an acquaintance of Ethel's, or even a past resident wishing to drop by without garnering undue attention.

The patch of static in the kitchen pulsed.

"Ethel? Is that you?" Taylin pulled back into the house and closed the door.

Great Aunt Ethel had never before displayed the ability to scrub herself from Taylin's empathic senses but the woman was fae and incredibly ancient; if she'd wanted to have some kind of clandestine meeting inside the house without alerting Taylin, this would be the perfect way to do it.

Releasing her grip on the wards, she smoothed her hands down the soft cotton of her pyjama pants and let out a long breath.

More jumping at shadows. When would she ever learn?

When Taylin entered the kitchen, Great Aunt Ethel was standing in her favourite spot by the far window, where a crack in the curtains allowed a perfect view of the courtyard beyond. That she didn't turn when Taylin flicked on the kettle was no oddity, and with her empathic senses now retracted as far as they could go, the strange static that had felt so grating before was almost unnoticeable.

"Tea or coffee?" Taylin pulled two mugs from the overhead cupboard and arranged them just so on the smooth wooden bench. "Ethel?"

When the fae who was nobody's Great Aunt and therefore everybody's Great Aunt didn't answer, Taylin swung to face her. Ethel remained as she'd been; still and silent. Shadows concealed most of her form, only the faintest illumination leaking in from the partially opened curtains to glint off the deep carmine velvet of her favourite robe.

Except … velvet didn't glint.

"Great Aunt Ethel?" Goosebumps rose in a wave as Taylin sidled closer. Ethel's iron-grey hair was in the long, loose braid she often wore for sleeping but it looked flat somehow, as though painted on.

Taking care to be gentle, Taylin put a hand on Ethel's shoulder.

It crinkled.

She drew back as though burnt, breath sawing in her lungs. That was the sound – the sound that had woken her. Crinkling, like … foil.

Swallowing her dread, Taylin illuminated her skin from within. The glow was gentle and soft, tinted blue-white like the moonlight it imitated, but it was more than enough to see by. More than enough to make out the shape of Great Aunt Ethel, her edges curiously rounded and her stance unchanging.

Taylin brushed her senses against the grating static that lingered in the air. As before, there were no signs of life, nothing to say that the shape in front of her was a person. But if it wasn't Great Aunt Ethel, who, or what, *was* it?

Shifting so she could see the front of the strange figure, Taylin slapped a hand over her mouth, catching her scream. Before her was a painstakingly precise sculpture of Great Aunt Ethel, her face set in an almost comical caricature of shock. The features were correct to the finest detail whilst remaining unnaturally flat, as though someone had taken the real Ethel and transformed her into a parody of herself. When Taylin laid a hand softly, so softly, against the effigy's outer surface, the crinkling of foil set bile bubbling at the back of her throat.

Swallowing the revulsion that threatened to overwhelm, Taylin opened her empathic senses as far as they would go. Beneath the static, almost impossible to detect, was a whisper of emotional resonance as unique as a fingerprint. The kind of resonance that allowed Taylin to say beyond any shadow of a doubt that the odd, foil-covered statue in front of her *was* Great Aunt Ethel.

Taylin's fingers twitched and the foil crinkled and tore. She leapt back with a squeak, staring at the tear for a moment before slamming her hand down on the panic button at the end of the kitchen bench. No alarm split the night, but she knew that in the guardhouse across the estate, warnings and lights would be going off like crazy.

In the meantime, Taylin couldn't help but bend to examine the rip she'd put in the foil. For all the hammering of her heart, she was the Sentinel here and it was her job to keep Aunt Ethel – and the rest of Evergreen Waters – safe. With careful fingers, she peeled the foil aside and stared.

It was … It looked like … No.

Surely not.

Shaking her head, Taylin tugged open the curtain to make sure she could see clearly, and when nothing changed, turned on every single light in the kitchen.

Beneath Ethel's foil wrapping was not a body. No flesh. No blood. Not even stone.

It was chocolate.

2

IT'S TIME TO GO BACK

There was someone at the door.

Not unusual; unless of course you were in exile and weren't supposed to have visitors. Drift stared until the knock became a distinct thump, at which point he decided he wasn't imagining it, pushed back his chair and went to answer. A man hulked on the doorstep; black jeans, black sweater, long black jacket ... and only one hand.

"Tyr?" Drift's voice cracked from disuse and he cleared his throat. "What are you doing here?"

The Norse God of Justice – fallen, just like he was, and even harder to locate since he didn't live in a single, convenient location – stared down at Drift from eyes that leaked silver flames. "The staff is gone."

"The staff is *gone*?"

"Stolen." Tyr dipped his head, the glow of his eyes hidden by the lip of his dark hood. "I came as soon as I heard."

Drift's grin was slow, wide and completely feral. "I owe you one."

"Yes." Tyr held out his hand.

Drift took it.

Magic surged and when he blinked next, they stood in a thick bank of trees. Instead of the ragged linen tunic and soft breeches that were his customary mode of dress, Drift found himself in torn jeans a shade tighter than he was accustomed to, a fitted black t-shirt and a wide, black leather belt with an oversized buckle whose silver accents matched those on his heavy black boots.

When he raised a brow at Tyr, the god shrugged. "You looked like a hobo."

Drift didn't need a mirror to know he now looked dark, edgy and every inch the wild creature he was. "Ears?"

"A small glamour. It'll wear off in a few hours."

"Good." With a sharp smile, Drift peered between the trees to see a verdant estate crawling with all manner of peoples. Most were humanoid and dressed in plain clothes, escorting or wheeling others in hospital gowns from one building to another. "Where are we?"

"Evergreen Waters Retreat." Tyr rolled his shoulders, the hem of his hood dropping even lower over his face. "A healing facility specialising in rare maladies of body, mind and magic."

"Huh." Drift examined the scenery anew, lips twisting as he spotted a number of rabbits wearing quaint, tailored outfits amongst the Retreat staff and their clients. The vast majority stood on their hind legs and carried clipboards or woven baskets, with a rare few scurrying hither and thither on all fours, whiskers twitching and little pink noses close to the ground. "The EBC is already here."

"Aye, but it's no matter; they're as lost without you now as then."

Drift took in a pretty brown rabbit in a frothy sundress and snorted. "They don't look it."

"Appearances can be deceiving." Tyr released Drift's hand to grip his shoulder. "This is your chance to set things right. Make it count."

"Justice." Drift inclined his head to the god – who disappeared without another word.

A look upward confirmed the moon was almost set, dawn a mauve promise on the horizon. Judging by the way the sky streaked and dipped without reason, he figured he wasn't on Earth but in Mu, where the weather was apt to be odd and the environment so rich in magic that it dripped off every leaf and petal.

Not that he could feel it any more.

Narrowing his eyes on the heels of that thought, Drift stepped out of the trees and began a slow, purposeful stalk across the lawn. None of the plain-clothed beings nor their patients stopped to question him – but when a rabbit wearing a waistcoat and a monocle gasped and dropped the clipboard in his paw, Drift knew he'd been made.

He smiled.

Wide.

Abandoning all pretence at civilised behaviour, the rabbit turned and fled, cotton-ball tail bobbing behind him. Drift continued towards the back of the property, where a two-story cottage stood in the eye of the chaotic storm. Situated beside an ornamental pond, the building was a mixture of natural materials that looked to have been slotted into the walls in their raw state. Branches poked out at odd angles, some with their leaves still attached. The thatching of an old bird's nest skirted one window. Sheets of shale were laid side by side with pebbles mosaiced in mud, and flowers grew from cracks in the mortar in several places. Despite the haphazard construction, the house maintained an air of understated elegance that screamed fae, and if Drift had been able to sniff the magic in the air, he was sure it'd carry the floral cadence that accompanied all fae enchantments.

"You!" A pair of rabbits wearing bow ties and tailored shorts tumbled to a stop in the cottage's open doorway. "You can't be here – this is the site of an official EBC investigation!"

Drift paused with one boot on the bottom step. Lemurian rabbits were significantly larger than their Earth counterparts, meaning that these were about knee height. One had pale grey fur and the other a tawny kind of caramel, with which his yellow accessory clashed horrendously. Caramel clutched a clipboard while Grey drew himself up to his full, astoundingly unimpressive height and crossed furry paws over his chest.

Bracing one arm on his raised knee, Drift leant down until the rabbits' whiskers tickled his cheeks. *"Boo."*

Caramel shrieked, throwing his clipboard up in the air as he bolted out onto the lawn. Grey flattened his body on the ground, eyes squeezed shut and paws over his head as though the sky was falling. Drift straightened, caught the falling clipboard and stepped inside the house before either rabbit had finished shitting themselves.

Pathetic.

Drift stalked through the darkened interior, glancing at the clipboard in his hand. In writing more suited to a child than an adult were scrawled a list of basic investigative questions of no interest whatsoever. Underneath that, underlined several times, were the words 'wards again intact'.

Lifting a brow at that little nugget, Drift stepped into a spacious kitchen well-lit by lace-covered windows. The place was teeming with rabbits in pastel outfits, voices frantic as they swarmed around a—

Drift froze.

He didn't need enhanced senses to know the thing by the window had once been the fae woman who ran the estate. Instinct drew him forward, his pace as inexorable as the tides and impossible for the rabbits to stop, no matter that several of them screeched and attached themselves to his legs like tiny, furry anchors.

Once, twice, he circled the life-sized chocolate figure wrapped in brightly coloured foil, before extending one finger to prod the section of chocolate exposed by a small tear. Energy zinged up his arm, the feeling so familiar he had to stifle a gasp and retract his hand.

"You're not supposed to be here."

Drift glanced up as a diminutive woman in a mauve bo-peep outfit stormed into the room. Spring-green ringlets poked from beneath a ribboned bonnet, a smattering of freckles dusting cheeks slapped with righteous indignation.

"And you are?" He stepped into her space, glaring down the length of his nose. "All bets were off the minute someone stole my staff."

She flinched at his tone, dark eyes skittering away from potential contact. "That staff is the property of the Easter Bunny Conglomerate, and we—"

"Fuck off, Gedenna." Drift jabbed his finger at the tall, sweet treat which had once been a living, breathing person. "Don't give me your bullshit when someone is using *my staff* to murder people."

"Murder?"

Drift spun on one heel as a second woman glided into the room. His momentum sent several of the EBC's rabbits flying but he paid little mind, enthralled by a voice smooth and cool as moonlight, her single uttered word more melodic than an entire choir. He catalogued a pair of plain navy cotton lounge pants, shapely hips and a slender waist whose navel peeped out beneath a matching cropped navy tank. Long black hair curled around a finely boned face, flawless pale skin the perfect canvas for—

The air punched out of him.

Her left eye was a bright sapphire and her right either false or blind, the featureless orb milky white but for a faint, glacial blue shimmer. A trail of fae characters dripped down from that white eye, symbols for containment and protection done in delicate black inkwork that tapered to a single string finishing at her jaw. A crescent moon was tattooed between her brows, additional fae symbols tripping across the bridge of her nose to finish halfway to the softly rounded tip. Her lips were full and firm, cheeks sharp in contrast to a sweeping jaw, and those eyes, those *eyes*, were enormous. Not only was she eerily, heart-wrenchingly beautiful, her skin gave off a faint, blue-white luminescence that was visible even beneath the kitchen's artificial globes.

Moonlight.

Drift had extended an awed hand before he realised and caught it back, shaking his head to clear the spell. "What?"

"Murder," she repeated, her voice thrumming through his veins in such a way it set his heart thumping out of time. "What do you mean by murder?"

"It's not really murder," Gedenna said desperately, making throat-cutting motions with one finger. "Once we have the staff—"

"So it's not here." Drift blew out a sharp breath, struggling against a surge of disappointment. He brushed a second touch over the exposed chocolate but whatever energy had lingered was gone, leaving little more than the sugary parody of a living, breathing person. "I didn't think it was possible for someone to misuse my staff more thoroughly than it has been already. I was wrong."

"It is *not* your staff!" Gedenna stomped one foot, face screwed up as though to hold back tears. "Don't do this, Drift. Leave now, while you still can."

"Wait." The other woman's voice never changed volume, but the weight behind it was impossible to ignore. "Drift, is it?"

And oh, though he'd vowed never to be caught by a woman again, his name on her lips was impossible to resist. Jaw clenched tight lest he say something stupid, he nodded.

"Taylin." She extended a hand in the human way, drawing his attention to the three thick navy bands etched into her skin just below the elbow.

"Taylin," Drift repeated, accepting the handshake and shivering at the silken perfection of her skin. Her inner light caressed the inside of his wrist, the energy of the moon so potent and pure that he swallowed. Hard. "You're human. A mage."

Her gaze dropped to the triple banding on her upper forearm, marks formed by the magic that was an intrinsic part of her. Each line was three fingers thick, so close together there was barely a gap between them. Drift might have been in exile a long time, but he'd been watching the world from his eyrie and knew that mage marks ranged from single to triple bands, their abilities further defined by the width of the lines. Whilst Taylin's skill set remained to be seen, one thing was certain – she was powerful.

"Good spotting."

The dry humour gave Drift the strength he didn't know he needed; he broke the clasp and stepped back, shaking his head. "Sorry. I don't get out much."

"Maybe because you're an *exile*?" Gedenna jabbed a finger in his direction. "Coming here was a mistake."

Drift looked down at the collection of pastel-clad rabbits slowly climbing his legs, and quirked just enough lip to show the tip of a fang. "Are your bunnies going to throw me out?"

They all flinched.

"Enough." Taylin held up a hand to forestall Gedenna's response. "You two clearly know each other and what's going on, but I'm very confused." She faced Drift, squaring her shoulders. "I'm the Sentinel of this estate and with Great Aunt Ethel indisposed, that puts me in charge. All I care about is that someone turned a powerful fae healer into chocolate and now you're saying ... what? That she can't be turned back? That she's *dead*?"

"She isn't dead." Gedenna fisted both hands in her skirts. "As I said before, the staff suspended her vitals during the transformation."

"I wasn't asking you, Handmaiden. I was asking Drift."

He took his time to answer, enjoying all over again the sound of his name in that cool, smooth voice – and the scandalised look on Gedenna's face as she was so summarily dismissed. "Your Aunt isn't dead, but neither is she alive. Her vitals are indeed suspended, but without my staff ..."

"That staff is no longer yours," Gedenna gritted out. "It is the acknowledged property of the Easter Bunny Conglomerate, who operate under the full authority of Ostara, Goddess of the Spring and the Dawn."

Drift cocked a brow. "Acknowledged is a strange word for 'ill-gotten.'"

"Wait." Taylin held up a slender hand. "It sounds as though the EBC is more concerned with a magical staff than whether Ethel lives or dies."

"Oh, no," Gedenna cooed, touching her fingertips to her heart. "It's simply that—"

"If you recover the staff, can you turn her back?"

Every rabbit in the kitchen froze.

Drift grinned. "Go on, Handmaiden. Answer the question."

"I ..." Gedenna's face twitched. "Uh."

Taylin's eyes narrowed. "You can't, can you?"

"Well." The Handmaiden of Ostara patted at the springtime flowers arranged across her bonnet. "It's critical to understand that the staff fulfils a specific purpose for the Easter Bunny Conglomerate

– to ensure there's a sufficient amount of chocolate available to spread joy at Easter in the name of Ostara, Goddess of Spring and Dawn, bringer of light and life—"

Gedenna squeaked as Taylin's fingers latched around one delicate wrist. "If you had the staff in your custody, could you use it to turn Ethel back?"

"No," Gedenna choked out.

"Finally, something truthful." Drift shook his head. "I didn't know you had it in you."

"Don't give her credit she hasn't earned." Taylin pointed at the chocolate effigy with her free hand. "Can anyone in the EBC turn Ethel back?"

"No." Sweat broke out across Gedenna's brow.

"Ostara?"

"No."

Taylin squeezed, her knuckles whitening. "*Can* she be turned back?"

Gedenna shook her head, green ringlets flying, but her mouth, it said, "Yes!"

"By ...?"

"Drift! If Drift had the staff, he could do it!" Gedenna was tugging desperately at her arm, but Taylin didn't budge in the slightest. "How are you doing this? Stop it! I'm not supposed to tell you these things!"

Taylin frowned, her sapphire eye tracing the length of Drift's body – and though her white eye was a featureless orb that appeared blind, he had the strangest feeling that it, too, was staring at him. "So the staff *does* belong to Drift?"

"It did, once," Gedenna panted, bracing her entire body against the kitchen table as she tried to pull away. "But Ostara claimed the Staff of Easter as the spoils of war. It's *hers* now – and he's breaking the terms of his exile simply by being here!"

Drift snorted. "Am I? Perhaps you've forgotten the exact wording, after all this time."

When Taylin held out her other hand, he didn't hesitate to lay his skin against hers, didn't fight when her fingers curled over his, the contrast between her pale colouring and his light brown compelling. Magic washed over him, the cool kiss of the moon, as she said, "Tell me who you really are."

"I'm the Osterhase." Drift's voice dropped until it was a vicious growl that rattled the crockery in the cupboards and had the fur of the rabbits clinging to his legs standing on end. "The staff was stripped from me during an ambush, the resulting wounds so great I had little choice but to accept exile rather than wrest it back."

A pale thumb stroked the back of his knuckles, the motion smoothing his jagged temper until the hard knot in his throat eased. Taylin hummed a soft note under her breath. "And now you're not exiled?"

"The answer is both yes and no. The terms of my exile are thus: 'As long as the staff remains in the custody of Ostara, Goddess of Spring and Dawn, so shall the Osterhase be confined to his home.'"

Taylin tipped her head to one side. "Meaning that while the staff is at large, you're free to roam. All right. What does this have to do with Ethel?"

"Nothing." Drift rolled his shoulders in a shrug. "I'm here for what's mine. Your Great Aunt's fate is nothing more than a side effect of the EBC's mismanagement." He turned his face away, determined not to see the rough slap of his words hit home. No matter how beautiful her appearance or how much her magic sang to him, he'd die before he showed his belly to another living being ever, ever, *ever* again. Lips pressing firmly together on that thought, Drift's gaze wandered over the kitchen, landing on the clipboard he'd liberated earlier. "I read the notes. Ethel's not the first victim, is she?"

"Hnnnngh," Gedenna gave up trying to escape and slapped her free hand over her mouth, eyes wet with unshed tears.

Taylin tsked deep in her throat and released Drift so that she could corral both Gedenna's wrists and draw her hands from her mouth. "I have accepted you into my home, you who proclaim yourself Handmaiden to a goddess. I have given you welcome and let your Easter Bunnies put their paws all over my belongings. All the while, the woman to whom I owe an unpayable debt stands frozen by the window, turned to chocolate, of all things – and I will do whatever it takes to save her. Now. You. Will. Tell. Me. The. Truth."

"He's right." Gedenna's response was no more than a broken sob, bonnet askew and body sagging in Taylin's grip. "This is the third time someone has been turned to chocolate since the staff disappeared."

Drift didn't bother smiling; he bared his teeth instead. "I told you once you'd reap what you'd sown. Neither you or Ostara chose to listen and now innocent people are suffering."

"The fate of Ethel Blueraven is regrettable, but not our main concern." Gedenna's mouth dropped open in horror at her own words. "There's little more than a month until Easter. The EBC *must* retrieve the staff, or there won't be enough chocolate to distribute in Ostara's name." Gedenna glared at Drift. "Why am I sharing this? Have you cast some sort of spell?"

He spread his arms wide. "You, of all people, know that I am powerless. How could I?"

"The staff doesn't have the full range of your abilities," Gedenna snapped. "It only turns things to chocolate. Who knows what you're truly capable of?"

"I do." Drift's claws sliced out of his fingertips. "And I'm more than willing to demonstrate."

"If you even *think* about laying a hand on me, Ostara will—"

"Oh, for the heaven's sakes." Taylin released Gedenna with a push, sending the Handmaiden of Ostara stumbling backward. "Drift, cover your ears."

He did, folding them flat against his head and laying both hands on top. Taylin whispered a single word and clapped her hands. Though Drift didn't hear anything, he felt the ripple of magic that spread from her like the shockwave of an explosion, causing everyone else in the room to collapse.

When she tugged a small, rectangular device from her pocket and began speaking into it, Drift chanced lifting his hands and straightening his ears.

"Raucous? I need a cleanup team in here. Yeah, the whole house." Taylin bit her lip as she listened. "Oh, really? No, that won't be necessary. Put them in a clearing beyond the estate's borders and send word to the EBC to collect them at their earliest convenience." Another pause. "No, they won't wake. I hit them pretty hard." Her lips curled in the faintest of smiles. "Yeah, thanks. I knew I could count on you."

Drift carefully extracted one booted foot from the small pile of rabbits puddled on the floor. "You put them to sleep."

"Yes." She grimaced. "All over the estate, apparently."

"Why not me?"

"Because I'm not finished with you." Taylin's mouth set into a grim line. "The EBC's official stance is that someone broke into the house and used a magic staff – *your* magic staff – to turn Great Aunt Ethel to chocolate, for reasons unknown. Is that correct?"

"I have no idea. I'm not with the EBC."

"Fair enough. If you get the staff back, can you really return Ethel to her normal state?"

"If she's in one piece, yes. If she melts, is broken or eaten, no."

Taylin grunted, then tapped at the rectangular device in her hands for a few moments.

"You took my words at face value." Drift drank in her every movement as she tossed the device onto the scarred tabletop. He might've learnt his lesson where affairs of the heart were concerned but there was nothing wrong with looking, and Taylin moved with a slow deliberation that was mesmerising.

"I knew these EBC cretins were lying the minute they showed up. Every word out of that Handmaiden's mouth was empty fluff – she only gave me the truth when I forced her." Taylin's brows beetled, the crescent moon tattooed between them standing out in stark relief. "I don't enjoy having to force someone."

"But you will."

Taylin nodded, and though she turned towards the sleeping Handmaiden, he had the curious certainty that her milky-white eye was watching him. "You, meanwhile, have spoken nothing but the truth since the moment you stalked through the door. I don't know what events led to the loss of your staff and subsequent exile, but if you can save Great Aunt Ethel, I don't care."

The foundations of Drift's reality bucked and shifted, and he fought with teeth-gritting determination to prevent this incredible woman becoming the centre of his universe. Taylin was a stranger, albeit one who moved like a dancer underwater, all strength and grace and effortless poise. No matter how the moon-kissed song of her magic beckoned to his parched soul, he couldn't afford to forget the past. It wouldn't be the first time he'd been presented with danger in a pretty package, though certainly never one so perfectly attuned to him as this.

And wasn't that, in and of itself, worth noting? What were the chances of coming face to face with someone so tempting within an hour of breaking exile? It wasn't impossible for Ostara to have planted Taylin Colkannis at Evergreen Waters, knowing Drift would investigate the staff's disappearance – and with her energy so alluring, it'd be easy to become distracted from his purpose. His gut churned. He'd been a fool once before, and it had cost him everything. There would be no second time, no matter how sweetly honeyed the trap.

"Ostara will send the EBC after the staff," he snapped, making no effort to conceal his temper. "If they get it first, there will be nothing I can do for your aunt."

Taylin backed up and he followed, stepping over the pile of fallen rabbits and into a clear section of the kitchen. They stood close enough that the gentle glow of her skin washed over his clothes, causing the tiny hairs on his arms to stand on end and his heart to stutter. Drift took a deep breath, longing mixing with the deep-seated fury burning in his gut – and her scent invaded his lungs, soft and sweet and so deeply reminiscent of what grew in his own garden that he couldn't help but close his eyes and breathe again.

"What are you doing?"

He lifted his lashes to find his face in her hair, fingers curled over her bare shoulders. "You smell like home. Jasmine and vanilla."

Taylin crinkled her nose and sniffed loudly. Despite the gravity of the situation, Drift fought the urge to laugh. "You smell like … like … wood and herbs. Cedarwood, maybe? And sage. As if you've been rolling around on the floor of a forest."

"Is that good?"

One black brow ratcheted skyward. "You might be in exile, but I have no doubt you're aware that's an inappropriate question."

Drift narrowed his eyes. "I don't have the same rules on etiquette as you do. I'm not human."

"The rabbit ears gave that away already."

"They're not rabbit ears." He jerked back, flattening the ears in question. Either Tyr had become sloppy with his glamour over the years, or Drift had underestimated the amount of power Taylin possessed, even with the triple-banded mage mark to warn him. "I'm the Osterhase."

She put both hands on her hips, the perfect portrait of irritation. "You said that before, but I still don't understand what it means."

"It translates to Easter Hare."

"Easter *Hare?* Like some kind of Easter Bunny ripoff?"

"No." The growl punched out of him, and Drift's fingers were tipped in claws when he waved at the sleeping rabbits curled together on the floor. "They came later. Ostara created the EBC once she appropriated my staff and ensured I'd faded into obscurity."

Taylin studied the top of his head. "In my experience, hares don't have antlers."

"I'm one of a kind." Drift glanced over his shoulder at the chocolate effigy. "Did you see whoever did this? Catch some clue of where they might have gone?"

"Nothing, apart from a sense of rage and desperation that was as short as it was sharp. The wards are intact, which leads me to believe that Ethel may have known her attacker – or, at the very least, didn't see them as a threat."

"The EBC noted the wards, too." Drift wandered to the other side of the kitchen, where a spring-themed wicker basket – Gedenna's, no doubt – held yet another clipboard with the same underlined note at the bottom. "I wonder if the previous effigies were also found in places with undisturbed wards."

"I have no idea." Taylin sighed, surveying the sleeping bodies in the kitchen. "It's a little late to ask them."

"It doesn't matter." Drift tossed the clipboard back into the basket. "All I care about is finding a clue that will point me in the direction of the staff – and if the EBC are fucking around to this degree, they don't have one."

"Gedenna said as much when she arrived." Taylin's lashes lowered to half mast, her expression a cool mask. "I might be able to help, though. For a price."

A price.

The words reminded him so strongly of Ostara, of her endless litany of checks and balances, debts and favours, that Drift took an involuntary step back. "In my experience, the cost is almost always too high."

"Yet you'll listen," Taylin predicted. "Because you're desperate."

A growl rattled in the base of Drift's throat, but she didn't so much as flinch. After a long moment staring at her mesmerising mismatched eyes, he thumped his fist on the table. "I'll listen – but I make no promises."

The front door swung open, loud voices echoing down the hall. Taylin glanced briefly towards the noise, then back to Drift. "Not here. Follow me."

Drift wanted nothing more than to slam her against the wall and demand answers, but he had no idea which were the right questions to ask. She appeared well entrenched at Evergreen Waters, yet had been co-operating with Gedenna rather than consumed by the grief of losing her patroness. She appeared dedicated to rescuing Ethel, but spoke with an attitude that many of Ostara's followers had adopted from their goddess. Was it mere coincidence, or were her motivations more sinister? It was impossible to tell – but on the offchance she could, in fact, help him, Drift trailed her into the hall without protest. She moved with calculated purpose, hips swinging and body poised, not an ounce of energy wasted. It was only once they'd ascended the stairs and stepped into a bedroom that Drift realised he was in her private haven.

Oblivious to the way his skin tightened and his eyes roved the space for signs of an ambush, Taylin closed the door behind them.

With the curtains down the room should have been dark, but the illumination coming from her skin increased until it was almost as bright as turning on a lamp.

"Moonlight." Drift turned his hands back and forth in the blue-white glow, arrested by the phenomenon. "You give off moonlight."

"I'm one of a kind."

His head snapped up at the repetition of his own words but she merely offered a half-smile.

She's probably a trap. Do not forget.

Except … he wanted to.

For just one moment, he wanted to forget the mistakes he'd made, the things he'd lost, the love he'd offered only to be irrevocably burned. He wanted to forget the gaping hole inside of him, the cracked glass upon which he walked day in and out, and immerse himself in the moonlit perfection of Taylin Colkannis, triple-banded mage and Sentinel of Evergreen Waters Retreat. He itched to peel her clothes from her elegant limbs and worship the flawless satin of her skin with lips and tongue and teeth, to clench his fists in her hair as she surrendered to the primal fury of his need.

Do not forget.

Struggling to breathe through the dichotomy of conflicting urges, Drift ran his gaze the length of Taylin's body and back again. Their eyes locked and he was struck anew by the notion that the milky white of her right eye was watching as avidly as the sapphire of her left.

Do. Not. Forget.

"What aid do you possibly think to offer that I would accept?" His voice was cracked and hoarse, lips curling around every word. "I prefer to work alone, and for good reason."

Taylin's lips thinned. "I can track the Staff of Easter."

Her declaration sounded in his mind like a gong, the syllables reverberating back against one another until they became unintelligible – and still they stared at one another, gazes bound as though there were nothing more important in all the Merged Worlds than the connection brokered by that simple, stark contact. There was surely some sort of societal convention condemning their behaviour – only Drift wasn't human and didn't have it in himself to care. In that instant, she was the only thing holding his feet to the ground, her words a lifeline he'd never thought to have extended.

"You can track the staff," he repeated, testing the sentence for himself. "How?"

"One of my abilities is … to recover part of oneself that has been lost. Often the truest part." Taylin smoothed her palms over her pyjama pants. "I know that sounds vague, but when I touch you, I feel it. The staff, I mean."

"It is an extension of me." Drift knocked on his own breastbone. "The temple housing all that I've lost. In that, you are correct."

"I could lead you to it." She swallowed, and his gaze snapped to the flexing of her throat. "With my help, you'd be able to reach the Staff of Easter before Ostara."

"What makes you so sure?"

"You said it yourself." She pointed at the floor, where the EBC slumbered beneath their feet. "Ostara and her followers have no clue as to the staff's whereabouts."

"Why not just tell me where it is?"

"I can't. It doesn't work that way – when we make contact, I can sense the direction and no more."

"So we'd have to go together, with me blindly following your lead." Drift blew out a long breath. "Forgive me for not dancing with joy at the prospect."

"It's more than you had before. I might not be perfect, but I'm willing to do whatever it takes to help you reclaim your staff." Taylin held out her hand. "All I ask in return is that you swear to do everything in your power to save Great Aunt Ethel once you have it back."

"That's it? That's your price?"

"That's my price, Osterhase. My help in exchange for Ethel's life."

Drift stared at her outstretched palm. His every instinct screamed that this was yet more honey for whatever trap Ostara had created, for who in their right mind would offer such a one-sided bargain? Although … Maybe the answer wasn't to avoid the trap, but to walk into it with eyes wide open. If he let Taylin, and by extension Ostara, believe him as naïve as he'd once been, he could turn the situation to his advantage, indulging in the decadent temptation this beguiling mage presented even as he caught her red-handed. And once it was done, he'd claim not only his staff but the justice he'd been owed for millennia.

Drift couldn't help the way his lips hitched into a grin as he slid his palm against Taylin's, the cool wash of her moon-kissed magic breathing life into all his cobwebbed corners. "I swear."

3

———

HEAVY

aucous was pissed.

"You can't *leave*," he thundered, feet braced and fists propped on his hips.

The force of his voice whipped up a wind that flattened the lush grass outside Ethel's house, loose gravel from the drive swirling into a vortex that pinged off the windows and clattered against the weathered walls. Staff and patients alike scurried for cover as the sky turned a shade darker, the promise of dawn eclipsed by boiling dark clouds.

"Stop." Taylin laid her palm flat against her friend's breastbone and shoved. "You're a Sentinel of Evergreen Waters – your job is to protect these vulnerable people, not frighten them."

Raucous collapsed to his knees, head bowed. The nascent storm died a swift death, taking with it the enchanted wind which had scattered debris across the lawn and ruined Taylin's hasty braid.

"You can't leave." He glared from between long hanks of chocolate hair, magic roiling beneath his skin. "You're *the* Sentinel. Everyone looks up to you, needs you. I'm just one of your minions, Tay. I'm not ready to take point."

It was second nature to project an air of calm, pushing the emotion across the space between them until the tension drained from

160

Raucous' muscles and the clouds boiling beneath his skin melted away. Taylin slid her hands into the back pockets of her jeans and gave him a firm look. "Yes you are."

"The wards—"

"Won't need charging for months." When he didn't answer, Taylin crossed the distance between them to thread her fingers through his hair. Raucous leaned his forehead against her thighs, wrapping both arms around her knees. "Do you remember when we first came here?"

He snorted. "Me, so angry at the world I had to be sedated to stop the storms and you, almost turned to stone? Pretty hard to forget."

"And Ethel put me in your room because I had the empathic ability to tame that fierce temper long enough for you to think. By working together, you remained calm enough to let the healers close and I gained a purpose."

"Which is exactly why you should stay – we're a team." Raucous tilted his head to pin her with his ochre eyes, the magic inherent to his nature causing them to flicker like the embers in a dying fire.

"Why are we a team?"

"Huh?"

"Why, Raucous? Why are we a team?"

His fingers flexed on the back of her legs. "Because we trust each other."

"Exactly. We trust each other – and it's that trust I'm leaning on now." She tapped the crown of his head in affectionate reprimand. "If not for Ethel, who took us in when everyone else in the world had given up hope, we'd both be dead. Now she's the one in need and I have the means to save her; don't ask me to sit by and do nothing. Trust me to get the job done and come back. More importantly, trust yourself."

Raucous humphed. "That's why you're the lead Sentinel, you know. All those pretty words."

"As I recall, it's because I lost the coin toss when old Veesh retired." Taylin paused, and when he snorted a laugh, her lips creased in an answering smile. "So?"

"All right. But I want to meet this guy you're going on a wild goose chase with."

Taylin rolled her eyes. "You're as bad as I always imagined a big brother would be. Drift was just overseeing the healers as they moved Ethel into the basement so she won't melt. He'll be here any second."

"Hmmm." Raucous unlatched his arms and rose slowly to his feet, eyes glued to Ethel's front door. "Now, actually. Nobody else here walks like that."

Taylin didn't have the sharp hearing her friend did, but she didn't need it; the hairs on the back of her neck rose, a sense of primal wildness whispering over her skin. She turned as Drift stepped onto the front porch, his long body as sleek as it was strong. This wasn't a man who'd ever trip and fall – every breath was a symphony of instinctive co-ordination, even the slightest of movements hypnotising to watch. "Raucous, this is Drift. The … Osterhase?"

"Oss-terr-haa-za," Drift corrected. Tight jeans and a black tee clung to warm brown skin, his body an exquisite sculpture of lean muscle and coiled energy. His hair was a thick mid-brown darkening to black at the tips, and stuck off his head in a way more reminiscent of fur than human hair. Two brown hare ears poked up from the mass, their tips black in the same way as his hair, and set just inside of them were a pair of deer antlers approximately six inches long, their colour so dark a brown as to be almost black. Both ears and antlers shimmered in a way that told Taylin his glamour was still in effect, meaning Raucous would see a man rather than a … whatever he was, but even without the obvious animal traits, Drift would never be mistaken for human. When he smiled, it showed off fangs and his eyes were a touch too rounded to be anything but otherworldly. The effect was mitigated somewhat by long, thick lashes and bright hazel irises with a gleam that hinted at laughter – but it was the laughter of an apex predator who'd sighted prey and decided it was time for lunch.

"What the hell is an Osterhase?" Raucous took a half step in front of Taylin, examining Drift through the veil of his hair.

"Obsolete." Drift's voice carried a rolling growl that gave a barely leashed quality to every word he spoke. When he'd first entered the cottage, Taylin thought it'd been his temper engendering the effect but the more she listened, the more she was certain it was just how he sounded; as though his vocal chords were born to speak some other language and he'd adapted them to hers instead. "Just call me Drift. It's good enough."

He held out a hand; not in the way humans did but with the palm down and fingertips faintly curled so that the back of his knuckles were exposed. Raucous stared at Drift's fingers for a long while, then finally shook his head. "I don't know what that means."

"An old greeting." Drift retracted his hand with the faintest of shrugs, and though the movement was a study in serenity, the skin over his cheekbones pulled taut. "Like I said, obsolete."

There was something so remote about him that Taylin's throat restricted and it took concerted effort not to send him calm the way she'd done Raucous. Where her friend welcomed the support, she had the distinct impression Drift would not, his bearing stiff and his expression cool and distant. None of that did anything to mitigate the sheer draw of him; he commanded the immediate space through a weight of character that was borderline overwhelming. It made Taylin glad his emotional resonance was so muted – at full strength, she'd be a melted puddle of pheromones.

"The weapon which transformed Ethel originally belonged to Drift." Taylin shook her head, clearing the cobwebs even as she drew a firm mental line between herself and the unfairly attractive Osterhase. They'd struck a deal of mutual benefit and nothing more; admiring his sculpted muscles and primal energy would only lead to trouble. "I'm going to help him recover it and in return, he's going to turn Ethel back into herself. I have no idea how long we'll be gone, so you need to be prepared to hold the fort indefinitely."

Raucous frowned, clouds blooming beneath his skin. "I don't like the idea that you'll be out of contact."

"There's not much choice; any technology we take provides an opportunity for the EBC to track us." Taylin squeezed his arm. "I know this seems daunting, but you have an entire team of Sentinels to support you, as well as the senior healing staff. This isn't a task you need to shoulder alone."

"I know." Raucous' eyes fluttered shut and he drew an unsteady breath. "Sorry, Tay. There's something in the air that's ruffling my feathers."

"Me."

Taylin glanced up in surprise. The early morning sunlight kissed the strong planes of Drift's face, highlighting the sweeping angles of his cheeks and jaw. A faint dusting of scruff turned him from gorgeous to gorgeously gritty, and in that moment, with the dawn breaking behind him, he was wild and untamed as the wind.

"You?" Raucous' voice, familiar and safe in a way Taylin didn't think Drift would ever be, roused her enough that she could blink and angle her face away, cheeks tingling with heat.

When Drift spoke, the rolling growl in his voice was thicker, each syllable a decadent caress. "Your feathers are ruffled because you sense the disconnect."

Raucous glanced at Taylin, who lifted one shoulder in a shrug and hoped the movement disguised the shiver that trekked down her spine. Since Drift had stormed into her life an hour or so earlier, she'd had a constant case of butterflies in her stomach. Every time she thought she'd contained them, he'd look her way or speak in that growling voice and the damned creatures escaped all over again, wings brushing her insides and goosebumps whispering over her skin.

To top it off, the more minutes ticked by, the more her fingers itched with the inexplicable craving to touch him again, to seek the faint hint of an emotional imprint she'd sensed in the kitchen; because without the tactile contact, he was almost invisible to her empathic senses. It wasn't a disguise so much as the odd certainty that there *should* be something there ... as if some intrinsic part of him had been excised and all that remained was a shell that would ring hollow when knocked upon.

"Are you saying we shouldn't trust you?" Taylin asked, shifting so that she and Raucous stood shoulder to shoulder. It'd been months since she'd seen her friend so tense, and if the Osterhase was to blame …

"You shouldn't trust anyone," Drift muttered, and Taylin bit her cheek as his pain pattered across her senses like a sprinkling of rain. "In this case, it isn't me that's the problem so much as the dissonance I put out." He tipped his head back, the muscles in his neck and shoulders bunching as he searched the greyish-blue of the early morning sky. "The longer I'm here, the more those with animal natures will feel the itch." His ears, not quite as long as a rabbit's but equally as agile, swivelled in Raucous' direction. "A thunderbird is not a creature I wish to antagonise without reason. I'll wait in the forest."

Taylin gaped as he loped over the lawn and out of the gate, disappearing into the overgrown wilderness that bordered Evergreen Waters Retreat in a matter of seconds.

"How did he know what I am?" Raucous' hands clenched to fists, ochre eyes glued on the place Drift had disappeared.

"I have no idea." Taylin shook her head. Raucous' true form was certainly no secret, but neither was it clearly advertised. "He must have sensed it somehow."

Raucous gave himself a shake, as though waking from a deep sleep. When he glanced down at her from behind the curtain of his hair, he'd lost the sharp edge of near-panic that had been riding him – but his expression remained troubled. "I still don't like this. Or him."

"You don't like anyone you haven't personally vetted," Taylin pointed out. "I saw Drift confront the EBC earlier – he's only after the staff. Once he's got it and Aunt Ethel is safe, he'll leave us be."

Raucous raised a single brow. "Are you sure about that?"

"What? Of course." Taylin caught the knowing glint in her friend's eye and blushed. "Stop it. It's not like that. I don't even know him."

"Doesn't mean you're not window shopping. Or that he's not." Raucous hesitated, a muscle tightening in his jaw. "Taylin, I hate to say this, but he doesn't seem the kind to settle on just one person. If you—"

"There's nothing going on," Taylin said firmly, crossing her arms over her chest. "I'll acknowledge that Drift's attractive – but being attracted *to* him is so many different kinds of stupid, I don't have a name for them all. He's fiercely elemental, while I'm ..."

"Calm and collected," Raucous murmured, squeezing her shoulder. "I know, Taylin. I know. The problem is people tend to take your generous nature for granted. I don't want to watch Drift step on you on his way to greener pastures." He grimaced. "Besides, I'm not sure if I could take him in a fight."

Taylin laughed, covering his hand with her own. "You're being ridiculous. Yeah, okay, my heart is far more fragile than the rest of me, but I've known him for a sum total of seventy-five minutes. I learned my lesson with Logan. I promise."

"Okay." Raucous searched her face, then nodded and let go. "I'll keep things ticking over here as long as you promise to be careful out there."

"I promise." Taylin glanced back at the house which had been her haven for more than a decade. "The EBC won't let the staff go without a fight. I'm pretty sure they'll be back to ask questions as soon as they wake."

The thunderbird snorted. "They'll get nothing from me; I have no idea where you're going."

Neither did Taylin.

Lips twisting on that thought, she shouldered the pack she'd propped against the porch and opened her arms. Raucous stepped into her embrace, squeezing as tightly as he could while she patted his back with gentle hands.

"Be careful," Raucous murmured, his cheek pressing hard against her own.

"You too." They separated on an arm clasp and though Taylin smiled, she spun away a little faster than necessary, an odd lump in her throat.

She didn't look back as she passed between the gates marking the edge of the estate, her feet carrying her steadily down the road until she reached a cluster of berry bushes. Her memory insisted Drift had turned into the forest right here, but there was nothing to prove it – not even a muddied bootprint.

"Drift?" Taylin pushed onto her toes, squinting into the forest. "Where are you?"

"Here."

She pushed carefully through the undergrowth, feeling out the uneven ground with her boots and using gentle hands to separate entangled branches that blocked the way. After a couple of minutes, Taylin emerged at the bank of a stream, water rushing swiftly over tumbled rocks and a downed tree creating a natural bridge over the gap. On the opposite bank, Drift lay on his back in a lush patch of grass, face shaded by the branches of the fallen tree and torso covered by … Taylin blinked. Rubbed her eyes. Blinked again.

The image didn't change, the creatures barely larger than her spread hand. At first glance, they looked like tiny hares – if tiny hares had feathered wings and miniature antlers. Some of them were curled up on Drift's chest and abdomen, heads buried beneath their wings as they slept. Others shuffled in the grass close to his body or climbed on his outstretched limbs, while several more sat on their haunches at the top of his chest, tiny paws braced on his chin and cheeks as they looked into his face. The soft, rolling growl of Drift's voice carried faintly through the air, and from the way it stopped and started, Taylin gathered he was talking to the little … hare-deer-birds.

Water sloshed and she glanced down in surprise. Absorbed by the sight of such a breathtaking man covered in such cute fluffiness, she'd forgotten to pay attention to her surroundings, but the area at the bank of the stream was clear, and she'd done no more harm than sinking her boots into the moist earth by the water.

"Sorry about the show; they haven't seen me in a long time." Drift's growling voice carried a hint of laughter and Taylin looked up to see him watching her through bright hazel eyes just a shade too large for his face. There was a warmth to his expression that hadn't been there before, and the half-smile he wore was a visceral blow to her senses. "I'd offer to carry you, but I'm somewhat indisposed. You can cross with the tree."

Taylin took an unconscious step backward, flattening one hand over the ridiculous fluttering in her belly. "That's not a good idea. I'm … heavy."

"I'm twice your size and I made it," Drift said easily. "It's sturdy."

He *wasn't* twice her size, despite having a good foot on her in height and the definite edge when it came to shoulder width and basic musculature – but it wasn't physical size that was the problem.

"What's the worst that can happen, Taylin?" she whispered, edging up to the tree and rapping her knuckles against the bark. "You get wet."

Aware of Drift's gaze on her, she set a foot gingerly atop the largest tree root and used it to lever onto the trunk. The wood creaked under her weight but held, and with her heart in her mouth, Taylin pushed to her feet.

Slow and steady. That was the key; the way she'd navigated her life from the moment she'd woken at Evergreen Waters with the startling realisation that she was still alive. Slow and steady, like her recovery. Slow and steady, like each breath she drew. Slow and steady, like each foot she placed with infinite care on the aged bark.

The trunk creaked and groaned with every step, Taylin testing with her toes before she eased her full weight forward. She was just past halfway when a sharp crack split the silence, causing several of the tiny creatures on Drift's chest to jump and Taylin to close her eyes on a sigh. The trunk had swallowed her foot up to the ankle.

"Are you all right?"

Rather than answer, she forced her eyes open to concentrate on her footing – or lack thereof. Leaning her weight backward, Taylin yanked on her leg to free it … and the tree broke in half, a snapping chorus of splintering wood and splashing water accompanying Taylin as she toppled unceremoniously into the stream.

It was as cold as she'd feared.

She came up spluttering, shaking her head to clear bits of wood and bark from her braid. The water shoved at her from one side, the current faster where it flowed through the break in the trunk, but she was too heavy to be tossed off her feet. Instead, she turned into the flow and let it cleanse the last of the debris from her clothing – and, with any luck, cool her face so that when she waded to the shore, Drift wouldn't see the way she was blushing like a schoolgirl.

"Taylin?"

Gods above, why did her name sound so good on his lips? Goosebumps raised over her skin that had nothing to do with the cold, and for a long moment, Taylin considered simply becoming a fixture of the stream for the rest of her life. Surely that would be easier than turning ninety degrees to the right?

Only ... Drift's voice pulled at her, a siren call she was powerless to ignore. She angled her head first, spotted him crouched on the bank of the stream just out of arm's reach. His head was cocked, one ear standing straight up while the other drooped slightly, turning him from gorgeously gritty to adorable. Those hazel eyes were filled with concern, nose twitching as he sniffed in a way reminiscent of a rabbit – or a hare, she supposed, since he'd been so terribly offended when she'd asked if he was an Easter Bunny.

"What happened?"

She considered the question, trying desperately not to notice the play of muscles up his arms as he braced his weight on the earth. This man, with his perfect features and wild spirit, was not ever going to be for her. "I got wet."

"I can see that." The corners of his eyes crinkled and Taylin had the distinct impression he was trying not to laugh. At that moment, one of the adorable creatures who'd been arrayed across his chest hippity-hopped to the edge of the stream. It regarded her with twitching whiskers and deep brown eyes before turning to Drift and placing a teensy paw on his forearm.

"No," Drift said, his eyes on the whatever-it-was. "She's not hurt."

A small silence, those whiskers twitching.

He raised an eyebrow. "If I go in there, we're both wet. That makes no sense."

Tiny brown eyes narrowed, and two delicate wings covered in white feathers snapped rather pointedly open.

"I can't," Drift said, running a fingertip down the leading edge of one wing. "Not any more."

Tiny wings drooped, the air filled with such sadness that Taylin's breath stalled in her lungs and her eyes prickled. As one, the cluster of little creatures behind Drift lowered their ears and looked unutterably miserable.

"What can't you do?" Taylin asked, the words popping out between her chattering teeth. It was a rude enough question that she slapped a hand over her own mouth. "I'm sorry. I don't mean to pry."

"Come out of the water and I'll tell you." He scooped up the tiny creature and backed away from the stream to give her room. Since it *was* cold, Taylin plodded her way through the waist-high water and made slow, careful progress up the bank on the other side.

The tiny fluffball in Drift's arms put a paw to his chest.

"I'm aware." His gaze made a slow, languorous journey from the top of her head to the tip of her boots and back again. When their gazes locked afterwards, there was a predatory glint in the hazel depths. "You're beautiful."

Heat slapped Taylin's cheeks and she angled her face away, wishing she could call him a liar – except her magic sensed he was telling the truth. The man clearly needed his head read. Determined not to break the promise she'd made Raucous, she ignored the statement in favour of studying the curious creatures now perched in the branches of the fallen tree. "What are they?"

"Wolpertingers."

"I'm sorry, Wolper-what?"

"Wolpertingers," he repeated. "The body of a hare, the wings of an owl, the antlers of a deer and the teeth and claws of a wolf."

Taylin stared at the tiny creatures until they began to blur, their fluffy bodies becoming translucent. Because *of course* the hare-owl-deer-wolf creatures could turn invisible.

"I can still see you," she told them.

"Even when they're faded?"

Taylin let her gaze track sideways, watching Drift out of the corner of her eye. She didn't want to bare herself to this man, so clearly an apex predator, but if they were to work together ... "My white eye can see through illusion."

"Huh." He examined said eye with laser-like focus. "I used to be able to change shape."

"Before you went into exile?"

"Yes."

Taylin bit her lip, noting afresh the similarities between Drift and the creature cradled in his arms. "You're a … were-wolpertinger?"

He threw back his head and laughed, the sound rich and rolling. It wrapped around Taylin like a cloak, thick and warm and as real as if he'd touched her with his hands. She clenched her teeth and counted to five, breathing through the punch of delight until the emotion – and the sound that went with it – faded to silence.

"I'm the Osterhase," Drift said at last, eyes dancing, "and the wolpertingers are my … friends."

"Osterhase." Taylin shook her head. "You keep saying that, and it's the truth, but it's only *a* truth, isn't it? Who are you, really?"

"How did you break the log?"

So, it was to be like that, was it? A truth for a truth. Taylin cleared her throat, bracing for the inevitable reaction, and then dove in head-first. "My bones are made of moonstone."

He blinked, but didn't baulk. "I'm a god."

A *god*?

"God of what?"

"Not that kind of god." Drift waved an irritated hand. "I'm … different. Even more so now that I've fallen."

"The staff," she murmured. The sadness suffusing the clearing turned swiftly to anger, several of the wolpertingers curling their lips to expose long, pointed wolves' teeth in their adorable hare mouths. "The part of you that's been lost."

He nodded. "I'm known as the Osterhase, but in reality I'm the Primal God of the Vernal Equinox. I'm just not as I once was."

Taylin ran her hands over her hair, was reminded quite suddenly that she was soaked, and pulled the length of her braid over one shoulder to squeeze the water out. No doubt Drift thought his reply made perfect sense, but she was only left with more questions. The problem was …

"Why are your bones made of moonstone?"

… for every question she answered, her companion expected the same in return. It made sense, since information was power and they were strangers. The more they knew of each other, the better they could work together – and the swifter they could defend themselves if something went awry.

Taylin squeezed her hair a final time, then flipped it over her shoulder. "Magic."

"Oh?" His gaze lowered to the triple-banded mage mark now visible through the sodden fabric of her long-sleeve top.

"My power is that of moonstone, but when my magic came in as a teenager, it was too strong for my body to handle. It began to turn *me* into moonstone." She swallowed, shuddering at the memory of her own slow petrifaction. "My parents took me to every doctor, healer, shaman and medic they could find. Nobody could do anything. Eventually, the story of my plight reached Great Aunt Ethel, the gifted fae healer who runs Evergreen Waters Retreat. I'd slipped into a coma by the time she arrived unannounced at my parents' door, and in desperation, they handed me over." Taylin's fingers raised to her right cheek, where fae characters tumbled towards her jaw like tears. "She was able to save my life … but not before I was irrevocably changed. My entire skeleton is solid moonstone crystal, as is my right eye." Taylin jerked her chin at the broken tree. "It means I'm very heavy."

"And the moonlight in your skin?"

"It's not in my skin." Taylin bit her lip as Drift stepped close enough that she could feel the primal heat of his body, the wolpertinger's silken white wings fluttering against her throat. "The light comes from my bones. I can make it brighter or dimmer, but it never truly goes away."

He lifted a hand, hesitated.

Feeling unaccountably vulnerable, Taylin nonetheless increased the glow until blue-white light filtered over the pale brown skin of his fingers. Wonder and longing suffused Drift's expression, turning him from adorable to alluring in a way Taylin found as tempting as she did terrifying.

"I am of the moon," he whispered, breath puffing over her cheek. When had he lowered his head? "It's in every fibre of my being. Every breath I take. Every pounding beat of my heart. You are made of the very thing which gave me life."

She was caught, surrounded by his heat and the hypnotic intensity of those vivid hazel eyes. When Drift's hand cupped her face, Taylin thought she'd never breathe again no matter how hard her lungs worked. His skin scalded hers, warming her in ways she'd never before been warm even as every hair on her body rose in primal warning.

A tiny paw touched her jaw.

Hello.

Taylin choked out a strangled laugh as the wolpertinger in Drift's other hand snuffled at her chin, shattering the moment like so much frosted glass. "Hello."

"You heard that?" Drift jerked backward so quickly that the wolpertinger toppled, spreading elegant wings to catch itself before it fell. Rather than chase after him, the little creature flapped up to perch on top of Taylin's head.

"I can't hear it now," Taylin said, because from the tension in the wolpertinger's slight weight atop her head, the little creature was making its opinion known.

Frowning, Drift held out a hand. It was a perfunctory gesture, but still Taylin hesitated before she touched the tips of her fingers to his palm.

—broken a wing, all broken, never fly! Bad Drift think with downstairs. Use brain.

Taylin coughed and pulled away. "I heard that."

"My brain works just fine," Drift told the wolpertinger. "Just like your wings. You were in no danger."

The tiny creature hunkered down, and Taylin felt the prick of claws in her scalp. Reaching up, she dared to pluck it from her hair. "Careful. My bones are hard, but not my skin."

Tiny wings and whiskers drooped, and though she couldn't hear its voice any longer, she could feel the swift rush of regret and remorse. Unable to resist, Taylin pressed a kiss to the wolpertinger's little pink nose.

"All right, all right, you're sorry." Drift retrieved the cute creature from her grasp and glared at it. "It's time for us to keep moving. You know what to do."

Tiny brown eyes narrowed, the wolpertinger staying firmly put.

Drift sighed and flicked a glance at Taylin. "He says his name is Bay."

"Nice to meet you, Bay. I'm Taylin."

Bay's ears perked up, and he gave Drift what could only be described as a saucy look before spreading tiny wings and flapping off, the rest of the wolpertingers taking flight in his wake.

"He'll be insufferable for eternity now," Drift muttered, eyes on the trees where his little flock of followers had disappeared.

"He's adorable."

"*I'm* adorable."

Yes. As well as a host of other things that made Taylin's blood fizz in her veins, but she smothered that response before it could mortify her by coming out of her mouth. Instead, she said, "We should formulate some kind of plan."

"We have one – you lead, I follow." Drift hitched one shoulder. "I was going to suggest a little four-legged transport, but something tells me you'll refuse to ride."

Taylin nodded. "I'm too heavy."

"And I can't teleport without my powers." He grimaced. "Speeder?"

"Ethel only keeps one, and it's for emergencies." Taylin glanced in the direction of the Retreat. "I'd also assume that if Ostara can track a phone, she'd have no trouble locating non-organic forms of transport."

"You assume correctly."

"So we walk." Taylin covered the tremble in her voice with a cough. It seemed only yesterday that getting out of bed was a triumph; the concept of traversing Mu on foot was something she'd never have thought possible when Ethel had explained her bones had turned to crystal, their weight so incredible that even lifting her head could be deemed a superhuman feat. Part of her wanted to explain that to the impatient god in front of her, but the larger, more cautious part held back. "It'll still be faster than waiting for the staff to materialise in front of you."

"I'm not sure I agree." He scrubbed both hands over his face, frustration etched into the line of his shoulders. "If Ostara catches even a whiff of the staff's location, we're doomed."

"Lucky she doesn't have someone to point her in the right direction, isn't it?" When he didn't respond, Taylin swallowed the flicker of hurt and added, "We should keep moving."

"You're still wet."

"I'll dry as we go."

Drift turned to face her then, and there was nothing innocent about the way he looked her over. "Not if I have anything to say about it."

4

WHAT ARE YOU MADE OF?

If Taylin Colkannis was a trap, she was the most unusual one Drift had ever seen. He pushed into her space without a hint of guilt, revelling in the moonlit magic that permeated the atmosphere. Shock made her eyes round, the effect emphasised by the wet hair clinging doggedly to her cheeks. Her clothing sucked tight to sinful curves and her lips were pressed into a thin line, her body quivering with banked emotion as she wrapped her hands in his t-shirt and yanked him even closer.

Gods, she was so perfect. Every dream he didn't know he'd had, poured into a single, spellbinding form that threatened to undo the brutal lessons he'd learnt at Ostara's knee. Despite the niggling suspicion that Taylin's sole purpose was to lead him astray, he wanted to eat her up, one bite at a time. He'd start by peeling each and every sodden layer off, kissing his way across her skin until—

Cold water closed overhead and Drift came up spluttering, the imprint of Taylin's hearty shove lingering in his breastbone. "What—"

"We made a deal to work together, and I expect you to stick to it," Taylin snapped, shaking her finger as though he were a naughty child. "I'm a guide, not a toy. Get your head in the game."

Drift gaped as she stormed off into the thick undergrowth without so much as a second glance, leaving him to flounder out of the stream on his own.

They spent the rest of the day in stony silence, and when Drift built a fire later that night, Taylin sat on the opposite side of it, nibbling granola bars from her pack and staring at the stars above.

"So." He dropped to a crouch, arms draped loosely over his knees. "I imagine you have questions."

"Not really." She stashed empty wrappers in a side pocket of her pack, somehow managing to ignore the penetrating stare which had never before failed to garner Drift the attention he required. "I suppose I do, on a larger scale: why would someone want to steal the Staff of Easter, why would that someone use it to turn people into chocolate, how will you go about turning them back once you have it … but none of the answers to those questions will speed up the process of finding the staff, so they end up rather pointless."

Drift pursed his lips. "Well, *I* have questions."

"Oh?"

"You said you can track the staff, yet you've barely touched me all day. How can you be sure we're going in the right direction?"

She looked at him then, the corners of her eyes crinkling in reluctant amusement as one long arm lifted, pointing off at the horizon. "The Staff of Easter is as bright as any beacon I've ever followed, and it's not changed direction since you stomped into Ethel's kitchen this morning. Whoever took it is moving in as straight a line as possible in that direction, and I don't need more than a brush of skin against skin to feel the tug. Where a bloodhound might need his nose constantly to the ground, all I need is the odd reminder here and there."

"That doesn't make a lot of sense," Drift muttered, pushing to his feet.

"It doesn't have to make sense. It's magic." Taylin pulled a blanket from her pack and wrapped it around her shoulders. "I'd suggest you eat something, Osterhase, or you're going to be hungry tomorrow. Unless I miss my guess, we've a lot more walking to do."

Drift watched in silence as she curled up on the ground with her back to him. When her breathing eased into the rhythm of slumber, he snatched several granola bars and a packet of beef jerky from the pile by the fire and shoved to his feet. The forest was quiet and still, nothing so much as a bat or a bird rustling in the trees. Rather than put him at ease, the silence only served to increase the tension tightening Drift's muscles.

Ostara had to know he was after the staff by now. He couldn't afford to dismiss the notion that she'd be hunting him, or that Taylin was leaving some kind of trail for the EBC to follow. It was that specific concern that had Drift going back over their trail, erasing bootprints and straightening bent branches. Without Taylin to slow him down he covered half a day's distance in a matter of hours, returning to camp shortly after midnight with sweat slicking his skin and unease pricking the nape of his neck.

The next day was much the same, long hours of trekking broken by sharp looks and cool responses to anything that tumbled past his lips. Drift came to hate the forest as much as he loved it, chafing at every fallen trunk or overgrown bramble that slowed them down even as he used those same obstacles to mask their passage. He tried to draw her out that evening but Taylin only shrugged in response to his questions, finished the jerky she'd taken from their supplies and bedded down for the night.

Drift lay on his back for some time, letting the fire die down to maximise the chill in the air. If Taylin were sent by Ostara to tempt him, she'd surely capitalise on the opportunity – but she didn't even have the decency to complain about the temperature so that he could offer to keep her warm. When he finally did drop off, it was to fevered dreams and a fine coating of dew that made rest almost impossible.

His irritation the next morning seemed to thaw Taylin somewhat, and she favoured him with soft-voiced conversation and a few reluctant smiles before they broke camp to resume walking. With every step, Drift's determination to unravel the mystery she presented grew. There was no denying the attraction he felt, both physical and metaphysical; if only he could reconcile his guide's behaviour with the scheming Ostara was so good at, he'd be well on his way to under-standing—

"We're here."

Drift's head jerked up at the smooth, cool sound of Taylin's voice. She stood at the edge of a copse of trees whose leaves were shaded in copper and rust, peering out at a simple log cabin built by the side of a slow-moving river. A water wheel turned ponderously in the shallows, the rhythmic creaking of the mechanism accompanied by the soft thump of a little wooden boat tethered to an equally quaint dock.

"The staff is here?"

"I'm not sure."

"What do you mean, you're not sure?" Drift glanced at her, then back at the quaint little cabin, suspicion curdling his breakfast. "We've spent days following your internal compass, and you literally just said 'we're here.'"

"'We're here' is not the same as 'the staff is here.'" She shook her head, long black braid wriggling to and fro. "I sense … the staff has left a strong imprint on this place. If it's not here, it *was*, and recently. I won't be able to tell for sure until we get closer."

Drift stared as though the sheer magnitude of his gaze could decipher the mystery Taylin presented but, as always, her façade remained immaculate. From his current angle, he could only see the right side of her face, with that incredible moonstone eye that was blind to natural sight but wide open to the arcane. Though the sun was well up, both the eye and her skin emitted a faint luminescence which, when teamed with the fae characters tattooed down her cheek, made her look as though she'd just stepped from the pages of a fairy tale. Every slow, measured movement was a work of art, and Drift's heart beat out of time as he imagined shaping the swell of her breasts, the dip of her waist and the curve of her behind. Simple jeans and a clinging sweater highlighted a silhouette he'd paid extremely close attention to when she'd been soaked to the skin, her clothing pasted against her frame in such a way it left little to the imagination.

He had a very good imagination.

"Stop it." Taylin didn't take her gaze from their destination, but colour slapped her cheeks nonetheless.

"Stop what?"

"I can feel it." Her eyes narrowed, her throat working to swallow. "Your desire."

Well, now. Maybe they were getting somewhere after all – although in typical Taylin fashion, in nowhere near the manner he'd expected. Drift considered her words, constructing an answering smile that was slow and wide and wicked. "You're an empath."

She stiffened, fingers curling against the rough bark of the tree.

"I am of the moon, remember? And *you* are made of moonstone, a crystal known for enhancing empathic connection – and encouraging the truth." Drift coaxed her pack from her back, smothering his grin when she immediately snatched it from his grip and stowed it beneath a thick bush. "You forced Gedenna to tell the truth when she desperately wanted to lie. That's it, isn't it? Your mage powers are derived from the qualities of moonstone."

"I told you that already."

Drift forced his attention off the constant lure that was Taylin Colkannis and searched his memories for her instead. "So you did. I didn't understand it until now." He blinked. "You can put people to sleep, and moonstone is known to help with sleep issues. How many of the stone's innate qualities have you inherited as active magic?"

"Enough to get by."

"Moonstone assists in finding the part of oneself that is lost, and you're tracking the staff." Drift stalked closer and she slid away, putting the trunk of the tree between them. Oh, no, that wouldn't do. Now that he'd prised a tiny hole in that armour, no way was he letting her patch it. Drift came hard up against the bark, fingers digging into the rough surface a bare inch from her paler ones. He peered around the trunk, taking in Taylin's fluttering pulse and flushed cheeks before locking his gaze to hers. "Moonstone is known to have a calming effect on those around it, and you pulled your colleague back from the brink of panic."

"Raucous isn't my colleague, he's my friend."

Drift's lips curled back from his teeth. His decision to walk away from the thunderbird had been part practicality – he did, after all, put out an energy dissonance since he'd fallen, one Taylin seemed conveniently immune to – and part instinct. Trap or not, if he'd torn Raucous' arms off for touching Taylin, it would have made recovering the staff that much more difficult … and no matter his compulsive fascination with this moonlit woman whose curves were built for the contours of his palms, he *had* to get the staff back.

He was tired of no longer being whole.

"You heard Bay's voice when we touched by the stream." Drift forced his hackles to smooth by inching his fingertips closer to her own, dropping his voice to a hypnotic murmur. "Moonstone can connect to the energies of others and even amplify them, if it so chooses. That's what you did, isn't it?"

Taylin's expression hardened. "If you want even another second of my assistance, you'll swear to keep that to yourself."

Drift blinked, drawing back to rest his cheek against the bark of the tree. "I'll swear, but I don't understand."

Something about the ease of his capitulation worked to calm her, her face softening as her breath exhaled in a long, slow gust that tickled the back of Drift's knuckles. Her lashes came down, thick and dark, and he took advantage of her distraction to ease his fingers even closer to her own, the moonlight from her bones seeping into his skin. With the soft light came peace, a soothing of his torn and ragged places that made way for his blood to fizz and pop, for his body to twitch. It took everything Drift had not to beg her to strip him to the skin so he could bathe in the otherworldly glow that every instinct screamed was his and his alone.

"I am *made* from moonstone," Taylin said eventually, and there was a tremble in her voice that drew Drift's gaze back to her face. "Can you imagine how much my bones are worth, for that alone?"

Ice doused all traces of his ardour. Drift opened his mouth to say he'd slaughter anyone who thought they had the right to peel the flesh from her body, but stopped. If circumstances revealed Taylin to be an agent of Ostara's, *he* might be the one peeling the flesh from her bones. Drift baulked, the idea so very abhorrent it made his gorge rise, the effort required to focus on Taylin's next words monumental.

"Death, however, would be the least of my worries. Think how useful a tool I'd be – to light the darkness, to force the truth." Taylin's moonstone eye opened, and he knew, he *knew*, it was focussed on him. "My petrified eye cannot see as your eyes see, but it sees that which is hidden or false – like the glamour Tyr placed over your ears and antlers." Her voice lowered. "Now imagine if the world knew I was a walking battery. That touching me could elevate a person's existing power into the stratosphere." Taylin's other eye opened, the brilliant sapphire drilling him right in the heart. "Tell me there's no one on Earth or in Mu, mortal or immortal, who wouldn't covet such a thing."

He couldn't. If people worked out the truth of Taylin, she'd be hunted for the entirety of her days. The possibility caused Drift's claws to shoot out the ends of his fingers, thudding into the trunk in the spaces between Taylin's own. He knew what it was like to be hunted, and no matter the reasons that brought them together, he'd never willingly consign her to such a fate. "Your secrets are safe with me."

She searched his face, then nodded and pushed away from the tree.

It wasn't the ringing endorsement Drift needed, his eyes narrowing to slits as he watched her walk away. Evergreen Waters didn't seem the kind of place capable of providing the refuge Taylin needed, particularly if it was peopled by healers rather than warriors. Had Taylin agreed to work for Ostara to keep the true extent of her powers a secret, or was Drift jumping at his own shadow? Whatever the truth, one thing was certain – Taylin was like no other creature he'd ever come across. Despite the difference in years and life experience between them, he was a newborn pup when it came to dealing with her.

"Stop looking at my ass," she called over her shoulder.

Drift jerked his eyes up to the back of her head. "I can't help it. It's a nice ass."

He jogged to meet her by the door of the log cabin but where Drift would have pushed right on in, Taylin lifted her hand to knock. The sound echoed through the interior once, twice, three times, before falling to oppressive silence.

"If there's anyone home, you just let them know we're here." Drift pressed his face to the old-fashioned keyhole and sniffed. Sunshine, linen, floor wax … no sign of another living creature having been inside for days. As an empath, surely Taylin would be able to sense that? If so, was her knock at the door an ingrained habit, or a signal to someone lying in wait? Drift's heart grew heavy as he sniffed again, confirming beyond doubt that the cabin was empty and hammering another nail in the Taylin-is-a-trap coffin. He thumped his head against the door, grappling with the pitiful inner voice that pleaded her innocence in spite of the evidence asserting otherwise. When he straightened, Taylin was watching him with her lips pressed into a thin line, withheld laughter causing her shoulders to tremble. He frowned. "What?"

She cleared her throat, a thrumming, half-chuckle of a sound that matched the sparkle in her eye. "It's the nose twitching. It's … cute."

"*Cute?*"

"Uh oh, are you too big and scary to handle a word like that?" Taylin's lips pulled into a smile that her fingers immediately tried to cover. "Oops."

Drift stalked in close, caging her against the door with an arm either side of her head. Another crack had formed in that cool armour – one his tortured heart had no compunction pouncing on. He felt like a volcano poised to erupt, smoke streaming from every pore to blot out the sun. The compulsion to shake the truth from her was as strong as his craving for her touch, for the release they could gift to each other. It was only Taylin's palm on his chest that stopped him from closing the distance between them, the immovable strength of her moonstone skeleton far outweighing the slight nature of her frame.

Drift lowered his head until they were eye height. "I want your laughter in my blood." He shifted so she'd feel the thunderous racing of his heart through her palm. "Why won't you give in?"

"That's my business, not yours."

Aware he'd lost the laughter he'd so very nearly coaxed free, Drift dropped his arms and took a deliberate step back. "If I'm trying to seduce you, then it's every inch my business."

"*This* is your idea of seduction?" Taylin choked and shook her head. "Gods above, you're about as subtle as a sledgehammer. But then, looking like you do, I don't imagine you've ever had to try very hard."

"And why should I?" He thought back over her words and offered a wolfish grin. "So you *do* find me attractive. Come on, Taylin – we're two people with a spark between us and nothing but empty road ahead. There's no reason not to indulge in our desire."

"No reason—" She blinked, cool armour sliding back into place between one breath and the next. "Whatever you think you've seen, you've misinterpreted. I'm not going to sleep with you, Drift. I barely know you."

"I fail to see how that's relevant." He fought the urge to bare his teeth and failed. "Sex is natural. It's a part of life; the ultimate celebration of joy and desire."

"So you're a god of sex now?"

"I'm not a god *of* anything." Drift prowled back and forth in front of the cabin, wishing he could fist his hand in her braid and yank her hard against his body – while being well aware that to try it would end in bloodshed. "I told you, I'm a primal god."

Taylin lifted a single brow. "I don't understand what that means."

"We don't have the time for me to explain it."

"Oh, but we can waste precious minutes plumbing the depths of my capabilities?" She snorted and reached for the latch on the door. "I'm more comfortable with my decision not to sleep with you with every passing moment."

"Wait." Drift slammed a palm against the wall of the log cabin hard enough that the windows rattled in their frames. He drew a deep breath as Taylin paused, uncertain why this was so important to him but unwilling to let it go. "The other gods are gods *of* something. A being with power that gives them a title. God of Storms, who makes lightning. Goddess of Sight, who has visions of the future. All the gods and all the goddesses – at the heart of it, they're just people with extraordinary powers they can choose to use, or not, as they wish." The claws he'd never sheathed dug into the wood of the cabin's walls. "Like I said before, I'm made from the moon. I wasn't born to a mother and father; I'm a creature constructed of wild, primal energy – that of both Earth and Mu. I'm the Primal God of the Vernal Equinox because I am the personification of that delicate balance, the dark and the light and all things in between. I am the bridge between Mu and Earth. I am the wolf. The deer. The owl, the hare, the frog, the cow, the bat, the rabbit – all the creatures who look to the moon for guidance and protection. I am life in the rawest of forms. I am wild. I am blood. I am sex." His voice lowered until it was little more than a gritty growl. "I do not have magic, Taylin. I *am* magic."

"None of that makes me the least interested in having sex with you."

"What?" Drift blinked. "Why not?"

Taylin glared from slitted eyes. "Even if I were going to explain – which I'm not – it wouldn't be here. Anyone could be listening."

"Cut the bullshit." He jabbed a clawed finger in her direction. "You know as well as I do that this cabin is empty – if the staff was ever here, it's long gone. There's nothing inside but dust."

"Dust and clues." She caught at his outstretched finger, curling her own around the length of it. The motion spiked Drift's pulse, sending his blood shooting south with unprecedented speed. Rather than defuse the tension she'd so artfully created, Taylin's eyes glazed over in a way reminiscent of a seer. "The staff is gone. In that, you're correct."

"See? Coming here was a complete waste of time."

Taylin released her grip on his pointer finger, face hardening. "If you can't see the value in gathering as much information on the thief as possible, you're dumber than I thought. No wonder you lost the Staff of Easter to an ambush." With her expression frosty and her movements measured and steady as always, she opened the door. "Oh, and for the record? Your nose is wrong, Osterhase. The cabin's not empty at all."

Drift opened his mouth to reply but she was gone, leaving him alone on the threshold with his thoughts in chaos and a half-formed erection rubbing uncomfortably at the front of his jeans.

5

BY BONE'S LIGHT

uted shafts of sunlight filtered through the log cabin's windows, causing dust motes to dance in the beams and casting the rest of the interior in thick shadow. Taylin left the front door open for when Drift inevitably decided to follow and moved through the formal lounge, running a finger over the sheets that covered the furniture. There were no doors, only open archways that led to the kitchen and washroom respectively. Each surface was as pristine as the next, the furniture precisely aligned and the rooms as soulless as a cheap motel.

Taylin paused by the sink, watching through the window as Drift prowled the yard, a frown darkening his expression. He was liquid grace and wicked sin, exuding an aura of sensuality just shy of intoxicating. The more time she spent in his company, the harder it was to keep Raucous' warnings at the forefront of her mind – particularly when Drift wielded a heated glance with the same predatory dedication as a sword.

Taylin sighed and made her way slowly back into the lounge, listening to the floorboards creak underfoot. She'd been alone a long time; not just romantically but in all areas of her life. Oh, she spoke regularly with her parents and interacted with the other staff at Evergreen Waters, but nobody had come close to the secret heart of her since Logan. Drift was twice as enticing as her ex-lover, his primal energy edged with a soft vulnerability – but the kind of casual encounter he'd suggested was impossible. Her body was irrevocably linked to her heart and she couldn't countenance the sharing of one without giving the other; a lesson she'd learnt the hard way when Logan had left a much younger, far more naive Taylin in tatters. It was only Raucous' friendship that had pulled her through, the two of them working together to build stronger versions of themselves. Now ... to willingly open herself to Drift, knowing he'd dust out her corners and empty her closets, scatter her fragile remains to the wind and then leave her with nothing but empty echoes?

No.

Blinking to dispel the heated prickling in her eyes, Taylin turned resolutely from the view out the window and made her way back into the formal lounge. She recited the alphabet inside her head until her heart rate calmed and the flutter in her belly resided. By the time Drift ventured inside, the fractures in her armour were visible only to herself.

"All right, I don't get it." He waved a hand at the dusty log cabin. "The interior looks like it's never been lived in while the exterior has clear indication that someone was here as recently as this morning."

Taylin forced her mind off the way Drift's hair tumbled across his forehead and cleared her throat. "They're underneath us."

"Underneath?" Two neat lines formed between his brows. "Like a burrow?"

"I'm betting lair." She jerked her chin towards the other rooms. "There's a kitchen but the cupboards are bare and there's no bedroom, only basic facilities. This upstairs level is entirely for show." Taylin hesitated. "I'm not sure how far removed from the world your exile makes you, but it's a common thing for Nightstalker vampires to do."

"Though we both enjoy the dark, I've never spent much time with Nightstalkers." Drift peered around as though expecting a vampire to leap out from behind the couch. "All I know is they're more powerful than their Daywalker brethren, but cannot tolerate the sunlight."

"More powerful is a misnomer – as in any species, some are stronger than others. In this case, though, it's not going to matter." She pointed straight down, unable to suppress the shiver tripping along her spine. "There are no emotional signatures here, only the same static I sensed in Great Aunt Ethel. We're too late."

"Of course we are," Drift muttered, shaking his head. "If we were moving any slower, we'd be standing still."

Hurt as sharp as any blade speared through Taylin's middle, stealing her breath and curling her fingers into fists. "With bones made of moonstone, it's impossible to do anything fast. I assumed you'd have worked that out by now."

"If you can lift your bones well enough to get out of bed, let alone trek through a forest for several days, then I don't see why you can't jog, at the very least."

Since explaining would involve opening herself up even further than she had already, Taylin turned to the fireplace and lowered her weight to one knee, peering into the cavity. True to what she'd learnt of Nightstalker homes, there was a discreet ceramic pressure plate just inside the chimney. When pressed, the base of the hearth slid seamlessly into the space under the floor, revealing a narrow set of stairs leading into thick, inky darkness.

"You know a lot about vampires." Drift was suddenly so close behind her that Taylin could feel the heat from his body even through the layers of her clothing.

"Great Aunt Ethel has them as patients from time to time." Taylin pushed to her feet and dusted both hands on her jeans. "As for your commentary on the speed of our journey, slow, steady and thorough is how I do things. If you don't like it, you're welcome to leave."

Never, as long as she lived, would she admit to relief when the faint rustle of denim announced him following her down the stairs. Instead, Taylin increased the glow coming from her bones and kept walking. Thirty narrow, twisting steps later, she arrived in a neat stone tunnel with wood-panelled walls and a plush strip of artificial grass running down the centre of the floor. At the far end was a heavy wooden door with an old-fashioned iron knocker and handle. The door stood ajar, the only clue to the room beyond a wadded-up piece of shimmering fabric that prevented the wood from sitting flush against the jamb.

Taylin crouched by the fabric only to discover it was a foil tube with a patterned cuff at the open end. When she lifted it for a closer look, a fine shower of dirt pattered onto the floor.

"It's a sleeve." Taylin dropped the foil as though it were on fire. "That's not dirt – it's pulverised chocolate. This was a *person*."

"A person trying to escape," Drift added, reaching around her to grip the edge of the door. "If they were running for the hall when they fell, that's how they'd land."

Taylin swallowed and pushed to her feet. "You go first. I'll follow."

"Are you sure? There's no shame in waiting out here." Drift motioned to the mess on the ground. "Unlike Ethel, whoever this was cannot be saved. They're dead."

"I'm fine," Taylin lied, lifting her chin. "It's just chocolate."

Except that chocolate was once someone who had lived and laughed and maybe even loved. Taylin did her best to breathe steadily while Drift examined her face, then nodded and pulled open the door.

Beyond the threshold was a single, open-plan abode. A cracked bamboo screen separated the sleeping area from a messy lounge, which in turn bled into a kitchenette whose open cupboards revealed shattered crockery, a refrigeration unit with a broken door and a dented dishwasher. The kitchen table had been overturned, one chair on the far side of the room and the other in pieces over the back of a shredded couch. Shelves lined the walls but the books, jars and sundries that had been stacked inside littered the space as though a hurricane had hit.

In the middle of it all, slumped over the arm of the couch, was a pair of foil jeans and a foil sweater in burnt orange. Large shards of chocolate were spread across the upholstery and scattered on the tapestry rug that insulated the room from the stone flooring, some of them large enough to be visibly recognisable as fingers, a knee and part of a face.

At Taylin's feet lay the person whose arm had blocked the door, their foil hoodie worn over a brightly patterned pair of foil leggings and misshapen foil slippers. This body was more recognisable than the other, with whole sections of the legs and torso intact – though both feet and the arm that had been trapped in the door were pulverised to crumbs.

"There was a fight." Drift prowled the room, sniffing at cracked jars and crushed plants that seemed irrelevant to Taylin, but made him frown ever deeper the further he went.

"I don't understand." She bent closer to the effigy at her feet, only to shy away, heart racing. "Gods above, her face."

The foil that had once been a woman's skin reflected a rictus of terror, mouth open in a scream. The material had split clean down the centre and shards of chocolate spilled out, the piece closest to Taylin's foot etched with the shape of a wide, staring eye.

"Here." Drift thrust out a deep wooden bowl as she swung around, gorge rising. Taylin clung to his waist as she retched, tears blurring her vision. All the while, Drift smoothed a hand along the length of her spine, murmuring gently in a language she didn't recognise. When it was over, he helped her to the sink and turned on the tap before leaving to dispose of her vomit.

"Sorry," she said when she sensed his return. "I'm usually made of sterner stuff."

He hummed deep in his throat and Taylin clutched the rim of the sink lest she do something foolish, like press her face into his chest and beg him to hold her until this eerie reality faded. Only it wasn't going to fade, and pressing up against that sleek, muscular body was going to send exactly the sort of signal Taylin needed to avoid – no matter how badly she craved his warmth.

So she closed her eyes and let her head hang, concentrating on her breathing until her stomach settled and she was able to rebuild some semblance of composure. When she finally opened her eyes and faced the carnage, Drift was staring avidly into the contents of a shallow tray he'd placed on the rumpled bedspread.

Taylin frowned. "What is it?"

"Bones."

"Actual bones?"

"Yes." He poked at the contents of the tray. "A vampire lived here, and also a … witch doctor? Shaman? I'm not sure what term humans use."

"Oh. You mean scrying bones." Taylin blew out a shuddering breath. "For a minute I thought you meant … You know …"

He turned just enough for her to catch his incredulous expression. "You do realise witch doctors deal in blood magic? These are still actual bones."

"Yes, I know, I just – never mind." She moved to join him, looking down at the tray. As promised, there were a selection of bones painted with runes and patterns. There was also a pearlescent shell, a small selection of crystals, a piece of broken pottery with time-smoothed edges and an old copper coin. "Bone scrying isn't limited to witch doctors. What makes you think these tools belonged to one?"

"The other reagents." Drift waved a hand towards a mess of shattered glass, plants and other unidentifiable bits and pieces that looked distinctly fleshy and stank of vinegar.

Taylin screwed up her nose. "Okay. Yeah. Witch doctor."

"The emphasis, I think, being on doctor." Drift nudged the tray with one knee. "Most of these characters pertain to ailments and healing."

"Great Aunt Ethel is a healer, too," Taylin murmured. "Renowned for her success with rare maladies."

Drift nodded. "The EBC said there were three other victims before Ethel, which makes this latest scene the fifth. I'm willing to bet they were also healers."

"Why, though?" Taylin propped both hands on her hips. "What possible use could removing healers from the world have?"

"Nothing good, that's for sure." Drift prodded at the bones before rolling one between his fingers. "This is a very complex scrying set, meant to assist with a variety of difficult magics in addition to pure divination." He rubbed a thumb over a smooth indentation in his chosen bone, then pocketed it. "Whoever came here was either asking for assistance the witch doctor couldn't give, or trying to prevent them extending aid to someone else. An argument ensued, and ..."

"Death by chocolate." Taylin shuddered. "Whoever stole your staff must be powerful if they can overcome an experienced witch doctor and a Nightstalker vampire."

"Not really – the staff alone is enough to do the job. All someone has to do is touch it, and they'll transform into chocolate." He tossed the tray back on the bed with a hiss. "Convenient. Too fucking convenient."

"What?"

"This entire charade." He swung an arm outward, claws glinting at the tips of his fingers. "The Staff of Easter has sat dormant in Ostara's sanctuary for millennia. Now, out of the blue, someone up and steals it mere weeks out from Easter – and rather than ransom it off or hide it away, they're murdering healers who specialise in rare maladies. Why?"

Taylin shook her head. "I don't know."

"Like fuck you don't." Drift blew out hard through his nostrils, and for a moment Taylin wondered if he would actually breathe fire. "The terms of my exile mean I can't enter the world while the staff resides in Ostara's domain. Having it 'stolen' means I'm free to chase it – but in doing so, I leave the safety of my sanctuary; the one place no god or goddess can enter without my express permission, the one place protected by a power greater even than what I lost."

"So ... you think Ostara arranged for the staff to be stolen? Why would she do that, if she already had it?"

He gave her an incredulous look. "To finish what she started when she first used the staff to siphon out half my soul, stealing my magic in the process. Domination."

"Wait. She took half your soul?" Taylin's jaw dropped, stomach twisting anew. "*That's* why your emotional resonance is so muted?"

"For an empath, you're pretty bad at reading people."

Taylin flinched as though struck. "I believe in the sanctity of a person's privacy, and I try to preserve it wherever possible."

"Of course." Drift choked out a bitter laugh. "Yet another convenient coincidence in a long line of convenient coincidences. But I'm not done; oh, no. Once Ostara uses the staff's disappearance to lure me out of hiding, she muddies her tracks by putting the ever-dithering EBC on the case and sets the thief a new task: visit the best healers in the Merged Worlds and help them shuffle off their mortal coils. Not only do the trail of chocolate effigies lead the poor, wounded Osterhase a merry chase, he gets to witness the loss of every single healer who might possess the necessary skills to repair his soul should he ever recover the Staff of Easter. Using that very staff to do the job only adds layers to an already clever taunt, don't you think?"

"I … that's a lot to take in. What happened to make her want you so badly?"

He bent until they were eye level, his breath fanning Taylin's cheeks. "You already know the answer to that question."

"Excuse me?" She reared back in shock. "How would I know that?"

"I tried, Taylin. For what it's worth, I really tried – but there's just too many coincidences to let slide." The corner of his lip quirked, but there was no joy in the motion, none of the wicked, teasing heat to which she'd become so accustomed. "Answer me this: if you were Ostara, and you wanted to lead someone to the perfect place for an ambush, somewhere well away from prying eyes and intervening hands, how would you do it?"

The nausea in Taylin's gut intensified. "I don't know."

"Funnily enough, I thought you'd say that." He straightened abruptly. "When you see your mistress, let her know her agent lacks finesse. These effigies don't look like the work of a criminal genius – they're nothing more than the leavings of an idiot with a pair of gloves and a misaligned moral compass."

Taylin gaped as he stormed out, heedless of the chocolate he crushed beneath his boots as he went. Her hand flattened over her stomach, as though that simple gesture would quell the rising of her gorge. She waited until Drift's emotional signature faded from her senses, then stumbled to the kitchen sink and leant over it, gasping for breath.

With only a partial grasp on Drift's history, many of the things he'd said made little sense, but one fact stood out with all the brilliance of a dying star.

He thought she was a spy.

The implications were too enormous to contemplate. Rather than try, Taylin gagged and retched over the sink until her stomach realised it had nothing left to give. She rinsed her mouth under the tap and hung her head, lashes drifting to rest on her cheeks.

Exactly how Drift had reached his strange conclusion, Taylin had no idea – but if he truly believed her an agent of Ostara, then he believed she'd been complicit in the attack on Great Aunt Ethel. Taylin's eyes narrowed, and she turned towards the door. There were many things she would weather … but an accusation of that magnitude?

No.

Taylin picked her way into the hall, the nausea she'd succumbed to fading in the face of her temper. She was halfway to the stairs when something tiny and soft bounced off her chest, landing in her outstretched hands in a tangle of feathers and fur.

"Bay!" Taylin carefully righted the fluffy creature, mindful of his fragile wings. "What's wrong?"

Since she couldn't hear his voice inside her head without touching Drift, and his assholishness was currently elsewhere, Taylin was forced to try and interpret the wolpertinger's waving paws and wild eyes – a feat that proved nothing short of impossible.

"Stop," she said at last, using the firm, calm tone she'd developed over her time at Evergreen Waters Retreat.

The wolpertinger fluffed out his fur, then settled with a squeak.

"All right, let's try again. Did Drift send you?"

Bay nodded furiously.

Taylin snorted. "If he thinks you're going to deliver messages on his behalf—"

The wolpertinger cut her off with a shrill squeak.

"He didn't send you with a message?"

One tiny paw see-sawed from side to side.

"He … sort of sent you with a message?"

More nodding, followed by some paw waving.

"You want me to go with you? I don't see what—" Taylin broke off as Bay started tugging on his ears. "The EBC are here, aren't they?"

He nodded.

Taylin bit her lip. "Drift didn't send you here to warn me, did he? He sent you to trap me, so that he could deal with one perceived threat at a time."

Bay's wings drooped, his expression so incredibly forlorn Taylin knew she'd been right.

"I'm not working for Ostara."

The wolpertinger snorted and rolled his eyes.

"You never thought so?"

A firm shake of the head, the simple gesture warming Taylin's heart from the inside out.

"Thank you for believing in me, Bay. I suppose the question is, what do we do now?" Taylin screwed up her face. "I don't much like the idea of waiting down here for whoever's victorious to come and claim, that's for sure."

Bay spread his wings in answer and Taylin launched the little creature into the air, following him back up the stairs. When she hauled herself out of the fireplace, Bay immediately flew into her chest, nudging and squeaking until she crouched in the shadows by the window.

Taylin peered over the sill to see Drift outside by the river, arms crossed and frown dark. In the middle of the yard, surrounded by a veritable cloud of Easter Bunnies in pastel outfits, was a short, voluptuous woman with a cascade of golden ringlets and a confection of a dress in layers of pale blue chiffon and lace. Her face was round, skin flawless and lips prettily pursed. Unlike Drift, power radiated from her in waves.

Taylin swallowed. "Is that ... Ostara?"

Bay squeaked an affirmative, ears drooping as he pointed again.

The two gods were speaking, though from the hard lines etched into Drift's face and the way Ostara's perfectly manicured hands were waving about, the conversation wasn't a pleasant one. Taylin edged closer to the window in the hopes she could make out their words, but Bay tangled his tiny paws in her braid and tugged decisively in the opposite direction.

"What?" Taylin pressed back against the fireplace. "If they're arguing about me, I have every right to eavesdrop."

Bay shook his head frantically, tugging again.

Taylin caught the end of her braid lest he yank her hair out by the roots. "What are you—"

She cut off as the cabin's wooden floor buckled. A sapling erupted in the middle of the room, sprouting roots with barbed tips that smashed nearby furniture. Taylin sidled along the wall, weighing the urge to run against the inevitability of her heavy footsteps giving away her location. She was almost in the kitchen before there was a loud crash, and shards of glass peppered her back and legs. Most of the projectiles were deflected by her jeans and sweater but several larger pieces sliced through, digging painfully into her flesh.

Bay peered around the curve of her ribs and resumed his frantic tugging. Taylin glanced back as another tree erupted directly beneath the windows, sprouting thorny branches that scraped over the stone fireplace like nails on a blackboard. When Bay squeaked and yanked again, Taylin didn't argue. She curled her fingers around the edge of a sideboard and used it to propel her body forward as fast as it would go. She was barely halfway across the room when branches punched through the kitchen wall, blocking access to the laundry and the back door. Taylin slammed into the spiky growth, barely managing to get her palms up to protect her face from the thorns. Her head was still spinning when the thick, barbed branches wrapped tight around both wrists, cutting off her escape.

"Bay!" Taylin gasped, tears blurring her vision. She blinked furiously, her breath coming in sobs as the thorns squeezed with enough pressure that if she'd been any other human, she'd have splintered. "*Bay!*"

The wolpertinger used her braid like a rope, pulling himself out of the circle of her arms until he sat on one shoulder, whiskers twitching nervously.

"I need you to get outside, where it's safe." Taylin did her best to project a calm she didn't feel, making direct eye contact to enhance the empathic connection. When the wolpertinger squeaked and tightened his hold on her hair, she sent him an extra spurt of courage. "Please, Bay. It's important."

A thick, thorny branch wrapped around her waist and began to squeeze. Taylin bit her lip to keep from crying out, certain Bay would stay if she made the slightest sound of distress. After a protracted moment, the wolpertinger lifted off, dodging falling plaster and waving branches until he zipped out of a hole in the wall and disappeared from sight. Taylin counted to five, prayed he was far enough away, then closed her eyes and let out the emotion that was foremost in her thoughts: fear.

Without the leash of her will, the feeling pulsed out in waves, echoing the thunderous beat of her heart. The plants hesitated and Taylin dug deeper into her emotional repertoire, pumping revulsion into the atmosphere until the thorns pulled free from her wrists and the vines began to loosen. When she had enough slack, she slipped her hands from the noose and gave one loud, sharp clap, backed with her full magical strength. "*Sleep.*"

The plants sagged, dormant between one blink and the next. Moving as quickly as she dared, Taylin unwrapped her waist and backed away from the wall of thorns. Years of meticulous practice allowed her to tiptoe past slumbering branches and dodge inert roots until she reached the large hole in the brickwork where the kitchen sink had once been. Once outside, she crept towards the meagre cover of a copse of fruit trees, making sure to keep the log cabin between herself and the gods on the front lawn. Bay popped out from behind one of the trunks as she approached, and Taylin's eyes misted when he threw his tiny body into her arms. She held him as gently as she knew how, running her fingers through his soft fur while he nuzzled her neck without care for the sweat that slicked her skin.

"Oh, Bay," she whispered. "What am I going to do?"

He squeaked mournfully, burrowing harder into her chest.

Taylin wiped her eyes on her sleeve and took a deep breath. "First thing's first; we can't stay here."

"You're not going anywhere."

Taylin swivelled to face the log cabin, breath catching in her throat. Ostara stood by the rear of the building, her voice as sugary as her appearance.

"You have no right to detain me, Goddess of the Spring and Dawn." Taylin swallowed her nerves and lifted her chin. "I've broken no laws, whereas you just destroyed a crime scene."

Ostara's jaw dropped, her spring-green eyes wide and dewy. Several rabbits clung to the hem of her voluminous gown, noses twitching as they looked from the ruined log cabin to their mistress and back again.

"She makes a good point." Drift wandered into view, hands thrust casually in his pockets. "As I was saying before you swept off to intercept Taylin, the responsibility for this entire shit show rests solely on your shoulders. Blaming a servant is low, even for you."

"My servant?" Ostara covered her mouth with one hand, her tittering laugh far too syrupy to be anything but manufactured. "Really? *Look* at her. Those ghastly markings are better suited to a crypt than a springtime garden and her outfit is just horrid. Is that eye *blind*?" The goddess shuddered. "I have no idea why you'd think I'd make a deal with ... whatever this is. Not to mention what she did to my poor plants. Just look at them!"

Drift snorted. "Cut the theatrics. I suspected Taylin was working for you from the beginning."

He'd suspected her from the beginning? Taylin froze as memories of the last few days tumbled through her head, each one more cutting than the last. If what Drift said was true, then every question he'd asked ... every scrap of information he'd drip fed her ... every heated glance and wicked word ... it'd all been a ruse, and she'd been stupid enough to fall for it.

Raucous had been right to doubt the Osterhase.

The guy was a dick.

Fire began to burn in the pit of Taylin's gut, spreading through her veins. She squared her shoulders and glared at the Goddess of Spring and Dawn. "Your plants tried to kill me. They deserved what they got."

"How dare you!" Ostara drew a dramatic breath, looking more like an indignant cake topper than an irate goddess. "First you ally yourself with my recalcitrant lover, and now you speak to me with blatant disrespect. Why aren't you crushed to a bloody pulp like I wanted?"

Lover? Ostara and Drift were *lovers*? Taylin narrowed her eyes, using the fresh wave of pain to fuel her temper. "I'm tougher than I look."

"Wait." Drift took a step forward, shaking his head. "Taylin's really not working for you?"

"Didn't I just say that?" Ostara tossed her golden curls. "Why would she be?"

"The moonlight. The way my skin tingles when we touch. Her proximity to the staff and her ability to lead me to it. The slow progress of our journey... the fact you didn't show up until she'd led me to the perfect place for an ambush." He swallowed, shifting from foot to foot. "She's the perfect trap."

Taylin stared, aghast. "You asshole. You absolute, self-entitled, egotistical *asshole*."

Drift's lips thinned but he remained silent, his focus on Ostara.

"My dear, sweet, foolish Drift." The Goddess of Spring and Dawn let out a long-suffering sigh. "If you think I waste my days laying excessively elaborate traps involving hideous humans when I can simply take whatever I want, then you're stupider than I thought. I wasn't led here at all; once I heard you were pursuing the staff so rudely stolen from me, I simply paid a portal mage to make a stone attuned to your personal signature." She lifted a hand and a smooth, ovular stone the same colour as Drift's eyes materialised in her palm. "A shame it's single use, but at least I finally found a purpose for the underwear you never bothered to clean off the bedroom floor."

Taylin choked, flinching when they both turned her way.

"What is it, little mage?" Ostara's lips twitched. "Only now realising you can't possibly measure up against a goddess?"

"Enough," Drift growled, voice lowering until it was barely understandable. "Leave Taylin out of this."

"I'm afraid I can't do that, my love." Ostara laughed and this time, it had a barbed edge. "I'll do whatever it takes to reclaim the Staff of Easter – starting with the slaughter of your human bloodhound."

The ground beneath Taylin's feet rippled as long runners of grass spiralled up her legs, binding them together and strapping both arms to her body. The more she pushed against them, the tighter they wound, ignoring the emotional lashing that had freed her from a similar trap only minutes earlier.

"No!" Drift lurched forward but the grass wrapped around his body too, cocooning him from the base of his neck to the tips of his toes. "Stop!"

"What is it, Osterhase? *Now* you choose to care? Too little, too late, I think." The Goddess of Spring and Dawn laughed as she swept across the yard, halting directly in front of Taylin.

"Leave her be!" Drift strained against his bindings. "Taylin!"

The sound of her name on his lips tore at Taylin until she looked away, her heart a chaotic mess of anger and fear. Raucous had warned her Drift was dangerous; more so, she'd warned herself. In spite of it all, she'd allowed him to sneak under her skin. What if they'd slept together? If she'd given him full access to her body, her heart, her mind, what then? Would he have killed her with his own two hands once he had what he wanted, or simply laughed and walked away as Logan had done?

"You made a bad bargain, human." Ostara gripped Taylin's jaw, forcing her head around. "Drift was, is, and always will be only one thing. Mine."

The goddess shoved hard, toppling Taylin backwards into the stream. Water frothed wildly before it closed overhead, the grass wrapped so tight that not even Bay's sharp teeth were able to cut through the bindings. In the end, the wolpertinger was forced to abandon his efforts and swim for the surface, leaving her with nothing but her broken heart for company.

Taylin closed her eyes as she settled at the bottom of the stream like a stone, completely and utterly helpless.

6

WELL, THIS IS EMBARRASSING

Taylin wasn't a trap.

The connection Drift had felt, the pull between them that made him want to scream mine, mine, *mine* – it had all been real. And like a fool, he'd thrown it away, too scared of deceit to see the truth in the moonlight she'd shed across his skin.

Oh, he'd been deceived all right.

By himself.

Rage boiled as Taylin sank deeper underwater, Bay clinging to the grass that bound her, desperately trying to chew through. Drift strained against his own grass bindings but it was no use; the shattered remnants of his magic left him barely stronger than a human.

"Bay!" Drift craned his neck, no longer able to see either Taylin or the tiny wolpertinger who was valiantly trying to save her. "*Bay!*"

Ostara chuckled. "I wonder how long humans can hold their breath? Or flying rats, for that matter?"

Bay erupted from the stream on the heels of her words, tiny wings beating frantically. *Bindings too strong. Taylin too heavy. Will drown.*

"No, no, no." Drift swallowed his panic lest it overwhelm him. "There must be a way."

"We both know there's not." Ostara's throaty purr turned to a squeal as Bay swooped at her head. "Get away from me, you little vermin!"

Filthy thief! You not goddess worthy of worship. Bay evaded Ostara's swatting hands and faded out, his body invisible to everyone except Drift – and Taylin, were she not helpless at the bottom of the stream. His wings brushed Drift's cheek as he fluttered by, his next words a private murmur. *Will be back. Keep fighting.*

Bunching every muscle he had, Drift shoved at the grass cocoon while Ostara watched and laughed. Her hands painted a dainty pattern in the air and the earth at her feet cracked, thick roots punching through to the surface. They began to twine together, collecting the grassed earth and moulding it into new shapes until a hulking golem stood in the yard. Damp loam clung to the wooden skeleton, forming a lumpy body, lumbering feet and crushing fists.

"I'm afraid I can't stay." Ostara curved one hand around the side of Drift's neck and leant in close, her lips brushing his jaw. "I have a staff to retrieve, after all."

"You'll never find it," he hissed, straining against her grip. "You have no way to track it down."

Ostara shrugged. "Sooner or later, whoever stole the staff will make a mistake – and once I have word of that mistake, a simple snap of my fingers will take me wherever I need to go." Glittery lashes tickled the skin of Drift's cheek. "Unless you'd like to end this farce, here and now? A few simple words is all it would take, you know. That has never changed."

"I'd rather die."

"I don't think so." All traces of warmth faded from Ostara's face, her grip turning cruel. "Once I have the staff, you'll have broken the terms of your exile and I'll be free to do as I wish without reprise from the other gods ... and we both know I have a far better use for you than death."

"Fuck the other gods. If Taylin comes to any harm, you'll pay for it from your own flesh, treatises and exiles be damned." Drift snapped his teeth in her face, darkly satisfied when she flinched. "I bared my throat to you once; I won't do it again."

"You're in no position to make threats, lover." Ostara dropped her hand and turned to face the golem. "Ensure the Osterhase doesn't leave this place."

The golem groaned in a voice of tortured wood and grinding earth, stepping through the shower of blossoms Ostara left behind as she disappeared. It swung a ponderous arm, hitting Drift squarely in the gut with enough force to knock the wind from his lungs and send him soaring across the yard, where he thumped unceremoniously onto the bank of the stream.

Drift coughed and choked, water seeping through the grass bindings to soak his feet and ankles. All he could think about was Taylin – how long had she been under? A minute, perhaps two? How long could a human hold their breath? He didn't know; he'd never needed to know.

The ground shook as the golem approached and Drift braced himself for the inevitable blow. It came in the form of an earthy foot, shoving him far enough into the water that his legs began to float. He strained against the grass, hope surging as his hands shifted the slightest amount – just enough that when he sliced his claws out, they cut into the bindings that held him immobile.

"Come on, you ugly motherfucker," he growled, glaring up at the golem as it hesitated on the bank of the stream. "What's the matter? Water doesn't agree with you?"

The construct teetered uncertainly as Drift dragged his claws across the grass cocoon, gaining more ground with every flex of his fingers. With a loud snapping sound, the bindings gave way and he shoved his hands into the muddy water, rolling aside as the golem aimed a second clumsy kick in his direction.

Drift! Bay erupted from the trees on the opposite side of the clearing, a flock of wolpertingers winging in behind him. The tiny creatures swept forward, attacking the golem in relentless waves that drove it slowly, step by step, back from the water's edge. *Will stall creature. Go!*

Drift used his claws to slice through the remains of Ostara's grass prison, kicking his legs to speed the process. As soon as he was free, he took as deep a breath as his lungs would allow and dove under the water. The stream was cloudy from recent agitation but a faint blue glow led him straight to where Taylin lay on the sandy bottom. Thick strands of grass trapped her limbs, some bearing marks from Bay's teeth. Her eyes were closed, lips parted as though for a kiss – but the water's embrace was a dangerous one, and the distinct lack of bubbles trailing from her mouth stalled Drift's heart inside his chest.

Tangling a clawed hand in the grass ropes, he tugged – and was promptly dragged downwards, thumping into Taylin hard enough to see stars.

She hadn't been joking when she said she was heavy.

Shaking his head to clear it, Drift burrowed his hands through the soft earth at Taylin's back until she was clasped in his arms, and braced himself against the bottom of the stream. He tried again to lift her, but no matter how he struggled or strained, she didn't budge an inch.

Come on, Taylin. Drift laid his forehead against her own, lungs burning from the effort of staying underwater so long. *Help me. Please.*

Water flowed and silence reigned, thick and overwhelming as a tomb. But then ... the barest tickle in his veins, a stirring of energy so faint that if not for the sudden shift in Taylin's weight, Drift might never have believed it to be real. He leaned back, realising the soft glow from her skin coated his face and neck.

Moonlight, emanating from her bones.

Moonlight, from which Drift was made.

Moonlight, the source of his every breath ... and the foundation of his power.

Drift bunched his muscles and heaved.

They erupted from the water amidst a fountain of spray, the waves created by their passage carrying Drift partway to the shore. Taylin's weight increased as the moments slipped by but he made it to solid ground, laying her out on the grass beyond the water's reach.

"Taylin?" Drift pressed a finger to her neck, where her pulse should have beat in time with his own. "Gods, no. *Taylin.*"

Driven by desperation, he interlaced his fingers and thumped clubbed fists against her sternum. Agony radiated up his arms, the shockwave catapulting him backward – into the legs of the golem. The construct toppled, ricocheting off Drift to land hard on Taylin's chest. She bucked under the blow, water shooting from her mouth with explosive force that left her coughing and wheezing. Buoyed by the sound, Drift dug his claws into the construct's shoulder and used the momentum generated by its struggles to push it onto the grass.

Bay and his wolpertingers dove with ear-splitting shrieks and Drift left them to handle the golem while he scrambled back to Taylin, heart in his throat as he checked her over. Her eyes remained closed but no more water trickled from her mouth … and most importantly, she was breathing.

Alive.

Scalding tears blurred Drift's vision as he shredded her grass bindings with his claws. "Taylin? Can you hear—"

A giant earthen fist hit him square in the side, stealing the air from his lungs even as it sent him flying across the clearing. Drift hit the remains of the log cabin and then slammed into the earth, agony turning him limp.

Did learn nothing from first time? Fists are big. Hurt much. Bay landed on his shoulder, tugging hard on one of Drift's soggy ears. *Up! It comes.*

"I thought you were holding it off!"

Not strong enough to keep away forever. Another sharp tug. *If Ostara come back, she kick our ass into next week and kill Taylin. Again.* The wolpertinger growled, sharp teeth grazing the edge of the ear he was trying so valiantly to remove. *Get off ground before Bay does golem job and bury Drift so deep nobody find, ever.*

"You know, I liked you better before I was exiled for thousands of years." Drift pushed to his knees, groaning as his ribs reported that several of their brethren were decisively broken. "I can't fight like this."

Must. Golem keep coming until ordered to stop, or destroyed.

"Dammit, Bay! Even if I wasn't injured, I don't have the strength or the magic to destroy it." Drift closed his eyes against the nauseating pain and tried to think. "Was there anything else in the forest?"

Bay's wings rustled as he shifted uneasily. *Wolves. They watch, but they may not help.*

"It's worth a shot." Hope a lead weight in his gut, Drift lifted his head and coughed out a howl. The action sent fresh pain shooting through his midsection and he flattened a hand over his ribs, his voice trailing into an agonised wheeze.

When an answering howl echoed from the woods – then two, three – Drift almost laughed in relief. Using the remains of the log cabin's wall for support, he clawed his way upright and faced the golem.

Ostara's creation was standing, too, although one leg was at an unusual angle. It shambled slowly towards Drift with misshapen arms outstretched, ignorant of the three large wolves that emerged from the trees. They stalked their enemy as a unit, heads down and hackles up.

Though every instinct screamed otherwise, Drift forced his feet to stay in place as the golem shambled closer, the wolves following with lips pulled back from pointed teeth. When the earthen construct raised giant fists for another shattering blow, the wolves leaped, hitting the construct in the back and shoulders. Drift barely managed to stagger out of the way as the golem went down, the trio of wolves ripping and tearing until Ostara's creation was reduced to little more than muddy splinters.

Huh. Bay fluttered down to check the remains. *Wish my teeth were big enough for that.*

Drift wheezed out a chuckle. "It's not the size that counts; it's how you use them."

One by one, the wolves raised their heads. The alpha's tail twitched as though he might have wagged it, but his ears flattened to his skull and a growl rattled in his throat.

"It's all right." Drift pressed a hand to his heart. "The dissonance hurts me, too."

The alpha dipped his head and the other two wolves followed suit.

They listen. Bay paused as the alpha chuffed deep in his chest. *He says the bond is tattered but not broken. Wolves will always answer the call.*

With slow, steady movements, Drift lowered himself to one knee and offered his hand, palm down and fingers curled slightly to expose the back of his knuckles. "Thank you."

The alpha growled again but when Bay growled back, the sound diverted into a whine. After several nudges from his fellows, the alpha leaned forward to gently sniff Drift's exposed knuckles.

For now, it was enough.

Bay hopped over and put his paws on the alpha's foreleg. *Be safe.*

The wolf huffed an affirmative and melted back into the trees, his companions following without a backwards glance. Drift looked down at Bay, his heart both full and heavy at the same time. "It's all right if you leave, too. I know the dissonance builds up over time."

Diss-oh-nance hurts like teeth under skin, Bay agreed, spreading his wings with a snap. *But I stay long enough to see Taylin.*

"All right."

With his ribs afire, it was all Drift could do to stagger to her side. She flopped onto her back as they approached, her skin so pale that the fae characters tattooed on her face stood out even more than normal.

"Taylin," he rasped, kneeling to cup her face. "I thought I'd lost you."

She glared up at him, jaw tight beneath his palms, and said nothing.

Panic filtered into Drift's heart. How did her truth magic work? Surely, with his skin flush against her own, she'd understand he meant what he said?

"I was an idiot." His voice wobbled but he pressed on, determined to make things right. "Ostara and I have a history, and I thought … gods, Taylin, I'm so sorry."

She sat up, and he shifted to give her room. Sodden hair clung to her face, making her mismatched eyes all the more prominent. Even bruised and bloody she was glorious, and Drift's fingers twitched with the need to touch her again, to draw her into his arms and kiss away the distance in her expression.

"The accusations I made were out of line." He swallowed heavily. "I was so busy twisting your words and actions to suit Ostara's aims that I never stopped to actually think. Now … I'll fix this, I swear. Can you forgive me?"

Taylin tilted her head to one side, examining his muddy, broken body before locking her gaze with his. Bracing one hand on the soggy earth, she leaned in until they were almost close enough to rub noses.

"No," she whispered, her voice a strangled rasp. "You're an arrogant, slimy, traitorous asshole. Apology rejected."

For the first time, Drift noticed tears running down her cheeks, mingling with the water from the stream. He opened his mouth to reply, but Taylin lifted one slender hand, curled it into a fist and punched him straight in the face.

Hard.

Everything went black.

7

THAT'S GONNA LEAVE A MARK

aylin stared down at Drift's unconscious body and shook out her fist. Her knuckles would bear the mark of her temper for a while yet, but it was the shattered glass of her heart that caused the most pain. "I'm so stupid."

Bay fluttered down to land in her lap, reaching out to put a paw on Drift's exposed forearm. *You not stupid, Osterhase stupid. Deserves to find staff without help. Bay show way home?*

Home. Where Raucous would be waiting with his best I-told-you-so expression and Great Aunt Ethel …

"No." Taylin tugged the remains of the grass rope from her body and tossed them aside. "I need the staff to restore Great Aunt Ethel to her former self – and if Ostara's recent performance is anything to go by, she's not likely to help anyone who's been transmuted by the thief."

Not without price. Bay shivered, ears drooping. *Ostara price always too high.*

"That's what I figured. Which means, much as I hate to admit it, that I need Drift as much as he needs me." Taylin frowned at the traitorous wretch sprawled in the soggy grass. "He's not much of a god, if a single punch knocked him out cold."

Lost strength when lost power. Not much power, not much use. Bay's whiskers twitched, and a sharp gleam entered his eye. *Osterhase deserved smack.*

Taylin laughed, the weight on her chest lightening considerably. She reached out to ruffle the fur between the wolpertinger's antlers. "I'm glad you agree."

Been saying he deserves smack for long time. You first to see sense. The wolpertinger gave Drift's shoulder a prod with his paw. *Must go. Dissonance hurts.*

The idea of being left along to deal with the fallout of Ostara's attack had Taylin's breath turning choppy. Tears pricked the corners of her eyes and she blinked them furiously away, determined not to falter so far into the journey.

"Okay. I can do this on my own, surely." She bit her lip to hide the way it wobbled. "I'll have to; we can't stay here."

No. Bitch goddess come back sooner or later. Bay gave Drift a poke. *Will carry?*

"It's probably the only way." Taylin let out a long sigh. "Raucous showed me a technique once for lifting and carrying someone in an emergency. As long as I can get Drift across my shoulders, the inherent strength in my bones should keep us upright … I think."

Worth risk. Even if bitch goddess not come back in person, she might send others to check on golem.

"Exactly. The only positive of the situation is that if Ostara and the EBC showed up here, it means they don't have any idea of where the staff is either. Wait." Taylin's eyes narrowed. "She said she tracked Drift here. Can she do that again?"

Only if she creepy enough to hoard more dirty underneath-pants. Bay's tiny face screwed up. *Never thought Drift wore those. One more stupid mistake he make.*

Taylin choked. "I really don't want to think about whether or not Drift wears underwear, Bay."

Such pretty lies you tell self. The wolpertinger chittered a sound suspiciously like a laugh. *Ah, don't make sad face. Drift say mean things that hurt, but Drift also hurt by Ostara long ago.*

"That's no excuse for what he did and you know it."

Bay knows. Just saying that when in pain, revert to base instinct ... and base instinct is most dumb instinct of all. He spread his wings and fluttered into the air. *Sorry, Taylin. Diss-oh-nance means I cannot stay.*

"It's all right. I understand."

Will be back soon. Good luck. He nuzzled a quick kiss to her cheek and then was gone, leaving Taylin alone by the wreckage of the log cabin with an unconscious god at her feet.

Grief and hurt immediately welled, but she pushed them resolutely down again. She needed to get herself and Drift to safety; then and only then did she have the luxury of falling apart.

After a quick check of her injuries, Taylin rose unsteadily to her feet and moved to retrieve her pack from the clump of bushes she'd stashed it in earlier. A rummage around inside yielded the antiseptic and bandages she needed to treat the nasty cuts and punctures left by the cabin's shattered windows and Ostara's vengeful plants. It was an awkward job on her own but once Taylin was satisfied, she donned the bag and returned to Drift.

When a splash of cold water didn't rouse him, she slung one of his arms around her neck the way Raucous had once shown her and straightened, dragging the Osterhase across the width of her shoulders. Adding his weight to her own made walking difficult, but as she'd hoped, her bones held strong – so Taylin concentrated on putting one foot in front of the other and forced her aching body to keep moving, eating the ground up with steady, measured paces and deep, slow breaths.

By sunset she stood at the edge of yet another treeline, looking out over a vast inland sea. Since Mu was divided haphazardly into territories whose climates and terrains were each unique, there was a distinct demarcation line between the end of the autumnal forest and the start of the mist-wreathed lake, with golden grasses becoming a sheer edge at which the gentle waters lapped peacefully.

Backing away from the border, Taylin deposited Drift in the lee of a tree whose weeping branches created a sort of pavilion. His breathing was even and his heart rate steady, unconsciousness having given way to sleep at some point during the ride on her shoulders.

Not in the least inclined to attempt waking him, Taylin dumped her pack at his side and returned to the lake. The water proved tepid and salty, not in the least drinkable or useful for bathing. Long-stemmed weeds roiled beneath the darkened surface, and the air, when she stuck her head and shoulders over the border, was thick and humid.

Gross.

Tabling the lake as a problem for Future Taylin, she canvassed the nearby area and discovered a Lemurian orange tree laden with fruit several shades darker than the sunset. Climbing trees was certainly not her forte but some of the branches hung low enough that she could pick a couple of oranges without even having to stretch. She pocketed them and returned to camp as the final coppery rays of sunset faded.

Dusk's silence was a peaceful one, settling over Taylin with the same soft comfort as a favourite blanket. Since lighting a fire wasn't the most sensible idea if she wanted to remain unseen, she navigated by the faint moonlight emanating from her skin. Using her pack as a stool, she broke the oranges into segments and ate one at a time, allowing the familiar routine of food and rest to continue distracting her from the myriad of things she didn't want to think – or feel.

"Where are we?"

Taylin flinched as Drift's voice rasped across her skin, the growl as deep and mysterious as the first time she'd heard it. Only this time, it brought not a visceral thrill but the sharp reminder that he'd viewed her as an enemy from the moment they met.

When she didn't immediately answer, Drift raised shaking hands to rub his face and tousle his hair, the black-tipped brown strands standing up at odd angles. "I'm sorry. I thought … I just … ah, fuck."

Taylin stared hard at the half-eaten orange in her hand, eyes hot. That was the problem with being an empath; she knew beyond doubt that Drift's remorse and regret were real. Too bad it didn't mitigate the unrelenting throb of her broken heart. Or the self-directed fury she'd been struggling with the entire afternoon.

"I don't know where we are," she said at last, hating the wobble in her voice almost as much as the sharp spike of grief it caused in Drift.

"I'm not familiar with this part of Mu. I followed the trail the staff left behind and hoped for the best."

"You're still following the staff?"

"You swore you'd save Great Aunt Ethel if I helped you find it." Suddenly nauseous, Taylin set the remaining orange segments down on the grass beside her. "Unless that, too, was just for show?"

Drift was silent for a long moment, during which Taylin stared determinedly in the opposite direction, taking in the gentle sweep of the tree's hanging boughs and the deep burgundy of its foliage. She could feel his eyes on her face, skin prickling as his gaze swept slowly over her ruined clothing and back again. When she didn't surrender to the sheer draw of his longing, Drift crawled across the clearing until he knelt at her feet.

"Take my hand."

"I'm not tracking the staff any further tonight."

"Forget the staff – I want you to know I'm telling the truth."

"Here's the funny thing about life, Osterhase. You don't always get what you want." Taylin slapped his hand aside only for Drift to catch hold of her wrist. "Let go."

A low growl crawled out of his throat, so deep and threatening Taylin had no choice but to look his way. Drift was bent over her arm, nostrils dilating as he sniffed the dressing she'd applied earlier. The ones at her wrist were soaked with blood and she had a sneaking suspicion the bandage around her waist looked much the same.

"What happened?" He began to unravel the bandage, ignoring her attempts to pull free. When Taylin yanked as hard as she could, the weight of her bones giving her the upper hand, Drift followed the momentum of her pull so that their bodies toppled into the soft grass.

"Get off me!" Taylin rolled but Drift straddled her waist, deft fingers making short work of the bandage in spite of her struggles. He hissed at the heavy bruising trekking up her forearm, framing a perfect ring of punctures that, while no longer oozing blood, were painfully raw. "*Stop!*"

Drift froze, blinking down at her through his fury – an anger Taylin could feel like a fist in her gut. "Taylin?"

"Move," she hissed, hot tears trickling down her face. "You have no right to put your hands on me for any reason."

His anger fractured, then, shifting through shock to regret in an instant. "I didn't mean to—"

"If you don't like what you see, perhaps you should consider I might've been spared these injuries if the person I trusted hadn't hung me out to dry like last week's washing." She shoved him hard in the chest and was gratified to see him flinch. "Now get off me before I put you into a sleep so deep you won't even wake when the night scavengers come to peck out your eyeballs."

Drift released her arm and moved to the side, holding up both hands for peace. "You have every right to be angry; I acted without thinking. I'm sorry."

"I don't care." Taylin rolled to her knees and upended her pack, digging out clean clothes and what remained of her med-kit. "I don't care what you think, what you like, what you hate. I don't care what you want, or what you feel. You served me up to that … that … *bitch* of a goddess without a care in the world, like some sort of ritual sacrifice! Oh, and let's not forget the part where you believed I was working for her." She choked out a dry laugh. "Earth to the Osterhase – not everything is about you."

"Taylin, please. It's not—"

"I don't care!" She snatched the closest item at hand – a bar of home-made soap – and threw it at his head as hard as she could. The motion and wind-up were slow, but her moonstone bones carried enough weight that even though Drift caught the bar before it hit, he was toppled onto his backside. "The only reason I'm still here is for Ethel. I have no interest in your lover's tiff with Ostara."

Fresh tears tracked down her face but Taylin refused to acknowledge them. Instead, she bundled up her chosen supplies and what remained of her dignity and stormed out of camp, dimming her bones' glow until it was little more than a shimmer under her skin. Shoving a fist in her mouth so Drift wouldn't hear the shards of her broken heart grinding against one another, she made steady progress to a small copse of tress. After a cursory check for any unwanted pursuit – namely, a certain god who would discover she was serious about her sleep threat – Taylin stripped to the skin, using a pack of wipes to wash as best she could. With clean underwear and a fresh bra on, she tugged on her only remaining pair of jeans and set about cleansing and re-bandaging the worst of her wounds. After rolling her dirty things into a small bag, she dragged on a long-sleeve top and a tunic-length hoodie, pulling the hood up so that she was cocooned in the soft, dark interior.

Feeling no less angry but far cleaner, she returned to camp on bare feet, muddy boots dangling from her fingers. Drift sat cross-legged with his back to the willow's trunk, her pack at his side. Since clothes and sundries no longer littered the grassy space, Taylin assumed he'd taken it upon himself to re-pack it – but since checking would involve getting close, she set her dirty things on the opposite side of the trunk and lay down in the grass with her back to the Osterhase.

"Are you hungry?" Drift's voice floated through the night and Taylin belatedly realised that in her current outfit, she'd condemned him to existing in inky darkness. Guilt flashed through her until she recalled the way her pack had been neatened, proving the night was clearly no impediment to Drift, broken god or not.

Trusting her silence to speak for her, she shut down her empathic senses and closed her eyes.

"I could hunt for you," he offered, his tone pitched low and gentle. When Taylin only scrunched her shoulders tighter, Drift sighed. "Ostara's not my lover. At least, not any more."

"I told you, I don't care." It was an outright lie – in spite of the way her breath caught with every inhale, Taylin couldn't deny the draw she felt, the indefinable spark that yet lingered between them.

Gods above, she was so stupid.

With that thought uppermost in her mind, she curled her hands deep into her sleeves, nestled them under her chin and commanded her body to sleep.

Except…

"You'd be more comfortable with a pillow, at the very least."

Taylin huffed out a breath, eyes snapping open. "Retrieving something suitable enough to use as a pillow would also involve getting close to you. No thanks."

He made a sound that might have been a growl or a truncated laugh, and then the clearing was filled with the rustle of fabric. A moment later, something soft and warm landed on her head, the scent of cedarwood and sage etched into every fibre of the fabric.

"Is this your t-shirt?"

This time, it was definitely a laugh. "Maybe."

"What are you wearing, then?"

"Not a t-shirt?" His tone took on a wicked edge. "I don't get as cold as you. I won't need it."

"Stop flirting with me." The last word broke as it tumbled over her lips, and Taylin clenched her teeth on a fresh wave of tears. "I trusted you. I liked you. Worse, I thought you liked me. But it was all an act, and I just … I can't do that. I'm not like that."

"I *do* like you. That part wasn't an act, Taylin. You're strong and smart and funny and—"

"Don't. I'm not interested."

"Then why are we still having this conversation?"

"Because you won't shut up!" Taylin rolled onto her back, balling the t-shirt up behind her head – to get it out of the way, not because she craved his scent even as she wanted to hit him all over again. "Whether Ostara is your lover or not is none of my business. All I care about is retrieving the staff so you can return Great Aunt Ethel to normal and then leave me in peace."

"Are you sure that's all you care about?"

"If you're implying that I might still harbour some semblance of positive emotion towards you, then you're about to be disappointed. Raucous warned me away from you before we left Evergreen Waters – all you've done is prove him right." Taylin draped one arm over her face, blocking out the world. "Just leave me alone, Drift. Please."

He didn't answer, and Taylin spent several moments torn between relief and disappointment before her mind gave up and her body shut down, seeking the dubious escape of sleep and whatever dreams awaited in the depths of her subconscious.

8

THE ILLUSION OF CHOICE

*D*rift watched Taylin sleep, his heart heavier than the cloak of night that blanketed the world. Now that he'd released the notion of her being a tool to orchestrate his untimely demise, his empty spaces breathed in time to the syllables of her name. His soul keened for her touch, his skin craving the moonlight he'd rejected in a fit of suspicious pique.

Bay was right – he was an idiot.

As midnight came and went, Drift tucked his knees to his chest and settled his chin on top, never once looking away from the slight form on the grass. He was used to getting what he wanted – even his exile had been by choice, rather than force. Yet barely a body length away lay a woman more intriguing, mysterious and complex than anyone he'd ever met and he wasn't allowed to touch. To hold. To cherish and protect.

"I trusted you. I liked you. Worse, I thought you liked me. But it was all an act, and I just ... I can't do that. I'm not like that."

Drift winced as Taylin's words echoed in his skull. He didn't blame her; he'd looked her in the eye and announced he was blood and sex and magic, not a man with a heart beating inside his chest that, if he could, he'd tear out and offer her on bent knee.

Taylin shifted on the ground, a shiver tracing the length of her spine. Opening the pack he'd kept deliberately close in an attempt to lure her near, Drift pulled out items one at a time until he came to the thin blanket folded at the bottom. It was only light, but someone had embroidered heat sigils onto it in wonky stitches. Crooked though they were, the sigils were active, the fabric warm in Drift's fingers as he recalled the way Taylin had tucked herself under it on previous nights.

It was big enough for two, but he'd given up the right to ask – so instead, he pushed unsteadily to his feet and crept close enough to drape it over her body. She mumbled in her sleep, curling contentedly into the blanket with a half-smile that hit him straight in the solar plexus. Drift spread a hand over his heart as though that would somehow keep it inside his chest and backed up until his spine hit the willow.

What had he done?

Try to ruin only good thing to come into miserable life since go into exile, that's what. Bay appeared as though summoned, tumbling into Drift's lap where he proceeded to wave his legs about in silent amusement. *You doomed. Taylin so mad at you.*

"How did you know what I was thinking about?"

Can tell from sad look on your face. Bay cocked his head. *Also, you said, 'what have I done', so that was good clue.*

Drift grunted. "I didn't think I said that out loud."

Want advice?

"From *you*?"

One of us has mate. It's not you. Bay paused. *Who else you going to ask? Fallen God of Justice is only friend, and he too busy being miserable.*

"Tyr is not my only friend." Drift glared at the ball of fur in his lap. When Bay remained unrepentant, he sighed. "All right, then. Go ahead."

You like Taylin? You want her? Think like Drift, not like Osterhase. Bay rolled upright, resting his forepaws on Drift's chest. *Don't take. Ask. Don't expect. Earn. And don't abandon to nasty goddess who wants to put you on a leash and parade around for all to see.*

"I feel like that last part goes without saying."

Me too, but you still did it.

Drift swallowed, glanced at Taylin's sleeping form, and bent to place his lips against one of Bay's floppy ears. "What if she still doesn't like me?"

Silly Drift. The wolpertinger nuzzled a gentle kiss to his chin. *If Taylin didn't like, Taylin wouldn't be sad. More she hurts, more she cares. Now is turn for* **you** *to care, and show that Drift is safe heart to share.*

Taylin stirred, turning onto her side with a sigh. Dawn was beginning to lighten the world beyond the pavilion and Drift knew from their short time together that she'd wake with the sun, ready to face the day ahead with the same stoic determination she did everything.

It was highly unlikely that his face was the first thing she wanted to see upon lifting her lashes.

With that thought foremost in his mind, Drift lifted Bay to perch on one shoulder and rolled to his feet, shaking out stiffened limbs and testing newly healed ribs. His face was still sore from where Taylin had punched it but the healing sleep she'd inadvertently put him into had mended his bones until only a lingering ache remained.

The same couldn't be said for Taylin's own injuries.

Drift frowned as he slipped out of the pavilion, her furious withdrawal from his touch more unwelcome each time he thought about it. There was only one thing for it – he'd have to earn back both her trust and her affection. Then he'd do what he'd been longing to since the moment they met; kiss her until their hearts took up residence in the other's chest.

Satisfied with his plan, Drift followed his nose to the edge of an enormous inland sea. The fractal magic of Mu made the change from crisp autumn air to swampish humidity a shocking one, but he pushed down his reaction and knelt, scooping up a handful of tepid seawater. Magic immediately soaked into his skin, the water carrying a presence almost as familiar as Bay's.

Drift watched the water drip from his fingers, making tiny ripples as it returned to the ocean. Earning back Taylin's trust would take more than lowering his defences; it would take courage and action, loyalty not just to her but to the worlds he'd turned his back on when he went into exile.

"Here goes nothing." Drift scooped up another handful of seawater and took a sip, grimacing at the taste. As the salt of the ocean coated his throat, he tossed the remaining water up in the air, whispering soft words in the language of his birth – a language spoken by very few living beings on either Earth or Mu.

Will she come? Bay's claws dug in as he leaned over the water, wings spread for balance.

"I don't know. I hope so."

The sky lightened by several degrees before the water began to ripple. Foliage rustled behind Drift and he caught hints of jasmine and vanilla on the morning air. Much as he wanted to, he didn't turn to look at Taylin; instead, he focussed on the pale shape rising from the depths.

"What is *that?*" Taylin whispered, coming to a halt at the edge of the lake. She stood just out of arm's reach, hood pushed back to reveal her rumpled black braid and mysterious, tattooed face, the skin yet creased with the marks of sleep. Beneath the jasmine and vanilla that was her own unique scent, Drift could smell fresh blood soaking into the bandages she wore.

"A friend." Though it went against everything in his nature, Drift kept his thoughts – and hands – to himself. "I'm hoping she can help us."

The pale shape grew bigger and bigger, until by the time it crested the surface of the water, the creature was large enough to swallow both Drift and Taylin in a single bite.

"Oooooosterhaaaaaaase," the whale bugled, staring out at Drift from an eye the deep blue-green of the inland sea. Her hide was a striking white, a spiralling horn longer than he was tall protruding from her upper lip. "Drrrrrriiiiiiffffffffft."

Heart a hammer in his chest, Drift extended his hand, palm down, fingers curled to display the backs of his knuckles. "My lady Ataraxia. It's been a long time."

"Hmmmmmmmmmmmmmmmmmmmmmmmmmm." The narwhal tilted

sideways, fixing her eye on Taylin. "I sennnnnnse the moooooooon in thissss onnnnne."

Taylin knelt and bowed her head. "Taylin Colkannis, Sentinel of Evergreen Waters Retreat, at your service."

"Reeeeeeeeeeally." Ataraxia surged forward, her enormous horn shooting through the space between Taylin and Drift so that her body could rest against the sea's edge.

"My apologies for the dissonance." Drift dared to lay his palm flat against the side of her nose. "I know it hurts."

Like teeth under the skin, Bay added, launching from Drift's shoulder to resettle on the narwhal's horn.

Ataraxia let out a long, ululating sound that might have been a laugh. "Teeeeeeeeth indeeeeed. Tayyyyyyyyyyyyylinnnnn?"

Taylin jumped, then cleared her throat. "Yes, my lady?"

"Yoooooou willll fixxxxxxxxxxxx the dissssssssonannnnce."

"Uh ... I will?"

"Touuuuuuuch the Ooooooosterhaaaaaase."

"I'd really prefer not to—" Taylin cut off with a squeak as Ataraxia's tail slapped the water behind them, sending a spray of spume into the air. "All right. I'll touch him."

Drift edged towards her outstretched fingers, the siren song of Taylin's moonlit soul reeling him in like nothing else ever would. Her palm glowed faintly in the morning light, and the moment his fingers made contact, sparks shot up his arm and rainbows erupted in the space behind his eyes. His gasp and Taylin's came in unison but instead of letting go they clutched at each other, the energy transfer building from sparks into a storm.

Involuntary tears prickled as Ataraxia's energy crashed into his mind, her presence so huge that it filled him beyond bursting. Taylin cried out, leaning heavily on the narwhal's horn for support.

Give it time. Ataraxia's voice, pure and clear as a bell, tolled inside Drift's body until he shook with the force of it. *It will settle, little moon.*

"Oh, my gods," Taylin panted. Her eyes were unnaturally wide, the blue one glazed and the moonstone one glowing from within. When Drift stepped closer, their bodies flush but for Ataraxia's horn between them, she wrapped her free arm around his waist and pressed her face into his bare chest. "I'm going to explode."

Such little faith, Ataraxia chided. *You are an anchor like no other, my dear. It would take far more than I to sweep you away.*

"I don't understand."

Ataraxia's laughter thrummed through them both, and if not for her steadying horn between them, Drift fancied he'd have toppled. *Yes, you do – you give Drift the strength he needs to retrieve the staff and restore balance to both Earth and Mu.*

"I'm not here for Drift." Taylin shivered where she rested against his chest, the skin contact agony and ecstasy all at once. "I'm here to pay a debt I owe to the woman who saved my life."

And yet, just as the staff is not only a symbol of Easter, so has it become one by association. Ataraxia splashed her tail again, her song turning to one of anger. *The worlds suffer because of one goddess' selfish desire to be more than she ought. It is time to end this farce once and for all.*

"I can track the staff, but I'm nobody special." Taylin lifted her head from Drift's chest and he felt the loss to the core of his being. "Just a tool easily discarded."

That is your fear talking. Drift's actions were foolish, but they were also driven by a past trauma not entirely unlike your own. The narwhal nudged Taylin with the side of her horn. *I see it inside your memories. A man ... Logan? He was a patient at the healing centre where you serve, and took the care you offered for his own selfish satisfaction. What you saw as a beginning was no more than a game to pass the time until he moved on. "It's been fun, Tay. A really wild ride. If I'm ever in the area, I'll drop back in for a do-over."*

"Enough!" Drift's claws slid out to prick the narwhal's thick hide. "You're being unkind."

I am making a point, Ataraxia corrected. *Taylin believes herself naive and undeserving of love. A curiosity to be poked and prodded and discarded. Though you made a mistake, she isn't judging only your own bad behaviour, but the behaviour of Logan, who trod before you – and she is using her own fear as an excuse to rationalise pushing you away. Or am I wrong?*

"I ..." Taylin dropped her gaze. "Logan was a lot like Drift; deliciously wicked and unfairly handsome. He could make people laugh with a few short words and had the kind of charisma that put others at ease with nothing more than a wink and a smile. I had begun to dream of a future, but to him, I was just another notch on the bedpost. When I was no longer useful, he dusted his hands and walked away."

"Then I did the same thing." Drift reached to cup her jaw with his free hand, tilting her face until she looked him in the eye. "Gods, Taylin. I'm so sorry."

Long, thick lashes fluttered shut. "I know you're sorry. I can feel it with every fibre of my being; sorrow, regret, heartache. But Drift … that doesn't stop it hurting."

All wounds hurt – but once properly cleaned, they have the chance to heal, provided the proper care is applied. Where you are judging Drift based on your past, so did he judge you based on his. Both actions are unfair, and both situations must be released if either of you are to move forward. Ataraxia pinned Drift with her enormous marine-coloured eyes. *Taylin is not Ostara.*

"I know, I know," Drift muttered. "Believe me, if I could change what happened, I would."

Ataraxia loosed a long, low note that shivered across Drift's skin. *Waste no more time on regret. Instead, start afresh with each other – or the Goddess of Spring and Dawn has already won.*

"No," Taylin snapped. "I need that staff to rescue Great Aunt Ethel."

"And I am tired of no longer being whole." Drift pushed down the flare of hurt her words caused and set his jaw. "I called, Lady Ataraxia, in the hopes you've some knowledge of my staff. We need to recover it before Ostara does – and before any more people are turned to chocolate."

Indeed. Shall I take you to the staff, then?

Drift blinked. "You know where it is?"

More or less. It passed by more than a week ago, now. I followed, but I was not foolish enough to touch. I have no wish to be turned by Easter's curse. Ataraxia shivered, sending a large wave rippling across the surface of the ocean *The thief took a ship to the opposite shore and passed through a gate to Earth. I can carry you in their wake … but there is an underwater gate far closer that would shave several days off your travel time, should you choose to take it.*

"No." Drift shook his head. "Taylin recently survived a drowning; I won't force her underwater again."

"Shouldn't that be my decision?" Taylin's fingers brushed the line of his jaw. Throwing caution to the wind, Drift leant into the caress, lashes fluttering. She stilled at once. "Don't look at me like that."

"Might as well tell the ocean to be less wet, for all the good that will do."

Her eyes shot to his, the motion tipping her face up. With the dawn light painting her in shades of silver and gold, it was almost impossible not to indulge in her lips – but Drift had taken so much already. And her kiss?

He wanted to earn it.

So instead, he indulged in the pleasure of maintaining eye contact, dragging out the moment until her cheeks tinted with colour and she turned her face away.

"The staff is our priority." Taylin's voice was husky, and Drift swallowed the triumphant grin that wanted to stake a claim on his mouth. "If you can promise I won't drown again, then I'll travel to the water gate."

I will carry you, Ataraxia announced. *So long as you stay in contact with my skin, you will not drown. It is a small magic, but one I have no trouble extending to you both.*

"Both?" Taylin darted a glance back Drift's way, caught him still staring, and cleared her throat. "I thought ... I assumed you couldn't drown."

"I'm drowning right now," he whispered, leaning on Ataraxia's horn so that he could snap his teeth at a stray strand of her hair. "It's ever so painful."

Taylin's eyes narrowed and she swatted his chest hard enough to make him cough. "Be serious."

"All gods can die," Drift said, straightening at once. "Some of us are harder to kill than others, but it can still be done. Right now I'm practically mortal."

"Apart from living forever."

Drift raised an eyebrow. "Constantly renewing cells doesn't make me – or anyone – invincible."

Taylin dipped her chin in acknowledgment before returning her attention to their narwhal host. "And you're certain this won't overtax you? I'm … heavy."

My dear child, I assure you I am more than the measure of your unusual bones. Neither your weight nor the magic required to sustain you will bother me.

Taylin's lashes fluttered shut, her expression stark with a mixture of pain and relief that tore at Drift's resolve. He shoved both hands in his pockets and forced himself to watch and wait as Taylin took several measured breaths in and out.

When she opened her eyes again, her heart rate had calmed and her voice was steady. "How will we cross to Earth without a talisman? I was unconscious the last time I passed through a gate but I know the lore – we can't get through without a talisman."

You have no need of a talisman. Ataraxia's amusement was a crushing embrace. *You're with a god.*

"Of sorts." Drift screwed up his face. "I'm no longer god enough to cross when I will it, or to make talismans … but I can take others through an already active gate."

"All right." Taylin swallowed, the muscles in her throat contracting in a way Drift found mesmerising. "It's settled, then. We take the sea road."

9

IT'S US

After a short, poignant farewell to Bay – who flat-out refused to accompany them underwater – Taylin climbed onto Ataraxia's broad back. The urge to hold Drift's hand as the narwhal slid away from the shore was almost overwhelming, particularly when he settled down beside her with only inches between them. Having her feelings publicly examined by a magic whale was an experience Taylin didn't care to repeat, but she couldn't deny that Ataraxia's words made sense. The enormous ball of hurt, fear and fury that had been trapped behind her breastbone had already grown soft around the edges, and looking at Drift as the water closed overhead saw a return of the butterflies that had filled her gut since their first meeting.

Unsure what to do with her changing feelings, Taylin chose instead to concentrate on the wonder of the ocean depths. Blessed by whatever magic Ataraxia possessed while in contact with her skin, Taylin's lungs worked as though she were on dry land and she felt neither hunger nor thirst. The wounds she'd incurred at the log cabin ceased to ache a mere few hours in, and when Taylin carefully unwound her bandages, marvelling all the while at the way they streamed behind her in the water, she discovered her injuries were completely healed.

"How is this possible?" She rubbed a hand across her waist, the skin as smooth and pale as it had ever been.

Ataraxia's song reverberated through the water around them, her laughter a waterfall of effervescence against Taylin's empathic senses. *Consider it a gift – though you may need some extra sleep to complete the healing process.*

The narwhal's prediction proved true, and Taylin found herself curling into her hoodie only a short while later, exhausted by whatever magic had healed her. Drift remained by her side as she slept, never touching but never out of reach. When Taylin woke, it was to find him staring out at the underwater landscape, surprisingly silent for a man so vital and raw.

They kept conversation light, Drift's bright hazel eyes locking with her own as he listened to her speak, not just with his ears but his whole body. For the longest while, she thought he never slept, but on the third day Taylin woke from yet another nap to find Drift all-but pressed against her, long lashes cresting sharp cheeks and his head pillowed on one muscular arm. He'd wrapped her braid around his fist and held it so close to his face it was a wonder the long strands of hair weren't tickling his nose.

Unsure how to handle the situation – and the tenderness that bloomed because of it – Taylin closed her eyes again. A few minutes later the tension on her hair eased, and when next she dared peek, Drift had reassumed his polite distance, fingers interlaced behind his head as he watched the trail of bubbles left by Ataraxia's passage. It was in that surreal moment, his brown skin painted a muted marine and dark hair floating around his long ears, that the bitterness haunting Taylin's heart dissolved. In its place was a vulnerability so raw that even looking at the painful beauty of Drift's face was too abrasive, leaving little option but to roll in the opposite direction and wait until her suddenly hammering heart grew calm.

It is time. Ataraxia's crashing symphony of a voice cascaded through Taylin's brain, startling her out of her introspection. *We've reached the gate.*

Taylin sat up as the narwhal slowed, settling her enormous body gently on the bottom of the sea. As the eddying sand settled, a tumble of coral-wreathed rocks appeared, the unmistakable shimmer of a gateway stretched between two stones like a magical spiderweb.

I cannot cross this gate with you. It is here we will part ways. Ataraxia hummed a low, drawn-out note and the water trembled in response. *The vernal equinox is less than a week away now, Osterhase. There is no better time to set this to rights.*

"I'm done with hiding," Drift returned, the water making his growling voice all the deeper. "This will end, my lady. That I promise."

Then go with my blessing, and my magic; the spell that keeps you breathing will see you both through the gate.

When Drift held out his hand, Taylin hesitated only a moment before lacing her fingers through his. Energy raced over her skin the moment they touched and she shivered as all the hairs on her body stood on end.

"Thank you," she said to the narwhal, allowing Drift to tug her from Ataraxia's back. The weight of her bones dragged them steadily to the bottom of the sea, sand swirling around her ankles as she found her balance.

Go with grace, little moon. And remember – forgiveness is not just for others. It is also for yourself.

Taylin raised her free hand in farewell as she walked towards the gate, Drift floating along beside her. Though the narwhal had promised the magic would last, Taylin's recent drowning had her tightening her grip on Drift's fingers and hurrying through the shimmering gate to the other side.

The tone of the water changed immediately, the Earth side of the gate situated in a cleft in a sheer wall of rock. Taylin followed the line of the cleft until they emerged in a small pool, the shining surface of the water only half a body length overhead. They surfaced in a cave whose mouth framed a sunlit woodland, the pool's still surface broken only by the occasional moss-covered boulder and a smoothly sanded beach. Taylin drew a deep breath and immediately broke into a fit of coughing, the thinner atmosphere of Earth harsh after so many years in Mu. She staggered to the shore, bracing both hands on her knees until the coughing fit had passed.

"Here." Drift held out her water bottle. When and how he'd acquired her pack Taylin had no idea but it lay open on the ground, several items scattered on the sand nearby.

"Thank you," she murmured, accepting the bottle. Her voice came out croaky and she cleared it before taking a long drink. "I forgot the air would be different."

"How long have you been in Mu?"

Taylin capped the bottle, watching Drift from beneath her lashes. Dappled light and shade highlighted the different colours in his hair and brought a blazing brilliance to the hazel in his eyes. When he braced both hands on his hips, showing off a lithe figure sculpted with muscle, she forgot how to breathe. "You're beautiful."

"Huh?" He blinked, glanced down the length of his body and back up again, the slightest smile curving his lips. "Thank you."

"Um. I didn't mean to say that out loud." Cheeks hot, Taylin began scooping her belongings off the ground, focussing her entire being on returning everything to her pack, zipping it shut and pulling it back across her shoulders. "As for your question – I was a teenager when Ethel took me to Mu, and I've been there ever since."

"Really? Why?"

She risked another glance, and though his eyes were on her face, Taylin couldn't shake the notion that he'd been staring at her backside. Her blush deepened. "Instead of collecting physical payment for her aid, Ethel asks for service at Evergreen Waters in some capacity. I … well. She only asked four years of me and I think she'd have been happy to negotiate less, but what price can I really put on my own life? Not to mention, as I said once before, I'm worth a lot of money dead and possibly more alive. I decided to stay at the Retreat indefinitely."

"Fair enough." Drift ran a hand through the back of his hair, the shining mass fluffing out like fur and making him look even wilder than he had before. "Although, if you ask me, it sounds a lot like hiding."

"Says the one living in exile."

He grinned, sudden and wicked. "Caught." The expression faded, shadows shifting in those brilliant eyes. "At the time, it was exile or a war between gods. I thought I was making the right choice."

The burning desire to know Drift's story crashed against the walls Taylin had built between them. She teetered on the edge but the precipice still felt too steep, so she took a mental step backward and held out a hand instead. "The sooner we find your staff, the sooner you can fix whatever was broken."

"Of course." Something that might have been disappointment flashed over Drift's face, but his smile was light and easy as he dropped his hand into her own.

Energy surged through Taylin's veins the moment she opened her senses. She gasped, gripping Drift's wrist as her vision swam. "We're close. Very close."

"Which way?"

"Uh ..." Taylin staggered and Drift's arm slid around her waist. When her vision at last cleared, she found herself so close that little more than a deep inhale separated them. Butterflies took wing in her stomach and it was an effort to think through the cedarwood and sage scent that was uniquely his. "North."

"North it is, then." Drift's eyes dropped to her lips and the growl in his voice lingered, supercharging the air. "Just say the word."

Taylin's breath fluttered in her lungs, her free hand finding its way to his hip. She meant to push him away but the warmth of his skin was a brand and that soft growl deepened the moment she made contact. "Drift."

"I can't help it." He lowered his head oh-so-slowly, pausing just out of reach. "Tell me to stop."

When she opened her mouth to do exactly that, the words lodged in her throat. "Don't let go."

Was that her voice? That breathy, needy whisper?

Drift shifted until every sculpted line and ridge of him fitted against Taylin's curves and hollows, fingers spreading to cup the base of her spine.

"Whatever you need." His voice rumbled through their frames, soaking into Taylin's soul until she was certain that if someone cut her, Drift was the one who would bleed. "Whatever you want."

Little more than mortal, he'd called himself – but this close, Taylin could feel the tattered remnants of the god Drift had once been. A primal god, he had said, and primal was the only word Taylin had to describe the riot of torn threads and echoing shadows that made up his emotional resonance. His frayed edges sang a siren song she was powerless to resist, their energy blending in a way that set her spirit burning and her skin tingling.

Whatever she wanted.

Whatever she *needed*.

"It's you," Taylin whispered, looking up into those hazel eyes. The contact was searing, stripping her bare.

"No." His breath ghosted over her parted lips. "It's us."

The statement carried weight, and though Taylin didn't comprehend the hidden nuances, she couldn't argue with her magic, which insisted his every word was truer than the rising of the sun. With that certainty as her foundation, Taylin let go of everything else and pressed her lips to his.

Drift growled into her mouth, taking over the kiss with a surety that melted Taylin's bones. He curved his body over hers and proceeded to conquer with his tongue, the raw fury of him deliciously overwhelming.

She tugged at his jeans, pulling the evidence of his desire hard against her, and got a nip on the lower lip in response. Pleasure shot through her veins and Taylin's knees gave out. Drift tightened his arms but they stumbled nonetheless, slamming hard against the rock walls of the overhang. The impact broke the kiss and Taylin dropped her gaze as the fire in her soul snuffed out with painful finality. "Sorry."

"Why?" He nudged at her chin with the back of one knuckle. "What's the matter?"

"I ..." Taylin cleared her throat but the wobble in her voice remained. "I'm too heavy."

Drift's growl changed cadence, and suddenly he was pinning her to the rock, teeth bared. "You are *not*."

Ignoring the way his words rang true, Taylin shook her head. "If that wall hadn't been there, I'd have dragged us to the ground."

"Do I look like I care? I'm too busy fighting the urge to rip off your clothes with my teeth." He snapped said teeth in her face. "I don't care how heavy you are."

"You don't understand." Taylin closed her eyes so he wouldn't see the shimmer of her tears. "If we ... I could crush you."

Drift went very, very still, and when he spoke, there was not a single trace of humanity in his tone. "Who told you that?"

Taylin bit her lip.

"Logan?" Drift shoved harder against her. "Did Logan say that to you?"

Shame burned Taylin's cheeks and stole her words. A single tear escaped her lashes to streak across her skin. Drift cursed, the words harsh and the language guttural – but when he trailed his finger down the line left by her tear, his touch was so gentle Taylin's heart cracked open.

"I am a *god*," he breathed, lips hot on her jaw. "A broken god, but a god nonetheless." Drift kissed his way across her cheek, the caresses so exquisitely hot and possessive she couldn't help but turn into them, her entire body trembling when he brushed his lips back and forth over hers. "You won't hurt me, Taylin."

"Really? Because I checked you over after Ostara's golem was destroyed. You had at least three broken ribs."

He winced. "That thing packed a punch."

"And I'm easily as heavy, if not more so, than the golem was." She shook her head again. "I can't risk it."

"So it's a no?"

There was such a wealth of pain in his voice, in the very air she breathed, that Taylin couldn't help but open her eyes. The raw perfection of his face was twisted, their proximity allowing her to feel the rejection crushing his spirit as though it were her own. Taylin's heart stuttered as she realised Drift's attraction to her was more than sexual; he wanted *all* of her, every solid, mismatched piece – and he thought she was turning him away.

"It's not a no." Taylin feathered her fingers over the satiny skin of his chest and gathered the courage to offer the truth. "It's a 'not until I'm certain you're safe'. I couldn't handle it if you were hurt."

The clouds in his empathic resonance cleared, determination and elation wrapping around Taylin until she was dizzy with it. Oblivious to the emotions he was sharing, Drift leaned in until his antlers clunked against the stone overhead, shaping her ribs with his palms.

"Here's what's going to happen." Heat began to build anew, both in his eyes and in the cavernous space where his magic should have been; a place that felt more like home than any physical place Taylin had ever lived. "I'm going to kiss you until you've forgotten your tears, and then we're going to get my staff back. Once I'm returned to full strength ... we'll have this conversation again."

Taylin couldn't help the laugh that escaped. "You sound confident."

"I am."

"Because you're a god?"

"No." His fingers stopped short at the edge of her bra and despite her fears, Taylin burned in a way she'd never burned before. Drift traced tiny, ghostly kisses over her skin until she arched towards him, needing the contact he promised but never quite delivered. "I'm confident because I have you."

As his lips claimed hers at last, Taylin was glad they were still pressed hard against the rocks for support – because her legs gave out entirely, and the only thing in the world that made sense was the all-consuming kiss of a broken god.

10

FOLLOWING BREADCRUMBS

The lure of kissing Taylin until the sun burned out and turned the moon to dust was more tempting than Drift cared to admit, but at long last he pulled back to cup her face in his hands.

"I don't know if you ascribe to the idea of fate, but the dark hole inside of me that's ached for so many years ... you're filling it." He brushed his thumbs across her cheeks. "With your moonlight and your magic and your smile."

Her face, so beautifully dishevelled from his touch, softened with an emotion he dared label as affection. "Is that why you fought so hard to cast me aside?"

"I was afraid – and even gods make mistakes." Drift sighed and shook his head. "We think we're infallible, and then ..."

"Someone tears out your soul?"

"Something like that." He grimaced, rubbing a hand over his breastbone.

Taylin's gaze locked onto the motion. When she at last looked at him, her jaw was set with determination. "I think it's time you explained what happened between you and Ostara."

This woman. Drift's heart wanted to leap out of his chest and settle in her body forever more. He cleared his throat instead, using the time it took to cross the cave to gather his wits.

"How about I talk while we walk?" Shading his brow with one hand, he pointed at the overgrown landscape ahead. "This might take a while."

Taylin nodded and they set out, shoving through the thick tangle of shrubs and flowers that surrounded the cave. Sweat dotted Drift's brow by the time they discovered a cracked stone pathway, thick-leaved trees growing at regular intervals along either side.

"Look," Taylin murmured, bending to run her fingers over the rough black surface. "Pre-Merge asphalt. I wonder if this place used to be some kind of public garden?"

"I have no idea." Drift glanced up and down the avenue of trees, then shrugged. "I know little of the actual Merge; I slept through it."

"You *slept* through it?"

"Yes – but that's not the beginning." He offered a hand, and to his delight she took it, lacing their fingers together. "Ostara and I met while I was visiting her territory. I helped her out of a sticky situation with another god, and she gifted me the choice of anything from her domain in return."

Taylin snorted. "That's a proposition if I ever heard one."

"Probably, though I didn't realise it at the time." Drift followed when she tugged him forward, trusting Taylin's senses to lead them towards the staff. "I'd been drawn to the energy of one of her great alder trees, so I chose a branch that had fallen to the ground as my payment. When I mentioned carving a staff, Ostara asked to see it when I was finished."

"And you didn't recognise *that* for the trap it was?" Taylin chuckled, a husky sound that whispered over Drift's skin in subtle symphony with the gentle glow of her moonlit bones. "She wanted you from the first."

"Looking back now it's easy to see, but I knew only that she was pretty and attentive. I visited often to show her my progress, and we were well and truly lovers by the time I had the staff finished. I spent so much time by her side that I eventually became known as the

Osterhase – and I didn't object, because in many areas of both Earth and Mu, the equinox that marks the height of my powers falls in Ostara's season."

They came to a fork in the path and Taylin led him to the left, where the asphalt gave way to overgrown gravel. After a few minutes ducking branches and picking their way around tightly clumped bushes, she paused in the shade of a tree and pulled her water bottle from her pack.

"So the staff, and Easter, belonged to you – but in Ostara's eyes, you belonged to her." Taylin took a long drink and offered him the bottle. "Where did it go wrong?"

"There was a war between the gods, and Ostara and I chose opposite sides." Drift accepted the water bottle and leaned against the trunk of the tree, swallowing around the sudden lump in his throat. "It sounds simple put that way, but the reality was entirely the opposite. I loved her – or I thought I did – and assumed she felt the same. When the first tidings of conflict reached us, Ostara saw an opportunity for power and glory while I saw horror and injustice. The more we disagreed, the more her mask of civility slipped, and it wasn't long before I realised she saw me as little more than a pet whose only role was to perform at her whim."

"Did you leave, or did she throw you out?"

Drift snorted a laugh. "I left after I caught her screwing one of the gods on the opposing side. Gedenna – yes, that Gedenna – had been instructed to distract me with a lost wolpertinger kit but Bay revealed he'd seen the kit alive and well less than an hour earlier. When he added that Loki had arrived—"

"*Loki?*"

"Norse God of Mischief, yes." Drift's lip curled into a nasty grin. "I tore the lecherous wretch from between Ostara's legs and threw him out the window, then set about destroying her treasured temple while she screamed obscenities at me. It was very dramatic."

"It sounds like something from a book." Taylin shook her head. "So … you took the wolpertingers and you left. I'm assuming, since you destroyed her temple, that Ostara sought refuge with her new allies?"

"Correct." He sighed. "It was during that time she plotted revenge for what she saw as my humiliating and ungrateful betrayal. With Loki's assistance, she obtained a gemstone capable of storing someone's soul inside. Whoever possessed the stone was able to control the being bound to it."

"Oh gods," Taylin whispered, her face stark. "That's ... Something like that actually exists?"

"It does." He stashed the bottle in her pack and zipped it up. "They're incredibly rare but Ostara's new lover was close friends with the self-styled goddess who owned the stones."

Taylin frowned, the crescent moon between her brows puckering. "I don't see you simply handing your soul over."

"No." He grimaced. "I was on patrol with my friend Tyr, the Norse God of Justice. We were ambushed and though we fought, we were vastly outnumbered. Ostara had brought not only a squadron of naga, but Loki and his son, Fenrir – an enormous wolf whose soul had already been trapped in a stone." Drift stared into the canopy of the tree, his mind awash with blood and death. "Fenrir tried to bite off my face and Tyr intervened; he lost his hand in the process. It didn't take long before Loki had a sword at Tyr's throat, and I was given a choice: surrender the staff to Ostara, or watch my friend die."

"The staff? In return for a life?"

"Seems odd, doesn't it? Ostara claimed it was hers by right, since it had come from her territory in the beginning – and in my naivety, I assumed she was only demanding the staff in an attempt to humiliate me as I had supposedly humiliated her."

"So you gave it up."

"At once." Drift snapped his teeth. "I dropped it at Ostara's feet and rushed to Tyr's aid. While I was distracted, Loki fitted the soul gem into the staff and ... stabbed me in the back with it."

"Oh, Drift." Taylin pressed against his chest, wrapping her arms tight around him. The embrace melted the cold, hard knot that had formed in Drift's gut, anchoring him to the present.

"I fought, of course. By pure luck, I shredded Loki's face and neck with my claws – nothing fatal, but enough to put him down for the count. The last thing I remember is Ostara screaming while Fenrir tried to drag his father to safety." Drift took the length of Taylin's braid in his fingers, seeking solace in the silken strands. "When I woke, several months had passed. The war was over and though Tyr and I both survived, Ostara took my staff when she fled – along with whatever of my soul had been sucked into it. My only saving grace was that the transfer had been interrupted early enough that she wasn't able to control me. Whether due to the incomplete ritual or the primal nature of my energy, the soul stone had cracked, and anyone or anything who touched the staff was turned to chocolate."

"Meaning Ostara got your powers but couldn't use any of them." Taylin pressed a hand to her mouth. "I don't know whether to laugh or cry."

"I've done both." Drift shrugged. "As soon as she realised I wasn't going to spend eternity as a vegetable, and therefore might still be of use, Ostara made several attempts to have me kidnapped in order to finish the job. Tyr was prepared to retrieve the staff by force, but I was in no shape to be of assistance and couldn't bear the thought of people dying on my behalf."

"So you volunteered to go into exile?"

He nodded. "Tyr wrote up the terms, carefully wording things so that once I was recovered, I'd have a chance to reclaim the staff if Ostara was ever foolish enough to lose it. Since it meant I'd be spending the rest of my foreseeable future essentially at Ostara's mercy, she agreed and I took up my exile upon the moon. Not long afterward, Ostara formed the Easter Bunny Conglomerate, using the staff to create the chocolates her minions delivered."

"And hoarding the attendant credit like jewels, no doubt."

Drift snorted a soft laugh into her hair. "Naturally. I think, in her mind, she assumed I'd be so bereft without her and my magic that I'd eventually come crawling back, begging her to enslave me."

"She never knew you at all, then."

"No." He sighed. "If you'd told me once that my ability to create chocolate – little more than a party trick – would become the basis of another goddess' empire, I would have thought you insane."

"We'll get it back, Drift." Taylin pushed up on her toes, brushing a kiss to his lips that struck all the way to his very core. "It's time for you to be whole again."

He kissed her soft and sweet. Taylin's moonlight washed through him, cleansing the shadows left by centuries of pain and despair so that when Drift drew away, his mind was clear. "I'm ready."

They didn't speak for the rest of the journey, winding through overgrown flower beds until they arrived at last by a run-down gatehouse whose crumbling brick walls and bent iron fencing separated the wild garden from the rest of the world.

"It *was* a botanical garden." Taylin ran a hand over a faded metal sign, the letters barely discernible.

"Forget that – look across the road." Drift ushered her into the shelter of the gate house, where a missing section of wall offered a clear view of their surroundings.

Across the street stood an old-fashioned estate whose fencing was, unlike that of the abandoned botanical gardens, in immaculate condition. Swept paths and neatly trimmed lawns surrounded a four-story white brick house with a slate-grey roof, the architecture a mix of pre-Merge humanity and post-Merge repair work. Care had been taken to blend the two styles, allowing the mansion to retain an old-world feel that would have been enchanting if not for the fact that sunlight gleamed unnaturally off the walls, and the windows and doors appeared painted on.

Outside the front gate was a line of beings in matching black uniforms, their bearing distinctly military. A sizeable group of journalists gathered on the cracked path, some talking amongst themselves while others orated enthusiastically into their cameras.

"This has got to be the place." Drift slumped against the wall with a growl. "I don't know what I expected, but a media circus around a chocolate mansion was not it."

"A chocolate … Oh my gods, you're serious." Close enough beside him that he could feel the soft rise and fall of her chest, Taylin took in the scene across the street and shook her head. "The staff is definitely in there; I can feel it. But why transform the house? That's insane."

"At this point in the game, I don't think sanity is a quality our thief possesses."

"That's true enough." Taylin drew back, lower lip caught between her teeth. "Still, up until this point the thief has made an effort to keep their head down. Transforming the house and garnering not only media but military attention seems counter-intuitive."

"Maybe." Drift swallowed his frustration and tried to think. "We still don't know why the staff was stolen in the first place; there's every possibility that this is simply the next step in the thief's plan."

"Hmm. I guess, as long as we retrieve the staff, it doesn't really matt – wait. What if your energy reintegrates with your body the moment you touch the staff? Will you still be able to save Great Aunt Ethel?"

"In theory." Drift shoved both hands in his pockets, a feat made all the more difficult thanks to Tyr's decision to create them so insufferably tight. "Most of my abilities are instinctive; changing shape, moving through time and dimensions, communicating with animals, and so on. The few powers I have that can be used externally – such as the creation of chocolate – were always difficult to control. That's why I created the staff in the first place; in the hopes that it would help focus my magic."

"That makes sense. Alder is an excellent wood for anchoring and channelling wild energy."

"Exactly." Drift glanced back at the mansion. "There are no real experts on how the soul stones work, but I've spoken with the god who knows more than most. Normally, once a soul is sealed completely inside the stone, it cannot be retrieved. Smashing the stone means the loss of the soul – and, consequently, the death of the person to whom it was linked."

"But ... you said the stone cracked when you interrupted the ritual."

Drift nodded. "It was theorised that because the stone cracked before my entire soul was sealed inside, I retain a connection to the portion I lost. It can be regained as long as the stone has access to the same pathway via which it drained the magical energy in the first place."

"Wait. Just wait." Taylin's face blanched. "Are you saying you need to be stabbed in the back with the staff to reclaim your soul?"

"Yes." Drift blew out a sharp breath. "Given the process will likely destroy the staff, I'm not sure how well I'll be able to control my magic once it's returned to my body. We'll rescue Ethel and the other victims before I try."

"Every second you wait increases the risk of Ostara attempting to steal the staff all over again." Taylin shook her head. "Why risk it?"

He smiled down at her, his heart full. "Because I promised you I would."

"Gods, Drift." Taylin's eyes overflowed with tears, and he couldn't help but bend to kiss them from her cheeks. "I didn't know what I was asking. I take it ba—"

"No." Drift nipped at the tip of her nose. "You may not have understood, but I did and I'm at peace with my decision. What we need to do now is act."

"All right." Taylin dropped her head against his breastbone and for a brief moment, they simply existed. "First problem: a chocolate house will never hold my weight."

"No – but it won't hold mine, either." Drift smoothed his hand up the length of her spine, revelling in the way she shivered at his touch. "My guess is our thief has only transformed the outer walls."

"Is that even possible?"

"Yes." His hands clenched in her clothes. "By my guess, the thief's been here a week at most – nowhere near long enough to transmute the entire house, but more than enough time to present a convincing façade."

"Okay. That makes sense." Taylin clicked her tongue against her teeth. "Our next problem is getting past the media and the guards. I'm getting snatches of emotional resonance all around the fence line, which leads me to believe there are guards posted the entire circumference of the estate."

"Sneaking in is going to be difficult, then."

"Very." Taylin slid off her pack and dropped it on the ground. "Which is why we're going straight in through the front door. You're a god come to claim what is rightfully yours, and I'm your Evergreen Waters escort."

"Taylin, no." Drift gripped her shoulders. "That'll out you – and your powers – to anyone watching the myriad of news networks broadcasting from the mansion. I can't let you do that."

"We don't have a choice. With every passing second, we run the risk that someone from the EBC reports that chocolate mansion to Ostara." She covered his hands with her own and squeezed gently. "You might not have come to Evergreen Waters for healing, but the fact remains that you're injured nonetheless. Saving Ethel is important, but returning the staff to you … erasing that great, gaping chasm inside of you … that's become just as important to me. You're willing to risk the healing of your soul for me, Drift. The exposure of my powers is nothing in comparison."

All he could do was stare, his tongue too thick in his mouth to shape words. When Taylin pressed a kiss to his forehead and stepped back, Drift followed her out of the guardhouse and across the street, every step cementing his respect for the woman by his side. Nobody paid attention as they threaded through the throng, and it wasn't long before he could see the mansion's wrought iron gate – and the warriors who stood guard over it.

The gate itself was chained shut, a hand-lettered board on the front that read 'Trespassers Will Be Dealt With.' An immaculately coiffed journalist stood in front of one of the guards, a russet-winged angel wearing black body armour and a sour expression.

"… an elaborate pre-Easter prank, but this suggests a far darker undercurrent. Professor Nichols' colleagues are adamant he's not the pranking kind. What say you, Special Agent?"

The angel's eyes locked on Taylin and Drift. Ignoring the journalist entirely, he held out a hand to halt their progress. "This is a crime scene – state your name and business."

"Primal God of the Vernal Equinox." Drift flicked one of his antlers, then gestured at the mansion ahead. "I'm here to reclaim a stolen item."

"A god?" The journalist rounded on Drift at once, almost losing one of her patent leather shoes in the process. "I've never heard of a primal god before, let alone one of the vernal equinox."

The angel, meanwhile, went pale. "Osterhase. Please excuse my manners."

"Of course. I imagine you've had plenty of curious onlookers trying to sneak past." Drift gestured to Taylin, her bearing not quite as militant as the angel's but far more warrior-like than he'd yet seen. "This is Sentinel Taylin Colkannis, triple-banded mage and representative of Evergreen Waters Retreat. She's here as my escort."

"A Sentinel?" The journalist's smile turned wolf-wide, showing off a pair of perfectly polished vampire fangs. "Vanessa Von Klanhorn, Vampire News Network. A few questions, if I may?"

"I'm afraid we're running on a tight schedule, Ms Von Klanhorn." Taylin laid a proprietary hand on Drift's arm, sending shivers of moonlit magic racing over his skin. "Perhaps another time."

"This won't take long." The vampire motioned her camera crew a little closer. "My viewers are going to be fascinated by your arrival, given this situation is already incredibly mysterious. What, exactly, does a missing mythology professor have to do with a chocolate house and an obscure god?"

A mythology professor? Drift frowned. If the professor and the thief were one and the same, it would explain how the thief had known where to find the staff in the first place. He caught Taylin's sapphire eye and she gave him the subtlest of nods.

"I'm not at liberty to discuss those details with you, Ms Von Klanhorn." Taylin's expression was as smooth and flawless as marble, leaving no room for disagreement. "My charge's business is his own."

"I see." Vanessa gave Drift a swift once over, barely blinking when he bared his teeth. "As far as I'm aware, Evergreen Waters Retreat is a secure facility in the depths of Mu, home to patients requiring intense physical or psychiatric care. Since you're providing an escort, am I to assume your charge is an inmate of the asylum? Is it safe to have a mentally ill god wandering the streets with only a single Sentinel holding his leash?"

Drift made to step forward, but Taylin's fingers tightened on his arm and when she spoke, her voice was limned with frost. "Evergreen Waters Retreat is neither an asylum nor a prison, Ms Von Klanhorn. It's a haven for those who need the kind of care the rest of the Merged Worlds cannot provide." Taylin cocked her head, giving Vanessa the full effect of her moonstone eye and the strange, ethereal tattoos that covered her cheek and nose. "In fact, since I believe Great Aunt Ethel assisted VNN's CEO only last winter, insulting our sacred healing space could be … what's the term? A career-ending mistake."

Vanessa Von Klanhorn gasped. "Is that a threat?"

"Merely an observation." Taylin dismissed the journalist with a roll of her shoulders, turning to the angel on guard. "Do our credentials suffice, Special Agent?"

"Now, wait just a minute." Vanessa stepped in front of Taylin, blocking her way to the gate. "The VNN prides itself on ferreting out the truth, and our viewers deserve answers. If you're bringing someone dangerous to— What are you doing?"

"Giving your viewers the truth, as requested." Taylin's fingers clamped tight around the reporter's wrist. "Why don't you tell the lovely people watching why you really approached us, Ms Von Klanhorn?"

"Because stirring up the hornet's nest always gets higher ratings." The reporter's eyes widened, her words picking up speed. "If I can get someone to lose their composure on camera, it'll guarantee me the prime time slot on tonight's broadcast. Anchoring for prime time comes with some serious credibility, which I need, since the producer I was sleeping with got fired last week. Oh my gods, why am I saying this? Turn that camera off, right now!"

The vampire tore free from Taylin's grip and raced off in tears, her camera crew following behind. Drift bared his teeth at the rest of the media. "Anyone else?"

The crowd dispersed at once, leaving Drift alone with Taylin and the Agents guarding the gate. The russet-winged angel propped both fists on his hips, awe painted across his angular features. "That was incredible."

"All part of the service." Taylin's eyes danced with amusement. "What a shame they didn't want to stick around."

"For that alone, I'd let you both pass – but since one of you is a god, it's my duty to ascertain whether the surrounding neighbourhood is in immediate danger first." The angel produced a slim key from somewhere behind his armoured vest. "If so, I'll arrange an evacuation."

"That won't be necessary, Special Agent." A woman rounded the corner, a half-smile creasing her face. Her skin was white as fresh-driven snow and her eyes pools of inky black with no white, iris or pupil. Equally black hair hung straight and sleek to her waist, the only adornment a string of feathers and charms braided in at one temple. Though she was shorter than Taylin and wore jeans and a pale grey sweater rather than the Agents' body armour, power pulsed from her in waves so strong that Drift took an involuntary step backward. She caught the movement, the corners of her eyes crinkling in amusement. "Any damage will be contained to the mansion and grounds; I'll make sure of it."

"Of course, Grand Sorceress. We'll stand by in case you have need of assistance." The angel slapped a fist against his heart.

"Thank you." The woman inclined her head, her voice smooth and melodic. "Go with grace, Osterhase."

Drift's polite response stuck in his throat when the Grand Sorceress locked gazes with him, the bottomless wells of her eyes making his skin prickle and his muscles lock. After a long moment she blinked, breaking the contact – and while Drift struggled to catch his breath, the stranger turned and walked away.

"Shit," Taylin whispered. "I couldn't … She was …"

"Don't worry, that happens to everyone." The angel drew the chain aside and pushed the gate open. "I'm Osprey."

"Drift." Exchanging a swift forearm grip with the angel, he stepped back so Taylin could do the same. "My thanks."

"Not at all, Osterhase. Good luck." Osprey winked at Taylin, then flinched when a growl rattled in Drift's chest. "Uh. Thanks again for your help with the media, Sentinel Colkannis."

"You're welcome, Osprey. See you soon." Taylin gave the guards a little wave and then started up the mansion's drive, leaving Drift to jog after her. "What was that about?"

"What?"

She cut him a sharp look. "The growl. I have ears, you know."

"Instinct." Drift scuffed a boot in the gravel, sending stones clattering up the driveway ahead of them. "I'm not as civilised as I look, and he was eyeing you off like a prime cut of meat."

The Taylin he'd met at Evergreen Waters would have boxed his ears for the admission – or shoved him into a stream – but this Taylin, who'd chosen to trust him in spite of his mistakes, merely laughed. "More like he was staring at the strange mage with mismatched eyes and a tattooed face and wondering if she posed a threat."

Drift opened his mouth to reply when the ground crunched underfoot. He looked down to discover his boot had gone clean through the porch steps, tearing the brightly coloured foil and revealing the chocolate within.

"Time to test your theory." Taylin bulldozed her way through what had once been a verandah, making no effort to mask the heft of her bones. When she drew level with the outer wall of the mansion, she punched out a small hole at head height. "You were right – the interior looks normal. Only the outer walls have been transformed."

"Let's go, then." Drift moved to her side and together they widened the hole until it was big enough to admit a person.

Taylin braced her weight on the tiled floor of the lobby, giving a grunt of satisfaction before she pulled herself into the mansion proper. "The staff is almost directly overhead. I sense two emotional signatures – one larger and more chaotic, one smaller. Faint. Either asleep or unconscious."

"An accomplice? A prisoner?" Drift leaped up beside her, straining his ears. "Whoever's here, they're very quiet."

"They can't have missed our arrival."

"No." Drift padded down the hall, where a grand marble staircase wound upward to the second floor. He paused at the bottom to inhale, sidelining the familiar strains of jasmine and vanilla that belonged to Taylin and parsing through what remained. "Nothing out of the ordinary. Stay alert."

The staircase ascended to a carpeted landing, the wood-panelled walls stained dark. Taylin pointed towards the first of the doors and Drift laid a finger against his lips as he crept close enough to listen.

"I know you're out there, Osterhase." The new voice carried easily through the silence, each word clearly enunciated. "If you value the life of innocents as much as my research suggests, then you'll enter the room very, very slowly."

"All right." Drift pushed the door open, staying well back from the entryway.

The room beyond was a blend of soft greys and pinks, dotted with white-washed furniture and polished silver. Floor-to-ceiling windows occupied half of the outer wall and in the far corner stood an enormous four-poster bed, the pink hangings tied back with a silver cord. Propped against a nest of pillows was a middle-aged man wearing tailored trousers, leather loafers and a plaid shirt open over a white t-shirt. A sleeping, pale-faced child lay in his lap, all manner of wires running from the adhesive pads on her body to the medical unit built into the head of the bed. As Drift edged into the room, the stranger lifted an intricately carved staff from the mattress and held it near the girl's too-pale throat.

"Don't." Drift held his arms out wide. "Don't harm her."

"Oh, I won't harm her, Osterhase." The man's gloved fingers tightened on the pale wood. "Her immediate safety is entirely in your hands."

Drift growled low in his throat. Now that the staff was within reach, all he wanted to do was lunge at it – but doing so meant risking the frail girl. He sidled further into the room, choosing a position where he could see the man clearly without appearing to come too close.

"I know there's a woman," the man said in the same calm, firm tone. "Come in where I can see you, please."

"Of course." Taylin moved slowly to Drift's side. "I heard mention that you're a professor."

"And I know nothing of you."

She smiled, wide and reassuring. "I beg your pardon; my name is Taylin Colkannis, Sentinel of Evergreen Waters Retreat."

"Evergreen Waters. Of course." The man sighed. "I felt bad about what happened to Ethel Blueraven. She was the only one who tried to help me."

"Perhaps, if I had more information, I might be able to assist in her place." Taylin inclined her head, as calm as though they were sitting down to afternoon tea. "Starting with your name, and why you need the stolen staff of a broken god?"

Drift tried not to wince at her words, but judging from the way the thieving professor's eyes darted his way, he wasn't entirely successful. The man considered both he and Taylin a long moment before lifting his chin, eyes bright with defiance.

"I'm Professor Jeffrey Nichols, Head of Mythological Lore at United Earth University – and I need the Staff of Easter to save my daughter's life."

11

FOILED

Taylin eyed the little girl cradled in Jeffrey's lap. In a perfect world she'd clap her hands and send the professor to sleep, enabling Drift to retrieve his staff while Taylin whisked the child to safety – but Jeffrey's gloved hand held the staff so close to his daughter's throat that putting him into an enchanted sleep would seal the tiny child's fate as surely as if Taylin had swung the staff herself.

So she forced herself to smile instead, projecting a subtle aura of calm throughout the room. "Stealing the Staff of Easter is a terrible risk to take, Professor. How could it possibly help your daughter?"

"Lara has a condition called Earlemurinism." Jeffrey kissed his daughter's strawberry hair. The little girl mumbled in her sleep, sharp cheekbones pushing against skin stretched far too tight across the bones of one so young. Shadows circled her eyes and lines of pain marked her brow, lingering even after her breathing settled into a more even rhythm. "Earlemurinism is a rare genetic disorder that shows up from time to time in humans and has no known cure."

Taylin nodded, her heart aching. "Great Aunt Ethel has seen a few cases. People whose core DNA hails from a time before the Merge, making it impossible to handle the magical energies permeating Earth and Mu."

"Correct." Tears gathered in the corners of Jeffrey's eyes, his grief whispering against Taylin's senses. "The speed with which a patient's body breaks down is dictated by how esoteric their genetic makeup is. At this point in time, Lara's life is numbered in weeks rather than months."

Drift didn't move from his place at Taylin's side, but the bright spike of pain in his emotional signature made her vision swim. She laid a hand on his arm. "Are you all right?"

"She's just a child."

"Unfair, isn't it? Lara's mother and I tried everything the healers offered but they only served to prolong the inevitable." Jeffrey's face twisted. "I immersed myself in books, using my position at the university to research more … alternative options. It was during this time that I came across the tale of a magical staff purported to contain the life force of a god."

"And you saw an opportunity." Drift rubbed both hands over his face. "I know what you're thinking, Professor. It won't work."

Taylin shook her head. "I don't understand."

"Lara doesn't need to be healed; she needs her DNA rewritten." Drift dropped his hands, hazel eyes burning as he stared at the sick girl on the bed. "Jeffrey wants to use the soul energy trapped within the staff to remake his daughter – but that energy is mine and will respond only to me. It can't be passed around like a stuffed doll and it certainly can't be transferred into Lara's body."

Jeffrey's jaw set like granite. "That's what the other healers said, too. I didn't believe them then, and I don't believe you now."

"Is that why you attacked? Because they refused to help you?" Drift's voice thickened, fury vibrating through his frame and leaking into the air until Taylin's throat was coated in it. "I saw what you did in that vampire's home. The way you smashed the effigies to pieces. That wasn't altruism or even self defence; it was murder, pure and simple."

"I did what I had to." Jeffrey cocked his head. "Ethel Blueraven was the only one who offered her assistance – she even volunteered to extract the soul energy from the staff."

"But the moment she touched it, she turned to chocolate." Drift turned his blazing glare on Taylin. "Would Ethel really agree to something like that?"

"Of course not." Taylin spread a hand across her stomach, feeling suddenly ill. "She'd never condone the desecration of another's soul."

"I didn't think so." Drift's claws sliced from his fingers, muscles bunching as though in preparation for a strike. "I'll give you one chance at redemption, Professor. Return the staff to me and I'll call in every god and goddess I know who might be able to help your daughter."

"No." Jeffrey drew a jagged breath, blinking rapidly behind his spectacles. "I've done the research; the only way to save Lara is by making her into a goddess – and I don't need you for that, Osterhase. I need your mistress."

"*Ostara?*" Drift's voice was high with incredulity, laughter feathering the edges of his words. "First of all, she has no hold over me. Second, what makes you think she would ever give up what she perceives is her property?"

"I wouldn't." A woman in a voluminous green ballgown swept through the door, emeralds winking at her wrists, throat and in the twisted branch crown upon her head. "I am a goddess and I answer to no one."

Jeffrey's jaw dropped and for the first time, his composure wavered. "Goddess of the Spring and Dawn."

"Great." Taylin edged closer to Drift. "Now what?"

Drift bared his teeth at the rabbits that peeked from beneath the hem of Ostara's skirts. "No matter what happens, she cannot get her hands on the staff."

"Oh, but it's too late for that, my love. You should have claimed it while you had the chance." Ostara lifted a hand and long, waving grasses sprouted from the floor, crawling up the legs of the bed to bind Jeffrey and his daughter in place. "You always were too kind. Now, your soft heart will seal your fate."

"Wait!" Jeffrey lifted the staff towards the ceiling, straining against the grass that coiled tighter around his chest with every passing moment. "Turn my daughter into a goddess with the energy inside this staff, or I'll tell the world you're responsible for the deaths of everyone it's transmuted to this point!"

Ostara laughed, filling the room with syrupy mirth and setting Taylin's teeth on edge. A thick vine punched through the ceiling, snatching the staff from Jeffrey's fingers and extending it towards the goddess in the centre of the room. The plant immediately began to stiffen, chocolate spreading down from the staff in a wave, followed swiftly by a coating of garish green foil.

Drift leapt into the air, snatching the staff from the petrified vine and landing neatly atop the canopy of the four-poster bed – only for an enormous branch to tear through the roof, swatting him aside with such force that the snap of bone cracked like a gunshot. The Staff of Easter clattered to the ground, rolling to a stop on a plush pink rug that promptly transformed into chocolate.

"Drift!" Taylin lurched forward, her heart in her throat. She'd barely taken two steps when the same branch collided with her chest, tossing her onto the floor beside the bed.

"You deranged, stupid little man." Ostara patted her perfect golden ringlets. "You think I care about the life of a single, dying mortal?"

Taylin craned her neck, trying to catch Drift's eye – but he lay limp on the floor, eyes closed. His emotional resonance was little more than a whisper against her senses, a sure sign he was out cold.

Great. Just what she needed; to face down a vindictive goddess all by herself.

Again.

"But ... but ..." Jeffrey's voice was thready with disbelief, and Taylin glanced up to find him pale with shock. "She's a child."

"If your mortal chit is too weak to manage on her own, that's no business of mine." Ostara smiled, beautiful and cruel. "I am a goddess. You are little more than insects to be crushed beneath my magnificence."

The Goddess of Spring and Dawn crooked a finger and Jeffrey screamed as the grasses poured into his nose and mouth. Taylin pushed onto her knees, tearing Lara from his lap and snapping the lines that attached the frail child to the bed's monitoring system. Screeching alarms rent the air, drowning out Jeffrey's dying gurgles and causing Lara to wake with a gasp.

Hunkering down behind the dubious shelter of the bed, Taylin gathered her magic and snapped her fingers. "Sleep."

Lara's lashes dropped, the blaring alarms no match for the strength of the spell. Moving as carefully as she knew how, Taylin slid the sick little girl under the bed and rocked back into a crouch so she could peek over the lip of the mattress.

Jeffrey's eyes were wide open, bloodied vines hanging from empty sockets. His body was a mess of greenery and torn flesh, and Taylin gagged at the stench that assailed her nostrils.

"You."

The hiss carried on a wave of fury that bludgeoned Taylin's senses hard enough that she saw stars. Ostara stood in the middle of the room, the Easter Bunnies that accompanied her asleep on the ground at her feet. Her voluminous emerald gown was splattered with blood, her cheeks slapped with fury and her green eyes aglow with power. She curled her fingers into claws and myriad grass tendrils wove their way into the bed's complex monitoring mechanism, writhing and choking until the alarms gave a discordant squeal and cut off.

"Your pathetic human magic might affect these weaklings, but it won't work on me." The goddess jabbed a shaking finger in Taylin's direction. "I don't know how you survived your swim in the river, and I don't care. Rest assured I won't make the same mistake this time."

"I believe you." Taylin edged backward, away from the bed and the child sleeping beneath it. She kept her gaze locked with Ostara's, one hand on the ground for balance while the other groped blindly behind her. The slick, cool texture of foil met her fingers and she smiled. "Too bad you've made several new ones instead."

Gathering the last of her courage, Taylin wrapped her fingers around the Staff of Easter and surged to her feet.

"What are you doing?" Ostara shrieked. "Give that to me!"

"No." Magic frissoned up Taylin's arm, numbing her fingers. "This doesn't belong to you."

Grass erupted from the floor to twine around her ankles, but a single touch from the staff turned the entire lot to chocolate. Taylin's face began to burn, the fae tattoos Ethel had etched into her skin stuttering to life as the staff's spell spread up her arm. She kept moving, jabbing at the writhing vines until each and every one had turned into foil-covered chocolate. The giant branch that had disabled Drift swept down from the ceiling; she lifted the staff to meet it and the plant shattered on contact, chocolate leaves clattering across the hardwood floor.

"Stop!" Ostara lunged forward, drawing up short when Taylin turned the staff in her direction. "You stupid mortal; I don't know how you're resisting the staff's magic, but you can't win. Soon you'll be little more than a chocolate effigy – one I'll take great delight in smashing."

"I know." Taylin didn't spare a glance for the slow tide of chocolate creeping across her chest and down her torso. "But it'll do the same to you, won't it? That's why you're standing back."

"How *dare* you." Ostara fisted both hands in her bloodied skirts, hatred pulsing in the air like a heartbeat. "The Osterhase was little more than an animal before I took him in – and that staff you hold came from my territory. Drift's strength, his powers and his glory belong to *me*."

"Drift belongs to no one but himself." Taylin forced her feet to move, bringing her the last few paces to the broken god's side. He lay face down on the floor, limbs bent at unnatural angles and breathing shallow – but he lived, and that was all that mattered. Taylin bared her teeth at the Goddess of Spring and Dawn. "I hope he bites your face off."

She plunged the staff into Drift's back, forcing the alder as deep as it would go. The Osterhase's emotional resonance flared to life, blistering Taylin's senses, while cracks raced up and down the pale wood, golden light spearing from the core. The staff gave a tortured groan before disintegrating in a shower of sparks, the tiny fireworks settling over Drift's body like a blanket. The energy soaked into his skin, his body glowing so bright Taylin's eyes began to water – until, all at once, it cut off.

"What have you done?" Ostara jerked back a step, raising a trembling hand to her lips. "*What have you done?!*"

"Ossssssstaaaaaaaraaaaaaaa." Drift's bones snapped and popped, returning to their rightful place with gut-wrenching speed. Muscles flexed as he pushed upright, hazel eyes lit by a golden glow. Raw energy hummed against Taylin's senses, the back of her neck prickling in primal warning. She wanted to scream, to run, to laugh, to dance, to throw back her head and howl at the moon until the moon howled back.

Drift had warned her, oh, how he'd warned her – but it was only in that shimmering, golden moment that she truly understood.

The gods had power.

Drift *was* power.

When he stepped in front of Taylin, the whole mansion shook. Clothing shredded as his body grew, brown fur sweeping over his skin and taking all pretence of humanity with it.

"*I used to be able to change shape.*"

"*Before you were exiled?*"

"*Yes.*"

Taylin bit her lip, noting afresh the similarities between Drift and the creature cradled in his arms. "You're a ... were-wolpertinger?"

How right and yet how wrong she'd been in that moment. This was no sweet, fluffy creature like Bay – this was the Primal God of the Vernal Equinox in all his terrifying glory. He stood on a hare's hind legs, his body covered in fur and his hands tipped in long, wicked claws. His antler rack curved sharp and deadly from the top of his head, far more magnificent than Taylin had seen on any stag in either Earth or Mu. Drift's eyes were the same brilliant hazel but his head was that of a hare, matching at last the black-tipped ears he wore no matter what form he took. The bushy tail of a wolf swept back and forth behind him and a wolf's sharp teeth filled his open mouth. When Drift hunched on a bestial roar, a pair of enormous white owl's wings sprouted from his shoulders, spanning so wide that even the generously sized bedroom wasn't large enough to contain them.

"No." Ostara stumbled backward, face pale. "Wait."

Drift swung a clawed hand, opening four long gashes across Ostara's face and neck. Blood spurted and she screamed, tripping over the pile of sleeping Easter Bunnies in her haste to flee. Drift caught up in a single stride, curling his fist in that mass of golden ringlets and lifting the Goddess of Spring and Dawn into the air.

"Come now, my love. We can talk about this." Ostara's feet kicked wildly, her embroidered slippers dropping to the floor. "I only wanted to help you ach—"

"You *bitch*." Drift shook the goddess like a doll, sending her crown flying across the room. "I should have ended you millennia ago."

Ostara sobbed and struggled, but her strength was nothing in comparison to Drift's. His wild fury crackled in the air, wrapping Taylin tight ... and then faded as the magic that had almost killed her as a teen slipped from her grasp like so much fine sand, overpowered by the chocolate slowly swallowing her whole.

"Papa?"

Silence, clear and sharp as cut crystal.

A tiny, waif-like face peered out from beneath the bed on the opposite side of the room, two enormous brown eyes staring straight up at Drift. His ears flattened, then stood straight up; his teeth snapped shut an inch from Ostara's nose. The air in the room distorted as though the very fabric of existence were twisting into a different shape – and between one blink and the next, the Goddess of Spring and Dawn was gone.

"Lara." The Osterhase crouched before the tiny girl, long wings spread on the floor behind him. "How are you feeling?"

"Tired," Lara whispered, staring up into his face. "Is Papa here?"

Drift glanced at the twisted corpse on the bed. "Uh ..."

"He locked Mama away," the little girl continued, her face sad. "She screamed at first, but Papa said it was just bad dreams. He went to see her and then she was quiet. Is she still sleeping?"

Drift turned to look at Taylin – and froze, the golden light in his eyes fading to familiar hazel as they locked onto her.

"Stay there," he told Lara, using his giant, clawed hands to tuck her ever so carefully back under the bed. "When I return, we'll find your Mama together."

Taylin didn't hear the child's answer, reality fading in and out. The floor shook, forcing her to open eyes she didn't remember closing. Drift dropped to his knees before her, running enormous, claw-tipped hands over her chocolate body.

"Taylin." His gravelly voice cracked with an emotion she could no longer feel. "What did you do?"

"What I had to." She forced the words out through a throat gone tight. "You're free."

"Not like this." Drift shook his head. "Oh, gods, not like this. Taylin, I – I don't know how to turn you back without the staff!"

"It's all right." She smiled and her lips fused in that position, sole indicator of the incredible warmth blossoming deep inside. When the chocolate closed over the top of her head, Taylin didn't feel grief, or pain, or regret – because there, in her final moments, she acknowledged the only truth that mattered.

She was in love with Drift, and she'd gladly give everything to keep him safe.

12

LOVE AND MAGIC

Drift stared at the effigy in his arms, heart shattering inside his chest. A small hand tugged at the fur on his arm, and a moment later, a tiny floral handkerchief popped into view.

"Here," Lara whispered. "Don't cry."

The tiny waif swayed on her feet, her skin so pale as to be almost translucent. Broken wires trailed across the floor in her wake, a stark reminder of the impending death Drift could smell seeping from her pores.

He accepted the handkerchief between thumb and forefinger and blotted both eyes with it. "Thank you."

"Welcome." Lara looked him up and down, doe eyes wide. "Are you the Easter Bunny?"

"Hare," he corrected without thinking. "I'm the Easter Hare." Drift glanced over his shoulder. "They're Easter Bunnies."

She turned in the direction he indicated, giving the yawning rabbits a delicate frown. "Why are they dressed so silly?"

In spite of it all, Drift snorted a laugh. "Apparently it makes them more approachable."

"Well, I think you're better," Lara announced. "You saved us from the bad lady."

"At what cost?" Drift ran a finger over Taylin's foil-wrapped face, the tattoos he adored now little more than cartoon squiggles. "I'm incandescent with power and I can't fix what matters most."

Lara gave his fur another tug. "It's not power that matters, Easter Hare. It's love."

"Love?"

"That's what my Mummy says – and she's always right."

"How do you know?"

Tiny eyebrows shot up. "Because she's my Mummy."

"Love," Drift repeated. "I'm not sure how that can help."

Poor Osterhase, all fixed and still stupid.

"Bay?" Drift lifted his head as the air beside Taylin warped. Bay appeared, perched on the shoulder of a man dressed head to toe in black – though this time, the hood on his jacket was lowered to reveal fair skin, icy eyes that flickered with silver flames and platinum hair hanging in waves to his shoulders. Silver charms dotted the braids at each temple, emphasising the pale scruff that lined a hard, square jaw and lips pressed almost perpetually into a line. "Tyr."

The fallen Norse God of Justice lifted his chin in the barest of acknowledgements. "The healing of your soul has righted the balance that was broken. Where is the Bitch of Spring and Dawn?"

"I …" Drift's voice cracked and he cleared his throat. "I sent her away."

"Don't tell me that after all this time, after everything she's done, you didn't have the balls to—"

"*Tyr.*" Drift ushered Lara out from behind his body. "I had my reasons."

The other god's gaze landed on the frail child and he coughed. "Indeed."

Bay fluttered down to Lara's face level. *Hello, small human.*

"Hello, tiny Easter Hare."

Name is Bay, he announced, brushing a wing against Lara's cheek. *Not Easter Hare – only Drift is Easter Hare. Am a wolpertinger.*

"A woppertinner?" Lara screwed up her face. "What's that?"

Bay drifted close enough to set his tiny paws on the tip of her chin. *Magic.*

"I love magic!" Lara scooped Bay into her arms, smile luminous. "Will you be my friend?"

Yes, but came a long way through magic door. Very tired. Bay curled into the girl's skinny body and affected an enormous yawn. *Can Lara rest with me?*

"Oh, yes! My bed is very big – we can both fit!" Lara took a step backward and staggered. While Drift caught her in his clawed hands, Tyr snapped his fingers and Jeffrey's grass-riddled corpse disappeared, replaced by fresh pink linens with bright white unicorns dancing amongst stars of palest grey.

Lara gave Drift a trembling smile. "Sorry."

"It's all right. Thank you for taking care of Bay for me." He set her gently on her feet. "Can you make it to the bed?"

She squared her shoulders. "Of course!"

Bay peered over Lara's shoulder as the child took slow, shaky steps towards the bed. *Will keep her safe. You fix Taylin.*

Drift swallowed heavily. *The staff—*

Staff is stick, no more, no less. Bay's ears twitched back and forth. *Drift doesn't need staff for magic. Drift **is** magic.*

Drift gaped, recalling a similar speech he'd given Taylin what felt like eons ago. "I'm magic."

Bay snorted and turned away, snuggling into Lara's arms as she climbed onto the bed. *Osterhase so dumb. Be dead if not for Bay. Really.*

The silver cords holding the bed's canopy open unravelled by themselves, and the curtains swished shut with all the finality of a slamming door.

Drift stared at Taylin's effigy, then up at Tyr. "I …"

"Your hurting heart prevents you seeing the path forward." Tyr squeezed Drift's shoulder with his single hand, icy eyes softening. "Bay is right, however; the staff was merely a focus. The power is yours, and always has been."

"I know that," Drift growled. "The fact remains that the staff served a purpose. If I couldn't control the power properly without an anchor back then, how am I supposed to do it now?"

"Without an audience, for a start." Tyr's gaze strayed to the cluster of Easter Bunnies huddled in the centre of the room. "You there, creatures of Mu and magic. Ostara's hold over you ended with the return of the Osterhase. You are no longer bound to the EBC, nor the goddess who aspired to build a kingdom upon thievery and deceit. What will you do now?"

"Um." A little grey rabbit in a frilly skirt shuffled forward. "We'd like to earn the Osterhase's forgiveness and return to the sanctuary he once offered."

Tyr's brows shot up. "Prove it. Guard the door."

Drift watched the rabbits scurry into the hall, waiting until the door clicked shut. Only then did he close his eyes and draw a deep, steadying breath. "Thank you."

"I'm not done." Tyr's hand tightened again, fingers digging into the fur at Drift's shoulder. "I cannot fix this for you, but I will say this: you already have a far more suitable anchor than the staff ever was. All you have to do is reach for it."

Understanding dawned like the sun after winter's longest night. Drift turned his focus inwards, embracing the maelstrom that churned inside him. He sank through the newly mended layers of himself, reclaiming forgotten skills and sharpening instincts long dulled until he reached the calm centre. A soft blue glow filled the space, pulsing in time with each beat of his heart. He latched onto that connection and felt his fur melt away, bones shifting and shrinking until, when he opened his eyes, he was as close to man-shaped as he would ever get.

"Love and magic, Taylin. That's all I have to offer." Power surged and ebbed but rather than try to catch it, Drift rode the waves, anchoring himself in the moonlit essence that had invaded his very core. Settling his forehead against Taylin's, he exhaled magic in a slow, steady stream. "Come back to me. Tell me that's enough."

Foil crinkled. Drift jerked back as the shell over Taylin's ribs shattered with a sharp crack, the hand that had been draped across her abdomen lifting to press against his bare chest. Another crack preceded the bending of her knees and by the time her second arm broke free, Drift was yanking shards of chocolate from her face.

One sapphire eye and one moonstone eye stared back at him. Fae characters dripped down her cheek like tears, trailing to a stop at her jaw. A crescent moon took up the space between her brows, tiny fae characters spilling across the bridge of her nose. Black hair formed a messy braid and moonlight leaked from her skin, bathing Drift in the same pale light that resided deep inside his chest.

Taylin blinked, and smiled. "There you are."

Drift pressed his lips to hers, kissing her through the sobs that shook his frame, worshipping her with the storm of emotion that swirled inside him. He kissed her while she laughed, her arms looping around his neck. He kissed her until she gasped and melted in his arms, opening her mouth to let him claim her as she had so definitively claimed him.

"I thought I lost you." He whispered the words against her lips, crushing her tight against his chest. "Gods, Taylin, I thought—"

"It's all right." She framed his face with her hands, the touch infinitely gentle. "It's all right, Drift."

"I ... I ..." he choked, squeezing his eyes shut until the smothering intensity of his panic subsided. When he opened them again, she was waiting, the steady beat of her magic anchoring the primal chaos of his own. Drift kissed her as tenderly as he could, a lingering caress that held everything he was. "I love you."

"Oh, my gods, that's a relief." Taylin let out a laugh, kissing him back. "I love you, too."

Drift grinned, sweeping her up in his arms. "In that case—"

"Wait." Taylin's fingers clenched in his hair. "You're carrying me."

"Yes?"

"But I ... I'm so heavy." She bit her lip, and he nipped at it until she released it to his care. "You couldn't even support me before. How is this possible?"

"I'm a primal god – my magic is my life and my life is my magic. Thanks to you, I'm no longer broken." Drift brushed kisses across her cheeks, her eyelids, down her nose. "I could carry you to the stars and never tire."

Tears glistened in her eyes. "Don't let go."

"Never," Drift promised, dropping a kiss to her forehead. The loud rattle of a clearing throat curved his lips into a smile. "Before we celebrate, I should introduce you to a friend of mine."

Taylin twisted in his arms but rather than set her down, Drift angled his body so they could face the other god in the room.

"Tyr," said Tyr, inclining his head with the grace of a king. "It's a pleasure."

"God of Justice," Taylin breathed.

Tyr grimaced. "Once, perhaps."

"But—" Taylin cut off when Drift squeezed her hip in warning. "Thank you for helping Drift in his hour of need."

"The honour was mine." Tyr stiffened, his gaze turning distant. "I must go."

"Wait." Drift thumped a fist against his chest. "Justice."

The fallen god pulled his hood up to cover his face, the silver flames that flickered in his eyes casting shadows over the interior. "Justice."

With the barest stretch of time and space, Tyr disappeared.

"Wow." Taylin huffed a laugh. "He's …"

"Yes."

She stiffened in his arms, craning her neck. "Where's Lara?"

"Resting on the bed with Bay." Drift lowered his voice. "Tyr removed Jeffrey's body before she saw it."

"Good." Taylin shuddered. "I witnessed his final moments. They weren't pleasant."

"Karma, perhaps."

"Perhaps." Sadness suffused her expression. "Is there nothing we can do to help her?"

"I have a few ideas." Drift closed his eyes, revelling in the swirling storm of energy he'd regained. Connections long severed blossomed in his mind and it was the work of a moment to find the one he wanted, wrap a mental hand around it and tug. "Anubis."

Shadows flickered throughout the room, as though a fire guttered in the hearth. A man appeared, skin dark as charcoal and eyes a sparkling hazel not too dissimilar from Drift's own. Long, straight black hair framed an elegantly pointed face and trailed over the shoulders of the gold leather armour he wore, beneath which rippled a well-muscled chest. Black-furred ears swept up from his hair, a match for the jackal's hind legs he walked upon and the plush tail swishing back and forth behind him.

"Osterhase." Anubis' voice was a sibilant, seductive thrum, his smile delighted. "You're whole."

"Soulcatcher." Drift inclined his head to the Egyptian God of the Dead. "It's been a long time."

"It has." Anubis blinked at Taylin. "Well, now."

"Enough of that, you meddlesome old wolf – I need your help."

Anubis raised an eyebrow, half turning to indicate the ruined room. "I'm afraid my interior decorating skills leave something to be desired."

"No, you ass." Drift jerked his chin towards the bed. "Don't pretend you can't sense the child. Or her Earlemurinism."

Taylin swung her legs to the floor, shifting to block the path to the bed. "If you're planning to take that girl's soul, you'll have to go through me to do it."

"Easy." Anubis lifted both hands in a gesture of peace. "I have other talents than death and the ferrying of souls. I swear, I mean the girl no harm."

"Taylin." Drift slid his hand down her arm and twined their fingers together. "Trust me."

"Oh, I do." She narrowed her eyes at the jackal god opposite. "It's him I'm not sure about."

"Please." Drift tugged on her hand, and Taylin sighed and stepped aside.

Anubis wasted no time loping over to the bed, ducking to poke his head through the curtain. The soft, velvet whisper of his voice was barely audible beyond, the drowsy answer even quieter. The exchange continued for several minutes before the Soulcatcher reached into the canopy and emerged with Lara snuggled in the cradle of his arms, Bay perched regally in her lap.

"I can help her," Anubis announced, crossing to Drift's side. "If my senses are correct, you'll find her mother downstairs. When she wakes, reassure her that I'll return Lara as soon as I've fixed the problem."

Drift inclined his head. "I owe you."

"No, Osterhase." The God of the Dead shook his head. "If anything, it is we who owe you; the situation with Ostara should never have spiralled so far out of hand."

Since there was nothing to say that would change the past, Drift merely shrugged.

"One thing, however, I can offer." Anubis snapped his fingers and loose linen trousers appeared on Drift's lower body. "There are some things that should remain a mystery, even between old friends."

Drift grinned. "Too bad you've seen it all."

"And cannot unsee it." Anubis made a face, then accorded Taylin a half-bow. "Thank you, my lady, for your courage. You've mended something too-long broken, and for that, you have the thanks of … about eighty-five percent of the gods."

Taylin's jaw dropped. "Eighty-five percent?"

"Indeed." Anubis sighed. "The other fifteen percent are either assholes, or don't care. Can't win 'em all, I'm afraid."

"Oh." Taylin cleared her throat. "Of course. Uh. You're welcome?"

"Oobis?" Lara's tiny hand patted the god's charcoal jaw. "You said ice cream."

"That I did." Anubis beamed down at the child, his smile bright enough to eclipse the sun. "With my mother, no less. Shall we go?"

Lara squealed in delight. "Yes! No. Wait. Bay come?"

Bay belongs here. The wolpertinger nuzzled Lara's throat, then fluttered over to perch on Drift's shoulder. *When you're better, Bay will visit again.*

"Promise?"

Promise.

The little girl nodded slowly, then laid her head against Anubis' chest. "Ready for ice cream now, Oobis."

"Very well. Hold tight." With a wink in Drift's direction, the shadows flared and the God of the Dead disappeared.

Taylin pointed at the space where Anubis had been. "What. Just. Happened?"

Drift laughed. "If you think that was odd, you should see Anubis and Horus together. Do you know they once made a god by accident?"

"By *accident?*"

"Nobody's sure who was more surprised; Horus and Anubis, or the poor sop who suddenly ascended from angel to deity." Drift looked down at his billowing linen trousers and sighed. "I didn't like the tight jeans Tyr conjured but I think, in comparison, they were much better than these."

"Oh, I don't know." Taylin gave him a heated once over. "It gives you a harem feel."

"Would you like that?" Drift growled, dropping his voice as deep as it would go. "For me to be your harem?"

Taylin curled her fingers in the waistband of his pants and gave a light tug. "The sooner we rescue those who've been transformed by the staff, the sooner you'll find out."

PRIMAL GOD OF THE VERNAL EQUINOX

In the cool, earthy basement of Great Aunt Ethel's house, the darkness broken only by the soft glow coming from Taylin's bones, the circle of foil effigies looked even more eerie than in the full light of day. Healers moved quietly through the room, assisted by the ex-EBC rabbits who'd chosen to stay in Drift's service. Minus their extravagant outfits and overbearing mistress, they proved dedicated and capable, having transferred all of Jeffrey's victims to Evergreen Waters Retreat in a matter of hours – with the exception of the vampire and his witch-doctor lover, who would remain buried beneath the ruins of their log cabin.

"If I bit one of those, would it taste like chocolate, or like person?" Raucous propped himself against the wall, shoving both hands in the pockets of his loose jeans.

"Chocolate," Drift called from where he knelt by one of the effigies. "But anything in your stomach will revert to raw meat when the spell is absolved."

Raucous made a face and Taylin laughed. "You two seem to be getting along much better."

"I can't explain it." The thunderbird shook his head. "Before, his presence was like … like …"

Like teeth under your skin, Bay volunteered, swooping in to land on Taylin's shoulder.

"Yes. But now he feels ..."

Taylin glanced up at her friend and was astonished to discover him blushing. "Like what?"

Raucous cleared his throat. "Like home."

Drift Primal God of Vernal Equinox. Bay pulled down one of his ears and began grooming the fur like a cat. *Ostara saw only Easter, cared only for accolades and attention. Missed most important part.*

"I don't understand," Taylin admitted. "I don't feel anything different about Drift – except, of course, that his emotional resonance is restored."

And wasn't that the understatement of a lifetime? Drift blazed with the brilliance of a star, his unique signature so deeply imprinted upon her senses that Taylin was certain she'd be able to locate him no matter the distance that separated them.

"You don't feel the difference because you don't have an animal spirit." Drift pushed to his feet, dusting his palms on his jeans. "It's impossible to entirely explain – but as a thunderbird, Raucous can feel the energy I give off. While I was broken, that energy was painful and discordant, but now that I'm whole, it's ..."

Comfort. Power. Safety. Love. Nurturing. Gratitude. Respect. Courage. Strength. Bay puffed out his feathers, then settled them with a rustle. *Home.*

A lump formed in Taylin's throat and she scuffed at the dirt floor with the toe of her boot. "I don't fit any of that."

"On the contrary." Drift prowled closer, liquid grace and wicked sin. "The moon is my lifeblood, the source of the magic I embody. And you ... you carry the moon's grace in your very bones. We were made for each other; two halves of a whole." Taking her hands in both of his, Drift tugged Taylin into the centre of the circle of effigies. "Your moonlight anchors my soul."

His lashes fluttered closed and Taylin felt a tug deep in the centre of her chest. She didn't stop to think; she opened herself to Drift's vast energy, letting it soak every cell in her body. Her magic hummed as it mingled with his, flowing back through the connection to create a synergy the likes of which she'd never felt in all her life.

"Do you see?" Drift's growling undertone rippled across her skin. "It's us."

"Yes." Taylin flattened her palms against his chest, anchoring Drift's magic as it spiralled outwards. One by one, the circle of chocolate effigies began to glow – not with the golden light of the Osterhase but with the shimmering pale blue of the moon. "It's us."

Drift rumbled deep in his throat, the vibration striking a chord in Taylin's bones so that they flared impossibly bright, limning the room in silver. "*Wake.*"

Chocolate cracked, sharp and loud. Groans filled the room as people stumbled from their shells, collapsing into the arms of the waiting healers. Gentle hands gripped Taylin's arm and it took all her effort to tear her gaze from Drift's.

"My dear." A woman stood at her side; tall and slender with pointed ears, lavender eyes and long, iron-grey hair caught in a loose braid. "That's enough now. You can let go."

It was Drift who had the strength to break the connection, pulling his hands free and taking a measured step backwards.

"Great Aunt Ethel." Taylin threw herself into her mentor's arms. "Thank the gods."

Ethel chuckled and shook her head. "No, thank *you*."

Taylin dropped her gaze, heat suffusing her cheeks. "Great Aunt Ethel, this is Drift, Primal God of the Vernal Equinox. He's the one responsible for reversing the chocolate spell."

"Ah, the Osterhase." With one arm around Taylin's shoulders, Ethel extended her hand with the palm facing down, fingers slightly curled to expose the back of her knuckles. "Ethel Blueraven, patroness of Evergreen Waters Retreat. Most people call me Great Aunt Ethel."

"A pleasure to meet you in the flesh." Drift took Ethel's hand and bent over it, sniffing at the knuckles she'd offered. "It's nice to find someone who remembers the old ways."

"When one is as old as the old ways, they become harder to forget." Ethel's eyes crinkled at the corners. "I rather wondered when you were going to get the one-up on Ostara; I see now it was a case of the right time, the right place and, unless my magic deceives me, the right person?"

Drift's eyes locked with Taylin's, his warmth shifting deep inside her. "Yes."

"I see. In that case, I absolve Taylin Colkannis of any obligation to Evergreen Waters Retreat." Ethel pressed a kiss to Taylin's temple and gave her a gentle push in Drift's direction. "I have loved having you here, my dear, but the time has come to go home."

Home. Taylin took one faltering step, then another. Drift met her halfway, sweeping her into his arms as though she weighed little more than a feather. Tears pricked the corners of her eyes and he kissed them away, sending shivers down her spine and igniting a tingling heat at the juncture of her thighs.

"Gods, I love you." He breathed the words against her skin, the simple, shining truth whispering down the bond they'd created.

"I love you, too." Taylin tightened her arms around his neck, heart hammering. "Take me home, Drift."

Magic surged and Evergreen Waters disappeared, replaced by a simple bedroom with wooden walls, a hand-woven rug and a solid bed dressed in earthen tones. Subtle strains of jasmine and vanilla drifted through the bedroom's open window, twining with the cedarwood and sage that was Drift's own.

The Osterhase set her on her feet by the bed, his lips on hers less than a second later. His kiss was voracious and Taylin clung to his shoulders as the warmth inside her caught alight, heating her blood until it thrummed with need.

"Wait." He broke the kiss on a gasping breath, hazel eyes wild with the same desperation Taylin felt. "Before we do this, I want you to know something. What I said to you back at the log cabin about sex and magic and instinct and … I mean, it's true, but I love the entirety of you and what we share will never be something I take for granted. I know I breached your trust and said some awful things, but I need you to understand that I'll never do it again. I swear it."

"I believe you." Taylin cupped his face, brushing her thumbs over the sharp angles of his cheeks. "And as wonderful as it is that you're being honest with me, this moment has been building since the first time we laid eyes on each other. If you don't start undressing in the next five seconds, I'm going to lose my mind."

His answering grin was wicked, uncertainty fading as Drift gripped the hem of his t-shirt and pulled the entire thing off in one swift, strong motion. Taylin wasted no time shaping his pectorals with her hands, running her nails lightly through his faint dusting of chest hair and then over sculpted abdominals until she was fumbling with his jeans. Drift lost patience somewhere during the lowering of his zipper, shoving at the waistband until they were low enough to be kicked aside.

"Gods, Taylin." His lips took hers, fierce and demanding. Fabric shredded, clawed hands reducing her clothing to tatters between one hungry breath and the next. The moment they were both naked, he pressed his body against hers, unravelling her braid to clench both fists in her ebony hair.

When Drift nudged her backward to the bed, Taylin shook her head. "I'll break it."

"No, you won't – everything here is bolstered by my magic." He tossed her onto the mattress, pouncing to land neatly between her knees. "You can't break the furniture here, and now that I'm whole, you can't hurt me, either. No more leash, Taylin. We're both free."

Free.

Taylin stared down the length of her naked body to drink in the sight of his; acres of brown skin, tumbled hair and a sinful smile that had her body aching in the best possible way. "Drift."

"I know."

He scooped his hands beneath her backside and lifted, sealing his mouth over her core. There was no gentle build, no warning – Drift knew exactly how to get what he wanted and in less than a minute Taylin was clawing at the bedclothes, her breath coming in gasps. Changing the angle of his tongue, Drift slid a finger deep inside her body and curled it ever so slightly. Taylin exploded on a wave of ecstasy that was violent in its intensity, clutching at his antlers while the rest of the world trembled around her. Drift growled against her needy flesh, drawing the orgasm out with his hands and his tongue until she was limp and panting.

"Better?" He kissed his way across her belly, nipping at the underside of her breasts until she arched impatiently towards him. "Or do I need to do that again?"

"Gods, Drift, if you don't stick your—" Taylin cried out as he took her breast in his mouth, swirling his tongue around the nipple with as much talent as he'd shown lower.

"You're not the only one who's been thinking about this since the moment we met." He shifted to the other breast, teasing the nipple with his tongue and his teeth. "I laid awake every night wondering how you'd taste." Wicked hazel eyes locked with her own. "How you'd feel."

Drift surged inside her with one long, firm thrust, the fit so perfect Taylin was lost for words. Bracing one hand on the bed, he curved the other around her hip and urged her legs around his waist. The razor-sharp tips of his claws whispered over her skin, feather-light caresses that had her lifting her hips to meet every wild thrust.

"Taylin." Her name became a chant, his lips and teeth blazing a trail across her jaw and down her throat. "Now."

There was nothing to do but oblige, Taylin's orgasm dragging a scream from the very core of her being. Drift's spine stiffened, his release slamming into her empathic senses on a wave of shuddering ecstasy that sent her tumbling all over again. When he collapsed on top of her, Taylin held him close, revelling in the way his body moulded to her own.

Drift nipped at the soft skin beneath her jaw. "Mine."

"How did you know what I was thinking?"

His laughter vibrated through them both. "Lucky guess."

"If you tell me, after all this time, that you can read minds—"

"No, no." Drift laughed harder, lifting his head to pepper her face with kisses. "I can feel you through the connection we initiated back at Evergreen Waters Retreat, though, so maybe I cheated a little."

Taylin narrowed her eyes but it was impossible to keep a straight face surrounded by so much joy. Drift rolled them over while she laughed, tucking her against his side as though they'd always lain that way.

"So what now?" She traced a lazy finger over his pectorals, savouring the satin heat of his skin.

He cracked a yawn. "I'm tempted to admit I have the same failings as most other males and need a nap, but I'm actually pretty hungry. How do pancakes sound?"

"Pancakes sound amazing, but that's not what I meant."

"Cheese and bacon pancakes." Drift pursed his lips. "With butter. Lots and lots of butter."

"*Drift.*"

"All right, all right." He sighed, fluffing the pillow behind his head. "The short answer is that I don't know. Ostara has capitalised on Easter for thousands upon thousands of years – I need to find a way to reclaim what's mine without disappointing people who have certain expectations."

"You know … people are generally more resilient than we give them credit for." Taylin drummed her fingers on his chest. "I can think of a certain news network that'll be eager to redeem their image after one of their anchors behaved so badly on camera. What if we set up a live broadcast where you tell the real story of what happened between you and Ostara; the exile, the staff, all of it – and then wrap up by explaining that you're taking Easter back?"

Drift was silent for so long she thought he'd gone to sleep but when Taylin levered up on her elbow, he was staring at her in slack-jawed astonishment.

"That's brilliant," he breathed. "Not only do I reintroduce myself to the Merged Worlds, but Ostara loses the credibility she stole those long years ago."

Taylin winked. "So that's a yes?"

"Anything with you is a yes – but this one is a double yes." Drift let out a long breath. "Easter's only a few weeks away. If we orchestrate this correctly, by the time it hits, everyone will know the truth."

"Exactly." Taylin brushed her lips over his, pouring her heart into the caress.

Drift growled into her mouth, deepening the kiss until they were both panting when they broke apart. "I need you."

"I thought you needed a nap and some pancakes."

He rolled towards her, his erection long and thick against her belly. "I need those, too, but not like I need you."

"Well, excuse me, but I'm a mere mortal. We get hungry, you know." Taylin slung a leg over his waist, frowning as he froze. "What's wrong?"

"About the mere mortal part." Drift cleared his throat. "We might have ... um. When we blended our energies at Ethel's. It. Well, I'm pretty sure that blend is permanent."

"Of course it is. I feel you in here." Taylin pressed a hand to her chest. "Why? What does that mean?"

"It means that your life force is bound to mine."

"So ...?"

"So."

"*Drift.*"

"You're immortal," he blurted. "Like me."

Taylin's stomach flipped over, her breath catching in her lungs. "Oh."

"I didn't know ... I didn't mean—"

"Hey." She shushed him with a kiss. "It's okay."

Drift blinked. "It is?"

"Getting a chance at forever with you? That's more than okay." Taylin kissed him again, coaxing with lips and tongue until he relaxed in her arms and kissed her back. "In fact, we should celebrate. Hurry up and make love to me before I pass out from hunger."

His hand slid down her spine, angling her hips even as he laughed. "*Now* you want pancakes?"

"No, now I want you. But after that, yeah. I want pancakes." Taylin groaned as he pushed inside her, every exquisite inch making it harder to think. "What did you promise? Cheese and bacon? With lots of – oh gods, don't stop – butter!"

"Let's make a bet." Drift began to thrust in earnest, sliding one hand between their bodies to stroke her clitoris. "First person to orgasm has to cook."

"I'm going to … I'm going to … *Drift!*" Taylin shattered in his arms and he joined her a scant few thrusts later, growling into her skin while they rode the waves of pleasure.

"I win," he panted. "You definitely came first."

"I've never been so glad to lose a bet in my entire life."

He laughed, stroking her hair back from her face. "I'll take that as a compliment."

"You should." She cut him a coy look. "Even if you cheated – again."

"Maybe." He winked. "In that case, how about I cook anyway? The pancakes were my idea, after all."

"Deal. While you do, I'll put in a call to the news network." Taylin grinned. "We're going to make a good team, Osterhase."

Drift pressed a kiss to the tip of her nose. "We already do."

~ THE END ~

♥

Thanks so much for reading!

I hope you enjoyed Taylin and Drift's story. This was the most challenging novella I've written to date, but I love how it turned out and with any luck, you did too.

So ... do I write other stuff? You bet I do! Keep up to date with all the latest shenanigans at:

www.sliceofsammy.com

Learn to let go... or burn.

Dating Noah Acheson has always been gentle, predictable and above all, safe – but when the softly spoken foxkin breaks the rules of their carefully crafted relationship, Deanna cuts him off, retreating to her private sanctuary deep in the Australian bush.

Stinging from Deanna's rejection, Noah returns from a brief stint fighting fires in New South Wales to face an infinitely more vicious fire front in Victoria. Though his broken heart still very much belongs to Deanna Schellponte, he's determined not to chase her – until the wind changes, turning the fires towards pack land, and Deanna is reported missing.

With fire raging all around, Noah races into the bush to find the wolfkin he loves. To survive, Deanna and Noah must confront not only the fury of Mother Nature... but the ghost whose memory tore them apart.

ALSO BY SAMANTHA MARSHALL

ABOUT SAMANTHA

Hi, I'm Sam!

I've been writing my whole life, scribbling stories on anything close to hand – from the shopping list to napkins to post-it notes (don't mention post-its to hubby haha).

I grew up reading fantasy of the likes of Anne McCaffrey, Terry Pratchett, and their peers. I'm also a lifelong vampire fan, along with all things spooky. In my late teens I was introduced to paranormal romance and discovered a whole new layer of storytelling with a bit of a spicy edge! Taking what I learnt from all of the above, I devoted myself to creating full-bodied characters, meaty plots, epic adventure, and a little bit of naughty sauce on the side.

I completed a Diploma of Professional Writing and Editing after high school and spent the next several years in my writing cave, working on a novel that is now in a drawer somewhere, followed by a couple of others who shared the same fate. (What can I say? I'm a recovering perfectionist.)

I came close to debuting my novel career in 2009, then ended up pregnant and took some time off to have kids. I debuted for real in 2019 with *Sorcery and Stardust* and won ARRA's Favourite Debut Romance Author for 2019, which was extremely cool!

I write speculative fiction that is a fusion of multiple sub-genres and therefore doesn't fit particularly well into any of them, but after many years and a lot of angst, I'm okay with that. I love all my characters and their stories for different reasons, but have a soft spot for an excellent villain and a tortured protagonist.

I currently live in southeast Melbourne, Victoria, with my hubby, two kids, a Golden Retriever, and a turtle. I volunteer with the Romance Writers of Australia, and I'm passionate about great writing, interesting characters, chai tea and happily ever afters.

And if you want to get to know the Perfectly Paranormal Anthology authors a bit more, get sneak peeks of what's coming up for the APP Anthologies, as well as giveaways, special offers and just some PNR fun, then join our Perfectly Paranormal Paramours Facebook Group.

Find us here:

https://www.facebook.com/groups/251663560162131

ACKNOWLEDGEMENTS

When I first set out to write a story about Easter, I had no idea how little mythology there was surrounding the holiday, nor how vague the existing mythology was. I was intrigued, but I also spent days looking for a spark to light my imaginative fire – because even though it wasn't necessary to have a link to our commonly accepted mythology, the Merged Worlds has always contained snippets here and there and I wanted to keep that trend going wherever possible.

Every time I started digging, I kept coming back to the Osterhase and became fascinated by the idea of him. Drift was born from that fascination, closely followed by his conflict with Ostara and the exile that has led him to fade into the background of our current myths and legends.

While the idea was amorphous to begin with, the characters were not and in the early drafts, Taylin and Drift carried the story when I wasn't sure exactly where it was going. So, in that respect, the biggest thanks goes to them!

I had a blast working in a few cameos from other Merged Worlds books (did you spot them?) and even though this was a bumpy road, I love the tale we ended up with. Even though *Foiled* isn't as laugh out loud funny as the previous novellas have been, it packs a heavy punch right in the feels that is due, in large part, to the enormous hearts that both Taylin and Drift possess. Exploring their worlds has been an honour.

If you enjoyed this latest peek into the magical Merged Worlds, then I'd love it if you would leave a review – not only does it help an author out, it lets me know that I've hit the mark and put a smile on your wonderful face. So, please and thank you in advance!

♥

BLIZZARDS AND BEGINNINGS

HELLUCY HOWE

BLIZZARDS AND BEGINNINGS

Tales from the Fae Court
Book Three

~

Hellucy Howe

ABOUT BLIZZARDS AND BEGINNINGS

What would you do if winter grew teeth and claws?

Lady Lyssica Aphiski, unexpected heir to the Duke of Papillion, is driven to prove to her father she is capable of fulfilling her role – even if it means juggling her estate duties with her secret and sacred responsibility as Handmaiden to the Unseelie Goddess, Ostara. Everything is going swimmingly until the first snow of winter arrives weeks ahead of schedule. If that wasn't enough, the participants for the Tri-moon training program arrive, bringing with them a scourge from Lyssica's past.

When Lord Emryn Phengaris agreed to represent his Changeling Clan in the Tri-moon program, he had no idea he'd end up as personal bodyguard to the gorgeous Lady Lyssica Aphiski. To make matters worse, his animal side insists she's their mate, which is impossible because, despite his fascination with her steel spine and shimmering smile, she's not changeling.

Then a Tri-moon apprentice is murdered by an ancient evil determined to bring about eternal winter. Only one thing stands in his way – the magic Lyssica has kept secret since childhood. With her world thrown into chaos and danger at every turn, Emryn proves the anchor Lyssica never knew she needed. Together, they must find the strength to vanquish not only the demons threatening the Queendom, but the ones inside their hearts.

DEDICATION

For my fellow authors, interested family members and all those folk who love fairy tales, as I do.

1

LYSSICA

Face pressed to the window, Lady Lyssica Aphiski stared at the soft falling snow, a moue of dismay twisting her mouth. Each new flake drifted on the wind's sigh, before inexorably dropping to freshen the ground's rapidly whitening carpet.

Winter's first snow? Already?

The frosty evidence was undeniable, even though leaves remained on most trees, and Juberd, the first moon of winter, was yet two weeks away.

"Goddess blast it." Lyssica pressed frustrated fingers to the glass – the tips forming claws – as if she could grab fistfuls of the wet stuff and somehow dispose of it. The early seasonal change would play havoc with the Duchy's horticultural plans; she'd have to adapt her timelines, bring some tasks forward and postpone others. Biting her bottom lip, she fought to swallow annoyance at firm evidence of the Cailleach's impatience to launch her season. But would she want to maintain the balance and leave early at winter's end? Lyssica huffed a laugh. Winter's Queen had never been known for half measures, but perhaps she'd entered into an agreement with Modron, the Autumn Goddess.

Swinging back to her mirror, Lyssica thrust more jewelled pins into her chignon. It was as well the Tri-moon apprentices were arriving today, because, if snow continued, travel would become difficult. Speaking of – she needed to hurry, or the apprentices would arrive at the front door before she did, and wouldn't Papan be thrilled about that?

The chignon's upsweep captured her wild mass of ebony hair, although the swathe of emerald above her left temple and swirl of lavender near her right ear were still prominent. If she turned her head, she'd see cobalt streaks which—

The antique Godfather clock in the downstairs antechamber gonged, the reverberations clanging through her revery. *Shite, Lyssica, get a move on!* Snatching up her makeup kit, she flicked it open and grabbed an applicator.

"Tig, could you please bring my mulberry cling-boots from the dressing room?" The words had barely left her lips when Antigony Lyonetti appeared in the mirror's background; her hair slightly dishevelled, but mouth curved with satisfaction, she brandished said footwear, trophy style.

"One step ahead of you, Lady Lyss."

"Excellent." Lyssica swept blush powder across her cheeks, pausing to contemplate the effect. Nodded. The peach was the perfect colour for her. Using a fingertip, she framed her aquamarine eyes with kohl and the lids with glimmering deep purple before wiping her fingers clean with a soft cloth. Smoothing her fitted violet silken shell, she assessed her outfit; the golden accents on the tunic-length garment went a long way to elevate the outfit from stark simplicity. Just below her hips, the tailored violet and gold trousers flowed down her legs to bell slightly around the lower leg and cuff at the ankle. "What do you think, Tig? I'm trying to look like a professional without losing femininity." She twisted this way and that.

"Everyone will fall at your feet, Lady Lyss." Antigony nodded as she proffered the shin-high boots. "And these will be the perfect finishing touch. Your Papan can't fail to be impressed."

Lyssica grimaced. "Let's hope you're right."

Rattling noises had Antigony hurrying to the window. "Carriages coming up the driveway Lady Lyss!"

"Goddess blast it!" Lyssica slid one foot into a boot, tabbing the side clasp shut as she hobbled for the stairway.

"Your cloak, milady!" Antigony chased after her, the indigo-coloured velvet garment held wide. Glancing back, Lyssica was startled by the cloak's resemblance to a storm sweeping in, then the soft folds enveloped her and the gold fastener clicked into place at her throat.

"Thanks, Tig." She reeled down the tower staircase, the cloak billowing. At the bottom, Lyssica clutched the railing with one hand, lifted her stocking clad foot, positioned her boot, fumbled with the buckle and – hissed as it slipped from her grasp.

"Hell's horns!" Closing her eyes, she mentally counted out her frustration ... *One duskit, two bunnies, three squizzles and – everything's fine, so slow the hell down.* Opening her eyes, she discovered Entanglit, the Papillion Estate's major-domo, proffering her errant boot.

A smile stretched her lips. "Thank you, Entanglit." She wobbled to a nearby chair, sat, thrust her foot inside and tabbed it closed. Regaining her feet, she hastened out through the foyer to the wide, wisteria-entwined verandah.

Maman's face lit up. "There you are, Lyssica sweetie. You're looking lovely."

Papan, the almighty Duke Yanvian Aphiski, flicked her a stern glance. "Beginning to think you wouldn't make it. The carriages are close."

Lyssica clenched her teeth. Convincing him to accept her as heir, a position left empty by her brother, DeMaksim, departing on Joint Queendom business, was something she'd had to fight for – and continued to – on a daily basis. Drumming her fingers on the porch railing, she refused to dignify Papan's barb with an answer, but memories flooded in.

Papan's refusal to include a nineteen-year-old Lyssica in the estate management lessons alongside DeMaksim. "You are a Fae-female and a lady. The position is above your ability."

"But I want to learn, Papan."

"You misunderstand me, Lyssica. Young ladies don't have the capability or intelligence. Stay within your limits and enjoy yourself."

The words had stung like darts; sharp stabs flaying her skin, allowing the polluted slime of hurt and anger to seep out. Reacting to the poison, she'd taken his advice and gone on a pleasure-seeking spree. Flirting with anything male, drinking to excess and partying her days away – boring but harmless, until she'd fallen victim to a predator.

She sighed, hating the idea of reliving those memories; afterwards, the only thing to save her from her self-loathing and heartache was her sworn oath to the Goddess Ostara. Completing the promised daily ritual became the light of her life, keeping her afloat in a quagmire of toxic ooze where her companions turned out to be users and abusers and her father thought her nothing but a pretty frippery.

It wasn't really his fault, she knew. The Seelie Fae had been a patriarchal society for thousands of years despite being ruled by a Queen. Stupid really. The Unseelie Fae weren't so ridiculously hidebound. Secretly, Lyssica had always admired their attitude. If you possessed the power or the skill, the Unseelie didn't care if you were female, male, or of some alternate persuasion. If you could do the job, it was win-win and you were in.

But things had recently begun to change and the uniting of the Queendoms under singular joint rule was a sign of new times ahead. She hoped.

Despite the fact that Seelie and Unseelie were now supposed to be one, the changes went against the traditions of several hundred years and there were those who struggled with the new status quo; and some who openly rebelled.

"This first Tri-moon program is very important." Duke Yanvian's voice brought her back to the moment at hand. Lyssica listened. Kind of. She'd heard it all before. A nearby grime-rose bush was much more interesting. Were the leaves bruised?

He waved a hand. "The level of success we attain will set the tone for the programs of future years."

Well accustomed to her father's love of rambling lectures, Lyssica reached to cup a leaf in her hand and was startled into dropping it when electricity zapped her palm. Mouth agape, she stared at the faint leafy imprint singed into her soft skin, then blew on her hand and shook it briskly.

Papan nodded, rocking back on his heels, as usual, completely oblivious to the fact she wasn't fully listening. "So everything we say and do must be carefully thought out in advance."

She peered at the plant – was there a blue glow overshadowing it? Instinctively, she began humming; leaning over the railing as she sang faintly, aiming her goddess power at the roots of the grime-rose bush. It sizzled, so she crooned a few more words of healing and encouragement.

Papan twisted, hands snapping to hips. "Lyssica! Are you even listening?"

The trembling bush sagged, before her quiet words imbued strength and life back into it. Then it brightened. She turned her head, regarded him coolly. "Absolutely Papan. As always you make perfect sense."

A few feet away, Maman chuckled. "You're always humming and singing. I never quite hear what you're singing about, but the plants seem to love your voice. It's no wonder our Papillion Duchy gardens are admired and envied by visitors."

Lyssica stiffened, flicked her mother an innocent glance. Did Maman suspect something? She dug her nails into her palms. That wouldn't do. "Oh? You think they hear and respond, Maman?" She laughed. "It's not very likely, but wouldn't it be fantastic? I'd adore being able to help them like that." She did adore it. "But really, it's just our marvellous gardening staff and my fancies. When I tell the plants how beautiful they are, surely they understand?"

She didn't admit how much of the gardens' beauty actually was due to her nurturing. Couldn't admit it even if she wanted to; Ostara had enspelled Lyssica's silence for her own protection.

But Lyssica found there were folk who wanted a reason for everything. *You must have a green thumb!* Was a comment she'd heard several times, when her thumb had nothing to do with it – the wonderful results were a direct response to the use of her goddess-given power. Her *Unseelie* goddess-given power. In a territory where the worshipped spring deity had always been the Seelie Goddess, Olwen, Lyssica was a handmaiden of Ostara.

Her father's hand clasping her arm jolted her into the moment. "Stop that infernal singing and look sharp; we've a reputation to uphold, Lyssica."

She wrenched her arm free and, holding her father's gaze, pointed. "Those plants aren't thriving in this early cold snap. Last night's snowfall was untimely, and unnatural."

Duke Yanvian beetled his brows. "Maybe Modron, the Autumn Goddess, wanted to leave early, she is female after all. The phrase 'changeable as the weather' is often used to describe the unsettled minds of females; neither easily explained. Early winters are never a good thing for crops and everyone will be in the same predicament. We can't be held accountable for the weather, Lyssica. We'll do the best we can."

Lyssica clasped her fingers together tightly. "Heavy snow three weeks early has nothing to do with the workings of female minds. With what promises to be a harsh winter looming, forage in the forest will diminish quickly and survival for any living being will become difficult."

"Oh, don't worry." Duke Yanvian waved a hand as the first carriage floated to a stop at the base of the colonnaded portico, popped out supporting legs, and settled. The second conveyance drifted to a stop and planted itself close behind. "We'll feed any deer seeking shelter on the estate, as we've always done."

Lyssica bit her lip; she worried for more than the deer, but their argument must wait. Below them, carriage doors opened, their inbuilt steps automatically descending. Shivering, she clutched at the edges of her velvet cloak; her dracon genetics responded to her unconscious prompt and upped her internal furnace until the cold vanished from her system. Smoothing her hands down her tunic, she drew a deep breath. Winter wasn't going to leave and neither were the new arrivals.

The candidates were engaging in the programme of reciprocal sponsorships discussed and approved at the last United Queendom's Summer Council. Selected single adult children of participating families were to spend the three moons of winter as apprentices at other properties. Some larger estates had accepted several apprentices and agreed to send more than one of their offspring elsewhere. It was embraced as a way to extend skills, promote cooperation, encourage friendships and see if any parties located suitable mates or consorts. Lyssica grimaced; a training program yes, but also a marriage market. Now, five Fae-males and one Fae-female stood on the lower steps.

Duchesse Azura entwined her gloved hands. "I hope our girls have arrived at their destinations safely."

Her consort flashed her a smile. "I'm certain they have. You needn't worry so, my dear." His smile faded. "It's a pity Trey refused. I think it would've benefitted him."

The Duchesse tilted her hand, palm upward. "You know he can't process things on short notice. At least he agreed to join next year's program."

Duke Yanvian nodded. "Better than absolute repudiation, which we all know he's capable of."

Their Tri-moon guests climbed the steps, their features becoming easier to pick out. Staring in consternation, Lyssica tuned her parents out. *Is that...? No, surely not.* But it was. In the advancing group were two faces she'd wished never to see again. Lord Perris Momphiday and Lord Venaday Tortrician. The first regarded her with a sly smile and one elevated eyebrow, the second rubbed his hands while grinning hugely.

Shite, bugger, and hell's horns! *I'm going to be sick.* No, no, she wouldn't. She couldn't. Swallowing harshly, she tried to rope in her errant emotions and thoughts. *Should have paid more attention when Papan showed me the lists! At least I'd have been more prepared. Maybe.* She dug fingernails into palms. *Don't look at him.* She turned her attention to the other four Fae-folk. She didn't recognise any of them; their wings were either tightly furled against the snow or tucked under cloaks so she there were no wing markings to help her.

Duke Yanvian spread his hands. "Welcome all!"

Duchesse Azura smiled widely. "You must be chilled. Let's retire to the salon for refreshments. The house is infinitely warmer."

Lyssica forced a smile. "So pleased." *Not.* At least, not to see— She shook her head internally. "Don't worry about your luggage, it will be taken to your rooms."

Cutting ruthlessly across the path of his companions to halt in front of her, Lord Venaday swept Lyssica a bow. "Lady Lyssica! Such a thrill to be in your delightful company again. Perhaps we can play cards as we used to? You remember the 'Swig or Strip' parties, don't you?"

"Oh! I can't say I do." *More than I'd like to.* "Are you sure I was involved? We were all very young back then and these days my time is filled with important tasks." Lyssica forced a smile. "As I'm certain your life is, Lord Venaday. I hope we have all changed and matured."

"Not too much change, I hope," he said, waggling his brows at her before moving to follow her mother.

Left by herself, Lyssica wasn't certain whether to laugh hysterically, hiss with anger, or cry in despair. Of course, she couldn't do any of those until she was safely back in her room and away from— She shuddered then pinched the bridge of her nose. How was she going to go in there and pretend like everything was normal?

Goddess help me, please. A zing shot through her body, electrifying every hair; she was left with the uneasy feeling that her words had been answered.

But what was her answer?

2

EMRYN

*E*mryn made a mental note to thank the Duke and Duchesse of Garadenya for sending the coach which drastically shortened his lengthy trip from the Kynthcat domains. Despite the fact his inner Kynthcat preferred to run rather than ride inside a stuffy carriage, even at top speed, it would take more than a week to travel on foot. The comfortable leather seats became more welcome the further they travelled from the heat of the Destrion Changeling Territory to the colder southern lands.

Even so, as they neared their destination, Emryn, awed by the massive trees of the forest lining both sides of the road, pulled the internal carriage cord for the driver to stop the coach. Grabbing his change-bag, he jumped out of the carriage and onto the road, consumed by the urge to explore despite the chill.

"I wish to finish the journey four-pawed, Brandon."

The coach driver wasn't the least bit bothered. "Sure, just continue on down this road. The entrance to the island estate is on the bridge you'll come to in a few leagues. I'll advise the gate guards to look out for you." He waved. "See you at Garadenya, Lord Emryn."

Emryn watched the carriage disappear around the next bend before he stepped off the road behind some bushes, stripped, stashed his clothing in the bag then tucked it into the crook of a tree branch. Even thus engaged, he was unable to stop staring at the lush beauty of the place. The forest thrilled both sides of him. As a Fae-male, he was awed by the massive wooden trunks with their canopies of branches and leaves, bulbous roots hugging the earth and the decaying litter of many seasons. His changeling animal wanted to get in amongst it all.

'Want to come out and see.'

'In a few moments.' He wandered deeper into the woods, shivering at the unaccustomed cool climate feathering his naked skin, but revelled in the chill for the same reason. It was so different to the hot dryness he was used to and he craned his head, soaking up the forest's peaceful ambience. Finally, regardless of the cold, he lay down to stare meditatively up into the greenery above him.

His dual senses were awash with sensation and each side of him wanted to manage the inundation differently. The change shimmered over them within seconds and Fae-male, Emryn, became a very large wildcat, his blissful awe eclipsed by a cat's curiosity.

'We play!' Kynthcat shushed his prowling paws through the rustling leaves while marvelling at the lack of sandy desert and towering monoliths of their home territory. His entrancement when he discovered an effervescent spring, leaping and burbling until it overflowed into a tinkling creek, had him springing about like a kitten. He stalked the dancing creek cutting through the ancient woods; his paws slipped on stones as he poked at bubbles with a claw.

A squawking bird with bright plumage winged over him. Head high he pranced after it. Too bad it was soon lost to view in the forest – but there was so much to see and scent. His interest was quickly reclaimed by the magic of the deep woods. His playfulness gave way to careful exploration and the training of years took over. As he padded carefully on through the leafy mulch of the treed wilderness, he kept to hard ground to ensure his large paws left little sign of his passage.

Wending around the bole of a forest giant, he leapt over a gnarled root and made for the game trail twisting away through the under-growth. The stench of a skunweasel assaulted his nostrils and he veered from the path, shaking his head and sneezing. His rich brown mane waved wildly, the braided lengths flopping in front of his beleaguered muzzle as he lifted a paw to bat away the disgusting odour.

"Blech!" The exclamation emerged as a snarling cough. *'Not that way!'* Emryn fully agreed; even though his horns, claws and fangs would make short work of the creature, the varmint's revolting smell would cling for days. It was better not to endure a face to face with such a one. Changing course, he bypassed the trail left by the foul skunweasel, steering clear of its pervading rottenness as he stalked regally between the trees and circled in a different direction to return to the water course.

Senses alert, he lowered his muzzle to the water, tonguing up the chilly liquid; even were he in familiar territory, relaxed vigilance was never a good choice. Concealed by the undergrowth flanking the creek, Kynthcat wove his way downstream towards the Rubiconia River. When the creek met up with the larger waterway, he turned upstream, picking up his pace along the river bank.

Much as he'd enjoyed the day, the urge to rest weary paws got stronger with each step. It had been a long trip and this exploration of the stand of forest on the Unseelie side of the river – *Oops, can't forget it's meant to be called the Northern Provinces now.*

No care. Kynthcat shrugged off the politics – he'd had fun, despite the skunweasel. When the road came into view he was grateful. Taking stock of their surroundings, he soon identified the jagged tree just short of the road where he'd stowed his travel bag.

Morphing from four legs to two, Emryn reached into the crook of the tree for his bag and dropped to the ground to open it. He pulled his neatly folded clothes out and wasted no time donning pants, shirt, jacket and boots. Running fingers through his long hair, he twisted the strands into a queue, tying the length off with the string he'd stashed in a pocket. Lifting his bag, he slipped through the undergrowth and headed for the road.

Setting a brisk pace, it took Emryn little time to reach the bridge. Part way across the first span, he halted, gazing over the stone parapet to the steadily flowing river. The flows and eddies of water had always fascinated him, regardless of whether he was Kynthcat or Fae-male. He'd been thrilled to discover that the site of his apprenticeship-exchange was on an island. Turning reluctantly away he continued his bridge crossing. They were here for three-and-a-half moons, plenty of time to explore the river.

The gated entrance to the Duchy of Garadenya appeared on the right, a break between the two spans of the arching bridge. He strode in through the opening, promising Kynthcat they'd continue across the bridge's second span to the Southern Provinces – the former Seelie lands – to explore, another day.

As expected, he found two guards both tall, blonde and muscled. Kynthcat bristled. *'We can take them.'*

Emryn sighed. *'We've no need to – we're honoured guests, remember?'*

A thickset, blue-eyed Fae-male blocked their way. "This is the Duchy of Garadenya, a private estate. Please state your purpose." A second, slimmer Fae-male stood at his shoulder, his green eyes wary, sword at the ready. Both wore grey pants, black boots and belted dark green tunics with a 'G' rune on the left breast, their Lepidopter-fae wings tightly furled.

"Good afternoon." Emryn nodded. "I'm expected – Lord Emryn Phengaris, on an extended visit to the Duke and Duchesse of Garadenya. Here's my writ, signed and sealed by both Queens."

After inspecting his paperwork, the heavyset, blue-eyed guard relaxed. "Welcome, my lord. Your baggage has already been delivered. Permit me to escort you to the castle. I'm Naseem."

"Thank you." Emryn smiled. "I'd appreciate it."

"A moment, my lord." Naseem turned to his comrade. "Jarith, I'll escort Lord Phengaris to the keep. Won't be long."

"Aye, captain. Welcome Lord Phengaris." Jarith nodded, sheathing his sword at his hip. "I'll just roust Vingle from his break. He can assist me till you return."

He kept up with the brisk pace set by Naseem as they traversed the tree-lined driveway but slowed as they rounded a bend and the Garadenya fortress came into view. It was impressive.

Built of cream stone, the massive square keep boasted four large, crenelated corner turrets and two smaller ones facing the extensive, cobbled forecourt. The cobblestoned area was surrounded by a variety of lawns and gardens stretching back to the island's forest. The driveway ended where the cobblestones began, so travellers were forced to cross the open forecourt to reach the keep's entry.

Emryn nodded; he recognised a good security measure when he saw one. Centred in the front facing wall, and bracketed by the pair of smaller towers, two arched metal gates waited, one containing a smaller door, which stood ajar. Another pair of guards waited there. One stood inside the keep, backing up the one framed in the opening.

Naseem saluted the first guard and nodded at the second. "Evening Captain Britha, Cyrano. I have with me Lord Emryn Phengaris. He's the apprentice staying for the next three-and-a-bit moons."

"Thank you Naseem." Captain Britha's chestnut hair was multi-braided and beaded then gathered in a loose band at the nape of her neck. Her sleeveless brown jerkin, again marked with the 'G' rune, swept down over black pants and tucked into black boots. Her waist was cinched by a belt from which a few pouches of various sizes hung. She held a spear, not quite relaxed, but neither was it aggressive. Cyrano, dressed similarly, stood rear guard, his longbow holding a loosely nocked arrow. Britha accorded Emryn a short bow then stood aside, gesturing for him to enter. As Emryn watched, the bowman relaxed and eased aside to make room for them.

"Welcome Lord Phengaris. Please come with me. Naseem, please wait here with Cyrano until I return." Naseem saluted and assumed his temporary position.

Emryn walked through the gates. "My thanks, Captain." She turned to lead him through the archway separating the walls of the barbican, a depth of about fifty paces, before they stepped into the courtyard of the outer bailey. As they walked, Captain Britha explained the layout.

"The curtain walls at the front and sides of this courtyard contain rooms for guards and other workers, plus stables for horses." She pointed ahead to the large central tower they were strolling towards. "That is the donjon, the heart of the keep." It was in a wall of buildings on the far side of the outer bailey, directly in line with the main gate. "It houses the great hall and banquet chamber which was the scene for Queen Maerovana's famous birthday feast over a year ago."

Emryn hadn't attended the ball, but senior members of his clan had and they'd described it often and well at full moon gatherings, so he was certain he'd find it familiar. He eyed the Fae-folk working in, and crossing, the Garadenya bailey this way and that.

"The place is a hive of activity."

"Always plenty to do and it's approaching dinner bell time – when the bell sounds, everyone has ten minutes to reach the dining room before the food does."

He looked around. "Are the kitchens and dining hall here too?"

Britha nodded. "The dining hall is in the wall stretching to the right of the donjon, along with storage chambers and the entrance to the dungeons. There's an archway at the end of the storage chambers which takes you through to the inner bailey, a square courtyard with a well. Around the inner bailey are the kitchens and the blacksmith's forge, plus some other work areas."

"And the building stretching to the left from the donjon?"

"The picture gallery, the library, the offices. They front the remaining quarter of the keep, given over to private and guest quarters plus the smaller garden courtyard I mentioned earlier." She pointed as she explained. "Their Graces said they'd await you in the library."

They mounted the steps to the donjon door which opened just before they reached it, revealing a Fae-male who waved them inside.

Captain Britha smiled. "Good evening, Minksalt. May I introduce Lord Emryn Phengaris, our guest for the next three moons? Lord Phengaris, this is our major-domo, Minksalt."

"Greetings Lord Phengaris, welcome to Garadenya." Minksalt bowed. "Thank you Captain Britha."

She turned to Emryn. "I bid you good evening, Lord Phengaris. Minksalt will escort you from here."

Emryn nodded. "My thanks, Captain. I'm sure we'll cross paths again during my stay." She acknowledged him with a smile as she retreated down the steps and strode away. Turning, Emryn met the eyes of the major-domo. "A pleasure to meet you, Minksalt."

"The pleasure is mine, my lord." Minksalt bowed again. "Would you care to freshen up before you meet our Duke and Duchesse? There is a guest refresh-room nearby."

Emryn knew when to take a hint. "Absolutely." He followed Minksalt through the large, stone foyer, noting the tapestries he'd like to inspect better at another time, and into the great hall. To one side of the entrance was a side corridor.

"Through there, my lord. I shall wait for you here."

"Thank you." At the end of the small corridor, Emryn pushed through a doorway into the refresh room. He used the facilities, washed, straightened and brushed down his clothing, checked the state of his hair – still neatly tied in its queue – then returned to where the major-domo waited. "Would you have my pack conveyed to my room please, Minksalt?"

"Certainly, my lord. I'll have it done as soon as I show you to the library." He accepted Emryn's small bag, then led him back to the foyer and into the right-hand passage way. He opened the second door and gestured for Emryn to enter. "Your Graces, Lord Emryn Phengaris has arrived. Lord Emryn, their graces, the Duke and Duchesse of Garadenya."

Moving forward, Emryn bowed, then straightened to inspect his hosts. He was not expecting to see the grey-eyed Fae-male with the shock of crimson, black and silver hair who stepped forward to clasp forearms. "Dario?"

"Great to see you, Emryn." The Fae-male grinned. "Didn't you know whose home you were coming to?"

"No, I hadn't made the connection between Lord Dario Eribifax and the Duke of Garadenya." Emryn shook his head, grinning. "When the special invitation from the Queens came to the clan, requesting a beta changeling to take part in the exchange program, we had no idea who was going, or where. The Sand Seers consulted, selected me, and handed over the second message advising the destination, your title and the arrival day, but, that the Duke of Garadenya was you?" His nose wrinkled. "I'd no idea; I was too busy resenting my selection to even think about it."

Dario frowned. "Are you saying you don't really want to be here?"

"Time sands no! And that goes double now I know I'm staying with you." Emryn shook his head. "It's just that my father isn't happy that I'm content being a beta in our clan and he wants to 'upskill' me, then mate me into another clan with a view to becoming a future alpha. I enjoy working with and helping others, but I don't wish to lead. I never have; nor do I wish to have my mating choices dictated by my father. Plus, I confess to some annoyance at being forced to leave home; not all outsiders are comfortable with shapeshifters, but as I said, now I see who my host is, the situation is far more palatable."

Nodding, Dario clapped a companionable hand on Emryn's shoulder. "The time away will give you a chance to clear your head and consider how to deal with your father when you go back. New skills never go astray – the things you'll learn in this program will be just as useful for a beta as an alpha. This apprenticeship will stand you in good stead regardless of where your path takes you."

Emryn tilted his head. "When you put it like that, I can see value in my presence. I appreciate your counsel – thank you." Emryn's eyes strayed over Dario's shoulder to where a gorgeous lady, with green-violet eyes and hair a combination of black and purple, watched them, smiling. "May I have an introduction to your lovely lady?"

Dario swung around. "Emryn Phengaris, meet my darling mate, Zhulija Aphiski Eribifax. Zhu, this is my friend, Emryn Phengaris of the Destrion Kynthcat Changeling Clan."

The duchesse stepped to meet him, ruby mouth smiling, eyes a-sparkle. "Greetings, friend of my mate." She held a hand out.

He bowed over her knuckles. "Duchesse Zhulija, the pleasure is definitely mine."

She laughed. "Just call me Zhu. I'm more comfortable with that. We're so pleased you could come and stay with us, Emryn, and as for the shape shifting? Well, that's no problem, either."

"It's not?"

"Of course not." She waggled her eyebrows. "You must know Dario catches fire when he wants to and I can be rather unusual too. Plus my brother is a shapeshifter, so we've no issues with your alter ego."

Emryn stared. "Your brother is a shapeshifter? Doesn't that mean you and all of your family, are?"

"No."

"Whisky-nectar?" Dario held out a glass. "It's all about genetics. In most of the family it's watered down. My bro-in-law, Mak, is a throwback – the only one who can change fully. So far, anyway."

Accepting the glass, Emryn took a sip. His eyes flowed between Dario and Zhu. "That's unusual. What animal?"

"Dracon."

In the process of taking another mouthful, Emryn spluttered. "What?" His hosts laughed so much they had to hold each other up.

3

LYSSICA

The melting snow had become muddy slush, but Lyssica was beyond caring; she needed fresh air and a break from paperwork. Sitting on one of two wooden benches in the mudroom, she kicked off her slippers, replaced them with snow-boots, then nestled into her heavy weather cloak waiting impatiently on a nearby hook. Once outside, the crisp chill of the air prickled her face with invigorating freshness.

Picking her way along the path leading to the stables, she waved to Vinny; judging by his armful of dried growth, the youngster was on fresh straw duty. He grinned and nodded, unable to do more with the handicap of his load, but the happy grin he shared lightened her dull mood.

The chaos of the new arrivals – with two of them unexpected and unwanted, by her – had stolen her ability to concentrate. Lyssica sighed and kicked at a flurry of leaves on the track to the water gardens. Yesterday had been filled with the flurry of her sisters' excited departures and now, of her siblings, only Treymeron was still home. She wasn't surprised he'd said no to an exchange this year, although he'd tentatively agreed to take part next year.

Never disappointed by nature's display, the shallow ponds

bedecked with lily pads soothed Lyssica with various colours of blooming lilies. Pleased the plants were looking healthy despite the early fall of snow, she moved slowly along the jade bridge, basking in the weak sunlight even as she checked the plants for the grime-rose's frozen blue blight. Finding nothing of worry in any of the separate ponds, Lyssica continued to traverse the series of ornate bridges linking the gravel paths, until she reached the cottage garden. In front of her rambling roses spread over wide pergolas, framing beds of hollyhock, foxglove, catmint, delphinium, phlox, peonies, cosmos, and other varieties.

Eventually, the sprawling gardens gave way to hedged lawns; beyond the hedges were the trees dividing the gardens from the gravel driveway. Lyssica paused as the sound of yet another carriage arriving reinforced her decision to avoid the drive. Slipping between the trees to the open area between, she spread her wings and flitted to the blue-stone gatehouse.

"On your afternoon trip to the forest, Lady Lyssica?" A smiling Fae-woman rose from her seat.

"Good afternoon, Bardia." She flashed the guard a return smile. "Yes I am – could you make a note in the day's records?"

"Sure thing, my Lady. Too bad you'll miss tea with the Countess of Cossidae." Her voice full of sympathy, Bardia reached for a quill. "Take care."

"So that's who just arrived. You're right, I'll be sorry to have missed her." Lyssica waved from the doorway, holding in her shudder until she was out of Bardia's sight. She was so not in the right frame of mind for the gossiping Countess. The postern gate was a smaller side exit, separated from the main driveway gates by two body lengths and a line of shrubbery, which allowed Lyssica to slip out unseen by their visitor or anyone greeting her. Carefully re-latching it, she crossed the road to weave a path between the small plants and bushes bordering the forest.

Walking quickly towards the tree line, she inhaled deeply of the cold, fresh air. Around her large trunks stood straight and tall while, above her head, a plethora of partly bare tree limbs reached for the sky. Her booted feet tramped the leaf strewn ground, damp after the snow, but the mulched thickness of many years prevented the forest floor descending into mud. Her swinging hand touched several limp looking bushes and she paused to direct little bursts of well-being into them. As she progressed, she noticed another shrub with the faint blue glow she'd seen in the garden the previous day. Frowning, she stopped to dowse it with power until the plant regained a healthy appearance, before walking slowly on. The blight she'd seen in the garden yesterday was also in the forest – where had it come from? She'd have to investigate further.

As a familiar clearing came into view, Lyssica sighed and flung her cloak behind her shoulders. Her breath steamed hotly in the frigid air as she inspected Ostara's Circle. Different sized stones sprinkled through it in a roughly elliptic layout, some low enough to sit on, others waist, chest and shoulder high.

When Maman had first brought her and her siblings here, many of the stones had been taller than her. She'd jumped, played and danced between and around them, intensely fascinated, unwilling to leave when her Maman had said it was time. The impression left by the glade had lured her back as soon as she could manage it. Sneaking away a few days later, she'd made her way unerringly back to the stone-filled clearing to explore. Inexplicable joy had filled her as she'd sung and danced.

Surprised when another voice had joined her song, Lyssica discovered a fairy on the topmost stone, singing and dancing along with her. Enchanted, Lyssica had drawn closer to the fairy, even as she continued singing her favourite song about sunshine dawning on a new morning of fresh opportunities.

"It's a beautiful day…" When the song finished, she'd been too awestruck to start another. The gauzy-winged little creature had tilted her head, meeting her gaze fearlessly.

"Hello." Lyssica had whispered, trying not to frighten the fairy. "You shine, just like my song. I'm Lyssica, what's your name?"

The fairy smiled. "Nice to meet you Lyssica. You may call me Ostara. I'm a Spring Fairy."

"Ooh, I love Spring! The flowers are so pretty and the new little animals are adorable. I could cuddle them forever!"

"Hmm. I've got lots of places to look after as the Spring Fairy and I'm tiny – it's hard to reach them all in time for Spring's beginning. I think I need helpers. Do you know where I might find some?"

"Ooh, yes!" Lyssica clapped her hands. "I know I'm little, but I can help you, Ostara Spring Fairy. Please, would you choose me?"

"You'd like to be a handmaiden of the Spring Fairy, Lyssica?" The little creature watched her with huge, serious, sky-blue eyes. "It's a large, forever kind of job – are you sure you want this?"

"Oh yes! I really do! I'll be a wonderful helper. You'll see how good I am when you come back – if you tell me what to do at the start. I'm a very good learner and it'll make me super happy, Ostara. It really will."

"The fairy pursed her lips. "I'm an Unseelie fairy and your family is Seelie – don't you think that's important?"

Little Lyssica's brows knitted. "Why? Maman told me there's been changes happening for years and years, something called you-ni-tee, I think. It means we're all one people." Her lip quivered. "Unless it matters to you, Ostara fairy?"

The gauzy, green and gold beauty laughed softly. "Goddess, no. And if it doesn't bother you, we're fine. Come closer, Lyssica." The Spring Fairy beckoned and Lyssica eased right up to the large rock, thrilling as the delightful being put a hand on her head. "I accept your pledge of service and hereby anoint you as a Handmaiden of Ostara." A tingle flowed through her from the top of her head to the tips of her toes, leaving her giddy with joy.

"Thank you." She beamed at Ostara. "I won't let you down."

"Here, Lyssica." Ostara held out a few tiny berries. "Share these berries with me to seal our bargain."

Those tiny fruits had numbered amongst the most delicious things she'd ever eaten ...

With the memory of the bonding uppermost in her mind, Lyssica executed a couple of simple dance steps, moved into a pirouette as she entered the clearing, then waltzed from one stone to the next until she'd made the full circuit. Even though she'd been too young to understand the full truth of the meeting back then, she certainly knew now.

Ostara, the Spring Fairy, was actually the Unseelie Goddess of Spring, Dawn and Fertility. She was the deity whom the festival of Ostara was centred around – the Unseelie form of the Seelie Goddess Olwen – and Lyssica had become her sacred handmaiden. The magical berries she'd eaten had enhanced her natural empathy into powerful regenerative skills. With it she could share her gift with any animal or plant, enhance their wellbeing or bring about fertile growth. Despite not truly knowing what she was signing up for, Lyssica had never regretted her choice.

As promised, Ostara returned regularly to teach, showing Lyssica, as her Handmaiden, new aspects of her power and position. She arrived every year with armfuls of blossoms and a basket of painted egg-shaped stones. When she flung the blossoms, they'd somehow take root in the ground and the randomly distributed painted stones were filled with warmth and good luck for the recipients.

It didn't matter what time of year it was to Lyssica, as a Hand-maiden of Ostara she'd promised to look after the welfare of animals and plants and that's what she did. The power wasn't something she could turn on and off, nor did she want to – it was a part of her and she protected the flora and fauna no matter the season. To her it wasn't a job; it was something she loved. It was an additional reason why she'd been eager to help in the running of the Papillion Estate – in her mind, the two positions complemented each other perfectly.

Pausing in her dance, Lyssica closed her eyes, raised her face to the sky, and took several enlivening breaths. The fresh air filled her lungs and each time she breathed out, she forced the stale greyness of her upsetting morning out as well.

Opening her eyes on the Goddess Circle, she felt familiar joy reclaim her and spun into a second round of dancing to salute Ostara. From a nearby tree warbled a familiar chorus. Glancing up, Lyssica identified two blush-cheeked chirpers, their pale green plumage framing their peach-coloured faces. A family of wood-bunnies crept out from between the bushes; the parents keeping a strict eye on the three youngsters as they swayed and jumped in time with her dancing.

Further around the clearing, a mother duskit brought out her four kits. Lyssica loved the purple, navy and white creatures with their huge ears, large eyes and bushy tails, but she continued on to complete her circle. Afterwards, moving to sit on one of the middle stones that was a good height for her, Lyssica hummed and waited.

One by one, from different points around the glade, a parade of animals cleared the undergrowth. They approached, chirping, mewing, squeaking or chittering, purring, huffing and whistling, but all wanting a touch from the fingers of Ostara's Handmaiden. For Lyssica, this never got old. She didn't care what sort of animal they were, if they came to her for a blessing, she gave it and, no matter the creature, there'd never been any trouble. Whether predator or prey, the animals seemed to know a visit here was sacrosanct, just as she was.

On other days, she'd wander the forest, or around the estate, touching the trees, plants and flowers, sharing Ostara's magical beneficence as her instincts demanded.

The weak afternoon sun was much lower in the sky when the line of animals dwindled. Lyssica rose and stretched, knowing it was time to return to the estate, clean up for dinner and re-don her heir's mantle. There was a welcome dinner to attend and if she wasn't exactly looking forward to it, at least she no longer hated the idea of having to pretend nothing was wrong to her parents and their six guests. No, seven. Zhu and Dario had taken one program apprentice and they were also coming to dinner. She smiled. Her home still contained Trey; Zhu and her mate, Dario, weren't far away. Her siblings, like her duties to Ostara, always gave her strength and courage.

Perhaps the winter wouldn't be as bad as she thought.

~

WHEN LYSSICA ENTERED the salon where the pre-dinner gathering was scheduled, she was informed all the new arrivals were already in attendance. Thankful for the tradition that saw her enter and be introduced with her parents and brother, she linked her arm with Treymeron's and followed the Duke and Duchesse into the room as Entanglit announced them to the room's occupants.

"This is everything I hate." Trey's voice was the barest mutter. She threw him an encouraging smile just as her father turned to place an arm around her shoulders.

"Why don't you do the honours, Lyssica?" Moving to her other side, Duchesse Azura dropped a kiss on her cheek. Treymeron rolled his eyes as he slid past her in the direction of Zhulija and Dario.

Summoning a smile, Lyssica clapped her hands lightly to gain everyone's attention. "Good evening all. I'm Heir-Lady Lyssica Aphiski. On behalf of my parents, the Duchesse Azura and Duke Yanvian and my brother Lord Treymeron, I welcome you all to the Papillion Duchy. We all wish you a pleasant stay and we plan for your apprenticeship to be successful. If you have any questions, please don't hesitate to ask. If there's anything we don't know, we'll either find out, or direct you to the correct party to assist you with your enquiry. Please feel free to approach us and introduce yourself. Entanglit, our major-domo will announce dinner shortly. Until then, feel free to mingle. Thank you."

The duke's arm tightened briefly around her before his arm fell away. "Well done." His smile was warm. "I couldn't have said anything better, Lyssica. Let's wander and give the new folk the opportunity to approach us." He offered his arm to the Duchesse and when she accepted it, escorted her deeper into the room.

A compliment from her father? Lyssica stared after him in surprise, then shook her head and moved to greet her sister who stood smiling in welcome. Beside Zhulija, Dario and Treymeron chatted with a tall Fae-male who had his back to her. All Lyssica could see was a head of rich brown hair neatly tied in a queue, before Zhulija drew her into a hug and they kissed each other's cheeks.

"Wow Lyss, that was great. Now come and meet our guest – he's an old friend of Dario."

"Of course." Lyssica nodded. "Zhu, you're looking lovely. That lavender shade really suits you."

"Thanks." Zhulija smiled again and tapped her mate's arm. "Introduction time, Dario."

Breaking off his conversation with Treymeron and the unknown, but solid-looking, Fae-male, Dario tugged Zhulija snugly under his arm and grinned at Lyssica. "Good evening Lyss. I thought your welcome was an excellent start to the programme. Allow me to introduce our Tri-moon apprentice, Kynth-lord Emryn Phengaris." He gestured to his companion.

Twisting to face the newcomer, there was a sharp *'snap' as* her shoe gave out from under her. Lurching forward, dignity at minus fifteen, she closed her eyes, expecting to face plant onto the hard floor. Instead, she slammed into a firm, unmoving body; solid arms curved supportively around her and brought her to an immediate halt. Flesh instead of stone – a definite improvement, but, oh my. She swallowed. Drew in a quivering breath. And found her olfactory senses inundated with a delightfully musky scent, redolent of the forest after rain had fallen. She re-opened her eyes.

To meet the molten silver gaze of Lord Emryn Phengaris. His glorious high cheekbones framed a blade of a nose, and swept down to firm, sensuous lips over a square chin. Melt in the mouth bronze skin was adorned by dreamy sable brown hair – and then came muscles. She could feel the taut musculature of his body curving, against her, around her – the muscles went for days. And nights. No wonder she'd stopped so suddenly. He was a rock-solid work of art. She swallowed again, dignity forgotten. Would anyone notice if she drooled? Or even, perhaps took a little taste?

4

EMRYN

Acting on instinct, Emryn braced his legs and tautened his body as Lady Lyssica cannoned into him. Closing his arms around her was equally instinctive as the breath 'oofed' out of her. Lifting her high against his chest, he cushioned her while she gasped and struggled for breath. He stared into her face, willing her to open her eyes. And then she did, the limpid aquamarine pools gazing dazedly. She blinked and her stare sharpened. He froze.

Paws spread wide, Kynthcat thudded to the front of his mind.

'Oh, yes! This one.'

Emryn's mind blanked. Intent on a conversation with Dario, he'd paid little attention to the lady while she was speaking. After all, a welcome was a welcome; they didn't change much and he wasn't staying at Papillion, so it was mostly irrelevant. But now the lady and he were up close and personal and … Lady Lyssica Aphiski's thickly lashed, blue-green eyes captivated him. Gulping, he mapped broad, high cheekbones flanking a pert nose, the whole softened by long wavy hair in swallowtail butterfly colours of ebony, emerald, cobalt, cream and lavender. Below that cute little nose, corners of enticing lips lifted in a weak, but bewitching, smile.

"Good evening Lord Emryn. A pleasure to meet you. I apologise for throwing myself at you."

Emryn's tongue was stuck to the roof of his mouth as if mired in caramel fudge. At last, he got his voice to work. "I think your shoe had a breakdown."

Another uncertain smile from dewy peach lips tantalised him. "Something certainly went inverted mushroom on me."

"Lyssica!" Duchesse Zhulija patted the goddess in his arms. "Are you alright? Does anything hurt? I heard a snapping noise." The hands moved down. "Oh, the heel of your shoe has broken off. I'll just remove both of them so you can stand."

Lyssica continued to meet Emryn's gaze, her breath came and went in faint, choppy pants; the aroma of freshly baked cookies tantalised him.

Kynthcat purred. *'Yum.'* Emryn had no argument.

Zhulija straightened with a shoe in each hand. "There you go, Lyss. Emryn? Can you lower her slowly, just in case of an ankle sprain or something?"

Gaze still locked with hers, Emryn gently let the lady down onto her feet. A slight wince, but Zhulija and Dario now supported her on each side.

"You've sprained an ankle!" Zhulija fussed.

"No, no, I don't ... The floor is cold." She blinked; the snapping of their visual connection drew a slight shudder from Emryn. *'Where'd that come from?'* His attention was riveted on Lyssica.

Still supported by Zhulija and Dario, Lyssica glanced his way again and her mouth curved up. Emryn mastered his scrambling brain enough to smile, trying not to appear obvious as he catalogued more of her.

She stole his breath – ravishingly wrapped in a long-sleeved, ebony dress, the inviting neckline dipping to delicious cleavage between plump breasts. He wanted to pounce; he yearned to lick; he ached to nip and nibble. Waves of hot and cold swept over him – what was this?

A brush of fur as Kynthcat prowled. Emryn coughed to swallow the faint growl bubbling up his throat; Kynthcat wanted to rub up against her. By fur and claw! She was slaying both halves of him, and if he didn't speak, she'd think him more of a dolt than he already appeared. "Are you certain you're okay?" A suppressed growl imbued his words with a guttural timbre.

She blinked. "I ... I think so."

Dario chuckled. "I was about to say: 'Emryn, meet Lady Lyssica Aphiski' but I think that's redundant."

A new voice intruded on their group. "Lady Lyssica. I trust you're unharmed after that spectacular lunge. A little clumsy of you, what?" His goddess stiffened. He glanced up to see one of the apprentice Fae-males approaching. "Allow me to introduce myself. Lord Perris Momphiday at your service."

Emryn bristled; Kynthcat's claws pricked, wanting to slash the rude upstart.

Lyssica nodded stiffly. "Greetings, Lord Perris." The unpleasant blue-eyed, blonde was followed by a Fae-lady and another four Fae-males.

A very tall, thin, male with ash-blonde hair tied at his nape bowed. "Greetings Lords and Ladies. I'm Tanjil Blastobarm and with me is Lady Kerrigold Helioden. Lady Lyssica, I sincerely hope you've sustained no serious harm."

"Welcome Lady Kerrigold, Lord Tanjil." Emryn catalogued the warm smile Lyssica bestowed on the pair. He memorised the way the smile lit her face; it would be even lovelier if it reached her eyes.

Kynthcat huffed. *'Something making our lady uncomfortable.'*

Lady Kerrigold clasped one of Lyssica's hands in hers. "Do you need to sit down, Lady Lyssica? That was almost a disaster if not for the quick thinking of Lord Emryn."

Lyssica's smile trembled. "Perhaps ..."

A snarky male voice drowned Lyssica out:

"She tripped across the ballroom floor

Her trip was quite fantastic

She heard a pop

But could not stop

She's wonderfully enthusiastic!"

The bad poetry-spouting Fae-male spread his arms, looking around and bowing as if expecting applause before he turned back to her. "Hello Lyssica."

Emryn disliked the russet-haired, brown-eyed smirker on sight, but he gave Lyssica credit for maintaining a smile, even if it was strained and flat. Who was this tactless swine?

"Venaday Tortrician! It's been a long time." Lyssica glanced from Lord Tortrician to the last two apprentices without extending him a welcome. Emryn bit his lip against a chuckle.

Kynthcat huffed again. *She no like him.* He sprawled with his head on his paws. *This very entertaining.*

"Melkaz Eriocraan and Roland Arrelgyre! How good of you both to join us." She clasped her hands and nodded. Emryn's superior olfactory sense enabled him to identify her polite insincerity; she wasn't keen on the second of the two Fae-males either. But she remained professional.

"Lady Kerrigold, Fae-lords, meet the Duke and Duchesse of Garadenya, namely my sister Zhulija and her true-mate Dario Eribifax, plus their apprentice, Lord Emryn Phengaris."

Duchesse Azura bustled up. "Oh dear, and to think I was in the dining room when you needed my help." She squeezed Lyssica's arm. "Come Lyssica, let's inspect that ankle and replace your footwear before dinner." Her gaze swept over the gathering. "I'm certain you all have plenty to discuss while Zhulija and I attend to Lyssica's comfort."

Flashing another smile, Lyssica allowed herself to be assisted from the room.

Go too! Kynthcat paced inside him.

No. Emryn coughed into his hand, covering his growl of refusal. "How interesting." He joined the small talk, commenting on someone's trip details and ignored Kynthcat's subvocal grumbling.

Both he and Kynthcat jolted in recognition the moment the absent trio of Aphiski ladies returned to the room, Lyssica limping slightly.

She in pain.

'*Not our problem.*' But Emryn sagged with relief as much as she did when the doors to the dining room opened to reveal Entanglit.

"Dinner is served, Ladies and Lords."

~

EMRYN WAS interested to see a round dining table, rather than the usual long rectangle.

Standing in the doorway, Duke Yanvian cleared his throat. "We hope everyone will forgive the informality, but as most of us will be eating together daily for the next few moons, we thought we'd start as we mean to continue. Please find your place and know that it will remain the same for the duration of your visit." Moving forward, the duke held a chair for his consort, then seated himself beside her.

Emryn took note of the seating arrangements – Duke Yanvian and Duchesse Azura were in ladder-backed, carver-style dining chairs, while everyone else was spread equidistant around the table in matching armless chairs. Lyssica sat to her father's right with Lord Perris next to her, followed by Lady Kerrigold, Lord Treymeron, Lord Roland, himself, Zhulija, Dario, Lord Venaday, Lord Melkaz and Lord Tanjil, then back to Duchesse Azura.

The round table meant Emryn could see his table companions easily, only needing to turn his head for those either side. As was expected in polite circles, he alternated between chatting with Zhulija and Lord Roland, despite the difficulty of keeping his gaze from Lyssica. If she caught him, he smiled, but otherwise he glanced away, not wanting to be caught staring. Even though he was. An unsettled Kynthcat paced within.

He savoured cream of watercress soup, which turned out to be the first of four courses. The soup was followed by a main of herb and vegetable salad with fish, a dessert of honey cheesecake and a final remove of lavender shortbread with candied fruits. It was delicious, even if the 'meat' was fish. Knowing most of the Fae were vegetarians, Emryn resigned himself to hunting to appease Kynthcat for the duration of their visit.

Zhulija turned his way. "Everything satisfactory?"

"Yes, thank you. A lovely meal." He paused. "Did I see Dario swap your name card with his, earlier?"

She chuckled. "Yes, I don't think he wanted me sitting next to Lord Venaday."

Emryn's mouth twitched. "I'm certain you can hold your own in most situations, Zhu."

Her eyes twinkled. "More than most, but I'm humouring him. It has its rewards."

He laughed as a low-voiced comment from Dario claimed Zhulija's attention. He picked up his glass of rosehip wine just as Lord Roland cleared his throat. "Have far to come, Lord Emryn?"

"Yes." Emryn played with the stem of his glass. "I'm glad last seven-day's snow melted before we all made the trip."

Roland swallowed some shortbread. "Absolutely. At least we'll have a comfortable winter." He flicked Emryn a look. "Although, Garadenya is an old stone fortress, so you mightn't be as warm."

"I've no complaints." Emryn met his gaze. "You've been there?"

"Yes." Roland fingered a crumb. "For Queen Maerovana's birthday ball last year when Duke Dario and Duchesse Zhulija completed their true-mating. You weren't in attendance?"

Emryn shook his head. "A representative of my clan was invited, of course, but it wasn't me, unfortunately. It would've been fun."

Roland snorted. "Some of it was fun, but we were forced to rub shoulders with all sorts of lowlife Unseelie creatures. Lowered the tone somewhat."

"Is that so?" Emryn knew there were Lepidopter-fae who consid-ered themselves the top of the Fae food chain. Looked like Lord Roland Arrelgyre was one of them. "Was there trouble?"

"Oh, it wasn't that." Roland shrugged. "Their Majesty's guards kept everyone in line – it's just that the creatures were *there*, mingling with those of us more well-bred."

Emryn cocked his head. "More well-bred? How do you define that? By district?"

"District?" Roland popped another piece of shortbread into his mouth, chewed and swallowed as he considered Emryn through narrowed eyes. "Are you talking Seelie or Unseelie? North or South of the Rubiconia River? Summer or Winter Court?"

"No. Are you?"

Roland curled his lip. "Of course not. I was referring to Fae-folk who turn into unnatural beings."

"Are not all Fae-folk unnatural beings?"

"You fail to understand, Lord Emryn." Roland glared. "We Lepidopter-fae are natural beings who remain ourselves no matter what. We wield magic. The unnatural Fae are those who become something other. They don't wield magic. They *are* magic."

"Ah, you refer to shape-changing Fae." Emryn's voice was a growl and he coughed to conceal the sound. "Now I understand."

Entanglit appeared at their shoulders. "Can I offer you more wine, my lords?"

Emryn shook his head. "Thank you, but could I have water instead, Entanglit?"

"Certainly, your lordship. I'll bring that momentarily." He refilled the wine glass Roland peremptorily tapped, before backing away.

"I've been trying to classify your colouring." Roland's head tilted. "Most of us sport our Lepidopter colours in our hair and wings. My family is from the Argyresthia moth, which birth in shades of bronze and cream, but your hair is simply brown and I haven't seen any wings. What type of Lepidopter do the Phengaris Clan hark back to, Lord Emryn? Are you an unusual type who can conceal their wings beneath clothing?" Roland sipped from his refreshed wine glass, his eyes sharply focused on Emryn.

"We don't have a connection to any Lepidopter Clan and you haven't seen any wings because there aren't any." Emryn looked Lord Roland Arrelgyre full in the face. "The Phengaris Clan are shapeshifters – we're some of those 'unnatural Fae' you referred to."

A tide of red swept up Roland's face. Combined with his upraised eyebrows, and the peaked quiff of his hair, Emryn was reminded of a startled beetroot.

"Your water, Lord Emryn." Entanglit returned to place a crystal glass beside Emryn's hand.

"Thank you, Entanglit." Emryn grasped the glass and raised it to his lips.

Roland's mouth opened, then closed again. His words, when they came, sounded strangled. "You – you're joking, aren't you?"

"No, I'm completely serious."

Lord Roland eased back in his chair, watching Emryn as if he were a bug.

"You'd better have a bath later, Roland." Emryn gestured between them. "Wouldn't want you to harbour any ill-bred, unnatural contaminants, would we?"

Roland's eyes narrowed. "How did a creature like you come to be in this exchange program? Are the Duke and Duchesse of Garadenya aware of this?"

"Of course, they are." Emryn shrugged. "I was invited, like everyone else."

Kynthcat paced in a swirl of indignation. *We eat this oaf!*

You know we can't. Anyway, he'd probably taste disgusting.

"You must have stolen the invitation! I can't believe the Queens would have approved—"

Emryn yawned. "But they did, Roland, they did."

"This is an outrage!" Although, their interaction had already become a focus to those nearby, Roland's shout drew everyone's attention.

Duchesse Azura's eyebrows elevated. "May I ask what the problem is, Lord Roland?"

"This … this … creature!" Roland pointed at Emryn, who calmly drank some water. "He's here under false pretences. He's not Lepidopter Fae, he's a low-bred shape-changer!"

"I beg your pardon." Emryn looked down his nose at Roland. "But you're quite wrong. My family has an excellent pedigree." On the other side of Roland, Treymeron Aphiski choked, then coughed into his hand.

Duke Yanvian looked to his son-in-law. "Dario? Lord Emryn is your guest – what say you?"

Dario sighed. "Lord Emryn has a legitimate invitation. He is a friend I have known for years and we have no issue with his abilities."

"No issue?" Roland trembled with anger. "How can you possibly welcome a shape-changer?"

"Lord Roland." Duchesse Azura's voice was cold. "Before you say one more word, I should like to advise you that your bigotry is unwelcome here."

Roland gaped, then recovered. "But you are Lepidopter-fae!"

"So we are." Duchesse Azura nodded. "A Lepidopter-fae family who also has shape-shifters in the bloodlines – as do many of the other Lepidopter-fae families and clans."

"You must be mistaken, Duchesse!" Roland shook his head. "Why would anyone breed with such creatures?"

Duke Yanvian rose swiftly. "Lord Roland! My mate warned you that bigotry is undesired, yet you persist. I regret to inform you that you've outstayed your invite. You may sleep here tonight, but in the morning you will leave."

Roland blanched. "You're throwing me out?"

"I am." The Duke of Papillion's stare was icy. "You'll also justify yourself to both Queen Dianathke and Queen Maerovana."

Red with rage, Lord Roland Arrelgyre flung the contents of his wineglass at Emryn. Beside Emryn, Zhulija hissed and flung up a hand – the liquid halted in mid-air, each droplet a perfect, light-reflecting ruby. Fisting her hand, she released her fingers in a forceful flicking motion. The wine reversed course to splatter Roland in the face, before dripping from his chin onto his clothes.

"You ... you ..."

"Shut up and leave." Zhulija made another gesture, and to the astonishment of all the guests, a cloud of plates, glasses, cutlery and scraps of food rose to hover around her. "Go before you end up wearing all of this."

Eyes bugging, Roland fled.

Fur fluffed inside Emryn as Kynthcat chuffed: *'One down.'*

Emryn concealed a smile behind his crystal tumbler. *'And we didn't have to eat him after all. Bonus!'*

5

LYSSICA

After breakfast the following morning, the five apprentices joined Lyssica in the foyer for the proposed orientation tour of the estate. She cleared her throat. "If nobody objects, we'll dispense with titles and move to first names." She was pleased to see nods of agreement.

Kerrigold smiled. "All the lord and lady-ing does become a tangle."

"Indeed it does." Lyssica clasped her hands. "Alright, Maman showed you around the manor last evening and Papan will talk about duties with each of you after luncheon. This morning, we'll flit around the grounds to acquaint everyone with the lay of the land." She smiled. "Let's start from the forecourt."

Limping slightly, she preceded the group out through the main doors, waiting at the top of the steps for them to regroup.

"Good morning!" The call had her shading her eyes to check the driveway. She waved at Dario and Emryn walking briskly towards them, finding it no hardship to keep her eyes fixed on the very handsome shapeshifter accompanying her brother-in-law.

"Back so soon, gentlemen?"

Dario grinned. "Emryn and I were up at the first blush of dawn.

We've already been around the island and now have business with Yanvian – you touring the estate?"

Lyssica nodded. "We are."

Emryn cleared his throat. "How's your ankle, Lady Lyssica? Are you up to the activity, physically speaking?"

She laughed. "Not if we had to walk, so we'll be flying."

"Oh, of course." He shook his head. "Being wingless, flying isn't my first thought, but I'll be sorry to miss the event – Zhu has been talking about your beautiful gardens since I arrived." Emryn's pale eyes glowed. She had first thought them silver, but maybe they were a frosty pearl? "Perhaps I could join you all later, Lady Lyssica?"

"Please call me Lyssica." She smiled again. "We've all agreed to dispense with titles amongst ourselves. If you've no objection?"

"Not in the slightest."

"Fine." She adjusted her feet. "You're most welcome to join our estate tour at any point, Emryn. I look forward to it." She glanced at her group. "If you're ready, we'll be going." Spreading her wings, she lifted off and led her fluttering charges down the drive. "First stop: the gatehouse to get you all registered and acquainted with procedure for leaving the estate, should you wish."

Kerrigold fell into flight beside her. "Forgive my bluntness, Lyssica, but does it feel strange being the heir?"

"Yes and no." Lyssica gestured with one hand. "The heir's always been my brother, DeMaksim, so that's the 'yes' part."

"And the 'no' part?" Kerrigold side-swooped a tree to snag an autumn leaf.

"Estate management is something I find interesting. I love nurturing animals and plants, and I see this as similar, so stepping into the heir's shoes was excellent for me."

Kerrigold nodded. "So you're happy in the role." She pleated the leaf between slim fingers. "I'm a craft artist, so managing an estate wouldn't suit me at all. I don't have the least interest in it, but my family believes learning new skills will broaden my appeal as a consort match. We made a deal that I give the program a go in exchange for some personal bonuses."

"You should talk with Zhu more – she's the artist in our family."

"Yes." Kerrigold's eyes sparkled. "I admire her work immensely and I'd love to make my art into a business. I agreed to this placement above all those I was offered because of your sister's proximity. With three moons of time here, I'm hoping to meet her informally and obtain professional artistic advice."

"I'm certain that can be organised." Lyssica landed outside the gate house and reached for the door, but a male hand beat her to it.

"Allow me, Lyssica." Venaday Tortrician smirked at her as he folded his wings. Lyssica restrained her urge to kick him with great difficulty. She'd been hurt the evening before and he'd seen it as a chance to recite trite poetry? He hadn't changed at all. Digging her fingernails into her palms, she kept her voice cool.

"My thanks, Venaday. Very nice of you to hold the door open for everyone." His smirk sagged as she swept past, as regally as one could while limping, and was followed by Kerrigold.

"But..."

"Thanks Ven." Melkaz Eriocraan breezed by, closely shadowed by Tanjil and Perris, leaving a scowling Venaday to bring up the rear. Forcing herself to keep a straight face, Lyssica shepherded her party to the reception desk.

"Greetings Lozito, how are you?"

"Very well, thanks, Lady Lyssica." The snub-nosed guard tucked a loose lock of flaxen hair behind a pointy ear then flipped open the day book. "I take it these are our Tri-moon guests?"

"Yes." Lyssica rearranged a vase of wilting flowers, righting a petal here and stretching to smooth a calyx on the other side. "Could you record their information please? Make a note they have live-in guest rights for the duration of their stay." Turning to her charges, she waved to encompass the office.

"This is where you come if you're wanting to leave the estate. You sign out and then sign in upon your return." She smiled. "It sounds straight forward, but search parties don't wish to have their time wasted. This kind of detail is important in the running of a large estate, as some of you may already know, so don't forget." One by one, they came up, provided their data and moved outside to wait. Lyssica was last out. Satisfaction filled her as her final glance at the vase of flowers showed them looking fresh and perky.

As she passed, Perris caught her arm. "We need to speak privately, Lyssica."

Fighting not to shudder, she pulled her arm free. "I'm certain we'll have the chance at some point." Smiling tightly, she turned away. "But for now, we'll cut through these woods to the summer house. It used to be Zhu's studio before she moved to Garadenya Estate with her true-mate." She took to the air, her group following one at a time.

As they flitted along a path between large pine trees, Lyssica was glad to see Perris had fallen back to play a game of tag with Tanjil using a pine cone flinging it at each other around trees and branches. Although conducting a low-voiced conversation, Melkaz and Venaday kept an eye on the wildly played game, ducking or dodging several times, to avoid being hit.

Drawing up outside the outlying building, Lyssica gestured. "The summer house was designed by famous Fae-architect, Sir Feragamo Notodonkae." She hovered at the bottom of the stairs. "Note the sliding door and large glass window in the 'valiant' style. Anyone wish to look inside? No? Okay then, let's keep going." She struck off through the small forest, a band of which bordered the estate on three sides. "This way to the formal gardens. The first one we'll come to is—"

"Aargh!" Lord Tanjil Blastobarm's yell came from behind a large pine tree. "Aargh! Aargh! By the Goddess, aargh!" With each screech his voice got louder and louder. Kerrigold froze, while Lyssica, Melkaz and Venaday all zoomed around the tree to discover the cause of his yelling.

Kneeling in a mass of muddy pine needles, Tanjil pointed at the base of a large tree trunk, eyes round with horror. A pale-faced Perris hovered nearby, pine cone in one hand, his mouth hanging open. From the narrow opening in the hollow cavity of an ancient tree, a white hand protruded, palm up, fingers pointing skyward. The ground was torn up and pockmarked with drag marks leading towards the trunk's gaping maw.

"Enough, Tanjil!" Lyssica shook his shoulder, but his mouth was a rictus of fear from which another wild bellow issued. Melkaz stepped closer and slapped Tanjil across the face. His eyes bulged even more, before he crumpled, a harsh sob escaping him. Lyssica's mouth twisted; the Fae were a long-lived race so death was often simply a word rather than a reality.

Perris lowered the pine cone, hand shaking, face pale as he stared at Lyssica. "Who is it?"

She sighed. "I've never made a study of hands, Perris. I'll have to look."

"It's got to be someone from your estate." He swallowed. "And you're the only one here familiar with all of your people."

Perhaps so, but really! From a hand? She flew across the messy ground and approached the trunk's narrow hollow, twisting to hover alongside. The body was stuffed into the cavity at an awkward angle. One arm thrust out from the torso, resulting in the hand extending through the opening. Lyssica recognised what she could see of the clothing as the outfit worn by Roland Arrelgyre the previous night, but he was lying face down. Further, the head was covered by a hood, making it impossible for a clear identification and, hadn't Roland left early this morning?

"Well?" Venaday's voice was sharp with demand. "Is there someone attached to the hand?"

Kerrigold's face appeared from beyond her concealing tree trunk. "Really Venaday! Do you think there are random hands lying around in the woods?"

"Well, there could be!" His hands went to his hips. "Art is done here, there might be hand statuary at random places."

Perris sighed. "I think Lyssica would've said something were that the case."

"You think?" Venaday pursed his lips and emitted a rasping blurt. "That's ridiculous and so are you."

"You mannerless oaf!"

"Get over it." Venaday shrugged. "Well Lyssica? Is there a body joined to the hand?"

"Yes." Lyssica shuddered, because there definitely *was* a body and Venaday Tortrician was a disrespectful, blithering idiot who'd grated on her every nerve from the instant they'd met several years ago. *Thank the Goddess Ostara, I only have to endure the fool for three moons.*

She bit her lip; she would've followed emergency procedures, but, since the unfortunate squashed into the hollow of the tree hadn't responded to the loud disagreement, she didn't think there was any point. "Kerrigold, would you return to the manor and get Papan, please?"

"Of course." Kerrigold flitted upwards, then put on a burst of speed and shot away between the trees.

Melkaz fluttered closer. "Should we try and pull the body out of that hollow?" His expression was uneasy, flicking from her to Venaday to Tanjil to Perris and back again.

"No. We touch nothing before Papan arrives."

Perris crouched down to check on Tanjil, who was now rocking himself to-and-fro.

"I know!" Venaday tapped his chest. "I'll start a business as a private investigator and this can be my first case." He grinned and swept a bow. "PI Venaday Tortrician at your service. Stand aside, Lyssica, let me study the body."

"No. Back off." Lyssica pinched the bridge of her nose. Was everything a performance, or a game, to this lackwit?

"But—"

She pinned him with a withering stare. "We'll await Papan." Turning away, she laid a hand on the tree trunk and almost hissed at the wrongness radiating from its heart. It was aware of something ugly befouling its space and wanted the thing removed. Like an infected splinter. She puzzled over a dead body classed as an ugly infection – was this connected to the infection problem she'd noticed in the garden and the forest? She had not arrived at an answer when the flutter of multiple wing-beats broke what had become an uneasy silence.

An instant later, her father, Dario, Kerrigold and two guards cleared the tops of the trees. They landed, one after the other, pausing to fold their wings before approaching. Bursting from the woods in a steady, ground eating lope came a large, maned wildcat with a pair of wicked looking horns. When none of the males paid attention, Lyssica deduced the huge brown and tan animal to be Emryn. She was disappointed when he stopped behind a large tree and reappeared a few moments later, a fully dressed Fae-male. He had a pack slung over one shoulder. A clothing bag? Either he'd carried it or someone had dropped it there for him to find; too bad it robbed her of what she was certain would be a very fine view of his naked muscled body.

Her father stopped beside her. "What's going on? Kerrigold said there's a body?"

"Yes, father."

Duke Yanvian absorbed Lyssica's report before moving to the tree for a closer look. "We'll have to bring the body out." He nodded at the two guards. "Vynstan, Brom would you assist me?"

Dario moved forward. "Let Emryn and I help in place of you, Yanvian. No offence meant, but we have the suppleness of youth on our side and four will make it even easier."

"Good points. I'm not offended." The duke stayed with Lyssica as the four Fae-males moved to liberate the body. Vynstan grasped the protruding hand, while Brom eased an arm into the hollow around the shoulders. The pair twisted and wriggled the torso until it came free, then Emryn came in on one side and Dario the other, to help free the hips and legs.

Laid flat on the ground, the limp figure drew everyone like iron filings to a magnet. Somebody whimpered; it could have been Tanjil.

Lyssica swallowed. "There's something strange here." Her goddess senses were shrieking and it wasn't simply because the head was completely encased in a hood.

Perris tugged an earlobe. "Well, those are the clothes Roland Arrelgyre was wearing last night, but what's with the hood?" The head covering was secured by wide ribbons tied in a bow under the chin.

"And the ribbon bow ..." Kerrigold's voice faded as Vynstan bent, untying the ribbons. The hood loosened and Brom put a hand under the head then drew the fabric free. They all stared down at the greyed, sunken face, wide staring eyes, the mouth ajar in a silent scream.

"It's definitely Roland." Melkaz sounded shaken. "But how'd he die?"

Tanjil's voice trembled. "I can't see any b-blood."

Leaning forward, Dario opened the shirt collar and eased the material aside to check the neck. "No bruising."

Kerrigold pointed at the hood. "Maybe that was used to suffocate him?" Before anyone could answer, a shaft of sunlight broke through the trees, illuminating the dimness and silhouetting Emryn against the bright glow.

Duke Yanvian gestured. "Could you move a little, Emryn? Give us better light?"

"Sure." He stepped aside, allowing the sunbeam to fully illuminate Roland's body; lifeless, waxy grey skin and distorted features on a body completely clothed, except for boots.

"What—"

The corpse brightened suddenly, sparks rising above it, flashing like fireflies. The guards near the body edged back, as did Dario. The grey face began to glow as if lit from within. The skin cracked, peeled and tore, allowing gleams of light to shoot through the gaps. The face sloughed off like serpent skin, the eyes popped out and one after another, the teeth shot out of the mouth as if propelled. Blond hair blackened and the darkness spread, over the forehead, down the blazing face and under the chin to disappear into the open neck of the shirt.

The creature sat up. The spears of light highlighted the flesh of the face, reforming it like moulded wax until it no longer resembled Roland Arrelgyre. White clawed paws pushed eyes back into sockets above a prominent, be-whiskered snout. The eyes swivelled to focus on the stunned and horrified watchers, assessing each one in turn. When it's malignant gaze landed on Lyssica, the hare-like creature grinned, revealing new sharp teeth, front and centre in the top jaw. It shook its head, tossing long, floppy ears to-and-fro, then scrabbled to stand upright. Filled with apprehension, Lyssica drew a cloak of Ostara's fertile life force around herself.

"Greetings, Chosen of Ostara, from the Bodach." The hare bowed, then straightened. Its head tilted, a white paw stroked long black whiskers as it regarded Lyssica almost slyly. "He hopes you enjoyed the show." The other paw tossed a cloud of glittering dust towards her, but Emryn leapt, grasped her arm and jerked her out of reach.

A fireball formed in the hand of Dario, the Unseelie Beast, and he flung it at the black and white furred thing. The rabbity creature gave Lyssica a wave and a smirking, toothy grin before the explosion knocked everyone flat.

When the dust cleared and they raised themselves to look, there was no trace – the rabbit-hare had vanished.

6

EMRYN

Emryn couldn't stop running his hands over Lyssica. Kynthcat, a surge of fur and claw within him, was also demanding to see and feel her. "Lyssica! Are you hurt?"

Her hands rose to bat at his, a shaky smile briefly curling her lips. "Thank you, I'm fine. You don't need to ..." She stopped, swallowing whatever she'd been about to say, then her voice emerged as a whisper. "That awful creature with its strange dust."

He shook his head. Voices floated to them on the ether.

"What just happened?"

"What in the name of the Goddess, was that?"

Dario snarled; a new fireball flaming on his fingertips. "By Old Mab's teeth and hair! It's gone!"

Kerrigold wrung her hands. "Your fire probably killed it!"

"Singed it maybe." Dario shook his head. "No, it got away."

Teeth clenched, Emryn joined everyone else in staring at the slightly scorched, bare ground. There was no body, no body parts, no discarded clothing, only blackened earth where the leaf litter and sparse blades of grass had exploded into a conflagration.

Engaging the heightened, but enraged senses of Kynthcat, Emryn moved closer, sniffing and pushing his tongue out to taste the air. A stench of black snow and putrid mud assailed him, overpowering the burnt smell. His tongue curled in disgust. He spat, then blinked his alternate vision into play – and there were the sparkling remnants of the glitter dust the creature had hurled at Lyssica. It was eating into the charred ground making the area worse by the second. Emryn could think of only one way to stop the blight.

"Dario!" He pointed. "Firebomb that black spot – the glitter dust that thing threw is disintegrating everything it touches."

Dario nodded. "Everyone, stand back." Body tense, he hurled another fireball.

Alternate vision still focusing, Emryn watched the firebomb land. A dark section in the middle of the blighted ground burst into flame. It roared high in a gout of black flame, lowered to a sullen grey, then changed to the colours of true fire before it finally snuffed out. Staring intently, Emryn realised the problem wasn't over yet. "Keep going Dario! Start where the edges meet the healthy ground and ring the entire portion of affected earth. What you did worked, but the blight is spreading outwards. We must stop it before the entire forest is ruined."

Mouth a thin line, Dario enflamed his second hand and took turns aiming fireballs in the pattern Emryn advised. Smoke wreathed the surrounds and coughing broke out amongst the watching Fae-folk.

Emryn's heavy exhaled breath was redolent with frustration; the stink of fear from the estate visitors combined with their macabre fascination, masked any other scents he might pick up. He glanced around, alert in case the thing returned.

Tanjil's back was plastered against a tree trunk; tears trickled down his cheeks as he rocked himself. Kerrigold talked to him quietly, gently clasping his arm.

Melkaz and Perris alternated glances between Dario, Emryn and the blighted ground. Venaday, mouth open, didn't stop staring at the fiery Dario. Duke Yanvian strode out from where he'd been searching among nearby trees. Meeting Emryn's gaze, he shook his head.

"No signs of the thing anywhere in the vicinity." Eyes widening, the Duke of Papillion stepped back as his son-in-law aimed and cast another fireball.

Hands still aflame, Dario strode closer to the blackened ground. "Emryn? Do I need to continue?" Emryn assessed the ground, looking for any further glitterdust. Lyssica answered before he could.

"It's all gone." Hands spread in front of her, eyes closed, she faced the blight. Her actions garnered everyone's attention.

Dario cast her an interested look; Yanvian awarded a dubious frown. They both raised eyebrows at Emryn, who nodded. "She's right."

Duke Yanvian confronted his eldest daughter. "Just exactly how do *you* know that, Lyssica? With your eyes shut?"

Lyssica nibbled on her bottom lip, then squinted at him, her gaze troubled.

The duke pinched the bridge of his nose. "Not to mention, I was summoned here because of a body in a hollow tree, believed to be Roland Arrelgyre. I thought that highly unlikely since I saw him out through the front gate and on his way home early this morning, yet here he was." He gestured violently at the scorched earth. "Him, or something that started off looking like him, until it became what? Some type of malevolent, bi-coloured, oversized rabbit thing?"

Lyssica stared at the blight, brows knit.

Dario peered at her. "Whatever it was, it seemed to recognise you, Lyss, and not in a good way. Judging by how the dust affected the ground, Emryn just saved your life."

Lyssica's troubled gaze lifted to tangle with Emryn's. "That's true." She didn't look away. "Thank you for that."

"More than a pleasure." Her eyes beckoned. Opening his senses wide, he reached for the link, wrapping himself in it. Their gazes held.

Kynthcat preened. '*She like us. Me like her, you do too.*'

Ignoring his outrageous cat, he cleared his throat and found his voice, enthralled by those captivating doe eyes. "It targeted you, that's for certain. If that's the case it'll be back."

Kerrigold swung around. "Why didn't you stop it?" Her sudden movement startled Emryn out of his private moment with Lyssica.

"We tried." Duke Yanvian shook his head. "It vanished using dark magic. The rest was smoke and mirrors with a finishing touch of poisonous dust."

Dario extinguished the flame of his Unseelie Beast, shook his hands out and straightened the cuffs of his jacket. "I agree."

Mclkaz cleared his throat. "Perhaps it wanted us to think it had died?"

"Ooh!" Venaday rubbed his palms together. "What a great thought, Melkaz – I'll include that in my notes later."

Duke Yanvian raised a supercilious eyebrow. "Notes?"

Venaday performed a flowery bow. "Venaday Tortrician, Private Investigator – my new career, you know." The Fae-male touched a finger to the side of his nose and winked. "Nothing to fear now that I'm on the case."

Grimacing as he looked away, Emryn discovered Dario smirking at him. His new mentor raised one hand to the side of his head and circled a finger several times, his gaze flicking to Venaday and back. Emryn hid his answering grin behind one hand.

Yanvian snorted. "Private investigations into this thing will get you killed, Venaday Tortrician. If you want to go home alive after this Tri-moon program, you'll refrain from doing anything so foolhardy. I have no wish to send home pieces of you in a coffin."

Dario studied the ground, head tilted. "I can't help wondering – was this really Roland Arrelgyre? Or simply a magical impersonation?"

Perris pressed fingers to his forehead, massaging. "If that's the case, it was an excellent impersonation of Roland."

Kerrigold nodded. "Therefore it had to have at least seen him, but was it the kind of creature to leave him traveling on undisturbed?"

Emryn snorted. "No. It was full of innate cunning, with a highlight of viciousness." His shudder was instinctive.

Melkaz studied him. "How do you know that?"

Emryn cast him a sidelong glance; he'd have to reveal a part of his nature to answer that question. "Empath."

An expression of outrage moulded Venaday's face. "So you constantly sense our feelings? Is there no privacy?"

"That's incorrect." Emryn frowned. Why did everyone always leap to that conclusion? "Generally, everybody has a personal mind shield through which I don't intrude unless invited, but violent or sudden feelings and thoughts are broadcast so loudly that they trample personal shields and in such situations I can't avoid hearing things." He nodded towards the scorch mark. "In the case of *that* creature, it didn't care who could hear it."

Duke Yanvian, hands at chest height, tapped fingertips together. "I'll need to send out search parties to look for Arrelgyre, or his belongings. We must ascertain whether the body here was really him, or a magical cover the creature superimposed over its true shape."

Lyssica wrinkled her nose. "You are assuming the nasty rabbit persona is its true shape."

Duke Yanvian's eyes narrowed. "And you don't?"

She tilted her head. "Well, maybe, but maybe not."

"Not very clear."

"It's more what the thing represents. Real rabbits don't behave like that. Ergo, it was a magical construct of some sort, sent by someone else."

Her father pursed his lips, still glaring. "Any idea who?"

Lyssica spread her hands. "It did mention the Bodach, but who knows if that is true or not. What is clear is, it *was* targeting me."

"Yes." Dario stroked his chin. "It recognised you, didn't it? Why might that be?"

Wincing, Lyssica studied the blackened ground.

"Lyssica?" Emryn placed a gentle hand on her arm. She rewarded him with a tiny smile. "There are lives at stake, so if you know anything that could help us, we would appreciate you sharing the information."

She sighed. "It's because of what I do." She glanced around the group.

Emryn did also, noting the prevalence of scowling faces. "You know, if frowns were people, there'd be a nasty crowd here right now."

Duke Yanvian folded his arms. "Keep going, Lyssica. That requires explaining."

She faced him; her mouth opened and closed, then she glanced around as if waiting for something. Finally she shrugged. "I'm a Handmaiden of Ostara. I have been since I was seven."

The Duke of Papillion looked like somebody had hit him over the head with a tree branch. "What! Why is this the first I've heard of it?"

Lyssica's throat worked; her voice emerged shaky and low. "Ostara bespelled me to silence for my own protection. The fact that I am now able to reveal the truth reinforces my belief that something is seriously wrong."

"That's right." Dario's hands went to his hips. "The rabbit thing called you 'Chosen of Ostara'. That's why you were the focus."

Emryn 's brow furrowed. "But it makes no sense. Rabbits are a symbol of Ostara and her fertility aspect, so why was the creature in rabbit form? A murderous rabbit? That's an antithesis."

Lyssica rubbed her temples. "Unless you're mocking the Goddess."

Duke Yanvian threw his hands in the air. "But you're Seelie and Ostara is an Unseelie Goddess!"

Emryn winced, but Lyssica pinned her father with a glare. "You forget yourself, Papan! Seelie and Unseelie are a United race under the joint Queendom and, if you recall, you fought in the Fae Wars for Fae Unity. You have both a son-in-law and a daughter-in-law who are both Unseelie. Your reaction is the very reason my silence on the matter was enforced by Ostara."

"Damn, you're right." Her father sighed as he focused on Dario, then glanced at Emryn. "My apologies. Old habits are harder to break than I realised."

Dario waved a hand. "Luckily I know you better than you think I do, old goat. I'm ignoring it."

Emryn nodded. "I'm taking Dario's answer for my own. If he says it's okay, then it is."

"Thank you." Yanvian swallowed as he turned to Lyssica again. "So, you're working for an Uns ... Ah, that is, you're working for a goddess and because of it, a monster is making you the object of its malevolence?"

Lyssica bared her teeth in a fierce smile. "That about sums it up, Papan." Emryn wanted to applaud. He hid his grin, but shite, she was a fierce little thing. She looked all fluffy and adorable like a kitten wanting to be stroked and cuddled, until her hidden claws came out to slash the unwary.

'Mmroww!' Kynthcat's tail flicked him. *'Fierce kitten ours.'*

7

LYSSICA

Flitting back to the manor house, Lyssica's thoughts were whirling. *Papan will want more information. How much should I explain? How much do I want to explain? How **can** I explain?* Her stomach twisted uneasily. Her role as Ostara's Handmaiden was a secret she'd been forced to conceal for years for her own protection. But the spell, which had stopped admissions on her part, whether inadvertent or purposeful, was gone. Now what?

Next to her, Papan bellowed orders even as he aimed for his personal study. "I want a squad of guards to search the Great West Road for Roland Arrelgyre! Brom, you're in charge of them. Vynstan, you take another squad and comb the estate for that rabbit-hare thing, or anything you think suspicious."

Lyssica combed fingers through her hair. Images of the horrible rabbit poking its eyes back in filled her mind; the creature's disrespectful use of Ostara's symbol sickened her, but it was also a warning. *I need to go to the Forest Circle as soon as I can, make my territory defences stronger. Even though I've already begun the winter protection rites, I must contact Ostara for further assistance and advice. This matter is so far beyond my expertise it's not funny.*

"Erm, Lyssica?"

Recognising Dario's voice, she glanced up. He surreptitiously indicated the five program apprentices milling uncertainly in the foyer, casting either anxious or speculative glances at her. She was pleased to have him and Emryn standing like sentinels on either side of her; two big, brawny males helping her feel safe, while Entanglit held his position at the entry. However, as the only family member here, it was time to play host.

Lyssica clapped her hands. "Right. Let's all go into the morning room and Entanglit will bring tea and biscuits. We can wind down and decide what's next on the agenda." She looked to their major-domo. "If you wouldn't mind, Entanglit?"

He bowed. "Certainly Lady Lyssica. Tea and biscuits in a jiffy." He strode off down the hallway.

The group adjourned to the morning room in silence and took seats where they could see her. Relief filled Lyssica as Emryn came to stand beside the chair she'd chosen while Dario took a position near the door. She scanned the uneasy faces, coming to Melkaz last. He pinned her with a stare. "Will the program continue now that one of us has been murdered?"

Lyssica dug fingernails into her palms. "I won't make any decisions without Papan's input. I'd like it to continue, but it may come back to personal preferences. For now, we're safe and every effort will be made to ensure that continues."

"But Roland—"

"Made his own path with his unrelenting bigotry." Emryn cut in. "That he came to grief afterwards is not something anyone expected or could have predicted." The electric silence that ensued was broken by a light tap at the door.

"Argh!" Tanjil Blastobarm started violently, then continued to shake like a leaf in wind. When the door opened for Entanglit to propel his tea trolley into the room, Tanjil sagged, his Adam's apple moving in an agitated swallow.

Lyssica hastily poured a cup of tea, added plenty of sugar and passed it over. "Here Tanjil, the tea will do you good. Would you like a biscuit too?" Entanglit proffered the biscuit tray to Tanjil, but he shook his head, clutching his tea cup like a lifeline.

"N-no thanks."

Lyssica continued to pour tea until everyone was served. Even with tea in hand, Emryn remained steadfast at her elbow; she cast him a grateful smile, unable to stop admiring him despite the circumstances. He was such a tower of strength and she'd been attracted from the beginning. She pulled a face – she'd fallen into his arms. Could a meeting be any more cliché than that? Turning, she watched Entanglit move from person to person with the biscuit tray, until the room was quiet except for the sipping of tea and the munching of cookies.

When the door opened to admit Papan, Tanjil trembled so much he dropped his cup.

"It's just the duke, Tanjil." Kerrigold patted his arm. Entanglit recovered the cup and mopped the few spilled drops.

Lyssica placed her cup on the trolley. "Tea, Papan?"

"Yes, thank you, Lyssica." He waited as she poured a cup, then paced to the nearby fireplace and set it on the mantelpiece. "I assume everyone has questions, so let's talk. I have sent guards to look for signs of Roland Arrelgyre in case the creature was impersonating him."

Melkaz cleared his throat. "I've already asked Lyssica, but she said to wait for your input, so I ask again: Will the program be continuing after this apparent murder of one of us?"

The duke clasped his hands behind his back. "I'll not stop anyone who wishes to leave and I'll provide an armed escort. Having said that, I'd like the program to continue – I'll remind you we all signed contracts—"

Perris frowned. "We did, but we had no idea a murder would happen."

Duke Yanvian inclined his head. "Correct. There is a clause in the contract to cover unexpected circumstances, so as I've just said, whoever wants to leave may do so."

"I can't stay here!" Tanjil's lips twisted. "I want to go home."

"Very well." Duke Yanvian looked from Kerrigold, to Perris, Melkaz, then Venaday. "Anyone else?"

"Oh, I'm definitely staying." Venaday leaned forward. "My PI investigation needs me to be front and centre."

When Emryn gently nudged her, Lyssica pressed her lips together, staring into her cup. Don't laugh. Once she had herself firmly under control, she looked up, only to meet Dario's grinning gaze; he pointed a finger at the side of his head and moved it in a circle. She choked and squeezed her eyes shut. Damn the pair of them!

Kerrigold's voice filled the room. "I'd like time to think about it."

Lyssica drew breath. "What if everyone takes the rest of the day to consider, then announces their choice over breakfast tomorrow?" Murmurs of agreement came.

The duke nodded. "An excellent idea. We'll leave it there, shall we?"

Perris looked between Lyssica and her father. "And you'll keep us apprised of anything you discover about Roland?"

"Don't doubt it." Duke Yanvian focused on Lyssica. "Now, we need to go to my office so you can you explain more about being a 'Handmaiden of Ostara', Lyssica."

She faced him. "I'm happy to talk about it, but we'll stay here." She'd prefer a public discussion. "I've nothing to hide, in fact I'm proud of my role, so what is it you wish to know?"

"How did she contact you?"

"I was seven, singing and dancing in the forest. Maman had taken all of us to the stone circle the previous day and I'd loved it so much I went back by myself. Ostara appeared as a tiny-winged Fae, joined in with me, then complimented me on my skills and introduced herself as Ostara, The Spring Fairy. She talked about how much work she had to do and I offered to help. She accepted my offer and I've been her Handmaiden ever since."

The duke rubbed his chin. "What does being a Handmaiden entail?"

"Looking after the flora and fauna in this region." Lyssica tilted her head. "I suppose you could say I'm her area representative."

Her father's frown deepened. "How do you do whatever it is you do? And where?"

Lyssica returned his frown. "There are some things that are between Ostara and me. As to where, I go to the forest outside our estate most afternoons to help any plants or animals in need. Ostara is the Goddess of Spring, Dawn and Fertility, with the hare as her symbol – but we've covered that already."

Papan gritted his teeth. "With that rabbit monster around, it's not safe. You will cease your visits to the forest."

Lyssica clenched her fists. "I will *not*. I swore an oath and I have responsibilities to fulfill. If you give me a moment I'll contact the Goddess Ostara for advice."

Her father's eyebrows raised. "We don't have time for you to set up some elaborate folderol ceremony with candles and scent sticks, then go into a trance, or whatever it is you do. The situation is critical and—"

"That's rubbish." Closing her eyes, Lyssica tuned her father out, took five deep breaths, envisaged their virtual meeting room in her mind and went inside. She created an image of Ostara's face, sent her mind call down their pathway, just as she always did, and waited.

And waited.

And waited some more.

'How strange. Ostara usually responds promptly.' She sent another call down their link, focusing more deeply in hope of an answer. The increased depth of her awareness revealed an unusual thick fog swallowing her calls, murky tendrils now reaching towards her. Uneasily, she backed out of the virtual meeting room and opened her eyes.

Everyone watched her, fascination written across their faces. Lyssica firmed her mouth and met her father's green and violet gaze.

"Well?"

She shook her head. "I couldn't reach her. I'm being blocked."

"What do you mean, 'blocked'?"

She drummed her fingers on the tea tray. "There was a fog and it was … in between me and where I wanted to go." Her frown deepened. "But it was also like I was being surrounded. Trapped even. It wasn't a pleasant sensation. I'll try again later."

"Is that wise?" Emryn asked.

Her gaze met his worried one. Instead of annoying her, his worry was like a balm. Even so, she spoke firmly. "I made a vow I have no wish to break."

Emryn nodded. "I admire your dedication." His words tingled pleasantly through her and she rewarded him with a smile.

Dario sauntered over and poured himself more tea. "There is something of deceit and trickery about all of this. What do you know about the Bodach?"

Lyssica's nose wrinkled. "The Bodach? He's the consort of the Cailleach."

Kerrigold leaned forward. "The Cailleach? You mean the Goddess of Winter?"

"Technically, she's Goddess of the Winds and the Cold, often called the Queen of Winter, or the Veiled One." Lyssica twisted her fingers in her skirts. "Her consort, the Bodach, is not a god, but he is a prankster. Unfortunately what he thinks amusing, others can find unpleasant, even deadly."

"And the Cailleach doesn't stop him?"

Lyssica shook her head. "She doesn't always know what he's doing. He's sly and secretive, and she's a fair and just deity, dedicated to doing right. I'm not sure how they came to be paired."

Melkaz lowered his teacup to his saucer. "If you're a Handmaiden of Ostara, how do you know so much about winter's deities?"

Lyssica shrugged. "Spring follows winter. Ostara takes over from the Cailleach and they talk. Sometimes they engage in contests which result in overlapping seasons. Ostara ushers in more clement weather and a thaw starts. The Cailleach responds by flinging more snow. Ostara organises warm winds and Spring rains. The Cailleach's answer is to force the temperature down and change the rain to sleet and ice. That sort of thing. You've all experienced such weather." She glanced around; they were all staring.

Suddenly Venaday rubbed his hands together. "This is wonderful! You're beautiful and you know two goddesses – it's perfect!"

Lyssica stared, fighting disbelief. What was the idiot warbling about? "Thank you for the compliment, but what's your point?"

He beamed. "I hadn't thought you'd be a good enough match for me. My family is quite exalted, you know. Pure bloodlines. We vet a prospect carefully before inviting them to join us. But you! Working with one goddess and knowing a second one – that elevates your importance well above the demarcation line. You qualify easily." He leapt from his seat, approached with firm strides and grasped a hand. "I offer myself to you. We won't want to waste any time, so I'm sure a consorting ceremony can be arranged easily and quickly." He patted her hand, started massaging her fingers.

A low growl came from behind her. Lyssica ignored it and withdrew her hand from his pawing clasp. He reached for it again, but she held it up between them, palm facing him. "No."

"No?" His mouth dropped open. He closed it with a snap. "What do you mean?"

"It's very kind of you to offer, but I have no desire to be your consort or have you as mine, so, no. Thank you."

He stared at her, brows so high they were covered by his hair. Then he relaxed, uttering a brief laugh. "I get it. You're shy. I've embarrassed you in front of all these onlookers. No matter. I'll approach the subject with you later, in private."

Lyssica sighed. "Lord Venaday, you force me to be blunt. I'm not currently seeking a consort, but even if I were, you're not whom I would choose. I'm sorry to disappoint you, but you don't have the qualities I want."

Before anything else could be said, Emryn moved purposefully forward, snarling. "This is irrelevant." The glare he aimed at Venaday promised blood. "Lyssica is in danger and must be protected and yet you mock her." His glowing eyes bounced from Duke Yanvian to Dario. "The Bodach named her – he has her in his sights and he's dangerous." His top lip wrinkled, then his smouldering gaze fastened on Lyssica and she fought a tremble of pleasure. It was like being exposed to a furnace – and it felt sooo good.

"Exactly!" Dario moved to flank Emryn. "She needs a guard."

"Excellent idea!" Duke Yanvian nodded firmly.

Lyssica wanted to protest, but she knew they were right. *The Bodach is up to something and I won't be able to protect myself properly while I'm engrossed in my duties. Papan already said he doesn't want me going to the forest – wait a minute.* She lowered her hand to cover the smile fighting to break free and cleared her throat.

Her father glowered. "No. Arguments."

"Have I argued?" She clasped a hand to the base of her throat. "I will happily accept and cooperate with a guard – if you stop trying to prevent me going to the forest to carry out my handmaiden duties." His eyes narrowed as he studied her. She stared resolutely back at him.

Finally he nodded. "Deal."

She smiled. "Thank you Papan." *I won't tell him I'd have done what I want regardless of his commands.*

Emryn took a step forward. "I will—"

Perris stepped in front of him. "I'd be happy to guard Lyssica."

"No!" Lyssica swallowed bile. She'd flee before ever again entrusting her safety to Perris.

His smile faltered. "What do you mean, no? There's nobody else here who could look after you like I can."

She shook her head, edging away from him when he reached for her. "No!"

Emryn stepped between them, body tense. "Are you always so rude Perris?" A low growl emanated from his chest.

Perris's Adam's apple bobbed. "Rude? It's not rude to state a truth. Lyssica needs—"

"You don't know what I need." Fingers clenching, her gaze flickered to Emryn then back to Perris. "I mean ... I ... we couldn't ask that of you," she finally managed to blurt out.

Papan studied her – she endeavoured not to tremble in the face of his assessing gaze. But after a moment he simply turned to Perris and said, "Thank you Perris, but I think Emryn would be our best choice. He's a warrior where you're not. I won't have someone with less than basic training protecting my daughter."

Perris shook his head. "I've had basic training!"

"It's not enough." Papan nodded as he turned to Emryn. "I'd like you to be Lyssica's guard, Emryn. Is that acceptable to you?"

Emryn pressed his chest with a clenched fist. "It would be my honour, Your Grace." Perris swung on his heel and stalked from the room; the door slammed behind him.

Lyssica heaved a sigh. *Thank the Goddess.* Hoping nobody noticed her hands trembling, she endeavoured to focus as her father continued.

"Dario, what say you?"

"It's a great idea; we'll need to work around Emryn's contractual expectations, though."

Papan steepled his fingers and tapped his thumbs together. "Fine. Let's hammer out the details."

Dario stroked his chin. "Okay, we know Emryn must spend time mentoring with me and Lyssica is involved with instructing the Papillion apprentices, so needs to be here. Then, there's her goddess-given tasks in the forest, a part of which stretches between our estates." Dario glanced from Yanvian to Lyssica and on to Emryn. "So, if the guarding is to be successful, Emryn must stay with Lyssica full time."

Lyssica's eyes widened. "What? Why? Surely, he could just come here early in the day while I do my work, then accompany me to the forest and back before he returns to Garadenya Island in the afternoon to complete his tasks?" Although whichever way things went, she'd get to spend a lot more time in Emryn's company and that pleased her no end. She fought to keep her smile hidden.

Papan frowned. "Will that work?"

Brows knit, Dario glanced between them. "I doubt it. I'm sorry Lyssica, but what you suggest wastes a lot of time. Besides, you can't possibly stay alone in your tower- it's too easy to access from the outside."

"Well, Papan could put guards—"

"And take them away from their other duties?" Emryn pursed his lips. "Or are you proposing they do longer hours, further exhausting them when your Papan needs them all more focused, rather than less?"

"I—"

Dario shook his head. "Emryn is right, Lyss,"

Papan crossed his arms. "Then how is this going to work?"

Dario clasped his hands behind his back. "I propose Lyss comes to stay with us."

Lyssica's eyes widened. "What? I can't possibly—"

Dario held up his hand. "Hear me out. If you come to stay with us, Emryn and I can do our work early in the morning while Lyss and Zhu keep each other company. Then Emryn and Lyssica can return here late morning." Dario raised his eyes to his father-in-law. "That's the time she'll help with your Tri-moon guests. Mid-afternoon, they both leave here and return to Garadenya via the forest where Lyssica can complete whatever responsibilities necessary before they return to Garadenya for the night. We have a suite with a bedroom only accessible through a smaller antechamber." He turned to Lyssica. "We'll put you in the bedroom and have Emryn in the antechamber to keep you safe."" He paused. "Thoughts?"

It really was quite sensible. And it would enable her to get away from … No. She wouldn't even think his name. But she would be able to keep her distance and feel safer at night. Plus she would get to spend more time with Zhu … and Emryn. Hoping nobody noticed the hot flush suffusing her body at that thought, she nodded primly. "That will work. Thank you Dario, I accept." She glanced across the room. "Emryn?"

Gleaming eyes meshed with hers. He inclined his head. "I also find these arrangements acceptable."

"Great!" Lyssica's smiled brightly. "When do we begin?"

The duke's voice was pure steel.

"Now."

8

―――――

EMRYN

*E*mryn braced against the cold winds blustering from a louring sky as he stood on the front verandah of the Papillion Estate manor house.. This last official day of autumn was bitter; he tasted oncoming snow within the chill gusts that whipped his cloak tighter around his legs. Although lunch was over and there were a few more hours before he and Lyssica usually set off to return to Garadenya Island, his senses warned him to leave early. Kynthcat agreed.

It was a good thing none of the other apprentices had decided to follow Tanjil's lead in scurrying home given the weather had turned colder and nastier the day after Roland Arrelgyre's unfortunate demise.

'He horrible male.'

'Yes – but nobody deserves to die that way.'

The guards had located his bags less than five leagues from the estate, ripped apart, the contents scattered. His wings had also been there, shredded and bloody, torn from his body by some unknown method. Arrelgyre had been flying home, but something had either dragged him from the sky or convinced him to land. Whether he'd been trapped or lured made little difference in the end. It had been a fatal choice, the cause of which continued to disturb them all.

Emryn had checked out the scene. The place was a mess of scent; Arrelgyre's was barely detectable over the revolting black snow and putrid mud smell of the devil-rabbit. There were other scents there, but Emryn was uneasy, because they were all a version of slimy wet fur, something with canine tendencies that he found unrecognisable. He pondered. Canine? Vulpine? He wasn't certain but the lingering presence of the stench indicated they were in league with the devil-rabbit and hence, the Bodach.

Anyone living on or near the estate had been warned of a killer on the loose. Descriptions of the magic using devil-rabbit had been circulated, with reports of any sightings requested and dispatches for the Queens, apprising them of the situation, had been sent along with a guard to the Arrelgyre family with a note from the duke and Roland's wings and belongings.

'*Bad weather come soon,*' Kynthcat reminded him. '*Need to take our lady and go.*'

Stalking back into the warmth of the Aphiski home, Emryn crossed to the work offices where Lyssica was seated at her desk with Kerrigold going over planning estimates and how she calculated them. He'd sat in on this lesson when she gave it to Perris, Venaday and Melkaz. Neither he nor Kynthcat liked the males near her, and there was no way he was leaving her alone with them like he did Kerrigold.

Melkaz wasn't so bad; he asked sensible questions and quickly grasped her teachings. Emryn was impressed at her knack of imparting information in an easily understood way. Perris had divided his attention between Lyssica and the watching Emryn, once even asking to see her privately. The question had been asked in a low voice, but Emryn, with his heightened shifter hearing, had no trouble picking it up. She had drawn Perris's notice back to the work and avoided answering.

Then, there was Venaday.

Emryn rolled his eyes. The obnoxious dolt made constant, annoying interruptions, questioned Lyssica's methods and implied her strategies were flawed because she was female. He continued to importune Lyssica to consort with him on a daily basis – perhaps he was hoping to wear her resistance away. Kynthcat itched to gore the smarmy bastard. A low growl rumbled in his chest; the numpty severely tested his patience, never mind his self-restraint.

Emryn coughed to swallow his ire-inspired rumbling as Lyssica looked up enquiringly.

"Sorry for the interruption, but the weather is deteriorating. We need to leave now so you can still perform your Handmaiden magic in the forest before the oncoming storm."

"Oh, of course." Lyssica rose, closed the workbook and stacked some maps into a leather folder. "Kerrigold, we'll finish this tomorrow, if that suits?"

Her prompt response to his advice smothered the rest of Emryn's low burning annoyance. The constant proximity engendered by their recent roles as guard and target had earned her, not only his trust, but his respect – and she had just returned the compliment.

Kerrigold pushed back her chair. "Sure. The break will allow me to digest what you've already explained." She rubbed the back of her neck. "It's fascinating, but complicated. So much to consider. Thanks Lyssica. I'll see you tomorrow. You too, Emryn." She flashed a smile and left.

"I'd better inform Papan and grab my bag."

Emryn crossed to the inner door to Duke Yanvian's attached study. He knocked, opening the door almost simultaneously. The duke raised his head from paperwork, one brow lifting in enquiry.

"Lyssica and I are leaving now. There's a blizzard coming."

Yanvian stood immediately. "Thanks for the warning. I will tell my people to prepare. Make certain you and Lyssica stay safe. We may not have seen any new signs of the devil-rabbit or the Bodach in the last two weeks, but you can be sure they're still out there."

Emryn nodded. "Any new reports?"

Duke Yanvian snorted. "The creature's been seen in several different places at the same time. Either my Fae-folk are seeing things or there's a herd of the damned things on the loose."

Emryn shook his head. "Probably the first option. Folk are afraid."

"Yes." The duke dropped his pen and rubbed his eyes. "Go in safety."

"See you tomorrow, Papan." Lyssica called out as Emryn re-joined her.

"Ready?"

She nodded and led the way out of her office. In the foyer, they found Entanglit seated at his desk.

"I took the liberty of fetching your bag, Lady Lyssica. Miss Antigony had it packed and ready."

Lyssica smiled warmly. "Thank you, Entanglit. You're a gem. And would you please thank Tig for me?"

As she approached her pack on a table adjacent to the doors, Emryn ducked into an anteroom, stripped, stuffed his clothes in a waiting satchel and morphed into Kynthcat. The magic whisked through him, a flurry of light and nerve pulses that always left him alert and ready for anything.

'My turn.' Kynthcat gripped the satchel between his teeth, padded around the screen in place for his use and exited the anteroom.

Lyssica stood so that she could see both the anteroom door and Entanglit, to whom she was speaking. "Emryn sensed the bad weather approaching. A blizzard he said." She smiled as they appeared and relieved them of their satchel. "Papan is sending out warnings."

"I'll alert the household." Entanglit nodded. "And bar the doors after you leave. The weather already has an unpleasant aspect."

Indeed it did.

Lyssica must have felt it too as she stopped on top of the porch steps, tapping her pursed lips and studied the filthy sky. The wind buffeted her and ruffled Kynthcat's fur as he moved to place her on his lee side. He nudged her. She looked across, meeting his glowing silvery eyes. As Kynthcat, the top of his head was level with hers. He rumbled, waved a paw at the sky and shook his shaggy head.

She sighed. "You're right. The wind is already too strong for flying." Emryn had imposed the rule of low altitude flying very early in the arrangement, so Kynthcat could lope along beneath and still be close enough to protect her. In the two weeks since the guarding had begun, they'd worked out a steady, league covering pace which suited them both. Emryn had also planned strategies to follow should they be attacked, or some other emergency arise. He was pleased when she cooperated and put full effort into practising the strategies with him. And his strange fascination with her continued to grow.

Rubbing a paw over one ear, he watched as she delved into her bag, pulled out her cloak and donned it. If she was flying, she preferred not to wear it, despite the wing-slits it contained. When she bent to pick up their bags, he uttered another low growl.

"Okay, okay." Leaning over him, she threaded a strap around his chest and buckled the bags in place. "I'll walk to the forest; it's not far." He grunted; he could deal with that.

Descending the steps, they set off down the driveway to the gate-house. Even the postern gate was closed full time now, with a round-the-clock guard, the same as the main gates.

The curly headed Brom was on duty inside the building. "Leaving early today Lady Lyssica, Lord Emryn, Kynthcat?" Kynthcat rumbled a greeting.

"Snow storm on the way." Lyssica scribbled their names in the register. "We're trying to race it back to Garadenya. Spread the word about the weather amongst the guards, would you, Brom?"

"Absolutely, my lady." Brom casually saluted them as they went outside again.

Kynthcat flanked her on the short path to the postern exit but pulled ahead as Lozito saw them coming and opened the small gate. *'The dolt didn't even check outside! Anything could be waiting out there.'* He growled. *'Poorly trained.'*

Ensuring he was between Lyssica and the exit, Kynthcat opened his mouth, tasting the air as he listened intently. Slightly mollified when he sensed no danger, he eased forward until they could do a visual check of the road outside. When he was satisfied all was as it should be, he paced through the opening, waiting for Lyssica to finish her chat with Lozito.

Crossing the road to the forest and the now familiar narrow path, they moved in single file with Kynthcat leading, senses on full alert. By now, they knew which way took them to Ostara's circle and when they reached it, Lyssica wasted no time. She spun around the perimeter, breaking into immediate, low-voiced song as she moved though the impromptu steps of her power dance.

Kynthcat shadowed her; he'd no wish to be distant if trouble found them. Opening his senses wide, he kept one eye on her and another on their surroundings. Even not paying full attention, he couldn't help responding to her ceremony, as he had since the first day. It was like she opened a bag and started flinging handfuls of love, well-being and reassurance for all the animals and plants. The feeling was amazing and he revelled in it. Not only the power she held, but that it came from her, although he wished he could work out why it made him want to pounce on her and made him putty in her hands.

But the way it made him feel … No wonder so many varieties of fauna flocked here for the 'hands-on' part of Lyssica's duties.

A variety of animals were now flowing around him on their way to Lyssica. The creatures showed no fear of Kynthcat's large form, hadn't even on the first day, despite his fangs, claws and the twisted twin horns on his skull. He was peripherally pleased that none of the smaller creatures showed any fear of Kynthcat. Perhaps some of Lyssica's scent lingered in his fur? And why did he like that idea so much?

Finally, his circuit brought him to a clear section stretching several ells back from the Ostara Circle until it reached two gnarled bushes. The space was devoid of animal presence. He cocked his head, studying the area. What was different about it? The branches of the bushes were spindly, and what was left of the leaves drooped in an unhealthy manner. As he stared at the bushes, he started to notice the emanations of an icy-blue glow. He paced closer, uneasiness growing.

Crouching down to lie flat, he twisted his huge head sideways to peer under the lowest branches of one bush. Wrapped around the base of the trunk was a solid looking, frosty blue growth. When he checked, the second bush revealed the same stuff. The attachments glowed with an ugly, unwholesome light and looked tight enough to strangle. In addition, glowing blue filaments snaked out of the parasitic mass, stretching glacial claws up the trunks. Extending a paw, he prodded at the blue mass with a claw tip. Quick as lightning, a frigid tendril extruded from the growth, darting at his paw. He snatched it back. The thread barely brushed his fur, but still caused a brief painful jolt of frozen electricity. Every hair on his paw stood on end. Oh, hell, no. This wasn't good.

Shaking his paw out, he turned his head in Lyssica's direction and emitted a low coughing roar. She and the group of animals with her all looked up. Lyssica's brows rose. Using the afflicted paw, he beckoned.

He took another look under the attack bush as he waited. The vicious icy tendril was still poised, waving around as if searching for what had annoyed it. Without any prompts from him, Lyssica lowered herself to the ground.

"By my Goddess! What is that abomination? It's killing these bushes, but it looks sort of frosty." She glanced at him. "Did you touch it? Is that why it's acting defensive?" He rumbled an assent, shaking his paw. "Let me see." She clasped both hands around it, inspected the singed spot, then sang softly, aiming her words into the fur. The goddess power flowed into his paw through her hands. It was augmented by her song and immediately eased the cold ache.

He leaned in and nuzzled her cheek. She smiled, then turned her attention back to the tree, smile fading. Wearing an expression of determination, Lyssica re-commenced singing, the words louder and more forceful. She held her hands, palms out, focusing on the strangling cankers. The malignant bulges shivered. Higher up in the bushes, the icy-blue shimmer stuttered and began to fade. Next the tips of the reaching tendrils shrank back towards the main swelling until the serpentine strands had pulled back completely.

Lyssica kept singing until the lumps were reduced to tiny nodules and then even those were gone. Still she sung, lowering her hands to focus on the roots. The ground quivered a little, but slowly settled and stilled. Lyssica changed her song and alternated moving her hands between the roots and back to the trunks of the bushes. Before long the plants were vibrant and healthy, getting even more so when

Lyssica touched them. When she stopped singing and eased back, she was mobbed by little furry creatures, who keened in delight as she cuddled and stroked them all.

He watched in awe. She was simply amazing. He could come up with no other appropriate words. Although, gorgeous also came to mind when he thought of her.

9

LYSSICA

"The forest sprawls over a large tract of land and we've patrolled widely." Lyssica frowned, her gaze drifting between tree trunks, hands on hips. "I doubt it's a coincidence that these killer growths are focused only in the area between Papillion and Garadenya."

Beside her, Kynthcat snorted. His mouth opened, his tongue curling out to taste the ether. "Mmroww."

Clutching a handful of fluffy mane, Lyssica grinned. "I can't get over you being able to 'taste' their smell – like rotten blueberries, you said?" She grimaced. "Nasty."

He worked his tongue, then hissed. "Gssst." In the six weeks since they'd found the first growth, there'd been at least one every day and, in a wonderful stroke of luck, his air-tasting sense traced them with unerring accuracy.

She tilted her head. "Can you sense any more infestations? Or any signs of the devil-rabbit?" He shook his head, huge mane flopping from side to side. "Good." She eyed the building clouds. "At least it's not snowing, so far." Blizzards, sleet and snowfall had intensified over the Moon of Juberd and continued into the Moon of Julary.

Winter had set in with a vengeance. An occasional weak, sunny day reared its head, but the temperature had dropped to freezing and stayed there. The sky was mostly covered in either stark white or gloomy grey cloud. She and Emryn continued the daily routine they'd begun as best they could. The harshness of the weather resulted in Lyssica rarely being able to fly; her wings were too delicate for strong winds and didn't function once wet, but after six weeks, their pattern of dividing the day between Garadenya, Papillion and the forest was well set.

"Rrow." Kynthcat rumbled deep in his chest as he nudged her out of her revery. She turned as he dropped to lie flat.

"Yes, you're right." She swung her leg over his back and settled, tucking her feet around his rib cage and grasping strands of his mane in both fists. Surging to his feet, he loped towards the Rubiconia River, threading between the trees, only stopping every now and then to re-test the air.

Riding comfortably, Lyssica sang, her words tiny pieces of power which the breeze of their passage scattered through the forest like seeds on the wind. She loved this benefit of Emryn and Kynthcat's company. In past winters, spreading her Ostara given power had relied on very loud vocals and how far she could travel in the wintry conditions. Only on a good day was she able to use her wings.

Beneath her, the muscles of Kynthcat's powerfully moving frame bunched and released. She revelled in it. His musky scent of rain-soaked forest drifted up to her, something she now associated with safety. Yes, he was guarding her, but, to her delight, he'd also been actively assisting in her work. She'd never guessed how much she'd enjoy having someone's wholehearted support. She'd come to rely on him a lot in her Handmaidenly duties.

Who was she kidding? She didn't just rely on him for that. She adored *him*. Longed for this to continue. Was there any way she could get him to stay on after the end of the Tri-moon program? She sighed. Naturally he'd have a life, commitments within his pack, so he probably wasn't interested in a chance-met female. Especially one with hang-ups like hers.

She nosedived, getting a face full of fluffy mane as Kynthcat skidded to a halt. "Ouch!" Under her legs, his ribs vibrated, a continuous snarl rumbling from his muzzle. Spitting out a mouthful of hair, she shoved to a sitting position and blinked, focusing between his outward curled horns to see what had upset him.

"Is that a spider's web? It's huge. I've not seen anything like it before." Lyssica stared as she gingerly touched her squashed nose. "I can't see it properly." She slid from Kynthcat's back, intending to approach, but he was a solid wall between her and the over-sized web. "Hey, you lump of rock! Move it." She poked him in the ribs, expecting him to step aside. Instead, he growled at her, not only continuing to block her from reaching the unusual web but nudging her further away. She sighed.

"Okay, I know it's likely dangerous. I know you're protecting me, but I have a job to do and this is part of it. You know that too, Emryn." His snarl faded. He looked at the strange web again, then hissed. But he eased to one side so she could approach where it extended between two tree trunks.

From several paces away, solid strands of shiny white crystal shaped a larger than normal open weave, spiralling inward like a funnel. It was interconnected by spokes to keep the shape in one roughly circular piece – quite weblike – but it radiated coldness, which was odd. The funnel centre contained an obscuring density. Was something there?

Lyssica stepped closer, craning her neck for a better look. The structure rippled, energy surged and—

Kynthcat roared. He lunged, hitting the back of her knees, throwing her off balance. A second blow hit the side of her neck and waves of painful cold seared her flesh, the agony increasing second by second. Something clung to her skin. Tightened and dug in.

She gasped, gloved fingers rising to claw at the spot. "It hurts, it burns!"

Kynthcat's snarling face eclipsed the surrounding forest. Time slowed. A paw rose, curving to smack her; she was already screaming as his massive paw, sharp claws fully extended, obscured her vision. The icy wind of their passing chilled her face, fur brushed her flesh, then, wicked claws dug into her neck – she jerked under the impact. Flesh tore and liquid trickled, a macabre tickling sensation. Why was this happening? The blazing torment at her throat intensified. She shrieked her pain, fear and betrayal as—

He ripped her throat out.

~

CRACK, crack, crack! Shards of crystal sprayed as Kynthcat's paw completed its arc. Iridescent crystalline chunks splintered crisply as they hit the ground and cartwheeled across the uneven terrain. The intense cold searing her neck vanished, leaving a deep stinging ache.

Lyssica crumpled; the forest floor, heavy and solid, whacked her in the back. The sky whirled above her in sickening swirls of white and grey. A cold wetness smooshed against her neck, smothering the burning sensation until it diminished to a dull throb. Staring, senses reeling, her every breath strained and torturous, she could only blink mindlessly when the heavens were blotted out by a blur of deep brown. Strands of fur fell softly against her cheek. A warm dampness began to gently brush at her tortured throat. Again and again the soft stroke returned, soothing scraped skin, dulling the sting of pain and somehow … somehow … calming her panic. Her hands reached blindly and she clasped silky fur between her fingertips, felt it tickling gently under her palms.

"Emryn?" Screaming had reduced her voice to a hoarse whisper. Every breath rasped viciously in her chest and throat, her vision was compromised, but she recognised the feel of his fur. And he was tending her, which meant … He hadn't torn her neck open? Understanding washed over her. Relief followed hard on its heels. No, of course he hadn't; he'd saved her.

His low growl suddenly became words. "Some guard I am! I know you have to do your work, but now you're wounded and I can't stand—"

Lyssica closed her fingers in his hair and jerked him down. Her lips mashed into his, the kiss a rough, slightly off-centre joining which he squirmed to correct. His mouth tasted as delectable as his alluring scent suggested. Strong arms wormed beneath her, firmed, then she was raised, pulled against him. Sensations swamped – the touch of his mouth, the feel of his cradling arms, her hands in his hair – those were her only points of reference. His response was ardent, his lips as eager as hers. She licked her tongue against his upper lip, into his suddenly open mouth and his tongue surged to join, to twine with her own. It was wonderful. It was delicious.

It was crazy.

Pulling away, Lyssica turned her head and rested it against his cheek. Her neck stung and she swallowed heavily, wishing she could ignore the pain. She drew a breath and – Emryn's delicious scent was strong in her nostrils, helping her to re-image the kiss in her mind, bask in the return of being sexually attracted to another; something she'd never thought to enjoy again after the bitter pain left by—

"Lyssica? Tell me you're okay!" He peppered the top of her ear with tiny kisses.

Her voice was tremulous. "I-I think so. By the Goddess, what was that? It feels like I have a very painful sunburn." She was tilted away from him slightly and couldn't help her brittle murmur of protest. "N-nooo."

"It's okay, I just need to look at the wound." His husky reassurance calmed her. "How does it feel."

"Not as bad as it did, thank goodness. Whatever action you took and the substances you put on it were tremendously effective." Her swallow was painful. "I'm sorry, but I thought you were going to kill me. I saw your fangs then your claws and—"

"Little fool." The humour in his voice took the barb from his words. "I was doing my job, saving you."

"Your job?" She was drooling over him and he saw her as a duty? The warmth inside her was suddenly chill. "Oh, of course. My apologies. Your job, I—"

"Stop." His arms tightened. "Let's be clear before your get any crack-brained ideas. *You* are not a job, but I was given the job of keeping *you* safe. There is a huge contrast between the two and I'll not have you confused about it. Okay?"

"I ... yes, okay."

He kissed her ear again. "Do you understand the difference? I want to be sure."

She started to nod; the sting stopped her. "I do see the distinction." But she wasn't certain where it took them. "Ah, what exactly happened?"

He snorted. "That web thing is a weapon. I sensed it was dangerous, but I didn't know what it would do. Kynthcat can't talk so we were pushing you away, but you persisted and sprung the thing's trap. I bumped you aside, but too late to avoid it completely. A sort of web thingy ejected at high speed, landed on your neck, and was digging into your flesh when I hooked it away. That action also smashed it to pieces – peeled away from your body it became hard and crystalline – but if I hadn't pushed you when I did, it would have landed on your face."

Shuddering at the thought, Lyssica's fingers came up to feel her wound.

"No touching. The vile thing's caused a nasty burn and torn your skin with that ugly web."

"Which I triggered with my proximity."

"The hazards of the profession, I guess. But ..." He tilted her chin up, forcing her to stare at the cosmos again. "Even though it goes against my protective nature, I won't second-guess your skills. I know we're still learning the best ways to work together." His lips twisted. "Mistakes always happen when partners are still learning. Neither of us knew *that* was going to attack whatever came near it. However—"

It was her turn to snort. "However. Yeah, I should have been more careful. Approaching from the front? What was I thinking?"

"You were thinking to investigate an anomaly in your forest. We both made a mistake. You approaching it head on; me not recognising the level of the danger. But we live and learn. This time, we're fortunate you're not seriously injured." His fingers gently turned her jaw from side to side. "Pain level out of ten?"

She grimaced. "About four. How'd you help me? Was the cold stuff snow?"

"Yeah. After I ripped it from your neck and shattered it, I packed on snow to ease the pain, but it's time to return to Garadenya and get some burn salve on it. Are you okay to travel?"

She tilted her head, met his silvery-grey gaze. "Only snow? What was the soft repetitive drag?"

His eyebrows rose. "Did it hurt?"

"No, no, no." She smiled weakly. "It really helped."

He nodded. "Good. Kynthcat was frantic – it was his tongue. He feels better for helping and now, I'd better change back so we can get moving."

"Change back?" Great goddess! They were talking and cuddling and they'd kissed and, and he was not able to do any of that as Kynthcat. Which meant … "Ohmygoddess! You're naked! That's not your leg I can feel – or maybe it is! Is that your leg? Please tell me it's your leg!" She was on her feet, with her back to him without even realising she'd leapt from his lap.

His uncontrollable laughter suddenly became the chuffing of a highly amused Kynthcat. She turned around to see him rolling on the ground, paws mirthfully batting the air.

Glaring, Lyssica snatched up a fallen, but still leafy, branchlet and swatted him across the flank.

EMRYN

"*I* came across them several times, when hunting rogue Ice-trolls." Dario stopped pacing to eye them grimly. "You ran afoul of a Vulpiawolf attack-web."

Scrubbing his head tiredly, Emryn sighed. "Well, cat-crap."

Lyssica frowned. "Vulpiawolves? In our forest? I don't know much about them."

Emryn grimaced. "I'm from warm lands and they thrive in wintry conditions, so I have never come across any before. But I have heard of them. They're vicious apparently."

Picking up his whisky-nectar, Dario cradled the beaker between his palms. "Be glad you've not met up with them – they *are* vicious. They're also malicious and often destructive. The pack has probably come down from the Northern Ice Wastes." He took a sip. "But what would have drawn them here?"

Helping herself to a cookie from the tray on the table, Lyssica contemplated the cholickalate chips. "What do they look like? I need to be able to recognise them." She bit into the cookie. "Mmm."

Emryn was overcome with a sudden need for his own cookie.

Dario continued as he sat next to Zhulija. "Their fur is a light greenish grey, but spiky rather than soft. They're spotted with the same green through a darker grey fur on their backs, although their fur coats only cover their body. Their legs are smooth, having dark grey skin speckled with small pale green oval marks. Their paws are five-clawed. Add to that narrow-pointed muzzles and ears, and a spike-furred tail with barbed tip, and you can't mistake them for any other creature."

Still contemplating the cookies, Emryn made a snap decision and snatched two before dropping into a comfortable chair. "And the attack-webs? Do you know how they're constructed? We saw lots of them after Lyssica recovered. She smashed them, from the side, with a club while Kynthcat flung whatever his claws could scoop. We disarmed as many as we found."

Zhulija stirred. "My avalanche power of flinging objects from a distance would be useful."

"Yes, as we unfortunately discovered, the web darts are set off by the target's nearness." Emryn met Lyssica's gaze. "We're going to have to do a daily sweep."

Lyssica winced. "Any idea how the Vulpiawolves create the stuff?"

Dario drew Zhulija closer. "As far as I know, the web stuff somehow extrudes from their claws as a soft substance, before hardening to ice. The claws are thick and hollow, like a tube. They also use the stuff like rope, to bind things, without the missile centre, of course."

Emryn frowned. "It broke easily."

"Binding-web ice is much thicker and stronger than attack-web." Dario reached for a cookie and handed it to Zhulija, before taking another and eyeing it in a predatory manner. "Plus Vulpiawolves hunt in packs."

Lyssica's eyes widened. "So multiple Vulpiawolves could bind you at the same time. That's bad. I wonder if the ice burns like the dart from the attack-web." She fingered her bandage-wrapped neck, causing Emryn to stiffen, while Kynthcat hissed and paced; he hated that she'd been in pain. Although, she was more relaxed since Zhulija had treated the wound with healing salve, applied a bandage and given her a pain-relieving herbal draught.

Dario swallowed a mouthful of cookie. "It all burns, but with a cold burn because it's ice."

Emryn lifted his beaker of whisky-nectar, swirling the liquid. "Do you think they're in league with the Bodach? Another one of his tools like the devil-rabbit?"

Lyssica nodded. "I wondered about that; the Bodach is cunning."

Dario exhaled. "I'm forced to agree. It would be a huge coincidence and we all know there's no such thing."

Zhulija nodded. "Yes, we've endured the devil-rabbit as the Bodach's messenger, the cancerous blue plant growths and now the Vulpia-webs, courtesy of a probable invasion of Vulpiawolves. What's next?"

Lyssica met her sister's gaze. "I've been thinking about that. As a consort to the Goddess of Winter, he has a lot of choice and control. He can call on anything with a cold vibration or winter-link."

Zhulija nodded. "Then these events are not just random bad luck. If we can figure out why it's happening, we may gain clues on what to expect and how to counter it."

"Okay." Emryn gestured with half a cookie. "Actions are usually based on want or need. So, what's the Bodach seeking?"

Brows wrinkled, Lyssica nibbled a cholickalate chunk. "To answer that, we'll summarise what we know of him. First, he's consorted to the Goddess of Cold and Wind."

Zhulija pleated her skirt with restless fingers. "True, but is he the alpha in their relationship?"

"I doubt it." Lyssica shook crumbs onto her plate. "Because, although she's also known as the Queen of Winter, he's never been called King."

Zhulija nodded. "So maybe he wants to be King of Winter? What else do we know?"

Contemplating the cookie tray, Emryn rubbed his jaw. "The myths state he likes to play tricks on others for his own amusement. They're reputed to not always be pleasant tricks." His hand hovered over the tray. "Sending a devil-rabbit, killing Lord Roland and exploding his body is proof of that." He succumbed to the cookie temptation and bit into another one.

Dario placed his whisky-nectar glass on the table. "He did say he hoped Lyssica, as Ostara's representative, enjoyed the show, but I fail to see killing as a fun activity, unless you're insane." He tapped the glass. "Lyss, I recall you saying that the devil-rabbit may have been an assumed body too?"

"Yes." She licked a streak of cholickalate from her lower lip; Emryn shifted in his chair, trying to ignore suddenly tight pants. "I was thinking the rabbit thing could have *been* the Bodach."

Dario frowned. "It spoke as if it wasn't. It said: 'The Bodach hopes you enjoyed the show.' Or something similar, which indicates it wasn't the Bodach."

"Ye-esss." Lyssica reached for her teacup. "But it wouldn't be the first time a being has referred to themself in the third person."

"It's a possibility." Emryn tilted his head, still riveted on Lyssica's pink mouth. He cleared his throat, suppressed memories of their explosive kiss. "But, one would assume, since the Bodach is her consort, the Cailleach knows what he's up to."

Zhulija and Lyssica met each other's eyes and broke into laughter.

Emryn's brows arched. "What's so funny?"

Lyssica shook her head. "Just because a couple is consorted doesn't mean they know every little thing about their partner or what they do. Zhu and I were thinking about Maman and Papan in that light." Fingertips rising to cover her lips, she chuckled again. "Nope, just nope."

Even Dario was grinning. "When you take a mate Emryn, you'll see the funny side of that comment too."

"Alright." Emryn's hands turned palm out. "So, the Cailleach may not know what her consort is doing?"

Lyssica's mouth thinned. "That's more than likely."

Zhulija leaned forward. "Is that deliberate? Is he hiding something from her?"

Dario pursed his lips. "Or trying to achieve something without her knowledge?"

Lyssica nodded. "Yes, good point! Something like a present, or a surprise? Despite his sly nature, he is rumoured to adore her."

Emryn put his glass down. "I like that idea. He's been her consort for eons and there's never been rumours about him wanting to be King."

"That's true." Dario wagged a finger. "However, his dissatisfaction could have been building for a long time."

"Maybe." Emryn spread his hands. "But, not everyone wants to be in charge; some of us are content to back our leader, as I'm currently doing for Lyssica." *'And loving it.'*

"Hmm." Dario cupped Zhulija's shoulder and pulled her back into the circle of his arm. "Your pack life gives you a uniquely helpful viewpoint, Emryn. If we continue the line of thought of the Bodach not aiming to be alpha, then, we can accept the possibility he's doing something for the Cailleach's benefit. Even if she's in the dark."

"I wish I could communicate with Ostara." Lyssica ran a hand through her hair fretfully. "She could speak to the Cailleach and this business would be sorted very quickly."

Zhulija stared. "Could the block be deliberate?"

"To stop me bringing in Ostara? You could be right." Lyssica fanned her hands in frustration. "But whether it's deliberate or not, I still can't get through to her, which means I'm on my own – sorry, *we're* on our own."

Zhulija's brow wrinkled. "If you can't call for help, the Bodach has longer to achieve his purpose, doesn't he?"

Emryn's mouth twisted. "Which means he assumes his powers are stronger than those you possess, Lyssica."

She sighed. "They most likely are. After all, he's consort to a goddess while I'm merely Handmaiden of one."

Dario pointed. "Don't sell yourself short Lyssica Aphiski. From what both Zhu and Emryn say, you've quite amazing abilities. Admit he's more powerful and you're all but conceding defeat. Whatever he's up to, we can't afford to lose and you're our best hope."

Lyssica flung up her hands. "Wow! Way to stack the pressure on!

It's winter, which is their season, so he's super strong. I wield spring power and it's not spring, so I'm weaker."

"But winter is *always* vanquished by spring." Emryn tossed in. "You – we – can't lose."

"Thank goodness!" Zhulija shivered. "Can you imagine if it was always winter?"

An electric silence filled the room as they all stared at her.

"Oh!" Lyssica's hands flew to her mouth.

"That's it!" Emryn was on his feet. "That's got to be it."

Dario hugged his consort. "You're brilliant sweetheart! Eternal winter, tied up in a bow from the Bodach to his mate. What better gift is there?"

ESCORTING Lyssica through the halls of Garadenya Fortress to their shared suite, Emryn's eyes were riveted to Lyssica's svelte form. His mouth watered and his cock thickened. Inside him, fur ruffled and claws jabbed; Kynthcat prowled. *'Want her.'*

'So you keep saying.'

'You do too. Your prick on alert.'

Emryn huffed. *'She's gorgeous, but it's not possible.'*

Pausing in the doorway, Lyssica glanced at him. "Something wrong?"

He summoned a grin. "Just tired. Today was gruelling."

His cat persisted. *'She ours.'*

'We're only visiting for three moons!'

'Take her home with us.' Cat logic. Simple and direct.

Emryn massaged his forehead. *'We can't do that! Her job is a critical part of her make-up.'*

A fur driven shrug. *'We stay here then. It work well. Fulfil our directive to create connections between shifter tribes and outsider Fae.'*

'But we're bound to the pack! I can't ... we need ... you ... they'd never ... it's not...'

A warm palm touched his cheek. Jerked from his pointless

pronoun babbling, he peered between his cupped fingers, gulping as he registered the tender expression on Lyssica's face. *'There! See?'* A very smug Kynthcat preened his whiskers. *'She adore us as a mate should.'*

'Mate?!' A tide of red seeped up his neck and a deep gurgling sound choked him. His desperately seeking hand hit the nearby wall in direct response to the dizziness flooding him. He fought it, denied Kynthcat's instincts. *'What in time-sands are you talking about?'*

'You a silly kitbabe. Not know mate even when she loves on us. You want a Seer reading. Pah!' A paw waved dismissively. *'Who needs Seer when truth and our very own beauty, luscious and ripe in our face?'*

'You're wrong! She can't possibly be our mate. She's not changeling ...'

"Emryn?" Lyssica's eyebrows furrowed. "Are you alright?"

"Ah, ah, yes." He fought for words. "Nothing a good night's rest won't cure."

Kynthcat lay down and put both paws over his eyes. *'I in error. You not just a silly kitbabe, you a scared, silly, kitbabe dummy.'*

'You can take a long walk off a short time-sand pier!'

Kynthcat chuffed his mirth. *'Only problem with that, if I do what you say, I take you with me, scaredy kitbabe!'*

Staring up at him, brows still creased, Lyssica patted his cheek. "You're probably right, but there's something I'd like to discuss – if you're not too tired?" Her mouth quirked hopefully. "I could give your neck a massage. If that would help?"

Kynthcat snorted. *'Not neck muscles he want massaged, Lyss-mate.'*

"Um. Massage? Ah, maybe." Emryn swallowed convulsively, ignoring Kynthcat. "You're correct though, we do need to talk about ... Ah ... About things, yeah things ..."

"Good." Grasping his hand, Lyssica towed Emryn into the sitting room of their suite. She dropped to sit on the sofa he would be opening into a bed later, as he had every night since they'd taken up residence. She still held his hand, so he'd little choice but to sink down near her, unless he pulled his hand free and moved further away. *That would be extremely juvenile and he wasn't a child*, so he sat, trying to hide how much he wanted to pounce on her.

"Well." He scraped the palm of his free hand up and down his thigh. "Here we are."

"Yes." Lyssica twisted to face him, then tilted her head. "Is there something wrong with your hand?"

"My hand?" He lifted the offending limb and stared at it. "Er, I think it might be itchy. Yes! That's right. It's itchy."

She peered at him. "You seem uncomfortable. What is it?"

"Um." He shrugged, glanced around for inspiration. "Wow, when did it get so dark? I must have missed that. How about I light the lamps? I'll just do that, yeah?" As a shape shifter, he had excellent night vision, but she wouldn't know that. He half rose from the sofa, but her firm tug on his captured hand aborted the action. Still loath to pull free of her grip, Emryn cast her a desperate glance.

She smiled ruefully. "Looks like I need to apologise."

He gawked. "Apologise? For what?"

"You're suddenly uncomfortable with me." Her hands clasped together, gripping his hand firmly between her palms. "The only difference is, I kissed you today. I'm not sorry, but I'll apologise if it helps."

One swift indrawn breath and he planted himself firmly on the sofa, face close to hers. "Apology rejected, Lyssica. My problem, my discomfort, directly relates to my aching need for more of your kisses."

"Oh!" Heat flooded her cheeks. "In that case, what's stopping – mmf—"

Emryn's mouth slid across hers, effectively muffling the rest of her sentence.

11

LYSSICA

yssica's hands emptied as Emryn pulled from her grasp, but his palms returned to cup her cheeks, slide into her hair. His lips twisted deliciously against hers, nipping, nibbling, enticing ... She opened her mouth on a gasp allowing his tongue to surge inside, deepening their connection and overwhelming her with his decadently spicy essence. After the disaster that had brought her party years to a brutal close, she'd never expected to desire a male ever again – but here she was, falling into a haze of need. The combination of his musky, fresh rain scent, the caress of his seductive lips and hands and the glide of his tongue combining to befuddle her senses.

His mouth eased from hers, spread kisses along her jaw. You're adorable Lyssica." His voice rumbled against the side of her neck, just below her ear, before his seeking lips enveloped her ear lobe, sucking and licking, until she quaked with fiery arousal.

Her head tipped back, the pleasure gifted by Emryn's touch chasing away the lingering taint of her darkest memories. The demons which had haunted her for so many years were as nothing in the face of his honest passion, the wild strength of him buoying her confidence until she reached out blindly, shaping the muscles of his chest through the thin cloth of his shirt. "Need skin."

Leaning away, Emryn fisted the back of his top and hauled it over his head. Lyssica's eager fingers travelled over his pectoral muscles, massaging and stroking the taut leaf-brown skin, then his talented lips found hers, his tongue licking the seam of her mouth. The kiss became open-mouthed, their eager tongues seeking, exploring, wrestling, before his mouth moved to spread kisses along her jaw.

She petted up and over his shoulders, tugging him closer so their chests rubbed together in an attempt to assuage the tingling fullness swamping her breasts. "Oh, yes."

"Better skin to skin." Emryn's lips tickled the corner of her mouth. "Raise your hands." Lyssica did so, cloth rustled as her top was swept off over her head and eased around her wings. He licked his lips, eyes a lazy, sexy, burning brand as they roved, until her nipples hardened, drawing his focus. She basked in his molten silver gaze as it became riveted on her full breasts, which thrust high and firm against their gauzy breast-band. His head lowered, mouth nipping and kissing, tongue wetting both her breast-band and the aching nubs the cloth concealed.

"Oh." Her fingertips shaped claws, dug into his heavily muscled chest.

"Keep doing that!" The expulsion of hot breath as he gasped was a further delight to her breasts. They ached, they needed ... She rubbed them across his face, arched to push one point against his lips. His mouth opened, fusing hotly around the wanting pertness. Palms stroked up her body, feathered across her other impatient nipple. Fingers caressed, gathered the damp fabric of her breast-band to rub to-and-fro across the peak. Pleasure expanded, shot in a direct line to her groin where fire bloomed and dampness grew.

"Emrynnnn ..." Lyssica's voice sighed out of her; a direct contrast to the urgent raising of her hips as they sought, searched ... there! A warm hard bulge against her thigh. Wrong place. She twisted, wriggled, trying for a better connection.

"Lyss?" Her lover raised his head slightly, eyes like pools of silvery lava. So enticing, but he'd paused in his ministrations to both breasts and that wouldn't do. Not at all.

Surging forward, her arms wrapping around his neck, body sandwiching his, she shoved. Emryn's eyes widened as he fell backward into the sofa, Lyssica riding him all the way. Knees either side of his hips, skirts frothing around her, she squirmed to connect the firm ridge in his pants with the hot, heavy aching desire between her thighs. Achieving her goal, she writhed and rubbed against him, almost sobbing as the fire blossomed to an inferno of want, of need.

It was a revelation she'd never expected to experience. And she wasn't going to let it disappear before she'd gotten her chance to fully appreciate their togetherness. Her hands reached for his, brought palms back to aching breasts.

"This." Emryn wrestled with the breast band. "Off!" There was a ripping sound, then cool air bathed her upper body. He stroked up from her waist, cupped her heated, heavy breasts. "Time sands! You're so exquisite, my Lyss." His hands shaped, kneaded. Fingers plucked gently.

The sight of her firm mounds filling Emryn's hands, the feel of those hands against her straining bosom added fuel to the fire of desire. Lyssica squirmed against his groin, the action and the feelings it engendered drawing sounds of pleasure from them both. "I need you, Emryn. I can't go another day watching and wanting ..."

His chuckle was hoarse. "Not just me then. You've bewitched me from the very first. Best thing you did was fall into my arms. Only ..." He hesitated. "I can't make any promises, Lyss. When the program is over, I must return home to my pack." Her hips undulated against him, her mouth falling open at the intense pleasure.

Words dropped from ruby lips. "I want you, Emryn. This is for me and I want you. The future can take care of itself."

He shuddered beneath her and grasped her hips. "Then, I'm yours, love. Take what you want, give us what we both need."

His smile radiated all the way to the glory of her femininity, making it pulse with desire. "Pants." Her fingers scrabbled at his belt, unlatching it, then the fastenings of his trousers fell victim to her intent. "Lift." He obeyed and she pulled his pants down past his thighs.

"Now you." Stretching, he raised her skirts, holding them while she rose to her knees, shoved her tights down over her bottom, then sat sideways and twisted to yank them off completely. His hands were there, guiding her back over his thighs, as eager as she for their joining.

Lyssica clasped fingers around his rigid length. "Look at you! So long and thick." She ran fingers down to his balls and back, traced the contours of the swollen head, brought her fingers to her lips, slick with his pre-cum. "I'm burning for you, Emryn."

His words were a husky murmur. "I'm clean. Are you protected? Because I have nothing with me. Although, shifters can only get their mates pregnant, so there's no worry about that."

"Yes. Clean and protected, a side perk of my goddess power."

He frowned. "I thought one of Ostara's abilities was fertility?"

She grinned, still caressing him. "Two sides of the same coin. All's well."

"Good." His forefinger circled a nipple, repeated the action on the other before pulling her close, lashing the first one with his tongue. The action lodged the hot stiffness of his cock firmly between her thighs until it nestled against her pubes, flexed hungrily against her mons.

"Oh, oh, oh, yes!" She lifted slightly, easing her opening back and forth over his unyielding shaft. She was willing putty in his hands as he coaxed her up, then lowered her to engulf his rod in the depths of her wet channel. Pushing high and deep, he filled and stretched her in a tumult of blissful delight. Her sigh mirrored his gasp, both of them stilling as they adjusted to their intimate connection.

Emryn's fingers feathered delightfully on her skin. "You okay, my Lyss?"

Nodding joyfully, Lyssica kissed him. "You feel sooo wonderful Emryn." Her movement caused a delicious friction where they were joined, eliciting indrawn breaths. Seeking to repeat the feeling, Lyssica swivelled her hips; Emryn lunged to meet her, pressing and thrusting. Eyes locked, cheeks flushed, panting and entwined, they kept loving until the tiny muscles in Lyssica's passage began to flutter and quake.

"Shite yes!" Emryn's mutter combined with her wail of gratification; her climax milking him to fulfilment. Clutching each other, they shook and shuddered until Lyssica collapsed against his sweaty chest with a huge sigh. Snuggling her cheek against his skin, unable to muster enough strength to move, she revelled in the sensations of Emryn's warm hands stroking her back.

A little later, he pulled a blanket from the back of the sofa to cover them, before wrapping his arms around her. Warm and cosy, they drifted off to sleep.

～

THEY STIRRED TWICE MORE during the dark hours, to reach and caress and love again. Each time was equally as wonderful as their first joining.

Now, morning light filtered in through the window and Lyssica studied Emryn's sleeping face, licking her lips as she recalled the night's pleasures.

Will I ever get enough of him? Her heart said no.

A large hand began to stroke her spine, something he apparently enjoyed – as did she. One eye opened, peered lazily at her. "Lyssica, my sweet. I doubt I'll tire of looking at you under any circumstances; you're everything I've always wanted. I'd love us to be able to stay here forever, but unfortunately, the day calls."

Regret twisted her mouth. "Duties and responsibilities. Yep, still there waiting for us." She eased away. "I call first dibs on the shower."

He tilted his head, batted his eyelids. "We could share ..." Grinned as she started to giggle, but the grin faded and his eyes glazed over as her breasts jiggled enticingly. Lyssica gasped as his hand feathered up her body to stroke ...

The shower happened.

Eventually.

A very long shower.

~

AFTER THEIR MUTUAL satisfaction was achieved and both were washed, Emryn dried and dressed quickly. "Must go, sweeting. I'm late meeting Dario."

She winked. "I know – not sorry."

He kissed her. The press of his lips was meant to be brief, but Lyssica threw herself into the embrace and he was seduced into lingering for several scorching moments. "Unh." His eyes were closed as he drew back and, when they flicked open to pin her in smouldering silver whirlpools, his voice emerged a growl. "Hold that thought for later, beloved." This time his mouth found her cheek, her forehead and her other cheek, before he rushed out the doorway of their suite and was gone.

Sighing happily, Lyssica finished her morning toilette and left their quarters to join Zhulija in the breakfast room. Her sister was filling a plate from dishes arrayed on the sideboard as Lyssica entered.

Zhulija beamed a welcoming smile. "Good morning, Lyss. Looks like we're all late getting up this morning. Sleep well?"

A heated tide swept up Lyssica's neck into her cheeks. "Oh, um yes. Very well. I feel so rested. A lovely night ..." She trailed off as Zhulija grinned at her knowingly.

"If it was like our night, it probably was lovely. I imagine you're quite sore this morning."

Lyssica's mouth tightened. She busied herself by reaching for a clean plate and inspecting the trays of food. "Not like you're thinking – I wasn't virginal."

Zhulija stilled momentarily, then arranged a slice of toast beside her scrambled eggs and bacon. "Okayyy."

Lyssica's fingers clenched around the plate edges. "Whatever's in your mind right now is probably wrong." She drew a deep breath. "What happened between Emryn and I last night was special because it was the first time the *choice* was mine, and that's how I'm processing it, because—" Goddess! What had she just said? She hadn't meant to ever let anyone know.

The plate in her sister's hands was thrust to the table. Sick horror reflected in Zhulija's expression. "You've been forced – in the past?"

Lyssica shrugged, her mouth twisting bitterly. She didn't really want to talk about it, but then again, she'd already said too much to ever think Zhulija would let it go. She sighed. "I didn't resist." Her eyes were on the patterned wallpaper. "Hard to resist when you've been drugged into unconsciousness."

"Oh Goddess! Lyss! I'm so sorry." Zhulija removed Lyssica's plate from her clenching fingers, set it on the sideboard and drew her sister into a warm hug. "How did I not know this?"

Swallowing heavily, Lyssica burrowed into the affection; for some reason her acceptance of it freed her tongue. "I've never told anyone. It was my own fault; during that stupid rebellious phase when Papan told me I wasn't good enough to learn estate management beside DeMaksim. According to him, young Fae-females only have a place as pampered misses with nothing to do but party and enjoy themselves. So I did, only, some of the folk I met were well-disguised swine."

"Oh, Lyss! It happened more than once?" Moisture filled Zhulija's eyes.

"No, fortunately." Eyeing her sister, Lyssica flung up a hand. "Please, no tears. I've had lots of time to think about what happened and I've come to terms with it. I'd prefer to talk about pleasant matters. Which brings me to last night. It was wonderful and completely consensual and I never thought I'd ever experience anything like it. But now that I have, I'm not sorry."

"Sorry?" Zhulija frowned. "What do you mean?"

Lyssica sighed. "I know our society expects us to remain virginal until we consort, but in reality, that's an outmoded belief and, if it's fair to apply the restriction to females, then it's also applicable to males."

Lowering her arms, Zhulija nodded slowly. "That last is absolutely true, Lyss. Whether we're sexually active, or not, should be our own choice, no matter who we are." She drew back, studied Lyssica. "Even so, it must have been a big deal with Emryn last night after … I know you said you're not sorry for it but … Are you certain you're okay? You said you've come to terms with the events – your link, your duties with Ostara, did they help you?"

Lyssica nodded. "My Ostara commitment kept me sane, especially after the incident. I was hurt and confused; first because of Papan and then … about what happened. But I was the one who went partying, foolishly trusting the folk around me."

"You don't believe you got what you deserved, do you? Because that's—"

"No, no, of course not. That's not what I'm saying. I mean, nobody deserves what happened to me. But I'll admit I've rehashed my lifestyle enough times to see what I should've done differently and to wish I had not gone down the path I did. But please don't think that means my own behaviour excuses that bastard for what he did; what he took from me…" Her hands rose to Zhulija's hips. "There is something I've been meaning to say though, Zhu? And now, I can. I need to apologise for the time I tried making a move on Dario. It was awful. *I* was awful." She spread her hands. "At that point, I was a mess inside, still working through my emotional fallout, thinking all males were untrustworthy and trying to protect you. Poor excuses, I know, but they're all I've got."

Movement in the doorway caught her attention. She turned her head to discover Emryn and Dario frozen in the opening, each of them holding two mugs. Dario wore an expression of angry shock; Emryn's face was filled with murderous fury. Zhulija's hair tickled Lyssica's cheek as she also twisted to eye the Fae-males.

Oh Goddess – had they heard too? From the look on both of their faces, they had; Lyssica firmed her mouth. All of these years she'd kept her secret, but there was no going back now.

12

EMRYN

"You were sexually assaulted in the past?" Emryn's stomach turned over. "Why didn't you say something? If I'd known I could have made sure you were okay, Lyssica, I would have asked you—" Emryn broke off and thumped the mugs he'd been carrying on the sideboard, heedless of the slopping liquid. He advanced on Lyssica, wanting to touch her, to hug her, to hold her safe, but would she even invite his touch? Had he frightened or traumatised her with his lovemaking? He stared down at Lyssica's beautiful face, feeling helpless and angry on her behalf. "Are you alright?" His mind ran over their activities of the previous night. "We didn't do anything to hurt or upset you?"

Lyssica smiled. "No. No, I enjoyed everything we shared. Thank you for asking but, if you recall, I was with you all the way last night. I would definitely have spoken up if something didn't um, sit well with me."

Approaching slowly, hands also empty, Dario flanked Emryn. "Who did it?"

"Good question." Emryn's voice emerged a growl. "He needs to be taught a lesson and I'd be happy to be the teacher." Inside him Kynthcat raged, pacing to-and-fro, claws digging in with every step, his snarl a low and continuous threat. *'We tear and snap and rend this creature who hurt our female!'*

"I'm not sure giving up his name is wise." Lyssica cocked her head. "I've moved forward, I can't prove anything and he'll deny it."

Emryn's growl deepened. "You think that bothers me? He may deny it all he likes, but as an empath, I feel the truth and as a shapeshifter, I scent it."

Dario briefly tightened his fingers on Lyssica' shoulder. "Lyssica, think about this – you may not be his only victim. A bastard such as this will repeat actions he believes he can get away with. You can't change the past, but what about the future?"

Head rising quickly, Lyssica paled. "Oh! I've never thought about him targeting others." Her fingers covered her lips for a moment, then dropped to her throat. "But he would. Yes, indeed he would."

Zhulija clasped her hand. "So give us a name, Lyss. Help us stop him."

Mouth trembling, Lyssica shook her head. "You're all amazing. I thought maybe … you might blame me given what happened."

Emryn knelt in front of her and took her hands gently, revolted by the thought she had blamed herself in any way for that the actions of an honourless bastard. "No behaviour of yours excuses his. Ever. No male worth his salt would ever take your choices from you."

She looked behind him to see Dario and Zhu nodding in agreement. Zhu bit her lip. "He's right, Lyss. You can't blame yourself. Not even a little bit." There were tears in her sister's eyes.

Dario swallowed. "Please, tell us who it was so we can help you set it a little bit right."

She blinked away tears, sniffing a little before nodding decisively. "Very well. It was Perris Momphiday. Do with the knowledge as you will."

"What?" Zhulija stiffened. "The same one who is Tri-moon guesting at Papillion?"

"Yes."

Suddenly, Emryn vanished, Kynthcat ripping out of him. Roaring, the animal bolted for the door, shedding scraps of clothing as he went.

Lyssica straightened. "Emryn, stop!" Lips taut, Zhulija tightened her comforting grip on her sister's hand.

Dario smiled grimly. "Don't worry, the door's shut and his paws handicap him." He closed in on Emryn, prodding the stymied, snarling Kynthcat in his rump. "Change back! We'll get the bastard, but we'll get him at the right time. Going off like this isn't the answer."

'Rend and gut him!' Kynthcat paced, lips peeled back from his very large, sharp teeth. *'You can't stop me.'* He flicked a wicked glance at Dario then lowered his head, horns aimed at the door.

Zhulija gasped. Lyssica shook her head.

"Emryn, no!"

Baring his own teeth, Dario pointed at Emryn. A small fireball spat and sparked on the tip of his finger. "By Old Mab's teeth and hair! If you start goring my door, I'll singe your hide, Emryn Arion Phengaris! In this place and time, I'm your Alpha and I'm telling you to stand down and change back. *Now!*"

Unable to resist Dario's alpha voiced command, Kynthcat reshaped himself. Naked and furious, Emryn glared, hands digging into hips. "Need to shred him!" His eyes were wild, still glowing with changeling energy.

Dario grabbed a quilt from a nearby chair and flung it at Emryn. "Stop thinking like a predator; it'll do you no favours, right now. And wrap that coverlet around you – I'd much rather Zhu look at and think about my gonads than get an eyeful of yours!"

Muttering, Emryn covered himself. Heat crept up his neck and face. Zhulija emitted a burst of laughter and even Lyssica was grinning. The ladies' reactions also helped to settle all of them. For that alone, he'd forgive Dario's harsh slap of reality. Twisting one hand into his wild hair, he pulled his fingers through the entire length to his shoulder, calming Kynthcat and reining him in. "Sorry. Didn't mean to lose control. Strong emotion feeds our empathic side and extremes of both can trigger uncontrolled savagery in Kynthcat, to the point where neither of us can think straight."

Still chuckling, Zhulija waved one hand. "It's okay, but perhaps you could go and get into fresh clothes?"

Emryn nodded. "Yeah." He shifted his attention to Dario. "Thank you. My apologies." His gaze flickered to Lyssica brows raising.

She smiled tremulously. "Thank you for wanting to defend me."

"Always." He turned and noticed Dario still had the tiny fireball in his hands and was tossing it from one hand to the other. Emryn's eyes narrowed. "Were you really going to zap me?"

"I protect what's mine – even if it is just a door."

"Noted." Emryn finger-combed his hair again.

"Good." The tiny fireball winked out. "Apology accepted." Then Dario grinned. "Go get dressed. We'll make fresh tea and reheat the food."

~

"I've just realised you used my full name." Emryn lowered his fork to his empty plate, reached for his mug of tea.

Dario grinned, both hands wrapped around his own cup. "That should've told you how serious I was."

Zhulija shook her head, a grin also gracing her lips. "Using a full name is very parentish, my darling Dario. You'll be a great father one day." Pursing his lips, he blew a kiss her way. She pretended to catch it.

Emryn watched Lyssica push some food around her plate. She'd eaten about half of what Zhulija had served her. Inside him, a tail whipped from side to side. *'Our mate still upset. She upset with us?'*

'I keep telling you, she's not our mate.'

Lyssica slanted a glance across the table at him. "I don't think I can manage anymore." Had she heard them?

"Don't then." He stretched a hand out. "I'm sorry if our unruly display added to your distress."

Kynthcat hissed. *'We not unruly.'*

Lyssica dropped her cutlery, accepted the offer of his fingers and twined hers into them. "It's okay, really it is. It showed me I'm not as alone as I thought."

Dario sipped his drink, eyed her shrewdly. "You've never told anyone, you said?"

Lyssica grimaced. "No. I thought it was my trouble to deal with – I wasn't comfortable sharing the details with anyone."

Zhulija rubbed Lyssica's arm. "Not even Maman?"

"No, I thought she'd be ashamed of me. Not about my being molested. But about how I behaved back then – drinking and running with a crowd of people with no thought in their heads other than to have a good time. If I hadn't been with them, getting drunk and behaving rashly, it probably wouldn't have happened."

"Oh Lyss. I'm so sorry you felt like that." Zhulija frowned. "I wish you'd been able to talk to at least one of us. You should be able to." Her frown deepened. "I thought us a close-knit family, but not close enough apparently."

Drumming his fingers on the table, Dario looked at Emryn. "If you're agreeable, we'll skip today's Tri-moon program lesson. You're ahead anyway and we need to plan."

Emryn nodded. "That's fine. Our situation has become increasingly complicated every day since this began. Whenever we go into the forest it's to find more traps and infestations to spike, with no sign of the devil-rabbit or actual sightings of Vulpiawolves. It's frustrating."

Zhulija sighed. "And now there is Perris Momphiday to deal with. Has he bothered you Lyss?"

Lyssica's nose wrinkled. "He's asked for a private meeting several times. I've been ignoring him as best I can; I've no wish to be alone with the creep."

"I should think not!" A growl rattled Emryn's chest. "Bad enough he's at your home, somewhere you should feel safe. Make certain you neither eat nor drink anything he offers." He cocked his head. "I'm assuming that's how he administered the knock-out drug?"

"Yes. A drink." Lyssica massaged her temples. "His turn to pay, he told us and when I began to feel drowsy and unwell, he acted the well-mannered Fae-male and helped me to find a secluded room at the tavern we were partying at. He attacked me, tore my clothes ... I couldn't fight. Probably better that I passed out." She shuddered. "I was so naive."

"I'll kill him." Emryn hissed the words between clenched teeth. His clasp on her hand strengthened.

Lyssica stared, round-eyed. "Kill him? You'd do that?" Her voice emerged a squeak.

Dario leaned back in his chair. "He deserves it, but the action will only get you into serious trouble. We wouldn't want his family to start a vendetta." He pursed his lips. "What we should do is set him up as bait for the devil-rabbit or the Vulpiawolves. Let them do the dirty work, leaving no suspicion on us. Then we've only got to deal with the Bodach and his minions.

Emryn was nodding before Dario had finished speaking. "Great tactics."

An expression of horror crossed Zhulija's face. "You can't just sit there and plot to have someone killed!"

"Why not?" Emryn cocked his head. "We just agreed he's deserving of it."

Dario held up a finger. "Actually, I can. And so can you. The Queens appointed us their representatives. Meting out justice comes within our range of duties; we just have to get him onto Garadenya lands. Our Queens, if they got hold of him, would tear him apart."

"Oh, of course. Justice. That I fully support." Zhulija nodded. "What say you, Lyss?"

She shook her head. "You're wasting your time appealing to me. I've dreamed of shoving a blade into him, but ..." She nibbled her lower lip. "Using him as bait for the Bodach would be very satisfying; and save Emryn having to dirty his hands."

Dario speared her with a look. "That's all perfectly understandable and we do need to draw the Bodach out if we want to defeat him."

Zhulija pursed her lips. "Have you been able to connect with Ostara yet, Lyss?"

Lyssica rubbed the back of her neck. "No, but I'm not giving up, because without her, I don't have a chance."

Emryn squeezed her fingers gently. "You say that because you believe the Bodach more powerful than you."

"He is."

"Not necessarily. Not in the ways that count."

The look she gave him could have melted his heart. "Thank you for your faith in me – it means the world. But even if you're right, it still doesn't guarantee a win against the Bodach."

"What if we resort to trickery?"

Zhulija considered him. "*Is* it possible to trick a trickster?"

"I think so, only because he's so busy running his own scam, he won't expect to have the tables turned."

Dario tapped the side of his mug. "Think of it as attacking him where he least expects it – he'll be vulnerable."

Zhulija frowned. "Does anyone have jurisdiction over the forest between Papillion and Garadenya?"

"Crown land." Dario gestured vaguely. "At a pinch, anyone who is an appointed representative of the Dual Crowns, could exercise their authority there." His mouth formed an 'o' of understanding.

"Exactly. That means us." A sly smile crept over Zhulija's mouth. "Lyss, you should agree to meet with that bastard, Perris. Suggest the forest as neutral ground for the meeting. That's where we'll be waiting, listening as you draw a confession out; then we'll arrest him. He can be strung up as bait for the devil-rabbit. Disposing of that weirdo should draw out the Bodach and ..." She spread her hands.

Emryn grinned. "Oh yes, I like that plan."

"Me too." Dario winked at Zhulija. "Some of my cunning has clearly rubbed off."

Replacing her mug on the table, Lyssica wiped her mouth with a napkin. "Something just occurred to me. Ostara has shared a number of times how much she enjoys having hand-maidenly help. Because she loves what she does, but it's hard work and, essentially, just a job."

Frowning, Zhulija toyed with a fold of the table cloth. "But she's a goddess."

"Who is expected to come back, year after year, doing the same things, over and over." Lyssica steepled her fingers. "She enjoys it, yes and she's worshipped, again yes, but it's because she gives people what they want."

Emryn cocked his head. "So what happens when people don't get what they want? They stop worshipping her? What happens to a deity with no worshippers?"

Dario straightened. "I see the other side of that coin. What happens when a deity does not leave when their job is over? Are they feted, or reviled?"

"And there's another angle." Zhulija ran her fingers over a coloured thread in the cloth. "If the seasons are their work, it's reasonable to assume their 'off' time is for relaxation, or a holiday. What happens to a deity when they've no choice but to work full time?"

"Exactly!" Lyssica pointed a finger at her sister. "The Cailleach probably doesn't want to work non-stop. Who would?"

A smile spread across Dario's face. "And there we have the Bodach's weak spot. His gift of eternal winter won't be received with the joy he believes. His Cailleach will, more than likely, be angry with him, and there's little happiness, or satisfaction, in a relationship where your woman eyes you with fury." He blew Zhulija a kiss.

She poked her tongue out at him. "I'll sort you out later."

His smile broadened. "I can't wait, my darling." She blushed, but her eyes narrowed and she wagged a finger. He blew another kiss.

A brush of fur, a prick of claws. *'See! That how romance done. More than hot skin and driving, wet ding-dong. Although, that rrowwrr.'* A tide of raw red prickled up Emryn's neck and surged across his face. "Be quiet!" He kept his voice to a mutter, but everyone stared.

"What?" Came from Lyssica.

Emryn cleared his throat. "Nothing. Just responding to Kynthcat's internal musings." Dario's grin was knowing. Emryn bared a fang, something common to both his forms. "Getting back to the matter at hand—"

"Is it?" Dario elbowed him, grinning like a hyena. "At hand? Don't let us interrupt your private time."

Certain he was about to burst into flame from the heat in his cheeks, Emryn groaned and face palmed.

Lyssica looked to be fighting her own grin as she gave a laughing Zhulija a good-natured shove. "If I might interrupt—"

"I'm certain Emryn would love you to do so." Dario's voice was a suggestive purr.

"Oh!" A wide-eyed Lyssica was also overcome by a blush. "You're really very good at this, Dario."

Dario winked. "Practice. You just continue practicing with Emryn and you're well on your way to nirvana."

Both Zhulija's hands flattened on the table top. "I think that's enough, Dario. If you're trying to help Lyss see there's a much more enjoyable side to sex, I believe she's already discovering that."

"Yes." Lyssica nodded, cheeks still pink. "To be able to talk so openly about ..."

Dropping his hand from his face, Emryn reached to grasp her fingers again. "The good side and the bad? Yeah, it's cathartic, healing and healthy to speak and share and even joke; the sort of thing that abounds in loving relationships and amongst good friends." He twisted to look at Dario and Zhulija. "Although I've interacted with Dario in the past, I know we've only come to know each other properly since I arrived for the Tri-moon program, six and a half weeks ago. In that time, I've recognised you as friends I'd be happy to commit to for life and, I hope you might see me in the same light – or manage to, before I must return home."

"Oh, Emryn, that's so lovely." Zhulija sighed. "I'm pleased to be your friend for life."

Dario offered his right arm and Emryn raised his in answer. As they clasped arms, Dario looked at him squarely. "You know it. Eternal friendship between us. Wherever we are."

This time, Zhulija pointed at Emryn. "And you may have to leave, but you'd better come back – or else."

Emryn laughed. "Or else?"

She wagged her finger at him. "I can do unpleasant things with a storm of loose objects – any loose objects." She raised her eyebrows. "Consider yourself warned."

And even though she'd added a light hearted touch, Emryn didn't mistake her intent. He looked to Lyssica; she winked at him.

13

LYSSICA

Firmly astride Kynthcat's back, fingers wrapped in the strands of his mane as she peered between his gnarled horns, Lyssica recognised the final bend in the road to Papillion. Beneath her, muscles bunched as his loping gait slowed and he headed for a copse of witherbeech saplings at the side of the road. Circling to the rear, where saplings screened them from the road, Kynthcat crouched, allowing Lyssica to slide to the ground. As she steadied herself, his big head swung around and a large rasping tongue slurped wetly across her face.

"Emryn!" She shoved him. "Urrk, I'm drowning. Blargh." He chuffed, ribs shaking as she scrubbed her face against his shoulder. "Stand still, you fluffy buffoon." Grinning, she unlatched the strap holding their pack, pulled the satchel away and watched, spellbound, as a shimmering swirl of magical light enveloped Kynthcat. When the magic shimmer faded, Fae-male Emryn stood laughing at her. Naked Emryn. He looked so delicious she couldn't stop some very lustful thoughts from swamping her mind.

He winked. "I thought you liked my kisses."

Her eyes ran over him again and she licked her lips. "So, I do, just wasn't expecting Kynthcat's huge tongue bath." She thrust the bag towards him. "Here. Find some clothes and put them on before I get any ideas. We need to go home and work." Accepting the satchel, he dropped it to the ground, then reached for her.

"Ideas? I like the sound of that. How about some loving first? Having you snuggled on my back was very invigorating." He grinned as he folded his arms around her. "If you know what I mean."

She raised her face, her mouth as eager as his, their connection equally as wonderful as it'd been every time since their first night two weeks prior. His taste, his scent, the way he held her. It simply felt right, like tab A and slot B had found their perfect connection. Her fingers threaded into the hair at the nape of his neck, sifting through the strands to stroke the skin beneath.

He shuddered, rocking against her; his erection large and thick between them. Lyssica gasped and rubbed the peaks of her aching breasts across his bare chest.

"Time sands, you're a sweet delight, Lyss."

She kissed him again, a full flowering of her mouth over his, before drawing back for breath. "The idea of being in the open for our loving is strangely compelling, but I'd like to choose a time when we're not in a hurry. Also, it's cold and damp."

He sighed. "Much as I hate it, you're right." Bestowing another lingering kiss before he released her, Emryn bent to their pack. Pulling his trousers free, he sat and dragged them on. Lyssica licked her lips as a loose tunic concealed most of his gorgeous chest, the laces left untied. Next were socks and finally a pair of baggy-topped, calf boots. Standing, he shouldered the now closed bag and held out his hand. "Ready?"

Smiling, she grabbed hold and they returned to the road. Emryn halted them, his fingers tipping her chin up so they could look into each other's eyes. "Lyss, I've been thinking about this." His throat worked, then words rushed out of him. "I love being with you and I'll proudly acknowledge our relationship. Your choice, but I don't want you to feel uncomfortable or to have anyone think we're sneaking around. However, if you prefer to keep our closeness a secret ..."

Her smile was tender as she stood on tip toes and brushed her mouth over his. "I'm at the point where I don't care what anybody else thinks. I won't hide our connection – I've no wish to."

Emryn's kiss was firmer. "Excellent." He kissed her again, mouth lingering. "Thoughts of you consume my days, but I'm not going to embarrass you, or your family, by behaving in an unprofessional manner during work sessions."

Lyssica rested her head against the side of his neck, one hand smoothing the chest of his tunic. "I can't keep you out of my mind either." She sighed dreamily. "At least we're spending all our nights at Garadenya."

He nodded. "Yes, we can be ourselves with Zhu and Dario." He drew her hand up to his mouth, kissed the palm, then relinquished it. Bowing, he made a sweeping gesture. "Lead on my delightful Heir-Lady Aphiski."

~

"We're back, Papan." Lyssica joined her father in his inner sanctum. "Safe and sound."

He grunted, looking her over. "Better late than never, I suppose." The duke's gaze shifted to her partner. "Greetings Emryn."

"Morning." The rumble of Emryn's voice vibrated through the connection where his chest met her back. She wanted to rub herself against him; instead she shrugged.

"Things don't always go according to plan Papan."

Emryn turned a hand palm up. "Dario and I were making plans this morning for future lessons. Time got away from us. Our apologies, Yanvian."

Her father grunted, massaging his temple. "Probably not important today anyway. We need a break from the guests, so I gave them the day off. Tomorrow, two will go to the barn and two to the stables for the morning, then swap for the afternoon. They'll be learning animal husbandry and how it relates to the estate's occupants. That gives you almost two days off." He glanced between them. "So, no need to rush back to Papillion tomorrow, if you'd rather stay with Zhu and Dario and rest."

Lyssica blinked in surprise. "Oh. Thank you, Papan. A day of relaxation will be wonderful."

"Yes, well, it's been a long six weeks and you've been looking tired lately." He shuffled papers on his desk. "I know you've taken on a heavy schedule and it hasn't been easy." He paused, gaze sweeping both of them. "Also, the more I've come to know Perris Momphiday, the happier I am Emryn is guarding you."

Lyssica tensed. Beside her Emryn's tautness radiated through their shoulder connection. "What do you mean, Papan? He's said or done something to um, upset you?"

Duke Yanvian methodically stacked his papers inside a folder. "I'm watching all our guests closely. I've reports to provide on this program and I like to be thorough – I require your opinions, too."

A smile lit Lyssica's face. "I'm pleased to contribute. But what did you mean, about Perris?"

Her father's eyes narrowed. "I'll get to him. First, the others." He massaged his chin. "Kerrigold is strong and determined – her heart's not really in this type of learning, but she's giving it her all."

Lyssica nodded. "I agree with that. Plus she confessed to me she has an artistic bent and would really love to talk with Zhu before she goes home."

"Ah." Yanvian pursed his lips. "We can arrange that." He nodded. "Melkaz is keen and interested. He's got a brain and he'll be an excellent partner for whoever he ends up with in the future."

"Yes." Lyssica tilted her head. "Plus, he's insightful and always a gentleman."

"Good. Moving on to Venaday." The duke's mouth turned down. "Although he acts doltish, he's smarter than one would think. He's giving lip service to the lessons but is persisting with his Private Investigation goal. I've suggested he seek an apprenticeship in that field."

Lyssica frowned, clasping her hands in front of her. "Venaday gives lip service to anything he's not absolutely invested in, but, if he is interested, he'll give all of his attention. I sometimes think the doltish act is a cover up."

Her father nodded. "You could be right. I hadn't thought of that." He frowned. "So, then there's Perris. On the surface, he's friendly, affable, always smiling – talks well and listens attentively. But ..."

"But?"

Duke Yanvian's eyes moved from Emryn to Lyssica. "Don't ever turn your back on him. Don't rely on him, don't trust him and don't ever make the mistake of thinking he's your friend."

Lyssica could only stare at her father. She bit her tongue to refrain from revealing how correct he was.

Emryn's soft voice filled her silence. "That's a very definitive assessment."

Yanvian's mouth twisted. "Like I said, I've been observing. So has Entanglit, at my request. The actions and interactions of Perris Momphiday are concerning. His smiles fade quickly when no-one is looking. They never reach his eyes. He sneaks around and listens to conversations before he enters a room. He lies. He puts people down, denigrates them under the guise of camaraderie and jokes. In my opinion he's an unpleasant sort."

Lyssica swallowed, decided to be truthful. "I confess he makes my skin crawl."

A low growl vibrated from Emryn. "I have ensured Lyssica is never alone with anyone but Kerrigold. Be certain I'll take extra care with him."

"Good. I'm glad we're in agreement." Stepping away from his desk, Duke Yanvian approached. "Lunch was put back to await your arrival; let's go and eat before it becomes dinner."

Lyssica's eyes widened. "Oh, Papan, you didn't have to wait for us." To her surprise, her father linked one arm with hers and the other with Emryn's.

"We chose to. Your mother and I decided we'd rather eat with family instead of strangers, even if they are guests."

Used to her father's gruff solemnity, Lyssica couldn't believe her ears. *'Who are you and what have you done with Papan?'*

Two weeks later, Lyssica huffed out a frosty breath and eyed the snow drifts gloomily. Beneath her, Kynthcat's large paws forged a path through the forest's frozen undergrowth. The snow continued to fall with an increasing regularity of blizzards, even though Auguary's last winter moon was waning. In another week it'd be dark moon night – the official end of winter and the beginning of spring. The vernal Spring Equinox was six days later. *Ostara Day in two weeks and I've made no progress!* She swiped at the tiny ice crystals on the tips of her lashes.

Impatience was a live coal burning her gut. She'd given sodding Perris Momphiday plenty of opportunity to approach and ask to speak with her privately, but he'd remained distant. She didn't understand. He watched her all the time when she and Emryn were at Papillion. Early in the program he'd asked for meetings several times, unhappy when she'd brushed him off, so what was he playing at now?

It wasn't as if she could invite Perris to ask her for a private meeting – not without making him suspicious as to her motives. And then there was the devil-rabbit – was it waiting for an invitation to participate in skulduggery? No. On a daily basis, bodies of hibernating animals were found ripped from their dens and left lying broken and bloody in the snow. She'd been able to heal many of them with slow but steady bursts of power; the survivors conveyed images of night attacks by Vulpiawolves guided by a large, nasty smelling rabbit.

Kynthcat slowed at the sight of more Vulpia attack-webs. From a bag at her hip, Lyssica drew out some stones and lobbed them at web after web until all of them were tatters drifting on the wind. The ground became littered with acidic web scraps; luckily they'd disintegrate over the next several hours. Carefully navigating a way between the pieces, Kynthcat padded on, aiming for Ostara's circle, where Lyssica dismounted.

As she began her paean of song and dance in praise of Ostara, animals gathered. Squirrels, rabbits, duskits and possums rubbed shoulders with predatorial foxes, raccoons, badgers and even some skunweasels; Ostara blessed all of them equally. Emryn professed himself fascinated by the tiny duskits with their huge eyes, enormous ears and super fluffy tails on small bodies. There were none near his packlands and, to his mind, they looked to be a possum-fox hybrid. Throughout the ritual, Lyssica glimpsed him patrolling the borders of the circle; the animals now so used to his presence, Kynthcat was mostly ignored as he wove between them.

Sitting as she ended her final dance, Lyssica spread her arms in welcome. "Come little ones." She was immediately besieged by animals wanting to receive a goddess blessing. She kept the flow of power a continuous low wave, bathing all in affection, light and warmth. Her access to the power had slowed to a trickle, with the strange blockage and her inability to contact Ostara, but hadn't totally dried up, much to her relief.

Lyssica patted, cuddled, blessed and cooed while the afternoon waned, then allowed the power flow to die away. "I'm sorry, it's time for me to go. I'll be back tomorrow though." She was surprised to notice none of the animals had dispersed as they usually did. "You can go home now." Some sat down, others whined, but they continued to watch her, none of them departing. She hesitated, then looked up as Kynthcat appeared, making his way between the creatures. They moved for him, then closed in again. He looked at her, brows knitting; then chuffed, the sound low and questioning.

"I don't know why they're still here – do they want to see us off?" The fur of his shoulders rippled in a feline shrug before he lowered enough for her to swing astride. Straightening, he walked slowly through the crowd of animals. Lyssica turned to wave and froze. "Oh my Goddess! They're following us ..."

And they continued to follow all the way back to Garadenya, refusing to leave her vicinity.

~

LYSSICA GLANCED OVER HER SHOULDER, stunned by the horde of animals hurrying in their wake. More than previous days, the most since the exodus of animals from the forest had begun. Species which were normally enemies ran side by side, sometimes even helping each other. A baggage train of frightened, bewildered, hungry creatures, ill-equipped to survive the heavy winter and the persecution of the devil-rabbit with a pack of vicious Vulpiawolves.

Now, none of the animals who came to Ostara's circle for Lyssica's rituals left afterwards and, every day a new group came to participate, never leaving her side when she finished. After the first time, animals even waited by the side of the road to follow Lyssica and Emryn to the Papillion Estate in the morning, as well as to Garadenya in the late afternoon. Both estates had impromptu animal hostelries set up, with Duchesse Azura and Treymeron supervising the animals' welfare at Papillion, while Zhulija and Dario oversaw those who'd arrived at Garadenya. Lyssica marvelled at how many creatures the forest was home to.

Even more disquieting was the lack of actual confrontation with the devil-rabbit, particularly after the first terrible meeting through Roland Arrelgyre's body. There were no day sightings of Vulpiawolves either. It was as if they deliberately conducted their heinous violence, set their traps and poisoned the plant life in the dark hours of the night when Lyssica and Emryn were *not* in the forest. But during the day, it was a constant battle to undo as much harm as possible to the flora and fauna under siege.

Looking ahead, Lyssica sighed with relief as the Papillion gates appeared. A shout rose as they were sighted and one gate was opened for them. The gate guards stared past them, wide eyed at the number of animals in their retinue. Without prompting, Kynthcat headed directly for the stables at the back of the manor. That building, plus the barns, had been re-purposed to house the refugee wildlife.

It was no surprise to find Maman and Treymeron moving around the structures, directing volunteers from all over the estate in the care the animals required.

From the door of the stables, Treymeron waved. "Lyss! I need a word."

She waved acknowledgement and nudged Kynthcat. He halted,

letting her slide from his back; she rubbed his shoulders affectionately as she went. He turned his head, lowering it to nuzzle her cheek, then made his way past Treymeron, into the stable.

Treymeron's dark black and violet eyes catalogued her. "Good to see you're okay, sis." He shook his head. "I can't believe all these animals – they just keep coming." Smiling widely, he provided a rundown on how everyone was coping, regardless of whether they were Fae-folk or forest dweller. "Even when you're not here, they accept and trust us."

"They scent Lyss on you, that's why." A dressed, two-legged Emryn reached them. "Thanks for staying with her while I changed."

Lyssica smiled. "You're loving this, aren't you Trey?"

One of his hands did a side-to-side juggle. "Part of it. I love the ability to interact with them like this, but I'm angry at the reason for it. The winters here have never been so severe." He glanced around, sighed. "It's unnatural for them to be cooped up, but we're doing the best we can and they seem to understand."

A tiny duskit, it's variegated purple fur brilliant against the snow-covered ground, squeaked as it drew up at their feet, huge ears flickering and large eyes liquid. A tiny paw tugged at the hem of Treymeron's trouser leg. "Aw." Bending, he scooped the small creature up and snuggled it into his neck. "It's okay, little one. I know you miss your maman. I'll take you upstairs to join the others in a moment."

Reaching out, Lyssica stroked the duskit baby with one finger. "The others?"

"Yeah, Papan has a basket with a few duskit orphans in his office. He said it was the warmest place for them, but I don't know." One eyebrow wigged up and down. "I popped in late yesterday and he had them on his lap."

Lyssica goggled. "Papan? Are we talking about the same Fae-male who sired us?"

"Yeah." He grinned as Emryn broke into a coughing fit. "Not what I expected."

"I know, right?" Lyssica shook her head. "A couple of weeks ago he told me he'd prefer to spend time with family, instead of guests. I thought there was something wrong with him. Now, he's snuggling orphan duskits? Wow."

Her brother nodded. "I've noticed changes too. Perhaps he's mellowing? Who knows, but that's not what I wanted to talk about."

"What's up, Trey?"

He glanced around, sidled closer. "That Perris Momphiday ..." His lip curled. "I don't like him. He's a slimy bastard."

"Good instincts."

"Yeah, well, he's been trying to befriend me. He asks questions about you all the time. Wants to know your schedule. I dodge him as much as possible. Lately he's been saying there's something between you and him."

Disgust welled in Lyssica. "There's not."

"Didn't think so." He folded his arms." He says you knew him well a few years ago. That true?"

"Unfortunately, yes." Her voice barely carried above the rattling growl in Emryn's chest. "It's okay, Emryn." She swallowed. "Trey, I need your help."

"What is it, Lyss?"

She pressed her lips together, gathered her courage. "We knew each other during my party years. He – he took advantage of me and my foolishness." She couldn't look at her younger brother, just couldn't.

Fingers under her chin raised her face to meet Trey's concerned gaze. "He harmed you?"

"Yes, but I'm okay and I won't let him make a victim of me. I won't *be* a victim, ever again."

Trey narrowed his eyes. "Hell. I'll kill that piece of—"

A deep snarl from Emryn. "Get in line."

Trey's brows skyrocketed. "Get in line? What's that supposed to mean?"

Fingers over her lips, Lyssica blinked at her little brother. Since when had he faced-off against others like this?

Emryn's smiled mirthlessly. "It means Dario and I are way ahead of you."

Lyssica touched Trey's forearm, brought his gaze back to her. "That's where I'd like your help. Dario is a Queen's agent but not on private land, unless he has a warrant, which he doesn't."

Trey cocked his head. "So you need Momphiday on crown land. The forest?"

She nodded. "Would you be willing to tell him I'll be at Ostara's Circle tomorrow afternoon? And Emryn will be leaving me to go hunting because I feel safe there?"

"So, he'll think you're alone?" Trey rubbed his chin. "Yeah, I'll do that." He cast a sly look at Emryn. "Hunting, eh? I just won't tell him he's the prey."

14

EMRYN

"The swine fell for it!" Grinning, Treymeron punched the air as they met him at the postern gate later that afternoon. "I told Momphiday your schedule's busy and I wasn't sure when you could meet him, Lyss. He pressed for details, sprinkling his questions while we cared for the animals in the barn." He snorted. "I dropped information about your daily visits to Ostara's Circle where it's so safe, Emryn often wanders off hunting. He asked me how to find the circle and after I explained about the path, he left me alone."

Emryn clapped Treymeron's shoulder. "Good work."

The younger Fae-male flexed his wings, firmed his stance, then focused on his sister. "I'd like to help, Lyss. What more can I do?" A purple furry head with large ears and night dark eyes, popped out of the neck of his voluminous cloak and chittered.

Lyssica blinked. "Oh." Smiling, she stretched a cautious hand to stroke the tiny duskit. "Look at you." Her voice was a low croon. "So cute and innocent." She flicked her brother a look. "I thought you were taking this one to add to Papan's orphan group?"

Slight colour flushed Treymeron's cheeks. "Yeah, well, I did, but she wouldn't stay there. I tried a couple of times, but every time I left, she followed me." He shrugged. "I caved in. It was easier to keep her with me while I was working than to constantly run up to Papan's office. I fashioned a small sling against my chest and she seems warm and comfortable."

Emryn tickled the baby duskit under her chin, watching her in fascination. Eyes closed, she lapped up the combined attention of both he and Lyssica. "I'd never seen duskits until I came here. There's none in the hills and valleys of the Pack territories."

Treymeron pursed his mouth. "Maybe that's because the climate is too warm?"

Withdrawing his hand to adjust a strap on his pack, Emryn nodded. "As good a reason as any, I suppose." His gaze was drawn to Lyssica as she cooed at the baby duskit; she was so gorgeous, gentle and kind. He hated to break the moment but … "Time to go, Lyss. There's more snow coming."

She studied the sky. "No argument from me." Turning to Treymeron, she pursed her lips. "I don't know what other chores to give you, Trey. You're already doing a lot by helping the animals – maybe keep an eye on Perris for me?"

"Yeah." He nodded. "I'll certainly do that." Leaning to kiss her cheek, he tried a hug but it proved awkward with the duskit snuggled in between. "You be careful now." Treymeron pointed at Emryn. "And you, too, Mr Kynthcat – you're the biggest bonus to come out of this swap program."

Smiling widely, warmth pushing up inside him like a furnace, Emryn exchanged a warrior's arm clasp with Treymeron. "Thank you. I will be sad to return home when this is over."

"You're welcome here any time." Tucking the duskit into her sling and wrapping his cloak firmly about himself, Treymeron slipped into the bushes.

Outside the gate, Emryn escorted Lyssica across the road to the bushy undergrowth at the edge of the forest where he dropped his pack and began stripping. Lyssica grabbed the bag and undid the clasps, holding it open for Emryn's clothes. He tossed them in, then straightened, gratified to see her eyes moved boldly over his nakedness.

She licked her lips, then offered an uncertain smile. "It will be awful to see you go, but we knew our relationship was going to be short term."

He kissed her, even as his eyes reflected pain. "Never thought I'd say this, but I hate the idea of leaving – you're a delight I hadn't expected. How is it we mesh so well when we're from such different worlds?"

Her lips trembled. "I hadn't thought to ever meet someone as wonderful as you, but yes, our personal obligations have us at a disadvantage."

His Adam's apple bobbed. "We need to think how we might get around your commitments here, both to the estate as Heir-Lady and as Ostara's Handmaiden; or my tether and commitments to the pack." He feared there *wasn't* a way and his heart weighed heavy inside him.

Kynthcat hissed, clawing at him sharply. *'No leave our mate. We steal her.'* Emryn flinched, but shook his head, unable to take his eyes from Lyssica.

She closed the pack, fiddled with a clasp. "You've mentioned that tether before. What do you mean? What is it?"

"Fair question." Emryn nodded. "It's part of shape-changer magic. A psychic link to our Alpha and, through him, a tenuous connection to other pack mates. The Alpha has one with every member of the pack. It's a permanent bond ensuring personal and emotional safety; no-one is ever alone, lost, or feels like they don't belong. It also acts like a … leash, I guess, for want of a better word. Wherever we are, the link stretches, but after a time we have to go home to re-charge because we're Pack. We're one, we're connected." He scratched his head. "I'm not sure I'm explaining it very well; it's never been needed before."

Lyssica didn't meet his eyes. "I think I understand." She hesitated. "Is it ever broken?"

Emryn's nose wrinkled. "Sometimes, but only for extreme reasons and any loners eventually go mad. For some reason, shape-changers *need* that psychic link of belonging somewhere."

Kynthcat snarled inside him. *'NOT leave our mate!'*

'You keep saying 'mate', but you can't possibly be right.' Emryn sought his change and dropped to all fours, becoming Kynthcat. *'You know we only mate with other shape-changers.'*

But, now that he'd morphed, Kynthcat was in charge and he roared their anger and denial to the sky, coughed, then roared again. His heart throbbed with anguish, but they were helpless against the power of the Pack tether.

Lyssica thwacked their ribs with the satchel, her voice a hiss. "That's certainly making a statement, but was it a good idea to announce our presence so loudly? Get down and give me a chance to mount up, you big oaf." Recalled to their senses, the extra air gathered for another roar left his lungs in a rush and he dropped to lie prone on the ground. Lyssica slung the divided bag across his shoulders then slid into position behind it. Once she'd settled, Kynthcat rose, padding deeper into the forest, following the ribbon of track barely visible under a thin coat of snow.

When they reached Ostara's circle, Kynthcat waited for Lyssica to slide off, before stalking back into the brush at the circle's edge. Behind him, Lyssica burst into song, her voice soaring as she began her daily ritual.

Patrolling the boundaries as had become his habit, Kynthcat threaded between trees and around bushes. At the far side of the circle, a faint but nasty scent assailed his nostrils and saturated his tongue – that of black snow and putrid mud. He propped, spitting in an effort to vent the cloying nastiness. There was no mistaking it, the devil-rabbit had been here earlier. Uneasily, he cast around some more, also picking up the wet fur aroma of Vulpiawolves; a lot of them.

Casting a glance back towards the circle, he glimpsed Lyssica dancing around each of Ostara's blessed rock tors, crooning to the heavens, arms outstretched. Still safe. He nodded, confident enough in her safety to see if he could discover which way the devil-rabbit had gone. Following the smell, sometimes nosing the ground, other times tasting the air with his tongue, he realised it was strengthening. But he was now well out of sight of Lyssica, had gone further than he intended and that unsettled him. Time to return, but just as he turned back, the flutter of wings came from above.

"Psst! Emryn, Kynthcat!"

Glancing up, he was surprised to find Treymeron hovering, his sooty wings with their cream, violet, lavender and cobalt blue markings spread wide.

"Momphiday didn't stick to the script, he followed you *today*. Get to Lyss, the swine's nearly to the circle."

'Damn!' He morphed quickly from Kynthcat to Fae-male form. "Dario was meant to be here to apprehend the cretin. Can you fly to Garadenya while we hold the fort here?" He barely heard Treymeron's hasty agreement before again becoming Kynthcat and spinning to race for Ostara's rocks. His heart beat out her name with every stride. *'Lyssica! Lyssica! Lyssica!'*

No time to freak out, this was battle. Slowing, he forced himself to slink closer, stopping behind a large bush to survey the scene. Perris Momphiday had halted a few steps inside the circle, just beyond where the path truncated, watching Lyssica who swayed as she serenaded Ostara, arms reaching to the sky. Near her, animals had gathered, waiting for her attention. Slowly, Lyssica lowered her arms and dropped to her knees, facing the nearest creatures.

Her words tripped out, softly lilting. "I'm ready, sweet ones, come to me."

Perris grinned. "Oh, I have, dear Lyssica, I have."

Stiffening, Lyssica turned her head, pinning a narrow-eyed stare on the interloper. "You're not welcome here, Perris. This is goddess business. At least have the decency to wait until it's completed."

"Pfft!" Perris waved a dismissive hand. "No need to pretend. We both know that's a lot of twaddle you invented."

She shook her head. "Your opinion is irrelevant. What do you want?"

Perris' slow smile was all teeth. "You. I want you. Unless you agree to consort with me, I'll tell your father, mother, family—" He spread his arms. "Demonhells, why stop with them? I'll tell the world that you're an impure slut."

Her stare was icy. "You really are contemptible. I feel sorry for your parents. You don't need me. You've already taken what you wanted."

He shrugged. "I've no problem having it again. Who wouldn't want a cushy position in life with a beautiful Fae-female at his beck and call? Then you'll inherit that magnificent estate and I'll be in position to take it over."

She tilted her head. "My Papan may live for many more years, you realise?"

His lips twisted in a sneer. "Accidents happen."

"I'll stop you."

"Not if you know what's good for you."

Inspired by Lyssica's calm command, Kynthcat dug his claws into the earth, fighting to emulate her serenity, when all his savagery urged him to pounce, to rip and tear, to rend this poor excuse for a Fae-male into bloody bits. Struggling to mute the snarls rattling his chest, Kynthcat tensed with hatred. *Want kill male.*

This Fae-male was a low-life bastard who deserved to pay for hurting Lyssica – in the past and for the hurts he planned to commit. But Kynthcat held his naturally bloodthirsty nature in, watched and waited, eyes savage with promise. The ball was in Lyssica's court.

Animals clustered around her. Glancing over them, she stroked the fur of as many as she could reach, then clapped her hands softly. "Go and hide little ones. Be safe and we'll commune later." They obeyed, scampering away. Perris Momphiday cleared his throat loudly.

"I don't like being ignored by my future consort."

"I know what's good for me; it isn't you." Lyssica stood, dusting herself off, meeting her tormentor's gaze squarely. "I'm declining your less than generous offer, Perris."

His eyes widened. "What do you mean you decline? You can't! Didn't you hear me say I'd tell everyone of your shame?"

She laughed scornfully. "*Your* shame, not mine. Back then, I was a victim, drugged and helpless. I'm not one now. I don't care who you tell – I'm proud of who I am. I doubt you can say the same about yourself." Deliberately, she looked him up and down. "It's obvious you're nothing but a stinking sleazebag."

His expression turned ugly. "Why you!" He leapt towards her. Still crouched, Kynthcat sprang into the circle, but halted as Lyssica twisted into a sideways jump, extending her leg and angling her foot to create a sharp edge. Perris impaled himself, his forward motion ramming her bladed foot deep into his stomach. Her momentum, fuelled with the anger of years, drove him backwards; the air whooshing from him. He flew through the ether before landing heavily on the frozen ground where he flailed feebly, gasping for air. Lyssica landed lightly, followed through on her action and kept moving until she stood poised with her heel above his throat.

"I know what you are and you don't frighten me, Perris. Give me one good reason not to crush your windpipe."

Stunned but proud, Kynthcat didn't intervene. Lyssica had this. All they had to do now was wait for Dario to arrive and this thug would be dealt with. He heard a whisper of sound behind them and twisted, cursing his preoccupation. And went down under a storm of Vulpia-wolves, no match for their combined fangs, claws and webs.

15

LYSSICA

Positioned threateningly over Perris, Lyssica twisted her head towards the snarls and growls; horror swamped her as a tangle of fighting animals rolled out into the open clearing. The green and grey Vulpiawolves were easily recognised.

"No!" She caught glimpses of Kynthcat's coppery hide, the curl of a horn, a flash of his deep brown mane, but over, above and around him was a seething, ferocious sea of spiky green-grey fur, dark grey skin, and barbed tails. The snarling, biting, flailing mass writhed across the ground – there were so many. Anguish filled her, came out in the scream of her voice. "Emryn!"

Beneath her, the desperate hands of Perris scrabbled at her mid-air foot and pushed. Losing her balance, she toppled sideways, but recovered even as she landed, crouching on the balls of her feet, one knee resting on the ground, hands on either side of her.

Turning her head, she expected to see Perris advancing on her, but he hadn't moved.

Lyssica sucked in a breath. Over him stood the devil-rabbit, clawed paws digging into Perris's neck, lips peeled back over sharp fangs. Ignoring Perris' gurgles, the creature's gimlet eyes swivelled up to

Lyssica; it grinned, shaking its head, tossing the long, floppy ears to-and-fro.

Struggling with the black snow and putridly muddy aroma of the creature, Lyssica choked. Then the filthy miasma of its linked death magic wafted on the breeze and she instinctively jerked on her Ostara powers, covering herself in a cloak of Ostara's fertile life force as she'd done the last time they'd met. Her breathing eased instantly.

"We meet again, Chosen of Ostara." The devil-rabbit grinned, its head tilted, prominent snout wiggling. "I scent the perfidy of this male on the ground. He hunted you. We can't have that. You're *our* prey." Without taking its eyes off her, the devil-rabbit dug its claws deep into Perris's throat and ripped sideways. Blood gushed and Perris's whimpering died; he sagged like a wet airbag.

Adjusting to full height, the devil-rabbit licked a bloody claw, paused, then licked the rest of Perris's blood away and smiled. "No distraction now, is there, Chosen of Ostara?"

Deliberately, Lyssica flung her life-force cloak at the devil-rabbit, pushing the power of Ostara's fertile life at the abomination. It squealed as the power cloak, visible only to Lyssica, covered it completely. She kept on force feeding power into the cloak, while the creature shrilled and struggled, muzzle drawn back in a rictus of agony. Sinking to the ground under her onslaught, it began to draw in upon itself, shrinking rapidly.

Lyssica gulped, raising her hands to cover her ears, but she kept the pressure of power up as the devil-rabbit shrank until finally, the last handful of it poofed away in a noxious cloud of black smoke. All that remained was the taint of its vile odour.

Cutting the flow of power meant her life-force cloak vanished as well. She'd reform it later; Emryn needed help now and she frantically hoped she wasn't too late.

Pain flowering inside her at the thought, she shot to her feet, then stopped as the ether trembled where she'd destroyed the devil-rabbit. Staring transfixed at the air shimmering like a miniature heat wave, she clenched her fists as a new figure took shape. Dismay filled her.

Hovering in the air was the solid, thickly muscled figure of a much older male. He wore ragged clothing, chewed on a long straw of dried grass, and an ancient, broad brimmed hat perched low on his head, like a dark mushroom cap. Black, watchful eyes assessed her from under the hat's curled brim. "I felt the yank as my rabbit-golem was destroyed. That makes me unhappy, Chosen of Ostara." Long claws, deadly as scimitars, flashed out from the tips of his fingers, gleaming in the wintry light.

Swallowing, Lyssica danced backward, but the old male covered the distance she'd achieved in one powerful leap, forcing her to continue retreating. She only stopped when her spine thumped into one of Ostara's tall rocks, her intent to dart sideways foiled at the sensation of cold, hard claws at her throat. The long, dagger-sharp tips pricked her skin, while his mouth stretched into a grotesque rictus of pleasure.

"What fun you've been, little upstart Fae."

Lyssica stared defiantly down her nose. "Who *are* you?"

He grinned. "Why, I'm the Bodach, of course."

She glared at him. "The cause of this entire mess. I hope you realise never-ending winter is a curse not a gift."

He stared at her, eyebrows shooting up until they disappeared under his hat brim. "How do you know my plan?" He scowled. "Never mind, what's your meaning?"

Lyssica snorted her disgust. "You'll be making your Cailleach work. All the time. Non-stop. Do you think she'll thank you for that?" Over the terrible old creature's shoulder, she saw Kynthcat drag himself from beneath a furry mass, his gaze fixated on her, then he stumbled and went down under a fresh pile of Vulpiawolves. Drops of red sprinkled the snow.

"No!" She couldn't hold back her cry of horror and the blood drained from her face, leaving her light-headed. She swayed, feeling the dig of the Bodach's claws, then Kynthcat howled, his ringing call of defiance an indication he yet lived. She straightened, fisted her hands as he reappeared, a swirl of brown mane and copper fur, horns swiping viciously, even as the Vulpiawolf pack hemmed him in, snapping and lunging. Several attacked from behind, their weight combining to ride him to the ground. The pack swarmed again and this time when the melee cleared, Kynthcat's form was limp, great horned head lolling as they dragged him to the nearest tree and bound him to the trunk with their icy web.

Lyssica's heart sank. Emryn and Kynthcat were trapped and she was helpless at the mercy of the Bodach.

Perhaps she'd lost, but she still had words for weapons. "What a poor excuse for a consort you are. If the Cailleach only knew what you've been doing, she'd be so disappointed."

Mouth twisted with displeasure, the Bodach crooked a finger. A Vulpiawolf responded, closing in to slap some web across her mouth, cheeks and chin. It hardened, stinging icily, but at least it didn't hurt as much as the attack-web they produced. He smirked. "That's shut you up."

Panting and furious, Lyssica fought despair over a failure more than personal. She hadn't lived up to Ostara's trust, she'd failed Emryn and let her family, and everyone relying on her, down. Worse, her defeat left the world open to the Bodach's evil actions. Pictures of the Fae-Demesnes locked in a bitter eternal winter flashed through her mind. Scene after scene of hardship, persecution and despair – for the Fae-folk, for all the animals and plants. Winter forever meant no new plant life and any young animals birthed would either die of cold or be slaughtered indiscriminately by the Vulpiawolves for food and sport. Blood would stain the snow, flowing in rivers like the lashings of redberry syrup Treymeron loved on his ice cream.

Lump in her throat, Lyssica bit her lip to stop tears as she stared across the clearing towards Emryn; Kynthcat was now alert and thrashing at his icy Vulpia-web bindings. An anguished roar escaped him as their eyes locked and suddenly she was flooded with tangled feelings, a knotty mass that rocked her empathic senses with ferocious intensity. Within the mass, fear and despair battled for supremacy. He was afraid for *her*, terrified that she would die and he be unable to save her. Oh, how she loved him for that.

She faltered. She loved him? Yes! Of course she did. She'd never have committed so much of herself to him if ...

A sharp slap to both cheeks snapped her head askew and only the hard rock at her back kept her upright.

"None of that." Still gleeful, the Bodach shook his head. His claws still hovered at her neck but had retreated a little. "I'll not allow it. Lots of creatures try disassociation of the mind by hiding inside themselves – I thought you were braver than that, Chosen of Ostara."

She was. Oh yes, she was. She'd conceded defeat too soon, shouldn't have given up in the slightest. Thrusting her face over his dagger sharp claws, she snagged the Vulpia-web covering her mouth and yanked.

Snap!

Crisp shards of icy web splintered free, to fall in frozen spicules and spray across the snowy ground. Snatching a breath and her courage, Lyssica started to sing, words of sunlight, of growth, of spring welling up inside her, pouring out of her mouth. Her triumph swelled as the Bodach hissed and trembled in fury, as Kynthcat lifted his head in hope, as—

The Bodach snarled, thrust his paw between her open jaws, snagged claws into her tongue and yanked.

His longest dagger claw flashed.

There was a brief pain; she tasted blood ...

And time slowed as her tongue cartwheeled through the air in endless lazy spirals. With a loud splat, it hit the snow, bouncing and rolling before it came to rest – an almost obscene blob of pink flesh, bloody, forlorn and abandoned.

Lyssica's vision began to blacken at the edges, her legs trembled, then gave way and she slid down the stone to collapse on the ground. She was barely aware of Kynthcat's roars of rage and distress and the Bodach's howls of laughter. Prodding her with his foot, he rolled her to her back, still laughing as he stared down into her dazed eyes. "Tell me off now, Chosen of Ostara." His words mocked. "How about you sing for me." He tipped his head sideways. "What? You can't? Ostara must be so disappointed in you."

'Ostara, my Goddess.' Lyssica pushed back the pain, the dizziness in her mind to access their internal meeting place, not surprised to find it still surrounded by fog. For days, she'd come here, calling and calling, using her power to batter at the fog, needing advice and assistance from Ostara and each time she'd had no success. Now, dizzy, bloody and despairing, she aimed and sent a thin mental dart, a cry of distress. She envisioned the tiny sharp point finding a way through when solid battering had gotten her nowhere. *'Ostara, I need your help!'*

The power of Ostara's mental response was a burst of sunlight, dispersing the fog in seconds, reading Lyssica's open and willing mind, reliving her memories of the events through the winter, of the Bodach's perfidious plan and her current hopeless situation.

The Bodach prodded her again. "I'd expected more from you, but there it is. A Handmaiden is no match for a Demigod."

She didn't respond to his taunts. Couldn't. Her body was filling with power like she'd never felt before. It swept to her extremities, enervating her senses, imbuing her with joy and a strength beyond her imaginings. The process made her body spasm as magic flooded her body.

The Consort of the Winter Queen grinned down at her spasming form. "Looks like I win."

"Not just yet, Bodach." Despite her state, Lyssica recognised Dario's voice. "Come, feel my fire." Lyssica managed to force her eyes open. Closing in on them was a two-legged figure wreathed in flames.

The Bodach whistled. "Oho, what have we here? The infamous Unseelie Beast challenges me. Ouch!"

A second fireball followed the first. "You talk too much."

The Bodach howled. "I'll put your flames out, see if I don't!" He began muttering, then lifted his face and arms to the sky and broke into a loud chant. "Ice, I call you, snow I command you, storms, I summon you. Let this blizzard destroy my foes and herald the beginning of eternal winter. In the name of The Cailleach, I—"

"Nngh!" Lunging forward, Lyssica wrapped a hand around the Bodach's ankle and opened the floodgates on her new power. It sizzled through her fingertips and into his body.

Screaming incoherently, he toppled to the ground. Lyssica held tight and wriggled until her other hand touched his other leg. Her instincts urged her to sing, but her mouth was an empty cavity except for the blood. A thought bloomed: *I still have my vocal cords; I can make noise.*

Certain it was a message from Ostara, Lyssica opened her mouth and let sound flow out, despite the pain. The wordless song was intertwined with the power of spring, of flowers and growth, of sunshine and light rain showers, of fertility and rebirth. She let it pour out of her in a continuous stream, a paean of joy and beauty. To her amazement, the well of force was ceaseless, no matter how much she poured into her voice and then, through her hands – it just kept coming.

Eventually, a hand touched her arm. "Lyssica, amazing as this is, you can stop now. He's unconscious, and so are the Vulpiawolves." Dario's voice was gentle.

Cutting the flow of energy, Lyssica simply dropped her head to the ground and lay there. But the new power was still a volcano bubbling inside, blooming and circling in a constant joyous effervescence of life and spirit. Surging to her feet, she hugged Dario exuberantly, then bolted across the circle toward where Kynthcat lay bloody amidst a ring of prostrate Vulpiawolves. He stirred as she reached him, eyes blinking open dazedly. She ran her hands over him, cooing wordlessly and the sparkling, healing current flowed from her to him like water. His Vulpia-web bindings melted away under the onslaught, wounds began to knit and bare seconds later he morphed, jerked to a sitting position and grasped her arms.

"Lyssica!" Emryn stared at her urgently. "Thank the Goddess, you're alright. What happened? Your tongue! And Dario came and ..." He stared over her shoulder, his expression baffled. "Who in hell are those two women and where did *they* come from?"

16

EMRYN

mryn's grip on Lyssica's arms slackened enough for her to twist and see two females glowering over the Bodach's prone body. She heaved in a great breath; her exhale accompanied by a trill of delight. As her voice lilted through the air, both females turned their heads; the younger lady's smile lighting her face with incandescent pleasure.

"Lyssica!"

The older one simply nodded. She was white of skin and hair, with one grey eye and the other a brightly gleaming white. Those mismatched eyes were narrowed, her blood-red mouth pursed as she returned to studying the Bodach, motionless at her feet. Printed with all types of small white skulls, her dark red robe brushed the muddy ground; a small set of deer antlers separated the long snowy hair clipped back from her face with barrettes adorned by tiny, pointy snouted, animal skulls.

The younger female was gowned in a cream-etched satin dress, gathered close to her torso by a green corset. Her full skirts swept the leaf litter and broken snow of the forest floor but showed no evidence of being wet or stained. A full length, voluminous green velvet cloak, dotted with small purple blossoms, hung behind her shoulders but still managed to flow around and over the sides of her skirts in queen-like glory. Her luminous creamy skin, coupled with green eyes and long, wavy, golden hair, bearing a wreath of colourful blossoms and leaves, gave her ethereal beauty an eldritch radiance.

Emryn forgot to blink as this glowing vision drifted towards them. The lady's robe trailed across the ground, light welling around her like sunshine dispersing clouds. Her every step shed tiny flowers which took root as if they'd always been there. Reaching them, she gathered Lyssica into her arms, hugging and rocking her. Lyssica sighed and relaxed. Over her head the Lady's gaze swept Emryn in a brief assessment, leaving him feeling weighed and measured down to his very soul. Despite that, he didn't feel threatened.

Kynthcat's paws batted softly. *'She see me, too! Who she is?'*

The lady smiled, but her focus dropped to the Fae-female she held. "Lyssica, beloved child. I'm so pleased to see you well."

Emryn shook off his stupefaction, satisfied that this female meant Lyssica no harm. *'Don't know. Looks like I imagine a goddess would.'* The crone moved, drawing his attention – he wasn't so sure about her. She'd stooped to place her hands either side of the Bodach's temples and was muttering a constant, unintelligible litany of soft voiced sound. She stayed so for several moments, then straightened with a harsh grimace and followed in Ostara's footsteps.

Kynthcat grumbled, snarling unhappily. *'That evil creature dead? He should be.'*

'Doubt it.'

'He harmed our mate.'

'And she kicked his arse.'

A chuff. *'Ha! You not deny this time!'*

Grief over the insurmountable situation filled Emryn; why was Kynthcat persisting with the impossibility of this mate business when it couldn't possibly be true? Even if he wished it was with every fibre of his being. To find such a one as Lyssica and have to give her up, lose her—

A shake to his shoulder dragged him from his misery. Personal flame now quenched, Dario loomed over him. "Ready to stand?"

Without awaiting an answer, he stooped, positioned a shoulder under Emryn's armpit and hoisted. The action drew the attention of all three women. Ostara tilted her head.

"Lyssica could you introduce us to these delightful Fae-males?"

She beamed delightedly, but Emryn's heart hurt as she opened her mouth, then froze and let it fall shut. Her face filled with pain. Parting her lips, she uttered a hoarse noise and indicated her lack of tongue with one finger.

Ostara peered in, then frowned. "Tut, tut. We can't have that." She glanced back at her companion. "Cailli, your consort's worked overtime here." She placed one hand on the side of Lyssica's neck and the other high on her throat. Growling, the hag placed one hand atop Ostara's at throat position and her second on the opposite side of Lyssica's neck. Both ladies' hands glowed; Ostara's with green-gold light and the hag's a pearlescent white. The Goddess of Spring nodded at the crone beside her. "By the way, this lovely lady with me is the Cailleach. Cailleach meet Lyssica."

"And ye were right, young Lyssica." The hag's voice was soft as snow. "I've no wish to be saddled with permanent winter. My Bo wasn't using his brains for their true purpose." Her red lips peeled back to expose bare gums. "Nice of him to plan a gift, although ..." She shook her head, the smile fading. "I don't endorse any of his methods and so I'll tell him." Her mismatched eyes swept over them; the white one ice-crystal sharp, the grey as threatening as a winter storm. "I offer my sincerest apologies for the actions of my consort." She withdrew her hand from atop Ostara's and let the other fall from Lyssica's neck. Her voice emerged gratingly harsh and blizzard cold. "Because he meddled and instigated an early winter, I will end the season early. I also grant the three of ye, plus all people and things connected to ye, my full protection – my Bo can be mean when he's thwarted. Granted, I sent him to stand in for me when we goddesses decided on a meeting, but it wasn't to behave as he did and his reports to me did not paint a true picture, else I would've been here to stop him."

Running her hand down Lyssica's throat, Ostara tapped the centre of the clavicle then drew her hand away. "Try now, my dear."

Eyes round, Lyssica's fingers rose to her lips while she switched her gaze from Ostara, to the Cailleach, to Dario and finally to Emryn. "M-my tongue." A smile dawned. "It's regrown. I'm talking!"

Dario grinned. "Even the blood is gone,"

Emryn drank in her flushed and happy face. "Thank the Sands of Time!" Unable to resist, his hand cupping her cheek, he bent to kiss the temptation of her pretty mouth. Her lips flowered beneath his, clinging in full participation.

Next to Emryn, Dario cleared his throat. "My pardon, High Ladies of the Year's Cycle, but since Lyssica is, again, temporarily mute, permit me to introduce myself. Dario Eribifax, Duke of Garadenya at your service. And the person attached to Lyssica's mouth is Lord Emryn Phengaris, a beta Kynthcat of the Destrion Changeling Clan. It is our pleasure to meet such illustrious goddesses." He swept a deep bow.

Parting from Lyssica, Emryn slid his hand down to grip hers then bowed. "Dear Goddesses, my thanks for assisting Lyssica to regain her tongue, although I will not apologise for my distraction."

Inside him, Kynthcat preened. *A mate shouldn't have to.*

Ostara nodded. "She is dear to you then?"

He nodded. "She is an unexpected delight I would never have found without the winter exchange program instigated by the United Queendom of the Fae Demesnes." He sighed, spoke deliberately, as much for the goddesses as in warning to Kynthcat. "It is sad that our time together will end in just over in a week at the program's conclusion."

Ostara's gaze sharpened; she took note of Lyssica glancing away towards the forest. "You will leave?"

"I'd love to stay here and build a life with Lyssica." He cast her a beseeching look. "I *want* to stay." The corners of Emryn's mouth turned down. "But changelings are tethered to their Alpha and the pack; thus, we cannot be away for too long and because we *are* pack animals, we cannot break our tethers without becoming feral or mad. I have no choice but to return to my pack, like it or not." He glanced between Dario and Lyssica. "It has been a wonderful visit, and I hate even the thought of leaving." He swallowed, glanced from Lyssica to Dario and back. "I would really like permission to return."

'*I tell you we find our mate and you call it interesting visit?*' A snarl reverberated through his chest; he sucked in a hard breath as claws scored and slashed inside him. He gritted his teeth.

'*I keep telling you – she can't be our mate, however much we'd like her to be – she's not changeling. I'd be overjoyed if she were. I love her and want to be with her regardless of that.*'

His expression serious, Dario nodded. "We have enjoyed your visit also. Come back any time, Emryn."

Even though Lyssica smiled, the stretch of her mouth trembled with sadness. "You'll always be welcome, Emryn. We have worked together so well; your help has been invaluable and … and I care for you." The deep wells of her eyes shone with a combination of tears and love. Emryn clenched his fists and dropped his head. She loved him, just as he loved her.

"A fitting finish." The Cailleach clapped her hands, breaking the melancholy of the moment. "Ostara, I formally hand the seasonal reigns over to ye. May I have my potion?"

"My pleasure, Cailli." Reaching into her cloak, Ostara produced a small leather flask, waved her hand over it, then held it out. Taking the flask, the Cailleach unstoppered it and drank the contents in one continuous mouthful. She shuddered as she re-stoppered the empty container and returned it, then stiffened and closed her eyes as her face spasmed. Before the astonished gaze of all but Ostara, the Cailleach continued to spasm and shudder as her face and body changed from crone to middle aged matron, to young woman. She coughed, then her eyes re-opened.

"Thank ye Ostara. Wonderful to share time with ye, as always." She reached to touch Lyssica on the shoulder. "And I thank ye for all the hard work ye've put in, my dear, and for not giving up. Ye are a credit to yer line." She gave the males a smile and a nod, before tramping forcefully back to where the Bodach still lay. Bending, she touched a forefinger to the centre of his forehead, the hollow at the base of his throat and the place above his heart, muttering all the while, then she straightened, placing her hands on her hips. The Bodach began to stir immediately, arms and legs twitching. His head tilted, then he sighted the woman standing over him and stilled.

His gravelly voice carried to them. "Cailli, my dearest. You're here. A little early, but—"

She pointed a finger at him. "Be quiet, Bo. I know what ye've been doing and I'm not happy."

"Dear One, it was meant to be a gift."

She smacked her fist into her other hand. "No! I've no wish to work full time, to be forever old, to have no surcease. Ostara's Lady Lyssica tried to tell ye that – ye should've listened. Although by then all yer damage had been done." She glowered at him. "All the harm ye've caused, the blood ye've shed, aligning yerself with evil and death magic – what were ye thinking?"

"But Dear One, you are aligned with destruction—"

"Ye know it is something I *never* use lightly and then only after I've exhausted my options. And ..." She pointed again, her expression fiercely forbidding. "As the patroness of starving wolves, how dare ye align with the Vulpia breed? How double damn dare ye!"

"But Cailli, my dear—"

The Cailleach gave an exclamation of distaste, reached down, clasped a wrist and jerked him upright. "Life, and the respect of it, is a part of my work – am I not also a professional deer-herder? I cannot tell ye how disgusted I am with what ye've done here." Hand rising, she pinched his earlobe and started walking, ensuring he must follow or risk having the lobe ripped off. Follow he did, head on one side, voice raised in protest, his steps staggering as the Cailleach dragged him away. Eight steps later, a ground mist rose around their legs, wreathed their bodies, climbing up and up until they were obscured from view. Their voices, one protesting, the other angry, faded and when the mist cleared, the two were gone.

Ostara's laugh tinkled. "He will not dare set a foot wrong for a very long time."

Emryn snorted. "And that's it? All this death and destruction, and that's all? Forgive me if my sense of humour isn't the least bit tickled, Goddess."

Her expression sobered. "You are right, of course. Nothing he did is the least bit humorous – it is his immediate future which I find so amusing." She considered him. "And, no – that's not all. Lyssica nearly died, as did you. She healed you with the power I was finally able to despatch." She rubbed an eyebrow. "To my regret, I hadn't tried to check in – Lyssica's never had trouble before or been unable to contact me as necessary. I've always had full trust in her abilities."

Emryn spread his hands. "Yet, as a Handmaiden, her power and skills weren't even in the same league as those of the Bodach."

Ostara frowned. "He's the consort of a goddess, which makes him a Demigod with greater skills, but there was no way to anticipate his actions."

"And if he comes back?"

"He won't."

Dario stirred. "What if he seeks revenge? He's that type of personality, is he not?"

"He is." Ostara waved a hand in the direction of where they'd last seen the Cailleach and her spouse. "But, if you recall, the Cailleach put the three of you under her protection. You'll also be under my protection. You *will* be safe from reprisals. And now, Lord Emryn, I wish to give you a little power boost, which will ensure your full recovery. Is that agreeable to you?"

Conscious of Lyssica clutching his arm, eying him a trifle anxiously, Emryn didn't protest. "I accept, thank you." Ostara pressed a palm to each temple and began to hum. He gasped as a jolt of raw energy coursed into him, eyes shooting wide. He'd been healing faster after Lyssica's touch, but now an intense blizzard of raw power zapped through every part of his body and although it healed him, he had the sense that Ostara had weighed and measured his physical make-up, his worth and his character, all at the same time.

He sagged as she removed her hands. Lyssica and Dario each grabbed an arm, supporting him. Blinking owlishly, he stared at the goddess. "That was fierce. Was I suffering so much injury?"

Ostara considered him, green eyes lambent, skin glowing golden. "A few things needed sorting; you'll do fine, now." She turned to Lyssica, who was bouncing from foot to foot. "Ah, still juiced up. We need a private conversation, my dear. We've some goddessy things to work through. Let's step over to the last stone in my circle."

Lyssica smiled. "Of course, my Lady."

"Wait!" Emryn's body trembled. "I feel strange. Are you certain I'm okay?"

One corner of her lips lifting, Ostara nodded. "Absolutely, Lord Emryn. As perfect, as can be. Just exactly what you need to be, in fact."

17

LYSSICA

The last stone in the circle was not particularly high, but it stood furthest away from the males. Ostara smoothed Lyssica's hair back from her face. At the goddess's touch, the tingling in Lyssica's skin increased, as though she were primed to explode in a shower of sparkles. Fighting to hold the euphoria in, she focused on the goddess's words.

"Your male has enhanced hearing due to his changeling heritage so I've also enclosed us in a privacy bubble. What I have to tell you is *your* information. You may decide to keep it private, but you're at liberty to share with whomever you wish, although I'd choose those folk carefully." Ostara scanned Lyssica's face, her own illuminated with the joy of life. "You've done a superlative job, dear one, succeeding against all odds."

Lyssica grinned, her insides bubbling, almost overflowing with her joy and delight. "Only because I was finally able to break through the barrier to reach you." She tilted her head. "I don't understand why we were disconnected. Do you know the cause?"

"Aye." Ostara grimaced. "The Bodach placed a veil between us. It was subtly done and my attention was on the other goddesses attending our meeting, so I didn't notice. He chose his time well, but then, his actions were all cleverly planned."

Lyssica rocked on the balls of her feet, a smile of happiness lighting her features. "I'm so pleased I finally broke through." Why did she feel like she wanted to sing at the top of her lungs and dance until she dropped with exhaustion?

Ostara pursed her lips as she considered Lyssica. "Let's hope you still think so after what I've to tell you." She reached out to clasp both of Lyssica's hands. "When you reached me and I was able to see, through your mind and memories, what was being perpetrated by the Bodach, I blasted you with the force you needed to resist, to fight back and overcome the Bodach. In so doing I had no choice but to use my power to change you into a being strong enough to contain and manage the sheer amount of magic I was pouring into you."

Lyssica stared uncomprehendingly, fighting to hold down the effervescence inside her. "But I'm your Handmaiden. I have been for years."

"Yes, that's true." Ostara's hands gripped more tightly as Lyssica jigged up and down. "But, as my Handmaiden, you already contained as much of my power as you could hold, in your current form. To give you what you needed to triumph, I had to make you more."

Lyssica gulped. "In what way?" The hairs on her body stood on end. "How much more?"

"You had to become enough to overcome the Bodach."

"B-but he … he's a Demigod! He told me; bragged about it."

"He is." Ostara nibbled on her bottom lip. "Although The Cailleach has now placed a cap on his abilities in an effort to leash him somewhat."

"Oh." Lyssica tried to keep her feet still. "So, that makes me …"

"A Demigoddess."

"Ahh … I beg your pardon?" Lyssica paled, gaping, her eyes searching the emerald of Ostara's. A force inside her threatened to explode and shower the clearing with … what?

The goddess massaged Lyssica's fingers. "In fact, you are now a Demigoddess of Spring with a huge amount of magic, and the talent to take in more, from me or nature, as you need it. Plus, between us we've a more direct link which no-one but I can separate, or veil, as the Bodach did."

Sagging against the tor, Lyssica struggled against the incandescence threatening to burst from her, even as she took in the news. "Umm. I feel ..."

Ostara nodded. "Yes. You're awash with power while your body is adjusting to its new form. It will settle in a few days. In the meantime, you will be bubbling over with life, love and growth, shedding it in sparkles." The goddess patted her hand. "You'll be a veritable blizzard of joy and new beginnings for all those with whom you come in contact. It will help them through the terrible events brought about by the Bodach and usher them into a new, prosperous and rosy future. Do you understand, Lyssica, my daughter?"

"I-I think so." Lyssica licked her lips. "D-daughter?"

Ostara smiled. "Yes, indeed. With what I've done to you, it is as though you were born to me in the real sense; you're a piece of me."

"B-but ..."

Shaking her head, Ostara held up a hand. "It's okay. I don't wish to supplant your birth mother, Lyssica. Just think of me as your Fairy Goddess-mother, for in effect, that's what I am."

Quaking with the effort of holding the effervescence in, Lyssica managed a jerky nod. She swallowed and forced herself to say, "Okay Goddess-ma, I understand. I think."

A tinkle of laughter left Ostara's lips. "Goddess-ma. I like it." Her features softened. "Everything will settle and come right, you'll see." She sighed. "But now I must go, dear daughter. Although, I'll definitely be back. You're a delight to my ages-wearied senses." She leaned forward and kissed Lyssica's brow, waved at Emryn and Dario, who'd not taken their eyes off them, then vanished in a rainbow of green, gold and purple sparkles.

~

"WELL, Trey and I disarmed every Vulpia attack-web we could find, but we didn't see any Vulpiawolves." Lyssica turned at the sound of Zhulija's voice, watched as Treymeron followed Zhulija into the circle, then sped to them on energy-winged feet.

"That's because they were all here!" Lyssica hugged Zhulija, then moved to hug Treymeron as well. The neck of his jerkin wriggled and a baby duskit peeked out. He reared back.

"Don't squash Pinkerpush!"

"Okay, okay." Her hands came out, palms facing him in a warding gesture. "Wasn't aware you still had this little one – why do you?"

A sheepish expression flitted across his face. "She won't leave me. The three Papan has won't be parted from him either. It's like they form an emotional attachment somehow." Then, he scowled at her. "What's with you? You're bouncing like you're on jump juice and blow me down if you didn't just leave a trail of sparkling glittery stuff as you ran to us."

"Ooh, did I really?" Lyssica pranced in a circle trying to see the effect, which drew the attention of everyone else. "Ostara said I might do that." She giggled.

Dario raised an eyebrow. "You sound as if you're tipsy as all hell."

Emryn growled. "You're raining glittery stuff – what did Ostara do to you?"

She waved an airy hand. "Just a little overflow of the magic she shared to overcome the bad folk." Rising to her toes, she spun in a circle, spreading more tiny shimmer particles. "No nasties left now."

Treymeron scowled, gestured to the body of Perris. "Well, he's nasty and he's still here."

Grimacing briefly, Lyssica cast a look at the prone body. "We probably should check, but the devil-rabbit ripped his throat out, so he's more than likely dead."

"Oh!" Treymeron pursed his lips. "Well, I know I should say it's a terrible thing, but after what he did to you?" He shook his head. "I can't."

"The devil-rabbit was here?" Emryn stiffened. "What happened? Where'd he go?" He scanned the surrounding woods intently.

"I took care of him." Lyssica couldn't stop shifting from foot to foot as she brought everyone who hadn't been present, up to date. "And as for the Vulpiawolves, Cailleach took them when she dragged the Bodach off." Lyssica grinned pirouetting and causing a rainbow of tiny fireglows.

"I want to hear exactly what happened." Dario cleared his throat. "But probably best to wait until we're with everyone so you don't have to repeat it over and over. Plus, it's late and we must all get home."

Zhulija caught his arm. "Beloved, I believe it would be best if we all go back to Papillion for tonight – we've survived a fight, some of us are injured, we're all in need of winding down, especially Lyss, and it's the closest place."

Dario's fingers closed over her hand. "Excellent solution, my darling. Papillion it is."

"And I guess we should take you-know-who back." Treymeron jerked a thumb towards Perris.

Zhulija rolled her eyes. "Wow, Trey, your sensitivity is amazing."

He scowled. "He might be dead, but he's still a swine."

Emryn's voice rumbled dryly. "Maybe you could suggest that to his parents as an epitaph."

Thus, a strange cavalcade returned to the Papillion Estate. Kynthcat carried the body of Perris slung over his back. Treymeron, Zhulija and Dario flew, while Lyssica, still full of boundless energy, danced along at Kynthcat's side. The fliers landed as they reached the gates of the estate.

Treymeron shook his head. "I don't know if anyone else noticed, but those sparks Lyss is spreading around are amaze-balls. Some become flowers immediately upon touching the ground and if they land on plants, there's an instant reanimation or growth spurt. She's full of go-go juice."

Zhulija turned and stared. "Goddess bless, you're right Trey! Look at all those little blossoms."

Lyssica did another glitter spreading pirouette and beamed. "Ostara said it will settle – eventually."

Dario shook his head. "Just as well one of us kept an eye out for danger." Zhulija blew him a kiss and his hand shot up to snatch it out of the air. She giggled as he made a show of raising the captured kiss to his lips.

Signing in at the guard house, they made their way to a shed at the back of the manor where they could lay Perris' body. By then, a crowd had gathered, both animals and Fae-folk, all drawn to Lyssica and the energy she radiated. She was thrilled to share, bless and coo, a repeat of her sessions in the forest. Later, she walked through the barns and stables, attending to creatures too ill or injured to move.

She shared the news wherever she went. "I'm happy to announce Ostara has made a deal with the Cailleach and the unnatural winter is over. The Vulpiawolves, devil-rabbit and the Bodach have gone, so conditions will improve over the next week or so. By Ostara's Day at the Spring Equinox, good weather conditions will be here." She stroked a quivering fox. "Of course, everyone may stay as long as they need or wish."

Zhulija tapped shoulder. "Lyss, it's time to clean up for dinner." She gazed at the fox. "Sorry little Reynard, but she must leave now." The fox uttered a soft 'yip', licked Lyssica's hand and laid his head down on the blanket.

～

DINNER WAS TUMULTUOUS. Lyssica couldn't sit still and the report of the forest fight had to be repeated several times. Everyone had queries, while the answers and explanations only gave rise to more questions.

Lyssica's parents, plus Kerrigold, Melkaz and Venaday all watched her in amazement. Emryn blew her a kiss, Zhulija winked, while Treymeron and Dario simply grinned as they watched everyone's reaction to the gyrations inspired by her excess of energy.

Duke Yanvian patted his mouth with a napkin, then fed tiny

morsels of food to each of the three duskits in a basket at his feet. "So, Ostara filled you with enough power to take down the Bodach and now you have to wait for it to ease?"

Lyssica grinned. "That's correct, Papan." She danced at her plate, loaded her fork with food and popped it into her mouth.

"When will that happen?"

She shrugged. "No idea, Papan." She was keeping the truth quiet for now.

"Are you able to concentrate?" Her father eyed her searchingly. "There's something I wish to say."

Venaday wagged his finger. "It'd better be pleasant, your Grace. I want her in a good mood so she'll agree to be my consort."

Lyssica rolled her eyes. "Oh do give up, Venaday! There's no way I'll ever agree."

Duke Yanvian stood, glaring at Venaday. "And there's the first thing. You, Sir, will cease importuning my daughter for her hand. She's said 'no' more than once. Do you have a hearing problem?"

Venaday's mouth fell open. "B-but, you were the one who said she was available."

Zhulija's fingers went to her mouth. "Papan, you didn't!"

With both Lyssica and Duchesse Azura glaring at him, Yanvian reddened. "Unfortunately, I did, but I've come to realise the choice isn't up to me, never was, and it was wrong of me to imply otherwise." He met Lyssica's angry stare. "I'm sorry and I'm taking this chance to publicly apologise." He glanced around the table. "When Lyss first broached the idea of learning estate management, I found it impossible to look at my beautiful daughter and see anything other than my little girl who loved tea parties and frilly things. To my regret I told her to go and be a traditional female, a brainless, pampered socialite."

He sighed. "I conceived a plan of finding a consort for her, but when DeMaksim's life took a new turn, I agreed to give Lyss a chance at being the heir." He cleared his throat and took a sip of water. "To my surprise and delight, I've discovered that Lyssica's skills at estate management are nothing short of brilliant. I've also come to know her as an adult, something which has brought me nothing but joy. I'm forced to confess how mistaken I was to pre-judge her as I did." He scanned the table of watchers again. "Don't get me wrong, the wonderful discovery of my daughter being fully capable of running this estate, probably any estate, has thrilled me no end." He smiled at Lyssica, then spread his hands, palms upward. "I looked in the mirror and saw a fool."

She had her fingers over her mouth as she watched him while bouncing on restless feet. His gaze softened.

"Furthermore, if she takes a consort, it will be her decision and choice of partner."

He walked around the table towards a stunned Lyssica and extended his arms. "My dearest Lyssica, I now see I've been blessed to have you as my daughter and I would be overjoyed if you can please forgive my stupidity."

Her voice trembled, a wobbly smile gracing her lips. "Oh Papan, how lovely. I do forgive you. Thank you." Accepting his hug, she grasped his shoulders and danced around the room, accompanied by their onlookers' laughter and applause. As she spun with her father, her gaze found Emryn, staring with pride and something looking suspiciously like the love which filled her heart to overflowing. Her soul bloomed in the joy of the night.

18

EMRYN

At bedtime, Duchesse Azura, with Duke Yanvian in tow, sought Emryn out. "I've had the Peony Room prepared for you, Emryn." She smiled, then noticed Lyssica shaking her head.

"Something wrong, Lyss?"

"No, nothing is wrong." Lyssica spoke firmly. "But Emryn is sharing my room – we're in a relationship and have been for some weeks now."

Her mother cocked a knowing eyebrow. "Ah, I'd begun to suspect."

Duke Yanvian's brows snapped together. "In a relationship? That's not—" His Duchesse elbowed him. "Ah!" He visibly swallowed. "Um, would it be alright if I ask your reasons for such a choice? Considering our societal strictures?"

Emryn enclosed Lyssica's hand in one of his as she wet her lips. "Well Papan, during that party period we both now regret, something happened to alter my perception of life and those societal strictures you mentioned."

Yanvian's gaze sharpened. "Go on."

Lyssica forged on. "An unscrupulous bastard – you know him as Perris Momphiday – drugged me to insensibility then had his way with me." Her parents drew in harsh, shocked breaths. "I was uncomfortable talking about the event, at the time. I-I wasn't in a good place. I admit it was a hard path to walk alone, but I learned to value myself as more than a precept of imposed beliefs." Her fist pressed her chest. "At my core, I'm still the same Lyssica, regardless of the rules and behaviours of others. I've learned to listen to my instincts, do what I believe is right – since obeying the advice of others meant I didn't like who I was and left me in a horrible situation."

Releasing his grip on her hand, Emryn wrapped an arm around her; he was solidly in her corner, sick at the harm she'd endured. Too bad that bastard, Momphiday, was already dead. Then, Treymeron appeared beside him, Zhulija and Dario planting themselves on Lyssica's other side and the support settled him, warming his core. Glancing around, Lyssica identified her siblings' support; a smile curved her lips.

'Our female very brave.' Kynthcat preened.

Lyssica's body expanded on a deep breath. "Emryn and I were drawn to each other from the beginning. We acknowledged it and I—" She turned to Emryn, gaze tender. He smiled at her as she continued. "I needed the power to choose for myself, since such a selection had previously been torn from my grasp. I wanted the liberty to connect with someone on my terms – doing so has done wonders for my self-esteem." Her gaze returned to her parents. "I'll apologise to no-one for my choices. However, I understand if you find this reality difficult."

Duchesse Azura's eyes shone with tears. "Oh, my dearest Lyss! That you endured that terrible experience alone. I'm so sorry you didn't find us approachable. I told Yanvian I disagreed with his stance, but I wanted you both to find solutions without my intervention. What an awful mistake!" She held out her arms. "May I hug you?"

"Of course, Maman." Sagging with relief, Lyssica stepped out of Emryn's embrace and into her mother's. Beside them, the duke quivered with fury. Emryn waited for his explosion – would he refuse to acknowledge his blame in the matter and turn on Lyssica again?

"I can't believe this!" Yanvian's eyes were wild with bitter fury. "Momphiday?! How dare he! The nerve – coming here a program applicant, forcing his company on you after he'd ... he'd ... If he weren't already dead, I'd rip his man parts off and feed them to him. That no-good, lying, disgusting vart-demon! I just can't—" He broke off, hands clutching his hair. A harsh sob tore from him, the shards of sorrow in the sound almost tangible. Lyssica moved from her mother's arms to hug him.

"Oh, Papan."

His arms encircled her. "Oh, my sweet girl. Can you ever forgive me?"

Lyssica rocked him. "You didn't do it, Papan."

"No, but I manipulated you into a position where a predator hurt you." A tear trickled down the side of his nose. "I don't think I can forgive myself. I was a rigid, rule-structured fool and see where it's gotten us?"

"Shh, Papan. Shh. As I told Emryn, Zhu and Dario, I'm now telling you – I've come to terms with it. Yes the events were terrible, but I survived and I've come out the other side a stronger Fae-female. I like who I am. Do you hear me?"

He drew back a little. "I'm proud of you, daughter. So proud. You're wonderful and I support your right to choose anything in your life." Eyes wet, he looked directly at Emryn, then his mouth firmed and he nodded.

"You've picked a beautiful Fae-lady to share this visit with."

Emryn seized the opening. "I plan to spend a lot more than just my visit with Lyss."

Yanvian looked taken aback. "But you … you're leaving soon. Aren't you?"

"I am." Emryn confirmed. "Pack tethering means I don't have a choice, as I've discussed with Lyssica previously, but I'm coming back." He focused on his love. "I'm definitely coming back. My Kynthcat declared Lyssica our mate from the beginning."

Lyssica gasped. "He did?"

"Yes. But fool me … I was uncertain because there's never been a mating to someone outside the pack." He turned to face her father. "But I no longer care. I love Lyssica." He met her startled, overjoyed gaze. "Yes, you." His finger touched the tip of her nose as she stood within her father's grasp. "I love you Lyssica Aphiski." Tender warmth filled his smile. "I love you and wish to spend my life with you, however we can arrange it. What do you say?"

"Yes. I say yes!" Lyssica released her father and leaped towards him. He caught her, pulling her close, his breath catching as the heat of her gaze thrilled him and Kynthcat to their core. "My Emryn Kynthcat, I'm so in love with you, so very much. You're my every wish and dream made real and I'm keeping you."

He kissed her then, regardless of the onlookers, the hooting, the whistling, the applause. He kissed her with all of the love in his soul.

'Maybe not so stupid after all.' Kynthcat did a jiggy, bucking prance, purring with happiness.

After a while, Emryn drew back, looking for Lyssica's parents. He was pleased to see them smiling, their arms around each other.

Unable to bow while clutching Lyssica, Emryn nodded his head to them. "Your Graces, I seek your blessing. I'd like to talk with you about what I can offer Lyssica and, by extension, your family, but to do that I must travel back to my pack and sort matters out with my family. I need my Alpha's help and guidance about the best way forward. I know there's a week left of the program, since the contract was to end on Ostara's Day at Spring Equinox, but I'd like permission to leave tomorrow."

"Permission granted." Dario said, smiling just as widely as his mate.

"Thank you." He turned to everyone then to say, "Know, all of you, and bear witness. I vow myself bound to Lyssica Aphiski." He raised her hands to his lips, kissed her knuckles, met her shining eyes. "I promise you, I will return as soon as I can organise everything, but I'd be remiss if I didn't explain: the details could take several weeks. It'll be difficult without you, my love, but I seek to construct our future."

She stretched on tiptoes to kiss him, a brief, but sound meeting of their mouths, leaving him hungry for more. "I understand." Relieved, he hugged her. Over her head, her parents still smiled. Euphoria blossomed within him and Kynthcat batted imaginary hearts and flowers.

'*Like kissing. More of that.*' The large, twin horned, furry animal attempted to pucker his mouth, to make kiss lips.

Emryn choked on a cough, but didn't miss Duke Yanvian's extended forearm, the Fae-warriors' recognition of equals. He accepted gratefully; then watched a look of wonder and delight bloom on Lyssica's face as Yanvian offered his forearm to her. "Oh!" Slowly, she responded, her gaze scanning her father's features.

"I acknowledge you, Lyssica, in your own right – as your Father, I give my blessing to you both."

"As do I." Duchesse Azura reached out to hug all three of them, something which culminated in a mother-daughter embrace, as the two Fae-males eased aside.

Emryn and Yanvian eyed one another. Yanvian's mouth twisted. "Hidebound as I am by the old ways, I can't say this any other way. After coming to know you during this program, I'm more than pleased to pass my daughter and her care into your safekeeping."

"I accept in the spirit of the offer." This time Emryn did bow. "In my clan, I'm a beta Kynthcat, but not because I'm weak. It simply means I'm rock solid in support and protection of my Alpha. That's how my role with Lyssica will work. If she asks me, I'll suggest, maybe advise and we'll discuss options, but ultimately, I'll always have her back, no matter her choices. You understand?"

Yanvian returned the bow. "I do. Now that I have shrugged off the veil of my idiocy, I see how perfect you are for my daughter and I'm well content."

~

THE NIGHT WAS an explosion of love and joy. Emryn could keep neither lips nor hands from Lyssica's glowing, delectable body and she was equally as eager for him, overflowing with energy and joy. She'd confessed her new Demigoddess status to him, but it changed nothing – she'd been his goddess from the second she'd toppled into his arms at the welcome dinner.

Roused in the early light of dawn by Lyssica kissing and licking her way across his pecs and up to his neck, he drew her close.

"I adore your aroma, Emryn." Her voice was throaty and he smiled, fondly remembering the delighted screams he'd caused during their loving.

"And I, yours, my darling; your scent is home." He stroked the curve of her spine until he reached the swell of her bottom. Grasping the curves with both hands, he urged her to sit astride him – not for the first time. He adored seeing his Lyssica take what she wanted from him – a victory for them both.

She sighed delightedly as he surged up inside her. She was amazing, as was her delectable heat, the feeling of being snugly home within her; those sensations would draw him forever. Nothing, nobody, had ever felt so wonderful. Her hands were on his chest, massaging, digging fingernails in – once she grasped how much he loved the prick of fingernails, the sharp bite of her teeth, she didn't hold back. They'd discovered she enjoyed being bitten by him too; but was a little wary of his claws – after all, Kynthcat's were a heck of a lot sharper.

'Me never hurt our mate.' Kynthcat purred, wallowing in the sensations rolling through them.

'I know. She'll learn.'

Lyssica stilled suddenly, her fingers grazing a tender spot on his neck. "Your skin's broken there." Her eyes sought his. "I-I think I drew blood, Emryn."

He grinned. "Oh, I know you did. It was wonderful, mate."

"Am I?" Her brow furrowed. "Are we really mates? Being from two different cultures and all?"

His grin widened. "Oh yes, you'll see when I return the favour. We might be from separate cultures, but both of those are still Fae. I know your branch has some other rituals, but for us, sex, biting and blood are the sealers. Although I'll dance your Rhynfallia with you whenever you want."

"Hmm." The frown cleared. She swept her hair back behind one gorgeously pointed ear. "May I ask, what you're waiting for then?"

"Nothing." Without warning, he eased her torso forward, one hand fisted her hair and he sank fangs into the glowing tawny skin of her throat. The hard thrust of his cock into her sex, the rough upward pumping of his hips, catapulted them both sky-high. Emryn's vision whited out at the combined sensations of their mutual orgasm, the drops of Lyssica's blood sliding sweetly into his system. His guttural roar was matched by her cry as their mating bond snapped into place, coursing through their bodies with the force of a winter blizzard being blown away by the cyclonic beginnings of spring.

19

LYSSICA

*H*e'd been gone a day over four weeks and Lyssica missed Emryn so fiercely she felt sick. Taking a sip of hot, fortifying tea, she stared at her breakfast morosely. Surely he'd be back soon?

The rumble of her father's voice drew Lyssica's attention.

"Azura, are you alright?" Papan's brow furrowed as he watched his consort poke at a slice of toast. "You usually have eggs as well."

Duchesse Azura smiled at him. "I'm fine, Yanvian, my love." She nibbled an edge of her toast. His frown lightened, but he continued to watch. She chewed and swallowed. "I just feel like plain toast this morning."

Still sipping her tea, Lyssica absently observed their interchange. Ever since she'd received the massive energy charge from Ostara, the estate and surrounds were bursting with the new season's light and warmth.

The Spring Equinox had become a festival of joy and love; animals and Fae all mingling fearlessly while honouring Ostara, the Goddess of Spring, Fertility and New Beginnings. Ostara had graced them with Her presence, hugging Lyssica and kissing her on both cheeks in front of everyone. The action, normally something shared between family

443

members, brought Lyssica a recognition she hadn't been fully prepared for. So many animals flocked to her, she was in danger of tripping over them; Fae couples approached for her blessing – one she happily provided, despite how self-conscious the focus felt.

Still radiant with the magic Ostara had shared, she continued to leave a trail of sparkles and tiny blossoms. After overcoming her embarrassment at everyone's fascination with the phenomenon, it became fun to finger-flick the glitter of her new power over everyone who approached, to watch them glow with pleasure as shimmers and flowers enveloped them. To her secret delight, she could see the magic sink deep into their bodies; watch them heal from tiny maladies of flesh and spirit they'd previously taken in stride; and see them come alive with new energy.

But was it ethical to perform internal checks on folk if they weren't expecting it? Perhaps she should do it openly. Maybe she could offer a healing and helping clinic for a few hours weekly, open to anyone, with some folk specifically invited? She chewed her toast as she thought about it, finally deciding it was a good idea. For now, though, there was Maman to consider.

"Maman? Would you allow me to scan you? Make certain you're well?"

A warm smile lit the Duchesse's face. "Of course, Lyss. I'd love to be your practice partner."

Returning the smile, Lyssica assessed her mother through her screen of enhanced power. To her elation, the source of the discomfort was easily located, but the reason, oh, that reason ... She covered her lips with her fingertips, staring at her mother while contemplating the miracle she'd seen. Did Maman know?

"Well? Just tell me the issue, Lyssica. There's no need to blink at me like a stunned fallow deer."

"Um, Maman—" She scanned again, just to be sure.

The Duchesse rolled her eyes. "You did another magical inspection, didn't you?"

"Um, yes."

Azura sighed, smiling indulgently. "I suppose we'll get used to your new skills, but it'll take a while." She tipped her head to the side. "Did you find anything wrong?"

Lyssica smiled weakly. "Well, no. Nothing wrong. Per se. It's just ..."

Her mother stilled. "Just what?"

Lyssica cleared her throat. "You're expecting a baby." There was a brief, charged silence before Duke Yanvian leapt to his feet.

"What?!"

Maman's mouth had fallen open. She snapped it shut, staring wide-eyed at her toast. "Oh." She rolled her lips in and out, her gaze rising to meet Lyssica's. "Of course. My change of appetite, the way I ... Yes, it makes sense now." She swallowed, her face paler than earlier. "You sensed, or saw, the differences in me?"

Lyssica tilted her hand from side to side. "Well, yes, but I can also sense and see the baby."

"Baby?" Suddenly Treymeron's head shot up, the conversation having broken the barrier of his concentration. His fingers clamped the book he'd been reading. "There's a baby? We're going to have a new brother or sister?"

"Yes." Lyssica grinned.

A heavy thump emanated from her father's direction, but when Lyssica looked, she couldn't see him. She frowned. "Where's Papan?"

"On the floor." Duchesse Azura giggled, then covered her mouth with a trembling hand. "I think he passed out."

EVERYWHERE SHE WENT THAT DAY, Lyssica recognised the same state in many females at Papillion, be they Fae or animal. There were plenty of new pregnancies. She was stunned. Still in the barn with some of the recovering fauna, she somewhat nervously communed with Ostara.

'Goddess-ma, there's a blessing of new babies on the way.'

A wash of love flowed across the link. *'Lyssica, my dear. Yes, it's common in spring.'*

'I know, but there seems to be a lot. I mean, more than usual.'

'*An overflow from you, dear one.*' Amusement came. '*You've been spreading the power widely, haven't you?*'

'*Well, yes, Goddess-ma, but—*'

'*Lyssica, we're fertility goddesses, remember?*'

'*Oh. Yes.*'

'*Although the mother does have to indulge in some lovemaking with her mate or consort – doesn't she?*'

'*Lovemaking with her ...*' Suddenly, Lyssica was overcome by an urge to sit down. Muscles quivering, mouth dry, she checked, and gasped. Blindly, she reached out to grip some nearby railing.

'*Holy Mother Goddess, I'm pregnant!*'

'*Congratulations, my dear Lyssica.*'

'*You knew!*'

Ostara corrected her. '*I knew it would happen. It was quite inevitable with the combination of a new mate and your power flux.*'

'*You could've have warned me.*'

A tinkle of laughter. '*Would it have changed anything? Our magic is strong enough to realign female cycles – it's who we are.*'

Lyssica gulped. '*Are you saying I'm destined to be pregnant for the rest of my life?*'

More laughter. '*Only if you want that. As your magic settles and you discover more about it, you'll learn to fine tune and only be fertile when you wish it. Right now though, the huge influx meant you avoiding pregnancy was like a fish attempting to swim against an extremely strong current.*'

'*Little chance of success?*' Lyssica massaged her temples.

'*Not with an earthy new mate.*'

~

EMRYN DESERVED to be first to know their news, so Lyssica tried to appear as she usually did. With the spotlight heavily on her mother, it wasn't as difficult as she'd imagined.

Duchesse Azura twisted her fingers together as she paced the library. "I've seven adult children; I thought I was well past the time of bearing offspring."

From his reclining position on a window seat, Duke Yanvian shook his head. He wore a drunken expression of wondrous joy, despite having tossed back only one small, celebratory beaker of flamuisge.

"A baby at our age; it's a blessing I still can't believe." One of his three little duskit shadows chirruped softly, climbed his leg and scampered into the curve of his neck. To Lyssica's amusement, it snuggled in, mewing and patting him with one tiny paw.

A faint chuckle reached her; she turned, taking in Treymeron, sprawled on a second window seat, gently stroking the infant duskit on his chest with one long finger.

Lyssica sniggered. "Obviously, neither you nor Maman are too old and you're getting heaps of excellent practice with those duskit babies." Her hand wave encompassed both Fae-males. "They seem to have formed some sort of bond with both you and Trey – you're already surrogate mothers."

Spearing her with wide eyes, Treymeron clutched Pinkerpush firmly, but shook his head. "I'm no-one's mother!"

She snorted. "Okay, a father then, but you're still parenting her."

"Lyss's right, Trey," Duke Yanvian continued to watch his consort who was mumbling as she finger counted. When she stopped at the second last digit and gazed at him almost helplessly, he nodded.

"It's okay, my lovely one. When are we due?"

Azura smiled weakly. "I think, late in the Moon of Mayember."

Lyssica clapped her hands. "How wonderful!" *Oh, goody, a blessing of new babies at the end of Autumn – at the moment only I know just how wonderfully momentous that's going to be.*

A ruckus drifted from the front hall. Both Yanvian and Treymeron sat up, focusing on the outer door, just as a knock sounded. It opened. Entanglit appeared and bowed. "The Duke and Duchesse of Garadenya with guests, your Graces."

Zhulija burst in, radiating excitement; Dario followed closely, hand outstretched.

"Have a care, sweeting. Please?"

Treymeron's groan was heartfelt. "By the Goddess, Zhu! Don't tell me you're pregnant too?"

She stopped short, face falling. "What? Yes, I am. What's wrong with you, Trey? Aren't you thrilled for me? For us?" She waved blindly at Dario.

"Yeah, yeah, sorry – it's just that we're surrounded by fertile females apparently. It's exciting, but a little disconcerting, having everyone fall pregnant at the same time."

Zhulija stared first at her mother, then at her sister, then back to her brother. Beside her, Dario guided her further into the room. "Everyone? What do you mean, Trey? Lyss. Are you expecting too?"

"No, not her." Treymeron's blithe comment took the pressure off Lyssica. "But Maman, some other estate females and many of the animals."

"Maman?!" Zhulija's squeal was deafening. "Oh Maman, that's wonderful."

Dario glared at Treymeron. "I'm certain I heard you congratulating us just now, didn't I?"

Treymeron surged to stand, Pinkerpush vanishing inside the neck of his shirt. "Oh! Oh, absolutely! It's marvellous. Congratulations Zhu and you too, Dario!"

From the doorway, Entanglit coughed. "Excuse me, but I'd like to introduce Alpha Kynth-lord Bregal Phengaris, his mate Kynth-lady Renfa Urlnyth-Phengaris and their sons, Kynth-lords Delano, Tucker and Emryn Phengaris."

There was a bevy of excited greeting, to which Lyssica was oblivious as, incandescent with joy, she ran for Emryn. Equally as intent, he was half way across the room to meet her.

"Lyss, my beloved!"

"My Emryn, thank goodness!" Heedless of everyone in the room, they embraced passionately. The familiar feel of Emryn's large warm hand cupping the nape of her neck, while his other clutched her close and tight, heated an internal pit Lyssica hadn't realised was cold. Emryn was here – he'd come back to her. She clung to him, returning his kiss with every ounce of love permeating her soul. At the same time she felt her way along their mating bond, all the particles of her being yearning for connection with him. And somehow, he was there, reaching out, linking with her. She imaged a baby. He gasped, his hold on her still deliciously firm, but gentling.

They drew back, eying each other with untrammelled delight, then Lyssica heard her name called. She turned her head; knowing she wore an uncontrollable grin. Her parents grinned back, thrilled by her happiness. Emryn's family stared with various expressions of pleasure or surprise. The elder Fae-male pulled his earlobe.

"Well, Emryn, you told me, but until this moment I didn't believe; there's definitely a mate bond between you and your lady. It's very pleasing." He cast a glance at Duke Yanvian. "You and I have much to discuss, Yanvian."

Her father nodded. "I agree, Bregal."

Lyssica pointed at Emryn's father. "You also need to talk with me, Alpha Kynth-Papan. I'm Emryn's mate just as much as he's my consort, and I speak for myself."

Bregal cocked his head. "Ah, my new daughter is an Alpha too. That's brilliant. It means Emryn's pack tether can be adapted."

Lyssica narrowed her eyes. "Moved to me?"

"Yes, but not totally. A pack of two or three isn't enough for a healthy balance, so a minor link to the Destrion Changeling Clan must continue." Bregal rubbed his chin. "But your relationship provides enough stability for visits to be by choice and not because Emryn is forced to recharge his connection." Joy surged along the bond from Emryn to Lyssica and back again; the last hurdle in their relationship had been overcome.

"Wonderful!"

Bregal nodded and turned in Treymeron's direction. "Didn't catch your name during the earlier introductions, young lordling."

He took the hint. "Treymeron Aphiski, at your service, Kynth-lord Bregal."

Bregal nodded. "Well, I need to correct you on something you said about ... "

Emryn flung up a hand, interrupting. "Thank you Papan, but I believe it's my news to share."

"Sorry, son." His father smiled sheepishly.

"News?" Treymeron's eyebrows elevated.

Emryn met his gaze. "Yes, news." He swallowed, glanced at Lyssica in his arms. "You got one thing wrong, Trey. Lyssica *is* expecting our baby. She just told me."

A look of scepticism flashed across Treymeron's face. "She told you? When you've either been fused at the lips or talking with us the whole time?"

Emryn grinned. "Communication takes many forms, Trey. She definitely told me. Plus, I both sense and scent the changes in her."

Staring in chagrin, Treymeron thrust hands to hips. "Holy snapping swamp turtles! Another one? I can't believe it! What is with all this fertility going around? Can't anyone keep it in their pants?"

Duke Yanvian laughed. "Maybe it's catching?"

A look of horror crossed Treymeron's face. His hands came up to form an ancient sign of warding and turning, he bolted through a side door. As it slammed shut behind him, Lyssica nestled into Emryn's arms.

"Thank you for honouring your vows to me, Emryn."

His smile was tender. "I always will, my darling. I have your name engraved on my heart. From now until forever, it's you and me."

"Oh, Emryn, I love you." More than content, Lyssica sighed and cuddled deeper into the arms of her mate.

THE END

AUTHOR'S NOTE

Dear Reader,

Thank you for reading Lyssica and Emryns story. I hope you enjoyed it. The next instalment of my Fae Court Series will appear in A Perfectly Paranormal Christmas, out at the end of 2022.

Reader reviews are wonderful, so if you did enjoy the story, please leave a review. It will be gratefully appreciated.

If you wish to know more about me, I have a website:

www.hellucywrites.com

GLOSSARY

Main Characters in this story:

- Lady Lyssica Aphiski – Fae-lady from the Papillion family of the Lepidopter-fae
- Kynthlord Emryn Arion Phengaris – a beta of the Destrion Kynthcat changeling Clan.

Lyssica's Parents:

- Duke Papillion – Yanvian Cosmo Aphiski
- Duchesse Papillion -Azura Gracilla Neptulide Aphiski

Her siblings in birth order:

- DeMaksim Yanvian Aphiski (Hero of Book 2: 'Ancestors and Expectations'.)
- Lyssica Fern Aphiski (Heroine of Book 3: 'Blizzards and Beginnings'.)
- Janeska Lyria Aphiski – twin to Tindresse
- Tindresse Azura Aphiski – twin to Janeska
- Treymeron Cosmo Aphiski
- Armelle Gracilla Aphiski
- Zhulija Juniper Aphiski

Sibling mates:

- Dario Calaspon Eribifax a.k.a. The Unseelie Beast; Hero of Book 1: 'Filigree and Fate'; Zhulija's mate/consort

- Cherith Vanitheriel Beriaden (half Undine-Fae/half Eldwytch-Fae) and one of triplets; Heroine of Book 2: Ancestors and Expectations; DeMaksim's mate/consort.

Emryn's Parents:

- Kynth-lord and Clan Alpha Bregal Fangorn Phengaris
- Kynth-lady Renfa Urlnyth-Phengaris

Emryn's siblings:

- Delano Tarhee Phengaris – brother
- Tucker Rory Phengaris – brother

The Fae Queens, cousins who'd decided to unite the Queendom and rule jointly:

- Seelie Queen Dianathke Morgana (Castle Elrodel)
- Unseelie Queen Maerovana Titania (Castle Synternesse)

Random characters:

- Antigony Lyonetti – Lyssica's personal assistant
- Bardia – gate guard at the Papillion estate
- Brandon – coach driver from Garadenya Fortress/Duchy
- Britha – Captain of guard at Garadenya Fortress/Duchy.
- Brom – guard at Papillion estate
- Countess of Cossidae
- Cyrano – guard at Garadenya Fortress/Duchy
- Jarith – guard at Garadenya Fortress /Duchy
- Lorth Entanglit – Major-domo at Papillion estate
- Lozito – gate guard at Papillion

- Minksalt – Major domo at Garadenya Fortress/Duchy
- Naseem – guard at Garadenya Fortress/Duchy
- Vingle – guard at Garadenya Fortress/Duchy
- Vinny – stable youth at Papillion
- Vystan – guard at Papillion estate

The Visiting Tri-moon Folk at Papillion Estate:

- Lady Kerrigold Anaya Helioden
- Lord Melkaz Brayg Eriocraan
- Lord Perris Haragen Momphiday
- Lord Roland Jarn Arrelgyre.
- Lord Tanjil Rosset Blastobarm
- Lord Venaday Quartz Tortrician

Note:

This series is Speculative and based in Faery. The family around whom the stories are based are Lepidopter-fae: that is Fae-folk with butterfly/moth wings. Other Fae races also appear. So far in my series, these include:

- Dracons,
- Undine water-fae,
- Trolls,
- Redcap goblins,
- Eldwytch mages,
- Shapeshifters – in this story they're Kynthcats: a large, lion-like cat with a mocha coat, a chocolate mane, pale glowing eyes, gnarled, curving horns (like a goat) and a whip like tail.
- Shapeshifter Sand Seers – folk of the Changeling clans who practice divination
- Vart-demons – a type of demon

Various animals including some I have invented for my own purposes, including:

- Wood bunnies – as opposed to just bunnies or rabbits, an Easter connection of sorts
- Blush cheeked chirpers – little birds
- Devil-rabbit – an evil rabbit, minion of The Bodach
- Kynthcat – See shapeshifters
- Duskit – a purple blue multi coloured little creature. Cross between a kitten, a squirrel and a possum.
- Pinkerpush – Treymeron's duskit
- Dash, Splash and Crash – Yanvian's duskits.
- Vulpiawolf- a type of wolf with a spiky rough body pelt, legs without fur and a spiked tail tip. They're greenish grey in colour and smell like wet fur.

There are also appearances by Goddesses, Gods and their consorts:

- Ostara – also known as Eostre – Unseelie Goddess of Spring, fertility and new beginnings, renewal and rebirth. She represents the Spring Equinox, when night and day are of equal length, which in this story I've labelled Ostara Day. Her symbols are the hare, the egg, all Spring flowers, dragons/serpents, a Celtic cross in a circle and the colours of bright green, gold and purple.
- Olwen – Seelie Goddess of Sunlight and Spring
- Modron – Autumn Goddess
- The Cailleach (pronounced Kellyark) Goddess of the cold and winds. Also called The Veiled One and The Queen of Winter. A crone for half the year and young for the six months after Winter's end.
- The Bodach (pronounced bowdark) consort of Cailleach, a mischievous prankster, not always pleasant. Often appears as an old man dressed in poor farming clothes, chewing a straw, with an old hat perched low on his head.

ALSO BY HELLUCY HOWE

Filigree and Fate

Dario and Zhulija's story in:

A Perfectly Paranormal Valentine

Ancestors and Expectations

Cherith and DeMaksim's story in:

A Perfectly Paranormal Halloween

Blizzards and Beginnings

Lyssica and Emryn's story in:

A Perfectly Paranormal Easter

ABOUT HELLUCY

Meet Hellucy Howe, a Book Dragon who teethed on romantic fairy tales and went on to voraciously devour anything paranormal. Writing was also second nature but became something to do in secret when the stories of her young child mind were ridiculed. Homes were populated with books and hidden caches of story notebooks inspired by a fertile brain and a massive creative streak.

She became a Professional Reader and a Closet Scribbler, convinced no one would want to look at the mad ramblings of someone who hates getting dirt under her fingernails and knows ironing was invented as a torture method.

Nowadays, Helen loves inventing paranormal and fantasy romance from the comfort of her cosy study with a hot cup of tea beside her laptop and her little spaniel, Lexie, snoring at her feet. With her anthology contribution of 'Filigree and Fate', Helen was dragged kicking and screaming from her closet, into the deer-in-headlights world of being a Real Author.

And if you want to get to know the Perfectly Paranormal Anthology authors a bit more, get sneak peeks of what's coming up for the APP Anthologies, as well as giveaways, special offers and just some PNR fun, then join our Perfectly Paranormal Paramours Facebook Group.

Find us here:

ACKNOWLEDGMENTS

Thank you to:
1.   My imagination for getting me started
2.   My daughter, Samantha, for believing in me and for kicking me in the butt when I doubted myself
3.   Fellow APP anthology members: Leisl, Marnie and Samantha for their expertise, advice and constant encouragement
4.   My furry girl, Lexie, for all her cuddles
5.   Ice cream and tea, for always being available …

BLOOD CURSED

LEISL LEIGHTON

BLOOD CURSED

A Gods Cursed Novella
Book 3

Leisl Leighton

Published by Leisl Leighton as Permien Press. For more information, email: leisl@leislleighton.com

First published 2022 in the A Perfectly Paranormal Easter Anthology. Rewritten and republished 2022 as a single title novella by Permien Press.

Cover design – Samantha Marshall

Editor – Marnie St Clair

❀ Created with Vellum

ABOUT BLOOD CURSED

A secret blood curse; a love worth fighting for.

Failed witch Korinna Soteira needs to figure out how to control her power before the moon rises on the first night of Oestra. She can't allow the disaster that killed all the people of Pompeii 2,000 years ago to occur again. Especially if it endangers the life of her beloved Tamuel.

If it was up to her, she'd never use her magic, but if she and Tamuel are to release the trapped HeartsBlood Gem spirit and vanquish the evil witch Clodia, she will need every ounce of her power and more. The problem is the one spell that might allow her to control her magic – a spell she can only access with her cursed blood – is forbidden to her because of how dangerous it could be.

But Korinna will do anything to get her hands on that spell, even if the consequence might destroy the one thing worth living for: her love.

THE CURSE OF ILIA

Stolen and tricked and bound to the heart,
Yet blessed to use the power of home and hearth
Waiting and scheming for a way to depart
That which bound me by love's false start.
Only those like me, cursed yet kind,
Can help to break the bonds that bind,
Truth-seekers powered to free spirit and mind,
And question the false-certainty of Gods that blind:
That love is not that which will cause the fall,
But the thing that should succour and save us all.
This is my curse uttered unto thee,
Trapped, used and Gods-cursed, through eternity.
I await the soul and blood cursed to set me free
So I utter it to the universe, so mote it be.
Hidden incantation in the lost Eleusinian Mysteries Grimoire

1

Korinna Soteira kissed her soulmate, Tamuel, goodbye. "Good luck and take care," she said, lips lingering on his.

"Are you sure you don't want to come?"

Gods, she did. She hated being apart from him. Just as he hated being apart from her. Every time he had to track down a lead, he begged her to come with him, but ...

She glanced at the chronometer she'd placed on the wall next to Jules' train station clock. Only a month until the first day of Oestra. Twenty-eight days left to discover what they'd failed to discover in the last five months. She frowned. "It doesn't make sense for both of us to go off tracking down leads. Just as it doesn't make sense for both of us to stay and do research."

"Yeah, yeah. Divide and conquer – right? But it sucks."

She kissed his pouting lips. "I know." But they didn't have the time not to divide and conquer. They had to find a way to channel their powers together without endangering themselves and everyone else – especially when they added the energy of Oestra into the mix. If they didn't, they wouldn't be able to release the spirit from the Hearts-Blood Gem. And without her, they'd never defeat the evil Priestess-witch Clodia when she came out of the Void the first night of Oestra. But so far, nada. "Are you sure the gem's spirit hasn't told you anything?"

He touched the place in his chest where he'd magically spelled the gem to live so as to keep it safe after the events of Halloween. "Not anything we can use in regard to this."

"But she is talking to you? Has she told you more about how powerful Clodia is likely to be? She was strong when your mother fought her, and it took Jules sacrificing her power to defeat her and push her into the Void. But now … I mean, does she still have some of my power? Yours? Will she be able to use the power your mother sacrificed when she pushed her into the Void? Will she be able to draw on the power of Oestra as we will be doing?" She could feel the questions rushing out of her, but couldn't help it. There was just too much they still didn't know.

"I don't know." His hands smoothed down her arms in a calming motion.

"Ask her."

"I have," he said, raking his hand through his hair, ruffling his curls. "The only thing she says is that with our powers combined, plus what we can gather from Ostara rising, we should be able to defeat her."

"Should? Can't she give us more certainty than that?"

"Apparently not."

She bit her lip. "I thought when we started this, she'd be there to help us, to steer us in the right direction. But all she gave us was romanticised waffle that hasn't helped at all. *Your power is not the source of your grief, it is its salvation.* What the Hells does that really mean? And, *Strengthen yourself and all will be revealed.* She raised her hands and made an exasperated noise. "Completely. Fucking. Unhelpful. But who am I to talk?" She smacked at the book open on her desk. "So far, the sum total of my usefulness has been to send you on multiple fact-finding missions that have given us very few facts."

"We've learned much thanks to you."

"Not enough." She jabbed her finger at the chronometer. "28 days!

That's all we've got. How are we going to find what we need in 28 days when five months hasn't been enough?"

He cupped her face, thumbs stroking her cheeks. "You need to calm down, Rinna." His hands slid down her arms to cup her hands, holding them up so she could see the orange power sparking at her fingertips.

"Shit." Magic sparked out as she moved away from Tam, backing up as quickly as she could to put some distance between them – and the priceless books on the desks and in the stacks nearby. Desperately, she tried to control the unbidden power, but it wouldn't dissipate. This was a big part of the problem. And she worried that even if they did find a way to channel their powers together safely, she wouldn't be able to control hers and then … boom!

"Breathe, Rinna." Tam followed her, reaching for her hands.

"No. Don't touch. I might hurt you."

"You won't do that."

"I could."

"You won't. I'm certain of it. Just breathe. Your power is simply responding to your emotions. Mine does the same now it doesn't have my cupid power to temper it. Just calm down and everything will be okay."

"I am calm!"

He gave her a look.

Hells. He was right. She was behaving like a bloody novice.

"Given you haven't used your power for 2,000 years, it's only natural you'd be a bit rusty," Tam said softly, jumping to the conclusion she let everyone else jump to. "Especially given how quickly it's growing. You're stronger now than when we last faced Clodia."

"So are you – and you're not struggling."

He snorted. "I wouldn't say that." Before she could argue with him over that patently untrue statement, he put his finger on her lips. "You need to give yourself a break. We all think you're doing amazingly well and I'm confident both of us will be ready to do what must be done when the time comes."

"But we still don't know how we're supposed to use these greatly strengthened powers."

"We'll figure it out. It'll be fine. The HBG agrees with me."

It made her smile, his nickname for the HeartsBlood Gem. Only he would give a nickname to something so powerful. "How can you be so certain?"

"Why else would she have picked us to free her after the thousands of years she's been locked away?"

"Because we're just that kind of lucky?" she said, grimacing.

He chuckled and squeezed her hands. "No, because we're the ones she's been waiting for. We're destined to do it."

"I can't believe after all this, you're so keen to embrace this as destiny. You know destiny simply means we have no choice."

"Only if you view the path destiny chose for us as the only choice. I like to think of it more like my cupid arrows – I might have aimed them at potential lovers to make them notice each other, but what they do after that is their own choice. Destiny is only the path – it is up to us to decide how we walk it." He held up her hands. "And see, I'm right – you can do this."

The power no longer sparked on her fingers. She pursed her lips. "Don't be so smug about it."

"It's not smugness but certainty. I have faith in you. Faith in us. I know we will figure it out."

"How can you be so sure?"

He tugged her closer. The gem that was embedded in his chest glowed as their joint hands hovered over it. Warmth fizzled through her, alongside a sensation of rightness. "Because of this. There is a reason the three of us came together. Only all of us working as one can defeat Clodia. I know it deep in my soul. Don't you?"

She looked into his beautiful peridot eyes and wished, not for the first time, she had his faith. But he didn't know what she knew. That she was the weak link and if she didn't find some way of changing that, they'd lose.

She stared at him, chewing on her lip. She wanted to tell him.

Wanted his help, his advice, but … she couldn't worry him with this. So instead, she squeezed his fingers and said, "Okay."

"Okay what?"

"You better go. But first, kiss me again." He kissed her lightly on the nose, making her giggle. "I didn't mean like that."

He leaned back, eyes full of his love for her, and not a little mischief. "I hope your research is fruitful, my love. At least you've got the library to yourself for a while. Violetta just sent Jules a message this morning saying she won't be back today as promised – she's found another lead."

"I hope it's more useful than the last one. I could really use her help going through some of the older magical texts. Jules is great, but because of her old magical affliction, she doesn't know the older grimoires as well as Violetta."

"I know, but she had a 'knowing' and there's no talking her out of it. So, she won't be back today and Jules and Bas won't be back until this evening. They're seeing the OBGYN and then having a 'date night'. Except, it's during the day."

"Maybe we can have one of those when you get back."

"Promises, promises." He hauled her against him, kissing her hard and long. She melted into him, giving in to the pull of him, to the incredible desire that raced through her every nerve, muscle and bone, firing a desperate need inside to lose herself in the wonder of what she shared only with him. But thankfully – because they were running out of time – he broke the kiss before she sank too deep.

Panting, he said against her lips, "Stop worrying."

"I'm not."

"You can't fool me," he said, touching his chest above his heart. "I feel your worry."

She knew he could – which made it worse. She didn't want it standing between them and complete happiness; like the kind his parents shared. "I promise to stop worrying if you promise to stop worrying about me."

He chuckled. "Only you could ask the impossible and make it sound reasonable."

"I'm a worrier. You'll just have to get used to it."

"And I am happy to, as long as we share the burden. We both had to rely on ourselves for far too long, but neither of us have to take on everything alone anymore. We have each other. Okay?"

Her mouth twisted but she hid it with a nod. She wanted to share everything with him – Gods how she wanted that – but she just couldn't.

He bent down and pressed a sweet kiss to her lips. "I love you."

"I love you too."

He kissed her again then walked over to the free space between the kitchen and desks, opened a portal and stepped through.

Air displaced as the portal closed, ruffling the papers on the desks around her and cooling her hot face.

Hells! She had to do something soon or he'd begin to suspect exactly how dangerous her growing power was and how little control over it she really had. And she couldn't let him know that. The evil witch-bitch Clodia would break out of her prison in the Void using the rising power of Ostara and the magics she'd stolen, but the HBG assured them they would defeat her, melding their powers together with the spirit in the gem once they'd freed her. Korinna couldn't see how, given how things were right now, but Tam believed implicitly, and it was his total faith in what the HBG had told them that was holding them all up right now. Without it, everything could fall apart. The problem was, unless she did something drastic, that melding of their powers would end in pain and disaster and death.

Her track record spoke for itself after all.

If it was up to her, she'd step away and let Violetta or Bas take her place, but unfortunately, it didn't work that way. According to the HBG, she could only be freed with the active powers of two incredibly powerful magic-users who were bound soul and mind.

Not only that, but from everything they'd discovered – pitifully little – she was key in the HBG's plan not simply because of the strength of her magic and how it worked but because she was the only one amongst them who had torn open the fabric of space and time and gained access to the Void – even though that had been a horrible accident. The only other person who had done it that they knew of was Jules, when she'd torn open the Void and pushed Clodia in there over a year ago. Unfortunately, Jules had thrown all of her power at Clodia to do so, so she couldn't be the one who did it now.

So she was locked into this with no way out.

Which meant going behind Tam's back.

She rubbed her chest at the ache that thought caused. But there was no other option. The only spell she'd ever heard of that could give her the control she needed was in the Eleusinian Mysteries Grimoire – and Persephone had made him vow not to let her see the grimoire as he'd once promised. Thankfully, she'd not made Korinna vow not to go looking for it – she'd just made Tam go back on his promise. Not that she blamed him for that – he couldn't deny a Goddess, not to mention making the vow had meant he could keep the grimoire to use as a resource in the fight ahead. But still, it sucked that this was what it all led to – her sneaking around to take a peek at a grimoire that had been promised to her.

Bloody Persephone. She'd railed at Seph to change her mind, but the Goddess had been adamant.

"Oh, my love. If only you had been truthful with me all these years, this wouldn't be an issue. But how can I trust you with the Mysteries when, at your own admission, you sought to use the soul-transference spell? A spell you know would lead to your death."

"But it was to save the souls I caused to be lost in the Void."

Persephone cupped her face. "Your soul holds far greater value to me than all those souls put together. As does your life. Tamuel agrees."

"No, he doesn't. He knows I wouldn't use that spell now. Not if using it would hurt him. I would never hurt him. He's my soulmate."

"You would sacrifice yourself to save him."

"I would."

"Then I cannot trust you with that spell."

"What if I promise not to look for it?"

Persephone shook her head slowly. "You think I have forgotten you have an eidetic memory? One glance and you would be able to use it. So no, I cannot allow you to see the grimoire. But because you may need some of what is inside it to help fight Clodia, I have allowed Tamuel to keep it. You must be happy with that for now because it is all I can offer."

It was pointless fighting with the Goddess any further – Seph was one of the most stubborn people Korinna knew, and that was saying something.

So, she'd tried hard to find an alternative. But it was no use. And given she was finally alone for the rest of the day, she had to make her move now.

She had to break into Tam's secret hiding place and steal what had been forbidden to her.

She only hoped that when Tam found out – and she had no doubt eventually he would – he'd understand her decision and forgive her. Because if her soulmate didn't forgive her, she had no idea how she'd live with herself.

2

Samuel bent over double, hands on his knees, gulping in breaths. He looked back down at the steep incline he'd just ascended – half a mountain's worth – and then up. The darkness of the cave's entrance was about twenty metres above him as the crow flies. Pity he wasn't a crow and was forced to follow a steep and treacherous goat-trail.

Why couldn't the hermit-monk live on an idyllic beach? Why a cave high in the heart of the Carpathian Mountains? Of course, if his portal magic was working properly, where the monk lived wouldn't be a problem. Instead of opening up outside the monk's cave, it had dumped him half-way down the mountain. He'd been so good at portals when he'd had his cupid power – but all he had now was his warlock power and it didn't seem to like the way he'd always made portals. The only good thing was that it was strong and growing stronger every day, just as the HBG had said it would now it wasn't tamped down by his cupid power. Maybe it was just that this magic was different. Perhaps he had to figure out a different way of using it than the one he'd been trained in.

Maybe he should talk about it with Rinna. She'd done so much research into all sorts of magic over the years. She could probably help him. And maybe in helping him, she could help herself. He knew she was still struggling with her magic too. They were quite the pair.

"You will both figure it out," the HBG spirit said into his mind.

"I'm glad you're confident."

"It's not confidence. I know you use your combined magic to free me and then together we all defeat Clodia and complete your vows."

"I wish you'd let me tell Rinna that part. It might help ease her worry and doubt." He pressed his hand against his chest, where he could feel that worry and doubt – and fear – tainting the glory that was their bond.

"I can't. Her knowing would affect the outcome because she won't do what must be done."

"And that would be?"

"I cannot say."

"Full of information, aren't you?"

"I tell you what I can. If I could tell you more, believe me, I would."

"But the way she's feeling … you know it's a problem right?"

"All I can say is that it will resolve itself in the fullness of time. You have to trust me on this."

"I do. Although you make it difficult at times. She's my soulmate. I want to share everything with her and it burns that I can't. I'm pretty sure she can feel I'm keeping things from her."

"In time, that will be resolved as well. You just have to trust in the strength of your bond."

He did – although, even soul-bonds could be eroded by secrets and lies. He'd seen too much evidence of that in the relationships between Gods and Goddesses he'd once thought inseparable. But that wasn't going to happen to him and Rinna. He wouldn't let it.

He straightened, concentrating on breathing slow and deep – the air was thin this far up, not to mention cold, and given he no longer had his cupid power, it was taking him longer than usual to acclimatise and recover. After a moment, he had his breath back enough to restart the climb. "This better be worth it," he puffed. Rinna's lead suggested there was an extensive library here featuring unique texts on the old Gods and their mysteries, including the Goddess Ostara and the unique power released at Oestra. If he got up there and found nothing, he'd be pretty pissed.

"On the bright side, the view is breathtaking."

Cold wind whipped around him, snow crystals fluttering in his face, sticking to his eyelashes. He brushed them away and used his magic to dry his sweat-dampened clothes, thankful he'd thought to put on a ski-jacket and beanie before coming. He trudged on up the hill, the icy air like pricking knives in his lungs.

His thoughts returned to the issue of his portals and why they kept dumping him so far from his intended target. Kyria – his and Rinna's trainer at the Ceraunian Mountains training camp 2,000 years ago – had always said portal accuracy relied on both strength of power and strength of will – he had the will, but his warlock magic still couldn't hold a candle to his cupid one.

"Utter rubbish," the HBG growled.

"What do you mean?"

"Your warlock power isn't weaker. In fact, in many ways, it's stronger. Your trainers were idiots."

He almost chuckled. "You sound like Violetta."

"Sensible woman."

"She said they seriously undervalued the power I got from my mother's side of the family."

"And she would be right. But then, it does not surprise me they had such little foresight. This is where the Gods and Goddesses are truly up themselves, thinking that their powers are the bees-knees when the truth is something else entirely. If only you had been trained in full, we wouldn't have to go through this ridiculous charade now."

"Charade? What Rinna and I have been going through over the last five months is hardly a charade. It's exhaustingly real and difficult. And worrying, made worse by the fact you won't—"

"Not won't. Can't."

"Can't tell us exactly how we are supposed to do what you need us to do."

"I've told you, you must discover much of it yourself. The curse that binds me in this gem doesn't allow me to collude with others to help get me out. I've

found a small way around it because of who you and Rinna are, but there is much I cannot say. I wish I could, but I am quite literally unable to."

"Doesn't make it any less frustrating," he said as he continued to trudge up the steep path, the cold quickly stealing his breath again.

"Your frustration is a fraction of mine. Imagine being locked in a gem, unable to do anything to help free yourself even though you know exactly what must be done."

Tamuel stroked his chest where the gem lay under his skin. "I'm sorry. I saw what that did to my father and I wouldn't wish it on my worst enemy. But at least you know it can be broken. I didn't think mine could – until I met Rinna again."

"Neither situation is ideal. The Gods have much to repent for."

"I'm not angry with Eros – he cursed me to save me; and put in the loophole knowing one day I could be free. And it wasn't a God or Goddess who cursed my mother and father – that was all Clodia."

"Because she wanted a Goddess' power. You cannot convince me, Tamuel, that the Gods did not play their part in that. If they'd wanted to stop her, they could have, and yet they didn't. They were happy to see the misery that came from her grab for power, and someone somewhere is still revelling in the pain that is continuing because of it."

"You know, when you get out of there, you really are going to have to let go of your animosity against the Gods. You cannot take them on and win."

"We all have a path to walk. You must allow me to walk mine whatever that might be. But first, I need to help you walk yours."

"Bloody double standard," he panted as he rounded the switch-back in the trail, the steepness of the path making his legs feel like jelly.

"You need to work on your fitness."

"Not even … the fittest … mountain climber," he gasped, "would be able … to do this … without getting … winded. It's how quickly … I recover … that's the tell of … my fitness."

"And not passing out before you get there."

"That too," he said, chuckling – or, more correctly, wheezing – at her acerbic tone.

Finally, the path came to a flat surface of rock that jutted out before the cave, the entry of which was blocked by rockfall. He stepped closer, pulling his magic around him and into his hand, then waved it in the air.

Around the edge of the cave, runes and symbols, traced deep in the rock, began to glow. "This monk ... better be home," he panted, reaching out to touch a series of runes and symbols that Rinna's research had shown would allow him entry.

Deep in the mountain, a rumbling started. The earth around him shook. Slivers of stone and dirt came free and rained down from the rocks above. For a moment, he worried there might be an avalanche. He pulled his magic to him, ready to open a quick portal, not caring where it might spill him out as long as it got him away in case the mountain did start to come down. He was immortal, not invulnerable.

A door slid open in the rockfall.

A man stepped out of the opening, dark hood masking his features.

"Tamuel. My old friend. Welcome to my home." He pushed the hood back to reveal a face Tamuel hadn't seen for many centuries. A handsome face of chiselled lines and palest skin. Surrounded by the blackest of hair that matched black pupils that forever twinkled with mischief.

"Loki. What the fuck are you doing here? And what did you do with my hermit-monk?"

Loki actually blanched. "Ah, well. About that. I might have played a little trick on your beloved by putting a morsel of information in her way that would lead you here."

"You little bastard. Why would you do that?" Tamuel made a grab at him, but Loki jumped back, his laughter lighting the air around them.

"Now, now. No need for violence. There's a reason – a good reason – I did what I did. One meant to help, not hinder. Just come inside and let me explain." He pouted, his eyes still twinkling when Tamuel did nothing but glower at the God he'd once called friend many centuries ago, before relations between the pantheons got rocky. "Come on. Just hear me out. For old times' sake. You won't regret it."

"I've heard that before," Tamuel muttered. "And then I always end up in the worst trouble of my life."

Loki put one hand over his chest. "I swear on my eternal life, no harm will come to you. I only seek to help you and your beloved in your quest to stop the hated Clodia."

Tamuel stiffened. "What do you know about it?" Nobody was supposed to know anything.

"Whispers on the wind, my friend. They all speak to me." Loki waved expansively, his shoulder-length hair whipping back from his face in a fae wind Tamuel knew he used for effect.

"Loki. Stop the farce and just tell me what you know."

Loki dropped his hands and the wind died down. "You're a party-pooper, you know that? I didn't think losing your cupid power meant you'd lose your sense of humour."

"Loki, I swear to the Eternal Well ..."

"Sensitive much? But I get it. Nix-may on the losing the pupid-cowers-nay," he said, making a zipping motion across his mouth.

As the HBG chuckled in his head over the complete bastardisation of pidgin English, Tamuel muttered, "I don't have time for this," and did an about face.

But before he could take a step, Loki leapt forward and grabbed his arm, swinging him back around. "I'm sorry. I promise, I'll behave. Just come inside and share a drink and I will reveal all. Well, I'll reveal what I know and how I'm going to help you, which will be better than revealing the mysterious 'all'. And it starts with a valuable bit of information I have about a certain ring that might be the very thing to help you on your little task."

"A ring?" Had Loki finally gone insane? How could a ring help them?

"Hear him out."

"The ring is important?"

The HBG made a muffled sound – she was being forced to be quiet by the curse that bound her.

So it was important.

Crap.

"Come on, Tam." He fluttered his eyes. "You know you've never been able to say me nay."

Even though he knew it was probably a mistake – whatever Loki had to tell him would not come cheap – the HBG had indicated this was key. Besides, he did not want to go back to Rinna empty-handed. So, shaking his head, he said, "Fine. I'll come with you."

Smile widening, Loki gestured towards the entrance. It glimmered slightly around the edges with Loki's signature ruby red.

A portal. "Where are you taking me, because I know it's not into that cave."

"To my private home. It's far more comfortable than anywhere else in this godforsaken Realm."

Tamuel pointed a finger at him. "I won't be drinking any of your mead."

Loki blew a raspberry. "Spoilsport. But I understand. You want to stay all respectable for your one and only."

"Yes. I do."

"And you've got important things to do."

"Yes."

"So, follow, follow, my good ex-cupid, and discover what your old friend Loki can once again do for you." And so saying, he turned and skipped through the portal.

"Are you sure we can trust him?" he asked the gem.

"Trust? No. But follow him you must."

"Korinna will kill me if she finds out I'm dealing with Loki."

"It's not Korinna you should be worried about."

Shaking his head, Tamuel stepped through the portal.

3

*K*orinna came to stand in front of the section of wall Tam had shown her the day after the events of All Hallow's Eve – just before Persephone arrived and bound him to that stupid vow.

It looked no different from any of the other stones. Not unless you knew what you were looking for.

She put her trembling hand on it.

Light glowed under her palm, reacting to the magic inside her. She took in a jagged breath – it still worked! She thought Tam might have rescinded her access after Seph's visit, but for some reason, he hadn't. Probably because he trusted her to keep to her promise not to look for the grimoire.

Guilt slashed through her, its jagged barbs digging in around her heart. Ignoring the sensation – what choice did she have? – she pulled her hand back, revealing a glowing triangle. Blue lines of magic ran out from it, Tam's private sigil – one he'd magically engraved into the stone when he'd originally started working with Bas to break Clodia's curse.

Of course, she wasn't certain this was where he'd hidden the grimoire, but given it had to be a place where no other God or

Goddess could feel it, it made sense. It was the ultimate in safe-houses. Somehow – and she'd have to make him tell her how he'd done it after Oestra – he'd created a pocket universe in which he'd created a private space where he kept his most treasured items. He said he'd created it centuries ago to get a bit of peace and quiet from Eros and the other Gods, who were always on his back over one thing or another. Such an intricate piece of magic; one he'd keyed to open only for him. Nobody could scry into it. Nobody who did not have the spell-key could enter without his permission. To other beings of power, it did not exist.

But he'd given her the key. Such trust. It filled her heart to bursting with love for him even as the barbs of guilt dug deeper.

Lifting her chin and flexing her fingers, she touched parts of the sigil in a certain order, and as she did, said the words of activation Tam had taught her. Thankfully, the sigil was powered by Tam's magic and didn't need hers at all. The sigil lit up, glowing brightly purple – a sign it had been created with his cupid power – then blue before fading to lilac.

Her breath caught in her throat as she felt a reaching, a seeking, rush through her. A voice whispered inside her mind and then … Nothing.

Crap. Had she done it correctly? She was certain it had been instantaneous when Tam showed her—

The surface of the stone rippled like a wave in water, then the sigil cracked down the middle, peeling back bit by bit, exposing a purple-blue portal. Its glow was bright in this dim section of the library, lighting up the shelves behind her. Hells, she really hoped nobody came down now.

"Hurry, hurry," she said to the portal as it grew until it was tall and wide enough to walk through.

Taking a deep breath – she really hated portal travel – she stepped into the purple-blue glow. A sensation like walking through wet, warm bubbles chased over her skin, but then everything contracted, expanded, spun around and she was tossed forward. She clamped her mouth shut on a scream as it felt like everything in her was turned inside out and back again before spewing her out the other end.

She rolled across the floor, sweat-covered and trembling, and came up against something soft. Swallowing back the bile in her throat, she opened her eyes to glare at the glowing portal. She had no idea how Tam used portals as regularly as he did. But maybe they didn't do to him what they did to her – one more piece of proof that her magic didn't work correctly.

Gods, she hoped the spell she needed was in the grimoire. She didn't want to have gone through all this for nothing.

Unsteadily, she pushed herself upright, stumbled dizzily and plonked down into the sofa behind her – the soft thing she'd bumped up against.

When the room stopped spinning, she looked around.

She hadn't come through when Tam had shown her the portal – Seph's arrival had made Tam close it up quickly – so she'd had no idea what was here. She was surprised to see it was set up like a large open-plan apartment, with a comfortable lounge area complete with the sofa she sat on, side-tables, antique lamps that lit the space, a coffee table and a desk. The walls on three sides were covered with well-laden bookshelves and on the fourth was a galley-style kitchen. On either side of that stood two doors – one that led to a bedroom and the other a solid-looking door that had another sigil on it. Tam had mentioned he had a vault here. That must be it.

The grimoire better not be in there, because he hadn't told her how to open it.

Only one way to find out. Given the grimoire was a copy of the original, made by Demeter's favourite priestess, it should be spelled to come to the call of anyone close by with a like tie to the Goddess and her daughter. She held out her hand and said, "Come to me, Eleusinian Mysteries Grimoire. Obey Persephone's Soteira. Come to me."

Nothing happened.

She repeated the command.

Nothing again. She gritted her teeth and said it more firmly.

Books erupted out of the shelves to her left and a large, green leather-bound book flew across the space to land in her hands with a small thud. Breath exploded from her as she looked down at the grimoire that had eluded her for so many years.

There was a three-pointed emblem etched onto the front cover, one that had elements representing Demeter – a winged serpent, a cornucopia and a wheat-ear – her daughter, Persephone – a pomegranate, a torch and a deer – and their servant in the Mysteries, the demi-God Triptolemus – a scythe, a sheath of wheat and a winged chariot. The triangular emblem was held within a circle, signifying the miracle of the cycle of life – birth, death and rebirth. All things they had in common with Ostara, the Goddess of Birth and Rebirth.

Excitement bubbled in her chest.

Followed by a cold splash of reality.

She had no time to look for spells that might help them. She had to trust that Tam could find and read them all, and that if he couldn't, that Persephone would guide him to them.

She was here for one thing and one thing only. She couldn't break his trust more than that. Placing the grimoire carefully on the desk, she bit her lip, then carefully opened it to the first page.

It was beautiful, its pages a pristine white so bright they were almost pearlescent. Archaic scroll-work and detailed drawings sprawled across its pages in splashes of blue and green, red and purple, gold and brown. With reverence, she worked through it, trying hard to only look at the first line of each new section – the first line would be enough to tell her if the spell was on that page, given all grimoires laid out spells like with like for safety. Even so, she couldn't help marvel at the secrets held inside. The magic hinted at in each first few lines was incredible, with spells ranging from worship to crop maintenance to magic enhancement, healing and beyond. She found the spell Tam had used to get into the Underworld in corporeal form in the first few pages, and it was only a drop in the ocean of a world of magic she had not realised could be created. Triptolemus, the creator of the Mysteries and this grimoire, had been a genius.

Then suddenly she was at the last page. She frowned. The grimoire wasn't as long as she'd thought it would be. And the spell she was looking for wasn't there.

Maybe it was written as part of a larger spell, so might be in the middle of one of the sections. Damn, that meant she'd have to read more deeply. She wouldn't be able to help her eidetic memory taking it all in. But she would try to minimise its ability to remember every-thing she saw as much as she could. Turning back to the beginning, she started again, placing her hand under the section she read, only removing it as far as necessary until she'd determined the spell she was after couldn't be on that page.

And all the time, she was aware time was running out. She hadn't planned to be here so long. Tam would most likely be gone for at least half a day, possibly longer if the hermit's library wasn't properly archived, but she couldn't rely on more than four or five hours. And she needed to be out of here soon if she was to do the spell before he arrived home and have a chance of getting rid of all the evidence – both physical and magical.

She came to the last page again without finding anything.

"Damn it, where are you?"

It had to be here. She'd found too many references to a powerful control spell in this grimoire for it not to be true.

She turned back to the beginning and read again more deeply.

And became aware that there were parts of the grimoire missing. Many of the spells, while powerful, were only half-finished. She could feel it in the hum of her power as her eyes ran over the words and sigils. In the ache of emptiness in her chest that had nothing to do with how quiet her bond with Tam had gone when she'd come in here.

Something was missing, and yet, she had no idea how to access it.

Pushing back from her desk, she stood. Tam would be back soon and she was no closer to figuring it out.

Perhaps she needed to use magic to call the missing pieces to her? There were spells she'd learned from Persephone when she was younger, ones to reveal hidden things. They were spells unique to Persephone and her Soteira; an element of her power that Demeter had gifted her at her birth and that could be used by none but her and her Soteira. It would make sense that Triptolemus, their most trusted servant, would use something so secret and hidden to unveil the deeper secrets of this grimoire, and that the priestess who had then made this copy so faithfully from the original, would include as well.

Nervously, she put her hand on the cover and said the words taught to her a few thousand years ago. Green light glowed from the sigil under her hand. It was working!

Breath in her throat, she opened the grimoire again, delighted to see that writing had appeared like a border around each page. She picked it up, turning it to read the words, a jolt going through her as she did. By the Goddess. This wasn't a replica – it was the original written by Triptolemus himself. The version Zeus and Hades had destroyed must have been the copy while the original was spirited away by Demeter's favourite priestess. Did Demeter or Persephone know? She suspected not, or they would never have allowed Tam to keep it, no matter how much they might need what lay inside.

This was, astonishing. To be holding something Triptolemus himself had held!

Her fingers brushed over the border writing reverently as she turned the grimoire.

The writing glowed, brightly green under her fingertips, and her power leaped forward in response, sparking across the page, lighting the glowing green words with a golden edge.

"Oh!" She dropped the grimoire on the desk ... and noted it seemed to have grown in thickness. Had the spell of revealing caused that to happen? Or her spark of magic? Triptolemus had probably spelled it to respond to his followers; and while a Soteira wasn't strictly *his* follower, they were close enough.

What did it matter how it had happened? If it stayed like this, Tam would know someone had looked at it.

She bit her lip. It wasn't that much bigger. He might not notice. Perhaps she just needed to be more careful about where she touched it so it didn't grow any larger.

Gingerly, careful not to touch the words in the border of the first page, she flipped it over to see what had been revealed.

It took ten page flips before she came to a section she'd not seen before. However, the green-tinged writing on this page was too faded to make out, and when she kept flipping, every new spell that had appeared was the same.

Hells!

Should she try the spell of revealing again? She stared at the grimoire for long moments, her breath coming in pants. She didn't really want to let her magic out again – a small spell was one thing, but the uncontrolled spark that had leaped out unbidden was something else entirely. And what if the grimoire grew even bigger and she couldn't return it to its normal size after she found her spell?

But did she have a choice?

Hand trembling, she opened to her magic and put her hand square in the middle of the faded page.

For a moment nothing happened. Then the page glowed green and something that looked like a vine slithered from the edge of the page and wrapped around her wrist. As it did, there was a sharp, stabbing pain as barbs appeared and sliced into her skin. She hissed, tried to pull her hand back, but the magical vine held her tight.

Blood dripped across her skin and onto the page. "Oh. No, no, no!" She tried to pull her hand away but the vine held her in a death-grip. She pushed her magic at it, but that only made it grow thicker, stronger, the barbs slicing into her skin deeper, making the blood come faster, pooling and expanding to flow down the sides of the grimoire, sinking into all the pages.

No! It would damage the entire book. How could she explain this to Tam and Persephone? They couldn't fail to notice the grimoire was covered in blood and it wouldn't take them long to figure out it was hers – her blood was marked by her magical scent. Tam would know she'd broken her promise to him and Persephone would be furious – and maybe even punish Tam somehow for not making certain she couldn't get to the grimoire.

She had to do something. But what?

Hells and all their torments. She was so foolish. Foolish to think a grimoire of this import didn't have magical defences. Foolish to think—

A keening sound pierced the air. A fae wind whipped around her, carrying the scent of soil, of grass heating on a summer day, of the delicate perfume of a scented rose. The vine vanished, and she snatched her hand back, rubbing the healing sores where it had pricked her – sores that looked suspiciously like the ones that dark sorcerers sported after using blood magic. How would she explain these?

She didn't get to think further on it because the pages of the grimoire began to flip over, doubling again and again, each page glowing with a mix of green and gold as her blood sank into the papyrus.

Finally, it got to the last page then slammed closed, the impact vibrating the desk and shaking the walls.

Gasping, she reached for it slowly. She didn't want to touch it but couldn't make herself stop. She lifted it, turned it over. Drawings had appeared on the front – a sketch of a bird in the left top corner, its bright blue feathers standing out on the faded green leather, as did the vibrant red-green of the vines that had appeared in the bottom left corner, the golden yellow of the sheath of wheat in the bottom right corner and the umber and purple tones in the mountains carved into the top right corner.

"What is this?" she whispered.

As if in answer, the grimoire hummed, then flipped open so fast she almost dropped it. She held on tight as the movement of the pages vibrated up her arm, then stopped.

And she looked down at the spell she'd been searching for.

The grimoire had hidden it. And it had been released with her blood.

Blood magic!

Blood magic unlocked hidden things in the Eleusinian Mysteries Grimoire?

It had always been rumoured that Eleusinian priests and priestesses used sacrifice as part of their worship, but that had only been a rumour or something that had occurred in a bastardisation of the Mysteries in later iterations, centuries after Triptolemus went missing. Persephone and Demeter would never condone the use of blood magic in any service or worship to do with them – and Triptolemus would never have used it in his grimoire. Good things never came from blood magic. They had lectured her on that very topic many times when she was young.

But why had her blood opened secret, hidden sections of the grimoire? It made no sense. Not to mention she couldn't possibly use anything that had been revealed with blood magic – could she? Things opened with blood magic couldn't bode anything good.

She stared down at the spell, the words glowing green and gold before her.

Ah Hells. She had to use the spell. She could feel even looking at it that it would work.

Fingers curling around the edges of the book, she silently read the spell. A simple-seeming incantation over some herbs then a period of meditation. Not difficult. And certainly not dangerous. There wasn't anything about it that seemed evil. *I mean, we have every single one of these ingredients in the cupboards in the library kitchen.*

She closed the grimoire before anything else could happen and carried it to its hiding place. As she did, it returned to its normal size with no sign of the blood – her blood – that had temporarily marked and engorged it. Letting out a shuddering breath she hadn't even realised she'd been holding, she put it in its hidden spot at the back of the bookcase, then quickly used an old tidying spell to return everything back to how it was before she'd entered. Her magic slipped and bucked, threatening to slide out of her control – showing her just how much she needed this spell – but she held on until the spell was done. Then, without looking back, ran out the portal.

She skidded out the other side, somehow managing to keep to her feet despite her disorientation as the portal closed behind her, the stone folding back into place with a loud click.

Leaning over, hands on her knees, she took in some deep, calming breaths. She'd done it! She'd actually done it.

As she straightened, she couldn't help but notice the wounds still evident on her arm and hand. They had healed up almost completely, showing only a fine red mark, slightly raised, where the vine had dug into her skin to draw her blood. If she was lucky, they would be completely healed before anyone got back and they would never have to know how close to darkness she'd gone.

She glanced up at the clock on the wall. Two hours had passed since she'd entered the portal. She should have time to do the spell and get rid of the evidence before Tam got back. If she was quick.

Running to the library kitchen, the spell and its ingredients a picture in her mind, she began to get out everything she needed, praying with everything in her that the Fates would, at least this time, be on her side in healing her wounds and allowing her to do the spell. She'd touched darkness, but if she could gain some semblance of control, it would be worth it.

4

---

*K*orinna had just sat back at her desk, the spell completed and everything put back to rights – except the faint scent of lavender and sage that still clung to the air – when a red portal popped open at the bottom of the stairs.

She jumped to her feet, hands raised, prepared to fight whoever – or whatever – came out of it. When Tam sauntered through a second later, she stared in confusion, even as her heart seemed to stop at the sight of him then thumped hard and fast as he drew near.

He did that to her every time, befuddling her senses. She should hate it, but she didn't – she loved it. And him.

He strode towards her, lips widening in a knowing smile. "Hey, beautiful. Jumping up to greet your man? Can't say I'm surprised. I am pretty jumpable."

She pointed behind him where the portal still glimmered. "What … Where … That portal is red!"

He glanced over his shoulder just as the portal snapped closed, the force causing a breeze that fluttered Tam's dark auburn hair. "Is it?" he asked, voice dripping with innocence.

"Yes. It's red. Why is it red?" His portals were always bluey-purple or bluey-green – to do with the origin of the magic he wielded – Bas' portals were bluey-purple, and if Jules were to get her power back, hers would be bluey-green. Never red. Red signified a different kind of magic. "Is something wrong? Are you okay?" Her gaze roved over him, but apart from looking a bit wind-blown and damp, he seemed fine. "Who opened that portal? And why didn't you open your own?"

"Oh, yeah, that. It was nothing. I'm fine." He turned back to her, his peridot eyes sparking with the warmth and love that filled them every time he looked at her, his full lips open and wide in the smile she so loved. A smile he often used to distract her.

Taking a step away, fighting the pull she always felt for him, and only him, she held up her hands. "No you don't. You don't get to charm your way out of answering my question properly. Whose portal was that and why did they open it for you?"

"Umm, well, the hermit-monk," he said, not quite meeting her eyes. "When I explained what we were doing, he said he wanted to save me using my own energy for our exertions, so he opened one for me."

"Bump-bowmm," she said, imitating a game-show buzzer. "Try again. That hermit-monk has no magic. He couldn't open a portal."

"How can you know that?"

She put her hands on her hips. "I did the research on him, remember? It was my work that sent you there."

"Oh, yeah, right."

Why was he lying to her?

You're lying to him too.

She pushed the guilt-barbed thought aside as he moved over to her desk and played with a stack of her notes. "So, did you find anything while I was out." He sniffed the air. "Did you do a spell?"

Hells. He shouldn't be able to still smell it. She stomped over to him and snatched her notes from under his hand. "Answer my question first and then I'll answer yours." Although, she wouldn't. Not with the full truth at least. Luckily she'd done a small spell after she'd finished to test her control.

His eyes twinkled. "Ah, so a 'show me yours and I'll show you mine' proposition."

Before she could answer, he pulled her into his arms and kissed her.

Her breasts smooshed against his firm chest and she let out a moan at the delicious contact.

It was obviously a method of avoidance, but two could play at this game. He might want to avoid answering her but she also wanted to avoid answering him. So, she gave into her never-sated need for him, her tongue meeting his, stroking, tasting, and ran her hands down his back to cup his firm arse.

Ah ye Gods, she loved the taste of him! The feel of him. The warmth of him. The strength of him. She pulled him closer, deepening the kiss. He made a little sound in his throat – surprise, pleasure – and met her demands with more of his own.

It was so easy to forget everything in his arms; all her worries, all her doubts. He did that for her, every time he touched her, kissed her, made love to her. If it was up to her, they would never leave their bedchamber. It was her greatest wish to be able to stay there, tucked up with him, losing herself to him, with him, drowning in the pleasure only he had ever brought her, and never surfacing to face anything ever again. When she was with him like this, there were no problems that could pierce the shield of their love.

And miracle of miracles, the joy flaring down the bond told her that she did the same for him. He was her shield as she was his. Equals. Mirrors. As the prophecy-curse Eros had uttered two centuries ago had foretold.

Except, she'd broken his trust and her promise. And she'd used blood magic.

The guilt-barbs dug deeper.

He jerked back a little, gaze slamming into hers. "Are you okay? I can feel you worrying."

Hells! "Just worried someone might see us," she said, pushing the guilt far, far down.

"Bas and Jules won't be back for at least an hour," he said, lips running down her throat, tickling against her skin. "And I can be quick." He lifted her and pushed her against a wall.

"I prefer it when you're not," she said, wrapping her legs around his waist.

Eyes glinting, he slipped open one button on her shirt, then the next, fingers brushing seductively against her skin, making her gasp. "Making demands now, are we?"

She couldn't stop a smile from curling on her lips. "Always."

"Then I will make sure the next time I worship you for however long you wish."

"Promises, promises."

He tore open her shirt, the buttons popping off in all directions. "No, it is a vow." Then he covered her mouth with his again as he pushed her shirt from her shoulders.

"Bugger that," she said and waved her hand. Their clothes disappeared and she gasped as the fullness of him pushed against her damp core.

He blinked in surprise. "You haven't done that since the tunnels."

"I realised you were right. I was being stupidly afraid to use my magic when I don't need to be." It wasn't really a lie – not now she had the spell helping her to control it.

"By the Gods, it's sexy when you take control like that."

"Then you're going to love this." She grabbed his hand and put it over her breast as she moved against him, his thick length sliding against her clitoris. "Now lick my nipple."

"With pleasure." He did something with his tongue that made her gasp. "Like that?"

"Oh yes. Again. Please. Hurry."

"Now you want me to be fast?"

She smiled down at him – nobody had ever made her smile like he could. "I want you in any way I can get you."

"Really?" He shifted, the head of his cock to rubbing over her entrance. "How about slow?" He moved, the pleasure increasing as every slick, thick inch of him pushed up and into her, filling her with torturous slowness.

She made a strangled sound deep in her throat and grabbed his arse, trying to pull him, shift him, make him move faster.

But this time, he resisted her taking the control. "Now-now, don't be impatient," he muttered against her breast before he licked across the tip.

He was killing her. Killing her. With pleasure. Her eyes were actually rolling back into her head. Any further and they'd never come back down again.

He did that thing with his tongue again.

Lights exploded behind her eyes, shimmering down her body to her core. She was so close to orgasm – and he hadn't even entered her fully yet.

"Please. Please," she begged, hands scrabbling at his back. "I need … I need …"

"Far be it from me not to give you what you need," he said roughly against the pulse hammering in her neck. His lips clamped over that spot as he slid in to the hilt, giving her exactly what she'd pleaded for.

The shock-pleasure of it sent her over the edge. She clenched around him, wave after wave of bliss exploding through her. He stilled, hands on her face, demanding that she look at him as she found her pleasure. His eyes were black starlight as he used his warlock power to hold her up.

"Gods! You're so beautiful."

"Tamuel," she gasped. She wanted to tell him how much she loved him, how much he meant to her, what he did to her, but he kissed her again and began to move. And all she could do was ride him, helping him gain his pleasure as he ensured she reached hers again.

Up and up and more and more until the world shattered around them, a kaleidoscope of colours shooting behind her closed lids until she fell into peace.

She was at peace.

But only for so long as the spell lasts and you can control your magic. And only so long as Tam doesn't find out you broke your promise. And that you used blood magic to get what you wanted.

And with those thoughts, her peace was destroyed.

She stiffened.

Ah Hells, she wanted to cry. Not wanting Tam to see, she let her legs slide down, dislodging him from inside her, then she kissed him softly. "Thank you," she whispered against his lips. "I needed that."

"Glad I could be of assistance." He smoothed back her hair, forcing her to look up at him. "What's wrong?"

"Nothing." She kissed him swiftly again, noting his eyes were back to normal, then with a swipe of her hand – so easy now she had control of her magic – she had them clothed again.

He looked down at himself. "Thanks but … My shirt seems to be without its buttons."

"Oops." Her lips twitched as she ran her hand down his chest. "I think my magic likes your bare chest too."

He captured her hand, bent to kiss it but paused. "What's this?" He rubbed his thumb over her wrist and hand.

She glanced down and saw faint pink marks marring her skin where the vine had pierced. They were so faint, she almost couldn't see them in this light – but of course he had. He noticed everything about her. "Nothing." She drew her hand from his, wishing she was wearing long sleeves so she could hide it.

"It doesn't look like nothing. It looks like welts or old wounds that are almost healed."

Zeus' balls! Why was he looking at her like that? Was he making the connection like she had – between the faint scars and blood magic? No, his expression was curious and slightly concerned. But it was turning into more concern as she stood there gaping at him. Hells. She had to say something. "Um, it was nothing really."

"You're full of a lot of nothing today. Try again."

"That's because it truly is nothing. I-I didn't want you to worry. I was trying to learn something we might be able to use against Clodia to bind her and the spell went a little awry, that's all. Rather than the binding lashing out as I hoped, it lashed back at me and wrapped around my arm, cutting me here and there. I did a little healing on it, like Bas showed me, although not as good as him, obviously, given it's still there. Healing's not my thing, as you know." Hells, was she babbling? She hated lying to him like this, but how could she tell him the truth? What would he think of her? It could change everything.

Relief filled his expression. "Ah, that explains it."

"Explains what?" she asked, jaw so tight it was a wonder she got the words out.

"The strange sensation I felt through our bond while I was looking for the hermit-monk's cave."

He had felt that? She'd have to be more careful. Not that she was going to do blood magic again.

"How badly were you hurt?"

"Not badly at all – as you can see. Despite my inept attempt at healing, it's almost all fine now." She waved her arm around before shoving her hand in her pocket. "It was just a little mistake and … hold on." She frowned. "What do you mean 'looking for his cave'? Didn't your portal take you right there?"

He grimaced a smile at her. "Ah, yeah, that. I kind of haven't told you about the fact I don't seem to have a handle on portal travel."

"Since when?"

"Since I lost my cupid magic."

"Why didn't you say anything?"

"I didn't want you to worry." He captured her hand and kissed her knuckles. "My portals land me in the vicinity, so it's not too bad. They just don't take me right where I want to be."

"That's why you've been taking longer than I thought you would on each trip. And why I've rarely seen you return by portal."

"Yep."

She couldn't believe she'd not put it together before now. "I wish you'd told me."

"You already worry enough. Besides, I figure it's just about practice for both of us, right?"

"Um, yeah." By the Gods, she hated keeping this from him, but—

A wailing moan rang through the air, as all the library ghosts rushed out of the stacks towards them.

"What the Hells?" Tam said as the ghosts whirled around them, gibbering and gesturing wildly towards the back of the library.

"What is it?" she asked, peering down the length of the stacks. She couldn't see anything. Not surprising given the caverns that made up the library hidden under Stevens House – the library of the Great Coven of Melbourne; the greatest library of magical books and artifacts in the Southern Hemisphere – were huge and ... cavernous. She still hadn't seen every part of the library and she'd been here researching and training for months.

"I've never seen them behave like this before. We should go and check it out."

She nodded and took his outstretched hand, relieved at the interruption.

As they entered the closest row, an odd hiss and growl started up, echoing through the stacks from the depths of the library. It quickly turned into a deep moan that made the chandeliers rattle. The lights dimmed.

She glanced up. The chandeliers were being shrouded in a growing cloud of darkness.

"Hells and damnation. Someone's left the Black Magic and Dangerous Books section open and something is trying to get out," Tam said, starting into a run.

"How do you know?" she asked, following him.

"Because I know what that is. I was the one who brought that book here for safe-keeping."

"Do you know how to fight it?"

He nodded. "We're going to have to channel our magic to capture it and fight it back into the book it was caged in."

"But that could be more dangerous than the entity trying to escape. I mean, there's a reason we've been looking for a way to channel our magic together at Oestra without blowing us, and everything around us, up."

"We have to find a way. The HBG says we can do it, so let's just try."

The chandeliers rattled again as the moan increased, echoing all around them. The darkness thickened, swallowing up more light, quickly followed by a foul wind that swept through the library. She coughed at the stench. Fuck and damn it to Hells and back. Baptism by fire it was.

5

amuel ran through the stacks towards the T-intersection that led to the wings of the library. He gagged as the foul-smelling wind whipped around him and glanced over his shoulder at Rinna as she ran at his side.

Her face was pale yet determined as she kept pace with him. Despite everything he knew still worried her about her power, she ran with him right towards danger.

She had a right to be worried though – what they were about to do was crazy. To try to meld their powers and use it to overcome an entity as evil as the one in the book … He wished they'd found a solution before now, because right about now they could really use one. He scrambled for something they'd found so far that could work to make their powers compatible enough to be channelled through one of them and used to push the entity back, but there was nothing.

Whichever of them channelled the powers was in for a world of hurt, if not worse.

He would be the one to do it. "Rinna, I—" He gagged on the smell the wind pushed into his face.

Her gaze slipped to his and she made a face. "Smells worse than a cyclops' armpit."

He laughed, then choked on the horrible stench. She waved her hand. Two gas masks appeared floating in the air a few metres ahead of them. "Good thinking," he said. They each grabbed one as they ran past and put it on – although now he couldn't say what he'd been going to say. He'd just have to make her listen when they got there.

He took in a deep breath; his lungs filled at once with clean, fresh oxygen, but even so, the cloying scent of BO and rotten eggs clung to the inside of his nose and in his mouth.

Around them, the mahogany shelves filled with books, manuscripts, scrolls, grimoires and artifacts, some tens of thousands of years old, shook and swayed.

Far above, the chandeliers began to creak, swaying in the foul wind, their light growing dimmer. The stacks two rows ahead disappeared into stygian darkness. He pulled out his mobile phone and turned the torch function on – thank all the Gods for this particular mod-con – and kept running.

Their shoes slapped over the black stone floors, muffled only by the Persian rugs scattered haphazardly between one section and the next. The darkness, not content with swallowing the light from the chandeliers, began to descend just as they came to the T-intersection.

This was his moment. Slipping his mask from his face, he said hurriedly, "Let me be the one who takes the brunt of the channelled magic, okay?"

She slipped her mask off, gagging slightly before saying, "No."

"Look, Rinna—"

She held up her hand. "No, listen." She pointed at his chest where the HBG glowed brightly – strange given it rarely showed itself. "When I saw that start to glow as it got darker, it gave me an idea. The gem channels the spirit's magic through it."

"I know."

"What if we can do that too?"

"With the gem? You know we can't use it."

"No. With something else that's just as powerful."

"There isn't anything else as powerful as the HBG. You know that. We've tried gems before. They can't hold our combined power."

"I don't mean gems." There was a loud shriek that echoed around them. She glanced up. The darkness was almost upon them. She looked at him, pleading. "I've played with the thought before but haven't said anything because … it's kind of crazy."

"What are you thinking?"

"Titania's wand."

He'd shown it to her months ago. She'd mentioned she'd done research on it when she was looking into using magical artifacts as a way to open up the Void so as to get the lost souls of Pompeii out. Her research had come to naught – none of the artifacts she'd researched were strong enough to do what she wanted – but he knew she'd get a kick out of seeing it.

Of course, at the time, he hadn't thought about its conductive qualities because the magic that was at its heart was meant to be used by and for the Faery Queen. She'd created it to pull on the power of her people and the natural world around them, to fight an evil threatening to swallow their land. It wasn't designed to channel magic that was not Faery in origin. She was right – it was crazy. "It's not designed to work for us."

"I know. But our magics share a similar origin to Faery magic in that they favour Mother Nature and magics that centre on hearth and home."

"That might be true, but its magic isn't even from a pantheon."

"We have to try." She pointed at the darkness that was creeping lower. "Using it can't be as bad as if we don't use anything. We need something to channel through or the backlash of our powers could destroy us, the library and the surrounds. As you've said, gems – the things you would usually use to channel magic through – haven't worked. Maybe what we need is an item of power that can hold its own."

She was right. But there was still a danger in using another magical artifact with its own magical properties, even if it wasn't from a different magical source.

"Loki just told you about a thing that would work and is of the same source."

"No. That isn't a possibility and you know it."

"It will work, though," HBG whispered. *"Trust that she will be able to carry the burden of it."*

"No. There has to be another way." And maybe the wand was it. "Okay," he shouted at Rinna over the increasing wails of the entity as it spread over more and more of the library ceiling. "You get the wand. I'll try to hold this at bay. Hurry."

He shoved his mask back on his face as she ran off towards the Faery section then turned and threw up a shield, trying to stop the entity from encroaching any further into the library.

The entity recoiled as his shield pushed out, and for a moment, he was able to breathe a sigh of relief. Maybe it wasn't going to be as difficult as he'd heard it would be to push this thing back into the book that had been its prison for centuries.

He just hoped Rinna was right. If the wand didn't work to mesh their magic in a controlled manner, it could be disastrous. But maybe not as disastrous as going it alone without any channelling medium.

"You are soulmates. It's meant to mesh together."

"That isn't how magic works. Not when it comes from completely different sources." It was an inviolable law of magic – or at least, that's how he had been taught.

"You were taught wrong. Korinna's instincts are right on this."

"I hope so." He really didn't want to explain why the library and their house was a crumbling ruin when Bas and Jules got back.

The entity chose that moment to lash out at his shield. Sparks flew from the contact and he grunted. It was strong. But so was he. He pushed back. It screamed but didn't retreat, instead lashing out again.

His shield flickered for a moment but he pushed more power into it; it held.

Zeus! He really needed to practice his defensive and offensive spells; he was rusty – no wonder, given fighting wasn't really something he'd done a lot of as a cupid. But he'd studied it with everyone else, so he knew some, and there was one in the Eleusinian Mysteries Grimoire that he'd wanted to try. Now seemed like a good time.

Holding his shield with one hand, he made the signs of an air sigil, infused it with magic, then blasted it out through his shield at the entity.

White light surrounded it. It screamed and writhed and drew back.

Light began to glimmer in the chandelier above him.

He pushed harder, filling the spell with more power. The entity drew back, spitting and hissing.

He'd done it. They wouldn't need to use the wand or try to mesh their powers together.

The entity let out a mighty roar and surged forward, hitting the spell, breaking it into a thousand pieces.

"Fuck!" Tamuel staggered under the force and almost lost control of his shield but held on just in time. Zeus! Korinna better hurry up, because he didn't know how much longer he was going to be able to hold it back – especially now he'd made it angry.

~

LIGHT FLASHED behind her as she searched the shelves. Where the Hells was the wand? It had been here when Tam had shown it to her months ago. But the place where it was housed was empty. Damn! She'd forgotten it was supposed to have a mind of its own and often went visiting other Faery artifacts.

A roar, followed by an explosion, shook the shelves around her. A shower of rock and soil fell from the ceiling. Hells. She had to get back to Tam. He couldn't hold that thing by himself.

But without something to help channel their magics, even with her control spell, they would have to work separately – would that be enough? Another roar. Another explosive shockwave.

Damn. She turned, about to run back. The wand rolled out from under one stack and across the floor in front of her.

"Yes!" She dived for it, almost going nose-first into the floor in her enthusiasm, her knees and palms smarting as she skidded across the carpet. The wand buzzed and jumped in her hand, rubbing against the carpet burn on her palm, its magic sensing hers but bucking against it.

She held on tight, but rather than forcing it into submission, said,

"Please. I need your help." She filled her mind with an image of the entity swallowing the light and the book they had to get it back into. "You helped Titania with something similar. Now we need you to help us work together."

The wand buzzed and hummed, moving as if to jump out of her hand.

A spark of green magic, like a vine, came out of her wrist and wrapped around the end of the wand, smearing a little of her blood on it. The wand glowed, the humming getting louder, then it fell still and silent.

She stared at it. Panic rose inside her. Blood magic again? Had she lost control? Was the spell not working?

No. It was there, humming through her veins as strongly as before. Then what had just happened? Maybe it had something to do with the nature of the control spell – it was the same colour as the magic-vine that had drawn her blood and held her to the Eleusinian Mysteries Grimoire. Yes, that must be it. But why had it drawn her blood? And why had that quieted the wand, making it ready to do her bidding?

She knew she should put the wand down, not use it. But its power thrummed through her, stronger after her blood-tinged magic had touched it; and it felt good. Or, maybe not good, but something that could fight the evil entity at least when bound with Tam's power.

More light flashed from where Tam battled the entity.

She had no choice. She had to try the wand.

Turning, she raced back the way she'd come. "I'm coming, Tam. Hold on," she yelled – pointless really given her voice was muffled by the mask.

Then she was beside him – she must have run faster than she'd ever run before.

Holding out the wand, she yelled, "Here! I have to be the channel though. It's already bonded to me."

He blinked, as if surprised, but then joined her in holding the wand. "Holy crap!" he said, as power sparked between them before quickly settling.

Immediately, his shield strengthened, sparking with a green and gold hue alongside his bluey-green. "Push," he said through gritted teeth.

She lifted their joint hands and pushed their magic through the wand. The shield pressed forward, forcing the entity back, but even so, she could tell it wouldn't be enough. "It's not going to work," she yelled. "We need to surround the entity, whittle it down." But she didn't know any offensive spells – it had never really been part of her training all those years ago or something she'd spent time researching. She stupidly hadn't even thought of that as something she needed, her focus entirely on finding a way to control her power and mesh it with Tam's. But of course, they would need defensive and offensive spells to fight Clodia. It was something she needed to rectify.

Thankfully, Tam had more training to pull from. "I tried something earlier but didn't have enough power to keep it up. We should have more than enough now."

"Do it."

"No, you'll have to do it given you've got the control. I'll write the sigil, but you'll have to power it."

"Okay."

He drew the sigil in the air. As he did so, something clicked in her mind – she'd seen this. She knew what it was. A spell from the Eleusinian Mysteries Grimoire.

A feeling of rightness filled her, like she'd found home after being lost for so many years. Her power leaped against the barriers of the control spell, wanting out, but she gritted her teeth and tamped down. Immediately, it settled, ready to do her bidding in the way she wanted it to.

The control spell was good.

As Tam finished writing the sigil in the air, she touched the tip of the wand to it and pushed their combined powers into it.

It lit up the entity, showing its edges, the dull fog-grey of its eyes, the snapping teeth that had been hidden in shadow before. It hissed and roared but could do nothing to fight the light that was growing, pushing it back.

They were doing it! She threw a grin at Tam. He grinned back.

They had this. This was how they'd fight Clodia and win the day. Finally, with her magic under control, she knew they could do the task the HBG had set them. Hope and certainty flared inside them.

And with them, her magic.

A slicing sensation made her grimace and she glanced down at the hand holding the wand. A blood-tinged green frond had emerged from her wrist to wrap around the wand – she glanced at Tam to see if he'd noticed, but thankfully, his attention was fully on the entity.

Before she could even attempt to call it back – *Why would you want to?* a voice whispered in her mind – the blood, along with the magic in the frond, sank into the wood of the wand. Power surged and the light exploded.

The magical shock-wave hit the dark entity. Its moaning turned to screams. The wind roared and the darkness bucked against the wave. But the wave was inexorable and pushed it back, back, scooping up the tendrils that tried to escape its force.

She tried to pull back the surge of power – it had to be evil given it was created by her magic mixed with her blood – but Tam shouted, "No. Don't. It's working. And the wand is holding it together."

Korinna's palm burned where the wand touched it, and from the grimace on Tam's face, it was burning him too, but she did as he said, letting the enormity of both of their powers flow through her and into the wand. He was right. It *was* working, pushing the entity back, back. Maybe you could only fight true evil like this with something just as dark. But she didn't have to like it and she vowed to make certain it didn't happen again.

The entity was now the size of a large bear rearing in the doorway that led to the Black Magic and Dangerous Books section from which it was trying to escape.

She pushed more power through the wand. The entity folded in on itself, now the size of a large dog. Still, it fought them, holding on with dark tentacles to the edges of the door. Tam opened himself up further, offering more of his power; she used it.

The entity lost its hold on the doorway and tumbled back into the room. As it moved, she spied the book it was trying to escape from lying open on the floor, a thread of darkened fog wavering up out of it the only thing still holding the entity to the book.

It was frayed and looked like it might snap at any moment.

"Hurry," Tam yelled, obviously seeing the same thing.

She pushed more power through the wand. It began to smoulder, the tip bending under the pressure. But she didn't let go – couldn't let go. With a yell, she dug down deep inside, pulling on more of her magic and channelling it into Titania's wand, then gave the entity a final blast. The light surrounded it, folding it down into the size of a ball, then shoved it into the pages of the open book. The book shuddered, spun, then snapped closed.

A roar, followed by silence so thick it was almost smothering.

Tam let go of her hand and grabbed her up. "We did it," he said, giving her a smacking kiss and spinning her around.

She laughed with him, but when he pulled back, her laughter died.

The wand was a blackened twig in her hand. A whimpering twig.

"Hells. Did we do that?" Tam said, grimacing.

"Yes," she lied. "Our powers combined must have been too much for it." But it hadn't been their powers combined that had done the most damage. That had only occurred when she'd used blood magic to further power the spell. The good intent of working *with* the wand had been perverted, bending the wand and its magic to her will, just as dark sorcerers did. Thankfully Tam had been too busy to notice. She had no idea how she could explain the use of such magic to him. She couldn't even explain it to herself. *I'll never use it again, though.*

Why not? It worked. And it felt glorious.

She shoved the whisper from her subconscious away, throwing up a wall in her mind between it and her. She couldn't listen to it. It was madness to consider using it again. Despite the fact it had helped her twice, it was still evil. But she wasn't. She'd spent her entire life trying to do good and make up for the one horrible thing she'd done. There were many times she could have given into darkness and used its thrall to take the easy way out of the burdens she carried, but she hadn't. She was a good person. And she wasn't about to change that now. Especially not now she had Tam in her life.

Hells, he couldn't know what she'd done. She'd do anything to make certain he never found out.

She looked down at the blackened wand in her hand. She had to try to make it better too. "Maybe Bas can heal it?"

"I'm sure he can. Let's take it back—"

The wand jumped out of her hand and flew down the row towards where she'd found it.

She went to chase after it, but Tam's hand on her arm held her back. "Let it go. I'll get Bas and Jules to look for it when they get back. It's unlikely to come back for us right now."

He was right. But still, she hated that she'd hurt the wand like that. That it seemed to be frightened of her now – although no wonder.

Tam cupped her face, then flinched. She grabbed his hand. "Let me have a look at that." His palm was burned, the skin angry and red, blisters already forming. A response to the darkness of the magic she'd used?

"It's fine," he said. "It can't be worse than yours."

But when he turned over her hand, there was only a little redness and no sign of blood or where the magic frond had burst out of her skin.

"What? But I felt it burn," she said, turning her hand this way and that – but there was no burn. Nothing to explain the sensation she'd endured when using both their powers through the wand, boosted by her blood. What did this mean? Nothing good, she was certain.

"Maybe you didn't get burned because you were the centre-point of the magic."

"Yes. Yes, that must be it," she said, grabbing onto his suggestion with too much enthusiasm and earning a strange look from him. She forced a smile to her face. "It did feel rather odd."

"But kind of amazing too. Especially that burst at the end," he said, returning her smile. "I've never felt so alive."

"Y-yes. M-me too."

"It's something we'll have to investigate when we try other artifacts."

"Other artifacts?"

"Of course," he said, pointing towards where the wand had disappeared. "You were right about an artifact of power allowing us to channel our powers together through it. This was a success."

"I wouldn't call it that. Look what I did to the wand."

"*We* did to the wand."

"And what about your hand?"

"A learner's injury. Bas will heal it in a jiffy." He flashed an encouraging smile. "All in all, not too bad given it was our first time channelling our power together. I was expecting worse." He cupped her face with his uninjured hand. "We did it, Rinna. We found the way forward."

He was right. Except … "I doubt the wand will let us use it again."

"I'm sure there's other artifacts out there like it we can use. Maybe one even more closely aligned with our powers that won't burn up like the wand did. This is it, Rinna. You've found the solution that will let us free the HBG spirit, open the Void and take care of Clodia once and for all."

"Gods, I hope you're right." And that they would work without her having to use her blood to fully power-up again.

He kissed her and pulled her in for a hug. "I am. You'll see. Stop worrying."

She nodded, then keen to change the conversation, looked back at the Black Magic and Dangerous Books section. "Who do you think let that out?"

"One of the interns probably didn't close up properly. It wouldn't be the first time. They've been getting slack ever since Jules lost her allergy to magic. Don't worry. I'll have a word with them. It won't happen again. Although, right now, I'm bloody glad it did."

She nodded, although she couldn't be as excited as he was. A dark foreboding crawled over her and as they went about cleaning up the mess the entity had made, she couldn't shake it.

6

They ate dinner in silence. Usually they chatted about everything and anything, but somehow, every time he went to try to talk about what had happened and their plan, one look at Rinna as she moved her food around on her plate listlessly had the words dying on his lips.

It was probably nothing more than exhaustion. The spell they'd done on the entity had been huge and she'd been the fulcrum for it. "Perhaps you should go to bed soon," he suggested into the silence.

She looked up at him for the first time since they'd sat down. "Um … yeah. I think I might. I'm pretty tired." Her fork clattered to the plate and she got up without another word and left the table.

"I'll see you up there," he said to the empty doorway.

"That's strange," the HBG said.

He picked up their plates and threw the leftovers into the bin. "I thought she'd be excited. We finally have a plan."

"Maybe she senses it's not the right plan to use any old artifact. Tell her about the ring."

"No. It's not the right time." He put the plates in the dishwasher. "She's probably just tired."

"You're not. You're wired."

He was. He'd expected her to be the same. Had expected her to drag him up to their room as she'd done so many times before regardless of if they'd had a good day or bad – sex with him, she always said, made her feel better about everything.

"Maybe she's waiting for you to remind her of that."

"Maybe."

"I'll just go be elsewhere for a while," the HBG said, pulling out of his conscious mind and going wherever she went whenever she gave them privacy.

He ran up the stairs, but when he got there, it was to find his soulmate already curled up on her side of the bed in the darkened room. She didn't stir as he entered. Didn't stir as he shucked his clothes and climbed in behind her. Didn't even stir when he wrapped his arms around her and spooned her – something they always did after sex, not before.

She must be truly exhausted. He kissed her on the shoulder and nestled down. But as he lay there, too wired to sleep, he couldn't shake the feeling that she was as awake as he.

The next morning he got up as light began to touch the room and headed downstairs to wait for Jules and Bas to join him in the breakfast nook, as they did every morning.

By the time they came down, he had the eggs and bacon cooked, a plate of toast, and pastries on the table for Rinna – given she had an insane hatred of bacon – and the coffee on.

As they ate, he filled his parents in on everything that had happened, his gaze sliding to the door every time he heard a noise that might indicate Rinna was up and joining them. But she didn't appear until he came to the end of the tale.

"Morning, Sleepy-head," Bas said, hopping up to pour her a coffee.

"Tam has just filled us in on everything," Jules said.

Rinna sat at the table and picked up a berry-filled pastry. She looked pale and had dark bags under her eyes. "Sorry I'm late. I was pretty tired after yesterday."

"No wonder, given what you both did." Bas handed her a mug of black coffee. "I've added a little something extra in there to help you feel better."

"Thanks." She took a large sip even though it must have been hot, then took a bite of her pastry. "So, what do you think of the plan? I expect Tam told you about his idea to use an artifact."

"He did," Jules said. "And I think you're right. Even if Bas manages to heal the wand, we need to look for other artifacts that might be closer in source power to yours."

"My thoughts exactly," Tamuel said, trying to catch Rinna's gaze – but she was staring at her pastry.

"Of course," Jules said, smiling proudly at him. "I do think that Korinna is right in that it doesn't matter what pantheon the source magic comes from. If it did, the wand wouldn't have worked at all."

Rinna glanced up at Jules. "We need to concentrate on artifacts that are connected to Goddesses that have similar power bases to Ostara."

"I can help with that," Jules said. "Part of my thesis was on artifacts tied to certain Gods and Goddesses and the source they were bound to."

"I did similar research," Rinna said. "But the only ones I ever got my hands on were in the Underworld – and we can't get those until Persephone is free to come back up here. Which isn't until after Oestra begins."

"We already know of the perfect one," the HBG said.

"It's in the Underworld and as Rinna said, we can't get access to anything there until after Oestra, so drop it, okay?"

He focussed back on the discussion at hand.

"... your research was very helpful when I was doing mine," Jules was saying. "Of course, I thought it was Varagustus' research at the time. But thanks to it, I was able to track down where some of the artifacts had ended up."

"That's amazing, Jules, but can we get them here in time?" Rinna said, glancing once again at the chronometer on the wall. He was relieved to see a spark of excitement in her eyes.

"Some of them might be difficult, but I know of two off the top of my head that I can probably get here in a few days. One is with the Roman Coven and the other the Edinburgh. They'll want to bargain for them but I've got some things here both covens have been after to add to their collections for a while, so I don't think it will be a problem."

"You're the best, Mum," Tam said, getting up and giving her a hug to cover his self-consciousness. It still felt weird calling her Mum. But that wasn't so much to do with the fact she wasn't biologically his mother and more to do with the fact he'd never had the opportunity to call the soul reincarnated into her 'mum' before. But the tie to her was strong and he wanted her – and Bas, his father – to know how he truly felt about them.

When he pulled back she was blushing delightedly – was that because he'd called her 'mum' or because he'd hugged her? Maybe both. He didn't get a chance to ask, because she pushed back her chair, saying, "Help me up. I'll go make my calls and you go and find that wand so you can heal it."

As he helped her to her feet, Rinna said, "What can we do?"

"From the sounds of it, you two need a greater repertoire of spells to fight Clodia with," Bas said. "Once we've found the right artifact, you'll need to know how to use it to win against her."

"I was thinking the same thing," Tamuel said.

"There's some good texts on fighting spells in the Arthurian section."

"I'll go look for them." Rinna stood. "After I've cleaned up here."

"I'll help," Tam said. Bas and Jules left for their various tasks and he and Rinna cleaned up the coffee mugs and tidied the kitchen.

Silence fell. Normally it wouldn't bother him – he wasn't someone who felt uncomfortable in silence, especially with Rinna – but after last night, it was like an itch under the skin. He hated it, but at the same time, he couldn't seem to break it.

"Guilty conscience for not telling her about the ring."

"No."

"She's strong enough to handle everything Loki told us," the HBG said doggedly as they dried while Rinna washed.

He had to stop himself rolling his eyes as he replied to it in his mind. *"I said drop it."*

"If you can't make the other options work, I don't think you'll have a choice but to go down and get it."

"No. She already worries about so much. I can't have her worried about me going down to the Underworld again. Besides, she'd want to go with me and I can't ask her to do that. Her guilt is too tightly wound into that place."

"Are you sure this is about her?"

"What do you mean?" He glanced at Rinna. She looked up, smiled at him. He smiled back. They returned to their tasks.

"Are you sure it's not just because you don't want to go down to the Underworld again?"

He snorted in his mind. *"Why wouldn't I want to go to the Underworld again? It's not like Hades hates my guts or anything."* The HBG's chuckle filled his mind. *"Besides, how am I supposed to get down there? I used up nearly all the energy in the Ark under the library and the next celestial rising I could use is the first night of Oestra – and given I need the ring to use then, that doesn't work, does it?"*

"You could take Loki up on his offer."

"And owe him a favour?"

"Isn't he your friend?"

"Kind of. Loki can be tricky in that way. Besides, with how things are between the pantheons, even if I was one-hundred percent certain of him in the past, I couldn't be anymore."

The HBG sighed. *"I think this is a waste of time. The ring Persephone has in her keeping is exactly what we need. The artifacts Jules will bring here might be strong and of the same kind of magic, but unless they are tuned to the stronger of the magics that will wield it – Korinna's magic – they're likely to go the way of the wand."*

"You can't know that."

She snorted. *"I think I'm uniquely qualified to say if something is strong enough to channel power through or not. My entire existence in this state has been as a tool others have used to channel power through."*

"I still don't understand why we can't use the gem you're trapped in as a channelling medium."

"*Because it's not the gem that has power – it's me. And once I'm released, it will simply be a gem. Albeit a unique gem with a latticework structure that makes it the perfect vessel to imprison someone of power in.*"

"*Zeus! You're right. We might not be able to use it, but we can use it.*"

There was a heavy pause and then, "*Do you think maybe you could make some sense this century?*"

"*I mean, we could imprison Clodia in it. We could, couldn't we?*"

There was a stunned silence before the HBG spirit said, "*Of course. It's exactly what we need to do. I never ... she didn't say.*"

"*She? Who didn't say?*"

There was a strange pause and then, "*The Seer who I heard much of this from. However, it makes sense she couldn't see everything. But this will work. Karma truly is a bitch, isn't she? Clodia's avarice will be her undoing – and it seems fitting that the gem she was so ready to twist to her own evil purposes will end up being her prison.*"

"*I don't think I've ever heard you so ruthless before.*"

"*I have my own darkness and a right to it. But all of this will come to naught if you cannot find the right thing to channel yours and Rinna's powers through. I still think you should go for the ring.*"

"*Not yet. We need to try other things first.*"

"*Well hurry, because you are fast running out of time.*"

"Tam? Are you okay?" He realised he was standing there staring at a half-dried mug.

"Umm, fine. The HBG was just talking to me."

"Really? What's she saying? Are we on the right track?"

"She thinks so."

"*Liar liar, pants on fire.*"

He ignored the HBG and put the mug down as that feeling in his chest – that empty, lost one that had started yesterday – grew a little larger. He grabbed Rinna's hand and the feeling dissipated. "We can do this."

She leaned up and kissed him – the first time they'd kissed or touched romantically since their dalliance in the library yesterday – a kiss he felt down to his soul.

She pulled away, all the warmth going with her.

"Let's finish up here," she said, all practicality – the warmth and passion of their kiss hardly seemed to have affected her. "Then we can go look for more spells we can use to fight Clodia. Bas is right – I was annoyed with myself when we fought the entity that I didn't know enough defensive or offensive magic. It's time I righted that issue."

He nodded. She was right. It was time for practicality – not passion and desire. Her practicality was one of the things he loved about her. Although, why did it suddenly feel like she was using it to build a wall between them?

Or was it him building the wall? Could the HBG be right – that this was a guilty conscience? No. He truly didn't have anything to feel guilty over. It wasn't like any of the HBG's suggestions were practical or possible. Zeus would kill him if he made a deal with Loki.

No. This was the way it had to be. They had a plan and it was going to work.

"You hope."

"Shut up."

He finished wiping the last of the mugs, put it away and held out his hand. "Let's go find some fighting spells in the Arthurian section. I don't think I've actually looked at anything in there before."

She shook her head. "No. I'll go research the texts Bas suggested. I think it's a better use of our time if you go and look in the Eleusinian Mysteries Grimoire for more spells like the one we used against the entity."

A horrible prickle shot over his skin and down his spine. "How did you know that spell came from that grimoire?" She wouldn't have gone through his secret portal and found the grimoire – would she?

She picked up the tea towel he'd put on the bench and hung it on the rack. "Like how I knew the sigil spell you used to get into the Underworld was from there. I've done a lot of research and recognised its magical signature. Not to mention, like my magic, its power originally was sourced from Demeter and Persephone. There's a ... familiarity to it."

She turned back to face him, expression guileless. Of course it was. There was no way she'd do anything that would make things harder for him with Persephone and Hades. He *was* the one with the guilty conscience when it came to that. She *should* be allowed to look at the grimoire and use it as he'd promised – but he was bound by that stupid vow not to let her see it. It's why he'd hidden it in his secret room with a spell only someone with almost God-like powers could break.

The gentle touch on his cheek brought him from his thoughts. "Of course. That makes sense."

"As does using it. The grimoire is out of bounds for me, but not for you. And its magic is as closely bound to Oestra and Ostara as any other, so it's bound to have spells we can use. You can teach me the ones you think I should know and still keep your vow to Seph."

"Okay. I'll go do it now."

"Good. And I'll go see if Bas was right. We need as much ammunition to fight Clodia as we can get." She kissed him again, then left. He watched her until she disappeared.

"Stop worrying about her," Jules said coming back into the kitchen. "She is strong and powerful. She will get through this, as will you."

"I feel she's hiding something from me," he said, rubbing at the ache in his chest.

"We all have our secrets, Tamuel. Just because you're mated doesn't mean you get instantaneous entry to every nook and cranny of her mind and life. I'm sure there's things you're not telling her either – probably telling yourself it's to protect her."

He looked down and shoved his hands into his pockets.

She chuckled. "See! And I bet she's saying the same. That she's keeping some things from you because she wants to protect you. We all do it. It's part of loving others more than ourselves."

He looked up at her. "You and Dad don't do it. Your bond is stronger than anything I've ever witnessed."

She took his hand. "That's because we work at it. And sometimes it's bloody hard. We both brought scars into this relationship. But we give each other the room to carry our scars and the trust that we will unburden to the other with time and let the other help heal those scars." She squeezed his hand. "Don't push too fast, Tamuel. It takes time to get these things right."

He nodded, looking away from her gaze – afraid she'd see the desperate need in him to have everything he'd never thought to have and to have it now.

Jules let go of his hand and sighed. "You've both faced a lot and have a lot more to face. Let her get through this first, then tackle some of the issues you feel as a wedge between you."

Of course, she was right.

"The good news is, both my contacts at the Roman and Edinburgh Covens are willing to bargain for the artifacts we want. They're going to call me back later with an offer."

"That's amazing."

"It is. I really feel now that we will find the exact thing you need to get the HBG spirit free and defeat Clodia."

"And get your power back."

She waved dismissively. "I don't care about that. I'm happy with what I've got."

"Are you? Without your magic, you'll die." He hated to bring it up like this but she had to realise how the thought hurt him. "You might get your human lifespan, but in sixty or seventy years, you'll die and leave Bas and the baby and … me." He suddenly realised these must be the scars she'd alluded to between her and his father.

"I know," she whispered, her trembling hand cupping her stomach. "And I don't want that. I don't. But if it comes down to a choice between getting rid of Clodia and getting my power back, I want you to promise you will not choose the latter. Clodia cannot be allowed back into this world. I sacrificed my magic to make that so, and I will not see that undone for any reason. Do you understand?"

"So, you think I was wrong to sacrifice my magic and allow her to escape?"

"No." She cupped his face, her fingers firm on his cheeks, forcing him to look into her eyes. "No. You did it to save the woman you love. Your soulmate. I get that better than anyone because I did the same. The only difference was, I had you and your father there to help me and I was able to open the tear into the Void and push Clodia through. If I'd been alone as you were in that moment, it would have been very different; I would have done anything to save you and Bastien." She rubbed her hand over her stomach. "Just as I would do anything now to save this little one. So don't blame yourself for the choice you made that day. None of us do." She gestured down to where the library lay below them. "What we do now is to ensure nobody ever has to make that choice again. And if succeeding means never getting my magic back, then I'm okay with that, as your father is. I need you to be okay with that too."

He nodded, even though he could never be okay with it. Not only had he made a vow – heard and accepted by the Eternal Well – which could never be broken, he would not, could not, let his mother die again. Jules might not be his biological mother, but her soul was the same, so she felt like his mother. The mother he was always meant to have but was stolen from him at the moment of his birth. He couldn't suffer the thought of her dying – not if he could stop it.

And he could. He would.

Before she could see the lie in his eyes, he turned from her and said, "I've got some research to do."

He got no more than a few steps when she said, "Don't forget, Tamuel – you are no longer alone. And neither is Rinna. You have each other and you have us, and there is more power in that than in any artifact or offensive spell you could ever find. Clodia won't know what hit her."

She left the kitchen, leaving him staring after her, a burning sensation around his heart.

7

Korinna threw herself into her work over the next few days – or at least tried to – researching spells to use against Clodia while continuing to encourage Tam to work in his secret place learning spells from the Eleusinian Mysteries Grimoire. She thought having some distance from him – from the constant reminder of what she'd made him be a part of – would help, but it didn't. At night, they lay next to each other, barely touching, her silence, her reticence, her *shame*, a chasm between them.

Perhaps she should tell him. But then, what would she do when he looked at her – as he inevitably would – like she'd done something wrong; or worse, like *she* was evil?

After two days of hardly being able to concentrate, she slammed her hands on the desk. "Enough!" she said to herself.

"Are you talking to me?" Jules said, sticking her head out of the nearest stack.

Hells. When had Jules come into the library? She hadn't even noticed. Really, she needed to pull her shit together and just get on with things. "No. Just myself. I'm struggling to find any spells that might help." Which was true. It was difficult trying to figure out what might work best as she didn't really know what kind of magic Clodia would attack with – nobody seemed to know the source of her magic, other than it couldn't be from Vesta. If it had been, she would never have been able to do what she'd done.

"Try this one," Jules said, putting one of the old grimoires she was holding on the desk in front of Korinna.

"I didn't see that in the Arthurian section." She would know. She'd looked at every book of magic there.

"That's because it wasn't there. It's from the small selection of rare books and antiquities we managed to collect from Atlantis."

"Atlantis? But … wasn't all that lost?"

"Yes. But Tam found some things years ago – I swear my son is like a bloodhound for finding rare and lost things. He gave them to my grandmama for safe keeping. I'd actually forgotten about them – she doesn't keep them down here – but remembered her telling me about them, so I went searching for them in her room. Good thing I did too, because I've actually found something in this one." She waggled the other grimoire she was holding. "It's about the Void."

"The Void?" They'd barely found any information on that mysterious place between space and time.

"Yeah. This is written by a priest who heard it directly from their God, Poseidon. Listen to this: 'Not much is known about the Void. All Gods and Goddesses who can traverse it stay silent on the subject except to admit to three unassailable rules. One: only things on the spirit plane, or beings of great power, can enter the Void and not be destroyed. Two: what does enter can only exit from a tear near where they entered – unless carried by a being of greater power to another exit. And three: all things inside the Void gravitate quickly towards any new entryway. If you do not want something to exit, make certain to close it quickly, or better yet, do not open the Void.'"

"That's actually helpful."

"It is, isn't it? It tells us we were right in our supposition about where Clodia will try to break out." She shook her head as she closed the book and looked at Korinna. "We're going back to the Roman Forum."

"Are you okay with that?"

Jules shrugged. "I have to be, don't I?"

A purple-blue glow pulled their attention to Tam's portal as it opened in the wall and a moment later, Tam stepped out. When he saw Jules standing there, he stopped dead.

"I didn't think you could portal through a wall like that," Jules said. "Is it safe?"

"Oh, yeah, of course," he said, gaze crashing into Korinna's and widening slightly as if to say 'oops'.

Oops indeed. He wasn't usually so careless about opening that portal when others might be around – it was supposed to be secret after all.

But, like only Tam could, he smiled his 'butter-wouldn't-melt-in-his-mouth' charming smile and said brightly, "Hey, what are you two gorgeous and talented ladies talking about?"

"This," Jules said, showing him the information about the Void.

"Well, isn't that helpful?"

"That's what Korinna said."

"Great minds."

"Yeah. You two are really meant for each other."

Tam's gaze softened on hers and a smile that cut at her heart bloomed on his face. She looked away, unable to stand seeing the trust, the love, there – and felt his hurt deep in her heart.

She was being so cold and horrible to him – but how could she be anything else? He knew her too well not to work out the secret she was keeping and she just couldn't let him know yet. Not before Oestra, when they needed – she needed – his faith in her to be as strong as it could be. But she ached with her need to be with him; to kiss him and touch him and have him look at her in that way that told her she was his everything.

She had to be strong though. He couldn't know, so she had to keep him at a distance.

"Hey," Bas said as he appeared at the bottom of the stairs, two boxes piled in his arms. "Your deliveries have arrived."

"Ooh, goodie," Jules said, clapping her hands and following him as he headed to the kitchen table.

"That was good timing," Tam said. He held out his hand. She looked at it. He kept holding it out – a challenge? A plea? She took it and let him draw her to her feet, then side-by-side, walked with him to join his parents at the table.

"Rinna, why don't you do the honours?" Jules suggested.

There was a letter attached to the box nearest to Korinna. She opened it first. "It's from the Roman Coven."

"Ah," Jules said. "Well then, this is Asherah's Cornucopia, rumoured to have once been used in ancient spring rights."

She looked up at Jules. "The ancient Mesopotamian Goddess of Motherhood and Fertility?"

Jules nodded. "That's why I thought it might work. She's pretty close in many respects to Ostara."

"What did you have to barter for it?" Tam asked.

"Nothing that will be missed," she said, giving him her 'mum' look of 'that is for me to worry about'.

Korinna was stabbed by a sharp jab of jealousy. Not that she would ever want Tam to miss out on a relationship with his mother in whatever form it took, but moments like this made her realise just how much she had missed out on with her own mother. Or with any parent for that matter. Persephone was lovely, but she was more an aunt for all that she'd raised Korinna.

Tam must have felt something down the bond because his gaze whipped to her, but she shook her head at him and asked, "What's in the other box?"

Jules gestured to it. "Open it and you'll find out."

"I haven't opened this one yet."

"Actually, I think you might want to try the other one first," Jules said, a knowing smile on her face.

"Okay." There was no letter on the top of the box that had come from the Edinburgh Coven, so she began to dig through the packaging beans. "It must be pretty small," she said when she didn't immediately come across the item.

"It would be," Jules said, helping her to empty the beans into the bin by the handful, her face brimming with excitement. "It's a ring rumoured to be made out of the hair of Nantosuelta."

"Nantosuelta? I don't know her," Bas said.

"Probably because most people know her by the name she used in later years – The Morrigan."

"She's a good pick, Jules," Korinna muttered, still searching through the box.

"I thought so, given she's the ancient Celtic Goddess of Nature, Earth, Fire and Fertility. You're sure to get some results with it. Possibly better than the cornucopia."

"Yes," was all Rinna said, hope a tight fist in her chest. That hope had been there when Tam first suggested searching for other artifacts, but over the last few days, with all her doubts, it had begun to fade. It was good to feel it again. Maybe now Tam wouldn't keep looking at her like she'd kicked a puppy – and he was the puppy.

She unearthed a small box near the bottom and lifted it reverentially to set it on the table.

"Open it," Tam said.

She flipped open the lid.

Nestled in red velvet was a plaited ring made up of three different threads of colour. The largest thread was black – so black it seemed to suck in the light – and through it was twined threads of gold and green that, in opposition to the black, reflected the light and dazzled the eye if you looked too long. It appeared to be made out of some kind of metal, but on closer inspection, she could see that it was plaited hair, coated in something that made it as tough as steel. Or, maybe, that was just the hair itself. If rumour was correct, it was made out of The Morrigan's hair, and she was one of the toughest Goddesses around.

"Try it on," Tam said to Rinna, picking up the box and holding it out to her.

Cautiously – she feared the same reaction she had with the fairy wand – Korinna reached out and touched the hair-ring.

The moment she did, the green and gold threads began to glow.

She snatched her hand back – she didn't want that blood-tinged frond of magic to erupt from her hand in front of them all. She should have tried to touch it first in private to see what it would do.

Tam grabbed her hand. "What happened? Did it hurt?" he asked, turning it over.

Self-conscious, and afraid of looking foolish, she said, "No. I just didn't expect it to flare so quickly. You touch it now. See if it does the same thing for you."

His smile widened as the ring glowed for him like it had for her – except, white light streamed out of the black twists of hair instead of from the green and gold. If it reacted like that for him, maybe she didn't need to be so worried that what happened with the wand would happen again.

"Here," Tam said, placing it in her upturned hand. "I think you are meant to be the fulcrum again."

The green and gold strands glowed again and the power thrummed through her, but nothing else happened.

She almost melted in relief. Even more so when Tam looked up at her, eyes full of excitement. "It's going to work. We're going to make this work."

She smiled back at him, laughing as Bas and Jules let out a whoop. For the first time in days, her worry lifted and she felt almost free. "I think you're right. This is it."

8

"This isn't it," Korinna growled, shoving the Cup of Freyr, complete with little wisps of smoke rising from the rim, into the middle of the table. It rolled then clanged to a stop against the Diadem of Brigid – the previous failure. Like Nantosuelta's Ring, Asherah's Cornucopia and every other artifact they'd managed to track down and get here over the last few weeks, the cup had responded to their touch quite well, and Tam had managed to combine his magic with it, but when she tried – smoke, fires, explosions.

She didn't even want to think about what would happen if she tried to use blood magic as she'd done with the wand. Not that she would, of course.

"I don't understand what the problem is," Jules said. "These are some of the most powerful artifacts to ever exist. And yet, they don't seem to be able to handle your power at all."

"Our theory must be wrong," she said morosely, frowning at the items in the middle of the table.

"I don't think so." Jules picked up the still-smoking cup, turning it over in her hands. "It's like your power is completely incompatible with the items. But that doesn't make sense. Unless … but surely … no, that couldn't be it. Could it?"

"Unless what? Couldn't be it what?" she asked, sitting forward.

Before Jules could answer, an alarm rang through the room, echoing with a bell-like peel through the library. Korinna spun around and stared at the chronometer on the wall. "No," she said over the noise. "No, that can't be right." It couldn't be signalling that the Vernal Equinox was only one week away. "I must have set it wrong." Except, she never got mechanical things wrong.

Zeus' balls! She wasn't ready. Not even close. How could the HBG spirit have thought her capable of this?

"There's not enough time. It has to be wrong." Because if she didn't have more time, then they wouldn't succeed. And if they didn't succeed, Clodia would be out in the world with power not meant for her, and then Tam would go off after her and they would never be together. Although, at this point, that might already be true as far as their relationship was concerned. He wasn't even holding her as she pretended to sleep anymore – he lay on his side of the bed and she lay on hers. She was surprised he still shared a room with her. Not that she blamed him. She'd built a wall between them with all her worry and fear. The only way to fix it was to tell him the truth, which she just could not do.

"Rinna, what's wrong?" Tam said, appearing out of the stacks. After their latest failure, he'd gone in search of any information on channelling he could find, despite the fact they'd already gone through every source logged as being in the library. He rushed to her side. "You're shaking."

She pointed at the chronometer just as the alarm turned off. "We've only got a week! How are we ever going to manage this?"

"It will be fine. I promise."

Every agony from the last few weeks came crashing down on her with those words. She rounded on him, eyes full of tears she couldn't seem to hold back. "How can you promise that?" she yelled. "We're no closer to a proper plan or solution than we were when I put that up there." She jabbed her finger towards the chronometer. "When I set that, I thought we'd know what we were going to do and have it practiced down to a fine art by now. Even if we find an artifact that works for us in the next day or so," she said, her voice rising to the verge of hysteria, "we barely have enough time to work with it to get it right. So, excuse me for being just a little upset, especially given I seem to be the one blocking the entire process."

"Don't say that, Rinna," Tam said, stroking up and down her arms in a motion she'd always found soothing but right now, didn't even come close because it reminded her too vividly that he'd not touched her for days – and she couldn't let him touch her now because her *need* was screaming at her to tell him, to open up, to lean on his trust in her.

But she couldn't. She just couldn't. So she shrugged away from him, ignoring his hurt, and asked flatly, "Why not? It's true. All of these," she waved at the items in the middle of the table and then at the ones that had been put back in their boxes and stacked over by the wall. "All of them, without exception, almost blew up because of my power."

"That's not true."

"Yes, it is. They work fine when I gather your power and mesh it with the artifact power, but the moment I add mine – whether I do it first or last – it's like adding nitro-glycerine. I have no idea how to stop it from happening. And it shouldn't even be happening given I have that control spell in place—"

"You have what?" Jules asked.

She snapped her mouth closed, horrified she'd just blurted that out.

Tam gripped her shoulders again, fear tinging his eyes. "What did you do, Rinna? Don't tell me you put restrictions on your magic?"

Her lips trembled. She wanted to deny it but it was the lesser of the two horrible things she'd been keeping from him, and she just couldn't hold this one in anymore. "I used an old spell that helps me to rope my magic in a little," she said, her voice a harsh whisper.

"What old spell? Where from?"

"Maybe it's what is causing the problem," Jules proffered.

"No." She shook her head vehemently. "No, it can't be. It's helping. Without it, I'd do something even worse than what I did to the wand."

He went to argue with her again, but she made a chopping motion. "I promise, it's not the problem. It's helping me. I couldn't control my magic before and now I can."

"But any change to your magic like that, especially after you'd suppressed it for so long, could have dire consequences," Jules said at the same time Tam asked, "Why would you keep that from me?"

The horrible hurt in his tone was like a jab to the chest. On top of the hurt she'd caused him daily by pulling away …

She eased out of his grip and stepped back, unable to stop from going on the defensive even as she hated herself for it. "You wouldn't understand. You've always had such control over your power. You've got no idea what it feels like to lose your grip on it, to have it grow stronger and have no way of pulling it back." She swiped at the tears running down her cheeks, hating that she couldn't just be unemotional and logical right now, especially in front of Jules. "Bad things happen. Disastrous, terrible things. I can't be responsible for that again. I just can't." But oh Gods. She was responsible for it possibly happening again. Because Jules was right. The spell probably was stopping her from being able to work with any of the artifacts. But she couldn't give it up. She just couldn't. Which meant … she lurched back, trembling fingers against her lips. "It's my fault. She's going to get free and it's my fault."

"Rinna, Rinna. It's okay." Suddenly, she was in his arms, his hands stroking her hair, down her back, over and over. Even though she knew she didn't deserve it, she couldn't help leaning into him, arms snaking around him to hold him tight.

"I'm sorry," he said, pressing kisses to her hair. "I should have remembered. I didn't realise … I'm sorry. It's okay. We'll work it out. It will be fine. I promise."

"How? How can it be fine and how can you promise?" she sobbed against his chest. "I set her free. It's my fault if Clodia gets your mother's power and escapes from the Void. My fault if we can't stop her. I'm the one who can't control my magic properly. I'm the one who keeps causing disasters to happen. And despite all my trying, I just seem incapable of setting them to rights."

He set her away from him, staring straight into her eyes, his shadowed by guilt and something else she couldn't read. "You're not responsible. It's my fault this time. This is on me. It's my fault there's been this ... chasm between us. And I know exactly how to fix it."

"How is it your fault—"

"I love you, Rinna." He wiped the tears from her cheeks with his thumbs. "I promise, I will do what I have to, to set this right." Then he gave her swift kiss before letting her go and turning away.

He waved his hand to open a portal.

"What? Where are you going?"

He glanced over his shoulder. "I'll be back as soon as I can with exactly what we need."

"What? No. Wait. Let me come with—" But he was already gone, the portal closing behind him with a pop and a little suck of air. She stared blindly at the space he'd disappeared into. How could he leave her like this now?

You pushed him away.

Oh Gods. She had. She had.

"Are you okay?" Jules asked touching Korinna's shoulder.

She blinked rapidly, shrugging away from the caring touch. "Why didn't he want me to go with him? Is he that angry with me for using the control spell?"

"What? No." Jules moved to step in front of her. "It's more likely he's just gone to do something dangerous and didn't want you in the middle of it. Either that or he's doing something he knows you won't approve of."

"Oh, you're right." She touched her chest where she could feel his anxiety and stress – mixed with a flutter of healthy fear – through their bond. It was a sensation she'd felt from him once before when they were down in the Underworld together. She shouldn't be surprised he'd put himself in danger to help her – even though she'd been behaving like such a shit towards him. It was his signature move when it came to trying to help those he loved. "How could he be such an idiot?"

"Our males can be incredibly stupid when the protective instinct comes over them. I almost feel the need to crown Bas 'King of Idiots' sometimes, with the shit he does to protect me. Wait until you have a little one onboard," she said, stroking her stomach. "The protective idiocy triples. I swear, if we didn't love them so much, we'd have to kill them."

Korinna snorted but couldn't help touching her stomach. She'd never ever allowed herself to think of having children, especially with what was in front of them and what she'd been doing to their relationship, yet suddenly, there was a longing for exactly that in her heart. But it wouldn't happen if Tam got seriously injured – or killed – searching for a solution to the problem she'd caused. "Well, I'm not going to stand around and let my idiot get away with his idiocy." Despite the fact she'd pushed him away, she was going to reel him back.

"Usually I'd be all for that, but he's just portalled away. Even if one of us could use a portal, we have no idea where he's gone."

Her eyes widened as a thought hit her. "I think maybe I know where we could find something to help us figure it out." He'd told her of a homing spell he'd used to track Bas down a century ago after finding out about the curse that had been placed on his parents – a spell that was in one of the grimoires in his secret place.

"We?" Jules began to smile. "I like the sound of that. What do we have to do?"

9

"Thanks, Loki." Tamuel nodded at the God.

"Believe me, it's my pleasure. It's good to be doing something a little exciting for a change." Loki smiled as he leaned against the bare wall of the cave he'd brought Tam to, deep under a buried temple where he'd once been worshipped by the Vikings.

"You'll need to guard the portal until I'm back. You won't leave, will you?"

"Of course not," Loki said, hand to his heart, mock-hurt on his face. "What kind of friend do you take me for?"

"The kind that drives a hard bargain rather than doing something out of the goodness of his heart."

Loki nodded sagely. "Yes, well, if I had a good side to my heart, that might be something I'd do but …" He gestured at himself. "I am what I am and what I was made to be. Besides, this kind of hotness is far hotter being bad than good."

Tamuel shook his head. "I'll try and figure out the sense of that when I get back."

Loki waved his hand at the partial carving on Tamuel's arm. "Finish that and I'll power you up."

As Tamuel carved the final stroke of the sigil on his arm, Loki put

539

his hand over the bleeding wound and, whispering ancient words Tamuel couldn't quite catch, pushed power into the magic that could open the portal into the Underworld and allow the bearer to go through in corporeal form – something he'd need to be to bring the ring back.

The portal opened in front of him and he stepped through.

Light spun around him, pulling into the distance, creating a long bridge with a wavering light at its end. The bridge seemed longer than he remembered, but shrugging, he started walking swiftly across it.

As he walked, he couldn't help chastising himself. He should have known what was worrying Rinna. Should have figured out why she'd been so stiff – and fragile seeming – every time he tried to touch her. It had got so bad, he was afraid to even cuddle her in bed anymore. He'd thought it was because she sensed he was holding something back from her – but it wasn't that at all. Well, it might have been a very small part of the chasm between them, but it wouldn't have caused her to pull away quite like she had. He'd been stupid to think so and an absolute idiot for not pursuing the real reason. She'd been hurting badly – had put manacles on her magic for fuck's-sake and hurt herself further – all because he was too stupid to see what was right in front of him.

What kind of a soulmate was he to allow his mate to suffer so needlessly?

The worst of it was, he could have stopped her from worrying; stopped her from doing something as terrible as leashing her magic. He should have come and got the ring weeks ago after they failed with the first few artifacts. Except, like a stupid, cowardly fool, he'd told himself they'd find something else; something easier. Something without all the complications and obligations the ring held.

He'd ignored what he'd known the moment Loki told him about it – that the ring was the only thing that would work – and now look what had happened. Rinna had torn herself apart with worry and guilt and fear and all for nothing.

Why hadn't she told him how afraid she was? Probably thought he knew – like he should have. Or maybe she thought she was protecting him. Gods, he loved her for that but still … it hurt him to think she felt she needed a control spell.

He wished he could make her believe in herself like he believed in her. He thought she understood that what happened at Pompeii hadn't been her fault – some other being of power had caused that to happen. But from the sounds of things, she was still hung up on that too.

Fuck. How had he let that slip by him?

"You have had a few things on your mind," the HBG spirit said. *"Don't beat yourself up over it. I missed it too."*

"True. I just wish we had more time."

But they didn't and wishing for it wouldn't change anything.

"The ring will help."

"Yes." Once she got the ring, she'd feel the truth in what he had long known – that she was one of the greatest practitioners of magic he'd ever met. And that there was no need to fear something as beautiful as her magic.

He should have made her feel that way before. He really was a shit soulmate and needed to beg her forgiveness for letting her suffer.

And maybe, after she'd tried the ring and succeeded, after they'd freed the HBG and defeated Clodia, she would forgive him. There was no way her power would be too much for this ring. It had held the power of a God and two Goddesses when Triptolemus had used it in his duties and worship of Demeter and Persephone. With it, she could let go of that stupid control spell and allow her power free. At least, he hoped she could – he really needed to find out exactly what spell she'd used – because the ring might sense there was something wrong with her magic and not work for her.

Which would be a disaster. Because, despite the HBG saying it needed both their powers to release it and defeat Clodia, Rinna's power was really the essential ingredient in the mix now he didn't have his cupid power. They couldn't afford for it to be leashed.

But before he could deal with any of that, he had to get to Persephone without letting Hades know he was 'visiting' using the very spell that had got him into so much trouble last time and that he'd promised never to use again. He also had to hope that nobody would find out he'd bargained with Loki to power that spell because there'd be more than hell to pay from Zeus and Odin if they found out.

"None of that matters right now. Concentrate on the job at hand. You won't make it through the portal doorway if you don't."

He concentrated on the wavering light in front of him, putting the image of Persephone in his minds-eye. Then, hoping to all Hells she was alone in her painting studio as was her habit at this time of the day, he stepped through.

There was a slight pop as he landed, cat-like, on the black polished floor. He looked up, expecting to see Persephone's sumptuously appointed studio but was instead greeted by a black stone wall with veins of red, purple and green running chaotically through it. The same wall he'd found himself in front of last time – the wall of the main hall.

Shit! Not again. He looked down at the sigil carved on his wrist and shook it, little flecks of blood splattering from the injury as he did so. *Does this thing ever work properly?* It couldn't be his magic this time – Loki had given him the juice to get here. Maybe Persephone was warming herself by the fire. Alone.

Please, please, please let me find Persephone alone, if for no other reason than I don't need to be scarred again by what I witnessed last time.

Cautiously, he turned around.

The room was empty.

Yes!

The doors that led to Persephone's private studio were only a few metres to his left.

He began to creep across to them but didn't get more than halfway when Hades came strolling out of the doorway on the far side of the room.

Tamuel ducked behind a massive statue of the God of the Underworld that most definitely had not been there last time.

Ye Gods, it was a nude!

Trying not to touch the dangly bits, he peaked around the edges of the sculpture to see where Hades was going.

"Is he wearing a pink shower cap?"

The HBG's surprised exclamation almost made him jump, it was so loud in his mind. *"Shh,"* he said, afraid Hades might be able to hear such loud mind-speech.

Thankfully the God seemed to be tied up in his own thoughts as he sauntered across the room, humming what sounded like *Dulcinea* from *The Man of La Mancha*. He stopped when he got to the mirror that hung over the giant maw of a fireplace, pulled something out of the pocket of his black jeans and leaned closer to the mirror.

"Is he plucking his eyebrows? Oh Gods, not the nose hairs too – and with the same set of tweezers. Yuk! And is that scent hair dye? He dyes his hair?" The HBG started laughing, the sound ricocheting around his mind. *"What next? Is he going to paint his nails and have a facial? Not so scary now, is he! Bwahahaha!"*

"Stop it!" he said, quietly backing towards the door, trying to keep the massive nude statue between him and his uncle. *"You're going to get me into trouble. Hades is too vain to let anyone know he grooms himself like this! We have to slip out of here."*

"But he dyes his hair! And plucks his eyebrows and nose hairs! Isn't he all-powerful enough to make himself look however he likes? Oh how the mighty have fallen!" The HBG's laughter was even louder and more forceful this time.

Hades dropped the tweezers and spun around.

Shit!

"I thought I said I didn't want to be disturb—" His annoyed bark died, eyes widening as he saw Tamuel. "You!" White lines appeared around Hades' mouth and nostrils as he shouted, "What in all the Hells are you doing here? And in corporeal form too? How dare you defy me!"

Despite the ominous glower that made lesser beings cower and beg the God's forgiveness, Tamuel's lips twitched – it was really difficult to take Hades seriously with that pink shower cap on his head.

Hades' eyes turned from black to red. "Are you laughing at me?"

"No. No. Not me," Tamuel said, trying desperately to school his features into his most charming and deferential of smiles. "Nice stat-ue," he said, hand waving at it.

Hades stopped glowering as his gaze ran over the nude. "Do you like it? It's a present for Seph – something to remember me by in the months she's forced to be away from me."

"It's um … very life-like."

"Really? You don't think he's overestimated the size of his c—"

"Shut up!"

Hades lifted his chin, looking very much like the cat who got the cream. "It is very life-like, isn't it?" He went to brush his hand through his hair, but froze as he touched the shower cap. He blanched and snatched it from his head, wet, freshly died hair flopping down to his shoulders in unaccustomed disarray, a piece catching on his cheek. Power prickled in the air and wind whipped around him, hiding him momentarily in a swirling pool of grey smoke with red sparking on its surface. Before Tamuel could consider running – if he found Perse-phone quickly, she'd save him – the tornado of smoke dissipated. Hades stood there glowering, his long, glossy black hair waving around his shoulders in its usual blow-waved-yet-bed-tousled style.

"He blow-waves his hair!" He squelched another bark of laughter from the HBG – who seemed to suddenly want only to get him into trouble – but knew he hadn't done a good enough job when the God's red eyes sparked into flames.

He cleared his throat and tried to cover. "Seems I have a tickle." He cleared his throat again as Hades continued to glower at him. Best he just get on with it. "Um … Sorry to disturb you, Uncle. I was actually hoping to speak to Persephone. Unfortunately, the spell brought me here. Again." He waggled his arm, then, remembering Loki's power still glowed within it, shoved it behind him.

"You throw the use of that spell in my face! I swear by the Eternal Well, if Seph hadn't given you her protection, you wouldn't walk out of here with that thing on your arm. Maybe I should just remove it."

"The spell?"

"No, your arm."

Tamuel gulped. "I'm sure that won't be necessary. I just need to see

Persephone and then I'll go right back home. You'll hardly know I'm here."

Hades snorted. "Why do you assume Seph wants to see you? Especially after you stole her favourite Soteira away."

"I didn't steal Korinna."

"Asked her to go with you, did you? When she was fully conscious?"

Tamuel grimaced. "It was the only way to save her. She was dying. Persephone seemed fine about that when she visited just before she had to come down here."

"Of course my hunnee-bunnee said she was fine – she didn't want our dearest Korinna to feel badly. But in actuality, she was heartbroken that you took our ... *her* almost-daughter away without a by-your-leave."

Tamuel frowned. "But ... Persephone said she was glad—"

"She. Was. Heartbroken," Hades grated out, his eyes sparking again, his form growing bigger.

"It's not Persephone that's heartbroken."

"No shit, Sherlock."

"This is probably why she told you to stay clear for a bit."

Tamuel almost rolled his eyes but stopped himself just in time because Hades had started stalking across the room towards him.

"So what are you down here to steal from my pumpkin-pie this time?"

"I'm not here to steal anything. I'm here to ask Persephone for something I heard she's holding for Rinna."

Hades stiffened, face blanching, the red in his eyes stuttering. "You can't have it!"

"I don't think that's your call."

The red flared again and he seemed to grow taller, dark shadows whispering around him. "You would challenge me, you vapid ex-cupid! I am the Lord of the Underworld! King of all the Hells and I—"

"I think the Morningstar would have something to say about that particular statement, my hunnee-bunnee-pie."

Tamuel spun around, breathing a big sigh of relief to see Persephone standing in the doorway behind him. "Seph – you have the best timing ever."

"Tamuel," she said on a big sigh. "I should have known it was you. Nobody but Zeus can make my sugar-bear lose his temper like you can. Oh, is that for me?" she said, gaze landing on the statue. "I love it." She ran over to Hades and wrapped her arms around him, leaning up to kiss his chin and fondle his hair. The shadows around him rushed away and he returned to normal size.

"You do?"

"Of course. Especially …" Her eyes glinted as her hand landed on his crotch.

Hades groaned then grabbed her up and kissed her passionately.

I'm going to yak, the HBG said.

Tamuel wanted to look away but somehow he couldn't – it was kind of like that thing that made humans look at a car crash.

Thankfully, their passionate embrace went no further than a too-much-tongue-and-groping-he-wished-he-could-unsee kiss. After a very uncomfortable – for him – few minutes, Persephone pulled away from Hades and raised her brow at Tamuel. She stared at him for long minutes.

"I expect you want to know why I'm here," he said, breaking the silence.

She held up her hand. "No. I know exactly why you're here. You want the ring."

"How did you know that?" he asked at the same time Hades said, "You can't give it to him."

She turned to Hades and stroked his chest. "It's time, my love-monkey."

He breathed heavily for a moment as he stared down at her, but then nodded. "I'll leave you to it, then."

"Good idea."

He pointed a finger at Tamuel. "The next time I see you here, you better be dead – or no matter what my sugar-fairy says, I will make it so."

Very Captain Jean-Luc Picard of him.

Ignoring the HBG, Tamuel only nodded.

Hades turned to leave, then turned back, grabbed Persephone and kissed her, hard and fast, then with a wave of his hand, disappeared.

Persephone turned slowly back to Tamuel and gestured at the couch by the fireplace. "Come. Sit. There are some things I must tell you before you take it."

"I don't have much time."

"You will have time for this."

Blanching at her ominous tone, Tamuel took a seat.

10

Korinna closed the manuscript in front of her with a snap, then coughed as a cloud of dust wafted up from the old, musty pages.

"Sorry about that."

"I'm used to it." Jules waved her hand, eyes fixed on the grimoire she was pouring over on the other side of the desk. "Was there anything useful in it?"

"No." She shoved it aside and grasped for another book off the pile they'd made when they'd broken into Tam's secret space. "You?"

"Not for what we came in to look for, but it does mention something about the power of Ostara being used at Oestra as a source of release. It might help to guide you in how to release the spirit from the gem."

"If we find the correct artifact to channel through."

"Yes. Or maybe…"

Korinna looked up as the other woman's words died away. Jules was biting her lip, her face scrunched up in pain as she clutched her stomach. "Shit. Are you okay?" What was she thinking, bringing a pregnant woman through a portal? Bas and Tam would kill her if anything happened to Jules and the baby. Scratch that. She'd do the job herself first.

Jules waved her away as she jumped up and rounded the desk. "I'm fine. Just some Braxton-Hicks contractions."

"Contractions?" Korinna yipped so high it was possible only a dog could hear. "We need to get you back."

"No, no, I'm fine. They're just false birthing pains. My OBGYN says they're normal and that they help prepare me for the real thing."

"How do you know they're not the real thing?"

Jules shrugged. "My water hasn't broken yet. Also, they come and go at odd times. Consistency is key in childbirth."

"I'm glad you can be so calm about it."

Jules smiled. "Well, I have to be really. When the time actually comes, I'm pretty certain Bas will lose his cool."

"But he's been through this once before."

"Exactly. And that didn't go at all well. I think I'm going to be in for some freaking out and increased paranoia on top of the over-protective stuff I'm already enduring. It's why I jumped at the chance to help you with this. If Bas was here, he never would have let me take a step near that portal, let alone through it." She looked down at the book in front of her. "I'm sorry. I'm enjoying myself and I should be horribly worried about Tamuel. And I am." She looked back up, her eyes – so like Tam's despite the difference in colour – met Korinna's with a plea. "I've just not had much excitement in my life, and to have the chance to do something like this is making me a little giddy and thoughtless. Will you forgive me?"

"Of course. There's nothing to forgive. I totally understand."

Jules reached out, gripped Korinna's hand, squeezed. "I knew you would. In some ways, we're very similar in how we've been hidden away and kept powerless for so long."

Korinna nodded but looked away. Jules' comparison was true, but not equal. Jules had been forced by circumstance to stay hidden and powerless; Korinna had chosen both.

But no more. She had to put all that aside if she was to make amends for what she'd done. "If you're okay, we better get back to it."

She pressed her knuckles against the feeling in her chest that was more like a whisper than ever before. Where had Tam gone that she could hardly feel him at all now? "I'm afraid he really is doing something stupid. I have to find him."

Jules went back to studying the book before her. Korinna tried to do the same, but her gaze kept going back to the woman opposite. After a moment, she blurted, "Do you want your power back?"

"Why do you ask?"

"Well ... I get the whole not being immortal thing being a big reason for wanting them back, but ... do you know what you're asking for? Just how much power you will be getting? I mean, Goddess-given power ... are you certain that's something you want the burden of?"

Jules frowned before letting out a deep sigh. "Is that how you think of your power? Like a burden?"

Korinna looked away. "I ... My power, it's not Goddess-given and—"

"Isn't it?"

Her gaze snapped back to Jules. "What do you mean? Of course it's not!"

Jules folded her hands on the desk in front of her. "Maybe I'm wrong, but I had the thought earlier that the reason why your power keeps overwhelming powerful artifacts is because it's more than any of us think it is."

"I ... no ... that's ... but my mother was the one Demeter gifted with her power. When she died, Demeter took them back and vowed never to gift them to another. And no other Goddess I know of is so free with their power – aside from Vesta. And she gave her power to one person – you."

"Your mother had you when she still had the Goddess-given power."

"But ... I ... they don't transfer to the baby. That's not how it works."

"Do you know that for a certainty?"

"I ..." Did she? "Tam didn't get the Goddess Vesta's power that

Lianna had when she was pregnant with him. Besides, I'm just a powerful witch."

"Are you? Do you know who your father was?"

She shook her head. "Persephone said that when he left, he broke my mother's heart and theirs along with it. If I asked anything more, she just said my mother couldn't bear to talk about him and so Demeter promised, and made everyone else promise, not to speak of him ever again. Seph wouldn't break her promise, not even for me." She bit her lip. "I got the sense that he died a long time ago. So he couldn't have been anyone important."

"Okay. It was just a thought. One that seemed to make sense. To me, at least. I might have only had my power for a short time, but I thought maybe I sensed something familiar in yours. Just wishful thinking though."

"Why would you wish that kind of power on me?"

"Because, if you did have it, what we're going to do the first night of Oestra would not be so rife with danger. If you had that kind of power, I know we would succeed." She swallowed hard. "I would so love to be able to live for eternity with Bastien and Tamuel and this little one." She looked down, stroking her stomach in a way that brought a lump to Korinna's throat. "It's a horrible ache in my heart to think of only having one lifetime with them."

"I ... I'm so sorry. I wish I did have Goddess-given power so I could make sure of our success."

Jules smiled sadly at her. "I know you would – even as I know it terrifies you to think of power that big. But don't put that burden on yourself along with everything else. It's bad enough you and Tamuel have to risk your lives to stop Clodia and get my magic back."

"Tamuel and I have to ... it's our mess." My mess.

"Is it? I used to think I was to blame – Clodia did all this to get my powerful magic after all. But now I know where the blame truly lies, and it's not with any of us. It's that bitch-witch who should pay. I just wish I was the one who made certain of it, not you two." She swiped at a tear running down her cheek.

"Here," Korinna said, reaching for a box of tissues on the desk, but as she did, she bumped a pile of ancient manuscripts. They teetered and began to tumble off the edge. Jules cried out, but before they could hit the floor, a gold and amber light surrounded them and they froze mid-fall. Then slowly, they lifted and piled back on the desk – in the middle this time – in a pile far neater than the one Korinna had placed them in.

"Thank you," Jules breathed. "That was quick thinking."

Korinna stared at her. "It wasn't me."

"It had to be you. It certainly couldn't be me."

"It wasn't me. I assure you." The colour had been wrong. Besides, "The control spell is in place, so my magic doesn't work unless I will it to," – as long as she didn't use blood magic of course – "and I didn't will it just then. The only answer is ..." Korinna's gaze went down to Jules' stomach.

Jules' mouth popped open on a little 'oh' of sound. Then she began to shake her head. "It can't be. Can it? The baby hasn't shown any sign of having magic before now."

"Perhaps something happened when you went through the portal. Or maybe it's just at that state in its gestation?"

Jules took in a shuddering breath as she met Korinna's gaze. "But how can she have that kind of power inside the womb? That's not usual, is it? I mean, I only know what's usual for witch-kind. Does having a child with a demi-God change things?"

Korinna shrugged helplessly. "From everything I've ever read, the earliest power usually manifests is at three to four years of age, but more usually nearing puberty, even in demi-Gods. There are some that occur earlier, but it's rare for babies to manifest magic in the womb. She must be incredibly strong."

Jules stared at her stomach. "I don't like this. If anyone finds out – they'll come after her, won't they?"

Korinna touched the other woman's shoulder. "I don't think so. She would have to be more than incredibly strong. I don't mean to be rude, but you don't have your power, so there's no way she can share in them, and her father is only a demi-God. A child with such parentage wouldn't really be of interest to the Gods."

"They were interested in Tamuel."

"Tam's case was different. Not only was his birth unusual, *he* is unusual with his two equal powers onboard – cupid and warlock. And they countered that by not training him in his warlock power." She touched Jules' stomach.

"Are you sure?" the mother-to-be said, eyes searching her face.

"I can never be completely sure about these things, but from what I've read and heard and observed over the years, I think it very unlikely any God or Goddess will be interested in your baby and her fledgling power; even if they do show themselves from now."

Jules sat down with a plop. "Thank you. I just ... I'm sorry. I panicked."

"It's understandable."

Jules nodded rapidly then gestured at the neat pile of books. "We should get back to this. You need to go save our boy and I've already taken up too much of our time with useless speculation."

They returned to their work, but even as she tried to concentrate on the grimoire in front of her, Korinna couldn't help but worry about the questions Jules had asked her. She knew so little about her mother and father and had always assumed she was just like all the other Soteira.

But what if she wasn't?

What if the reason her father had broken her mother's heart was because he turned dark? Was that why using blood magic came so easily to her?

No. It was useless speculation that wouldn't help her track down Tam and stop him doing whatever stupid thing he was currently doing. She rubbed her chest where the feel of him through the bond had become nothing but a ghost-echo. Where the Hells was he?

Jules looked up. "You okay, Korinna?"

She nodded. "Just worried about Tam." Her gaze ran around the room. She had to get to him. This was taking too long. Where the Hells was the spell of homing that he'd used?

On the other side of the room, under the lamp next to the book-shelf the Eleusinian Mysteries Grimoire was hidden in, a paper fluttered and glowed. She leaped to her feet and raced over, pulling the paper out from under the lamp. Her gaze ran over the scrawl of writing that was definitely Tam's.

"What is it?" Jules said, coming to her side.

Korinna, smiling for the first time since Tam had left, held the paper out to her and said, "You don't happen to have any eye of newt back home, do you?"

"As a matter of fact, we do." Jules took the paper and shuddered. "You have to drink this?" She shook her head. "The things we do to protect our men from themselves."

"They're worth it."

"Yes, they are. Okay, let's tidy up here and then get to it."

11

Samuel stepped into the portal, blood dripping from the freshly carved sigil on his other wrist. Wind whipped around him, threatening to pick him up and toss him into the spinning maw that surrounded the bridge. Bloody Hells. This wasn't like the last few times he'd gone through it. Persephone said it would be difficult to get the ring out of the Underworld, even with it nestled inside the small rune-covered box she'd given him, but she trusted that he'd manage it, particularly with the help of the sigil spell from the Eleusinian Mysteries Grimoire carved into his arm.

It appeared Persephone was the queen of understatement.

He held on tight to the spell in his mind, clutching the box against his chest and, putting his head down, took one difficult step after another.

The wind tightened around the box, tendrils winding around his fingers, pulling. The box slipped. "No you don't." He clasped it in both hands, holding it firmly against his chest despite the HBG's protest. "I'm sorry, but there's no choice," he said to it.

When Persephone had shown him the ring, the magic in it had lanced out as soon as he'd touched it and pierced his chest right at the spot the HBG nestled, fingers of it pulling at the gem, trying to tear it from its seat in his sternum. He'd thought he was going to pass out from the pain and the HBG's screaming in his mind. Thankfully Persephone had quickly torn the ring from his grasp and returned it to the box with its runes carved into the wood acting as a shield – if she hadn't, he might not have made it back from the Underworld alive.

Had he thanked her? He wasn't sure. It had all been a bit of a blur after that. She'd mentioned a lot of dos and don'ts which were all a bit of a muddle in his mind right now – probably something to do with the remnants of pain in his chest, the whimpering of the HBG and this bloody wind.

How long to go? He glanced up. He was almost through the swirling void that was the bridge between places; the glowing oval of the exit portal was only a few feet ahead. Bent over almost double as the wind buffeted and pulled at him, he managed to take one step, then another, then another before, with a pop, he spilled out onto the floor of the cave.

The wind reached for him, threatening to pull him back in. He drew the line of completion through the sigil, cutting the magic. The portal snapped closed behind him with a crack of wind and power that sent him to his knees.

He took in a deep breath, the box clutched hard against his chest. "I hope you're worth it," he whispered to it.

"Did you get it?" The God of Mischief stood exactly where Tamuel had left him, lounging against the rough rock wall of the cave. "So, let's look at it then."

"Um ..."

Loki pouted. "Come on, Tamuel. Fair's fair. Given I gave you the power you needed to get down there so you could ask Persephone for it, I think giving me a little looksy is the least you owe me."

Eyes narrowed, Tamuel asked, "So, if I show you the ring, I don't have to pay you back for what you gave me?"

Loki's smile widened. "Good try, but no. You still owe me for the power boost. This is just a little something extra for old-time's sake. Come on. Show me." He wiggled his fingers, palm up.

Tamuel sighed and clambered to his feet. "I can't show you. Persephone had a list of dos and don'ts. And one of the 'don'ts' she was quite firm about is that the box shouldn't be opened for anyone but Rinna. She's not certain what it will do if exposed to the world it's been kept from for so long without the control of one of her Soteira to guide it."

Loki's brows rose. "Ooh, intriguing. Makes me want to see it more." He tried to snatch the box from Tamuel's hand.

"Damn it, Loki." Tamuel darted away. "It could be dangerous."

"Is that supposed to frighten me?"

"Not frighten you. Make you see reason."

"And here I thought you knew me well."

"I do. Which is why I didn't want you involved." He shoved the box in his jacket pocket and started to make a portal.

"Not so fast," Loki said, waving his hand; the portal dissipated before it could truly form. "I want to see the ring."

"No."

"No?" The Norse God's eyes narrowed. "Remember the wordage of our bargain?"

Crap.

"I told you to be more careful about the wording."

"I was." He ran over the words he'd bound himself with. *In exchange for the power to cross between Realms in corporeal form, I Tamuel, will give Loki anything that he asks for, or do anything he asks for, at any time in the future, with the exception of giving him, or hurting, a loved one, child or friend, or doing anything I find morally execrable, including breaking the law of man or Gods, murdering or hurting anyone or giving up a child.*

"See, I covered all the bases."

"Except keeping Loki from seeing the ring before Rinna has it under control."

"How could I know that was going to be an issue?"

He was about to try to argue his case further when the air shimmered in front of him and Rinna appeared – he had no idea she could apparate like that. It was similar to something he could do when he had his cupid power.

The HBG pulsed warmly in his chest at her presence at the same time his heart skipped a beat. *"Her magical abilities are as extraordinary as I thought, even with her power bound by that spell."*

"She is extraordinary." By all the Gods and all the Realms, he loved her. Just seeing her made him feel like a thousand suns had lit inside him. He wanted nothing more than to take her in his arms and kiss her until they were both breathless. Especially given how things had been between them. This might be the last time she looked at him like that, once she found out what he'd kept from her ... and what he'd just done.

"Thank Zeus you're okay." She grabbed his face, pulled it down to her, then electrified him with a kiss full of worry and relief and love and wonder.

And passion. Passion he'd missed so much in the last few weeks.

Heat rocked through him, then lightning zipped through his veins as she moved closer, her body touching him in all the right places. He let go of his suit coat, both arms going around her, hands running up and down her strong back, pressing her to him.

She'd come to him. Maybe things were going to be all right.

For a blissful, crazy moment, as their mouths tangled and his hands held her close, closer, and he lost himself to the feel, the taste, the scent that was Rinna, he let himself believe that was true.

A wolf-whistle echoed around them.

Rinna broke away from him and spun. Loki stood there, waggling his eyebrows at them, a shit-eating grin lighting his face.

"So, I presume this is the infamous Rinna who stole my friend's heart and sanity."

"Loki?" Her expression a storm cloud, she glared up at Tamuel. "What's he doing here?"

Uh-o! "What are *you* doing here?" he countered.

"You just up and left without telling me where you were going or what you were doing, and almost from the very moment you left, I felt something here." She dug her fist into her chest between her breasts. "It wasn't good. And then you ... faded. It was horrible. I knew you were doing something stupid and dangerous and I had to come and save you from your idiot self. Jules agreed with me." She whacked him on the arm. "That's why I'm here."

His lips twitched. "I missed you too."

For a moment the storm cloud lightened, but then Loki said, "How sweet," and made a yakking noise.

She spun to face the annoying arsehole, her brows almost meeting in the middle as she glared at him. "What are you doing here? Why would you – either of you – do anything to incur Zeus' or Odin's wrath by being in the same place like this?"

Tamuel tried to signal Loki over her shoulder by shaking his head, but the God of Mischief's smile just widened as he said, "Not that I care what Zeus or Odin want, but I was doing something nice."

Rinna snorted. "Like I believe that."

Loki's eyebrows rose. "I like you."

Rinna crossed her arms. "The feeling is not reciprocated."

"Maybe it would be if you knew what I was doing."

"I doubt that."

Tamuel stood behind Rinna, waving at Loki to stop, but his friend ignored him, saying, "For your information, I was helping your love get to another Realm."

"You did what?"

"Thanks a lot, friend."

Loki flashed a wide smile.

Rinna spun back to face him, her expression thunderous. "You asked *him* for help?"

Tamuel shrugged, ignoring the hurt in her eyes. "He's my friend. Who else was I supposed to ask?"

"Me. Bastien. Grandmama. Even Eros would be better."

"Eros," Loki snorted. "He's too busy cleaning up his own pile of shit to bother helping anyone but Psyche. Also, there's no way he'd help Tamuel get back down to the Underworld again in corporeal form."

"You went back to the Underworld? Without me? Why?"

"Show her the box," Loki whispered loudly.

"Box? What box?"

Loki darted forward, grabbed Tamuel's suit coat and pulled the box from the pocket. "This box."

Rinna gasped as Tamuel shouted, "No. Don't open—"

Loki flipped open the lid and a green light flashed out, bathing the cave in its blinding glow. Every place of rock or soil the light touched began to writhe and move as flora and fauna pushed up and out of the ground, growing in front of their eyes. Tamuel clapped his hand to his chest, trying to conjure a shield spell as the fingers of power began to tear the HBG from his chest, but it was hard to concentrate through the pain and the HBG's screams.

"Tam!" Rinna threw up a powerful shield. The flare died, leaving only a slight glow behind. "Are you okay?" she asked, her hands running over his chest, the sensation helping to stop the HBG's whimpering.

"I'm fine. It's fine. Don't worry—"

His mouth dropped open as behind her, the cave filled with plants and flowers of all different hues, turning it from a barren place into a mini Garden of Eden. She turned slowly, following his gaze, and gasped.

"By Odin's balls. That's one Hells of a ring," Loki said.

12

"That's the lost ring of Triptolemus," Rinna said breathlessly as she stared at the ring in Loki's hands.

Black hair a halo of spikey curls around his head, the God looked down at the large green ring that was nestled inside the square rune-covered box. "Seems that was a bit of a furfie."

"What are you talking about?"

"It wasn't lost. It was in Persephone's hot little hands all this time," Loki said. "Fancy that."

Tamuel shot the God a 'shut-the-fuck-up' look as he said, "Triptolemus gave it to her before he disappeared."

"That makes sense," she said. "He made it to help them, after all."

"Did he now? That's not what I heard," Loki chimed in again.

She crossed her arms as she glared at him. "Really? And just what did you hear?"

He winked at her. "That's for me to know and you to find out," he sing-songed. "Wish I could be a little birdy on the wall when you finally do find out, but that's not to be my role in all this." He pouted.

"Your role? What in all the Hells are you talking about?" Tamuel asked.

"Wouldn't you like to know." He grinned in a way that made Tamuel want to punch him.

"I'm sick of this. Just give us the ring and go," Rinna said, making a grab for the box.

Loki darted to the left, holding it above his head out of her reach. More light spilled out of the ring, this time covering the ceiling of the cave. Plants grew down like stalactites forcing them all to hunch over. "Oops." He snapped the lid closed. "Let me take care of that."

He waved his hand; red-tinged power arced out like a scythe, cutting off the heads of all the flowers and plants. Leaf-litter and blossoms rained down on them.

"Oh, for the Goddess' sake," Rinna snapped, lifting her hands in an arc. The shield she'd raised around them turned flaming green-gold; the mess created by Loki's spell became ash as it hit the sphere. Then holding out her hand, she said, "Come to me." Power crackled around her, and the ring and its box disappeared from Loki's hand to appear in hers.

"Hey! That's rude," Loki complained.

"It's not yours to begin with," Rinna said. "You have no idea what to do with its power or how to manage it."

"And you do?"

"Given I am the pre-eminent scholar on powerful gems, *and* I'm a servant of Demeter and Persephone, I do. And given Tam obviously made his foolish bargain with you to travel down to the Underworld to get this from Persephone so we can use it in the battle ahead, then once again, yes, I do. And finally, given Persephone gave it to Tam, she must think I have a good chance of working it properly."

"That's a given, you silly girl. You really have no idea what you hold in your hand."

"I'm pretty sure I do," she said, looking down at the box. "Thank you for your 'help' in getting it, but now it's time we go."

"Ah-ah-ah! There's the little matter of Tamuel's debt to me."

"And that is?"

"That he will give me whatever I ask for – with certain boring provisos to safeguard his morals and family and friends, yadda yadda." He yawned and patted his mouth.

"You agreed to what?" Rinna turned to Tamuel, her expression shocked and not a little angry.

"It was the only way to get the ring from Persephone in time."

"But ... how did you know about the ring anyway? It wasn't in any of our research."

Here it was. He had to tell her the truth. Looking her right in the eye, he said, "He told me about it a few weeks ago when I went to the hermit's cave."

"He ... what? You've been sitting on this information this entire time?"

"Well," he said, waving at Loki, wishing he could as easily have waved away her hurt. "I didn't think it was a good idea to try to get it, given making a deal with Loki was really my only way to get down there. And I didn't tell you about it because I knew you wouldn't agree to how I would need to get it. You know that only the power of a God or a heavenly confluence would give me enough power to get to the Underworld right now."

"But Eros ..."

"As Loki said, he isn't in a position to help. And we had hope that other artifacts might work for us. But then they didn't, and you were so upset—"

"You made a bargain with this idiot—"

"Hey!"

"—for me?"

"I'd do anything for you, Rinna."

"I ..." She blinked rapidly and touched his cheek. Her lip wobbled. "Tam. I-I don't deserve such a sacrifice."

"What are you talking about? Of course you do." The look in her eye – Gods! He thought by getting the ring it would make things better but it seemed like he'd just made them so much worse. "Rinna, what is it?"

"I ... I—"

Loki sighed loudly. "While this is fascinating, can we get back to the matter of me calling in my chit?"

"You've seen the ring. What else do you want?" Tamuel snapped, his arm going around Rinna, hating how stiffly she held herself.

"You didn't let me see it, so that doesn't count." He tipped his head, eyes glinting. "I'd like to be in on the action."

"What? Are you insane?" Rinna spat out. "Your God-energies are all wrong. You could completely screw up everything. He can't come." She looked up at Tamuel. "You have to tell him he can't come."

He leaned down and whispered, "Let me take care of this." Then he turned and shook his head at the God. "It's okay, Rinna. If that's what Loki truly wants, I can't say no because of the terms of our bargain, although ..." He smiled at Loki. "I have to say, I am a bit surprised you of all Gods would want to go back into the Void."

"The Void?" Loki said, his cocky grin slipping.

"Oh, didn't I mention that? Yep, that's right. One of the things Persephone told me was that we can't let Clodia out of the Void. Apparently a Seer she knows saw that if she did get out, even if we defeated her, she'd cause even more havoc. So, that means we have to go into the Void to fight her. But that's not a problem for you anymore, right?"

"Um," Loki said. "I ..."

"You're not afraid of the Void, are you?" Rinna asked, somehow knowing, despite her obvious upset, to play her part beautifully.

Tamuel leaned down to whisper loudly in her ear, "Thor and his friends played a trick on him when he was younger. The upshot was he got trapped inside the Void and couldn't get out. Odin had to go and rescue him. Apparently he was screaming about the dark nothing for days, and from what I heard, still sleeps with a nightlight to keep the nasty darkness away."

"That is supposed to be a secret," Loki said, eyes blazing, face completely white.

"Perhaps you should have a word to Heimdall about that. He's surprisingly loose-lipped when you get him drunk on tequila."

"Bastard. I'm going to kill him."

"Well, good luck with that. Of course, the killing of Heimdall would have to wait until after you came with us into the Void. You're still coming, right?"

"Ah," Loki said, backing up. "On second thoughts, I'm a bit busy at the moment, so I'll have to call my chit another time. See you both later."

He disappeared so quickly, there was a little pop and a suck of air that ruffled their hair.

"Thank the Gods for that," Rinna said, pushing her locks back off her face.

"Rinna, about me not telling you about the ring—"

She waved her hand. "Forget it. We've both done things ..." She shook her head. "It doesn't matter. What does matter – is what you said true?"

"About him getting stuck in the Void? Or about Heimdall—"

"No! About going into the Void."

"Yes. Unfortunately it is."

She blanched. "But ... nothing corporeal can live in there – except Gods and Goddesses. The moment we try to enter, it will suck our souls out of our bodies and kill us."

"Not if we use the spell in the Eleusinian Mysteries Grimoire," he said, pointing at his wrist where blood still seeped from the sigil he'd carved. "It will allow us to travel through the tear in space and time and into the Void in our corporeal form and help us to get back out again."

"Are you kidding? It wasn't made for that. It was designed to help someone travel to the Hell Realms and back, not cross into a place where time and space have no meaning."

"I know. But Persephone says that with a slight modification, it could allow us to travel into the Void for a short period."

"How short?"

He couldn't meet her eyes as he said, "Ten minutes. Maybe more."

"But time means nothing in there, so ten minutes out here could be forever in there. Or no time at all."

"Maybe if you made us a chronometer each to wear, one tied into the sigil-spell so it can cross those space-time boundaries, we'd be able to judge how long we have."

She stared at him for long moments before nodding. "That could work. Although, I'd have to make modifications to the sigil spell as well."

"You know how to do that?"

"I think so. Something like this should do it." She took his wrist and drew with her fingernail an addition on either end of the sigil design then added another rune to the circle of origin.

Prickles chased over his skin as he stared at the additions she'd made. A sinking feeling – denial mixed with realisation – descended from his chest to sit heavily in his stomach. "Where did you learn that from?"

She still wouldn't look at him, and he knew – Gods-damn-it! – what she'd done.

Fuck. He knew he should have rescinded the permission for her to open and enter the portal into his secret place after Persephone made him make that stupid vow, but he just couldn't do it. How could he ask for her trust if he didn't give it in return? With a sinking sensation he said, "You used my portal spell."

Her head whipped up, eyes awash with tears and determination. "I … I didn't want to go behind your back. But you'd made that vow and … You don't understand. I needed it."

"You should have told me. I would have looked for you."

"You would have looked for a spell I could use to control my magic?" She shook her head sadly.

"You don't need a spell of control!"

"But I do."

"Why?"

"To save you!" she shouted, eyes ablaze with fervour and not a little fear. "To keep you safe! And Jules and Bas and the baby and Violetta and everyone else too."

"But … what? For the Gods' sake, why?"

"You see …" She jabbed her finger in the air between them. "This is why I didn't come to you with this. Because you don't see the faults in me. You don't see the danger of me. In me."

"Danger? That's absurd."

"Is it?"

"I know you've had some problems with your magic, but you've never hurt me or any of my family with it."

"That's just luck."

He gripped her shoulders to stop her pacing. "No, it's not. It's you. All you. You would never hurt us, which means your power would never hurt us either."

She jerked out of his grip. "I would never have hurt all the people of Pompeii and yet I did. It was not only my job to see to their protection – I cared for them! And yet I hurt them in the most horrifying of ways."

"That wasn't your fault. You know some greater power manipulated you and your magic that day. We have proof of that. We just don't know who or why – but after this, I promise, we'll look into it. You can't blame yourself."

She shook her head, eyes brimming with unshed tears. "And yet, I do blame myself because that manipulation is only a part of the story. It would never have happened if I'd had control like I should. I've had a lot of time to think about this. My power, it's too big for me or I'm too weak for it. Either way, it's why whoever was behind that manipulation chose me."

"That's not—"

"They chose me; not you, not Dianna, not any of the others. Me!" She thumped her chest, the sound echoing, dead and hollow, around them. "They chose me because they knew they could use me. Because ultimately, the control I thought I had was an illusion."

Tamuel frowned at her in consternation. "Even if that was true then, it's not true now. You held your power in check for 2,000 years and then used it as precisely as a blade in the Underworld to protect us."

"No, I didn't. I didn't mean to use it any of those times and yet it came out of me anyway. And then when I meant to use it, I almost killed the both of us."

"I don't see it that way."

"I do."

He gaped at her. Was this why she'd been pushing him away? Hells. He raked his hand through his hair. This was all his fault and he needed to fix it. He cast around for something to say but could think of nothing.

"Her power is not the same as it was before she used it up."

The HBG was right! He took a slow step towards his love. "Rinna, listen to me. Even if all of what you said is true, now is different because you don't have all your power. You gave a great chunk of it so Clodia could escape and take on your vow. So even if you couldn't control it when it was at its height, you don't have that problem now."

She stared at him, chest heaving. Then words seemed to explode out of her. "It's all back and more. The HBG said to grow my power with training and self-reflection, but it was completely unnecessary to do so. It grew of its own accord. And its stronger than ever before."

"But why is that a problem? You've changed and grown too. You're one of the strongest people I know, don't you see th—"

"I couldn't control it all those years ago and I most definitely can't control it now."

He reached out to touch her, but she jerked away from him. A sound of frustration escaped him. "Rinna."

"No, Tam. I'm right." Her gaze blazed into his. "You've seen what I've done to all the artifacts even with the control spell. My power is too much for me, and despite everything I try, it just doesn't behave like it should. It's doing things ... I don't want it to do."

His mouth popped open on an exhalation as realisation hit him. Slowly, he said, "Maybe it's supposed to behave like that."

"What do you mean?" She looked horrified.

He rushed to explain, worried about what she thought he meant. "Maybe this isn't an issue of control but the fault of the training you were given."

"But ... our training was the same as thousands of others and none of you had problems."

"But our powers aren't the same. Yours was always unique, so maybe it reacts differently to how we were taught."

A strange expression crossed her face, almost like panic, as she said, "Mine isn't that unique. Besides, everyone's powers manifest a little differently."

"I'm not explaining this right." He waved his hand as if to rub out what he'd already said. "It's like the difference between my cupid and warlock powers. They're from a different source, so they behave completely differently. I've had to learn a new path – am still learning it – to make my warlock magic work properly because it doesn't respond to the cupid way. What if learning the Soteira way was the wrong way for you because your power is actually from a different source than what you've always thought?"

She made a strange sound. "Jules said something similar."

"She did?"

Rinna nodded quickly. "She suggested maybe it was Goddess-given because of how strong it is. But that's impossible."

He stared at her. "Maybe improbable, but not impossible. What if—"

"No. It's ridiculous to even begin to think it."

"Why?"

"Because it doesn't help!" She lifted her hands then dropped them. "Even if it was true – which it isn't – we would need to know which Goddess gifted me with power so as to even begin to structure a training program to teach me how to use it. And we don't even know if that Goddess is of good or evil intent!"

"What are you talking about? Why would your power be evil?"

She made a sound of frustration. "I don't know. It's as much a probability as anything else."

"No, it isn't," he said, grasping her hands tightly and staring into her eyes, trying with everything in him to make her see what he saw. "You are good. Your power is good."

"You can't know that. Not for certain."

"I am more than certain."

"Then you are fooling yourself. I mean, look at the evidence."

"Rinna ..."

"No. I can't hold my power inside myself and make it do what I want. It keeps slipping out and doing things without any direction. I used bl—" She turned paler if that was possible, tearing her hands out of his and turning away. "I almost destroyed the faery wand because of it."

"But you didn't. You pulled back in time and we managed to deal with an entity that would normally take a coven of witches to subdue."

She shook her head. "Luck. That was luck, and I can't trust in luck. Just like I can't trust my power – Goddess-given or not. I can't trust it with the enormity of what lies before us, and I most definitely can't trust it around you. I can't risk losing you. I can't. I just can't." She spun to face him. "So don't ask me to give up the control spell. Please. Because, I'll only disappoint you."

He stared at her, taking in the desperation in her eyes – a desperation tinged with fear. He wasn't going to be able to talk her out of this – certainly not now they knew they had to enter the Void. But there was one more thing he needed to say.

Holding up his hands in the sign of peace, he slowly edged towards her. "Okay. I won't ask you to undo the control spell. But I want you to think about this: The power is yours. It is a part of you as much as your heart and your lungs and your soul. The person who you are at your core holds all life to be precious – so why would your power be destructive – Goddess-given or not?"

Her brows pressed together as his words hit. "I ..."

"Think about it. And remember what Kyria said to us when she started our training: The Eternal Well would not give you what did not belong and what you cannot control."

13

His words a maelstrom in her head, making it throb, she cast about for something to say, somewhere else to look – because she couldn't look at him with his loving, trusting eyes and his 'you are good' when she knew there was a possibility that just wasn't true.

She'd used blood magic, for Zeus' sake! And she'd almost told him. Thank Hells she'd stopped herself. She just couldn't witness his look of trust and love turn to something else. Not right now. Not with what was coming.

Her gaze landed on the box in her hands. She'd almost forgotten about it. It was the one good thing to come out of today. Persephone wouldn't have given it to him if she thought Korinna couldn't handle it. "Let's test the ring and see if our combined powers can get us home," she said quietly.

Tam nodded. "Given my portal making is far from accurate, that might be a good idea."

She held it out, but he shook his head. "Persephone said you had to wear it and command it to do what you want. I only need to hold your hand when you do." He put his hand over his chest. "But first you need to command it not to try to tear the HBG out of my chest."

"Are you sure that will work?"

"Persephone said it would. Although, maybe I'll just go stand over the other side of the cave."

She waited for him to get as far from her as he could, then took the ring out of the box. Hesitantly she put it on her hand and … oh! The feeling that raced through her. All worries and negative thoughts disappeared. It was like coming home. "This feels amazing. I think … I think it will do anything I ask it to." It felt so good, she struggled to understand why she'd been so upset only moments ago.

"Great. So quick. Tell it not to take the HBG," Tam said, his voice hoarse as he held onto his chest.

She gave the command, and instantly, Tam sighed. "That's so much better. Seems Persephone knows her stuff." He walked over to her. "Are you okay?"

"I'm … I'm fine. No, better than fine."

"I'm so sorry."

"What for?"

He gave her a strange look. "For … for keeping the ring from you? If I'd known, I would have got it weeks ago."

She touched his cheek. "All that matters is we have it now."

He frowned at her. "Is that all that matters?"

"Yes." She held out her hand. "Let's go home."

With a grateful sigh, he placed his hand in hers. "Take us home, Dorothy."

She smiled at his silliness. "Okay, Scarecrow."

As she roped in their magic to create the portal, she wondered if it would be like this for all Soteira. It was no wonder Persephone had hidden the ring from them all if so – she could imagine that to many, it would be addictive. It filled her with such a sense of peace and surety – even more so than the control spell. She couldn't wait to see what else they could do with it.

The portal ride was so smooth, it was like stepping through a doorway, and then they were standing in front of Jules and Bas.

"You found him," Jules said, running forward to give them both a hug. "Thank the Goddess you're both safe."

"It wasn't just Tam I found." She held up her hand, and together, they told Tam's parents about the ring and going into the Void.

After a very heated discussion about the necessity of doing something so dangerous, she suggested they start to train with the ring.

"Umm, don't you think there's things we need to finish talking about?" Tam asked as he pulled her aside.

"Like what?"

"Like … I mean … the effect the ring has on you for one. It's almost like I was dealing with a pod-person back in the cave when you first put it on."

"What about now?"

"You seem … better?"

"I am. It just took me by surprise and made me feel a little giddy at first. It's probably why Persephone has kept it from us all these years. But I can handle it now I know its impact. I promise."

His gaze met hers like he was digging deep inside her soul. His frown deepened but then he nodded. "Okay, but that isn't the only issue. I mean, you said back there … you think your power might be evil! I know I said I'd drop asking you about the control spell and I said I'd let you think about what I said but … I just can't let that one slide. Rinna – why would you think that?"

His words were like a bucket of icy water dashing over the warmth the ring had imbued. It made her want to run away, to hide, because she didn't want to argue with him. She couldn't tell him about the blood magic. Things were already bad enough and they just weren't going to agree on this, or anything to do with her and her magic. She looked up into his eyes and said, "Please. Could we just concentrate on this for now? Oestra is only a few days away. I just … I need … I can't …" Inexplicably, she burst into tears.

He pulled her into his arms and buried his face in her hair. "Hells, Rinna. I'm sorry. I don't mean to push. I'm just worried."

"I know," she whispered, lifting her hands to swipe her shameful tears away. "But … can we do this after Oestra?" she asked shakily. "I just don't have the energy for more now."

He pulled back, his gaze delving into hers – she wanted to look away, to hide from him any truths he might see there, but she didn't. He deserved more than a cowardly response. "Okay. After Oestra."

Her legs almost buckled with relief. "Thank you."

Over the next few days, as Bas set them tasks ranging from easy to difficult, he kept his word, but she couldn't help but notice the way he looked at her as if scared she might vanish.

She tried to repair some of the damage she'd done. She made certain to touch him as often as she used to, to smile at him and try to share their little, bantering asides, but it wasn't the same. He held her at night – gently, carefully – but made no move to make love to her; and she couldn't seem to make herself break past his reticence.

She'd wounded their bond and she had no idea how to fix it given she couldn't tell him what he wanted to know.

The only good thing was the ring. The more she wore it, the less it affected her as it first did, and even better, it did everything they asked of it with ease and no signs of burning up. Even when they practiced with Bas – they needed his power on the night as well and had to get used to the resonance of his cupid magic – it coped. Better than coped.

But what she loved most of all was when she and Tam worked together. It almost felt like it had always felt between them. With his power wrapped around hers, she felt … whole.

This is how magic should feel.

So, she made certain they did far more practice than they actually needed, pretending it was harder for her than it actually was.

They transformed objects and then themselves – she loved being a bird the most; they made a forest grow in the library and then returned it to seed; they worked on their offensive and defensive spells and deflected everything Bas threw at them with his own magic, even vanquishing the six evil entities he released from the Black Magic and Dangerous Books section to set on them; they opened portals together, ones that transported them to the exact spot they placed in their minds, no matter how near or far.

It was astonishing. Amazing. Wonderful.

And best of all, she truly believed for the first time that they could do this. It was almost … exciting. And that feeling was almost enough to help her hide from the horribleness of what she kept from him and the way she caught him looking at her when he didn't think she was watching.

He was sick with worry. And it was all her fault.

~

OESTRA-EVE DAWNED. They spent the day training together again and going over the dregs of the plan multiple times, trying to bed it down more firmly. At close to 10 pm, Jules called a break. "We need to eat and rest – all of us," she said, doing her best mum-to-arguing-child look when she pointed at Tam and Korinna. "I've made a lasagne and salad. Eat and then go try and catch some sleep."

"We will leave at 7 am Melbourne time," Bas said. "That will get us there at 11 pm Roma time so we can reset the pentacle with power for the working. We'll meet in the library at 6 am to go over the plan one more time before we leave. Sound good?"

They all nodded and headed off. Bas and Jules had already eaten, so they went to their room to shower and get some rest.

Korinna managed to choke down half a piece of lasagne under Tam's watchful eye, the green of the ring glinting on her finger a constant reminder of what lay ahead. She should take it off, but something inside her told her not to – she needed to be as bonded with it as she could. Maybe it was because the Oestra moon was already rising in this part of the world and the power of Ostara was making itself felt. It buzzed through her, fizzing in her nerves, making her feel hot and … needy.

Finally, she threw down her fork and pushed her plate away.

"Finished?" Tam asked softly.

"I'll choke on it if I eat anymore."

He pushed his plate away – he'd done little better than her. "Let's go try and get some rest." He held out his hand and she took it.

The feel of his hand, warm and tender as his fingers wrapped around hers, almost made her cry and want to jump him at the same time. But when she looked at him, he wasn't looking at her. Staring firmly at her feet, she let him lead her upstairs.

When they got to their room, she was too edgy to even consider lying down – especially lying down next to him and doing no more than spooning.

She walked to the window to stare out at the rising moon, neediness and desire for him, and only him, a pressure under her skin, tightening her lungs, pressing on her heart.

"You okay?" Tam came up behind her, not touching her with anything other than the warmth of his body as he stood centimetres – yet what seemed like a chasm – away.

"Just thinking."

"About what?"

"Stuff."

He chuckled, hand twining with hers as he pulled her around to face him. She almost whimpered at the contact. "What stuff?"

"Stuff-stuff."

"We're about to save the world stuff? Or how could I be lucky enough to be mated to this handsome ex-cupid stuff?"

Her lips twitched. "Save the world stuff, of course."

"Of course." He tugged her closer and she melted against him.

Gods! She wanted to burrow into him, to feel all of him, skin-to-skin, against all of her. She wanted his hands and lips on her, driving her crazy as only he could, before finally, finally, slipping inside of her and becoming one. Whole.

But how could she ask that of him when she had dug this chasm between them? She'd ruined everything they had. Everything they could have. But how could she tell him about the blood magic without breaking what little was left?

Maybe if you gave up the control spell, things would be better between you?

She shoved the thought aside. It was foolish, dangerous even, to consider it. Given what her magic was already doing, if she gave up her control, she'd probably end up tearing him from her in the same way she'd torn the Pompeiians' souls from their bodies.

So, she forced herself to pull back, to resist the insane need driving her to give in, to give up, to give him exactly what he wanted if only she could have a moment of bliss in his arms. Possibly for the last time.

But, stubborn cupid-warlock that he was, he wouldn't let her go. "Rinna," he breathed before capturing her mouth with his. He pulled her close, hands firm on her back, tongue diving into her mouth, twining with hers in that way that made her whimper and plead for more. She tried to hold herself back – it was a lie, wasn't it? To do this without giving herself entirely to him? – but Gods forgive her, she couldn't.

She needed him too much to ever let go, even though holding him like this hurt him more. She could feel it as she removed their clothes with her magic, the warm silk of his skin sliding erotically against hers. He wanted the kind of relationship his mum and dad had, but despite how she felt about him, she knew she could never give him that, no matter how much she wanted to. Not while the issue of the nature of her power and what she was doing with it lay between them.

But she couldn't stop. Couldn't stop herself from dragging him to the bed and losing herself in sensation as his hands and lips and tongue moved on her skin, driving her crazy. She knew she should stop him when he suckled on her nipples, making her buck and moan. She knew she should stop him when he put his hand between her legs and drove his fingers inside her. She knew she should stop him as he kissed down her torso, replacing fingers with tongue, driving her to orgasm over and over. And she knew she should definitely stop when she flipped him over and returned the favour.

But she didn't. Couldn't. Even as he bucked under her, calling her name, saying words of love and passion she knew she didn't deserve.

Finally, when he groaned that he could take no more, he flipped her over, entering her in one swift move that drove her up the bed and had her screaming his name.

When they were finished, they started the madness all over again.

And each time they did, the chasm widened and there was nothing she could do to stop it.

Except let go.

14

Just over two hours before they were due to leave, they tore themselves away from each other, showered and dressed, then headed down to the library.

Despite having only had about an hour's sleep, Korinna was oddly energised. Well, perhaps not so oddly. Ostara's energy was all around, heightening her awareness of Tam even more than usual – as evidenced by how they'd gone at it like bunnies last night.

It made her hyper aware of every breath he took, every move he made down to the slightest twitch of muscle. He looked so handsome and buff in his black fighting gear, it made her want to grab him and start the madness of the last few hours all over again.

But she couldn't. They had a job to do. Her Oestra-driven hormones would just have to take a backseat.

It was difficult though, because while it was still a few hours before midnight in Roma when the moon would be at its zenith and the magical fluctuations of Oestra reached the level they would maintain for the next three days as the moon headed towards its renewal, Oestra was in full force here in the southern hemisphere. Its influence on her system was almost overwhelming. And despite the fact she knew she shouldn't have given into it like she had, she couldn't be sorry about it. It had stopped her from thinking too much – and stopped Tam from bringing up the issues between them. Although, he'd promised to leave it until after Oestra, and he was a male who kept his words.

The chasm she'd created was still there but making love had been like an ephemeral bridge built between them, making her feel one with him at least for that time.

Once we've succeeded. I'll tell him. I promise.

"Glad you two could join us," Bas said as they entered the library.

"It doesn't look like you got any sleep," Jules commented.

"We rested," Tam said, gaze flicking to her, a secret smile just for her curving the corner of his mouth. The warmth in his eyes, the memory of what they had just shared, should have filled her heart, but instead, it just made her feel worse, because when she did tell him, she'd probably never see that smile again.

Somehow though, she managed to return his smile just before they joined the others at the table.

"I want to go over the plan one more time," Bas said, gesturing at the board they'd written it on. "But before we do, there's something we want to say to you." He looked at Jules.

"I just wanted to remind—" She winced, clutching her stomach.

"You okay?" Korinna asked.

"Fine," Jules said, waving her hand at Bas as he moved to her side. "The baby is very energetic. It just kicked me in the rib then poked me in the kidney with its elbow. So stop fussing everyone and let me say what I want to say."

Tam went to her side and took her hand. "What is it, Mum?"

She blushed delightedly. "I just wanted to remind all of us why we are fighting tonight."

"I thought the fact we're trying to stop an evil bitch-witch from coming back into this Realm with stolen powers was reason enough," Korinna said.

Jules nodded. "Yes, that's important. But we are not fighting to simply stop her. We are fighting for something far more important."

"And that is?"

"Love. Happiness. Family. Friendship. Trust. All the things that we treasure and Clodia doesn't. She thinks they are weaknesses. But they are our strengths. It's what helped me win last time. And it is what you have in abundance. You are soulmates and lovers and friends – and you have us with you, your family. All of that together is a greater power than you can possibly imagine. So when you stand in place just before midnight tonight, I want you to hold that in your hearts and minds and not lose sight of it. Trust each other and trust yourselves. Promise me that you will."

"No. Vow it," Bas said.

Tam took Korinna's hand in his and, looking deep into her eyes, said, "We can do this."

Guilt spiked through her – what Jules said was true, but with her lies, with the fact things were not quite right between her and Tam, had she damaged it in some way? Even so, she could admit to none of those fears – if the others believed they had the power of love and family and friendship and trust to wield, then surely that would be enough? Belief powered the Gods and Goddesses after all. Surely it could make up for what she lacked.

So, despite all her doubts, and because she didn't want to worry him or let him down more than she knew she already had, she nodded.

Then, as if they'd practiced, they repeated the vow together.

Three loud knocks rolling in the distance showed their vow had been heard and accepted by the Eternal Well – the seat of all Godly power and the keeper of vows, prophecies and dreams.

Jules sighed a long sound of relief. "Good. You will not forget."

Bas clapped his hands together. "Now, the plan. Once more for good measure."

Tam nodded then pointed to the board, going through the steps.

Jules stopped him when he got to letting the spirit out of the gem. "Will that be enough time?" she asked, picking up a marker and drawing a ring around the time they'd set on the plan. "The spirit has been stuck in that gem for thousands of years – it could take some time to get her out."

Korinna shook her head. "All my research on gems of power suggests that if you aim the right concentration of magic at a time of heavenly confluence – like Oestra – right at the singular flaw that all such gems have, then it should take no more than a minute or two. And that time is mostly for gathering the power you need. Once the blow is struck, it should be but a moment's work."

"The tricky bit is if we have enough power." Tam shot her a look. She stared back at him and gave an almost imperceptible shake of her head. He sighed and looked away.

"I wish Grandmama was back already," Jules said, tapping the marker against the whiteboard as she stared at the plan. "We could do with her power to help make sure you can get the spirit out of the gem."

"Have you heard anything from her?"

She shook her head. "Nothing after the cryptic message telling us not to do anything until she got back."

"Well, that's not going to happen," Korinna said. "Even if she got back right now, whatever she's found out will have to keep. We can't afford to change anything now."

"Agreed," Bas said.

"Still," Jules said, twisting the marker in her fingers. "It would make me feel better if she was here. Just in case."

Bas took Jules' hand in his and kissed her knuckles. "She's okay."

"I know. I would have felt it if she wasn't. I just wish I knew where she was and why she isn't back yet. Not to mention, we could really use her help with all this."

"We'll be fine," Korinna said, smiling encouragingly at her. "The ring has given us both a boost in our powers and our ability to channel them. With Bas' help, I'm sure it will be enough." It had to be.

"I hope you're right because I can't help and we can't bring anyone else into this. It's too dangerous."

Tam flashed her a 'see – I'm not the only one' look, but true to his word, he didn't say anything. She firmed her jaw and shook her head, hating the look her denial put in his eyes.

Tam sighed and then said to Jules, "Rinna's right. We'll be fine."

"I agree. Okay, so, we break the spirit out of the gem," Bas said, returning their attention to the plan. "Who is going to take the broken pieces of the gem?"

Korinna put up her hand. "I will."

"Good. What comes next?"

They went through the rest of the plan until they came to the last point. "We know what we have to do in the Void, just not how to accomplish it."

They all looked at the document pinned to the board; the one Jules had found and translated about the nature of Voids – the only information they had. "Knowing this will have to be enough," Korinna said.

Tam took her hand and squeezed. "We'll figure it out."

"Yes, we will."

Jules winced again. "Don't worry," she said hurriedly before any of them could fuss. "Just a Braxton-Hicks. I'll be fine."

"Here," Bas said, starting to massage her back. "Is that better?"

She sighed. "The baby likes that. So do I."

"Perhaps you should stay here," he said softly.

She whipped around to face him – moving surprisingly fast for a woman about a month away from giving birth. "Not a chance. You need me to help release the HBG spirit."

"Maybe I could—"

"No. The gem is activated by female touch or the touch of someone aligned with Vesta, so either Korinna, Tam or I have to be the one holding it just before the power strikes. And given all of you must concentrate on the spell, I'm the only one free to do so. Besides, I have to be there so Tam and Korinna can channel my power into me when they get out of the Void. From everything Korinna has told us about gem-lore, the ring can only hold Goddess-given power for so long. Not to mention, portal travel could destabilise it faster."

"She's right," Korinna said softly, wishing it wasn't so – Jules did look very pale and tired.

Before anyone could argue further, the chronometer on the wall began to chime.

"It's time," Tam said, smiling at her once more, forgiveness and understanding in his eyes. How long that would last after he found out she'd used blood magic, she didn't know, but right now, she couldn't make herself care – she'd take what she could get for as much time as she could have it.

The others followed them over to the clear space between the kitchen and the study area.

"You ready?" he asked.

They all nodded.

Linking their magic through the ring, they opened a portal.

"After you," Tam said to Bas and Jules.

Bas put his arm around his soulmate and they stepped into the portal and vanished.

"I love you," Tam said.

With the wind of the portal on her face, blowing her hair back, Korinna said, "I love you too," then stepped through the portal with him.

15

They arrived and immediately set about preparing the pentacle, drawing power from the rising of Ostara above and the ley lines below, and funnelling them into it. It was ancient – it had first been drawn by Clodia 2,000 years before – but it had been rejuvenated last year when she'd tried to use it again, so, even though it was a bit sluggish to begin with, it eventually began to glow as it should.

"*One task completed,*" the HBG said.

The chronometer buzzed on Tamuel's arm. He glanced down at it, even though he didn't need to. He was hyper-aware of exactly what time it was.

He wished he hadn't promised Rinna not to press her about the control spell or why she thought her power might be evil. It wasn't something that should lay between them before going into the Void. But he had promised and so he kept silent, hoping that if they got through this … no, not if, *when* they got through this, they would finally be able to talk and he could find some way of showing her just how wrong she was to believe such a preposterous thing. And then they could heal what was broken between them.

Not that he blamed her reticence to trust him with her worries. He hadn't been truthful with her either. But after this night was over, that would stop. Jules had said in her speech to them that love and trust were powers of their own and he knew it to be true; he'd had them both with Rinna before he'd kept the secret of the ring from her, forcing her to use a control spell on her magic and making her think for some reason she might be evil.

He would make her listen to him and trust him again if it was the last thing he did.

He looked over at her now. She stood there, working magic into the pentacle, resolute and stalwart, wearing her black fighting gear, hair tied back in a tight bun that accentuated the angles of her cheekbones, brow and jaw. Just looking at her made him feel settled. Despite the … distance? disharmony? … between them, he knew that together, they could face anything.

She looked up as he joined her, pale face shining in the moonlight. "Ready?"

"I trust you, Rinna. With my life. As do we all." The expression of pain and devastation that crossed her face was like a knife to his heart. "I didn't mean to hurt you by saying that."

"I know," she said, sucking in a shaky breath. "It's just, I didn't expect …" She took another, steadier breath. "I love you too. I trust you with my life too."

She leaned up and kissed him with a need that touched him to his soul. He went to wrap his arms around her, pull her tighter, show him her need was mirrored in him.

"Activate the sigils, Tamuel," Bas said.

He wanted to tell his father to go to Hells, but Rinna pulled back, smiling slightly. "After."

"Yes, after."

She held her arm out and looked at him expectantly. "Do the honours."

Carefully, he carved the sigils into her arm, blood dripping over her pale skin, dark and thick, tainting the air with a copper tang; if he looked with his magic, he knew he'd see it glowing with the power of both her life-force and her magic – both beautiful and powerful and good. There was absolutely nothing evil about her or it – didn't she see that?

She didn't flinch once as he carved the design, with the changes Persephone had told him to make, into her flesh. When he turned to do his own, she grimaced.

Gods in all the heavens, how could she feel his pain more than her own?

Once he was done carving the sigil into his arm, he handed Bas the ceremonial knife and turned back to Rinna. "This won't hurt, but it will feel strange."

She simply nodded.

He took her arm and, pressing his fingers on the three points of congruence on the design, whispered the words that had been forbidden thousands of years before, but that he'd already used twice in the last six months. Three was the magic number, surely? Maybe the three in this would help to set things to right between them because it was about to bind them even more closely than they already were.

Korinna's body wavered for a few seconds, becoming almost like heat-haze on the horizon, before returning to normal.

"It itches," she said, rubbing just above the sigil, the green of Trip-tolemus' ring glowing in the light of the full moon that was almost at its zenith; the blood dripping across her skin looked like dark rubies.

"It does." He repeated the sequence for himself, the strange crawling sensation running over his skin and then sinking deep inside, anchoring his soul completely to his flesh and forging soul and body together in a way they usually weren't, making it so places like the Underworld – and hopefully the Void – couldn't make the distinc-tion between the corporeal and the spirit. He thought he was used to the sensation by now, but it was different this time. Of course it was – it had turned their bond into an almost-visible thing between them, thick and pulsing, joining them more tightly for their journey through the Void.

Jules gasped. "Together you're stronger."

"Yes." He knew they were, but did Rinna believe that? He could see from her expression she longed for it to be true but doubted it. Because she doubted herself or doubted him? He wished again he'd not made that promise but it was too late now.

The chronometer on his wrist buzzed again, signalling the next part of their plan was due to start. He followed Rinna to join Bas and Jules at the head point of the pentacle.

"This is it?" she asked when she got there, reaching out with her hand to push at the air.

Bas nodded. "This is where Clodia stood – twice now – in an effort to steal power that wasn't meant for her."

"So this should be where she exits the Void." She sucked in a breath, glancing at him briefly. "Can you feel that? It's already thinning. We don't have long."

He didn't need to touch it to know what she was talking about – he could feel the power growing there, responding to the heavenly forces as Ostara rose to prominence. Even so, he reached out, fingers tingling as he touched the place Jules had torn open just over a year ago, and with help from him and Bas, love for her family filling her, had thrust Clodia into the Void before trapping her in there for good.

Well, at the time they'd thought it was for good. Just as they'd thought they'd never have to open it again.

But here they were, about to do just that.

If you do not want something to exit, make certain to close it quickly, or better yet, do not open the Void.

The words from the grimoire Jules had found rang through his mind. He shook them away before the doubt in them could take hold and looked over at his soulmate.

She met his gaze, and as if she could feel what he needed, smiled.

"It's time," she said.

Pushing all his worries aside, he placed his hand over the spot where the HBG nestled in his chest – it had been suspiciously quiet since he and Rinna had started their Oestra-fuelled love-making fest last night – and intoned the counter-spell to the one he'd used to place it there.

He grunted at the strange sensation as the gem rose out of his chest and almost leaped into his hand – eager to get this done, obviously. He didn't blame her. He'd be eager too if he'd been locked up for thousands of years and used like she had.

Jules held her hand out for the gem. He hesitated. This was the part of the plan he really didn't like – and given most of the plan was insane, that was saying something.

She wiggled her fingers. "Hand it over."

"Are you sure about this?" Bas said, echoing Tam's worries. "I'm worried you won't be able to get out of the way in time."

She gave him an eviscerating look. "I know I'm as big as a whale, but I can still move fine." She glanced at Rinna and smiled. "Also, I trust Rinna not to miss."

Just before Tam let go, he sent a thought to the gem that had lived close to his heart for the last six months, *See you soon.*

"Thank you."

All sense of the gem in his mind disappeared the moment he released it into Jules' hand. He rubbed his chest where it had so recently been seated, frowning deeply as he watched his mother walk to the centre of the pentacle.

"You okay?" Rinna whispered as she leaned into him, her arm twining with his – maybe their loving last night had bridged the gap more than he'd thought. "Tam?"

He realised he hadn't answered her. "I'm fine. It just feels strange now that she's gone."

She leaned up and kissed his cheek. "Let's set her free."

16

He closed his fingers around hers, making sure to touch the ring as he did. Bas came to stand behind them and placed a hand on his shoulder, the other on Rinna's. Power tingled through him as his father opened himself to them. Then Rinna took that power, gathered his too, and channelled both, along with hers, into the ring.

The moon, full and glowing more brightly than it normally did, rose above them, close to the zenith. Magic gathered around them as nature responded to the rising of Ostara, Goddess of the coming Spring, of dawn and light, of birth and rebirth and fecundity. Within the pentacle, magic coalesced, starting as sparks of light that danced around until it gained form – a hare with an egg in one hand and a sheath of wheat in the other. His fingers tightened around Rinna, her touch a flame inside him as the magic fuelled the need he had for her.

More sparks of light danced and coalesced into a proliferation of hares, circling around Jules, drawing closer and closer to her. Jules stood in the midst of the magic, one hand on her stomach, the other holding the HBG, her eyes wide, delighted.

"What's happening?" she called.

"They're responding to your pregnancy," Rinna said.

"We should get her out of there," Bas said.

"No," Rinna said sharply before he could move. "They won't hurt her. They love her. They'll protect her. And her presence is bringing Ostara's magic into the pentacle, making it easier to use. She has to be there. It's meant to be. Hearth and home. Family and friend. The fire of eternal love to lift them all."

Tam glanced at her – her voice echoed through the space, her eyes glowing with a strange green light. And her expression – it was beatific. How could she think herself evil?

"It's okay, Dad. Korinna speaks the truth." He had no idea how he knew that, but he did. He felt it in the heart of him.

But before he could process it further, Rinna lifted the hand he held and said, "Come."

The magic-filled hares stopped capering around Jules and propelled themselves across the pentacle towards them. He expected the magic of Oestra, the power of Ostara, to fully enter them via the ring, but instead, it whirled around them, drawing closer, until, on the third time around, the hares leaped into their outstretched hands.

He gasped as the power hit them, surprised they weren't flung back by it. Bas grunted as some of the power leached into him.

"To me," Rinna said calmly, and the power returned in full to them. Maybe she was right about the control spell after all – because everything was clicking into place with an ease he hadn't imagined.

The magic swirled through them both, twining around their chests, their arms, their faces. The scent of it was a field full of flowers in spring; the taste of it was water from a mountain stream; and the feel of it … well, that wasn't anything he'd ever felt before. It fizzed and burbled like water through rapids but at the same time was as soft and soothing as a feather brushed over his skin.

"It's incredible," he said.

Rinna simply grunted.

He glanced at her – her face was drawn, lips tight and slightly blue, her jaw clenched. And her eyes – they were a fire of green and gold and orange and pink and the most astonishing blue; the colours of the greenest dew-tipped grass glowing in the dawn beside a crystal glacial lake.

It was astonishing, and yet, in that fire, he saw licks of pain. He'd been stupid to be fooled by how quickly she'd called the magic; stupid to think that maybe the control spell was a good thing. It wasn't. Fuck. He really should have made her see reason and not hampered himself with a stupid promise. "Rinna?"

"I'm okay," she gritted out.

He clenched his teeth at the sight of her pain. Would it really break his promise if he mentioned letting go of the control spell? The promise had been more about not asking why she thought herself evil – a main reason she thought she needed the spell. He hadn't specifically promised not to bring up her letting go of it again. Splitting hairs, but beggars couldn't be choosers and he just couldn't let this go. Not now. Not in the face of such agony. "You have to let go."

"No. Almost … there."

He wanted to yell at her, to shake her for being so stubborn, but could do nothing but stand there as she pulled the power in and in and in to her until he could barely feel its effects anymore.

"Rinna," he yelled, worried she was about to explode with the enormity of it all.

She grunted then gritted out, "Now!"

Somehow, Jules heard her, because she threw the HeartsBlood Gem into the air just as Rinna released all the power she'd collected and aimed it a place three metres above Jules' head.

"Run!" Bas yelled – not that he needed to, Jules was already running for the edges of the pentacle.

She got there just in time.

The power hit the gem as it reached the peak of its ascent. There was a loud, sharp clap and an explosion of light so bright he had to fling his free arm up to cover his eyes. A sound, high pitched and achingly beautiful, followed the thunderous clap and despite the brightness of the light, he couldn't help but peer over his arm to see its source.

The blood-coloured gem had split into two pieces above the

middle of the pentacle, a ghostly apparition rising from it – although, she was unlike any ghost he'd seen before.

Rather than a pale imitation of what she must have once been, she shone with green and blue and all the colours of the dawn. She was like light after passing through a prism. "Beautiful."

"Yes," Rinna breathed out beside him. "She is."

At the sound of their voices, the spirit that had been trapped in the HeartsBlood Gem for millennia, looked down at them.

Horror. Pain. Suffering. All of them in her eyes.

He would have cried out as the emotions stabbed through him, but then she smiled. "Tamuel. Korinna. Bastien. Julianna. Thank you. You have saved me where none have ever tried before."

She floated down to them, the two halves of the gem coming with her. She hissed at them as they hovered in front of her, her face contorting with fear and rage. "Get them away from me. They try to suck me back in."

Jules moved from where she'd stood transfixed on the other side of the pentacle, and plucked them from the air, holding a heart-shaped half in each hand. "Will this close again when you capture Clodia?"

"It will," the spirit said. "It's as angry with her as I am for what she tried to do with us. It longs to gobble her up."

Jules looked up at her. "Is it talking to you?"

The spirit shook her head. "I can feel it." She thumped her chest. "Here." Touched her head. "And here. Even though I am separate from it now, it appears I am still linked. Hopefully, after what we do tonight, I will be able to escape from the prison of it forever."

"For your sake alone, I hope that's true," Rinna said, letting go of Tam's hand to take the two halves from Jules. She tucked them inside her tunic pocket then looked down at her chronometer. "Two minutes." She swallowed hard. "I need to replenish myself. That took more than I thought it would."

"Undo the control spell," Tam said against her ear so the others wouldn't hear – he couldn't give up trying on this one thing at least.

As Rinna began to shake her head, the spirit floated close and said softly, "Tamuel is right, Korinna. You need to access your power in full to do what we must inside the Void."

Rinna's gaze darted between them, then she slowly shook her head.

"Please, Rinna. Trust me."

A look of hurt in her eyes so deep, he wanted to take back his words, she said, "I do trust you. But I don't trust my power. Please, stop asking me to do this."

"Don't you remember what Mum said? About trust? We made a vow."

"And I will keep that vow. I trust my power as long as it is contained inside the spell."

"Damn it, Rinna. Please. I felt how bad that was for you just then. Against Clodia it will be even worse."

She turned on him, eyes flaring. "I don't want to talk about this anymore, okay? I said no and I meant it. Let's move on." She made a hissing noise. "I'm wasting time. I need to gather more power so we can open the Void."

Before he could stop her, she moved to the middle of the pentacle and called the power of Ostara through Oestra to her again. Bursts of magic poured out of the earth and pranced around her in hare-form until she drew it inside herself.

Inside his mind he heard very faintly, *She will see. She will do what must be done. Blood calls to blood. Like calls to like. Soul calls to soul.*

He turned to look at the spirit. "You can still mind-speak to me?" he asked softly.

"What? No. We are no longer linked. Why? Did you hear something?"

"I did."

"Maybe Ostara spoke to you."

"I doubt that."

"Why?"

"I'm hardly to her usual taste." She tipped her head on the side. "I'm male," he said, gesturing at himself. "Ostara bestows more of her light on the feminine than the masculine."

"Ostara's dawn light can shine on all." Her eyes glowed brighter for a moment before fading to a more normal hue.

He glanced at Rinna. "Why can't I make her see?" About the control spell. About the goodness of her magic.

The spirit came to hover in front of him. "She will see in time."

"Will she?"

"Yes. What is certain is that right now, she will not listen to you on this or anything else to do with that spell and how she got it. I know this as well as I know my name."

He frowned. "What is your name by the way? Or can you still not tell me? It just seems wrong to keep calling you HBG spirit."

"Yes, it is no longer appropriate given I am not locked to the HeartsBlood Gem anymore."

"So what is your name?" Korinna asked, joining them.

The spirit stared at Korinna for a long moment before looking down at the space under their feet. "You can call me Ilia."

"Is that not your name?"

She sighed. "My name … it brought so much pain for so long. I do not wish anyone to call me by it any longer. Besides, uttering it might bring the unwanted attention of certain Gods."

"Who did you anger?"

Her jaw squared as she said, "I did nothing. It was they who saw a threat because of a prophecy based on the sons I bore. And because of it, I was cursed into that gem and caged for thousands of years, forced to the bidding of worthy and unworthy alike. Forgive me if I do not wish for that to happen ever again."

Korinna blanched. "You were locked in that gem because of a prophecy?" She glanced at Tam then back. "What prophecy? Who spoke it?"

"I do not know. All I know is that when it was heard, my life ended."

"I am so sorry."

Her lips twisted. "You helped when so many others didn't. For that, you have my eternal gratitude."

"I'm sorry I cannot give you your life back."

"You freed me and gave me the right to choose for myself once more, regardless of the form I might now be in. That's more than I thought to have again."

"So, breaking you out of the gem broke the curse?"

"It did. In part. I am here to take care of the other part. And to avenge what was done to me."

"Are you saying Clodia was part of what was done to you?"

"No. But she discovered the truth of who I was and what happened and she could have used her position and the power she'd leeched from Julianna to free me, but instead, like those who caged me, she chose to use me for her gain. Such a person does not belong in the world. I vowed many years ago that when I was free, I would see to it that anyone who sought power as she did would suffer in the same vein I suffered. I mean to see the completion of that vow begin today."

"Is that why you wanted to help us?"

She looked back at them. "Yes. She and others like her must pay."

"I won't argue with that," Tam said.

She turned quickly to face the place where they would tear open the Void. "It is almost time." Her ghostly voice carried across the pentacle, echoing off the ruins that surrounded them.

"I just want to take in a little more power," Rinna said, taking a small step away.

He wanted to tell her not to, but she was right. They needed as much power as they could get. So he forced himself to stand still as she gritted her teeth and pulled more and more power into her, pushing it into the ring. As she did, it glowed through her skin and eyes, pouring out between the strands of her hair, making it look like dawn-touched night. The ring glowed so brightly now, it was near to blinding – although the colour was no longer deepest emerald, but a green so light it almost looked golden-white.

When he thought she could take no more, she turned to him and held out her hand. He twined his fingers with hers and sucked in a breath as she filled him with power too.

Ye Gods. It was pain and pleasure entwined.

"Ilia, come," she gasped.

The spirit joined them, putting its ghostly hand over theirs, her index finger slipping through theirs to touch the ring. The moment she did, Oestra magic filled her, sparkling like light inside a diamond.

The chronometer alarm buzzed. Taking a deep breath, Rinna carved runes into the sigil to tie it to the chronometer. It sparked and chimed, signalling it worked.

Without saying a word, she and the spirit flung their combined hands out and shoved all the magic inside them to the point of the pentacle where time and space were already thinned from the last Void opening.

Tam groaned as the power burned through him, through their entwined hands, through the ring and at the rift-point.

A tear appeared, light spilling into it, making it seem like it was lit from within, but then, as the tear widened, they could see the swirling dull grey that was the Void where nothing of true light or life could live.

"It's working," Jules shouted.

He could barely hear her above the shrieking wind of the rift tearing open, wider, wider, until it was big enough for them to step through.

"Ready?" Rinna shouted at him.

"Always," he shouted back.

"Me too," Ilia said. "Let's get this bitch."

He heard Rinna's snort through the bond more than with his ears, the shrieking was so loud, but it made him smile. Then together, they walked towards the tear they'd made.

He lifted his foot to step inside and stumbled as something shot out of the Void.

Jules screamed, Bas' shout of horror following close on its heels.

Out of the corner of his eye, he saw Violetta step out of a portal just outside the pentacle, her hand raised, the other hand clutching a gem hanging between her breasts. Magic shot out of her hand, shoving the dark cloud that had escaped to the side. Her voice reached him somehow. "Jules, get away. It's going to—"

He didn't hear the rest. They were sucked inside.

17

Grey surrounded them in the nothing that was the Void. A nothing so profound, it stole her breath, her reason, her soul.

And her sight. She was blind. She was deaf. She felt nothing. She *was* nothing. Less than nothing. She was—

"Don't let it in. Fight it, Korinna."

Ilia's voice sounded in her head. Or next to her head? She wasn't sure. Nothing sounded like it should. Nothing looked like it should. Or felt like it should.

Tam's hand squeezed hers and she clicked into place.

She looked up at him. He was pale and grey-looking – as if seen through mist – but he was there. And so was she. And they weren't nothing. They were something. More than something. They were everything. Even with what she held between them, they were one. Whole. The power of Oestra last night had shown her that truth.

"Okay?" he asked, voice echoing and distant.

"Yes." Her voice an echoing husk. "I just lost myself for a moment."

"I know what you mean. This place ..." He gestured around him with his free hand. "It's so vast and yet feels like it's collapsing in on me at the same time."

She sucked in a desperate breath. "That's exactly it."

"We need to get ready," the spirit said. "And we need to block the exit. We can't let anything else escape from here."

"Gods, that's right. Did it attack Jules? I heard her scream. We have to go back and see." Tam turned, but Korinna tugged his hand, stopping him.

"No. Violetta was fighting it. Besides, we can't go back. We have to finish what we came here to do. We won't get a second chance."

He looked torn, but finally, he nodded. "I just hope she's alright."

"I am certain Bastien and Violetta have it in hand," Ilia said. The spirit's head jerked around and she took a long sniff of the air. "She's coming. Be ready."

There was nothing to see – everything was grey and foggy within a few feet of where they stood – but she too could feel it. A sense of something rushing towards them.

"How do you know it's her?"

"She used me for years. I know her feel and her scent. It's definitely her." She looked at Tam, taking a longer sniff. "I can smell your mother's power. It's with her, though not in her."

"That's one good thing. At least we won't have to fight against Jules' power," Korinna said.

"She couldn't have use of it until she exited the Void anyway. She cannot take Vesta's magic fully into herself until she is in the Earthly Realm because that is the heart and seat of that power. It will not activate until she is standing on your Earth."

"You seem to know a lot more about the Void than you told Tam," Korinna said.

"To speak of forbidden things is to bring attention where it is not wanted." She pointed behind her. "Out there, there is much I cannot say. In here, there is no one to hear but you."

"I wish I had more time to question you on what you have learned."

The feeling of something rushing towards them grew suddenly stronger. "I too wish for that, but we do not have time," Ilia said. "Gather your power. She is here. We cannot let her through."

Wind whipped around them, bringing with it a foul stench that made Korinna want to vomit. And with the stench, a sound like tens of thousands of voices screaming.

"What is that sound?" Tam said, putting his hand to his ear.

"Is it the Pompeiian souls?"

"She took on your vow," Ilia answered. "So it is possible that when she was returned to this place, the souls were thrust upon her so she would be able to complete the vow."

"Gods! They sound tortured. How can she stand it?" Tears in her eyes, Korinna wanted to put her hands to her ears to shut out the sound. But she didn't. She had done this to them, so she could bear their pain.

"I don't think she cares."

Tam gripped her hand tighter. "We will send them to Elysium soon."

"Yes, we will."

Clodia suddenly appeared before them, her face lighting with maniacal glee as she saw them. "Tamuel and Korinna! It had to be you that opened the tear early. Thank you for being too stupid for words and doing half my job for me. Now, step aside, or would you like me to drain you again?"

"I wouldn't be so gleeful if I were you," Ilia said. "Now!"

Her hands gripped around theirs – touch ghostly but firm – and her power surged into the ring. Korinna didn't even hesitate – she lifted their hands and pushed a stream of power right at Clodia, hitting her in the chest.

The witch screamed as she disappeared in a flare of bright light. When the light dissipated, she was no longer in sight.

"Where's she gone? It can't have been that easy," Tam said, glancing around.

"She's still here," Ilia said. "Watch out!"

Tamuel pushed his power into the ring and raised a shield just in time. The witch flew at them from the side, magic surging from her hands like black lightning. It hit the shield and sparks flew off it to be swallowed in the grey.

Clodia screamed in frustration and bombarded the shield with more black lightning so that it cascaded over its circumference, trying to find a way through. He didn't know how much longer he could hold against her bombardment, but then Rinna hit her with another blast of power that somehow went through his shield – maybe because it was the same kind of energy or from the same source of power. He didn't know, but it worked, forcing Clodia to defend rather than attack.

As Rinna fought Clodia with wave after wave of power garnered from Ilia and Ostara, he worked seamlessly alongside her, using the ring to channel and intensify their magics. He held the shield firm against the glancing blows Clodia managed to get through, and against the screaming soul-wind. And Rinna ... she fought like he'd never seen her fight before. She was magnificent as she brought up one spell after another – most of them the ones he'd taught her from the Eleusinian Mysteries Grimoire – keeping Clodia at bay, pushing her back. Kyria, their Amazonian trainer, would be proud.

Even so, as she fought, the toll began to show, the strain written on her face. He wished he could help, but all his attention went into keeping the shield up, protecting them not only from Clodia's strikes, but from the shrieking souls.

They were so loud now and getting stronger as they scratched and scraped at the edges of the shield closest to Rinna, trying to get to his love. Did they blame her or see her as their salvation? He couldn't take the risk and let them through to find out.

"How are we supposed to take them with us if they are fighting us too?" he yelled over the noise at Ilia.

She didn't answer, so he turned his head to look at her. By the Gods, how long could she last with Rinna pulling on her power like that? The prismatic colours that had been so bright out of the Void were now fainter and less distinct. "Are you okay?"

She nodded. "I will last, but we have to finish this fast. Too much time—"

The chronometer on his wrist began to buzz, signalling that the sigil spell was fast running out of juice. If they didn't get out of here soon, their souls would be ripped from them and they'd be as lost in the Void as the Pompeii spirits had been all these years.

"Rinna! You have to finish this."

Turning her head slightly, she spoke through gritted teeth. "I'm giving it all I've got. But she's too strong."

"She shouldn't be. She's not using either of our powers and she hasn't got my mother's magic either – you heard what Ilia said about that. Her power alone isn't enough to fight ours combined."

"I know it shouldn't be, but it is." Rinna's mouth pulled back in a grimace as she shot another bolt of power at Clodia, connecting a mighty blast with the black lightning the evil witch had just let loose. She shook, as if the magic had hit her, and stumbled, the green-gold light in the ring fluttering.

"Rinna!"

He wanted to help but had to keep the shield strong. Even as he thought it, the shield fluttered nearest Rinna. Holy Hells! The spirits bashed away at it, harder and harder. It was all he could do to tighten his control and push as much as he could of the power left to him into the shield nearest her.

Rinna trembled violently, her hands shaking so badly her spells went wide.

"Here, take this," Ilia yelled.

Suddenly golden light hit Rinna from behind and she snapped upright, gasping, but to her credit, didn't skip a beat. She pulled the power down through herself, twining it with hers and Ilia's power and what little Tam could still spare, then pushed it through the ring, but it wasn't quite enough.

"Ilia, she needs more."

Ilia gritted her teeth and cried out in pain, but then lit up like the morning dawn. "There. Use that. But hurry. It will not last for much longer."

"Why? Where are you pulling it from?"

She jerked her head back through the tear. "Ostara rises. And with her comes the dawn of a new life."

His eyes widened in horror. "Jules! The baby? Jules is having the baby?" She nodded. "And you're using the power of its birth?"

"She gives it freely. I would not take without asking."

Holy mother in all the Heavens. "Please, don't hurt my mother or the baby."

"Do not worry. She's incredibly strong. Stronger than she should be."

"She'll be even stronger when we get her power back to her."

"I wasn't talking about your mother."

Just then, Rinna shouted a spell – one that was horribly familiar. He'd only found half of it in the Eleusinian Mysteries Grimoire, but she'd found the entire thing.

He'd complained about all the incomplete spells to Persephone when he'd seen her in the Underworld; she'd said the only way the entirety of it could be opened was with a combination of a certain magic and blood – magic and blood with direct ties to its creator, Triptolemus.

He gasped.

That could only mean one thing.

He glanced at the ring on Korinna's hand, glowing with the power of the supposedly lesser God that had created it, a God who had lived in service to Demeter and Persephone and had created the Mysteries for them.

But had he?

No. He didn't think so now. Because, if only his magic and his blood – or magic and blood related to his – could fully open it, then he had created it for himself.

And his progeny.

To what end, he didn't know. But by all accounts, Triptolemus had been beloved by everyone; a lesser God who gave everything he was to better the lot of those around him, and who valued life and nature above all things.

The lesser God's blood, his magic, it ran in Rinna.

He was so stupid not to have seen it before. It explained so much about why she was able to work the ring so well.

It was meant to be her ring.

But even with the ring, she still struggled. Maybe, like the grimoire, it was meant to be accessed fully with her magic *and* her blood.

A barrage of black lightning slipped under Rinna's defensive spell and hit the shield with a massive crack. The shield shuddered and fine fault-lines began to show in its surface. "Rinna. I can't hold this for much longer."

"More power. I need more power."

Ilia nodded and bore down – Tamuel could swear he saw a faint dawn-coloured thread span from her and through the tear. It lit up and pulsed and power shot through them all. Rinna steadied once more, the ring's light strengthening. She threw another round of attacking spells – he couldn't remember them learning all those, nor some of the defensive spells she'd used to force Clodia's attacks aside. Was it instinct or something else? Something deep inside her that, despite herself, was slipping out.

Gods, he hoped so, because he was afraid that unless she did let all her power out, they weren't getting out of this alive. Ilia was almost translucent, her touch like the whisper of a cobweb. He was afraid she wasn't going to last much longer doing what she was doing. And he certainly was running out of juice.

So was Rinna. He could see it in the blue ringing her lips and the red around her eyes, the sweat dripping down her face. It was taking everything for her to just keep up with Clodia, let alone vanquish her.

And the evil witch herself – somehow, she seemed as strong as she'd been when she first came shrieking towards them out of the Void-grey.

They needed more power. And the only place they could get it from was buried deep inside Rinna. She had to let it out. Now.

"Rinna, we're losing. You have to let go of your control spell and use all your power. Now!"

She turned her head, eyes desperate and full of pain as they met his. "I can't."

"But you have to. Ilia is using birth power from Jules and Ostara combined, but she can't maintain the link for long. We're about to run out of the boost."

She shook her head. "You don't understand. I've already tried. I can't. The spell broke under the pressure of all the magic I've been using a few minutes ago. But still, my full power won't come."

"What do you mean it won't come?"

A tear of blood dripped from the corner of her eye. "I don't know. It's there, but it won't do what I want. I've damaged it. Or my link to it. I don't know what to do. I'm so sorry. I should have listened. I should have done what you asked." She cried out as Clodia sent another barrage that beat back Rinna's defensive spell until it hit the shield, causing more cracks. "Tam! I don't know what to do. We're going to lose."

"Not if you use your blood."

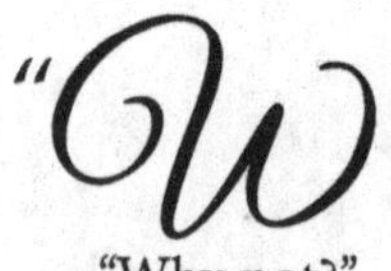

hat?" Why was he asking her to use blood magic? "I can't use blood magic!"

"Why not?"

"Because it's evil."

"No, it's not. It's life. It's love. Your blood will save us all."

"Are you insane?"

"No, I'm right. Use your blood, Rinna. It's the only way."

Tam stared at her as the shield cracked around them and Ilia slumped behind them, almost completely drained. The spirit had given her all, as had Tam – he was almost as pale as Ilia and lines of exhaustion dragged at his handsome face. They barely had anything more to give. She was the only one with an untapped source of magic. But because she'd been so afraid of it, of herself, she'd kept it trapped, beaten down, for so long, and now she needed to use it, wanted to use it, it wouldn't come to her call.

And Tam thought she could access it with her blood? Why? Why would he even think that? And what did he mean her blood would save them all?

Clodia sent another barrage at them and she managed just in time to throw up a repulsing spell, sending the power skittering into the grey of the Void.

"Rinna, you have to use your blood. Now."

"I can't, Tam. You don't know what you're asking."

"Of course I do. You opened the grimoire with your blood, didn't you?"

He knew? He knew. How did he know? Hells.

"And I saw you use it when we fought back the entity – it's what truly powered the wand. I just didn't put two and two together until now."

Gods – he'd known all this time? How was it he looked at her with anything close to love? She wanted to ask him, but nearly every shred of her energy went into fighting back Clodia's attacks, the evil witch strengthening as she weakened.

"It's why, isn't it? Why you think your power is evil? Because you used blood magic?"

"It is evil," she managed to gasp.

"Was it evil when I used this?" he held up his arm, showing the sigil that had allowed them to be here ... using magic powered by blood.

For a second, her mind blanked. How had she not thought of that before? Tam had used blood magic. Not once, but three times now – and he wasn't evil. His magic wasn't evil. Could it be ...?

Clodia's cackling and a fresh attack drowned out what Tam was yelling at her. Tapping into every ounce of what she had left, she managed to hold back the onslaught, only catching the end of what Tam was shouting.

"... Triptolemus. He used his blood as a key. With the grimoire. With the ring. You accessed the grimoire with your blood. You have to use it on the ring."

"But that doesn't make sense," she said through gritted teeth, trying to push more power into her repulsion spell as Clodia attacked again. "For my blood to work, that would mean ..."

"You are related to Triptolemus. Which means, your power is good. Don't you see?"

Oh Gods. She did. She did see. How could she not have seen it before? How Persephone and Demeter's reluctance to talk about their beloved Triptolemus, the lost lesser God, matched their reluctance to talk about her father. How her magic and blood had opened up the Eleusinian Mysteries Grimoire. How easy it was to use the spells from it. And how easy it was to use the ring – how putting it on felt like coming home. "I didn't realise. I didn't know. Oh Gods, I'm sorry. I'm so sorry." She could have stopped all this already if only she'd put it all together before now. Although, could she? Would her blood work?

The chronometer buzzed madly; the sigil spell had begun to fade at the edges as it was used up.

"Don't be sorry," Tam gasped, touching her face. "Fix it. You're the only one who can."

Words sprang into her mind, four verses from different parts of the grimoire, and yet, she knew they belonged together:

They who are earth
They who are fire
They who are water
They who are air

~

Power comes to the wearer.
Power comes from the bearer
Power comes through the carer
Powered by and for the sharer

~

For they who give in
For they who give all
For they who wait
For they who fall

~

The ring is blood kin
Powered by blood and the first
The ring is blood touched
Powered by the blood cursed

It didn't follow the form of most of the spells in the grimoire, and she suddenly realised why. It wasn't a spell.

It was a message.

A message for her. From the male who had created the Mysteries – not simply to celebrate his love of Demeter and Persephone, but for his progeny.

For her.

It had all been there, in the writings in the margins that had been exposed when she'd touched them. The writing – his writing – had reacted to her. She just hadn't been ready to understand.

Now she was.

She glanced down at the ring. Not Triptolemus' ring. Her ring. One he'd created in his ring's image for her. Because, for some reason, he was blood cursed and he needed his ring to help fully access his power. And because she was blood-kin, she too suffered under his curse – so she too needed the ring to help her access and fully control her magic.

And to work properly, it needed her blood.

She scraped it across the drying blood on her arm.

Nothing happened.

It needed fresh blood, just like the grimoire.

Turning the ring, she wrapped her fist around the sharp edges of the green gem. Tam, seeming to know what she needed, wrapped his hand around hers, squeezing hard. She winced as the gem cut into her palm – then cried out as the power, blood-cursed to be dormant, leaped to life and lit her up like a green and gold flame.

The glorious light of her power lit the space around them, turning Tam's eyes into reflective-flaming pools as it pulsed into him. It lit up Ilia where she stood behind them, snapping her upright, her grip no longer like cobwebs on her skin.

She had no idea why she'd been so afraid of this, her full power – it was love and wonder and friendship and joy. It tasted of the spring and new growth; it whispered of birth and death and birth again. It was of earth and fire and water and air.

And blood.

Her father's blood. Her blood.

Not evil.

Not good.

As Tam had said, it simply represented life and all that came with it. The good and the bad.

Blood flowed through her as her power flowed through her. It was up to her to decide what to do with both. Her blood might be cursed, but that didn't mean it or her power had to be evil.

It could fight evil.

It could fight for everything she held dear.

With a shout of exultation, she flung out her free hand and let go of everything that was inside her.

Light, brighter than before, twined with green and red and blue and gold, shot out of her and hit Clodia square in the chest. But rather than push her back, it expanded, threads of it capturing her arms and legs, tying them together; it reached out to grab the power she'd loosed and pulled that back too.

Clodia screamed and raged, fighting the power binding her, but it was no use – she was no match to what was truly inside Korinna.

The Pompeii spirits who'd been bashing at the shield, trying to get to her, stopped, hanging like a fog to her left.

"It is done," she shouted above Clodia's raging. "Now to take back what isn't yours." She opened her palm to show the ring. Her blood smeared it, but as they watched, it sank into the gem, making it glow more brightly than ever before.

Clodia's shouts died as she spied the ring. "How do you have that? Who are you?"

"I am the daughter of Innia and Triptolemus. This ring is mine by birth and by blood."

"No. You shouldn't have the power you do. Triptolemus was blood cursed. He Who is Unknown made certain neither that bastard nor his line could stop Him from taking what would eventually be His." She screamed as the power tightened around her.

Korinna wanted to ask her what she meant, but there wasn't time. "Talking of taking things that aren't yours ..." She reached out her hand and called Jules' power to her. Flickering like fire, it leapt across the grey of the Void and into the ring as Clodia screamed and raged. Sick of the sound of it, Korinna flicked her finger so a thread of power covered the ancient witch's mouth, cutting off all sound. Then she said, "And the cupid power too." Despite the fact Clodia hadn't used any of the power she'd stolen from Tam to escape from Tartarus against them, Korinna could feel an echo of it hiding deep inside Clodia's black heart. She reached out with her fingers and made a grabbing motion.

Threads of indigo light rose from Clodia's chest, the deepest red of the heart at their core, and like an arrow, flew across the gap to connect with Tam's chest. He grunted at the impact but then, as his power returned to where it was meant to be, he stood straighter, eyes glowing and flickering from indigo to black to peridot. Beautiful. So beautiful.

"And finally, I take back my vow. Drop the shield, Tam." He did as she bid, and before the spirits could react, she said, "Come with me, my friends. I will take you to Elysium, where you should always have been, and all these years of pain will be forgotten in the eternal bliss awaiting you there." She made a gathering motion with her hand and the fog that was tens of thousands of spirits sank into the ring and disappeared. "It is done," she said, smiling. "Now to finish this. Tam, prepare the HeartsBlood Gem."

He pulled it out of her pocket and placed it, both halves face up, in his palm. "Ready."

Clodia's eyes opened wide and she struggled harder against the power binding her.

"You took so much joy out of using this for your machinations," Ilia said. "Now you're going to find out exactly what it feels like to be used against your will."

Korinna gestured with her hand and fingers of power reached out towards Clodia.

"Mmph, mmph," she said, struggling harder. But it was no use, the deep-ruby light touched her, wrapped around her, and as it did, Korinna drew back her power. Then they watched as the ruby light pulled Clodia down and into the heart of the gem.

As she disappeared like smoke inside the halves, Ilia said:

"Trapped inside and fixed within

Your power owned by an owner's whim

Never to rest, always in pain

Punished forever for seeking to gain

That which was meant to be Goddess-given

Your hubris never to be forgiven

I speak these words from the heart of me

Three time three, so mote it be."

The gem's glow grew bright and the two halves snapped together, looking like it had never been broken.

They stared at it in silence for a moment, then Tam said, "We better get out of here. Our time is about to run out."

Korinna realised the chronometer buzzed madly against her wrist. Rather than waste time checking just how little time they had, she gripped Tam's hand. "Come on, let's go." But before they got to the tear, the final alarm sounded and the buzzing stopped.

Her gaze met Tam's.

They were out of time.

Staring into his eyes, she waited for her soul to be torn from her body by the Void.

19

*N*othing happened.

"What? Why aren't we dead?" Tam said softly.

"Look!"

Korinna's gaze followed where Ilia pointed. She gasped.

Threads of magic – the colour of darkest indigo mixed with the gold of dawn over a horizon – touched in the middle of Tam's back. He was staring at her back – one touched her too.

"Is this you?" she asked Ilia.

The spirit shook her head. "No. My magic is not nearly strong enough to do that."

"To do what?"

"It's keeping you in your corporeal forms."

"But how? Where is it coming from?"

"From there." She pointed and Korinna followed the path to the tear in the Void. The surface of the tear was now like the clearest pool of shimmering water. And through that pool, she saw Jules on the ground, sweaty and pale, leaning against Bas, Violetta at her side. She wasn't looking at the tear or at her mate or grandmama. She stared at the baby in her arms.

A baby that glowed with power the colour of the threads holding

613

their souls in place, despite the fact they'd run out of time and should be dead.

"It seems your sister has arrived," Ilia said to Tam.

"Gods. She's beautiful." He glanced at Korinna. "But I don't understand. How? She's only the daughter of a witch and a cupid. She shouldn't have power like that."

"And yet she does," she said softly. "She showed signs of it, but I had no idea she was this powerful."

"You knew about this?"

"Some. Not all. Certainly not that she would have the power to rival Ostara. It seems that she, like your mother, is Goddess-touched. It is the only reason she could hold us here like this."

Resignation filled his expression. "And so it starts again."

"Maybe. Maybe not. But we won't figure it out here. Let's go." She took his hand and they stepped towards the tear.

As they did, the HeartsBlood Gem was almost ripped from his hand. He cried out in surprise and Korinna helped him to hold onto it. "Try again," she said, wrapping her power around it.

But when he tried to go through the tear again, the gem didn't want to go with him.

"What can we do?" he asked. "We can't leave it."

"Give it to me," Ilia said, reaching out her hand. "I'll hide it in here with me."

"What? What do you mean?" Tam said at the same time Korinna asked, "You're not coming back?"

"No. I thought this might happen. You two have a life to lead – so the one to stay must be me."

"Why didn't you say something?" Tam asked as Korinna blurted, "We're not leaving you here."

Ilia looked at them sadly. "What if I want to be left here?"

"Why would you want that?" Korinna asked.

Ilia's ghostly lips trembled. "Because I have nothing to go back for. I have no life, no body. Even my boys, my precious boys, who were torn from me at birth, are gone, the legacy of the love I meant them to have for each other destroyed by betrayal. I am empty. It is fitting I remain here to be guardian of the prison we've put Clodia in."

"No. I do not accept that," Tam said, leaving Korinna's side and going over to where Ilia floated. "I did not keep you safe in my chest all these months only to lose you now."

"Be sensible, Tam," she said, reaching out to touch his face in the way a mother might. "There is no other choice."

"Yes there is. There is always a choice. If we've learned anything today, it's that. A choice for good. A choice for evil. A choice to die or a choice to live."

"And it is my choice to stay here."

"I will not let your choice be to sacrifice yourself to another prison."

"You cannot stay here. And neither can Korinna."

"And neither will you." He grabbed her arm, pressing the now-glowing sigil against her forearm, and intoned:

"By blood we saved, by blood we're bound,

By blood and life and love and ground

Return her to corporeal form

The dawn of life to be reborn."

Korinna gasped – he'd used the most forbidden part of the sigil spell – the reason Hades and Zeus had destroyed the Mysteries and everything to do with them. The spell that could return a spirit's corporeal form.

A pulse of the same indigo and dawn light that was in the thread holding them to their bodies shot out from the tear and wrapped around Ilia. She cried out as it lit her from the inside out.

"Tam, you genius!" Korinna said as the light brightened so that they could no longer see Ilia.

"I thought so." He gifted her his most cocky smile, the one that made her feel warm and alive. And loved.

"Thank the Gods for you." Ilia's pain – and her near-sacrifice – had touched something deep inside her; something so familiar, she knew she couldn't live with herself if not given the opportunity to make things right for her. Tam – wonderful Tam – had made that possible.

She wrapped her arms around him and hugged him tight, so glad for the magnificent heart of him that had never been darkened, no matter what happened to them; the heart of him who had figured out her secrets and turned them from bleak darkness into the brightest good. He would never let harm come to anyone he loved, especially if they were family, and she knew that's how he felt about Ilia.

The light died.

Standing before them was a woman, clothed only in the magic of dawn light that had given her form. She stared at them from liquid eyes of darkest purple lit by sunlight and said, "What did you do?"

"With my cupid and warlock power combined – and somehow with the power of Ostara – I saved you with the spell from the Eleusinian Mysteries Grimoire."

"Hades and Zeus will kill you for that."

"No, they won't. Because I used it how the spell was always meant to be used, not how they feared it would be. I brought life back to someone whose soul is eternally good."

"I …" Her gaze raked his before it fell to the gem in her hand. "But what of this?"

"Maybe I should take it inside me again," Tam suggested.

"No," Ilia said, and before either of them could stop her, jammed it against her chest, canting the spell Tam had used six months ago to meld it with his flesh. Slowly, it sank into Ilia's breast, disappearing below the skin, the only sign of its presence a dark-red glow.

"Why did you do that?" Tam asked. "I thought you hated it."

"It is my burden to bear, not yours. I will not allow you to be tainted by this any further. Now, let's get out of here."

"Here, let me clothe you first." Korinna waved her hand and clothing, similar to her own, appeared on Ilia's body.

"Thank you. Now we should go." Taking Korinna's outstretched hand, she led them out of the Void.

Unlike before, nothing tried to stop them from leaving. It was as simple as allowing the threads of magic that kept them anchored to the Earth Realm to reel them out of the Void, through the tear, to where they all belonged.

As soon as they were clear, Korinna turned, and saying the words of the reversing spell, used her magic – now as easy as breathing with the help of the ring – and closed the entrance into the Void.

"By the Goddess' grace! You're all okay," Violetta said, rushing towards them. "I thought I was too late, but you did it. You vanquished Clodia and saved us all from the disaster that would have occurred if Ria Silvia had stayed in the Void."

Korinna whipped around to face Ilia. "Ria Silvia? You're Ria Silvia?"

Ilia blanched. "I have not gone by that name for many thousands of years and do not wish to be called by it again."

"You are mother to Romulus and Remus."

She pressed her lips together and nodded.

"The boys you spoke of," Korinna said. "I should have realised."

"Why would you? Their legend has faded in the depths of time and I was never a very important part of their story."

"Not important," Jules said from where she still lay on the ground against Bas, clutching her newborn babe to her chest. "As a mother, I object to that statement. I think you are the most important part of their story – with a story of your own to tell."

Ilia's mouth twisted. "Please. I cannot talk about this now."

"Of course. When you are ready."

"I may never be ready."

"When you are," Bas said softly. "We are here to listen. And to help. Now that you're free and my son, with the help of my daughter's power, has returned you to corporeal form, I am certain that is something we can manage."

"But you are a God. Why would you want to help me?"

"Demi-god, thank you very much. And not all of us are so devoid of humanity as to walk past someone else's need and pain. Especially when we've all experienced our own and found help when it seemed there was no hope. When you're ready, allow us to help you do whatever you must to give you back hope. I promise you, there is something better for you in this world."

"Well said, Bas." Jules reached up to cup his cheek. He leaned down and gave her a soft kiss, then kissed the top of his baby's head.

Pain slashed across Ilia's face as she watched the new parents. Then she turned quickly and walked away. Tam moved as if to go after her, but Violetta rose from Jules' side to stop him. "She needs some time."

"We can't let her leave," Korinna said.

Violetta pointed to Ilia, her hand tracing a motion in the air that led back to the baby – and as she did, the faint trace of magic showed, a fine thread of indigo and dawn light leading from Ilia to the baby. "She can't go far."

Tam looked around them. "Are we still attached too?"

"No. Only Ilia."

"Why?" Korinna asked.

"I assume it's because she was remade and will need the power of the Goddess-touched that gave her life again to keep the process from reversing – for a time at least."

"It's lucky the baby has power like Ostara, or things could have turned out very differently."

Korinna looked at the baby and another knowing came over her. "I don't think luck had anything to do with it. I think the Eternal Well has plans for both the baby and Ilia. Only time will tell what, but it's something big. Something to save us all."

"From what?"

"Probably from the thing that slipped out of the Void when you opened it and tried to attack Jules and the baby," Violetta said.

"What happened to it?" Korinna asked. "I didn't see it re-enter the Void – although, we were a little busy."

"Bas and I fought it off, but we weren't strong enough to force it back. It got away."

Korinna frowned. "Do you think maybe it was responsible for why Clodia was so powerful?"

"That makes sense," Tam said slowly. "Do you think it poses a danger to the baby and Ilia?"

"I think there's a very good chance of that," Violetta said grimly.

Bas called out to her then and she rushed over to her granddaughter's side.

They watched as she held the baby while Bas helped Jules to her feet.

Korinna took Tam's hands in hers. "They'll be safe. We'll make sure of it."

"Damn right we will." He turned to smile down at her, hands stroking up her arms to cup her face. "Together, we can do anything."

"Yes. Equal and opposite, together we are whole."

"I love you."

"As I love you."

She went to pull him into her arms, but he held back a little. "I'm sorry, Rinna."

"For what?"

"For not seeing sooner just how lost in pain and despair you were. For not trying to look for the truth about who was behind what happened at Pompeii so that you fully believed it wasn't your fault. You said you understood something else had influenced you, but I didn't see that you still blamed yourself. That it was a large part of why, when you used the blood magic, you thought that meant your power is evil. I should have seen it. I let you down."

Horrified at the sadness and self-recrimination carving lines of stress on his handsome face, she wrapped her arms around him. "Tam, no. Don't blame yourself."

"But I'm your soulmate. I felt you were troubled but looked no further than the obvious – that you, like me, struggled to master power that was unfamiliar to you. I didn't—"

"No. The blame is not yours. At least, not solely. I didn't want to think too deeply about everything either. I kept it hidden – from you, from me. I should have taken the darkness inside me into the light and exposed it for what it was, but I was too afraid to do so for fear you might think differently of me." She put her fingers over his lips when he went to argue. "I should have known you never would look at me with anything but love. And trust. I won't make that mistake again. Just as you won't make the mistakes you made again."

"Never. I promise. Although," his lips quirked in chagrin. "I can't promise never to make mistakes again. This cupid ain't perfect."

"Neither is this Soteira – or daughter of Triptolemus or whatever I am."

He shook his head. "I can't believe Persephone didn't tell me that when she gave me the ring. It would have solved so many of our worries before we went in there tonight."

"I know, right? She and Demeter have some serious explaining to do."

"Do you think they will? Explain, I mean?"

She shrugged. "I hope so. Although I won't hold my breath. Even they do things in their own time."

"Can you wait? To find out?"

Her lips quirked up. "What do you think?"

"I think there's going to be a lot of very full-on research in our futures."

"Our futures – I love the sound of that."

They kissed a kiss of promise, of longing, of passion and trust with no need of Oestra to fuel any of it. He believed in her, and now, with him by her side, she believed in herself.

She wished she could disappear with him right then and there, but they still had not finished their tasks for the night. Slowly she pulled away from him, noting green and gold sparks like her magic glowing in his peridot eyes – as if somehow, part of her was inside him. She wondered if her eyes had taken on the glow of his dual powers too. She'd have to look in a mirror when they got home. "We'll finish this later," she whispered.

"Definitely. But first, you better send those souls to Elysium."

"Shouldn't we make sure your mum and sister are safe and then get Ilia settled in first? Besides, I'll need the spell from the Eleusinian Mysteries Grimoire to transfer them from the ring and into Elysium."

"No. I swore that you would never have to use that dangerous spell and I am not going back on my word now."

"But with you and the others to help – plus this ring – it won't kill me like it would have before."

"It's still dangerous. Besides, why do you need that spell when you've got all of us here, with the power of Ostara to boost you and two witches with Goddess-touched powers?"

"Two?" Her eyes opened wide as she realised what he was saying. "Your mother's power!"

"Exactly. Return it to her now and then we can all help you complete your vow. But quickly – or the full power of Ostara will be gone until the moon rises again tomorrow night."

They rushed to Jules and Korinna looked down at her and the baby. "She's beautiful."

"Yes – she is. Her name is Dawn." She glanced up at them both. "You will help me to keep her safe?"

"Of course. But you'll be able to do a lot of the keeping safe yourself after this. Ready?"

Jules gave a jerky nod and Korinna put her hand over the new mother's heart. Then tapping into the deepest recesses of her power, she opened the section of the ring that had taken in the Goddess-touched power Vesta had bestowed on Jules' soul over 2,000 years ago. As the power rushed from the ring and into the person they were made for, Jules closed her eyes and sighed, a sound of rightness, of acceptance.

Korinna staggered slightly as the last of the power settled into Jules – but Tam was there, holding her secure.

Jules opened her eyes and whispered, "Thank you." Her gratitude alone would have been enough, but the baby opened her indigo and dawn eyes and looked up at her, and she felt the gratitude down to her soul.

"Now we have to help Korinna," Tam said. "Are you right to do that, Mum?"

Jules smiled beatifically. "I've never felt so good." She bounced on her feet, the baby gurgling in her arms. "Let me help." She waved her hand and the pentacle glowed violet and white and green and gold. Light-hares rose from the ground again and began to caper around as each of them went to stand at a point of the pentacle. Then, as Korinna pointed her ring hand towards the centre of the pentacle, the hares rushed to the spot and began to swirl in a maelstrom of light and fire until a rift opened, a small pinprick to begin with, growing wider and wider until it was at least three feet around.

Without her having to say a word, the others pushed their powers at her, making her the focus through which the spirits in the ring could safely exit. She opened her mouth to say the words of release and the souls came rushing out.

No longer insane with anger and desperation, they were full of joy and excitement as they rushed towards the rift into Elysium.

As the last of them went through, the rift closed of its own accord with a little snap and a gasp of relief from all of her new family. A sense of peace, almost as wonderful as when she'd realised Tam was her soulmate, came over her. It was done. She'd completed her vow.

Now she got to live free with the man she loved with everything in her. And together, they'd look into the mysteries of her life and find the answers she longed for.

"Are you okay?" he asked, coming to her side.

She realised there were tears flowing down her face. She wiped them away and beamed up at him. "Never better. Now kiss me and take me home. I need to spend the rest of the night showing you just how grateful I am you're in my life."

He winked at her. "I have to say I'm a big fan of Oestra."

"It's not Oestra that compels me. It's you. And me."

"Us."

"Yes, us."

"Sounds good to me."

Taking her ring-hand, he used his powers to open a portal and took them all home.

Somehow they ended up in the kitchen instead of the library. "Damn," Tam said. "I thought that would have been fixed when I got my cupid power back."

"Maybe your warlock power is stronger than your cupid one now."

"I guess we'll see," he said wryly. Then as the others headed to their own rooms, he leaned down and waggled his brows at her. "In the meantime, do you want to check my GPS settings?"

She chuckled. "I'd love to." And opening a portal to their bedroom, she dropped them right on the bed naked – exactly how she intended them to be for the next few days at least. What better way to celebrate Oestra than with passion and love and the promise of a future that looked bright with renewal.

20

$\mathcal{P}$ersephone appeared behind her mother as she looked in her mirrored pool, scrying – or spying – on the woman they both loved like a daughter.

"You gave her the ring," Demeter said, not looking around.

"I had no choice after you set your secret lap-dog on her."

"Loki simply tested she was ready when he let that entity escape from its book."

"It could have been a disaster. Would have been if Tamuel had not been there. His presence was the only reason she thought of the wand."

"Loki was close by in case she didn't do what we knew she could. Besides, you well know it was the only path we could take to make her realise what must be done."

"I see that didn't stop you from getting Loki to whisper about it in Tamuel's ear as well."

Demeter waved her hand. "I did what I could to get the outcome we needed. Nobody would guess Loki is working with us." She glanced up at her daughter. "I thought you would be thankful."

Persephone shook her head. "You know there will be consequences."

"I know. But I couldn't risk losing her or Tamuel. Besides, it was time Ilia was released as well."

"Zeus won't be happy."

"Is he ever?

"Neither will Hades."

"I care little for what makes that beast happy or not." Demeter sighed and turned around, her light, spring-green eyes shadowed. "You don't have to worry about being the one to tell Korinna about her father. Ilia will take care of telling her about the origins of the blood-curse and what her father did to save us all."

"Another part of the Seer's vision you didn't tell me about?"

"No," Demeter said, waving her hand over the water again so it centred on the spirit, now reborn in corporeal form thanks to the spell their beloved Trip had devised. "I told her when I had the HeartsBlood Gem in my care before I allowed Clodia to steal it."

"But she hates all of us. How can you trust her? I don't want Rinna to hate us too."

Her mother flinched but said firmly, "What must be will be. It was fated she one day discover the truth and so I did what I could so that neither of us had to bear those tidings to her. Speaking of him, and what he had to do ..." Her mouth pulled tight as she visibly held back tears.

Persephone put her hand on her mother's shoulder, her throat tight with her own tears as she said, "It's too painful. I know. But I would have told Rinna, to save you that pain."

"And now neither of us have to," Demeter said, the smile she flashed Persephone a faded facsimile of its usual brilliance. Then she sighed, the smile falling away as if it was too much effort to hold on to. "Ilia, for all her faults, will not seek to hurt Rinna. In fact, she'll tell her out of a need to help. So, while Rinna might be angry with us for some time, she'll eventually come around."

"It's caused so much pain."

"It's going to cause more before we are done." Demeter looked back at the pool, waving her hand and bringing up the image of a man.

His hair was longer than the last time Persephone had seen him, his muscles even more well-defined, skin glistening with sweat in the sun as he toiled, hand-sowing seeds on his farm.

"He looks much as he did," Persephone noted. "Maybe a little more care-worn." But that was to be expected, given what they'd done to him.

"He's been gone too long from our service."

"And from your side. Will you awaken him soon?"

Demeter shook her head. "It is not for me to waken him." She waved her hand again and a new image of Ilia, face grief-torn and hate-filled as she stared at a statue of her sons, appeared next to the one of the man. "You know the prophecy as well as I."

Persephone nodded. But she had no idea how a woman who hated the Gods as much as Ilia did – and rightly so – would ever be able to awaken Triptolemus from the fake life they'd been forced to protect him with and bring him back to his former self.

But somehow, she had to – because if they were to fight the coming ancient evil, they would need him and her and Tam and Korinna and Jules and Bastien and yes, even little baby Dawn, to help them.

Even then, it might not be enough.

"What can we do to help?"

Demeter sighed, waved her hand so the water rippled and the images disappeared. She got up from her kneeling position, her lilac gown flowing around her as she began to walk to the edge of the cliff and looked out on the Earthly Realm below. "Nothing, for now. All will follow as fated."

"Your will, mother. I will do what must be done." As she always had – regardless of how much pain it brought to her, but more importantly, to those she most loved.

She only hoped that, once this was done, they would all be alive so she could beg their forgiveness and make amends for what she had done – and what was still to come.

~

I HOPE you've enjoyed the conclusion of Tamuel and Korinna's story … but rest assured, the saga continues with Ilia and Trip in *Hearts Cursed* – due out in A Perfectly Paranormal Christmas in late 2022.

IF YOU'VE GOT A MOMENT, I would love it if you could leave a review for ***Blood Cursed***. Reviews can help readers find books, and also help tell me where I'm going right and where I'm going wrong. I am grateful for all honest reviews. Thank you in advance for taking the time to let others know what you've read, and what you thought – you can leave your review at Goodreads, BookBub or the ebook retailer where you bought your copy. You can find links to the ebook retailers here:

https://www.leislleighton.com/paranormal-romance-novels/#APPE

the only one who can feel it. Unable to endure such unhappiness—even if he does call her Poison Ivy—she is determined to help him, no matter the cost. Because Pack McVale cannot survive without him, and curiously, neither can she ...

Simply sign up to my newsletter and I will email your free copy of Witch Bound to you. You will also receive the latest on upcoming books, sales, giveaways and relevant bookish news.

Get My Free Copy of Witch Bound Here:
https://www.subscribepage.com/w2g6b9

ALSO BY LEISL LEIGHTON

Gods Cursed Series

Love Cursed

Soul Cursed

Blood Cursed

Hearts Cursed

(Coming out Christmas 2022 in A Perfectly Paranormal Christmas
Anthology)

Fates Cursed

(Coming out mid 2023 in A Perfectly Paranormal Prophecy Anthology)

Pack Bound Series

Pack Bound

Moon Bound

Shifter Bound

Wolf Bound

Witch Bound

(A Pack Bound Series Prequel Novella)

Soul Bound

(Dawn of the Curse: Book 1

A Pack Bound Prequel Series)

As well as writing sexy, dark paranormal novels, I write mysterious and
emotional romantic suspense novels.

CoalCliff Stud Series

Climbing Fear: Book 1

Blazing Fear: Book 2

ECHO SPRINGS SERIES

Dangerous Echoes: Book 1

Books 2-4 in this series, (written by Daniel deLorne, TJ Hamilton and Shannon Curtis) are also available now at all ebook retailers.

ABOUT LEISL

Leisl Leighton is a tall red head with an overly large imagination. As a child, she identified strongly with Anne of Green Gables, and like Anne, is a voracious reader and born performer. It came as no surprise when she went on to a career as a performer, script writer, script doctor, stage manager and musical director for cabaret and theatre restaurants.

After starting a family, Leisl stopped performing and began writing the stories plaguing her dreams. She now writes emotional stories mixed with mystery and a little bit of what goes bump in the night. Her novels have won and placed in writing contests here and overseas. She is a passionate advocate for the romance genre, was President of Romance Writers of Australia from 2014-2017 and when she's not writing romantic stories of redemption, she is helping other authors reach their dreams with her Author Services.

You can contact Leisl through her website:

www.leislleighton.com

or sign up to her Newsletter:

https://www.subscribepage.com/w2g6b9

and be the first to find out about new releases, appearances, special deals and exclusive giveaways.

And if you want to get to know the Perfectly Paranormal Anthology authors a bit more, get sneak peeks of what's coming up for the APP Anthologies, as well as giveaways, special offers and just some PNR fun, then join our Perfectly Paranormal Paramours Facebook Group.

Find us here:
https://www.facebook.com/groups/251663560162131

facebook.com/LeislLeightonAuthor
twitter.com/LeislLeighton
instagram.com/leislleightonauthor
bookbub.com/authors/leisl-leighton

ACKNOWLEDGMENTS

Thanks go to all the usual people: my hubby, my boys, my mum and dad, my writing group friends—Anita, Marnie, Chris, Laura, Frana—for all their love and support through the years, especially over the last few terrible years. I couldn't do this without you all being in my corner, cheering me on and helping me move forward.

Thanks will always go to Helen and Liz—your counsel and amazing friendships will always be missed. You're both in my heart every day.

Thanks to my agent, Alex Adsett, for encouraging me to go off and pursue getting these stories out there myself.

Thanks to my editor, Marnie St Clair—working with you is always a joy, but you especially brought the goods on this one.

Thanks to Samantha Marshall for your amazing cover. It's always such a pleasure to work with you.

And a big thanks to my fellow A Perfectly Paranormal writers – every day working with you all is a joy I am so thankful for. You guys rock!

Finally, thanks to all the readers. You are a big part of why I do this crazy thing. I hope you enjoy my stories as much as I enjoyed writing them.